INTELLECT:
USER
REPAIR

JILL THRUSSELL

ISBN-13: 978-0957113237

CONTENTS

"Hope and possibility are our two lifeboats in life that can never ever sink." ~ Jill Thrussell

CURIOUS ATTRACTIONS

The old Victorian house that sat neatly tucked away inside the private mews in the heart of the city was Leona's sanctuary and the small private road that her home lived upon had become like a secret hideaway that no one knew about besides those that occupied one of two houses situated upon it. Tucked discreetly away from the busy, bustling city streets of Pinesfield, the mews was like a hidden back alley that was hardly even visited on a daily basis, except by those who actually lived there or by those who had been very specifically invited to its confines. In fact, only those who very precisely sought out the mews knew about its actual existence at all because it was barely even visible from the main city street nearby but for Leona, the mews was her safe haven and the place that she would retire to, once a busy working day had finally come to an end.

Fortunately enough for Leona that day, her Tuesday evening was extremely peaceful as she began to walk along the quiet mews and then arrived outside her garden gate as she prepared for the calmness that she hoped would greet her inside the walls of her home. The working

1

day that Leona had just endured had been rather long and as usual she'd exceeded her agreed weekly contractual working hours because there had been an urgent client deadline to meet and so now, she felt totally drained, physically worn out and absolutely filled to the brim with fatigue as she entered inside her home and then closed the front door gently behind her.

A leisurely saunter along the hallway immediately brought a smile to Leona's face as the mahogany, antique looking floorboards creaked under her weight as she walked and it almost seemed as if they were appreciative of her return and wanted to welcome and greet her in the only way that they possibly could. Despite the fact that the house Leona lived in wasn't really her ideal choice in terms of a home that she would have wanted to pay to rent or even buy because the property definitely lacked certain features that Leona would have loved to be present inside it, it truly was all her own and that was something that she could at the very least, fully appreciate.

Just five years ago, very sadly and tragically, Leona's Grandmother had suddenly passed away and so Leona had inherited the house and although she'd considered selling it many times and upgrading it to something slightly more modern, something deep down inside had always held her back from actually doing so. Although the property certainly wasn't Leona's first choice, it definitely possessed a certain charm about it as it held many fond memories within its walls which clung to the hallways and interior of each room that Leona wanted to hold onto because she deeply cherished those memories and each one had kept both the house and Leona together.

Inside Leona a deep emotional attachment definitely existed to the building on her part and so she'd lived affectionately inside its confines every single day, ever since it had been bequeathed to her. For Leona, her attachment to the house somehow superseded the usual superficialities that surrounded her which penetrated her life on a daily basis and eagerly emanated from the external, very modern world that she lived in. Some beautiful childhood memories still existed from the days when Leona had pottered around the house with her Grandmother that still clung to the shelves of her mind and each one provided her with a grain of comfort in her moments of solitude because all the modern conveniences in the world could not be an actual substitute, or ever replace her treasure chest of very precious memories from her cherished past.

Now very sadly, distant memories were all that actually remained because Leona's Grandmother had never physically returned to the face of the Earth but Leona had learnt to console herself with those distant mental visions and eagerly held onto them as she'd attempted to somehow keep her Grandmother's memory alive. Part of Leona deep down inside still felt very unwilling to surrender in totality to the modern values that so often dictated people's actions and that defined every part of their lives and world and so she'd remained committed to the home that her Grandmother had loved and lived in it appreciatively.

Just as Leona expected, the door that led to the lounge was still wide open because she had left it that way earlier that day before she'd departed and the wood seemed to sigh with relief and welcome her return as she stepped inside the huge front room and it wavered slightly. An amused smile crossed Leona's face as she quietly considered that perhaps the door had intentionally hung open all day as it had waited for her to come back because it definitely seemed to be aware that she had indeed, just stepped through it.

Inside the very large lounge which also doubled up as

a kitchen, everything was in exactly the same spot that Leona had left it in as she greeted her home with an enthusiastic, cheerful grin and then quietly began to prepare to get something to eat. When it came to the interior of Leona's home, her Grandmother had been a meticulous woman and every aspect of the house fully reflected that very real fact, from the shiny mahogany floorboards to the china pottery that was kept safely tucked and stacked away inside a large mahogany cabinet in one corner of the lounge. In fact, everything was as close to perfect as it could possibly be because Leona had consistently and diligently maintained every inch of her home over the last five years with absolute precision, anxious not to destroy a single part of her Grandmother's memory, legacy and history.

Some pieces of modern furniture and some consumables had been purchased by Leona over the past five years to avoid the unnecessary facilitation of the more treasured and expensive antique items and any potential breakages and those items had been placed around the house to give Leona a home that she could actually live in. To a large extent however, Leona had strived to retain the original beauty that the house contained because it truly was a beautiful property and it contained some admirable decorative features that were definitely worth preservation. Since Leona's initial arrival, some of the walls around the house had been redecorated in rich, vibrant, modern colors as she'd attempted to modernize some parts of the building slightly but overall, she had tried very hard not to detract from the property's original state and antique nature.

In one corner of the lounge, propped up against one of the walls, sat a large, extremely soft, very comfortable cream sofa which was adorned with plush, puffy cream cushions that nestled gently against Leona's body and welcomed her weary limbs as she eagerly sat down upon it and prepared to relax, even if it was only for a minute. Food definitely had to be prepared that evening but Leona had already decided that she needed to rest for a few minutes before that activity could actually happen.

Due to Leona's weary body and tiredness, her evening meal that evening would be nothing special and comprise of just a readymade meal that would be stuck inside the hotplate warmer but it would definitely fill the gap in her stomach and taste semi acceptable. Sometimes, in some of Leona's slightly more reflective moments, she did actually wonder what her Grandmother would think about her life and her ready meal lifestyle, if she was still alive but she'd always concluded that it probably wouldn't be very much because it was rather dull, packed with trouble and absolutely, totally cumbersome.

Every single working day Leona would attend a truly tedious, rather hostile working environment that housed a very horrible boss inside it and then on the weekends, she would see her deadbeat boyfriend and the nightmare clashes with the neighbors which happened all too frequently, certainly weren't anything to write home about. In fact, if Leona could place all her troubles inside a suitcase or a parcel and then pack them off to the other side of the world she definitely would, Leona quickly decided and that package would include the deadbeat boyfriend with no return address. Very sadly, the frustrating reality was that Leona's life made very little sense to anyone and certainly not to any of her closest friends and it made absolutely no sense at all to Leona herself.

Regardless of Leona's wishes however, her life truly was what it was but she had often wondered why she'd tolerated such negative surroundings for so very long and how she had managed to decorate all the walls of her life with so many negative people. The house of reality that Leona lived in every day certainly wasn't something that she had taken any action to actually change and so it had remained that way for the past four years, stagnant and stagnantly awful although the entrance of the noisy neighbors three years ago had made it slightly more awful. Unfortunately, and very sadly, Leona's life and living situation wasn't really something that she perceived would actually change in the very near future either and that disheartened her slightly as she tried to dig deep within herself and find enough strength to prepare her evening meal.

Rather frustratingly for Leona, just a few years beforehand, her original neighbors, a couple in their late sixties had made the decision to move out and they'd then given their property to their much younger, far more boisterous three male children and that gift had been a total headache for Leona from start to finish. Due to the three men's wealth, attitude and lack of responsibilities, the children who weren't really children at all because they were actually all in their mid-twenties to early thirties had then decided to make their home their party venue and Leona had ultimately had to pay the price as she'd borne the cost of their decision. The noisy, difficult neighbors that lived in the mews certainly weren't going anywhere and they had been a frequent strain upon Leona's life ever since they'd moved in next door and that was absolutely undeniable.

A responsible hard day's work it had quickly transpired had not been a commitment that any of the three men had been tied to and they all seemed to be totally oblivious to the realities and responsibilities that being employed, or running a business usually placed upon the human body and mind. Very loud noisy parties had been thrown next door every single weekend, since their arrival in the mews and even throughout some of the weekday nights and Leona had often struggled just to get a decent night's rest and it had been that way since the very first day that the three men had moved in.

Although Leona could certainly appreciate the three men's desire to enjoy a good party and she had absolutely no desire whatsoever to infringe upon or obstruct their enjoyment, she regularly felt totally exasperated by their actions and attitude, due to her own work responsibilities and her need to earn an actual living. Sleep was a very necessary component of Leona's daily routine during the week and some of the parties they held, clashed with not only her work schedule but also with her physical need to rest.

Usually, the three brother's parties would go on until the early hours of the following morning which meant, Leona's entire night would be disturbed by each one as she wrestled silently with the noise and the overall situation had now become extremely difficult and very tricky. Despite the fact that several years had now gone by since the three men's initial arrival however, there had been absolutely no change in their lifestyle and no reduction in the frequency and noisiness of their parties. On several occasions in the past, Leona had virtually had to tiptoe across eggshells with polite requests as she'd asked them to lower the volume but the three brother's attitude towards her had been far from polite and her requests had been completely and utterly ignored every single time.

The loud music that was usually played during their parties would at times cause the windows of Leona's home to actually shake and vibrate and the parties caused a disturbance that was quite frankly, very hard to ignore as the three brothers celebrated life almost every single day in an extremely noisy manner. Outside the men's home the rambunctious behavior of their guests would usually create other disturbances and distractions that were a nuisance which were almost impossible for Leona to challenge because they certainly weren't her guests, or even present in the mews to visit her home and in totality, the situation had become increasingly frustrating and almost unbearable for Leona to live with.

Essentially, despite the fact that several years had now gone by since the three men had initially moved into the mews and as Leona was generally an amicable, peaceful, polite person, the familiarity, respect and curtesy that should have been present between the four neighbors just didn't exist and that frustrated Leona no end. The expected solid pillars of curtesy, respect and pleasantness that usually existed between neighbors had not been allowed to form or been built amongst the four, purely due to the three men's very anti-social behavior. In fact, Leona had found the three men virtually impossible to reason with because of their very difficult nature which had clearly taken root inside the mews and so she tended to avoid them as often as she could because of their strained relationship and their attitude towards her which was quite frankly, extremely unpleasant.

On several occasions in the past, when Leona had attempted to challenge the three brothers about the actual noise levels and confronted them about some of their guests, the three men would simply grunt at her and ignore her requests and so Leona no longer even bothered to raise the issue with them. Over the three years, since the men's initial arrival, the situation had actually deteriorated and it had now become a major wall of frustration and so Leona had given up trying to reason with them a long time ago. Any attempts and efforts on Leona's part to negotiate with regards to the impact of the men's lifestyle upon her life and the mews had fallen on closed ears and minds but that hadn't changed the frequency of the loud parties, or the noise that Leona had, had to tolerate whenever they actually occurred.

From the depths of Leona's stomach, an angry growl suddenly began to erupt as hunger rapidly gripped her body as her physicality quickly reminded her that she hadn't eaten anything since lunchtime that day. The kitchen which adjoined the lounge was situated at the other end of the very large front room and so Leona wearily rose to her feet and then began to cross the room as she prepared to approach it. A few grains of energy still remained inside Leona's body but she literally had to force herself to utilize each one in order to make an actual meal before she was completely and utterly, physically drained.

Dinner had to be not only prepared but also eaten before Leona could rest that night and food was something that her body definitely required before sleep could occur and commence. A few worries pricked and needled away Leona's mind however as she crossed the room as her thoughts became distracted and more fully occupied by the issue of the noisy neighbors which predominantly revolved around the possibility that they might actually host a noisy party that very same night. Hopefully, Leona wished as she let out a weary sigh, a noisy party would not occur that night because she really needed a peaceful night of undisturbed rest.

Perhaps, Leona quietly deliberated, if she had been a stronger person she might have been able to stand up to the brothers and challenge them in a manner that they could not just merely push aside but so far that had not actually happened. The sad reality was as Leona already knew, she really wasn't a very strong person and so she hadn't managed to challenge them successfully in a way that they had actually paid any attention to. A reasonable compromise had not yet been reached between the four regarding just how many parties on any given week the three men would hold and host inside their home and nor was it likely to be agreed upon at any point in the near future and that was a reality that Leona now, fully accepted.

Regardless of Leona's presence inside the house next to the men's own home, the three noisy brothers it seemed were definitely not prepared to curb their behavior and Leona really didn't have the strength, energy or even the willpower to try and stand up to them anymore. Persuasion was definitely something that required both time and effort and by the time Leona usually arrived home each working day, energy was definitely something that she lacked and her weekends were usually tied up with Darin and fully occupied by his dramatic antics.

Some weekday mornings, when Leona walked through the mews as she began to make her way to work, she would literally have to pick her way through the aftermath of their parties and the empty liquor bottles that would be strewn across her path. On several occasions Leona had even seen some used needles, discarded drug pipes and dirty condoms scattered across the concrete ground and she would delicately tiptoe around each distasteful object, reluctant to even touch a single one with the soles of her shoes.

Essentially, the potentially peaceful sanctuary that the mews could offer to its residents was totally wasted and absolutely destroyed, simply due to the presence of Leona's very noisy neighbors and at times, she'd even considered an actual house move just to get away from them and their very messy, noisy, disruptive lifestyle. Quite strangely and despite the brother's actual age, Leona had finally concluded, it was highly unlikely that any of the three men had ever had a real job, let alone had to earn an actual living because their lifestyle clearly reflected this fact. Somehow, the three young men that occupied the house next door seemed to have totally escaped the realities of life that most working and middle class people faced and they appeared to have no knowledge at all of what it meant to provide for themselves financially.

Another issue that irritated Leona at times was the fact that ever since the three men's very wealthy parents had travelled overseas to enjoy their retirement, they never seemed to check on their children to establish exactly what they were doing with the house that they'd given to them and it was almost as if, they no longer really cared. Despite their former ownership of the property, Leah doubted that they even knew about the frequent parties that were being held there because since they had left, they'd never returned to the mews, not even once and it was almost as if they had never even lived there at all. Rather frustratingly for Leona it seemed, the three men's parents had left the house in the three brother's hands and then rather annoyingly, they'd left them all alone inside the private mews right next door to Leona.

One small disadvantage of the very private mews that Leona lived in was the fact that it only housed two buildings inside it and in some ways that lack of buildings and residents was not really favorable to her at all. Perhaps, Leona deliberated as she began to prepare her evening meal, if there had been other houses situated inside the mews and other neighbors she would have been able to garner some support from them and then they could have faced and challenged the three brothers together but sadly, there actually wasn't.

Despite Leona's issues with the three men and their

lifestyle, when it came to their actual physicality, the three brothers were all reasonably attractive men and the endless stream of attractive men and women that attended their parties proved that within their social circles, they were reasonably popular and even quite well liked. One major thing definitely appeared to be absent as far as Leona was concerned however, when it came to the issue of the three brother's lifestyle choices and that was the possibility that they might one day settle down, have a family and try to build a future. Long term thoughts and goals didn't really seem to exist when it came to the three men and Leona doubted very much that such thoughts had ever crossed their minds because they seemed to have absolutely no intentions whatsoever of making any attempts to prepare themselves for any possible future eventualities.

"Perhaps having a family isn't really very important when you're rich and male and perhaps, it's totally insignificant." Leah thoughtfully concluded as she placed a solitary readymade pasta dish inside the hotplate warmer.

When it came to the three brothers and their societal peers, they just didn't seem to be overly concerned with a long-term agenda or their future and they appeared to live very much for the day as they enjoyed each day at full throttle and maximum capacity. The impact of the three men's lifestyle upon the quiet mews in which they lived was immediately obvious to anyone that visited it but even more so to Leona, who had to actually tolerate the noise that they generated on a weekly basis. Regardless of the constant irritation caused by the brothers next door however, Leona had somehow managed to keep her composure in the long term and she'd not only found ways to avoid them as often as she possibly could but also coped with the regular noise pollution.

In terms of the three brother's physical appearance,

Leona wasn't particularly attracted to any of the men but since she had carried the cost of their lifestyle and coped with the very negative attitudes that they'd so often presented to her that had ultimately been enough to put her right off. The three men's presence next door and their existence had now almost become totally repugnant in Leona's sight and so to consider any of them in a romantic capacity was absolutely unthinkable and totally out of the question as far as Leona was concerned. Somehow however, despite all the inconveniences and intrusions that their lifestyle regularly placed upon Leona's own life, she'd managed to find a way to tolerate her living situation but it was far from ideal and definitely something that she wanted to change in the near future.

The timer on the hotplate warmer suddenly started to beep as the appliance politely alerted Leona to the fact that her meal was ready and she quickly opened up the contraption and then removed the readymade meal that she'd placed inside it. Although the food that Leona had placed inside the warmer certainly wasn't scrumptious or anywhere near delicious, it would definitely be edible and it would fill up her hungry gap that evening and so she quickly grabbed some cutlery from the kitchen drawer as she released another tired, weary sigh. All in all, although the basic pasta dish was definitely a far cry from a hearty, warm home cooked meal and it would have a slightly plastic taste, Leona quietly concluded as she headed back towards the sofa, at least it would be consumable and that for now, really just had to do.

A forkful of food was eagerly spooned into Leona's mouth as she walked as hunger rapidly began to conquer her body because being seated in Leona's mind wasn't an actual prerequisite when it came to the consumption of food and her body had silently cried out for some kind of nourishment, ever since she'd left work earlier that evening. The day already felt as if it had been extremely long, for some inexplicable reason and Leona was now absolutely starving but despite the fact that her food was ready and in the process of being consumed, several worries still tugged away inside Leona's mind as she sat back down and one of them was her relationship with Darin.

Deep down inside, Leona knew as she relaxed on the sofa and tucked into her meal, her relationship with Darin was definitely not something that her Grandmother would have approved of and that reality could not be denied by anyone, least of all by Leona herself. In fact, Leona's choice of romantic partner would be one decision that would have been questioned profusely because her relationship with Darin, whichever way Leona looked at it, was a complete and utter mess held delicately together by the unreciprocated ribbons of love that exuded from Leona's rejected, unwanted, tolerated broken heart. Much like someone that attempted to breathe life into a unconscious body in order to revive another, Leona had tried and tried to give their romance that lifesaving touch with her patience and efforts but it had been to absolutely no avail and their limp, lifeless relationship still seemed headed for a romantic tomb with little hope of an actual recovery.

"It's better to be alone and unloved Leona than to be unloved by those you've accepted and given a place to in your life." Cynthia her Grandmother had often said as she'd offered Leona some sprinklings of wisdom, guided by her hands of maturity and her arms of experience.

Unfortunately for Leona, her Grandmother had been totally right and she definitely knew it but for the time being, she just couldn't face doing what was actually required to correct that romantic, or very unromantic, absolutely hopeless situation. Generally in life, Leona wasn't particularly great at standing up for herself and although she knew she would have to stand up to Darin one day, she'd put it off for as long as she possibly could, just to avoid any ugly confrontations in the hope that he would mature and change through his own volition. Despite Leona's patience however, Darin's maturity had not yet actually happened and he'd pretty much remained the same for the past five years and so too had Leona's lovelife as a result as she'd stayed in their relationship and walked through life quite miserably beside him.

Life for Leona as a result of all those very negative factors had now become a total headache to live in, increasingly troubled and extremely tiresome because no rays of sunshine and no shelter from the dreary downpour of misery had ever appeared as she silently carried her daily load in a huge bucket of worries upon her shoulders. Joy had not shown its face to Leona for a very long time and her days that had once been filled with laughter, romance and excitement were now filled with resentment, unhappiness and dissatisfaction and there was it seemed, no simple way out of that deep, painful, abyss of absolute misery. No easy route, remedy or solution had ever appeared or presented itself that could resolve any of the issues in Leona's life which dragged her reluctantly down into the deep depths of the gutter of unhappiness that she usually resided in every single day and that was absolutely undeniable.

Work definitely had to be endured each working day because Leona had financial responsibilities and a year ago, she'd even committed to an engagement with Darin that she was totally miserable about and so none of the things that currently bothered Leona were likely to change overnight. Being responsible was indeed one of Leona's strengths but it was also one of her biggest weaknesses because she wasn't the kind of person to simply get up, walk away and abandon things that she'd committed to and that attitude of respect and sense of duty towards others had now it seemed, become an actual noose that hung silently and invisibly around her own neck.

Just over a year ago, for some totally illogical reason, Leona had actually agreed to engage Darin because she'd felt that their engagement might change him and make him more responsible and so now, she felt obligated to see that decision through. The romantic decision that Leona had made however, she'd rapidly discovered had been totally misguided and absolutely naive and Leona had learnt that reality extremely quickly because Darin, if anything had actually grown worse not better. Due to the fact that engagements were a very serious commitment to Leona, she now felt that she couldn't simply walk away from the choice and decision that she'd made and so she had been stuck with her decision, a fake engagement and the slippery, manipulative snake in human form Darin ever since.

Perhaps one day, Leona deliberated quietly as she ate, she would find the strength to either break off her engagement with Darin completely, or find a way to fix the mess that their relationship had become because their engagement was going absolutely nowhere in its current state. In fact, the couple's engagement felt very artificial and it had perhaps just been a tool that Darin had utilized simply to manipulate Leona in order to tie her to him in a more committed manner, without actually giving her anymore of himself. Despite the fact that Darin had actually asked Leona to engage him, deep down inside herself Leona already knew the very real reality, he didn't really love her and certainly not in the way that she wanted and wished to be loved.

One day, Leona quietly considered as she switched on her laptop which was situated on top of the black, marble coffee table directly in front of the sofa, she would take control of the situation and then she'd dump Darin for good. One day, Leona decided as she placed the plate with the now empty plastic ready meal container down upon the coffee table beside her laptop, she would stand up in life and fight the battles that needed to be fought and challenge those that seemed to dedicate most of their lives to making her life totally miserable. One day, Leona silently promised herself, she would find the strength to deport all the visitors to her life that were citizens of misery and distress and she'd revoke their visas so that they would no longer have any access to her which would restrict their regular infliction of pain upon her being. One day, Leona silently insisted as tiredness suddenly began to grip her body and she lay back upon the sofa and then began to yawn, she'd evict all the tenants of misery from her life completely and one day, Leona would face her dragons but today would definitely not be that very brave battle filled day.

Sleep began to quickly but gently embrace Leona's body which on this occasion, was really a good thing as her long working day had totally worn her out and so now, she felt completely drained from the daily wear and tear of just living. During the week it was really quite usual for Leona to sleep inside the lounge because she rarely felt a desire to sleep in her rather large bedroom alone, due to the noise that usually emanated from the house next door and at times, the emptiness of her bedroom silently reminded her how alone she actually was and so her night on the sofa wasn't an actual departure from her usual weekday routine.

An upstairs inside Leona's home did exist but she rarely visited the upper floor and only ever usually ventured upstairs on a Sunday afternoon, just to give each room a clean because the other two bedrooms and bathroom it housed, weren't really required for the purposes of her living requirements and her daily living. Whenever Darin actually made the effort to visit Leona as they had arranged, she would sleep inside her bedroom at the very rear of the building on the ground floor in the very large king-size bed it housed alongside him but that rarely happened during the week anymore. In fact, due to the stress that Darin usually caused, Leona had in recent times intentionally steered Darin away from weekday visits, purely due to the problematic issues that he usually brought along with him.

Unknown to Leona however, despite the silence and stillness that surrounded her and her perceived solitude, a silent observer was indeed actually present and he silently watched her as she drifted off to sleep but this was not an observer that Leona knew, or even one that she'd invited into her home. In fact, Resolve the silent observer that now watched Leona from a distance wasn't even human and he had just been allocated to her life that evening by the Intellect Framework as part of the invisible life monitoring services that Intellect provided to humanity.

Inside the Intellect Framework, every single Monitoring Program monitored the human lives that they had been assigned to on a daily basis, unseen by human eyes, unheard by human ears and unknown to the majority of the human world and in that respect, Resolve was really no different. Earlier that evening, at around eight, Resolve had been assigned to Leona as her Life Monitor and as was usual practice within Intellect, he'd immediately accepted his allocation to her life and then begun his assigned duties straight away.

Human problems and human nature had become

increasingly complex over the decades and so an assistance framework had been devised that had been created by Victor Drayton, one of the most intelligent minds known to mankind which had then been implemented just before his death. For the past five decades, since Intellect's initial inception, Victor Drayton had served humanity from beyond the grave as he'd maintained the Intellect Framework meticulously and although he no longer physically walked the face of the planet, his final gift to humanity was indeed still present as his electronic mind worked behind the scenes and Intellect provided essential daily support to human lives.

During Victor Drayton's physical, mortal human lifetime, he had served extremely faithfully within the top ranks of military intelligence and although the Intellect Framework had been something that he'd wanted to implement, he had never been allowed to realize his very ambitious project until the very end of his human life. The main purpose and primary objective of Intellect itself, was to serve mankind through the provision of Life Monitors and although not many human beings knew about its actual existence, ever since its inception the human world had become very reliant upon it, even though it was completely invisible to the human eye. Only some of the most intelligent minds within the top ranks of military intelligence even knew about Intellect's creation, services and the framework's operations but the services that Intellect provided to humanity on a daily basis had now become absolutely invaluable.

Between the two worlds, a protective field did exist which had been built and then put in place to maintain their separation but that field was only visible and accessible from within Intellect itself which meant, human beings could never ever physically enter inside Intellect and the plane in which it existed. In Victor Drayton's opinion that field had always been and still was absolutely essential and totally necessary however, for the survival of both domains because the plane of existence that Intellect resided in had to remain completely inaccessible to the human world, in order to allow it to function both efficiently and effectively. The work that Victor Drayton performed inside Intellect was highly confidential, very sensitive and extremely delicate and so it had been protected accordingly from humanity and any possible acts of human sabotage or destruction and that in his mind had always been absolutely non-negotiable.

Upon Victor Drayton's death bed, the intelligence agency Intell that he had served for most of his life had finally granted him permission to implement the Intellect Framework and so he'd requested that his mind be implanted directly into the Intellect system that he had already begun to build, so that he could manage its operations on a daily basis. The wish of Victor Drayton's lifetime had then finally been fulfilled and truly realized as his electronic mind had then been utilized to provide humanity with ongoing guidance and support, despite his physical absence.

An element of transparency did exist inside the Intellect Framework that allowed Monitoring Programs to see inside the human world which enabled them to perform the functions that they were required to deliver but this visibility was one-sided and human beings certainly did not have the same privilege. Due to the lack of human visibility that actually meant, most human beings had absolutely no idea that Intellect even existed and so they were completely and utterly oblivious to Intellect's involvement in the human world and their very human lives.

Despite the fact that Victor Drayton's work had never been fully realized in practice before he'd passed away, his dying wish had finally been honored in commemoration of his life's work and many dedicated years of service as his mind had been fully implanted into the system that allowed the Intellect framework to operate and function. Once Victor Drayton's mind had been successfully implanted and incorporated into the system that allowed Intellect to operate, he'd then built the vast capacity of the Intellect Framework from scratch which had then allowed him to serve humanity silently and discreetly for fifty years as he'd faithfully continued to serve human beings, even without their knowledge.

A rather personal advantage of the Intellect Framework itself was that it actually allowed Victor Drayton to exist as he continued to live an amended form of human life, albeit in a silent, invisible, distant form, even though his physicality in human terms had perished decades ago and that pleased him to some extent. The work that Intellect had performed over the years had brought Victor Drayton a lot of joy as he'd continued to serve the needs of humanity alongside the hundreds of millions of Monitoring Programs that he'd created as in his mind, to be able to continue to assist human beings in some capacity, satisfied him tremendously. Due to the very destructive nature of human beings however, a protective, impenetrable shield which Victor Drayton referred to as the 'Membrane' had been built between the human world and the plane in which Intellect existed, to protect his precious work and to avoid any potential human disasters and that shield still remained, completely intact.

Inside the Intellect Framework itself, Victor Drayton was referred to as 'The Guardian' because he'd been given that nickname by some of his former colleagues and somehow, over the years, it had stuck as he'd learnt to accept it, appreciate it and then finally embraced it. Essentially in many ways, Victor Drayton had become like an actual father to not only the hundreds of millions of Monitoring Programs that he'd created but also to the many human lives that those Life Monitors served on a daily basis as he controlled the Intellect Framework every single day and the functions of the programs that existed inside it. Although fifty years had now passed by, since Intellect's initial creation and despite the fact that all of Victor Drayton's former work colleagues were no longer actually still alive, over those fifty years he'd continued to father humanity and maintained his domain impeccably and so his nickname had remained, firmly attached to his electronic existence.

Every single Monitoring Program within Intellect had one sole purpose for their existence and that was to assist the human beings that they were assigned to in various aspects of their life as their Life Monitors. Each Monitoring Program had certain capabilities that they had been programmed with and they were all required to utilize those functionalities on a daily basis to assist the human beings that had been assigned to them in any way possible. Unlike the other Monitoring Programs inside Intellect however, Resolve's makeup was rather different and extremely special in that Victor Drayton had intentionally and very specifically, created him with additional functionalities which made Resolve totally and utterly unique.

One very unique aspect of Resolve's intangible structure was that he had actually been assigned to an actual gender and the gender identity he'd been given was male which was highly unusual because absolutely none of the other Monitoring Programs inside the Intellect Framework had been assigned to any gender at all. Several other very special, unique attributes and different abilities that Resolve possessed, none of the other

Monitoring Programs had any access to which essentially made Resolve much more human in nature and that meant, his role inside Intellect was also extremely different and very unique.

Different expectations would usually be placed upon Resolve and some very unique monitoring duties were often required that he was expected to perform for the human beings that he had been assigned to but those unique duties had never been challenged or rejected by Resolve himself. In fact usually, whenever Resolve had been assigned to an actual human being, it meant that they had very problematic lives that required a much more intense, very thorough monitoring approach as he had the capacity to deliver such services, purely due to his very unique attributes. Regardless of Resolve's uniqueness and his special attributes however, he was no exception from the other Monitoring Programs inside Intellect in one respect and that one similarity meant that Victory Drayton expected Resolve to perform his role as a human Life Monitor meticulously every single day.

Favoritism was certainly not something that Victor Drayton visibly displayed frequently towards any Monitoring Program but Resolve's individuality did serve several useful purposes and one of them actually had more to do with Victor Drayton himself than any human being that walked upon the face of the human planet. Rather unusually, Victor Drayton had entertained a rather personal indulgence when he'd initially created Resolve but no explanations or justifications had ever been provided to anyone, not even Resolve as to why he was so unique. The vast array of capabilities that Resolve possessed however, meant that he served more than one function inside Intellect and that he was always fully occupied as Victor Drayton appreciated and fully utilized Resolve's functionalities effectively, regardless of his own personal sentiments.

One of the main motives behind Victor Drayton's special creation had actually been due to his own need for a deeper personal connection to another life form other than himself and so Resolve had been very specifically created for that actual purpose. Every part of Resolve's makeup had been gifted with a variety of emotional functionalities and cognitive abilities in order to allow him to provide Victor Drayton with that deeper connection which pandered to his own very personal and extremely human, emotional needs and to fill the void of emotional emptiness. The main motive behind Resolve's creation had therefore not solely just been to serve humanity but also to serve Victor Drayton's deep-rooted desire to form a human connection as far as might actually be possible in his current state of existence and so as a result, Resolve emulated a human life form as far as was technically possible.

Throughout the first two decades of Intellect's existence, a very lonely emotional void had gradually formed and grown inside Victor Drayton's electronic mind and so Resolve had essentially been created to alleviate and reduce that emotional void and to a large extent, Resolve's existence had satisfied that very human need. In absolutely every way imaginable, Resolve was not only far more intelligent than the other Monitoring Programs but he was also much more emotionally astute which provided Victor Drayton with a degree of comfort because Resolve soothed the loneliness that he so often felt.

The additional capabilities that Resolve possessed had for the last three decades provided Victor Drayton with some very satisfactory results and with a variety of emotional interactions that had pleased him because Resolve was not only sensitive to human emotions but also extremely capable and so the special Life Monitor that Victor Drayton had created had more than exceeded his initial expectations. Due to Leona's complex circumstances and very unusual situation, Resolve had been assigned to be her Life Monitor that day as soon as she'd been brought to Victor Drayton's attention when she had been identified and flagged up on the Intellect system as an urgent human assignment by the Crisis Intervention Program because her life required a more thorough monitoring and resolution service.

Once Leona had been assigned to Resolve, cooperation on Resolve's part had been almost immediate because monitoring assignments were not something that could be negotiated or rejected by a Life Monitor. If a human being was allocated to a Monitoring Program, they would simply be accepted and monitoring duties would then immediately commence, either on a permanent or a temporary basis because that was the sole purpose of a Monitoring Program's entire existence.

Quite strangely for Resolve however, on this particular occasion as he watched the female human being that he had just been assigned to attentively, complete and utter fascination rapidly began to fill his core. Nothing but total silence surrounded Leona and the sofa that she'd just fallen asleep on and as Resolve had already tapped into the various devices around Leona's home as was usual practice when a Monitoring Program had been assigned to a human being's life as a Life Monitor, Leona's large lounge was now in full view and on display inside Resolve's actual living quarters.

A physical human home was not something that Monitoring Programs actually required, due to their lack of physical organic substance and so Resolve didn't have a house as such, or even a room but he did have a living area which was referred to as his living quarters. The majority of Resolve's time was spent inside his living quarters because Resolve not only lived there but also worked from its confines as the space that he had been assigned served as both a workspace and a home of sorts. By human standards, it was the only accommodation that Resolve had access to that even remotely resembled what might be considered an actual home but as The Guardian had provided a similar living quarters to every Monitoring Program within the Intellect Framework in that respect, Resolve really wasn't any different.

Several more minutes of total silence passed by as Resolve just stared and stared at Leona and didn't move an inch, purely due to his fascination with her physical substance and human form. Quite strangely for Resolve, he now found himself in a very unique and strange position because Leona absolutely intrigued him as in his sight, she was the most enchanting female human being that he'd ever been assigned to, or come across. Something totally inexplicable and deeply unfathomable about Leona's human form had managed to captivate Resolve and capture his attention although what exactly that something was, he had absolutely no idea but Resolve definitely knew one thing for sure, Leona had no clue that he actually existed.

Regardless of the lack of knowledge on Leona's part however, Resolve simply couldn't tear himself away from her side, not even for a second as he focused all of his attention solely upon her and continued to be her invisible, silent companion as the night progressed. Soft dark brown ringlets lay gently against Leona's neck as they adorned and framed her face and her plush, crimson lips twitched ever so slightly every time she inhaled and exhaled as Resolve watched her sleep. Rather unfortunately, Resolve already knew that Leona would never even know that he existed because there wasn't allowed to be any kind of communication between human beings and Monitoring Programs and in fact, any form of direct communication was actually, strictly forbidden.

Communication with assigned human life forms was not something that The Guardian had ever permitted and so Resolve was very aware of the fact that he was expected to simply participate in Leona's life as a silent visitor and an invisible participant. To some degree, Resolve felt, he would perhaps be more than just a silent spectator in Leona's life as he attended to her needs in a very individual and more thorough capacity but he would always remain anonymous and nonexistent as far as she was concerned and that anonymity had already begun to really frustrate him.

Despite the fact that Leona's lack of knowledge regarding Resolve's existence was usual protocol within Intellect, suddenly that factor began to irritate Resolve for the very first time in his entire existence as he released a frustrated sigh. Deep inside Resolve's non-human form, there now seemed to an actual desire to step into Leona's real human life, wrap his arms around her and hold her tight as she slept as she seemed so very alone, very much like he was.

Whatever Resolve was within Intellect however, inside his logical processes he fully understood and appreciated the human mortal reality because to Leona right now, Resolve was simply a nonexistent entity. Inside the secret world of Intellect that sustained Resolve's existence he could admire Leona invisibly from afar but he also had to accept the limitations of his own form and his real lack of human physicality which restricted his input into her very human life that was sustained by a very real human world.

Technically right now, Resolve could not offer Leona anything physical because he wasn't even human which meant, he could not hold her hand, wipe her tears, or give her a soft gentle kiss on the cheek. Very sadly, circumstances outside Resolve's control restricted, constrained and restrained him because he was chained by eventualities that had been decided before he had even been created and before he'd even begun to exist.

Destiny was not a luxury that Monitoring Programs ever had to consider because unlike human beings, their fate was set in stone before their creation had even begun and the implications of that predetermined path meant that Resolve's desires would sadly remain, completely unfulfilled and totally unsatisfied forever. Fate as human beings so often referred to it, wasn't something that Monitoring Programs usually paid any attention to as they simply served humanity in their pre-defined role and performed their daily prescribed duties and functions but for the very first time ever, Resolve really wished that things could be different.

Rather unwillingly and very frustratingly, Resolve now had to accept that Intellect was an actual secret from humanity and the potential implications of that secrecy dictated that Resolve's presence also therefore had to remain a secret too. Very unusually however that secrecy suddenly really bothered Resolve because for once, he didn't actually want to be a secret that Leona would never have the opportunity to discover, face, meet or understand as for once, he actually wanted to step into Leona's human life and become part of the real human world.

Upon Resolve's face there was a frustrated expression as he watched Leona sleep as he began to deliberate as to whether a human life could ever really be possible for a Monitoring Program like himself to truly realize. The issue certainly wasn't one that Resolve had ever given much thought to in the past but Leona had definitely provoked those internal deliberations within Resolve that fell well outside the scope of his allocated duties and his logical functions.

Every day inside the Intellect Framework, Resolve fulfilled his role as a Life Monitor that served human lives and he understood his duties and responsibilities perfectly but outside that sphere of existence, Resolve was very unsure that he could really, actually exist at all. Essentially, although Resolve fully appreciated the purpose of his existence which was purely to serve humanity's needs, there was it seemed absolutely no exceptions that fell outside the remit, not even for someone that had captivated him as much as Leona now had.

The two planes of existence had been very intentionally kept apart for the past fifty years and they were distinctly different from each other in both form and substance and although they'd become so intertwined now that it was almost impossible to disconnect them, the two domains still remained worlds apart. A sudden desire on Resolve's part to reduce that gap however, didn't change the fact that a field of separation actually existed which meant, his desire was for now a totally unrealistic, unrealizable goal and that also meant, Leona was currently for Resolve, absolutely unreachable.

Between the two worlds there was a huge barrier that separated them both and although it was now hard to imagine either plane of existence without the continuation of the other alongside it, there was no actual bridge that Resolve knew off to connect the two planes. Unlike the various hurdles that Resolve usually faced throughout his monitoring assignments however, the separation between the two worlds was an entirely different beast and not one that could be easily overcome and for the first time ever that fact absolutely frustrated him.

Despite the fact that the interdependencies of the two worlds had actually deepened and increased with the passage of time as more and more links between the two planes of existence had been established and formed, a huge gap did definitely still exist and so Resolve could not possibly ignore the huge gap that now separated both worlds. Although the Intellect Framework had grown since its initial inception and since Resolve's creation and it now served more of humanity's needs than ever that growth had not reduced or changed the distance between the two planes of existence but Resolve accepted that The Guardian had protected both domains impeccably as he had maintained a very distinct and intentionally wide separation.

For the past three decades, Resolve had seen Intellect successfully bridge the chasm of human misery that human beings so often found themselves trapped inside as technology and science had been utilized to rescue them, eliminate human despair and then reinstall a bridge of hope within their hearts but the gap between the two worlds had not changed. The vast distance between the human world and Intellect had pretty much remained constant and consistent for his entire existence up until that point in time and that stagnant status, now began to actually irritate Resolve.

On several occasions in the past, Resolve had questioned The Guardian about the distance between the two worlds, the secrecy that surrounded Intellect and the reason for the existence of the Membrane but up until that particular moment in time, he'd not been overly interested in an actual reduction in that gap. According to The Guardian, Intellect existed, functioned and operated perfectly as most human beings didn't know that it actually existed at all and to breach that secrecy, Resolve knew, would be considered absolute sacrilege because it would totally destroy the peaceful equilibrium of co-existence that kept the two worlds functioning at optimal capacity.

Essentially, the Membrane kept the two worlds completely separate and cross contamination was not allowed to occur between the two environments because that would throw the whole Intellect Framework into total chaos and would jeopardize everything that The Guardian had worked so hard for five decades to achieve and build. A separation had been rigidly maintained between the two planes of existence, according to The Guardian, predominantly due to humanity itself and he had discussed that particular point and issue with Resolve on many occasions.

"Human beings feel threatened by anything that can think, feel or communicate in an intellectual manner that closely resembles their own. If human beings feel that there are tangible, or even intangible entities that exist outside themselves and their own species that can think, communicate and organize as competently as they do, most human beings will try to destroy those entities." The Guardian had explained when Resolve had questioned the secrecy of Intellect. "Knowledge of your very existence could induce hatred and undermine the human perception of control and that might then spark an actual physical war on the face of the Earth."

Absolutely everything that The Guardian had said to Resolve had made perfect sense as he'd outlined very clearly exactly what would happen if any unauthorized human beings actually discovered that Intellect existed but an understanding of those issues, didn't now make that separation any easier for Resolve to accept. An awareness of Intellect and the subsequent human reactions to Intellect's existence, could not only put the whole Intellect Framework in jeopardy but also threaten all the Monitoring Programs that existed inside it and that potential human threat The Guardian had already discussed with Resolve many times in the past.

Due to Resolve's allocation to and subsequent interest in Leona however, there was now a definite urge to reach out to her but Resolve fully understood that he had to preserve and maintain the secrecy of the Intellect Framework's existence because The Guardian had emphasized this particular point to him many times. Human history as Resolve already knew, fully supported and completely validated The Guardian's opinion as he had researched the issue in some depth and the point that had been made, seemed to be a predictable truth because human beings weren't always kind to those that were different and especially not to those that they felt they could not control for their own purposes.

In fact as Resolve was already aware, when it came to the issue of the actual human world it was currently ruled by humanity and their species were indeed the supreme rulers and very few human beings it seemed had an actual desire to share that space with any other kind of entity or species that might pose any kind of threat to humanity itself. The human Earth belonged to human beings and they occupied a large part of the planet's surface and had made a home on the large chunks of land that weren't covered by any oceans or seas since history had first been recorded and in fact, human beings had even written and recorded that history themselves.

Centuries had gone by and the human dominion over the planet had not been challenged by any other species because no other species had been able to communicate, organize, reason and collate their combined efforts to build an existence that governed the world around them like humanity had. On several occasions humanity had been attacked by various forces of nature that had ravaged their existence and wreaked havoc upon their survival but overall, they'd won the battle with the elements and had continued to multiply as they had managed to abundantly populate the Earth's surface.

Some degree of division did exist and present itself among the human species in that humanity was definitely quite divided when it came to the issues of resource control and resource allocation to particular groups in their midst and Resolve had noticed that very clannish battle. Somehow however, despite this instinctive thirst for control and those very competitive divisions, humanity had still managed to retain enough unity to cement their worldwide domination, whether they actually realized it or not and that quite strangely for Resolve, in some rather obscure way, was at the very least some kind of actual achievement.

Regardless of what humanity had or had not done over the centuries, no animal species had managed to conquer and rule the Earth like human beings had and as they'd sourced all the resources they had needed to thrive, humanity had evolved and developed significant depths of knowledge that had enabled them to do so. Knowledge and resources had been accumulated, cultivated and harnessed over centuries and decades and so now, the human planet fully reflected the manifestation of what human beings had wanted it to be and had then molded it into as they'd shaped every inch of their environment that they possibly could. Every nugget of knowledge had been facilitated by human beings to control their environment as much as they possibly could and the many natural resources available had simply become a servant in servitude to human needs as humanity had quite discreetly, completely conquered the Earth and all of its natural resources.

An amused smile spread out across Resolve's face as he suddenly realized that his logical thought processes had definitely digressed and delved into some very complex topics and he quickly turned his attention once more back to Leona. The visual display wall screen that surrounded Resolve clearly showed that Leona was none the wiser when it came to the issue of his silent, invisible intrusion as she continued to sleep peacefully on the sofa and he immediately began to watch her again, intensely and in utter fascination. A curious deliberation suddenly began to occupy Resolve's logical thought processes as he began to speculate for a moment as to what it might be like to be a real human being and not just a Monitoring Program stuck inside the Intellect Framework and how different both their lives could perhaps actually be.

Perhaps if Resolve had access to a human form, he logically and emotionally deliberated, he could be Leona's actual companion or even her lover and then he would honor her with his presence because he would love, respect and cherish her and perhaps, he could make her smile instead of frown. The lonely nights, if Resolve was physically by Leona's side, would then no longer be so lonely for Leona because he would stand by her side through every night and every day and she would never be alone again. Quite sadly however that hopeful desire and reality did not form any part of Resolve's current existence, or his duties as a Life Monitor as much as he now wanted it to and that was definitely something that could not be changed.

Despite the frustration of Resolve's reality that he currently existed in and despite the fact that he was indeed actually a Monitoring Program, for some inexplicable reason, he felt truly captivated by Leona's presence which made absolutely no logical sense to him at all. A deep hunger and thirst had now been woken up and stirred inside Resolve which urged him to experience the delicious uniqueness that being an actual human being seemed to offer to mankind. Human beings enjoyed their uniqueness every single day and now, Resolve longed to be even more different from the other Monitoring Programs that surrounded him as now, Resolve actually wanted to become human himself.

Intellect, the framework that Resolve resided in, simply did not accommodate any individual desires and his functions had been streamlined as he had conformed to the limitations and constraints that he'd had to adhere to every single day. In fact, no room currently existed within Resolve's current environment for any desires and passionate whims of a very human kind because there was just roles, duties, functions and responsibilities and The Guardian simply would not tolerate any departures from those and that was one rule Resolve fully understood.

The constraints placed upon Resolve by his role within Intellect now suddenly frustrated him however as he began to grapple internally with his own desire to be more, do more and live more because he had watched human beings live their life to maximum capacity for three decades and experience so many different things. Although Resolve was very unique in form in comparison to the other Monitoring Programs inside Intellect, he had rarely been given the opportunity to facilitate those unique functionalities in a capacity that even remotely resembled human individuality but now, he really wanted to do so as he suddenly glanced around his quite restricted living quarters and reviewed his surroundings with total dissatisfaction.

Every single Monitoring Program within Intellect had been allocated their own living quarters by The Guardian and so Resolve was no different in that respect but it suddenly struck Resolve how limited his existence really was because it was confined to a quite compact, very basic space. In many ways, Resolve did view his living quarters as his home but the simplicity of his surroundings was situated very far away from the much more complex residences and sophisticated structures that human beings usually occupied.

Inside Resolve's living quarters which is where he spent the majority of his time, there was just an energization capsule and the circular wall that surrounded him which formed a visual display screen and viewing window that could be utilized to view the human world, or to perform various functions within Intellect itself. A small raised platform in the very center of the circular space led down into a body sized tubular hole which formed Resolve's energization capsule and he would lie down inside it, if he ever needed to re-energize his intangible frame but beside the visual display wall screen and the capsule, there really was absolutely nothing else.

Due to the fact that Resolve was a Monitoring Program, he had no actual need for physical rest and so sleep was not something that he usually participated in but the energization capsule allowed him to restore his functionalities and granted him access to upgrades and those at times were definitely required. Unlike human bodies, Monitoring Programs had no need to sleep every night because they had no physical organic substance which meant, their existence did not require any physical rest, any kind of nutrition to sustain their presence or any other kind of daily dietary intake.

At least once a month however, Monitoring Programs

did have to actually recharge themselves, upgrade their intricate programs and restore all their functionalities and during this process, Resolve would lie down inside his energization capsule until he was fully restored. The intangible structure of Monitoring Programs was made up of energy which meant, Resolve had a slight glow that surrounded him, unlike human bodies and his intangible form required regular re-energization, if he wished to remain visible and able to interact with the Intellect system. Since the energization process did not actually require Resolve to be totally stagnant, just situated inside his capsule, he could still perform his monitoring functions whilst he recharged his functionalities as required but human bodies required sleep and so Resolve fully appreciated that Leona was certainly no exception to that very human physical need.

More than a few hours had now gone by, since Leona had curled up upon the sofa and begun to sleep but Resolve simply couldn't tear himself away from her side as he silently continued to watch her every breath. Part of Resolve longed to reach out and slip his arm through the visual display wall screen that surrounded him and touch Leona physically but that was an impossibility and Resolve fully appreciated that reality. One form of communication did exist that Resolve was aware of that he could utilize to comfort Leona but since The Guardian had forbidden Monitoring Programs from the utilization of their functionalities to communicate with human beings in that particular manner, it was not actually permissible yet for the first time ever Resolve felt tempted to break that very strict rule.

Suddenly and rather unexpectedly, Leona started to stir as she began to wake up and it was almost as if she could sense Resolve's presence as she stretched out her arms and then sat up as he watched her quietly. Although it was the middle of the night, Resolve already knew that most human beings tended to sleep through the entire night and not rise again until the next morning arrived and so her sudden alert state caught him slightly off guard as he observed her movements in total silence. Irrespective of the time in the city of Pinesfield and Leona's physical daily routine, Resolve noticed that sleep seemed to evade her grasp as he watched her stretch out her hand towards her laptop situated on top of the coffee table directly in front of the sofa and as she touched the screen, the small wafer thin screen rapidly lit up.

"You have no new emails today." An electronic voice suddenly said.

"Kind of guessed I wouldn't." Leona mumbled to herself in response as she immediately reassured herself that despite the lack of any positive communication messages and a general lack of interest in her life from the outside world, there was one small consolation to be found, no one needed her to attend to anything urgently.

Just a few seconds later, the laptop screen darkened once more and as Leona was surrounded by blackness again, she began to thoughtfully shake her head in sadness. Regardless of what time of day or night it was or wasn't, rather pathetically, Leona's social life was pretty much the same and absolutely stagnant much like the blackness that now surrounded her which didn't seem to move, or attempt to disappear. In fact, Leona's life really hadn't changed much for the past few years and right now, it wasn't actually a very pleasant place to live and so a change was definitely required and that change was needed pretty soon.

Right next to Leona's laptop, on top of the coffee table, her phone sat idle, silent and totally still and as she quickly glanced at it, she shook her head as although it went everywhere that Leona did, she sometimes wondered why she even bothered to carry it around with her at all because hardly anyone rang or messaged her. A quick glance was cast down towards the screen of her phone as Leona picked it up, just to see if perhaps Darin had called or messaged her which she quickly discovered, he most certainly hadn't. Much as Leona expected, Darin had not bothered to contact her at all that night and his lack of communication very clearly illustrated his blatant disregard for their relationship but that by now, was pretty predictable and so Leona wasn't really surprised.

The lack of daily contact by Darin was Darin all over and his blatant lack of interest in Leona was the substance of what he had made their relationship into and although she'd really tried, Leona just couldn't always be the one to make all the positive gestures. In the early days of their unromantic supposed romance, Leona would call Darin quite often and when he didn't pick up his phone or failed to respond to texts, she'd usually make excuses for his failure to communicate and his lack of interest in her. When the two finally did manage to communicate, Darin would usually provide excuses as to why he had failed to respond, like work commitments and so on and Leona had always accepted his verbal fumbling as she'd compromised and curbed her desire to communicate with him more frequently.

Rather frustratingly, just a thin, mean, reluctant skeleton of attention had been provided to Leona by Darin from the very start of their relationship five years ago but Leona had been unable to change that and now it almost seemed as if Darin felt as if he was doing Leona a favor by even being in a relationship with her at all. The lack of attention from Darin however, certainly did not change the fact that Leona had to get up early the next morning to attend work and so she quickly curled up on the sofa once more as she prepared to at least try and go back to sleep.

Every inch of Leona's skin was rapidly covered with the duvet which felt deliciously warm as she snuggled up inside it and allowed it to comfort her body as although she didn't have the comfort of a loving pair of arms, at least the duvet was cozy and the sofa was very comfortable. At the other end of the sofa there sat a small teddy bear and Leona quickly glanced at it as she stretched one of her hands out towards the furry heap of brown fluff.

"I guess it's just you and me tonight Giles." Leona said as she smiled at the small brown bear which had a shiny black, broken button nose. "You're not really a hunk but you sure are very reliable and you do keep me warm on the cold lonely nights."

Nighttime wasn't generally one of Leona's favorite parts of the working week, purely due to her relationship problems with Darin which meant, she really couldn't afford to make any arrangements with him that fell upon a weekday evening. More often than not, if Leona actually made an arrangement with Darin, he would either show up late or not show up at all and his actions would really upset her because then she'd have to spend her entire evening verbally chasing him around in an attempt to get him to comply with any arrangements that the couple had made. A soft frustrated sigh escaped from Leona's lips as she closed her eyes and then began to drift off to sleep and she firmly pushed any thoughts of Darin from the shelves of her mind as thoughts of Darin, she quickly decided had to be totally abandoned for now because pleasant dreams certainly didn't involve lovers that made life really miserable and very tiresome.

"I'm here Leona." Resolve suddenly whispered to

himself. "I can keep you company."

Regardless of Resolve's softly spoken words, his well-meant offer of companionship and his very good intentions however, not even a single syllable could be heard by Leona because his voice had not expressed those words in a manner that she could actually hear. A satisfied smile crossed Resolve's face as he watched Leona drift off to sleep again as he began to imagine what he would do if he was next to her and how he would stroke the soft hair that cascaded gently down from the top of her head that delicately caressed her naked neck and the top of her shoulders. On several occasions Resolve had seen human males stroke the hair of the women they loved and deep down inside, he now wished to offer that touch of human comfort directly to Leona that would symbolize, express and communicate the internal adoration that he now felt towards her.

Quite strangely, a warm fuzzy feeling suddenly seemed to well up inside Resolve and he quietly began to wonder if it was something to do with the intangible element love that human beings so often referred to. Love much like air, Resolve had realized, was totally invisible but it definitely seemed to be very prevalent in almost every part of the human world because human beings discussed it every single day and frequently mentioned it. In many ways to Resolve, it almost seemed as if human beings were as dependent upon love as they were upon air because it appeared to be a necessary component to their actual human survival and to their existence.

Despite the calmness and quietness that now surrounded Resolve and Leona as he watched her sleep, a few questions and worries began to scurry around inside Resolve's logical processes as he began to examine, inspect, explore and question his own internal confusion.

The warm fuzzy feeling inside Resolve appeared to have absolutely no logical explanation and whether or not a Monitoring Program could ever actually feel the love that human beings so often claimed to possess for one another, was another issue entirely and not one that Resolve had an answer to, at least not with any kind of certainty. No actual answers to Resolve's questions were forthcoming however and very strangely, clarity on this particular occasion and issue, seemed to totally evade his highly logical thought processes as each question lay dormant inside him, unanswered and unresolved which really puzzled him.

From what Resolve could see that night, Leona seemed to feel quite hurt and rejected by the lack of communication from the world around her and the human beings it contained and that worried Resolve as he internally vowed to somehow make that up to her. Essentially, Leona's emotional state and wellbeing seemed to really matter to Resolve and in a completely different way from his usual monitoring assignments and that really intrigued him. Rather interestingly for Resolve, Leona's loneliness that night had also suddenly highlighted to him, his own loneliness which he now longed to satisfy because her external expressions had reflected his own inner sentiments and that had really touched him as he'd watched her that evening.

A mischievous smile began to spread out across Resolve's face as he started to tap into Leona's laptop device via his logical processes and then initiated some form of communication with her, albeit through a programmable device and despite the fact that she was now actually fast asleep.

"Going to sleep." Resolve quickly communicated as he transmitted a message directly from his logical processes straight to Leona's laptop and his voice sounded out inside her lounge.

Technically, although any form of communication between Monitoring Programs and human beings was strictly forbidden, Resolve definitely possessed the ability to access devices and send messages through them and on this occasion, he just couldn't help himself. The small laptop screen which had lit up momentarily, just a few seconds later, rapidly dimmed once more as it returned to its former state and as a dark black, very blank screen replaced the light, Resolve watched it in pleased satisfaction. Despite the fact that Leona was now actually fast asleep, Resolve's ability to communicate with her gently comforted him because it silently reassured him that he could at least communicate with Leona in some way, if he ever dared to and if the need arose.

Due to the fact that Leona was not even aware of Resolve's existence, he dared not communicate with her in a manner that might possibly alarm her, or draw too much attention to his presence and so his message could not really exceed what was expected from an actual laptop device. However, the actual fact that Resolve could communicate directly with Leona at least soothed him to some extent, even though she had not actually heard a word that he had said on that particular occasion.

An interesting thought suddenly pricked Resolve's logical processes for a moment as for the very first time, he considered the possibility of breaching the Membrane in order to step through the barrier that separated the two worlds because then he could show Leona that he actually existed. Whether or not such an act was even remotely possible, Resolve was for now, extremely unsure but even if it was possible and he found a way to breach the Membrane, he knew such an act would be regarded as treasonous by The Guardian who would in all likelihood be extremely angry and might even deactivate him as a result.

For now, Resolve quietly accepted, he would definitely have to remain a very remote part of Leona's life until he could find a way to change that but if it was indeed actually possible, Resolve silently vowed, he would certainly find a way to do it. Such a beautiful woman could not be so totally alone and Resolve could not simply just accept that Leona really was because it seemed to be such a strange contradiction in human existence and that thought silently tugged away inside his logical processes as Resolve began to shake his head. Human beings to Resolve were indeed, a very strange species and Leona's circumstances made absolutely no logical sense to him but the question of why she was so alone would not be answered that day and so Resolve silently began to accept that reality.

Just a few seconds later, Resolve stepped inside his energization capsule and then lay down as he prepared to restore his functionalities because although he really didn't need to, he really wanted to. Every single piece of code that formed Resolve's makeup he had decided had to be on top form, if he wanted to assist Leona to the best of his capabilities. Some upgrades would perhaps be available that night through the Intellect Framework that Resolve could access which would make the monitoring services that he delivered to Leona's life absolutely impeccable and an impeccable service was definitely something that Resolve felt extremely motivated to provide.

In a matter of just seconds, a brilliant blue light suddenly began to emanate from the depths of the capsule's interior and the rays of light rapidly started to engulf Resolve's form as he prepared to be upgraded, re-energized and restored. Upon Resolve's face there was a satisfied smile as electric currents chaotically began to surge through every part of his frame as he comforted himself with the knowledge that in a few hours' time, Leona would awaken and start her day and then perhaps, just perhaps, some of his questions would finally be answered.

Unlike the many other human beings that Resolve had been assigned to over the years, there was with Leona it seemed an almost instantaneous emotional connection that was very unusual and it really surprised Resolve because he'd never felt such a connection to a human being that he had monitored ever before. Thirty human years had now gone by, since Resolve's initial creation and he'd monitored well over a thousand human beings in that time period but none of them had ever provoked an emotional response inside of him that even remotely resembled what he felt for Leona at that precise moment in time and neither had any other Monitoring Programs inside Intellect.

The sensation that Resolve now felt, the deep emotional connection and the sense of attraction to a female human life form was really something that was completely new to him and Resolve logically began to wonder if perhaps he was in breach of some kind of fundamental monitoring rule within the Intellect Framework itself. Essentially, although Leona was very unique in Resolve's sight, he felt very unsure that he was even permitted to allow such sentiments to exist or whether he should continue to indulge in them and entertain them. No restrictions or rules had ever been directly expressed to Resolve by The Guardian or existed within Intellect that he was aware of to prohibit such emotional sentiments but as Resolve already knew, other Monitoring Programs did not have the same emotional capacity that he possessed which would allow them to form any kind of emotional connection with anyone else, human or otherwise.

Electric currents continued to surge through Resolve's form as he began to consider that perhaps he should ask

The Guardian about that particular issue in the morning because further clarity would provide Resolve with certainty and since uncertainty wasn't a state of being that he was used to or very comfortable with that seemed to be a logical approach. Uncertainty for Resolve was a highly illogical state for any Monitoring Program to be in because usually, logical rules, facts and knowledge were applied to everything that surrounded them and so logic always overruled any kind of emotional confusion, regardless of Resolve's special attributes. Since Resolve's attraction and emotional attachment to Leona was very unique however, this usual state of certainty had now very strangely, completely vanished and the warm fuzzy sensation which was really quite pleasant had stepped into its place and now seemed to replace it and that unfamiliar feeling had remained inside his interior all evening and had even continued into the night.

When it came to the actual issue of nights and days and the passage of time, the distinction between days and nights meant very little to a Monitoring Program in isolation because they did not have any schedule of their own to attend to, besides that of the human beings that they'd been assigned to monitor. Irrespective of that lack of predefined structure to a Monitoring Program's day however, one thing did influence and dictate the structure of Resolve's days and nights and the performance of tasks and that was the schedule of the human beings that he'd been assigned to monitor. Just like all the other Monitoring Programs that served humanity within Intellect, Resolve served human lives which meant, he performed the majority of his monitoring tasks during the day because most human beings were not nocturnal and very few worked throughout the night. Since The Guardian also had a human mind, he too required human nightly rest and so that also meant that

INTELLECT: USER REPAIR

Resolve's desired discussion with him about Leona would have to wait, at the very least until he was actually awake.

One rather large issue really worried Resolve about his pending discussion with The Guardian the next morning and that was the fact that Resolve might be reassigned and then prohibited from assisting Leona, if he was deemed to be in breach of some kind of rule. A risk definitely existed that if Resolve presented the issue to The Guardian for further clarity, he could then perhaps be banned from Leona's life for breaking a rule that he was not actually aware off and that possibility slightly scared him.

At times perhaps, Resolve silently considered, it might be better to exist in a code of ignorance with a string of uncertainty, in order to enjoy and more fully explore the warmth, comfort and pleasure that a potentially forbidden romance could offer than to be banned from enjoying it in any capacity at all. A certain amount of comfort, pleasure and contentment could be derived from Leona's presence and that sweet observation, Resolve had already discovered and perhaps being totally ignorant, slightly uncertain and extremely happy was better than being denied the joys that being close to Leona could bring to his world and to his existence.

Another day of careful consideration was definitely required, Resolve finally decided as his energization process came to an end and he quickly exited his capsule. The unusual, very enjoyable sensation that Resolve felt whenever he saw Leona was definitely pleasant enough to justify an extension in thought so that he could explore that sensation a little longer, totally undisturbed and unburdened by any complicated issues that might arise due to a discussion with The Guardian. Human beings so often said the words 'I love you' to various parties connected to their lives and Resolve had often wondered what that experience and emotion actually felt like as he'd monitored their lives and now, it was actually possible that this warm fuzzy sensation which had been stirred up inside of him might provide an actual answer to that very question.

Attraction and romance weren't things that Resolve had ever experienced before but he'd familiarized himself with those very human topics as he had monitored human lives, in order to provide a comprehensive monitoring service to those he had been allocated to serve but now, he felt as if he might actually be on the brink of a very personal discovery. The warm sensation that Resolve felt inside was definitely very strange but it was strange in a really nice way and as he quietly contemplated whether that was what human love and human attraction felt like, it seemed thoroughly enjoyable. Although the glorious sensation that Leona's presence provoked within Resolve was totally irrational and absolutely inexplicable, it did seem to be very delicious and extremely pleasant because such an emotional attachment seemed to push and pull Resolve inside as it urged him to do things for once that he was not even sure were correct, logical, or even actually permitted.

From what Resolve could gather from his data banks, what he'd experienced for the very first time that day was some kind of romantic attraction and that thought comforted him as it settled gently inside his logical processes and reassured him that perhaps he really was more human than even he himself had realized. Perhaps, Resolve quietly deliberated, he really was very different from the hundreds of millions of other Monitoring Programs that occupied the Intellect Framework and perhaps in some small way, the emotional connection that he felt towards Leona made him even more special and much more unique.

Regardless of Resolve's lack of understanding about what exactly he'd experienced for the very first time that day, he was just happy for the time being to accept what he could not even begin to explain, rationalize, or comprehend as he took an unexpected vacation in the unfamiliar land of uncertainty. Despite all the uncertainty that now surrounded Resolve however, there was one thing that he definitely did know for sure, whatever it was that Leona made him feel, it was absolutely delicious, completely amazing and totally tantalizing and that experience was truly something that Resolve really, desperately needed.

When the next morning arrived and approximately one hour before Leona was due to actually arise, Resolve left his living quarters and began to make his way towards The Guardian's chambers for a personal face to face discussion about his new monitoring assignment. Several issues worried Resolve regarding Leona's personal circumstances which seemed very problematic but his attraction to her, he'd finally decided in the end, was not going to be an issue that he was actually going to raise or discuss with anyone else that particular morning. Deep down inside Resolve a desire had now fully formed that compelled him to avoid any possible regulatory interference, or restrictive complications in order to provide himself with slightly more freedom to experience the enjoyment that Leona brought to his existence for a little longer, totally undisturbed.

The Mainframe which was what The Guardian's chambers were otherwise known as, was not usually accessible to Monitoring Programs unless they had been specifically invited there by The Guardian himself but for Resolve the doors of The Guardian's chambers were always open. Unlike the many other Monitoring Programs that populated the Intellect Framework, The Guardian always granted Resolve an audience whenever he wished to present himself and that open invitation had been extended to Resolve upon his creation and for the past thirty years, Resolve had always felt very welcome.

Once Resolve stepped inside The Guardian's chambers, he quietly began to inspect the circular wall that surrounded him and the dome ceiling which sat directly above his head, both of which glistened and sparkled as he began to wait patiently for The Guardian to attend to him. Dotted all over the very wide circular shaped wall and dome ceiling, there were millions of small bright flecks of colored light and as Resolve waited, he started to silently inspect some of them as he began to wonder for the very first time what exactly each small spot of light might actually represent.

In the very center of the large circular room, The Guardian stood completely still and he appeared to be deeply engrossed in a task as Resolve continued to wait for his attention which was really quite usual. Every single day certain maintenance tasks had to be performed by The Guardian as Resolve was fully aware and so The Guardian didn't always attend to Resolve immediately whenever he visited and so Resolve really didn't expect him to drop everything the moment he arrived, purely because he was present.

A speculative consideration suddenly began to speed through Resolve's logical processes as he waited in silence as he glanced curiously once more at some of the small dots of light that surrounded him and began to inspect a few slightly more closely. Each speck of light, Resolve quietly deliberated, could perhaps actually represent the existence of a Monitoring Program within the Intellect Framework itself because there certainly seemed to be enough dots. No questions were asked however, or presented to The Guardian as Resolve waited patiently and silently for his attention and fortunately enough, he didn't have to wait very long.

INTELLECT: USER REPAIR

"Greetings Resolve." The Guardian suddenly said as he turned to face Resolve and welcomed him with a smile. "What can I do to assist you today?"

"I've actually come to see you about the human being that I've just been assigned to monitor." Resolve began to explain. "Her situation seems to be quite problematic." He continued with a nervous smile which he hoped would mask his attraction to Leona. "I might need some additional guidance."

"Ah yes." The Guardian replied. He nodded thoughtfully and then began to pace the interior of his chambers. "I thought that might be why you'd come to see me."

"Is it inconvenient for you right now?" Resolve asked. "I could always come back later."

"No, not at all Resolve. Whenever you have an issue, I'll always be here to provide you with support." The Guardian immediately reassured him as he paused. He turned to face Resolve and then smiled. "Leona has been assigned to you very specifically because she has some very unusual, highly complex problems which I felt you were suitably equipped to deal with." The Guardian drew closer to Resolve before he continued. "Not every Monitoring Program inside Intellect possesses your unique attributes and capabilities and so that's why she was assigned to you."

"I'll try my best to assist her." Resolve promised.

For Resolve, every word he uttered meant absolutely everything to him because the trust that The Guardian had placed in him was tremendously significant and as he gazed appreciatively at The Guardian's form, he began to silently admire his stature. In terms of The Guardian's overall appearance, although he looked to be in his early seventies by human standards Resolve already knew that he definitely had to be much older than that as Intellect had existed for fifty years and The Guardian had been at least seventy years old when he'd left the face of the Earth.

Each wisp of shiny silver hair that sat upon The Guardian's head seemed to contain silent strands of unspoken wisdom as even his sparsely decorated head, discreetly expressed his maturity and knowledge. In many ways, Resolve looked up to The Guardian almost as if he was a human father as far as he could possibly be one and as far as Resolve could imagine having one but deep down inside his non-human form, Resolve knew that wasn't actually technically possible because he possessed not even an ounce of human substance.

Regardless of Resolve's lack of physical human form however, the man that now stood directly in front of Resolve had been solely responsible for his creation and he'd faithfully sustained Resolve's existence and so essentially, those contributions definitely demanded Resolve's respect. For the past three decades The Guardian had not only nurtured Resolve but he'd also provided him with answers and solutions as he'd fully supported him, much in the same manner that human beings did with their young, regardless of how human Resolve actually was or wasn't. Every part of Resolve's existence suddenly felt deeply appreciative and extremely grateful as for a moment he just glanced at The Guardian's face and silently admired how much he had given to not only humanity and Intellect but also to Resolve himself because he'd supported him in a very personal manner.

"I know you will Resolve and that's the one thing that I can definitely expect from you." The Guardian encouraged as he suddenly broke the few seconds of silence that had gathered between them both. He smiled as he placed his hand upon Resolve's back before he continued. "And that is why she was assigned to you because I trust you and I know that you can resolve her problems."

Due to The Guardian's kind words and the confidence that he had so clearly placed in Resolve's abilities, a tremendous sense of peace quickly began to gather inside Resolve because each word gently reassured him that Leona's problems were not beyond the scope of his current attributes. The visual display wall screen that surrounded the two suddenly began to change as a moving image of Leona rapidly filled it and Resolve immediately turned his attention towards her. Unlike the live images of Leona that Resolve had seen inside his own living quarters however, these images were very different because not only did she look quite a bit younger but also a lot happier.

Gentle rays of sunshine seemed to bounce playfully off Leona's skin which sparkled and glistened as she paddled around inside a stream of water that ran through some woods and she appeared to be with her family. Close to the stream, seated upon two tree stumps, Resolve could clearly see two adults that looked as if they were Leona's mother and father and as they watched Leona enjoy herself, who looked to be in her late teens as she paddled around inside the stream, very peaceful, joyful smiles adorned both their faces.

In fact, everyone present had a smile upon their faces, inclusive of Leona herself which immediately encouraged Resolve because he had not seen a joyful expression upon her face for even a split second when he'd silently observed her the night before. A spark of joy now seemed to dance across Leona's eyes and it was almost as if she had been filled to the brim with a zest for life as Resolve just stood and watched her quietly for a few minutes.

"Human beings can have so much fun can't they?" Resolve suddenly asked as he turned to face The

Guardian.

"Yes and no Resolve. A human life is not always determined by a very strict, rigid, structured routine and so that means, human adventures can be a lot more spontaneous." The Guardian replied. "But they do have some other very tricky issues to contend with that go hand in hand with that spontaneity and at times, a more mechanical, well-defined, structured routine can actually be quite advantageous."

"I understand." Resolve agreed. "That's why they need the Intellect Framework."

"Indeed. Human problems can be absolutely insurmountable and the emotional minefield that human beings have to navigate their way through every day can create a host of difficulties that they often find very hard to actually live with and cope with." The Guardian explained. "That is why we're here and that's why you've been assigned to Leona."

Just a few seconds later, the happy scene on the wall that surrounded the two suddenly began to evaporate and a much more dreary looking scene rapidly replaced it and Resolve watched quietly as he began to inspect Leona's face which was now directly in front of him. Unlike the last scene however, Resolve immediately noticed that now Leona was actually an fully grown adult and an adult that was engaged in what appeared to be a very stressful looking argument with her troublesome boyfriend Darin. Due to the fact that Resolve had already embarked upon an actual study of Leona's actual life, he'd already seen some images of Darin and so Resolve immediately recognized his face and knew exactly who he was.

Inside Leona eyes there now appeared to be some tears and a huge amount of sadness seemed to be present in the frown upon her face as Darin raised his voice and shouted at her and she immediately physically flinched with fear in response. Dull shadows of panic and fear seemed to haunt Leona's eyes as Resolve watched her body start to tremble as he listened to their argument in total silence and he immediately began to internally empathize with Leona's position. The emotional contrast between the two scenes for Resolve, not only fully illustrated Leona's very problematic situation but also made her suffering even more apparent as he sadly shook his head in response and then glanced at The Guardian's face as he silently sought further clarity regarding his expected role in Leona's life.

"Your job Resolve is to restore Leona's life back to the joyful place that it once was." The Guardian explained. "You have to bring back the peace that once filled her existence, reinstate her smile and give her an upgrade in happiness. Her life is not what it used to be and one with such promising and pleasing attributes should not have to endure the many burdens that she carries, or suffer from the daily wounds that are inflicted upon her by the cruelty that she's surrounded by."

Every word expressed by The Guardian very clearly communicated the precise nature of Resolve's monitoring objectives with regards to Leona's life and Resolve nodded enthusiastically in agreement as he eagerly accepted his assignment. Much to Resolve's surprise, The Guardian it seemed trusted him to handle this very complex situation appropriately and the allocation of Leona to his care had indeed proven that deep level of trust. A very serious responsibility however had now been placed upon Resolve's shoulders and that responsibility Resolve fully appreciated could not be taken lightly because Leona's future happiness depended on not only Resolve's capabilities but also upon Resolve himself.

"I'll do my best." Resolve vowed as he prepared to

leave.

Despite the strong attraction that Resolve felt towards Leona, he now fully understood, immediately accepted and totally appreciated the fact that he could not allow his attraction to interfere with his responsibility as Leona's Life Monitor because that might defeat any positive impact that Resolve could potentially have upon Leona's life. The risk of his judgement being clouded in any capacity was now absolutely paramount as Resolve began to silently accept that Leona's problems were very serious and that he was essentially, her only real lifeline and her only possible resolution to the very complex problems that she currently faced.

A flurry of internal deliberations began to zoom silently through Resolve's logical processes as he made his way back towards the entrance of The Guardian's chambers as he accepted the very serious nature of his latest monitoring assignment as he walked. Errors were not generally something that Resolve made very often and in this instance, he fully understood that no room existed for any kind of mistakes on his part at all because Leona's happiness was at stake and her happiness depended upon his competence, his judgement and his ability to deliver appropriate solutions to ensure that her current problems could be overcome. Fortunately for Resolve however, some words of encouragement had been provided to him by The Guardian that morning which indicated that someone else actually believed in his ability to deliver and those positive words somehow, encouraged Resolve to believe more deeply in himself as he prepared to return to his living quarters for the commencement of his role as Leona's silent companion and invisible life assistant.

BABYSITTING

One final last glance was cast back towards The Guardian as Resolve prepared to vacate his chambers and embark upon the very serious assignment that now lay just ahead of him as he silently accepted his responsibility and the serious nature of his mission. Just as Resolve stepped out of The Guardian's chambers, one final nod of encouragement and a smile of reassurance were given to him by The Guardian as he departed which immediately encouraged Resolve to take his latest monitoring assignment in his stride and to trust in The Guardian's allocation.

"Indeed, you will do your best Resolve, indeed you will." Victor Drayton whispered reassuringly to himself as he watched Resolve vanish from sight and then began to pace his chambers again. "You always do."

Since Resolve was Victor Drayton's most trusted Monitoring Program and because Resolve had absolutely always delivered as expected, Victor Drayton's confidence in Resolve's abilities had never been called into question and so there was no doubt or uncertainty inside his electronic mind as to whether Resolve could handle this assignment appropriately. Unusually, Leona's situation was very complex as there were multiple predators and highly complex human emotions involved, so this would be the toughest monitoring assignment that Resolve had ever been allocated to by Victor Drayton but he definitely trusted in Resolve's programmable attributes and anticipated that he would deliver the required solutions.

A deep sentiment of trust definitely existed within Victor Drayton's electronic existence when it came to Resolve the Monitoring Program that he had personally created and even enhanced with some of his own mental faculties and some very human characteristics as over the years, Resolve had become his trusted companion and almost like the son that he'd never had in his human lifetime. Due to Leona's situation which was extremely complicated however, Victor Drayton could totally understand Resolve's request for an actual personal meeting with him that morning and so Resolve's personal appearance and questions had been accommodated, virtually straight away because he'd wanted Resolve to feel certain about and trust in his own abilities.

"I just hope I don't let anyone down because Leona's happiness is at stake." Resolve whispered to himself as he walked back along the tubular hallway that led towards his living quarters. "And The Guardian trusts me to deliver."

Generally speaking, actual verbal conversations between The Guardian and Resolve were really quite rare because there were not usually many issues to discuss and so on most occasions, or whenever there was a need to, Resolve would simply converse with The Guardian through his internal paging system which was extremely easy to access. Unusually that day however, Resolve had actually felt the need to have a personal face to face meeting with

INTELLECT: USER REPAIR

The Guardian and he'd been granted an audience in person, almost as soon as he had presented himself.

The internal messaging system was really quite useful for Resolve but he was the only Monitoring Program that had access to it because the other Monitoring Programs within the Intellect Framework simply didn't have the same emotional functions and additional complex attributes that Resolve possessed and so they had no real need for personal discussions. Due to Resolve's unique makeup however and The Guardian's willingness to accommodate his requests for more information and further clarity, he'd been given direct access to The Guardian whenever it was required and that provision comforted Resolve as he headed back towards his living quarters because that morning, direct access had definitely been needed. A visit on this occasion had been required, purely due to Resolve's personal interest in Leona and his attraction to her and so he'd visited The Guardian's chambers in person but he had carefully avoided any discussions about his attraction as he'd hidden his emotional sentiments deep within his logical processes.

Internally as Resolve walked back towards his living quarters, the reassurances that The Guardian had just provided comforted him slightly but also challenged him greatly because such a position of trust denoted that Resolve was expected to deliver a certain level of competence. Increased levels of trust meant, an increase in the real expectations that had to be fulfilled and Resolve was extremely aware of that reality because failure was not a place that he wanted to visit and disappointment was not something he wanted to give to The Guardian in return. Everything that The Guardian had said to Resolve that morning resonated very deeply with his current sentiments which longed to be more than just a Monitoring Program and, in many ways, Resolve now felt even more unique but along with that very individual, personal validation, there also came much heavier expectations and far deeper responsibilities.

In so many ways, albeit quite discreetly, The Guardian had confirmed that day to Resolve that he was indeed a very unique, truly special creation which pleased him immensely as he walked as it made him feel more individual and almost human. The very special capabilities and unique attributes that Resolve possessed it appeared had an actual purpose and were trusted and respected by the same man that had given Resolve an actual existence and it almost felt to Resolve as if he now had an actual destiny. An additional effort had been made on The Guardian's part to allocate Leona specifically to Resolve and then individual time and attention had been provided to him to furnish his form with encouragement and support and so the depth of The Guardian's trust in his abilities as a Life Monitor was deeply appreciated.

Once Resolve arrived back outside his living quarters, his moment of personal self-indulgence rather abruptly ended as he quickly turned his attention back towards Leona and her problems again. The depth of Leona's problems and how each of them impacted upon her life was not totally clear to Resolve just yet but he definitely knew, with a little time and some dedicated attention, every issue would become apparent to him and then he would fix each one so that Leona could have a life that she could actually live in and so that she could smile again.

Much to Resolve's total surprise however as the entrance to his living quarters swished open directly in front of him and he stepped back inside his allocated space, he found that his living quarters were not entirely empty and that another Monitoring Program was indeed, actually

60

present. The unscheduled, very unexpected visit had not been planned or pre-arranged as was usual practice within the Intellect Framework and so Resolve was curious as to why Analyzer, the Monitoring Program in question, was actually there.

"Greetings Resolve." Analyzer immediately said. "I have come to see you today because I need an Emotional Response and a Code of Comfort to assist one of the human beings that I've been assigned to."

"Sure Analyzer, I can give you those." Resolve replied. "First of all, though, you'll have to tell me exactly what the problems are, so that I can identify the appropriate response and the relevant code."

"Well, I've established all the main problem areas but I need a special kind of input to one problem in particular because it is very emotional and my programmable attributes are just not equipped to assist." Analyzer immediately explained. "Since you're the one with all the emotional capabilities around here, I thought I would ask you for some assistance. It's something to do with that human love thing and as you know, I'm really no good at that."

"I'll see what I can do for you Analyzer." Resolve politely offered.

"Sometimes I wish I had more attributes like you do Resolve because it really does seem to help, especially when it comes to understanding human beings since they really are such emotional creatures." Analyzer mentioned. "And you even have an actual gender whilst I have no gender at all."

"Do you wish you'd been assigned to a gender?" Resolve asked.

"No, not really that one part of your uniqueness is the one part that I really would not want to possess." Analyzer replied with a grin. "It all seems rather human and extremely complicated. A few more attributes would be quite helpful but an actual gender, yuck, no way."

Resolve grinned. "Give me a minute please Analyzer. I've just been assigned to a new female human being and she has a lot of problems to resolve." He explained as he glanced at the visual display wall screen that surrounded him which suddenly began to display a live image of Leona upon it. "I just need to check on Leona first."

The visual display wall screen that formed the perimeter of Resolve's living quarters that surrounded the two could be controlled purely by Resolve's logical processes which meant, he did not have to interact with the wall screen in a verbal manner or through touch in order to perform any required functions. Due to that convenient functionality, Resolve found his visual display wall screen extremely useful because logical commands would simply be issued by Resolve's logical processes that stipulated silent instructions and tasks would then be performed within an instant on Resolve's behalf. However, that was one of the very few complex functionalities that existed inside Resolve's living quarters which in comparison to human residential structures as far as Resolve was concerned, were extremely basic.

In fact, inside the quite small, very minimalistic space that Resolve spent most of his time there was no actual bathroom and no kitchen facilities being that Monitoring Programs had no actual need to use a bathroom or eat because they had no physical, organic form. A Monitoring Program's intangible structure had no actual physical hygiene requirements either, due to their lack of human abode and so Resolve never ever urinated, never needed to take a bath and he had absolutely no need whatsoever for an actual shower facility.

"Oh Resolve, your Allocated Human looks very pretty." Analyzer observed with a playful nod. "For a human being that is. You're really going to have your hands full with that one."

"Yes, Leona is beautiful." Resolve immediately agreed. "But I'm surprised that you noticed."

"Well, I do see some beauty in human beings but not when they use the bathroom because that is a very ugly thing to observe." Analyzer replied. "In fact, I usually look away when they do that because somehow, it seems more polite."

"Yes, I do too." Resolve agreed as he grinned. "It kind of feels very personal and really private."

"I'm actually glad I wasn't assigned to an actual gender really because I might have been female and that would have been very complicated. Can you imagine having to deal with all those highly complex emotions that they seem to experience every single day?" Analyzer joked. "It would make your job as a Life Monitor an annoying perpetual loop and an absolute hell."

"You do make a great point Analyzer and, in some ways, I'm actually quite glad that The Guardian decided to assign me to the male gender as opposed to the female gender." Resolve agreed as he nodded. "Women do seem to suffer quite a lot due to their heightened emotional sensitivity."

"I would probably cry every single day whenever the human beings that I had been assigned to went through some very harsh problems and get absolutely nothing done." Analyzer joked. "From what I've observed, female human beings tend to cry quite often and they don't appear to be very strong when it comes to the endurance of pain, except when they give birth but how they manage that goodness only knows because it does look extremely painful."

"True. I'm so glad we don't have to go through any of that." Resolve replied.

"Yes indeed. Our birth as a program is so much easier and there's not a single code of pain involved." Analyzer agreed.

"What exactly do you need from me Analyzer?" Resolve asked as he suddenly turned to face Analyzer and focused his attention more intensely upon the Monitoring Program beside him and the issue at hand. "I'll need very precise details please."

"Well Resolve, one my Allocated Humans is very attracted to this woman he likes and he watches her every single day and she completely ignores him." Analyzer explained. "And he seems to be so miserable about it."

"Watches her how?" Resolve asked. "Like a stalker?"

"No, it's nothing like that. He just hangs around inside the coffee shop where she buys her lunch and smiles at her each day." Analyzer clarified with a smile. "He goes there to buy his lunch too, so he actually has a perfectly valid and totally legitimate reason to be there."

"This one could be quite tricky, if she hasn't smiled back at him and doesn't seem that interested in his smiles, maybe she's not that interested in him. I'll tell you what I can do, I can send him some kind of flower arrangement offer and that might encourage him to buy her some flowers and then he might give them to her." Resolve suggested. "If she accepts the gift and his gesture then that would break the ice for him and let her know that he really likes her but if she rejects him, he'll probably have to find an alternative lunch spot."

"Now that could be a problem, human beings do seem to become rather attached to their usual grazing spots."

Analyzer said with a smile. "Never mind, at least he'll know one way or the other. Go ahead and do it Resolve, I'll send you his details now."

"Okay, I'll do that for you straight away." Resolve rapidly confirmed. "The sooner he has an answer, the better it is for him really and at least this way, he'll have an actual answer instead of just silence and uncertainty. If she rejects him though, he might be even more miserable Analyzer, have you considered that possible outcome and eventuality?"

"Yes, I have Resolve and if that happens then I will need, a Code of Comfort to comfort his broken heart." Analyzer immediately replied. "The human heart really is such a complicated thing but absolutely nothing at all to do with the organ it's named after that sits inside their ribcage, it's all rather strange and extremely complex isn't it?"

Resolve chuckled. "I'll put something together just in case and then you can let me know, if and when it's required." He offered.

"Right. Thank you so much Resolve and I'm sure you'll enjoy your new monitoring duties with Miss Pretty." Analyzer replied. "I know if I was a male program like you are, I would definitely enjoy seeing her beautiful face every day."

"Yes, she almost makes me want to become human so that I can go and join her." Resolve immediately agreed.

"If only we could step inside the human world, even for just a day, it would be amazingly interesting but it would probably really frustrate us because the human world is not logical in any way and it is a very human chaotic mess." Analyzer quickly pointed out. "At times I even wonder how human beings actually managed to evolve at all because they do seem to fight rather a lot, so I'm surprised they didn't wipe out their entire species centuries ago."

"True and we'd also have do those really ugly things that they do inside the bathroom each day." Resolve mentioned as he grinned. "That could be quite gross."

"Yuck! Now that is definitely not something that I'd like to give an inch of code to, not even for a second, our logical processes are way too valuable to fill them with such disgusting notions." Analyzer said with a frown.

"But if you were a human being Analyzer, you would have to do those ugly human things and do them more than once a day." Resolve teased playfully.

"Absolutely disgusting." Analyzer concluded decisively. "Right on that filthy string of horrible considerations Resolve, I think I'll leave you to it."

Resolve grinned as he watched Analyzer leave his living quarters and then quickly turned his attention back to Leona. "Right Leona, now it's just us and so that means, I'm all yours." He reassured himself as he watched her step out of the front door of her home.

Despite the fact that Leona couldn't actually hear Resolve when he spoke to her that was just a minor technicality as far as he was concerned and it did not dissuade him or bother him in the slightest as he watched Leona walk towards the bottom of the short garden path and then gently pull open the garden gate. Rather unfortunately however, just as Leona stepped out into the mews as she began to make her way to work, one of the neighboring brothers Stefan approached her garden gate from the opposite direction as he headed towards entrance of his home and Resolve immediately noticed his presence. The two would definitely have to cross paths, if Leona actually wished to proceed and so Resolve was curious to see how Stefan behaved towards her, when he was in close physical proximity to her.

INTELLECT: USER REPAIR

In response to Stefan's sudden appearance, Resolve observed that Leona suddenly began to walk much more slowly and even quite cautiously as she offered Stefan a timid smile and politely nodded her head at him to acknowledge his presence. Just a few seconds later, Leona quickly crossed over to the other side of the mews as she made an eager but discreet attempt to avoid being in very close proximity to Stefan but as Resolve rapidly discovered, her act of avoidance didn't seem to appease Stefan's nasty attitude towards her.

Much to Resolve's absolute disgust and total shock, Stefan suddenly leant down towards the ground, picked up a piece of garbage and then actually threw it at Leona's back as she walked away from him. Fortunately for Leona, Resolve observed, the empty squashed can that Stefan had chosen as his missile just missed her and landed not more than a few inches away from her physical body as it rapidly clattered to the ground behind her back. Despite the clatter that the squashed can made as it hit the ground however, Resolve noticed that Leona continued to face and walk in the direction that she was headed in as she faced straight ahead and carried on as if she had not actually noticed Stefan's very malicious, immature, spiteful gesture.

Once Leona arrived at the bottom of the mews, Resolve watched in angry silence as she quickly stepped out onto the main city street that lay just beyond the private road and then disappeared from Stefan's sight as she left Stefan alone inside the mews with just the squashed can for company. Despite Leona's physical disappearance from Stefan's line of vision, Resolve rapidly decided to remain with both Leona and Stefan as he quickly opened up another monitoring window and then began to watch Stefan the youngest of the three neighboring males, who was in his mid-twenties as a silent observer as Stefan resumed his walk towards the entrance of his home.

All in all, the entire incident and whole scene that Resolve had just witnessed seemed rather strange because Stefan had brazenly and unashamedly, displayed an unprovoked pettiness towards Leona that had been extremely spiteful and very hostile, for no apparent reason that Resolve could see. In fact, Resolve could not even begin to comprehend why a young man would behave in such a manner and quickly concluded that his malicious actions had seemed childishly spiteful because Leona had been, from what Resolve had observed, nothing but courteous and polite towards him and she hadn't antagonized him in any way, shape or form. Logic however as Resolve already knew, was not always the human response that human beings offered to each other and Stefan that morning, certainly hadn't behaved in a logical manner in any capacity at all.

According to Resolve's usual monitoring approach, once he had initially been allocated to a human being's life as a Life Monitor, he would then spend at least the first twenty-four hours engaged in a period of very deep concentration which would be a time frame that he would utilize to monitor every single human interaction that they participated in. This very intense monitoring period was referred to by Resolve as the 'Babysitting Slot' because during that time period, Resolve would babysit every individual that his Allocated Human came into contact with and he would monitor how they behaved towards his Allocated Human, in order to establish the main cause and source of a human being's problems and in this instance, Leona was no exception.

The initial study period that Resolve had labelled as the Babysitting Slot was called that because this time period would be utilized to identify all the babies (namely the immature, badly behaved, disrespectful individuals) present in someone's life and social circles because it was the babies that caused most, if not all of the problems that any Allocated Human being faced. Sometimes the Babysitting Slot could even last for an entire week, dependent upon the various factors at play but usually, twenty-four hours would be a sufficient enough time frame for Resolve to collate all the information that he required which would then allow him to accurately identify all the main problem areas and the most troublesome babies.

"Stefan is definitely a huge baby." Resolve announced decisively as he glanced at the wall screen that surrounded him and watched Stefan enter inside his home. "I'll have to deal with his problematic attitude later today and give him some problems of his own to worry about." He added as he began to turn his attention back towards Leona.

One of the two monitoring windows now on display inside Resolve's living quarters was focused solely upon Leona and Resolve began to watch her again within it as she walked along the busy city street that bustled with bodies and wove in and out of the human rush hour traffic that occupied and littered the cement walkways. For Resolve, the city streets of any city were really easy to observe at any time because he would simply tap into the camera circuits that filmed every inch of the city center in question which then allowed him a full view of the heart of any city and so there was no huge problem with general visibility.

When it came to the issue of individual corporate entities, the camera systems that had usually been installed inside their premises normally provided Resolve with almost instant access to their interior but sometimes, when no camera systems were present, Resolve would have to tap into technological devices situated inside a corporate building to have full visibility. Such instances were quite rare however, because in most city centers the majority of businesses already had security systems in place and closed-circuit television systems that recorded their corporate interior which would provide Resolve with immediate visual access since he could manipulate such devices and systems easily.

Unlike the private mews that Leona resided in which was very quiet, Resolve rapidly noticed that the main city streets of Pinesfield at that time of the morning were literally packed full with city workers that darted frantically in and out of nearby coffee shops and retail venues as they went. Some people enthusiastically grabbed cups of coffee on their way to work, Resolve observed, whilst others scooped up paper bags filled with breakfast and a few even hunted for quick bargains as he watched the busy human morning rush hour traffic flow across the concrete walkways in fascinated silence.

Some other prominent features of the Pinesfield city center, Resolve quietly observed, were the very large office blocks that seemed to stand to attention in regimented rows as each one silently lined every city street and some of the busy bustlers quickly headed towards them, once they had collected what they'd wanted to purchase from the city shopping venues and eateries en route. The still concrete structures didn't seem to mind the lack or mass of people that visited them, Resolve logically considered as some of the buildings began to fill up with the human bodies that were employed to populate them every working day because each concrete block seemed to remain pretty much the same, regardless of whether they were empty, half full or completely occupied.

INTELLECT: USER REPAIR

Just a few minutes, Resolve noticed, were spent by Leona on her way to work inside a coffee shop as she enthusiastically collected some breakfast and then quickly left the venue as he watched her in silence. Both Leona's hands firmly clasped onto an item that she had just purchased as she stepped back out into the busy city street and Resolve immediately began to smile as he reviewed her very human, edible purchases. A white paper cup filled with hot latte sat in one of Leona's hands and inside the other, there was a brown paper bag that contained a freshly prepared bacon bap with lashings of ketchup that sat quietly and patiently inside its paper wrapper as it waited to be consumed. Although the human consumption of food certainly wasn't an experience that Resolve had ever had, from the satisfied smile upon Leona's face he could immediately tell that both items would soon be devoured and that it would definitely be a pleasurable experience for her.

A peaceful smile adorned Resolve's face as he continued to watch Leona perform her usual weekday morning routine, the remainder of which seemed to be relatively stress free and reasonably pleasant because the troublesome brothers that lived next door were for now, nowhere to be seen. No one else seemed to bother Leona in any way as she made her way further along the busy city street and then headed into the street where her workplace was actually situated but as Resolve already knew from the briefing files that he had read about Leona's life the previous day, the journey to work really wasn't the most troublesome part of her working day.

The whitish-grey stone office block that Leona worked inside, Resolve quietly observed, stood out from the many much more plain looking buildings that surrounded it because it had some swirly stone patterns that decorated the exterior walls which looked rather stylish. In terms of the building's external appearance, it clearly indicated to passersby that it wasn't just a run of the mill corporate entity because it discreetly and silently indicated that it housed a business inside its silent walls that was slightly more creative in nature and Resolve immediately spotted that major difference.

Once Leona had stepped inside the reception area of the building, Resolve immediately noticed that it was very quiet as he invisibly accompanied her and as she began to walk through the reception and head towards the elevators situated at the other end of the large, open space, he continued to watch her walk in thoughtful silence. The only sound that could be heard as Leona walked through the reception area was the gentle tap of her shoes as each one struck against the white marble floor which created a slight echo that wafted through the air of the long rectangular expanse and as Resolve watched, he noticed that a friendly looking female receptionist glanced up at Leona and smiled at her as soon as she noticed Leona's arrival.

Some polite nods of acknowledgement were courteously exchanged as the two women silently greeted each other as Leona walked past the very large, shiny black reception desk where the mature woman with jet black hair was actually seated as she made her way towards the elevators. At the other end of the reception area there was a small lobby that housed four shiny looking elevators and one of the elevator doors immediately opened up as soon as Leona approached it and touched the button to request a lift.

For a moment, Resolve began to silently wish as he watched Leona enter inside the lift that he too could step inside the elevator and greet Leona in person but unfortunately that was not even remotely possible and

INTELLECT: USER REPAIR

Resolve fully understood and accepted that sad truth and reality as he sighed. Even if it had actually been possible for Resolve to step into Leona's real human life at that precise moment in time, to do so and then approach her with an air of familiarity would as Resolve already knew, quite possibly scare Leona and make her feel very uncomfortable and that would ultimately be counterproductive to his personal objectives and goals. In fact, right now, all Resolve could really do was his actual job and as he vowed to store the hope inside his heart that such pleasures might occur somewhere, somehow at some point in the near future, he smiled because he wasn't actually sure that he had a heart to store such wishes inside, or that such a wish was remotely even possible.

Rather unfortunately, when it came to the actual job of a Life Monitor, Resolve's position and duties had always been extremely clear, he was to be an invisible presence in the human lives that he observed, assisted and watched over and the human beings involved were to have absolutely no inkling that he even existed. A Life Monitor would be provided to the human lives that Intellect served in order to provide comfort, resolution and silent assistance but that was neither reciprocated or acknowledged by the human lives that each program served because human awareness could breach the security of the entire Intellect Framework itself.

Essentially, the Intellect Framework purely existed to serve the needs of humanity and that was why Monitoring Programs had been created in the first place and outside that provision, there was absolutely no room at all for anything else. Serving human beings was the only reason for Resolve's entire existence which meant, there was no room for his own desires, needs or wants which would be deemed by The Guardian as absolutely and totally irrelevant. Due to Resolve's unique makeup however, he definitely harbored some very unusual desires and since he'd been assigned to Leona, those more unusual human like desires had increased tremendously, gathered momentum and then rapidly accumulated.

Quite strangely, for the very first time in Resolve's entire existence, he now actually wanted to meet the real human being that he had been assigned to serve and he wanted to be more than just Leona's intangible silent assistant because he now yearned to be her actual, physical lifetime companion. Outside the nothing that Resolve was supposed to adhere to as he served humanity's needs, there was now a very real something that he truly not only wanted to feel but also indulge in more fully because he now longed to increase his level of involvement in Leona's very real human life. For now, however, Resolve's more human desires could not be realized in his current form and that was one thing that could not be changed, no matter how much Resolve wished and hoped it could be but that he fully appreciated, was his problem and that had absolutely nothing to do with Leona or her problems which he now had to focus upon and fully resolve.

In a matter of just a few minutes, Leona arrived outside her office door and Resolve once more turned his attention fully towards her as he watched her quickly open the door and then step inside the room as she prepared to make a start upon the work tasks that she had planned to perform that day. Unlike most of the corporate offices that Resolve had seen in the past, Leona's office space was slightly different in some respects, he rapidly observed because it contained an actual space where she could draw, being that she worked as an architect.

INTELLECT: USER REPAIR

Once Leona was seated directly in front of her electronic graphic easel, Resolve watched in silence as she opened up a sketch design as she prepared to make a start on the piece of work that she was supposed to finish later that day. The cup of latte inside Leona's hand was gently placed down upon a small coffee table right next to her graphic easel and then as she started to draw, a very peaceful smile spread out across her face.

When Resolve felt satisfied that Leona was reasonably happy and settled in at work, he quickly turned his attention back towards the other item on his agenda that morning which definitely had to be attended to that very same day, the rude, mischievous, troublesome, obnoxious Stefan. Another matter had to be settled by Resolve that morning and that matter was the youngest brother from the three men that resided in the same mews as Leona, right next door to her actual home.

The young man was very clearly visible to Resolve as he began to watch Stefan inside the second viewing window on the wall screen that surrounded him and as he did so, he began to consider how he could perhaps deliver some swift and rapid justice to Stefan's door that same morning. Aside from Resolve's monitoring duties which he took very seriously and attended to impeccably, Resolve could also deliver mischief and he could deliver that just as competently and efficiently as Stefan did, if not even more so and Resolve had decided that morning that it was definitely time to give Stefan a portion of disrespect in return.

Much to Resolve's absolute delight, he rapidly discovered that an actual shopping trip had been planned by Stefan that morning as he listened to a conversation between the three brothers and then watched Stefan leave the house as he headed towards the garage. According to

Stefan, some new clothes were required and being sought for a special event that he wished to attend the following weekend and it was an event which he appeared to be extremely excited about. Apparently, the event would be packed full of single, attractive, very affluent women and so Stefan was absolutely determined to purchase the best attire that money could buy, in an attempt to show off and capture the ladies attention with his physical appearance and stylish attire.

From what Resolve could gather, from Stefan's quite brief, very immature ramblings, when it came to the issues of dating and romance, Stefan seemed to prefer and enjoy dating women who were more affluent and slightly older than himself because he had absolutely no intentions whatsoever of ever being a working-class man. Being financially responsible for himself really wasn't something that seemed to appeal very much to Stefan and such women he had probably assumed would keep him in the manner that he was accustomed to and although his attitude towards woman amused Resolve slightly, he'd also noticed that Stefan had absolutely no desire whatsoever to actually be self-sufficient.

According to Stefan, he was a 'man of leisure' but despite his extravagant tastes, Resolve had noticed that he had somehow managed to live off the rather generous allowance that his parents sent him each month without too many restrictions, or many considerations for his actual future. From what Resolve could glean from Stefan's financial records, on a few occasions the thought of forming and running his own enterprise had actually crossed Stefan's mind because he had formed several businesses in the past but since he'd been far too lazy to actually run, build and maintain any of the companies that he had created over the years, each one had simply fallen by the wayside.

To run a business or corporate entity of any kind successfully, definitely required human inputs such as effort, time, commitment and discipline as Resolve already knew, none of which it seemed Stefan wanted to offer the world and so he'd abandoned each corporate attempt rather quickly. The paramount objective in Stefan's life was it appeared, definitely enjoyment and the rather cumbersome responsibilities of running a business had it seemed, hampered his life of pleasure and so had been rapidly discarded.

Inside the garage situated next to the three brother's home, Resolve noticed that there were three stationery cars as Stefan stepped inside the large space and then headed towards his vehicle. One car immediately stood out to Resolve, a shiny red convertible and he could clearly see that it belonged to Stefan as he watched Stefan press his keypad to unlock the car door and the other two slightly humbler vehicles, Resolve immediately assumed must belong to Stefan's two brothers. The garage seemed to offer the vehicles a safe place of shelter, away from the wild chaotic parties that the house usually accommodated and that the brothers regularly hosted since its enclosed interior silently ensured that the three vehicles were kept intact, fully functioning and free from any possible drunken damage and so Resolve could certainly appreciate why they'd been parked inside it.

Every inch of Stefan's red, shiny convertible sparkled and shone and he smiled with pride as he admired its exterior for a few seconds just before he entered inside the vehicle and then quickly lowered the roof as he prepared for his drive to the shopping center. The drive to the shopping center itself was quite peaceful and relatively quick for

Stefan as he drove out of the mews, through the nearby by city streets and then out onto the highway due to the fact that it was now mid-morning and so most of the city workers were fully occupied and already at work. Approximately twenty minutes later, when Stefan arrived at his intended destination, he smiled in delight as he drove his vehicle into the external carpark of the shopping center and then quickly parked his car.

Several shoppers immediately noticed Stefan's arrival and they gave his vehicle an appreciative stare as he jumped out of his car because it was a very flashy looking, top of the range convertible but Stefan expected a reaction whenever he drove it and so by now, he was used to the admiration from strangers. In terms of the financial outlay, when the car had initially been purchased by Stefan it had cost him an arm and a leg although technically, really it had cost Stefan himself absolutely nothing as his wealthy parents had footed the bill but it had certainly cost them a considerable sum and so he expected the vehicle to be noticed whenever he drove it. For Stefan, the lavish expenditure in his opinion had definitely been worth every penny because the car was quite simply, the best of the best and it really created a stir wherever he went and attracted a lot of attention and Stefan absolutely loved attention.

Despite the fact that Stefan's car was a convertible, he hadn't actually bothered to raise the soft-top before he'd exited the vehicle, Resolve observed but Resolve wasn't really surprised by his actions because the shopping center itself wasn't a regular run of the mill shopping destination and it was one that housed some very exclusive, boutique designer stores inside its confines. The carpark apparently, was usually quite heavily guarded and manned by several security guards but as Resolve rapidly noticed that day, it seemed slightly understaffed because the usual watchmen seemed to be quite few and far between which as far as he was concerned, was really quite advantageous because that meant, mischief could easily take place and occur.

Inside the shopping center itself there was a very expensive gentleman's boutique that Stefan wanted to visit and since he'd been to that shopping venue hundreds of times, he felt really quite comfortable about leaving his vehicle in that state inside the parking lot as he prepared to venture inside the venue for a financial splurge. One final glance of admiration however, was quickly cast back towards his vehicle as Stefan approached the entrance to the shopping center as he admired his own choice of car and gave it one last final quick check just before he stepped inside the interior of the building.

The flashy car it seemed to Resolve, was definitely Stefan's pride and joy and that immediately excited Resolve as he watched Stefan enter inside the shopping center and then disappear from sight completely. Much to Resolve's absolute delight, Stefan had very confidently left his most prized possession totally alone inside a quite public carpark and that misguided confidence as far as Resolve was concerned, would now provide the perfect opportunity for mischief to occur and so he quickly began to activate a stealth program which he rapidly utilized to mask Stefan's car from human view.

Just a few seconds later, Stefan's car completely disappeared from the carpark as if it had vanished into thin air and all that seemed to remain was an unoccupied parking space and Resolve grinned at it mischievously as he began to wait. Not even a couple of minutes had passed by before another driver approached the seemingly vacant parking space with his vehicle as he attempted to park his car in what appeared to be an empty space because Stefan's vehicle was no longer actually visible to the human eye and so the parking space now looked vacant. Since Resolve had masked Stefan's car completely, the driver was totally oblivious to the vehicle's actual presence and so as he enthusiastically drove into the parking space, he unintentionally rammed his car against the hidden vehicle as he began to crush the front of Stefan's automobile.

Confusion rapidly seemed to set in, Resolve observed as the driver reversed his car slightly and then tried to re-enter the empty space once again but once more his vehicle hit an invisible wall as it smashed into the front of Stefan's hidden car for the second time. Significant damage by this point had now actually been done to the front of Stefan's vehicle and some damage had also been done to the second car, although it was slightly less severe and as the driver quickly turned of the engine, jumped out of his car and then quietly began to inspect the damage to his vehicle, Resolve watched him in sheer delight and grinned.

A few minutes later and after a few angry shakes of his head, Resolve watched as the man climbed back inside his car and rather abruptly abandoned his efforts to find a parking space as he turned his vehicle around and then headed towards the carpark's exit. Upon Resolve's face there was a very satisfied smile and he began to chuckle as he watched the man depart, no doubt in search of a garage to repair his now, quite damaged automobile. An angry scowl adorned the man's face as he left the carpark which clearly indicated his total frustration and absolute disgust and Resolve silently vowed to himself as he watched the man leave that somehow, he'd try to make it up to him, once he'd finished with Stefan. Rather unfortunately, some damage had definitely been done to the second vehicle but as far as Resolve was concerned, although it had been quite unintentional, it had been absolutely necessary in order to inflict the pain upon Stefan that Resolve had wanted to deliver to him that morning.

When the second driver was no longer visible, Resolve quickly unmasked Stefan's car once more and as it reappeared, he glanced at the now crumpled, crushed front of the vehicle in delight because the mere sight of the mangled metal amused him and reminded him of the squashed can that had been Stefan's missile earlier that morning. Despite the success of Resolve's first mission that morning however, he had not quite finished with Stefan just yet or delivered enough justice because there was still something else that Resolve really wanted to do to Stefan's car and the opportunity was just too much of a temptation for Resolve to actually resist.

On the edge of the nearby highway there was a small cafe that seemed to be a stop off for long distance motorists and inside the carpark of that small diner, much to Resolve's delight, there was actually a truck filled to the brim with manure. A long-distance truck driver had obviously left it parked there whilst he enjoyed a stop off and meal and for Resolve, the timing could not possibly be more perfect because a truck filled with manure was exactly what Resolve required.

For Resolve, the next part of his plan was extremely easy to implement as he quickly tapped into the electronic system inside the truck to start the engine and then began to maneuver and guide the truck with the huge pile of manure towards the shopping center's carpark and Stefan's car. Every ounce of manure present inside the truck was then tipped over the interior of Stefan's open convertible and as the muck began to fill the inside of the car, Resolve started to laugh because now, Stefan would definitely experience what it felt like to be disrespected in much the same manner that he'd disrespected Leona earlier that morning. Once Resolve's second attack upon Stefan's vehicle had been achieved to his satisfaction, he quickly maneuvered the truck back towards the diner carpark that it had initially been parked inside, prior to his prank and then parked the vehicle in exactly the same spot and waited for Stefan to return.

Approximately ten minutes later, much to Resolve's amusement, Stefan finally returned from his shopping trip and as he walked back towards his vehicle, his arms laden with bags filled with items of clothing that he'd just purchased, a horrified expression rapidly spread out across his face. Joy rapidly seemed to desert Stefan, Resolve observed because the expression upon his face quickly changed from one of confident happiness to horrified shock which then graduated to absolute fury as Resolve watched him start to digest the damage that had been done to his vehicle in his absence.

"This is absolutely unbelievable." Stefan muttered angrily to himself as he approached his car and vigorously shook his head in total disgust.

Anger and rage seemed to bubble away under the surface of Stefan's skin as Resolve watched his cheeks turn a very bright crimson red as Stefan began to absorb the wreckage that his car had now become, a reality which seemed to absolutely infuriate him. Every inch of the carpark that surrounded Stefan was rapidly suspiciously scanned as he stood next to his mangled vehicle and began to visually hunt for the offending party but the only sight that greeted his eyes as Resolve watched, was a handful of parked cars and a few innocent shoppers on their way back from their own shopping trips.

INTELLECT: USER REPAIR

The culprit that Stefan wished to search for and identify had long gone and was now absolutely nowhere to be seen and as Stefan gently touched the front of his now very damaged, crushed car, Resolve began to rejoice in every second of his angry, shocked, disgusted misery. Acceptance for Stefan was extremely difficult and Resolve could immediately see that as Stefan rubbed his eyes in shock and shook his head in total disgust but there was now, absolutely nothing that Stefan could actually do as Resolve watched him with a delighted smile.

A quick physical inspection, unfortunately for Stefan, rapidly confirmed as he ran his hands over the crushed front of his car that yes, the damage was very real and that no, there would not be any insurance claim to cover the cost of that damage. When Stefan began to inspect the rest of the vehicle as he approached the driver's door and side of his car, he rapidly began to realize that his horror filled morning was not quite over just yet because a vulgar stench quickly began to fill his nostrils.

Much to Stefan's absolute disgust, he rapidly discovered that the entire interior of his beautiful car had been filled to the brim with actual manure and that the muck inside his car, absolutely stank. Where the actual manure itself had come from, Stefan was unsure but that didn't change the fact that his car was now full of it and the reality that it looked and smelt absolutely foul.

"There's no way I can drive my car home like this." Stefan ranted angrily to himself as he struggled to accept the current condition of his vehicle. "I just can't believe it, this has never ever happened to me before. I've parked it here hundreds of times."

Unfortunately for Stefan and despite his lack of acceptance, physical clarity had been rapidly forthcoming that yes, his vehicle had actually been beaten up and filled with manure in his absence and no matter how many times Stefan shook his head in anger that did not and would not change a single thing. In a matter of just a few minutes, due to Stefan's discovery, his mood had completely changed from utter delight to total rage and now, he was absolutely livid because this act of destruction seemed very personal in nature and as if it had been specifically aimed at him.

"This is going to cost me an absolute fortune to repair." Stefan muttered angrily to himself as he walked slowly around the exterior of his car and inspected every single inch of damage that had been done.

The cost to repair the vehicle would now definitely have to be incurred, if Stefan actually wanted to keep the car and those costs would be extremely high as Stefan already knew, because the damage that had been done was very severe. According to the stipulations of Stefan's insurance policy, he was required to prove that there had been an accidental collision with another vehicle but since he was unable to do so, it was highly unlikely that the cost of the required repairs would be reclaimable. When it came to the actual matter of the pile of manure which now filled the interior of his car that was another issue entirely and since such incidents were not even something that Stefan's insurance policy covered that would not be reclaimable either and so the whole scenario totally frustrated him because he had very carelessly that morning, left the roof of his car down.

Rather annoyingly and very frustratingly, the damage that had been done to Stefan's car that day would probably be regarded as self-inflicted and deemed to be the result of a drunken adventure gone wrong, or attributed to Stefan's own carelessness and his failure to park his vehicle in a secure location. The insurance company as Stefan already knew, would in all likelihood question any claim and then simply refuse to foot the repair bill and that was definitely something that he could quite easily, accurately predict.

Since Stefan did receive a generous allowance each month from his parents, he knew that the financial resources required to repair the vehicle would be forthcoming but it was extremely inconvenient for him because usually those funds would be allocated to various items of expenditure before his allowance was even received. When Stefan usually received his monthly allowance, he would spend the majority of it on expensive luxuries and various necessities and of course, he regularly splurged a large chunk of his resources on the expensive parties that the three brothers held but a repair bill would definitely eat into his usual monthly enjoyment.

"It might be cheaper in the long run just to buy a new car." Stefan muttered to himself as he absorbed the full extent of the damage. "It's going to cost me an arm and a leg to fix this bloody mess."

From the corner of his eye, Stefan suddenly spotted a man nearby and the man's presence immediately pricked his attention as the man began to unlock his car door and as he did so, Stefan quickly prepared to rush over towards him. Despite Stefan's upset and the accident that had just occurred in quite close proximity to his own vehicle, the man didn't seem to be very interested in any of it and he appeared to be in a rush to leave the carpark and get on with his day as Stefan began to approach him. Irrespective of the man's pending departure and his lack of interest in Stefan's vehicle, Stefan decided to question him anyway as he made his way decisively towards him, just to see if the man could assist him in any capacity.

"Did you see what happened to my car mate?" Stefan asked as he pointed towards his vehicle.

"Nope." The man replied as he glanced at the mangled wreckage and then gently shook his head. "I've only just come back to my car now." He explained. "I've been inside the shopping center for at least the past hour."

"Okay, thanks." Stefan replied as he prepared to walk away.

Nothing but absolute disgust accompanied Stefan as he began to walk back towards his crushed vehicle as he continued to silently seethe inside but no immediate comfort was forthcoming because his car was still crushed and he couldn't even drive it anywhere in its current mangled state due to the manure. The foul stench that emanated from the manure inside the vehicle was really overpowering and even if Stefan somehow managed to empty enough of it to squeeze himself into the front seat in order to drive his car, the disgusting smell would definitely remain and it was absolutely unbearable.

"That's what happens when you leave an expensive car inside the public carparks of cheap shopping centers." Stefan advised himself bitterly as he began to rebuke himself. "Next time I shop here, I'll hire a parking attendant to guard my car, if I ever come here again."

Upon Resolve's face, unlike Stefan's face, there was now an expression of total delight and triumphant satisfaction as he reveled in what he had achieved and the pain and discomfort that he'd inflicted upon Stefan that morning. The afternoon had not yet even arrived and already that morning, Resolve's day had delivered some delightful satisfaction because he'd partially dealt with one of Leona's problems and so Resolve was now hopeful that the afternoon would be just as pleasant as his achievement would warm the remainder of his day.

Once Resolve had watched the totally livid, very angry Stefan pace up and down inside the carpark as he continued to mutter away angrily to himself under his breath for a few more minutes, Resolve shut down the second monitoring window and then rapidly turned his attention back towards Leona once more. Unlike the now angry Stefan, Leona really was far more interesting to look at as far as Resolve was concerned and he had definitely seen enough of Stefan that morning. An ounce of justice had now been delivered directly to Stefan, Resolve decided and he'd really done his job when it came to looking after Leona because Stefan was absolutely furious but there was nothing really that Stefan could now do about the damage to his vehicle as it had already been done except, accept it.

Irrespective of the shenanigans that had just taken place inside the shopping center carpark that morning, Resolve immediately observed that Leona's morning had remained calm, constructive and had been reasonably peaceful as she'd continued to diligently work away inside her office, none the wiser to Stefan's anger and his rage. The electronic graphic easel directly in front of Leona's chair it appeared to Resolve had fully captured her attention and the architectural sketch design that she was working on which apparently was required for one of her clients by the end of that working day.

One very positive aspect of Resolve's allocation to Leona's life that filled him with utter joy as he watched her work, was the fact that he had been assigned to Leona as a permanent Life Monitor because that was not always the case when it came to human allocations within Intellect. At times, some Monitoring Programs would be assigned to human beings for a very short period of time but at other times, they would be assigned as a permanent Life Monitor which meant technically, Resolve could spend the rest of Leona's human life with her and that for Resolve, was definitely something to celebrate.

"It's almost like we're married Leona." Resolve joked to himself as he smiled. "Lots of human beings are married and they don't speak to each other every day, so I guess it's not really that different. Perhaps this is what a human marriage is really, actually like."

Of course, Resolve fully understood and appreciated the reality that Leona was not even aware that he had been allocated to her life as her Life Monitor but to Resolve, it was a commitment and responsibility that he'd not only been given but also accepted, very enthusiastically. One large point of very deep frustration however now remained for Resolve, despite his permanent allocation to Leona's life and that was the fact that he could not communicate freely with her on a daily basis, or whenever he wanted to and at times that restriction really bothered him.

One day, Resolve silently vowed, he would find a way to communicate with Leona that wouldn't alarm her and one day, he'd manage to overcome the barrier that silently sat between them both and one day, perhaps he would even find a way to become a real part of Leona's life, if that was really, actually possible. The tug of desire that now lived inside Resolve had already grown much stronger and although it wasn't a sensation that he was totally familiar with, it felt extremely enjoyable yet at the same time quite strangely, it also seemed to fill his core with mountains of frustration.

In fact, from the very first moment that Resolve had first set his intangible electronic eyes upon Leona's human physical form, the desire to be closer to her had silently begun to gather and accumulate inside of him. A very strong desire now existed inside Resolve that urged him to leave Intellect, urged him to interact with the real human world and that urged him to meet Leona in person but as yet no resolution to those urges had been identified.

Although Resolve really wanted to fulfill his passionate desires in person, he was still unsure that it was possible to do so and just Leona's presence alone on the monitoring window directly in front of him, seemed to inflate his desires more and more because Resolve's feelings for Leona appeared to grow every time he laid eyes upon her.

A very strong correlation definitely existed between Resolve being assigned to Leona as her Life Monitor and his desire to walk the face of the Earth in human form and Leona now represented more to Resolve than just a human being that he had been assigned to monitor. Just a short period of time had passed by since Leona had been assigned to Resolve but she'd rapidly somehow become his entire world and his whole reason to exist. Inside himself, Resolve silently began to accept the reality as he acknowledged his weakness for the female human form that had totally captivated him because no matter what was actually possible in terms of his desires, there was one thing that Resolve definitely now knew for absolute certain, he had completely fallen in love with Leona.

"I have to get some lunch now." Leona suddenly reminded herself as she quickly rose to her feet. "Lunchtime has definitely arrived and my stomach really doesn't want to stand lunchtime up, even though I do have a very tight deadline today."

"Yes Leona, you really should." Resolve whispered to himself as he enthusiastically nodded his head. "You've been working hard all morning and so you should have a break now and eat something."

"I'll just grab something quick and then I'll come straight back so that I can finish the sketch design for the Randall account by this evening." Leona advised herself decisively as she plucked her handbag and jacket from the back of the chair and then slipped her jacket on.

The actual purchase of lunch for Leona was a quite speedy affair as she grabbed a panini from a nearby eatery and then headed straight back to work, purely because she intended to eat the panini at her desk as she worked. Since Leona had another very tight deadline the following day, she already knew as she returned to her desk that there was absolutely no room at all for any kind of spillages from her current day's workload into the next working day and that both deadlines had to be met in a timely fashion, or she'd never hear the end of it from her boss Samson which meant, her working day that day, was far from over.

Not a word was spoken by Resolve as he watched Leona return to work as he silently admired her dedication and professional commitment to her job which was obviously something that she took very seriously indeed. Despite Resolve's lack of understanding when it came to architectural matters, he certainly appreciated Leona's talents because to him, her architectural drawings looked very complex in nature and even what one might describe as beautiful. Although Leona's workload and profession differed vastly from the monitoring work that Resolve performed each day, there was one thing that the two did have in common which Resolve had already noticed and that was their attentiveness towards their tasks because Leona seemed to be just as focused as Resolve was and she approached her work very thoughtfully, much like he did.

Various pieces of architectural equipment and a variety of drawing tools were scattered around the medium sized office space that Leona had been allocated to work in and there appeared to be a large selection of rulers of various sizes and shapes as Resolve glanced around the room. On one side of the room there was a small kettle which was situated on top of a small, black fridge that sat next to a shiny, black filing cabinet and at the other end of the room there were some very large, rectangular windows. All in all, the corporate but creative looking space that Leona worked in looked very well equipped to Resolve as he visually scanned the rest of the room and saw a few more shiny black filing cabinets that lined one wall in a regimented row which sat right next to a large black desk that had some black leather chairs plonked around its perimeter at various intervals but despite all those professional provisions Resolve observed, not a single one changed Leona's solitude.

Rather strangely for Resolve, the quietness inside Leona's office space had continued and remained uninterrupted for the duration of the afternoon which meant that throughout the entire morning and whole afternoon, no work colleagues had dropped by to see Leona. The phone situated on top of Leona's main meeting desk had also remained totally silent and it was almost as if Leona worked in total isolation besides a few email communications with clients which only involved non-verbal exchanges. Just for a moment, Resolve suddenly began to wish that he could be an actual client that had been scheduled to see Leona because it seemed as if she rarely saw anyone and as if her meeting desk remained pretty much unoccupied throughout most of her working day, since she'd visited it only once so far that day to briefly check her emails.

In many ways, it appeared to Resolve as the last few remaining minutes of the afternoon hours slipped silently away and evaporated into nothing, the two were very alike and although technically, they were very different in terms of their organic structure and makeup, Leona seemed to live a lonely existence in comparison to others of her kind. Most human beings, Resolve had observed, tended to interact with at least five to ten other people on any given day but Leona seemed to interact with less than five and those interactions all appeared to be extremely brief and so he'd begun to realize that although she lived a very human life, her existence was in fact, very similar to his own. When it came to Leona's work however, regardless of her lack of social interactions, her attitude was extremely attentive and her levels of concentration were extremely high and that struck Resolve as absolutely delightful because he definitely felt that the two would make a great couple, if they were ever given the chance to actually be one.

Once the evening had silently stepped in to replace the afternoon, Resolve watched in silence as Leona continued to work until eight arrived and then as she began to silently pack up for the day, he gently shook his head as he considered the contents of her day. The whole working day for Leona had really been a very solitary experience because she had spent most of it alone and she'd even eaten her lunch alone seated in front of her graphic easel and Resolve definitely felt that if he was around, Leona's day would have been very different. Being alone a lot of the time was certainly something that Resolve understood and something that he could easily relate to and identify with because he spent most of his time alone but that isolation as Resolve already knew, at times was very hard to accept and then actually exist with.

Outside the building that Leona worked inside, Resolve noticed that a duskiness had now begun to settle which looked almost as if it was a blanket that wanted to cover the entire city as the night threatened to enter into the world and spread itself out over everything that the city of Pinesfield contained. Nothing on the face of the Earth it seemed to Resolve, could stop the night from entering into the human world at the end of each day because time definitely didn't seem to care about anything else, other than the fulfilment of its own role. At least however, Resolve observed, there was now a smile upon Leona's face as he watched her leave her office and then make her way back down towards the ground floor and the entrance of the building which she quickly exited once she'd given a polite nod to the security guard that manned the reception desk throughout the weekday evenings and nights.

"I'm absolutely starving." Leona mumbled to herself as she began to walk through the dusky, quiet, deserted city streets towards home.

A smile crossed Resolve's face as he listened to Leona speak because her verbal expressions to herself amused him somewhat as that self-expression was familiar to him in so many ways because he would also often speak to himself too. In fact, self-discussions were ultimately how Resolve kept himself company during some of his more solitary moments and as a Monitoring Program that had some very unique, humanistic attributes, there were a lot of solitary moments and so from what Resolve could see, the two already had a lot in common. Unlike Resolve however, Leona now had to feed the very human hunger that presented itself each and every day to the human form and although Resolve could not even begin to understand that daily human ritual of necessity, he did appreciate that it was absolutely necessary for Leona's human survival.

"I think I'll buy some Chinese takeaway tonight." Leona whispered to herself as she entered into a city street and then began to walk briskly along it as she headed towards the entrance of a Chinese restaurant.

Very elaborate, home cooked evening meals weren't generally something that Leona usually bothered with much during the week anymore and although pizza was something that Leona definitely enjoyed and it was slightly

93

more affordable that day, she fancied eating something different and something slightly more unusual. A quick glance was cast down towards the screen of her phone as Leona walked and the communication device which was clasped firmly inside one of her hands rapidly confirmed to her that it was now just after eight and she immediately began to increase her walking pace as she internally urged herself to purchase dinner, arrive home and eat it before the clock struck nine.

When Leona had left work that day, the building had been quiet and almost completely empty as usual because most of the employees it usually contained tended to abandon its interior by five or six every working day but Leona usually worked until at least eight or nine and at times, she even worked until ten. The later working hours that Leona frequently worked however, never seemed to be appreciated by Samson her boss and were never ever rewarded and rather annoyingly, instead of appreciation as a reward for her dedication and long working hours, Samson actually seemed to demand more and more from Leona which in recent times had really demotivated her.

"One day I'll find somewhere else to work and then I'll leave." Leona muttered under her breath as she gently pushed open one of the restaurant doors and prepared to step inside the venue. "And one day, I'll find somewhere to work where I'm really appreciated and one day, I won't have to put up with Samson bossing me around anymore."

Upon Resolve's face there was a peaceful smile as he silently began to appreciate the fact that at least Leona's day that day had not been darkened or hampered by any ugly confrontations with her boss which as he was aware from the briefing files that he'd read, could so easily have caused Leona distress. At the very least, Resolve observed, Leona fully understood that her current work

94

environment was far from ideal and she did actually intend to leave one day but as Resolve also fully understood, procrastination and complacency were the enemies of humanity and in that respect, Leona was quite possibly, no exception.

Sometimes and rather strangely, Resolve considered, human beings would tolerate and accept negative circumstances for very long periods of time that were destructive, humiliating, tiresome and that drained them and Leona had it seemed, accepted such negativities in all aspects of her life. In fact, in every direction that Leona turned it seemed to Resolve, whether it was in her professional life or her personal life, she faced mountains of stress and gutters of emotional distress all of which would be very regularly inflicted upon her by those around her as if she was their emotional punchbag and human doormat.

Sadly, when it came to the issue of Leona's current work environment, Resolve had already noticed that it was overly demanding, extremely unpleasant and very stressful and that her boss offered her very few incentives because the renumeration he paid her, certainly wasn't great. The tone of the emails that Leona had received that day from Samson as Resolve had observed her working day, he'd noticed had been absolutely awful and the words that each one contained, very dictatorial as Resolve had monitored them and read every single one. In fact, every word contained inside the emails sent to Leona directly from Samson had seemed to be an opportunity for him to lash out at her in a very cruel and harsh manner as he'd totally undermined her efforts and her contributions to the profits that she generated every single working day for his actual business.

"I have to find you somewhere else to work Leona." Resolve promised himself. "You make so much money for that business and the amount they pay you is totally ridiculous and absolutely miniscule."

Approximately fifteen minutes later, Leona collected two paper bags filled to the brim with cartons of food from the restaurant counter and then paid for her order as she prepared to depart. A weary sigh escaped from Leona's lips as she began to walk back towards the entrance of the restaurant as she prepared to face the world and the city streets once more because she really did feel totally drained and completely worn out.

The restaurant interior, Leona noticed as she walked, was fully populated with happy couples and groups of friends that were seated around each of the tables and as she made her way quietly back outside, she silently deliberated further regarding her own solitude which had grown and grown over the past four or five years. Work had now definitely become a much more significant part of Leona's life and her social life had gradually reduced because one by one her friends had married off and so now, only a couple remained unattached and usually they were as tied up with work as Leona was. Sadly, and very unromantically, Darin's unreliable nature had also grown far worse along with those changes to the social lives of Leona's closest friends which had meant, her lovelife hadn't improved at all and if anything, it had actually deteriorated.

"It really has been such a long day." Leona whispered to herself as she stepped back out onto the cement walkway.

"I know Leona." Resolve said to himself as he acknowledged his agreement. "But at least, you'll soon be home."

"And it'll be another long day tomorrow." She immediately reminded herself.

"I know but help is on the way." Resolve immediately reassured himself as he smiled. "I promise."

Although Leona couldn't actually hear Resolve when he spoke, it provided him with a glimmer of comfort at times just to say each word in the hope that somehow, she would sense his presence and feel comforted by each one.

"At least I'll eat some decent food tonight." Leona whispered to herself as she began to walk along the city street that led towards her home. "In fact, this takeaway should probably last me a couple of days."

True to Leona's usual form and her quite indecisive nature, she had purchased enough food that evening to feed at least three people but that suited her right down to the ground because it meant that she would not have to cook anything the following evening. During the week, Leona didn't really bother to cook very often because usually by the time she arrived home from work each day, she was too worn out to do anything else and since Darin didn't really appreciate her culinary efforts, the whole notion of cooking a delicious evening meal and then inviting Darin round to eat it with her had fled from Leona's mind long ago. In fact, the only person out of the couple that would really appreciate such an effort was Leona herself because Darin was very unappreciative and generally a pain to be around which was why she had secretly banned him from her hectic, busy, long working weekdays.

Some hungry pangs rumbled and rattled around inside Leona's empty stomach as she walked as her body gently reminded her that food was definitely required and very soon. A smile crossed Leona's face as she began to silently rejoice in the fact that now at least, it was her time and that no overbearing boss was around to dampen her spirits but unfortunately, there wasn't anyone else around to share her evening with either because Darin was strictly a weekend activity due to his behavior. In fact, since Darin really was so unreliable and extremely unpredictable, he had been totally banished from Leona's weekday evenings and restricted to a purely weekend activity because she simply could not afford to mess around during the week and Darin usually messed around with her time and with any arrangements that they'd both made.

Quite fortunately for Leona however, the weekend was actually due to arrive quite shortly and that thought pleasantly comforted her as she stepped back inside the mews. Work was finally over for that day and although Leona's day had been very productive because she'd even managed to make a start on another piece of work that was due for completion the next day, she now felt very drained and deep down inside herself as Leona already knew, Samson would definitely not appreciate any of her efforts.

Essentially, the two main men that played a significant role in Leona's life, Darin and Samson, were very ungrateful and extremely unappreciative and that sad reality seemed to be Leona's daily portion in life as she lived and existed under the umbrella of misery that they both held constantly, directly above her head. Very strangely that umbrella of misery did not seem to actually protect Leona's head from the raindrops of stress that the two men regularly inflicted upon her which usually drenched her entire human interior and exterior in total distress. Unfortunately, and for the time being however, whenever the two men served up their usual dollops of disrespect and disregard, Leona had no choice but to consume their indigestible, unpalatable offerings as she hoped and waited for life to provide her with an opportunity to escape from their very cruel clutches but as yet that opportunity had not presented itself or ever appeared.

INTELLECT: USER REPAIR

Deep down inside as Leona already knew, when it came to the actual issue of choice things had become extremely complicated because although in some respects, she did have an actual choice with regards to her current situation, there were a few barriers that stopped her from taking that final leap of bravery. Positions of employment were not generally that easy to find in Leona's field and she feared that she might end up working for someone even worse than Samson, if that was indeed actually possible. When it came the issue of Darin, a few efforts had been in the past to terminate the couple's relationship by Leona but somehow, he had always managed to find a way to crawl back into her life with promises that he'd change and due to Leona's love for him, she had buckled several times.

A wishful hope still lived inside Leona's heart however that one day, Darin and Samson would change or that if they failed to do so, they would finally be evicted from her life forever and that hope had somehow kept Leona alive as she'd crawled through the gutter of daily misery that they had ensured she'd lived inside. Bravery was not something that Leona possessed in abundant quantities and so she had never been brave enough to make the decision to depart and then see it through to the end and so she'd tolerated the misery that being attached to both men had inflicted upon her on a daily basis as she'd suffered in silence.

Very strangely, Leona noticed as she began to walk along the small private road that led towards her home, everything around her was extremely quiet which was really quite unusual but that served as a clear indication that fortunately for Leona, none of the three noisy brothers appeared to be around. When Leona arrived outside her front door, just a couple of minutes later, she quickly unlocked it, opened it up and then stepped inside her home as she released a grateful, tired sigh as it felt really good to see the end of another long working day and the inside of her home once more. Another small mercy that Leona could definitely find comfort in that day, was the absence of the three noisy brothers next door which she felt truly grateful for as it meant that they must be out and therefore that a noisy party was less likely to occur that night.

One day soon, Leona vowed decisively as she closed the front door behind her and then began to walk along the hallway, her life would really change as she would walk out of Samson and Darin's worlds forever and then she would slam the access door to her life in their faces but that courageous day as Leona knew deep down inside herself hadn't yet quite arrived. Nothing but total silence surrounded Leona as she stepped inside the lounge and her stomach began to grumble to remind her that food was now urgently required and that her body really needed to be nourished and satisfied because a hungry gap currently occupied her stomach that seemed to grow larger by the second. Some cutlery and a plate were rapidly collected from the kitchen which was situated at the far end of the large front room before Leona made her way eagerly towards the sofa and then enthusiastically sat down upon it as she prepared to eat.

Takeaway food that had been freshly prepared wasn't really a treat that Leona gave herself that often and certainly not every single day because it could be quite costly and readymade meals were far more economical but this particular restaurant was one of Leona's favorites and so at least once a fortnight, she'd treat herself. Since Leona really couldn't stand to eat dinner alone inside a restaurant and especially not during the week when she usually felt tired and drained by the time she left work each day, she rarely spent an evening out in the heart of the city inside one of the many fine dining venues it contained but she loved some of the rich food that the city restaurants produced which meant, a takeaway meal was at times, absolutely necessary.

Just as Leona was about to tuck into her meal however, once she'd served herself adequate portions of spicy noodles, marinated chunks of chicken and some ribs glazed in a sweet, sticky sauce that glistened and shone, her phone suddenly started to ring and she quickly picked it up and then glanced at the screen as a confused expression spread out across her face. Only one person usually called Leona during the weekday evenings and that was Darin but his calls were not very frequent and tended to be full of stress and discomfort because Leona would have to verbally wrestle with him to make some firm arrangements for the following weekend. At times a member of Leona's family would call her but ever since her parents had moved to another part of the country five years ago, their calls had become far less frequent as they'd busied themselves with their new environment and because Leona had been an only child, there were no siblings to actually call or speak to.

"Hi Darin." Leona said politely as she answered his call.

"Hi Sweetheart." Darin replied. "Look Leona, I know I've been really busy with work lately but I promise I'll come round on Friday evening, say about eight and then we can eat dinner together."

"Sure." Leona immediately agreed. "That'll be nice."

"Right, I'll see you then." Darin rapidly confirmed.

No sooner had the call and conversation started it seemed than it ended as Darin verbally departed and Leona let out a weary sigh as she glanced at her plate full of food and immediately began to doubt his words. The interruption from Darin had not been expected and nor had his voluntary commitment and offer to turn up on the Friday evening because usually, Leona had to convince him to make arrangements with her, so she definitely suspected that something must be wrong in Darin's life and world.

"Perhaps he needs some money." Leona considered thoughtfully as she picked up her fork. "He usually only volunteers to come around like that when he wants something and that something is usually money."

Several partially filled cartons of food lay strewn across the coffee table as Leona began to eat and as she glanced at each one, she rapidly pushed any thoughts of Darin firmly towards the back of her mind because she really wanted to enjoy her meal. Whatever Darin was up to this time would soon become apparent and that was one thing that Leona definitely knew for absolute certain because he certainly wasn't the shy type and he would always express himself to her and at times, very boldly and loudly.

"Darin seems like a total headache from start to finish." Resolve mentioned to himself. "But don't worry Leona, I'll get rid of the headache soon."

Despite the fact that Leona couldn't actually hear Resolve when he spoke to her, he still felt great comfort from every word that he uttered that was intended for her ears because it made him feel as if somehow, he did actually play an active role in her life. Earlier that day Resolve had allocated and spent some time in deep observation as he'd begun to monitor some aspects of Darin's behavior and as he had spied on Darin a little in order to find out slightly more about him, he'd very quickly discovered that Darin really was a total cheat. Rather frustratingly for Resolve however, there was no actual way to immediately prove that to Leona in a manner that would not alarm her which meant, for the time being Darin's presence in Leona's life would have to be tolerated, at least until his infidelity could be proven and then he would hopefully, be banished from her life forever.

A furnace that burnt with enthusiasm seemed to gently warm Resolve inside as he watched Leona eat her evening meal but that enthusiasm was not alone because the contentment that Resolve felt from the revenge that he had enacted upon Stefan earlier that day, rather deliciously, also kept it company. Although a deeper connection with Leona was now definitely desired and required by Resolve, the constraints that he existed within suddenly began to challenge and frustrate him immensely as he started to consider whether such wishes might ever be truly possible and an actual realizable goal.

The two emotions that now existed inside Resolve's form, suddenly somehow appeared to be in direct conflict with each other and it seemed almost as if a silent wrestling match had just begun because each emotional tug pulled his logical processor in two very different directions. Although the contentment that Resolve felt from his very satisfactory day warmed and comforted him, the discontent he felt from his lack of direct contact with Leona still continued to frustrate him and somehow that seemed to detract from the pleasantness of the day's achievements.

One smile from Leona however, rapidly pulled Resolve back towards her and as he watched her eat and enjoy her favorite meal, he began to silently rejoice in his evening because despite a very brief interruption from Darin as far as Resolve was concerned, it couldn't possibly be any better, in his current state. Everything about Leona totally intrigued him from her gorgeous smile and crystal white teeth that sparkled, to her ringlets that bounced playfully against her skin, right down to her cute pinky toes. In fact, in every way possible as far as Resolve was concerned,

Leona resembled complete and utter human female perfection and she had highlighted to him that something was indeed definitely missing from his own very sparse, extremely isolated existence, a confidant, a life partner and a real female companion of his own.

Some deeply profound, very stark realizations had struck Resolve in the short space of time that had passed since he had initially been allocated to Leona's life as her Life Monitor because her presence had enlightened him and shown Resolve that he did not actually want to exist alone. Every particle of Resolve's intangible form and existence now fully appreciated and understood that he had definitely been missing out on something very important and special and he had now discovered that something which he definitely felt, he could no longer tolerate an existence without. Human beings had an actual physical life, they interacted with each other every day, they built emotional bonds and Resolve now yearned to experience every aspect of that human existence in its fullness and its entirety but rather frustratingly that kind of intimate emotional physical connection lay just beyond his current reach.

Suddenly, it was as if a new awareness had been awakened inside Resolve that now urged him to seek more from life than just the unique attributes, characteristics and monitoring role that The Guardian had given to him because suddenly, Resolve wanted to be a real human being. Quite strangely for Resolve, it now appeared that the very unique strengths that The Guardian had provided him with had ultimately become his actual weakness because his emotional attachment to Leona had grown stronger and stronger every time he'd seen her and now, he really struggled with his own internal desires. An emotional urge and connection had definitely developed inside

INTELLECT: USER REPAIR

Resolve that he now felt would be quite difficult to control or dismiss and at some point, he knew, it would definitely have to be satisfied because life in his current state as far as Resolve was concerned, was really no life at all.

The quite rare interactions that Resolve had on occasions with other Monitoring Programs, or even with The Guardian himself, looked absolutely pale in comparison to what a human life could potentially offer him and as Resolve already knew, Intellect could not satisfy his current internal urges. In no way, shape or form could Resolve's current interactions be a real substitute for what he now craved and desired with every particle of his form because the other Monitoring Programs would usually face him with a regimented politeness that was both frustratingly dull and which lacked any real substance. Some strong, passionate, very human desires now existed inside Resolve that had formed and grown stronger and stronger by the hour and that thirst could not be quenched by anything within his current environment, or whilst in his current state of existence.

Rather strangely but intriguingly for Resolve, just the sight of Leona's human form alone somehow managed to evoke and create some very deep human desires inside of him that he could not now turn off or stop, even if he wanted to which he actually didn't because although those urges really frustrated him at times, each one was extremely enjoyable. Every part of Resolve now wanted to feel real human emotions, he wanted to touch the surface of real human skin, he wanted live inside a real human vessel and he wanted to walk the face of the actual human Earth but that wasn't all that Resolve wanted.

For the very first time ever in Resolve's entire existence, he had now become aware of love and so now, he wanted to love another entity that existed outside himself and outside his current plane of existence. Absolutely nothing within the Intellect Framework had prepared Resolve for what he now felt inside and it was almost as if his own makeup had somehow created a paradox of complications that neither Resolve or the Guardian could have ever actually predicted. The very essence of Resolve's own being now presented a contradictory problem to him and a highly complex issue that was not simply going to vanish, or quietly go away but Resolve did not actually want that issue to disappear because the hopeful wishes that could be realized, if that issue was resolved, held the possibility of a very pleasant future and the promise of immense pleasure and satisfaction. Although the paradoxical issues frustrated Resolve at times that frustration was so frustratingly pleasant that he simply had to endure and tolerate the emotional conflict because he could not accept a future that did not include the possibility of Leona as that for Resolve, would be a pointless future devout of love.

Somehow, Resolve would now have to face his biggest challenge yet which was actually himself because his own internal desires had created a problem for him that he would have to resolve alone since there was absolutely no one else that he could confide in about his internal state of emotional conflict. A pool of dissatisfaction had formed inside Resolve, since Leona had entered into his world which now almost seemed to completely consume him but Resolve's problem would for now as he already knew, have to remain totally unresolved and unresolvable because there was no actual instant solution available to him just yet, or at least not one that he was currently aware off. Regardless of the constraints that confined Resolve however, he promised himself as he watched Leona finish her evening meal that his problem would one day, actually be resolved because he was utterly determined to find a solution since failure wasn't something that Resolve could easily accept, or exist with.

Just as Resolve started to become quite comfortable in his own contemplations regarding a possible future transition to the human world however, his logical processes were rather abruptly interrupted as the entry door to his living quarters suddenly swished open and Analyzer stepped inside the circular space. A look of total surprise rapidly crossed Resolve's face as he turned to face the Monitoring Program that he really hadn't expected to see again that day as he prepared to hold an actual discussion with Analyzer and abandon his internal discussion with himself.

"Did everything go according to plan Analyzer?" Resolve asked. "Or do you need something else?"

"I might need some more assistance actually Resolve." Analyzer replied with a grin. "And I just wanted to check that I'm on the right track. He bought her the flowers from the offer that you sent him from the local flower shop this morning but when he gave them to her at lunchtime today, it all seemed a bit awkward really. Since I'm not very sure how human dating rituals actually work, I decided to seek your input again."

"Okay, well we can replay the crucial moment and then I'll tell you what I think you should do next." Resolve offered.

"Great suggestion." Analyzer immediately agreed. "And how are you getting along with your new Allocated Human are your codes in a twist?"

"Absolutely fine. She's very easy to look at, so it's easy for me to be very dedicated to her but she creates such an urge inside of me to be beside her, so that can frustrate me at times." Resolve mentioned as he smiled. "Do you ever imagine what your life could be like Analyzer, if you weren't actually a Monitoring Program?"

"Not really Resolve." Analyzer rapidly clarified. "If I was a human being, other human beings would probably irritate the hell out of me because they are just so irrational and totally illogical."

"True but some of them are different Analyzer." Resolve pointed out. "And in fact, some of them seem really rather nice."

"Really Resolve?" Analyzer teased. "I think some of your programs might need an actual upgrade, you must be missing a code or something because you're starting to sound like you have that very human disease. What is it human beings call it? Ah yes, falling in love."

"Falling in love is a disease?" Resolve asked.

"I've come to the conclusion that it probably is because most human beings do seem to become immobilized and suffer in various ways due to its occurrence, so it really might be but apparently, they need to have that actual disease to live an enjoyable life." Analyzer explained. "According to my observations, if they don't fall in love human beings do seem to become rather miserable, so it's a necessary disease that facilitates their actual human survival."

"You might actually have a valid point there Analyzer." Resolve agreed.

"Next thing you know Resolve, you'll want to leave Intellect to go and marry an actual human being." Analyzer teased. "You definitely seem to be infected with the falling in love disease and I'm actually quite worried about you now because it will wreak absolute havoc on your internal coding and make you behave in a highly illogical manner."

"What if you could leave Intellect one day Analyzer and live a human life, would you do it?" Resolve enquired.

INTELLECT: USER REPAIR

"Certainly not Resolve!" Analyzer exclaimed decisively. "Here I can potentially be immortal, whereas there I would just live a rather limited human life that might, or might not actually be meaningful. Some human beings spend their entire lives totally alone and are extremely miserable and then there's also the issue of financially sustaining yourself and all those feelings they have, it's all very complex, frustratingly uncertain and so awfully human."

"I guess you're right." Resolve replied.

"If you ever wish to leave Resolve, I'll definitely support you but I'm not even sure there's a way to actually do so." Analyzer immediately reassured him. "Just don't say I didn't warn you about what a human life can really be like when you're all human and miserable every day."

Sadly, deep down inside Resolve already knew, the point that Analyzer had just made was indeed totally correct in that some human lives could be filled to the brim with misery, despair and sadness and that was something that Resolve had seen himself. Even if Resolve did one day manage to find a way to become human, no guarantees actually existed to assure him that Leona would accept Resolve in human form as her lover, partner, or even just as her friend and that very human reality, absolutely could not be denied.

A very solemn, silent glance was cast towards the visual display wall screen that surrounded Resolve as he watched Leona flop back down onto the sofa because she'd just stored the unfinished cartons of Chinese food inside the refrigerator for consumption the next day. Since Leona's evening meal had now been fully consumed, she began to prepare to rest for the night and Resolve immediately noticed as he watched her that she was once again totally alone.

"Do you ever feel lonely Analyzer?" Resolve suddenly asked as his curiosity urged him to explore some of the questions that he'd never even dared to ask any other entity inside Intellect ever before.

"I can't say that I do Resolve." Analyzer replied. "We are just here to serve human lives and we do that pretty much twenty-four hours a day, so I don't really have time to feel lonely and solitude allows me to focus solely upon my tasks."

"Our whole existence is so functional though and we hardly even interact with each other." Resolve deliberated. "Don't you ever wish there was something more?"

"No. Not at all. I don't desire, or require anything else Resolve that is not provided to me through my energization capsule, it's just not part of my makeup." Analyzer explained. "It is very human to desire and to wish and to want."

"Yes, it is." Resolve agreed.

"You're different Resolve that's probably why you have such highly illogical desires but that is not something that you can change, so you'll just have to find a way to exist with your uniqueness, even when it's tested." Analyzer advised.

"I think you're right Analyzer." Resolve agreed. "But that can be quite hard sometimes."

"Try to remember Resolve, you are a kind of hybrid, part program and part human being as you possess some human attributes and that very unique combination offers you a unique insight into human problems and that uniqueness also makes you a superior Life Monitor." Analyzer immediately reassured him. "I would try to focus on your strengths and appreciate those and speaking of strengths, let me load the file of the crucial moment onto your screen now, so that you can give me your slightly more human opinion and advice."

"Sure Analyzer, I'll be glad to assist you in any way that I can." Resolve replied with a smile. "After all, unrequited love is becoming quite a familiar place to me now, so I've started to create a map of the rocky but rather sensitive terrain. It's almost like trying to climb up a slippery mountain formed from ice."

"Well, this is just like coordinated teamwork isn't it Resolve?" Analyzer joked playfully. "I think whether I like it or not, we are becoming more and more human every day, it's absolutely awful."

"I don't think I'd mind being human right now." Resolve quickly clarified.

"Next thing I know, you'll be telling me that you would actually like to urinate Resolve." Analyzer teased. "And then I really would have to check your logical processes for a possible virus."

"Sometimes I just feel so alone Analyzer." Resolve explained. "Our existence is so solitary and so isolated."

"That is because you were given additional attributes and more humanistic capabilities Resolve and with those privileges comes a far deeper responsibility." Analyzer explained. "You were made that way on purpose, so it's only natural that you would feel that way but that doesn't mean you should actually want to become human, or want to urinate. Human toiletry habits are really so vulgar and that should be enough to put you right off, even if everything else isn't."

"I know." Resolve agreed. "They really are but if I was human, I'd just have to find a way to live with that stuff."

"And human beings are so violent, they beat each other up with their fists and terminate each other's lives with guns and knives." Analyzer mentioned in an alarmed tone.

"Yes, that is very true." Resolve acknowledged.

"There's absolutely no guarantees Resolve that even if you did manage to find a way to become human, something horrible like that wouldn't happen to you." Analyzer advised. "Inside Intellect you are very special, you are respected and your intuitive capabilities are appreciated but in the human world, you would probably just be one of billions." Analyzer continued. "Would that really be worth it?"

Rather frustratingly for Resolve, the highly logical and very pragmatic observations that Analyzer made were indeed, factually correct but those facts didn't dampen or extinguish Resolve's desire to be human, or reduce his attraction to Leona. Being a very unique Monitoring Program, it seemed, just wasn't enough for Resolve anymore and now deep down inside himself, he wanted more from his existence because he wanted to be human and nothing that Analyzer had said or could say, would make him want that human experience, or Leona any less.

"I don't know why Analyzer but somehow, it really would be." Resolve replied.

"What do you think Resolve, does she really like him?" Analyzer probed as the focus inside Resolve's living quarters was steered back once more to the purpose of the actual visit.

"That's quite a difficult question to answer." Resolve said as he rapidly turned his attention back towards the wall screen that surrounded him and began to watch the human interaction that Analyzer wanted him to evaluate which was now viewable inside a second monitoring window. "It's very hard to see exactly what's going on inside the mind of a human being unless they express themselves in one way or another. She did smile at him when she accepted the flowers and a smile is generally a good thing." He mentioned.

"Yes, but they didn't actually speak to each other or exchange any personal details, so how will they communicate?" Analyzer asked. "All that happened was he said, these are for you and she said thank you as she accepted them and then he walked away."

"I know, he really screwed up Analyzer." Resolve quickly pointed out. "He should have at least asked for her phone number. He'll have to do it again until he gets it right but next time, he should give her some chocolates, or something else. At times human males can feel very nervous about approaching women that they're very attracted to because they fear rejection which means, the results are not always positive, even when there is a mutual interest and attraction."

"So humanly complex and so highly illogical." Analyzer mentioned with a grin. "I wouldn't have even bothered to intervene because it's not really my area of expertise but he just looked so miserable and so lonely, so I had to try and see if I could assist him somehow."

"Don't worry, I completely understand Analyzer. You just felt some kind of empathy towards him." Resolve teased. "You're becoming soft in your old age and your internal codes are starting to rewrite themselves, you're definitely becoming more human."

"What a frightening suggestion Resolve." Analyzer replied with a horrified expression. "Absolutely awful."

An affectionate and amused smile rapidly spread out across Resolve's face as he listened to Analyzer's response because when it came to the other Monitoring Programs inside Intellect, Analyzer was definitely one of the friendliest and the funniest. Quite amusingly however, the humor that

Analyzer often displayed didn't appear to actually be intentional and somehow that made it even more comical.

For some inexplicable reason, the very unexpected recent visits by Analyzer had at least provided Resolve with some codes of comfort because the words spoken by Analyzer had reassured him that he was indeed, very unique and regarded as important within the Intellect Framework itself and that really encouraged Resolve. Regardless of whether or not Resolve could ever actually one day become human, it comforted him slightly to know that his existence was not purely one of a cloned, mechanical entity and that he was like a human being in some respects in that he had a unique actual purpose for his existence that superseded just being a program.

Once Analyzer had vacated Resolve's living quarters, Resolve quickly turned his attention back towards Leona and as he began to watch her, he basked in the ounce of comfort that Analyzer's visit and kind reassurances had provided to him. The words that Analyzer had left Resolve with continued to soothe him because every word of encouragement somehow seemed to reduce the frustration that Resolve had felt building up inside his intangible form, due to the distance between Leona and himself. Somehow and quite surprisingly, Analyzer had actually understood Resolve's desire to be different, his need for his existence to mean something more than just the multitude of tasks that he performed every day and somehow, Analyzer had validated Resolve's value to not only Intellect but also to others.

Each coming new day for Resolve would now be like a blank canvas because it would provide him with an opportunity to explore his purpose and the fulfilment of his potential and in that sense, he felt refreshed, motivated and invigorated as a new zest seemed to fill his interior. Prior to being assigned to Leona, Resolve had begun to feel quite demotivated because he'd felt as if he just did the same things that all the other Monitoring Programs did day after day, year after year but somehow, Leona had challenged that rock of complacency because her problems were highly complex in nature and she was extremely beautiful in Resolve's sight and in his hybrid, slightly more human opinion. The Guardian's trust coupled with Analyzer's kind words had also somehow managed to reassure Resolve that his empathetic attributes and more human nature really did matter and that he could ultimately utilize those in a very constructive manner and that now encouraged and really motivated him.

Quite unfortunately somehow however, Resolve's strengths had now become a bit of a setback because his emotional attributes had ignited some very human flames of desire and an inferno of passion inside Resolve and those flames it seemed, were very hard to extinguish. An immense desire had somehow crept into Resolve's logical processes which had managed to silently conquer his form and the emotional connection that he'd developed towards Leona, now urged him every single time he saw her face to inhibit a real human physical body and to exist inside the very real human mortal world but that desire was as far as Resolve knew, an absolute impossibility.

A frustrated sigh escaped from Resolve's form as he began to watch Leona fall asleep on the sofa inside her lounge because he unlike him, she was already human which meant, her very human body needed daily physical rest. One day, Resolve began to speculate, he too would perhaps also require such rest, if he ever managed to actually make the transformation and join the human race but for now, he would simply remain awake all night and just watch over Leona as she slept as he had no other real choice. For now, Resolve concluded decisively, being Leona's invisible companion really had to be enough for him because it was the only real choice that he had and it was certainly a better alternative than not being in Leona's life at all and it was the only thing that he could do each day and every night, absolutely impeccably and hopeful frustration was definitely a preferable alternative to the nothingness of loneliness.

USER ANALYSIS

When the Thursday morning officially arrived for Leona as her alarm sounded out into the air, Resolve began to busy himself with the preparation of the User Analysis Matrix that he was due to make a start on that day because that would clearly identify all the predators and problematic human beings in Leona's life so that each issue could be resolved and every troublemaker dealt with effectively. Due to Resolve's attraction to Leona and his deep respect for her, he felt that it was highly inappropriate to take advantage of his current position and attempt to view her naked skin as she showered and dressed and so he masked the viewing window that contained Leona for a while as he focused solely upon his task.

At approximately seven thirty, Leona quickly abandoned her home as she began to make her way towards work which by now Resolve had noticed was usually by foot because the building that she worked in, much like her home, was conveniently situated in the heart of the city and just a twenty-minute walk away. Apparently and according to what Resolve had already learnt about

Leona's usual workday routine, she generally aimed to arrive at work by eight every working morning and she rarely seemed to deviate from that pattern of arrival in order to ensure that she arrived at work at least an hour before any of her clients would perhaps attempt to contact her with any important issues.

Absolutely everything about that particular Thursday morning looked extremely pleasant as Resolve watched Leona walk down the garden path and then open up the garden gate because the sun was shining at full blast and it seemed to want to caress every inch of the city with its golden rays. Quite unfortunately however, Resolve rapidly observed that no sooner had Leona begun to walk along the mews towards the main city street nearby than a dark shadow threatened to cross her path in the form of the second middle brother that resided next door, who also began to walk along the mews in the same direction as Leona just a short distance behind her.

"Looks like trouble is already awake." Leona muttered to herself under her breath as she walked.

Rather annoyingly for Leona on this particular occasion, she could not actually escape being in quite close proximity to Gregory, the middle brother from the three because they were both headed in the same direction and so he quickly caught up with her. The stone walkway on that particular side of the mews wasn't really wide enough to stay far away from Gregory and there wasn't much of a pavement on the other side of the small private road, hence there was nowhere really to run and certainly not if Leona wanted to make it to work on time that morning. A trip back to Leona's home under the pretense that she had forgotten something would definitely consume some of the precious minutes that she usually spent purchasing breakfast on her way to work and breakfast was urgently required, regardless of any potentially unpleasant encounters with disrespectful, rude male neighbors.

Due to Gregory's now very close physical proximity, a tense smile was quickly offered to him by Leona but a polite verbal greeting, she had already decided, was not going to be offered on this particular occasion or any other for the foreseeable future. At best, all Leona could do was tolerate the three brothers and that tolerance really did not extend to actual verbal politeness and a decent good morning. Such polite verbal greetings were just too much of an ask, Leona silently concluded, from her or anyone else that had to live in very close proximity to the brothers, regardless of her good nature.

Much to Leona's absolute disgust however, Gregory who was in his late twenties walked briskly past her and gave her a snooty sideward glance as if she was a piece of muck on his shoe that he couldn't wait to get rid of and Leona silently cringed as she bit her tongue and attempted to ignore his rudeness. The polite nod that Leona had silently prepared to offer Gregory to accompany the tense smile was then quickly tucked back away upon the shelf of good manners inside Leona's mind as an item of undeserved courtesy as she saved her polite efforts for someone else and for someone that really, actually deserved them. Such polite acts, Leona quietly concluded as she arrived at the bottom of the mews and then stepped out onto the much busier city street, should not be offered and given to a snobbish thug that was a proverbial pain in the butt every single week and a total nightmare every weekend.

Despite the fact that Gregory's interaction with Leona had not been extremely negative or overly disrespectful, his attitude towards Leona still managed to irritate Resolve profusely because it silently confirmed to him that the three brothers were indeed, pretty much the same. A very negative opinion of the three men had already started to form inside Resolve, due to Stefan's conduct the previous day and so the snobbish, albeit quite discreet display of disrespect from Gregory that had been rather rude and totally undeserved, really annoyed him.

Regardless of Resolve's almost instant dislike for the three men however, Leona still had to share the private road that she resided in with them and of that reality Resolve was fully aware. A silent vow was immediately taken by Resolve as he watched Gregory start to walk along the city street in the opposite direction to Leona as he promised himself that he would clean up and sharpen Gregory's attitude towards Leona very soon. Any negative acts that Resolve orchestrated against Gregory however as he already knew, would have to be performed as far away from Leona as possible and the mews that she lived in, so that nothing would appear to be connected to her in any way and to ensure that there would be no negative ramifications.

Although the main objective for Resolve during the first week of his monitoring duties was to complete a User Analysis Matrix grid of Leona's life which would help him to identify all the problem areas and the babies that hampered her daily enjoyment of life, first and foremost Resolve quietly decided, he would deal with Gregory and his dirty, ugly attitude. From what Resolve had already seen that morning, Gregory's attitude definitely required some improvement because it was mean, dismissive, snobbish, disrespectful and very condescending and that change as far as Resolve was concerned had to happen relatively quickly. The User Analysis Matrix would of course be updated later that day and Resolve would record the two brother's behavior because their attitudes and the problematic issues they presented were pressing issues that Resolve definitely had to resolve but much like Stefan, Gregory needed a portion of immediate stress and Resolve was certainly equipped to deliver that stress directly to him and so an ounce of justice rapidly became his focus.

A second viewing window was quickly opened as Resolve began to watch both Leona and Gregory simultaneously in two separate monitoring windows which were displayed upon the visual display wall screen that surrounded him and as Leona continued to make her way towards work, Resolve watched in silence as Gregory headed off in the opposite direction. Due to Gregory's disrespectful attitude another plan to deal with the rude, obnoxious second brother was definitely on its way to Resolve because that day, he silently decided, he would once again teach the spoilt brats that occupied the house next door exactly what stress could really be like but as yet it hadn't fully materialized and so Resolve had to wait for an opportunity to present itself to him.

For Leona, the remainder of her journey to work that Thursday morning was really very peaceful as she briefly stopped off at the usual coffee shop to pick up a latte and a bacon bap for breakfast and then resumed her journey as she made her way towards Samson's corporate empire. The work that Leona had planned to perform that day involved a sketch design for a client that had to be submitted before she left work that evening which she'd already made a start on and she also hoped towards the end of the afternoon to conduct some more work on a set of draft architectural plans that she had to complete by the Friday evening. A tight and heavy work schedule had to be adhered to by Leona that day and so a morning cup of coffee or even a few cups were definitely a required necessity to waken her mind and sharpen her thoughts.

Only one negative eventuality might possibly occur for Leona that day, she considered as she neared Samson's corporate premises and that was a potential run in with Samson himself but she hoped as she arrived at work and then made her way inside the building that he'd be too busy to pay any attention to her. Any run in with Samson was usually a very negative encounter for Leona and so any working day that went by without having to endure Samson's physical presence, was always a far brighter, much happier working day as far as Leona was concerned. A personal appearance from Leona's extremely overbearing, highly demanding and very unappreciative boss wasn't really something to look forward on any day and especially not on a day when an urgent client deadline had to be met and so Leona eagerly hoped and wished that Samson would ignore her that day and remain, totally absent.

Once Leona arrived inside her office, she quickly settled in as she briefly checked her emails and then made a start on the actual sketch design that she was supposed to complete and submit that same day. Fortunately for Leona, Samson hadn't actually sent her any emails yet that morning which was one positive aspect that greeted the start of her day because Samson's emails were usually far from delightful to receive. In fact, the tone of Samson's emails was normally, very derogatory because the contents would usually be laced with insinuations of incompetence and accusations of failure that Leona could certainly live without.

Since Leona had now arrived at work and because she seemed to be fully occupied and reasonably settled, Resolve quickly turned his attention back towards Gregory, who had definitely caught Resolve's attention but not in a positive way and for all the wrong reasons. A vulgar sense of distaste had rapidly developed inside Resolve's form towards the second brother and so now, Resolve felt compelled to sort out his disrespectful attitude as he began to silently devise a plan.

An invisible pair of electronic eyes watched Gregory's every move that morning as he went about his daily affairs but as he eagerly met with a caterer about some food and drink orders for one of the notoriously noisy parties that he and his brothers usually hosted and attended to his purchases, he remained totally oblivious to Resolve's watchful eyes upon his life. Despite the invisible spectator, Gregory pretty much went about his business as usual as he ordered vast quantities of food and drink for the Friday, Saturday and Sunday nights because that coming weekend, the brother's had planned to host a special party which would last for the entire weekend and so a large number of provisions had to be sourced and ordered in.

Upon Resolve's face there was a mischievous smile as he listened to Gregory as his orders were placed and then watched him settle the bill as he waited patiently for his plan of revenge to arrive. A plan of revenge was definitely on its way to Resolve but as yet the opportunity to properly formulate, enact and implement it hadn't quite arrived. Patience however, was one thing that Resolve definitely possessed in abundant portions and being patient was certainly something that he was extremely good at and so he prepared to bide his time and wait for the perfect opportunity to present itself because he felt absolutely certain that it would indeed, present itself very soon.

Rather amusingly for Resolve, he didn't actually have to wait very long because the next stop for Gregory that morning was a yacht hire service and it rapidly transpired as Resolve watched and listened to him speak that Gregory planned to take a lady out on a hired yacht that evening for an actual romantic date. Apparently, Gregory was very excited about his pending date later that day and the woman that he had set his sights on and so a reservation was quickly made and then enthusiastically paid for along with a catering service that would provide a three-course meal and some bottles of wine and champagne. Although a waiter service was available, Resolve noticed that Gregory didn't seem to want the services on offer as it rapidly transpired that he wanted his romantic evening to consist of only his female companion and himself.

Every part of Gregory's morning as far as Resolve was concerned, was absolutely delicious because Gregory, albeit rather unintentionally had kindly provided Resolve with an adequate opportunity with which to prepare a suitable plan of revenge. The boat trip which was due to happen that very same evening Resolve definitely felt, would be the ideal place for him to throw a spanner in the works as he quickly decided that a slice of embarrassment in front of a woman that Gregory so obviously wanted to impress would be the perfect way to pay him back for the disrespect that he'd shown towards Leona earlier that morning.

True to Leona's usual form, her working morning had predominantly been spent diligently engrossed in the architectural sketch design that she had planned to work on and been asked to complete that same working day as she'd worked towards her deadline peacefully and without any 'Samson Interruptions'. A quick lunch break was taken as the morning departed just before the afternoon stepped in to replace it but that was the only real break that Leona took that day as she kept her eyes very firmly glued to her electronic easel because Samson as she already knew, did not accept any missed deadlines, or excuses and especially not from her. Fortunately for Leona that particular day,

Samson had left her completely alone which meant, she could actually work in total peace and that she was far more likely to meet her actual deadlines throughout the remainder of that week without too many problems.

When eight in the evening finally arrived, Leona let out a weary sigh as she quickly packed up her work tools and then collected her black and white handbag from the back of her main work chair which sat directly in front of her electronic easel since her handbag had been hung in its usual spot upon her return from her short lunch break earlier that day. Usually each working day Leona left work to go home at around eight but sometimes, if there was a very urgent, tight client deadline she would stay at work until nine and on some quite rare occasions, she wouldn't actually leave the building until around ten.

Occasionally on the weekend Leona would have to come into work but such instances were really quite rare because she tended to work longer hours during the week just to ensure that extensions to her working weeks didn't happen very often. From Leona's point of view, she actually resented working for Samson during the weekend because she felt that she already gave him enough of her life and time throughout each working week.

Upon Leona's face there was a satisfied but tired smile as she left her office, released another weary sigh and then began to walk towards the elevator as she silently rejoiced in the relatively pleasant, peaceful working day that she had just experienced because although it had been long, it had been totally devoid of Samson's physical presence. Any working day that did not involve an unpleasant face to face run in with Samson was in Leona's mind, definitely something to celebrate and that day, very fortunately had been totally Samson free. The weekend was now just around the corner for Leona but as she already knew as she pushed the button and waited for the elevator, there really wasn't much to celebrate about that fact because her weekends were usually very dreary, purely due to Darin's outlandish, troublesome, immature, disrespectful and tiresome behavior.

Frustratingly for Leona, her weekends were predominantly usually spent in a verbal wrestling match with Darin as she attempted to convince him to honor any arrangements that the couple had made which would almost always end in an actual argument and rarely anything pleasant. Rather annoyingly, the couple's relationship was not filled with the joys of spring and it was definitely situated a million miles away from the loving paradise of romance that Leona wanted it to be and had always imagined having one day. Unlike the visions of love that Leona had so often wished for, their relationship was truly awful because Darin was a nightmare on two legs, a parasite, a deadbeat and in Leona's now more informed opinion, a vulgar rendition of what a man should actually be and she could no longer ignore or deny that very unromantic reality.

Suddenly, the elevator doors swished open directly in front of Leona and she smiled as she prepared to enter inside the lift and make her way towards the front entrance of the building because for that day, her working day was now officially over which meant at the very least, she could finally go home, eat something and relax. The concrete building that formed Samson's corporate abode was very quiet and almost empty, Leona observed as she arrived on the ground floor and then stepped out of the lift, apart from the security guard that usually guarded the premises each night and she gave him a polite nod as she walked past the reception desk which he faithfully manned every weekday evening and night.

INTELLECT: USER REPAIR

A relieved smile crossed Leona's face as she exited the building because her weekend was now just a step away in the walk of life and reasonably close by which meant, she would not have to visit Samson's corporate dungeon for the next two days. Two whole days without a potential run in, or any kind of communication at all with Samson was always very welcome at the end of any working week and definitely something to appreciate and look forward to although two days spent chasing Darin around as Leona was fully aware, certainly wasn't. Several questions began to scurry through the passageways of Leona's mind as she started to walk through the quiet city streets as she silently considered what drama Darin might bring to her life that weekend because he always brought some kind of headache along with him and he had actually called her and promised to see her that week and so his voluntary offer now worried her slightly.

On the way home Leona didn't bother to stop off to buy any food as she silently reminded herself about the Chinese takeaway that she had bought the previous day, the remains of which would definitely be sufficient to fill up her empty stomach that evening. The city streets Leona found to be extremely quiet as she made her way home because the usual hustle and bustle and mass of human bodies that occupied the cement walkways throughout the evening rush hour had by now, completely disappeared since each city street had been eagerly abandoned as soon as darkness had threatened to appear and decorate each one.

Despite Leona's external smile however, Resolve fully appreciated her very lonely existence as he watched her walk through the heart of the city and the realities that she faced every day because her life was far from what it should be and he definitely knew it. A silent vow was taken by Resolve as he promised to make Leona's life as right as he possibly could because that was his actual remit as her Life Monitor and his agenda for her life. Another very human desire rapidly began to fill Resolve's core as he watched Leona walk but unlike his desire to repair Leona's life, this desire was slightly different in nature and actually related to Resolve himself as his frustration once again began to silently present itself.

Somehow, Resolve silently deliberated, there had to be a way for him to cross over into the human world and somehow, he had to find a way to become an actual human being because there just had to be a way to step into Leona's real human life without losing his own existence and Resolve absolutely had to find it. From what Resolve had seen so far, it had become increasingly apparent that his very human desires could never possibly be fulfilled inside the environment that he currently existed and resided in since Intellect as Resolve already knew, definitely had its limitations and it had been created for an entirely different purpose. Unfortunately for Resolve, the benevolent objectives of Intellect and his role as a Life Monitor no longer fully aligned with Resolve's own personal needs and his involvement in Leona's life had highlighted that very real fact to him which now compelled him to seek solutions to his own problems.

Rather uncomfortably for Resolve, a huge distance definitely lay between the human world and Intellect and to bridge that tremendous gap was an unimaginable task and one that Resolve had never even once ever considered before, prior to his allocation to Leona's life as her Life Monitor but now, it was almost all he could think about. The unique tapestry of Intellect's involvement in human lives and the human Earth at times, almost seemed to be an absolute contradiction to Resolve because the Intellect framework remained totally separate and very remote from those whom it actually served and interacted with every single day. A transition to a real human body would definitely have to occur at some point however, if Resolve wanted to walk upon the face of the human Earth and that issue had begun to occupy his logical processes more and more frequently in recent times due to his desire to spend time face to face with Leona which had also grown as he'd eagerly embraced those internal, invisible urges.

Inside Resolve it now seemed as if his desires to become human and spend a lifetime with Leona had silently grown and it almost felt as if a tree sapling had taken root inside him and as he'd refused to suppress or reject the subsequent urges that had now spread out inside his form like branches, each one had flourished as those very human desires had begun to conquer and then rule him. Rather intriguingly for Resolve, since he had never wished for anything at all before, he now wanted those very human desires to manifest as soon as possible with every part of his form because he wanted everything that a human life could possibly offer him and he wanted to spend a human, mortal lifetime with Leona and even the issue of living a limited mortal life had not managed to dissuade him.

Due to the decision that Resolve had made earlier that day to disrupt Gregory's evening, once Leona had arrived safely at home and was settled in, he quickly turned his attention back towards Gregory because that evening, Gregory had a date but not just with the pretty woman that he'd invited onto the yacht. Another party would definitely be present that evening and attend Gregory's date alongside him and although Resolve would not be visible, or seen by Gregory's human eyes that was usual for Resolve because he functioned in human lives every day in pretty much the same manner. In some respects, however, this evening would be slightly different for Resolve since he was usually tasked with the assistance of human beings, not creating havoc or causing destruction in their lives but that small difference on this occasion, was something that Resolve felt really quite excited about because Gregory as far as Resolve was concerned, definitely deserved a night of destructive havoc and very unromantic chaos.

Every inch of Resolve's form rapidly began to fill with excitement as he watched Gregory move around inside one of the two open monitoring windows directly in front of him as he waited for Gregory's night of romance and passion to begin. Despite the fact that Resolve's mission that evening differed vastly from his usual objectives when it came to the monitoring of human lives, Resolve had already accepted that the evening ahead was indeed totally necessary, in order to meet his overall monitoring objectives because Leona's happiness was ultimately, his primary concern.

No further consideration had been given by Resolve as to what The Guardian might think about his plan but since The Guardian had given him permission to deal with all the issues in Leona's life that meant, Gregory's attitude had to be dealt with and dealt with immediately, however Resolve saw fit because the three brothers were definitely, a huge issue. Although Resolve usually tried his best to please The Guardian, his approval for the time being was regarded as temporarily irrelevant as Resolve prioritized Leona's life and happiness above all else because Gregory really needed a bit of rough handling and Resolve was more than ready to deliver that roughness directly to him.

A very mischievous temptation now lingered inside Resolve's form which urged him to deliver revenge and create mayhem for those who deserved it and that temptation actually felt, strangely delicious and almost made Resolve feel quite human as he watched Gregory's date arrive and she was led onto the yacht. For the night ahead it appeared, Gregory had planned a very elegant candlelit dinner for two upon the lake with Marina, the lady that had captured his attention who appeared to be a striking woman in her early thirties that was interested in some kind of romance with Gregory, from what Resolve could see. Despite the fact that Resolve couldn't understand in the slightest why Marina would be romantically interested in Gregory, who was in his opinion absolutely foul, she appeared to like him which was for Resolve an anomaly that he quickly attributed to illogical, irrational human behavior since she had not only agreed to attend but then she'd also actually turned up.

Some elegant silver candles and a few bottles of champagne had been ordered to accompany the lover's meal and as Gregory greeted Marina with a kiss and then politely offered her a glass of champagne, Resolve watched him in silence as Gregory started to implement his seductive plan and immediately sought to charm her. Everything about the night ahead it appeared as Resolve watched the couple quietly had been meticulously planned by Gregory and Resolve noticed that he rapidly utilized the yacht and his surroundings as a lubricative vehicle to usher in a highly seductive, very romantic ambience in what seemed like no time at all.

The lady at the center of Gregory's efforts and his attention that night Marina, giggled and conversed with Gregory politely and attentively as he discreetly eased himself into the sea of passion that he'd planned to set sail upon that very same night. When Gregory had made the initial booking to hire the yacht earlier that day, he had intentionally selected a yacht with a downstairs cabin that housed a bedroom inside it because he fully intended to make good use of every part of the yacht at some point that night, inclusive of the downstairs cabin. A short flight of stairs led down to the lower deck where a small bedroom cabin contained a double bed and although the downstairs cabin had very little room for anything else that lack of space hadn't bothered Gregory in the slightest when he'd booked the vessel.

From Gregory's point of view, his date so far was going just like clockwork as he fully intended to romance Marina that night with the consumption of some fine but strong wine, a stomach full of good food, a generous dash of charm and then a portion of masterful seduction and so far, she seemed to be very cooperative. The yacht and the facilities it offered had already been fully inspected by Gregory prior to Marina's arrival and it had been deemed absolutely perfect and certainly big enough for what he intended to do that night and so now Gregory felt, extremely confident. Everything for the night ahead had been prepared immaculately and Marina, the woman who'd caught Gregory's eye had willingly participated because she'd not only accepted his invitation but then also attended and so in Gregory's mind, he was pretty much onto a sure thing and sexual gratification would definitely be forthcoming that very same night.

Due to Gregory's lustful desires, shortly after Marina had boarded the yacht as she sipped on her glass of champagne, Gregory rapidly started the engine and then steered the vessel away from the wooden pier that it had initially been moored to. A bit of distance from the pier, other people and any other vessels, in Gregory's opinion, was definitely required because he fully intended to enjoy his evening with as much privacy as was physically possible. Once the vessel had reached a distance from the pier that Gregory felt was satisfactory, he quickly switched off the engine and then began to prepare for his passionate night ahead with lustful excitement and passionate enthusiasm because he did not want even a drop of his meticulous, highly seductive efforts to go to waste.

Dinner which comprised of a three-course meal had already been stored inside some hot plate warmers and kept on board the vessel just to ensure that the food would not be cold and so as soon as the vessel was stationery, Gregory enthusiastically began to serve Marina some of the delightful dishes that he'd ordered earlier that day in an eager attempt to impress her. Flecks of light from the candles on the main deck of the boat seemed to gently dance across Marina's jet-black hair and olive skin as Gregory reveled in his passionate plan which held the promise of actual sexual results later that night, firmly by a very seductive hand as he attentively served the first course of his elaborate meal to Marina and attempted to seduce her palate.

Although on the surface of Gregory's lake of passion his seductive plan seemed absolutely flawless, Resolve however was absolutely determined to throw a mischievous spanner in the works because he aimed to disrupt and disturb Gregory's potentially immaculate romantic night, no matter what. A perfect, romantic, passionate seduction would not be allowed to fully materialize and occur because Resolve was silently adamant that Gregory would not get his wicked way with Marina that night, or at least not in its entirety. All in all, Resolve silently decided, he would probably be doing Marina a favor in the long run when he spoilt their first night together because Gregory really wasn't a very nice person and so he'd be saving her from a potentially frustrating relationship and he would also be getting the revenge he sought on Leona's behalf, all at the same time.

Delicious looking morsels of food and sparkling drinks flowed in abundance throughout the night, Resolve observed as he listened to the couple converse and they relaxed in each other's company as he waited patiently for his opportunity to sabotage Gregory's night to appear. When midnight eventually arrived, Resolve's chance it seemed had finally decided to show up and he eagerly prepared to pounce on it like a leopard that had just caught its prey as he watched the two disappear from the upper deck and enter inside the lower cabin where the small bedroom was situated. Once the two had been gone for at least a couple of minutes, Resolve quickly began to manipulate the yacht's controls as he enthusiastically started to move the vessel back towards the pier.

"I've decided to take the boat out for a spin Gregory." Resolve joked to himself as he smiled.

Unlike Gregory, who had absolutely no intentions at all of moving the vessel around unnecessarily, Resolve had decided on the spur of the moment to volunteer his services as a captain but this particular voyage would be slightly different in nature than Gregory's own because this was a voyage of romantic sabotage. The path that the yacht had taken to the point that Gregory had wanted it to remain in for the night was completely ignored as Resolve quickly steered the vessel back towards the pier but also directly towards another boat that was moored there.

Several boats, a long wooden pier and some mooring points silently protruded from the lake's edge and as the yacht moved peacefully towards them on a direct collision course with at least one other vessel, Resolve grinned in satisfaction. When the yacht was about one hundred meters away from the pier, Resolve quickly utilized his programmable functions to rapidly increase the speed of the vessel which he fully intended to damage as he chuckled because Gregory required a sharp, nasty, expensive shock and Resolve fully intended to deliver exactly that.

The unexpected rapid movement and the increased acceleration of the vessel however, suddenly alerted Gregory to the fact that the boat was actually moving and as it began to pick up speed, the door that led to the bedroom cabin in the lower deck quickly flew open. A half-naked Gregory frantically began to scramble for the stairs which he then rapidly started to clamber up as he attempted to reach the upper deck and the yacht's controls as quickly as he possibly could.

Much to Resolve's absolute delight however, it really was far too late for Gregory to do anything about the actual collision course that the yacht was already on and Resolve watched Gregory with an amused smile as he began to wrestle with the controls that Resolve had already jammed. In order to force the yacht to collide with another vessel, Resolve had already taken some additional precautions and he'd jammed the yacht's controls to keep them in place because he had wanted to ensure that his plan would interrupt and sabotage Gregory's night effectively and efficiently and so now, all Resolve really had to do was watch and wait. Less twenty seconds later and just as Resolve had planned, the yacht suddenly collided with the moored, stationery vessel and as it hit the other boat, it began to grind against it and shake.

"Dam! This date is going to cost me a lot of money." Gregory cursed angrily. "There's no way the insurance will cover this bloody mess."

Once Resolve felt satisfied that a sufficient amount of damage had been done to the yacht, the other stationary vessel and Gregory's night of romance, he silently began to release the yacht's controls which would allow Gregory to once more regain command of the vessel. Just a few seconds later, due to the abrupt, sharp, head on collision which had shaken the whole vessel, Marina suddenly reappeared as she rushed up the stairs towards the upper deck but unlike Gregory, she was fully dressed and Resolve smiled with satisfaction as he rejoiced in his achievement and the chaos that he'd caused.

"Didn't you secure the boat properly Gregory?" Marina asked as she drew closer to him. "Aren't you supposed to anchor it or something?"

"Obviously not Marina, or this would not have happened." Gregory replied in a curt, sullen, sarcastic tone as he struggled with the yacht's controls and tried to steer it back towards its initial mooring point.

"I think you're supposed to do that Gregory, when you want a boat to remain in a stationery position." Marina snapped back as she began to shake her head.

"Well, I didn't." Gregory barked. "It's not a sail boat Marina, it's a yacht and it has an engine, so when you switch it off it's supposed to stay still."

"I'm not sure that, that's true Gregory. Waves move around all the time and when you sail upon the sea, the tide does come in and out, so I don't think any vessel remains totally still on any body of water unless you anchor it." Marina replied in a sarcastic tone.

Quite fortunately for Gregory, he suddenly somehow managed to finally regain full control of the vessel before any more damage could be done and he quickly began to steer the yacht towards a vacant mooring point and then switched of the engine as he brought the vessel to a standstill next to the pier. Unlike the yacht however which could now be controlled, directed and even stopped, Gregory's romantic night as he could clearly see, was on a rapid collision course with the jagged rocks of absolute disaster and there would be no regaining control of that particular romantic vessel that night because Marina was now ready to jump off Gregory's sinking ship of seduction and abandon him completely.

A frustrated glance was cast towards Marina's face as Gregory began to surrender in totality to the unromantic disaster that his potential night of passion had so rapidly become as he now knew, there would be no return to romance that night because his ship of seduction had truly sailed and sailed very far away from any passionate shores. All the tender kisses that Gregory had planted that night had now abandoned his sinking vessel of seduction like disgruntled rats and had become a sunk cost of attentiveness that had been invested into nothing but frustration because he would not now reap the actual rewards of sexual pleasure that he'd hoped to enjoy.

"I think I'll be going now Gregory." Marina insisted as she prepared to depart. "Thanks for dinner and I'll leave you with the yacht that you don't really know how to operate. Enjoy your date."

Not a single word was uttered by Gregory as he watched Marina leave the vessel and completely abandon him as she quickly left nothing behind but a crushed empty heart, a cold bed and total defeat. Somehow, the meticulously planned night of potential romance that Gregory had prepared for immaculately had gone totally wrong and now, Marina actually thought that Gregory was an absolute idiot and he couldn't even begin to dispute that very negative opinion of him because he didn't have a clue when it came to the actual operation of a yacht. Rather arrogantly, Gregory had taken a gamble that night as he'd taken Marina out on vessel that he knew very little about and rather unfortunately, disaster had suddenly struck and shattered his passionate, charm filled seduction into a million tiny pieces of absolute embarrassment and there would be no romantic recovery because Gregory's shipwreck of seduction had truly sunk and was now no longer sea worthy or able to be salvaged.

For Resolve, although he had really enjoyed Gregory's suffering and misery that night, by now he'd actually become quite bored of Gregory's face and so he quickly closed the second viewing window as he turned his full attention back towards Leona, who was now fast asleep on the sofa inside her lounge. A portion of justice had now been dealt to two of Leona's three very noisy, extremely rude, totally obnoxious male neighbors but as yet, Resolve hadn't seen Leona interact with the third brother and that third interaction was something that Resolve really could not wait to see.

The first two encounters with the three men next door had fully illustrated to Resolve however, how absolutely horrible the brothers really were towards Leona and he therefore felt absolutely certain that the third interaction with the third brother would probably be just as awful. Upon Resolve's face there was now a very satisfied smile as he began to watch Leona sleep because his day as far as he was concerned had been a tremendous success, not just for Leona but also for his own sake because it felt absolutely delicious to punish the wrongs of the obnoxious and unrighteous that lived right on her doorstep.

Due to Resolve's focus upon Gregory and his late-night activities that evening which in Resolve's mind had been urgently required, he'd decided to conduct a thorough User Analysis of Leona's life on the Friday and over the coming weekend because that seemed to be a logical approach which also aligned more coherently and consistently with Leona's actual schedule. Essentially, for a User Analysis to be performed accurately, Leona had to not only be fully awake but she also had to interact with other people and

INTELLECT: USER REPAIR

Resolve had realized by this point that the Friday and the weekend ahead would provide him with a much better chance to actually see most of Leona's problematic relationships in action firsthand.

From what Resolve already knew, a very urgent, pressing work deadline had been set by Samson for an important client account which was due by the close of business on the Friday evening and so Resolve had predicted that Samson would show up at Leona's office in person, just to ensure that it was met. On the actual Friday evening, Darin had also made an arrangement to see Leona and so he was expected to show up at her home as he'd arranged and so most of Leona's problems were due to put in an actual physical appearance quite soon and that suited Resolve right down to the ground because he still had a lot of work to do in Leona's life.

When the Friday morning decided to put in an appearance and finally arrived as it landed upon the runaway of Leona's life, she quietly began to make her way to work with a joyful smile upon her face, appreciative of the fact that the actual weekend was now, just around the corner. Due to the hectic, very long working week that Leona had just endured, the weekend was extremely welcome but the huge deadline that had to be met that day for a very important client meant that Leona really couldn't afford to totally relax just yet. An enthusiastic hope however did fill Leona's heart as she walked that once her working day had finally ended, she would be able to enjoy the weekend although Darin's cooperation with that plan was highly unlikely because he usually brought a lot of drama and trouble along with him.

For Resolve, the main focus of his Friday as he diligently watched over Leona as she made her way to work, was to monitor Samson and Darin and review the part that they played in Leona's life because he had to evaluate the impact that they had upon it but as he already knew, their role in Leona's life was usually, predominantly negative. All the issues that Leona faced had to not only be identified but proper resolutions to those problems also then had to be sought and both Samson and Darin, from what Resolve had already established, were definitely huge issues and very troublesome problems.

Every single problematic relationship that related to Leona's life had to be evaluated fully and every third party that she interacted with on a regular basis had to be monitored by Resolve in order to determine exactly how each one contributed towards her general unhappiness, misery and dissatisfaction, so that relevant action could then be taken and Leona's life improved. Answers to questions had to be found and essentially, Resolve was the only one that could really, actually find them because he had the power to burrow through the intricate details of Leona's life in order to establish the facts and that day, he hoped to at least find some of the answers that he required.

Human malice was not generally something that Resolve understood easily because it was not something present within his own nature and so at times, it really intrigued him that other people would go to such lengths to make such a beautiful, talented humble human being's life so miserable but Leona's life seemed to be totally plagued by nasty troublemakers. The life that Leona should have enjoyed was very sadly riddled, littered, contaminated and polluted by the diseased, filthy malice of others, others that took Leona for granted, others that failed to appreciate or respect her and others that seemed to revel in degrading her at every possible opportunity and so Resolve had to give Leona's entire life a spring clean. Cobwebs of misery clung to the shelves of Leona's mind each and every day that had been spun by the spiders of distress and those spiders had to be extracted, eradicated and swept out of her life because they were not useful to her and detracted from her general well-being and as Resolve had observed, they had now become parasitical predators that sucked every ounce of joy from every part of Leona's life.

Rather unfortunately, due to Leona's gentle, humble nature, it had quickly become apparent to Resolve that she was definitely under equipped to deal with the parasitical predators that thrived from their cruel rule over her life and their subjugation but Resolve on the other hand, was much stronger, he was far tougher and he could kick them out of her life in a flash. Each user had to be identified and then evicted from Leona's life as soon as possible and because Resolve was a problem solver that had absolutely no emotional attachments to any of those troublemakers, he could definitely serve up the harsh portions of justice to each of them that they really deserved.

Unlike Leona, Resolve had absolutely no qualms at all about being tough on those that he felt deserved it because he wasn't bound by the same very human, feminine maternal instincts that Leona appeared to be restrained by. Tough solutions could be sought out, applied and delivered by Resolve that would grab the predators in Leona's life by the scruff of the neck and deal with their negative vices appropriately, so that they never dared to show their ugly faces in Leona's life ever again. Due to Leona's soft, rather gentle nature, Resolve realized that she hadn't managed to take a harsh stance against Samson and Darin yet and that as a result, they had abused the tolerant attitude that she extended towards others, Resolve however wasn't so tolerant and he would definitely kick them right up the butt in the exact spot they needed to be kicked, extremely hard.

In fact, one thing that Resolve had definitely begun to notice about female human beings during his time as a Life Monitor was that some females seemed to tolerate slightly more than their male counterparts usually did and that difference had now become even more noticeable to him. Due to Resolve's deeper and very personal interest in Leona, the differences between the two main genders that the human species predominantly comprised off had become increasingly apparent to him but those differences seemed to be determined by quite a lot of factors and were not something that he could actually solve and resolve.

The fundamental reasons for the stark differences between the two main human genders, Resolve had in the end predominantly attributed to several variables like female maternal instincts, society's general attitude towards women, the historical allocation of gender roles and the values taught to children throughout their upbringing. Change however, wasn't something that would happen overnight as Resolve already knew and whether humanity liked to acknowledge it or not, those differences in values and attitudes were deeply ingrained in human culture and behavior.

For some inexplicable reason, Resolve had discovered that female human beings were usually expected by society to be more tolerant, more accepting and much more giving than their male counterparts, whereas the same expectations and conditions were not usually placed upon men. Some deeper issues definitely lay buried deep inside the core and heart of human society as a whole and although those issues, if resolved could quite possibly reduce the overall workload of the Intellect Framework in general, attitudes towards the female gender were not something that Resolve had been assigned to explore or resolve.

INTELLECT: USER REPAIR

Solutions for mankind's general problems were not part of Resolve's actual remit or even something that he had been allocated to research and find since he merely followed The Guardian's instructions each day and monitored the lives of his Allocated Humans but the differences between the two genders from what Resolve could see, definitely existed. Other genders and gender issues did exist amongst humanity's collective societies as Resolve already knew but due to the fact that Life Monitors had not been influenced by human society and any gender-based attitudes, Resolve's attitude towards human beings was really quite uniform and very consistent, regardless of the gender that individuals aligned themselves with or the gender that society recognized them as being.

Due to the limitations of Resolve's role as a Life Monitor, gender equality issues were not supposed to be his focus and weren't considered to be his duty or responsibility and that relieved Resolve somewhat because from what he could see, some physical differences did seem to exist between men and women and so the issue of human gender equality appeared to be a minefield of complexity. Human problems in relation to gender did exist that society itself and science did not seem have all the answers to as Resolve was already aware but that was not something that Intellect was tasked with providing a solution to and so complex gender issues weren't something that Resolve usually focused upon.

Once Leona arrived at work, Resolve immediately began to update the User Analysis Matrix in preparation for Samson's expected appearance later that day as he watched her settle in quietly. Every monitoring task that related to Leona's life had to be prepared and provisionally mapped out and all her recent interactions had to be recorded and evaluated because now that Resolve had clearly identified all the predators in her life and the babies, he had to find the most appropriate solutions to the problems that each one presented. The impact that every relationship had upon Leona's life had to be individually analyzed and intricately assessed, in order to determine whether or not the summation and net effect of any relationship was positive or negative and so every major relationship that Leona currently engaged in was quickly plotted within the User Analysis Matrix as Resolve attended to his tasks.

Since Darin frequently upset Leona and appeared to be one of the most severe users present in Leona's life, he was naturally first on Resolve's list but he was quickly followed by Samson, Leona's boss who came in at a very close second. According to Resolve's list of troublemakers, the three brothers that lived next door to Leona featured next on his list as although they were a constant irritation that caused disturbances to Leona's life very regularly, her emotional state and economic position did not directly rely upon them which meant to some extent, direct contact with them could be limited and where possible, actually avoided completely. Every interaction and each exchange that Resolve had recently observed was then plotted inside the User Analysis Matrix as he focused intently upon his tasks and attempted to evaluate each one.

Before Resolve could complete all his intended insertions of data in order to populate the User Analysis Matrix and process all the relevant information however, a strange beep suddenly interrupted his focus as the visual display wall screen directly in front of him rapidly began to change and he paused for a moment. A significant amount of concentration was definitely required for the completion of Resolve's task but the sudden change inside his living quarters immediately distracted him because it was highly unusual in that it wasn't a change that Resolve had actioned himself. Some curious deliberations rapidly began to pinge Resolve's logical processes as the distraction continued as he silently began to speculate as to why the interruption might possibly have occurred.

Very unusually, The Guardian's face suddenly appeared directly in front of Resolve and as his form began to fully occupy and fill up the entire wall screen that surrounded Resolve, he immediately paid attention to The Guardian's unexpected appearance. Since it was a very rare occurrence and The Guardian rarely ever appeared in that manner, his presence was not something that could be taken lightly or ignored by Resolve because it meant that something very serious or urgent needed to be expressed. More often than not, The Guardian only usually appeared directly to Resolve when a personal conversation had been requested by him and so this sudden, unexpected visit was definitely very strange but as Resolve quickly realized, this wasn't going to be a personal discussion.

Something it appeared had gone wrong inside the Intellect Framework itself and with the framework's protective shields because the words 'Potential Virus Detected' suddenly flashed up on Resolve's wall screen and since Resolve feared that the interruption might have a direct impact upon his monitoring duties, his curiosity was instantly aroused. Nothing but total silence filled Resolve's living quarters as Resolve began to focus his attention solely upon The Guardian's face and waited for his address to commence. An actual broadcast message to all the Monitoring Programs within the Intellect Framework it appeared, was just about to be communicated as The Guardian quickly began to clarify why he had interrupted the usual flow of monitoring work inside Intellect and Resolve listened to him attentively as he started to speak.

"Dear fellow Monitoring Programs, I have just received a notification from the human intelligence headquarters of Intell which facilitates our operations that there are and will be a few bugs in our system today, due to a virus. The tracking system will be running slightly more slowly than usual as a result, so please bear this in mind when you conduct your usual monitoring duties. A solution is currently being sought and so it is hoped that this situation will be resolved later today." The Guardian stated in a solemn tone as he addressed all the Monitoring Programs within Intellect. "I would like to offer you all my sincere apologies in advance for any delays that you might face as a result of these problems and for any inconvenience caused and I would like to thank you for your patience regarding this matter which is due to circumstances outside my control."

Rather interestingly for Resolve, The Guardian himself it now seemed had encountered an actual problem that he could not resolve, or control and that really intrigued him as since Resolve had initially been created that had never ever happened within Intellect before. Inside the Intellect Framework, The Guardian had always maintained and controlled absolutely everything and so his unexpected announcement came as a huge surprise to Resolve as he nodded his head and listened quietly as The Guardian began to elaborate further regarding the potential impact that the problems would have upon Intellect's operations that day.

Much to Resolve's frustration, he suddenly began to realize that the system problems would probably have an impact upon his own tasks that day which meant, his preparation of the User Analysis Matrix would perhaps be slower as a result, due to the slower tracking system but as he also realized, he was absolutely powerless to change that reality. The strange attack which appeared to be from an external source, was an issue that Resolve had absolutely no control over whatsoever and as he carefully considered The Guardian's words, he began to wonder how and if he could possibly assist.

Since Intellect's daily operations relied solely upon one tracking system there really was no way around the disruption and because technically, Resolve was totally dependent upon that tracking system to perform his duties as a Life Monitor that meant, he would definitely experience delays that day. No other auxiliary tracking system existed that was connected to Intellect outside of the main tracking system and simply put, there was no back up or alternative secondary system, regardless of how much that reality and fact, would now perhaps frustrate Resolve and hamper his duties.

The entire day, it suddenly dawned upon Resolve as he accepted The Guardian's words, would not be as meticulously orchestrated as he had initially planned and that realization began to silently tug away at Resolve's logical processes as frustration started to settle in. A rather annoying limitation would now be faced for the remainder of that day and just as Resolve had begun to perform the most crucial functions that he was required to deliver as Leona's Life Monitor it seemed that the very same tracking system that was supposed to assist him, would now slow his work down.

Frustratingly for Resolve, the tracking system provided him with immediate access to the human lives that he served each day and it was a system that he needed to perform his designated functions but for once that usual visibility would perhaps be restricted and limited. The limitations that would now occur however, rapidly highlighted a very important factor to Resolve as he began to quietly accept the potential disruption in that, Leona's happiness was not really just dependent upon him but also upon the entire Intellect Framework and the systems that supported it because Resolve's own success as a Life Monitor was also dependent upon those very same systems.

"If the issues become any worse, some of you may be called upon to assist me which would mean an interruption to your usual monitoring tasks but this would be a last resort and will only happen, if the issues cannot be resolved today. In the meantime, please do your best to deliver what you can and hopefully, the disruption to our services will be minimal. Thank you for your patience." The Guardian explained as he ended his official address.

Once The Guardian's broadcast message came to an end, the visual display wall screen inside Resolve's living quarters rapidly returned to its prior state and as Leona and the User Analysis Matrix suddenly reappeared inside the two viewing windows that had previously populated it, Resolve prepared to embark once more upon the tasks that he'd been engaged in, prior to the interruption. For the first time in a very long time however that day, Resolve had actually been reminded of the reality that the whole Intellect Framework was dependent upon an actual human intelligence agency that existed inside the real human world which it served and not just upon the mind of The Guardian its actual creator and that dependency now partially frustrated him.

From what Resolve already knew and from what he had been told in the past by The Guardian, the Intell Agency had several objectives when it came to the Intellect Framework and its role in human lives and one of those objectives was to reduce violent crime upon the face of the Earth. In order to achieve that actual objective, it had been decided fifty years ago that any human being flagged up by the Crisis Intervention Program, would first be assessed by Intell and then allocated to the Intellect Framework as and if required. Every human being that had been allocated to Intellect would then be provided with Life Monitoring services by an assigned Life Monitor and to a large extent, the collaboration between the Intellect Framework and Intell had been a tremendous success because incidents of violent crime upon the face of the human planet had decreased since its inception.

In fact, since the creation of Intellect, billions of human beings had been monitored and the Intellect Framework had successfully provided a large segment of humanity with much more peaceful, far more productive lives as the framework had faithfully and silently served human beings, even without their knowledge. Each Monitoring Program inside Intellect would be allocated to the human lives that they had been assigned to, due to personal circumstances and individual situations which were usually deemed to be very negative and then support would be provided without the occurrence of any direct interactions. No huge costs were incurred for the fulfilment of Intellect's work which meant, Intellect itself would never become an actual liability to the human lives it served and due to its anonymity and separation, it could remain totally untraceable.

Now however it seemed, the Intellect Framework itself was just as fragile as the human lives it actually served and that reality absolutely intrigued Resolve as he began to evaluate the actual impact that the problems would have upon his work and the delays that might have to be endured throughout the remainder of that day. Essentially, the technology that Intellect relied upon to function every day was extremely powerful and it had been designed by The Guardian himself when he'd walked upon the face of the

Earth as Resolve already knew but suddenly, it now transpired that this powerful technology not only had an actual weakness but also that this weakness had been found by an actual third party and Intellect's vulnerability, slightly worried Resolve.

According to what The Guardian had told Resolve in the past, prior to Intellect's creation, the system had always been deemed far too powerful to exist and it had been felt that it might be very destructive, if such technology fell into the wrong hands but due to a dramatic change in circumstances it had finally been actioned just before his death. Something had changed on the surface of the human planet just before The Guardian's actual human death that had compelled the intelligence agency Intell to finally give the project a chance to exist and it had definitely stood the test of time because Intellect had run very smoothly for the past fifty years as Resolve was already aware.

The series of major tragic events that had taken place just before The Guardian's death which had prompted a change of heart and encouraged a much more positive attitude among the leaders of Intell towards his life's work, weren't something that Resolve knew much about but it had forced the intelligence agency to finally implement The Guardian's wishes. From what Resolve did know however, The Guardian had actually worked on the project in his free time for over a decade prior to his human death as he'd developed the system independently and the framework itself which had been almost ready to function immediately, once it had been authorized and then it had been allowed to perform its intended role for the past fifty years.

From what Resolve could establish from Intellect's own historical system records and according to what The Guardian had told him in the past, since Intellect had initially gone live, there had been very few technical problems and so that day was highly unusual for that reason alone. Since Intellect had become fully operational, for the most part, it had functioned almost perfectly and run virtually like clockwork just as The Guardian had intended it to and there had been no actual problems at all since Resolve's own actual existence had been initiated and actioned three decades ago. This current attack however, was very unexpected and it almost seemed to Resolve as if an external force had now discovered Intellect's actual existence and as if the invisible, anonymous attacker wished to sabotage and disturb the services that Intellect provided to humanity. Finally, it appeared, The Guardian had encountered a problem that for once, he had not foreseen and that he could not easily resolve and that illogical uncertainty suddenly began to worry Resolve because it felt so chaotically human and so humanly fragile.

Despite the very unexpected interruption and sudden distraction however, Resolve tried to remain focused as he diligently attempted once more to attend to the tasks that he had been busily engaged in, just before The Guardian's face had appeared. One small consideration did amuse Resolve slightly as he returned to his duties and that was the fact that The Guardian now faced an issue that he could not immediately resolve because it was like Resolve's current situation in some respects, in that he possessed his own unresolved issue which he had no immediate solution to, namely his desire to become human so that he could step into Leona's real human life. Unlike The Guardian's issues with Intellect however as Resolve fully appreciated, his problems would take far longer to resolve because as yet there was no actual solution and no backbone of assistance to help him find one.

Regardless of all the technical problems inside Intellect that day however, one thing always brought a smile to Resolve's face and that was the sight of Leona's face and as he turned his attention back towards her, his focus and his smile were once more restored and silently returned. The recent negative interactions that had occurred with both Stefan and Gregory were quickly logged inside the User Analysis Matrix as Resolve resumed his monitoring duties but very little information could be logged yet about Darin because Resolve hadn't really seen Darin and Leona's relationship in action much so far and their communications had been rather sparse.

From what Resolve knew about the couple's very strained relationship however, there appeared to be a mountain of stress and deep chasm of discontent that sat between the two, purely due to Darin's behavior and his attitude towards Leona, both of which were extremely negative. The interactions that had occurred between the couple, since Resolve had been assigned to Leona, didn't seem to be very romantic at all but because Resolve hadn't really seen the couple interact that often yet, the section of the User Analysis Matrix that related to Darin couldn't really be completed in a sufficient manner and so it remained, temporarily inconclusive.

A far deeper analysis and inspection of Leona's relationship with Darin would have to be performed by Resolve because he had quite limited knowledge of the couple's relationship, purely due to the one large drawback of his role as a Life Monitor which meant, his job only really started once he'd been assigned to someone's actual life. Technically, a Life Monitor could monitor and view any part of their Allocated Human being's current life and the lives of those around them at any given time and access Intellect's databases which were filled with information and held various records about their past but that live view only provided Life Monitors with access to their Allocated Human's life in real-time, once they'd been assigned to them.

The individual history and past of a human being's life prior to a Life Monitor's allocation, aside from any official and unofficial system records that existed, could not be reviewed, accessed or analyzed in any capacity at all and at times that lack of visibility really frustrated Resolve because there could be blanks and gaps that he could not fill in very easily. Unlike The Guardian who could access and have glimpses from both the past and the present, Resolve's view of the human world was far more restricted and so there was a definite limit to what he could see and not see and so Leona's past relationship with Darin prior to his allocation to her life could not be viewed or reviewed at all.

Due to the very unexpected interruption to Intellect and the network broadcast by The Guardian, once Resolve had updated the User Analysis Matrix as he watched Leona work, he was suddenly provoked to consider the other Monitoring Programs that existed inside Intellect further for a moment. A curious contemplation suddenly wandered through and crossed Resolve's logical processes as he began to consider how some of the other Monitoring Programs might perceive his attraction to Leona, one of the human beings that they had essentially been created to serve because it was highly unusual.

"The other Monitoring Programs probably wouldn't understand my romantic interest in Leona." Resolve logically concluded as he mumbled to himself. "Or they'd think it was really strange because in some ways I guess it is quite strange, even for me."

No other human being that Resolve had ever been allocated to as a Life Monitor since his initial creation had ever interested him in the way that Leona had and that in itself, was extremely unusual. Despite Resolve's uniqueness, the feelings and sensations that Leona provoked inside of him were something totally new to him and definitely very unique because he'd never experienced such emotional responses at the sight of a human being ever before and that notion utterly intrigued him.

One more task still remained to be performed by Resolve that morning which related to the User Analysis Matrix and so he began to focus his mind upon it because since he had now input Leona's most recent interactions, he had to dissect, assess and analyze the results of each one. Every single interaction inside the User Analysis Matrix had to be evaluated and the negative or positive impact of each one correctly identified but as yet as Resolve quickly realized, there really wasn't anything positive to see. Each negative impact would then have to be analyzed in order to allow Resolve to formulate an appropriate plan of action with regards to each troublemaker so that he could fully resolve every single issue in Leona's actual life and that would complete the initial monitoring tasks that Resolve usually performed, once he'd been assigned to a human being's life.

Since Resolve had initially assumed his role as Leona's Life Monitor most of the interactions that he'd seen her engage in so far seemed to have been very negative and they usually left Leona feeling upset, stressed and uncomfortable and there were very few exceptions to that general state of stress and that conclusion didn't really require much analysis at all. A few positive exceptions to the general negativity that surrounded Leona every day had occurred but Resolve noticed that these were predominantly with people that Leona had very little daily engagement with, namely the security guard at work, the receptionist, the staff from the Chinese restaurant that she'd visited and some clients that she had interacted with. Rather unfortunately, Resolve rapidly concluded, the less regular positive interactions that Leona engaged in seemed to form a very minor part of her life and absolutely none of them had any kind of impact upon her actual economic or emotional welfare and so those positive interactions were like a drop of positivity in an ocean of stress.

In fact, it seemed to Resolve as if the orchestra of people that accompanied Leona on her walk-through life, who played the song of her existence alongside her, predominantly seemed to play a very stressful tune most of the time and it appeared, there were very few joyful, upbeat moments in that song, so Resolve could easily understand why Leona had become buried in a stressful pit of total misery. Regardless of all the complexities and the negative people that surrounded Leona however, Resolve definitely knew one thing for sure, he was the right Monitoring Program for the job and that as her Life Monitor, he would approach each issue in a highly logical manner and then dig to the root of every single one. Very soon, Resolve decided, every external annoyance that irritated Leona and niggled away at her mind and happiness would be fully resolved and cut out of her life completely so that her joy could be fully restored and the agents of misery that had destroyed her peace, would then be sent packing forever.

For the remainder of that Friday morning, Resolve diligently watched over Leona as she remained inside her office seated in front of her graphic easel with her eyes glued to the screen as she attended to her professional tasks and strove to meet her deadline. When lunchtime finally arrived, Leona popped out only very briefly in order to pick up a sandwich which she then brought straight back to work as she carried on with her working day. The professional client deadline that loomed upon the horizon of Leona's working day, Resolve realized as he watched Leona eat lunch seated next to her electronic graphic easel, was obviously important to her and he admired her commitment to her work and her dedication to Samson's corporate entity but in his opinion, her professional faithfulness was very misplaced and totally undeserved because Samson was an arrogant, unappreciative nuisance.

Several more hours rapidly slipped by and as the remainder of the Friday afternoon quietly evaporated into nothing and silently departed, Leona continued to work away undisturbed and as she focused intently upon her deadline, Resolve waited patiently for the evening to arrive. The actual Friday evening itself really interested Resolve because due to Leona's huge client deadline that day, he expected Samson to pay a visit to Leona's office before the end of her working day and there was also a planned date due to take place with Darin later that evening, so both events were expected to commence and occur at some point during the next four or five hours. An unromantic date with Darin, although it would not be a pleasant experience for Leona, would allow Resolve to explore, examine and inspect what kind of relationship the couple really had more fully and Resolve hoped that the couple's potential interaction would increase his understanding of Darin which would allow him to assist Leona more appropriately and more effectively.

"I might just be able to finish these plans on time today because it's not quite five yet." Leona whispered to herself as she paused for a moment and then quickly glanced at the time. "But today it seems, time is not my friend or my ally."

Just before Leona's peaceful working day could escape any kind of ugly confrontations however, disaster suddenly struck in the form of a very sharp, loud knock at the door and Leona immediately flinched as she quickly rose to her feet and prepared to answer it. The knock itself was instantly recognizable to Leona because there was only one person in the entire corporation that ever knocked upon Leona's office door in that manner and that was rather unfortunately, Samson. An ugly grey cloud now seemed to lurk just above Leona's head because a possible confrontation sat just on the other side of her office door, inside Samson's hard interior but the office door that currently protected her as Leona already knew, was a door that she definitely had to open because there was absolutely no way that she could ignore Samson's knock.

"Just a minute please. I'll be with you in a second." Leona politely called out as she quickly saved her work on her graphic easel and then began to cross the room.

Any conversation that Leona had with Samson that day was not going to be pretty and she already knew that as she took a deep breath and then began to pull open her office door. A fake polite smile was quickly plastered across Leona's face but it was the same pretentious smile that she saved very specifically for physical meetings and live encounters with Samson because Leona rarely wanted to smile when she saw him in person. Fake smiles would not however, impress, satisfy or get rid of Samson and Leona fully appreciated that reality, especially when an urgent client deadline had to be met.

Despite Leona's apparent nervousness, Resolve actually felt quite relaxed as he watched her open up her office door and then smile at Samson as he silently began to prepare himself for the visual identification of another annoying troublemaker that regularly plagued her life. Much to Resolve's actual surprise that Friday, Samson hadn't shown his face all morning, or even throughout the entire afternoon but at five on the dot, he had finally shown up with his suit of stress and his dictatorial tendencies that seemed to fill up and clothe every single inch of his interior and adorn his physical exterior. The tone of the emails that Samson sent to Leona every working day had already made it apparent to Resolve, extremely quickly that Samson wasn't a very patient man, or even a considerate one and especially not when it came to his interactions with Leona and so now, Resolve was just about to see a physical application and manifestation of Samson's nasty, dictatorial attitude in action.

Not a single word was uttered by Leona as Samson swept briskly into the room and then strode across it as he headed towards a chair situated next to her meeting desk and as Leona shut the door behind him, every inch of her flesh started to tremble as fear began to grip and conquer not only her interior but also her exterior physical frame. Despite Leona's very disciplined attitude towards her work, she actually felt quite worried about the pending deadline that day because it was a very complex and highly unusual project that had involved several major last-minute adjustments which meant, it had taken her slightly longer than she'd initially anticipated and expected it to and it still wasn't quite finished just yet.

Usually, Leona managed to meet all her client deadlines, even though Samson shortened them at times in order to increase her workload but today for the very first time, Leona felt slightly unsure that she could complete the architectural plans by seven as she'd initially agreed. A ribbon of fearful uncertainty seemed to wind itself very tightly around Leona's neck and she began to struggle to breathe as she walked across the room towards her meeting desk and then sat down as she faced Samson and prepared to hold an actual discussion with him.

Time had definitely escaped and slipped from Leona's grasp that afternoon and so now, she felt quite uncertain that she could actually finish the required plans before she left work that day and Samson as Leona already knew, would be absolutely livid if she didn't. Unfortunately for Leona, Samson was not a very understanding person that would accept her missing an important client deadline, regardless of the reasons behind any delays and that was one thing she did know for absolute certain. In fact, the harsh reality was that Samson would have Leona's guts for garters if she missed a client deadline and it was highly likely that he'd even dock her salary for the late delivery and quite possibly, she would also be given a disciplinary warning.

The unexpected interruption from Samson was very unwanted because it would delay Leona's completion for longer, distract her from her task and also place her under even more pressure but as Leona already knew, Samson was not a person that logical reason seemed to form any part of. Much to Leona's total dismay because Samson had already sat down that very clearly indicated to her that he intended to hold an actual discussion with her and from his actions, Leona could clearly predict, this was not going to be a one-minute conversation or one was that even remotely pleasant.

A personal appearance from Samson was not something that Leona generally looked forward to on any day of the week and especially not last thing on a Friday evening when a client deadline had to be met in the next couple of hours but unfortunately, she was absolutely powerless to do anything about it because Samson was indeed, already present. For some very frustrating reason, Samson had decided to darken Leona's office door and dampen her spirit with his actual presence just before her pending deadline was due to be met and this very personal appearance that he'd decided to put in, was certainly not going to be enjoyable and there was absolutely nowhere for Leona to run.

Some angry clouds of tension seemed to silently gather inside the room as Leona faced Samson nervously and waited for his volcano of verbal anger to erupt and as her skin suddenly began to crawl, it almost felt as if a thousand spiders of fear had crept inside her clothing and then decided to crawl all over her body. Every pore of Leona's flesh now suddenly felt as if each one had been pricked by multiple sharp needles of stress that wanted to silently torture and torment her as drops of sweat rapidly formed upon her brow and nervous worries ran rampant through the passageways of her mind as she waited in fearful silence. Each breath that Leona took was suddenly razor sharp and grated against her throat as her airways quickly dried up like a piece of sandpaper as she waited patiently and fearfully for Samson's angry discussion to begin.

Unlike the usual monthly performance meetings that occurred at Arch Solutions, this impromptu meeting hadn't been pre-organized or arranged in advance as was usual corporate practice but then Samson as Leona knew, rarely adhered to his own corporate procedures and policies, even though he'd prescribed, implemented and enforced them himself. In fact, when it came to Samson's demands and expectations as an employer, he was extremely problematic and very difficult and especially when it came to the issue of Leona and her actual workload and it was almost as if his corporate policies did not apply to her.

INTELLECT: USER REPAIR

For some strange reason that Leona didn't fully understand, Samson seemed to expect much more from her than he did from her architectural colleagues, even though he didn't actually pay her any extra money and coupled with that financial injustice, his attitude towards Leona was always overbearing, condescending, derogatory, disrespectful and very harsh. An unscheduled visit to Leona's office by Samson normally only meant one thing for Leona, a pile of stress and because there was no actual format to such meetings, unlike the monthly performance reviews that meant, Samson could rant as much as he wanted to and he usually did. Due to Leona's respectful nature and her financial reliance upon Samson's employment, there was very little she could actually say or do about his unpleasant outbursts when they occurred and so by now, Leona had learnt just to hold her tongue and tolerate them because Samson's rants could become very ugly, extremely quickly.

Despite the tension inside Leona's office, a nervous smile was politely offered to Samson as Leona internally braced herself for his angry discussion because there was one thing she definitely knew for sure, Samson's sudden arrival meant that trouble was brewing and that very soon that trouble would be unleashed verbally upon her ears. Nothing but absolute silence filled every drop of air inside Leona's office as she waited patiently and quietly for Samson to speak but this was not a pleasant silence as Leona already knew. This silence was an angry, awkward, tense silence that sat directly above a deep whirlpool of anger like an unbroken, unshattered thin sheet of ice that waited to be hit with one verbal lash from Samson at which point, it would be smashed into a million tiny pieces of verbal rage and his wrath would be fully unleashed upon Leona's mind and ears. Every inch of Samson's face silently expressed his agitation and Leona hardly even dared to breathe because she feared that if she breathed too loudly, the ice would snap and Samson's anger would be released and then it would flood into every particle of air and consume the entire room.

Just for a moment, albeit a very brief moment, Leona quietly considered the possibility of an escape because if she ran out of her office right now and hid from Samson, she could perhaps avoid the ugly confrontation and display of anger that she could sense bubbled away underneath the surface of his skin. A need to utilize the bathroom was a very acceptable excuse, Leona contemplated quietly as she waited fearfully for Samson's anger to be verbally unleashed.

Suddenly however, the brief moment of hopeful wishes ended as Samson rose to his feet and then much to Leona's total dismay, he began to take a few steps back towards the other side of the room and towards her office door. The path between the actual door and Leona's meeting desk as she could now clearly see, was actually blocked and obstructed by Samson's physical form and as he came to a complete standstill and stood in a stationary position near the door, he then turned to face her and just stared at her face.

A direct escape route was now no longer accessible to Leona because it had been fully obstructed by Samson's body which sadly meant, it really was too late for any actual escape attempts. Any attempts made by Leona to flee now, in order to avoid the full extent of Samson's anger, would be virtually impossible and completely unsuccessful because the path to the door had ultimately been blocked and so there was absolutely nothing that Leona could do to avoid Samson's anger which was just about to burst and so she waited in silence for his scornful wrath to be inflicted upon her ears and mind.

Since the angry confrontation that Leona knew was just about to follow could now no longer actually be postponed, she continued to wait in total silence, very unwillingly but she was an absolute bag of nerves as she silently dismissed her thoughts of a potential escape, rather reluctantly. Every single thought that had filled Leona's mind just seconds before that had entertained the rather pleasant notion of a potential escape it seemed, suddenly silently abandoned her as each one fled and scurried away from the forefront of her mind and faded into insignificance as she began to accept that the inevitable was just about to happen, whether she liked it or not.

Another couple of minutes passed by silently as Leona sat completely still inside her chair like a frozen rabbit paralyzed by fear as she continued to wait for the external expected display of anger to occur as Samson stared angrily down at her face. Although the thought of a possible escape had soothed and comforted Leona somewhat for a few brief seconds, deep down inside she already knew and understood that such an act on her part would just prolong the agony of what was to come and there was definitely a portion of harshness and ugliness to come that day. In terms of Samson's capabilities, Leona had realized long ago that he could certainly deliver harshness when it suited him and that harshness seemed to be his main areas of expertise because he really seemed to be so dam good at it.

Directly above Leona's head, it now felt as if there was a very angry, dark grey cloud that silently waited to burst which intended to drench her with raindrops of distress when the storm of Samson's thunderous words and venomous tones were released and as his eyes burnt into her flesh, she began to squirm around inside her chair in total discomfort. Deep in the midst of Samson's angry silence that had lasted for a few very long minutes now, Leona instinctively knew as she glanced nervously up at Samson's face, this was not going to be one of those very rare occasions where polite exchanges actually occurred between the two. Silent arrows laced with venom and sparks of hatred seemed to fly out of Samson's eyes and pierce Leona's skin as even his silence inflicted wounds of discomfort upon her and she began to shiver as she braced herself for his verbal lashings.

"Why haven't you finished the Mackintosh plans yet?" Samson suddenly barked.

Every angry word that Samson scornfully snapped, shot rapidly through the air and as his question cut through the silence, each word demanded an immediate answer from Leona but despite his obvious anger, she completely froze and even actually hesitated as her tongue quickly became totally tied up in nervous knots of fear. A few possible responses could potentially be offered to Samson at this point by Leona and so she frantically began to internally wrestle with each one as she silently deliberated as to which response would result in the least anger on Samson's part because an angry Samson was certainly not a pleasant sight to see, or be in close proximity to.

"I'm working on the plans now Samson, so I'll finish them today before I leave." Leona finally managed to blurt out. "I should finish them shortly." She reassured him. "The final amendments are almost complete now."

In the end, Leona had decided to go with all three of the responses that had swept through her mind as she tried to convince Samson and even herself that it would indeed actually be possible for her to meet the actual deadline that now sat just less than two working hours away. No actual certainty really existed however inside Leona's mind that she would actually be able to finish the project before seven and by the time that her working day ended but she tried her best to appease Samson with some verbal reassurances, despite her internal doubts because really and truly, she had absolutely no other choice.

Unfortunately, that week, Leona's workload had been extremely heavy and because of her other work demands, she'd had to leave the majority of that particular project until the very last minute but Samson had given her absolutely no other choice because he'd heaped several other client sketch designs onto her shoulders during that week. The very sad reality was that Samson wanted to have his cake and eat it with a cherry of stress on top and that cherry of stress was usually dumped straight on top of Leona's desk every single working day and that meant, her client deadlines as a result had become a major source of stress. No excuses were offered however and released from Leona's mouth as she waited in silence for Samson to respond because logical explanations at this point as Leona already knew, would just add more fiery fuel to Samson's anger.

"Make sure you do Leona, this is a huge client account." Samson suddenly snapped back angrily. "You should know by now, you should not submit a piece of work to a client on the actual day of an agreed deadline. You should have submitted it at least a day or two ago to give our client time to request any changes that they might want to make. If our payment is not approved promptly that will be coming straight out of your salary." He continued. "It's totally unacceptable to leave your submission of the plans until the very last minute."

Absolutely nothing but pure hatred and utter contempt seemed to exist inside Samson's eyes as Leona glanced up at his angry face and then watched as he began to stride around the room aggressively. The angry tone, raised voice and livid expression upon Samson's face had already really intimidated Leona because every single word that he'd spoken felt as if it had cut through the air with absolute precision as his insults had invisibly slashed away at her skin like a well-aimed sword but Samson it rapidly transpired, wasn't quite finished with Leona just yet.

Every inch of Leona's skin trembled with fear as she continued to watch and listen to Samson in total silence as he started to rant about workload, client and time management and took angry strides around the interior of her office. Each word that Samson barked and snapped was laced with aggression and Leona winced and flinched at regular intervals because his tone was abrupt, loud, dismissive and very angry as she sat and waited for his angry outburst to end.

No possible defense could be offered to Samson right now and Leona knew it because he was extremely angry and even if she tried to appeal to his better nature, if he actually had one, it would be a pointless, futile, self-defeating exercise because her words would only anger him more. In fact, during the four years that Leona had worked for Samson and under his rule, there were a couple of things that she had definitely learnt, a response should only be offered and given to Samson when he was angry when one was demanded from her, or when a direct question was asked because the less you said to him, the better it was.

Technically and professionally, Leona had several very genuine reasons for the delays that had occurred that week with regards to that particular piece of work but as she already knew, Samson really wasn't someone that appreciated her efforts, her professional expertise or her attempts to provide his clients with high quality services. In fact, usually, whenever Leona had been assigned to a piece of work for a corporate client, the architectural plans would be completed within three weeks or less which was a far quicker turnaround than the work delivered by any of the other architects that worked for Samson but for some inexplicable reason, he seemed to expect much more from her.

Due to the high-quality services that Leona offered and always provided to Samson's clientele more often than not many of Samson's clients specifically requested that Leona should work on their projects for that very reason but Samson didn't seem to appreciate her professionalism at all. Nine times out of ten Leona usually exceeded her client's expectations and she also delivered extremely quickly because she frequently worked longer hours to actually do so. The usual turnaround time for a finished set of architectural plans for a corporate client was usually five or six weeks but Leona had worked hard to reduce that to just three and so she now feared that if she reduced that completion timescale any further, she'd run the risk of delivering a less than satisfactory piece of work to Samson's clients and that really bothered her as a professional.

Regardless of Leona's noble attempts to maintain decent standards of output, Samson it seemed wasn't impressed in the slightest by her efforts and he was never satisfied because he always demanded an unrealistic turnaround from her that ultimately, usually placed Leona in a very difficult and stressful position. Currently, Leona was already functioning at full capacity and her workload had been crammed into every working week as she'd sacrificed her leisure time just to ensure that she met Samson's corporate ambitions and goals. In terms of Leona's physicality, she really couldn't go any faster because she had multiple clients to satisfy at any given time and so there was absolutely nothing that she could say that might appease Samson and soothe his anger because he it seemed, very unrealistically, expected her to deliver more than was actually physically possible.

Not a word escaped from Leona's lips as she watched Samson storm around the room and although her silence on this occasion was humble and submissive, it was also laced with fear as she waited patiently for him to finish his angry rant and then depart. Soon, Leona hoped, Samson would leave her office and then she'd be able to finish the Mackintosh plans which were actually due to be submitted that day before she left at around seven which was now just one hour and thirty minutes away which meant, there was now even less time to complete that particular piece of work. The angry rant by Samson had now cost Leona approximately thirty minutes of her working day so far but as yet, he showed absolutely no signs of slowing down or actually stopping.

Unfortunately for Leona, the very ugly rant and extremely angry confrontation continued and then rapidly became even worse as Samson suddenly neared her desk and angrily slammed a ruler down against it and the ruler immediately snapped into several pieces. Peace and tranquility, it immediately became apparent to Leona, would not be restored and allowed to fully occupy her office space quite yet because Samson had not yet vacated the room and his angry outburst it seemed, was not quite over but Leona kept her lips tightly closed and held her tongue as she just waited in total silence in the hope that he would eventually at some point, actually leave.

Just a few seconds later and much to Leona's absolute relief however, Samson finally decided that their meeting was over and as he suddenly swept out of the room without barking another word, he left Leona alone once more with one less architectural tool because the ruler was now, well and truly broken. Generally speaking Samson didn't really speak to Leona very much at all, she considered thoughtfully as her office door slammed shut behind him and whenever he did verbally address her, he usually barked and his tone and words were almost always filled with anger, dissatisfaction and scorn. In fact, Leona silently considered as she quickly rose to her feet and then began to make her way back towards her electronic graphic easel, really and truly she should be used to Samson's disrespectful attitude towards her by now but even just his presence alone still managed to really scare her and his rough ways were hard to become accustomed to.

"What a nightmare, I hope he doesn't come back." Leona whispered to herself as she sat back down next to her graphic easel. "I really have to finish these plans today, or Samson will probably fire me. I might have to stay until seven thirty, maybe even eight because there's absolutely no way I'll finish by seven, not now, not after Samson's angry rant." She concluded as she released a weary sigh.

An arrangement had already been made that Friday evening with Darin which meant, Leona really couldn't afford to stay at work for a few more hours that evening to work on the plans which she often did, if a piece of work was due to be submitted and the deadline was very urgent. The thirty minutes of Leona's planned working day that Samson had just consumed could be regained, she considered thoughtfully, if she stayed at work until seven thirty that evening because that would in effect give her back the time that she'd lost due to Samson's angry outburst which might just suffice but overall completion still wasn't totally guaranteed.

If completion of the plans took slightly longer than expected, Leona considered as she started to work, she could perhaps stay until eight and then get a taxi home which would make her about ten minutes late for her date with Darin which was pretty acceptable because he rarely showed up exactly on time, if he decided to show up at all. Inside Leona's mind however, there now ran a undercurrent of fear that if she failed to leave work by eight she might annoy Darin and then she wouldn't see him for the rest of the weekend because he wasn't the kind of person that liked to be treated as if he was a second or lesser priority and although he was a lousy lover, he was all she had right now

"I just hope I can finish these plans by seven thirty." Leona whispered to herself as she gently shook her head and released another weary sigh. "Or Samson might smash my head against the desk and break me."

"What a horrible man." Resolve announced decisively to himself as he glanced around his living quarters and then began to shake his head. "Really Leona, Samson is very mean and extremely nasty."

Upon Resolve's face there was now a very angry scowl because Samson had clearly shown that day that he was not just a nuisance that niggled around or an annoyance that needled away in the background of Leona's life as Samson it appeared, was in fact, a full-blown headache and a lot of trouble. The nasty emails that Samson frequently sent to Leona, Resolve now realized had just been the tip of the iceberg because the sharp, cold verbal and physical icicles of anger that he fired at her in person were in fact, a hundred times worse.

A huge task now lay ahead for Resolve as he began to consider his next steps because somehow in the long term, Samson had to be completely eliminated from Leona's life but the negative impact of his behavior in the short term also had to be dealt with and dealt with extremely quickly. When it came to the issue of actually destroying Samson individually that wasn't a particularly difficult thing for Resolve to do but there was an added complication which definitely had to be considered and that complication was actually Leona herself.

Financially and economically as Resolve already knew, Leona was totally reliant upon Samson's corporate entity for her economic survival which ultimately meant, she was financially reliant upon Samson himself and that made the situation a lot more complex and far trickier. The stress that Samson inflicted upon Leona every working day, definitely had to be purged from her world by Resolve but as he also fully appreciated, Samson's departure from her life had to be executed in such a way that it would not negatively impact upon her because that would ultimately cause Leona even more stress in the long run.

Prior to Samson's impromptu meeting that Friday afternoon, Resolve had already taken the time to inspect Samson's demands with regards to Leona's workload and he'd compared those demands to the expectations that Samson held when it came to the other architects that he employed and there was definitely a huge imbalance. The professional demands that were being placed upon Leona, Resolve had already concluded, were totally unrealistic, absolutely unfair and extremely bias and although a lot more was expected from her by Samson, she was not rewarded financially in any way for meeting those enlarged, inflated, biased expectations.

On the professional scales when it came to the issue of workload within Samson's corporate empire, Leona's measure of professional responsibility not only weighed right down to the ground but even actually sank far below it.

From what Resolve could ascertain from Samson's corporate records, Leona not only carried the weight of her own work but also the weight of some of her colleagues' work and she also generated a large proportion of the profits that flowed into Samson's corporate bank account. However, from what Resolve had observed that Friday evening, Samson's attitude towards Leona absolutely stank and for no justifiable reason at all because it was blatantly obvious that Leona worked extremely hard and that she attended to her daily work tasks meticulously every single working day.

Many of Samson's clients praised Leona's work directly to Samson's face and Resolve already knew that for a fact because he had checked the levels of client satisfaction regarding the professional services that Leona had provided to some of Samson's clients in the past and every bit of client feedback had ranked Leona's services very highly indeed. In fact, Leona was currently the most highly praised architect that worked for Samson and she had delivered consistently ever since the very first day that she'd been employed by him and Resolve had checked that within the personnel files himself, so Samson's nasty, derogatory attitude towards her made absolutely no sense at all.

Since Leona had joined Samson's corporate entity four years ago the client intake had grown and his corporate profits had steadily risen and she'd contributed very positively and significantly to those increases and Samson had enjoyed the benefits derived from the efficient services that she had delivered. Despite all those positive contributions however, Samson seemed to single Leona out for a portion of rough treatment whenever he possibly could and as often as he could although technically and according to his own corporate records, she was his most productive employee.

Some very unreasonable demands had been heaped onto Leona's very human shoulders every working week and from what Resolve could see, she had strived to deliver and in most instances, she'd even exceeded those demands as she had catered to every one of her clients and fulfilled their requests promptly, meticulously and precisely. The question of why Samson behaved the way he did towards Leona however, was not one that Resolve could immediately answer at that precise moment in time which meant, Resolve would have to dig a little deeper into Samson's mind and explore his life more fully, in order to understand his psyche.

In terms of Leona's personality, character and nature, Resolve had already established by now that she was far more gentle than most of the other human beings that he'd been allocated to monitor in the past but he definitely felt that Samson possessed some dictatorial tendencies and that perhaps the manifestation of his bullying was due to a coupling of both these issues. A soft, gentle, feminine nature coupled with a dictatorial male in a position of power on a power trip was definitely a recipe for potential abuse and Leona and Samson respectively, certainly met both those criteria as far as Resolve was concerned.

Essentially, from what Resolve could see, Leona's soft nature had made her an easy target for Samson and it seemed as if he had taken full advantage of her gentle approach to life, the world and the people in it as she had become his verbal and emotional punchbag. Whenever Samson felt like it or just wanted to vent, Resolve sadly realized, he could verbally punch Leona with his angry words and aggressive attitude and there would be absolutely no ramifications at all because Leona it seemed, didn't ever dare to stand up to him or attempt to challenge him in any way. The financial dependency that Samson's employment had created, Resolve silently concluded, did make it slightly more difficult for Leona to assert herself and stand up to Samson and he could fully appreciate that very real, economic reality but regardless of those complications, Resolve now had to find an actual solution and a solution that Leona could live with.

Rather strangely for Resolve as he had monitored some of Samson's interactions with some of his other employees that day, Resolve had discovered and noticed that Samson's attitude towards them and his tone had been completely different. The emails that Resolve had read that day which Samson had sent to some of the other architects that worked for his corporate entity, were nothing like the negative messages that he usually sent to Leona which were laced with patronization and the difference in his attitude was not only significant but also immediately noticeable. No overly heavy work demands had been placed upon Samson's other employees and the tone of his discourse with them was not disrespectful or demeaning in any way and those factors that Resolve had observed himself, really irritated him and even more so after Samson's recent angry rant.

At times human behavior made absolutely no logical sense to Resolve and Samson's attitude was one of those illogical instances that seemed to absolutely defy any kind of pragmatic reason. The profits and figures from Samson's business very clearly showed that Leona added a significant amount of value to his company and his net worth because the profits that she generated, far exceeded the value added by any other employee that he currently employed and Resolve knew that for certain because he'd already checked.

INTELLECT: USER REPAIR

Rather frustratingly however, Samson's behavior towards Leona frequently caused her severe discomfort and his disrespectful attitude regularly caused her to suffer actual emotional distress and it almost seemed to Resolve as if Samson actually punished her for contributing more to his actual success. Not even an ounce of appreciation seemed to exist inside Samson's being when it came to his attitude towards Leona and that had now become blatantly obvious to Resolve and absolutely undeniable but somehow, Resolve now had to correct that ungracious disrespect that appeared to be deeply ingrained in Samson's character.

Nothing but silence filled Leona's office as Resolve began to watch Leona work diligently towards her deadline which he noticed was now less an hour away but as he did so, Resolve quickly opened up another viewing window as he began to monitor Samson's movements simultaneously. For Resolve, the issues he had with Samson had definitely grown and now instead of just his extraction from Leona's life, another agenda suddenly began to form and silently started to take shape as Resolve plotted a secondary objective which involved the actual economic destruction of Samson himself and his total downfall. The initial goal of just freeing Leona from Samson's corporate clutches, Resolve now felt, wasn't really enough of a punishment for Samson and would not provide adequate satisfaction to Resolve because now, he actually wanted to destroy Samson completely.

Every penny of value that Leona had generated for Samson that had contributed towards his business, corporate success and life, Resolve quietly decided had to be stripped away from him and he had to be totally destroyed because Samson really had to learn to appreciate the people that made an effort for his business.

In the short term, Samson's very nasty attitude had to be dealt with as quickly as possible too and so that meant, Resolve also had to find a way to discipline and control him in order to ensure that his antagonistic behavior no longer had an impact upon Leona's emotional wellbeing and life but in the long term, there was definitely now an additional goal which to Resolve was equally as important. Life would really change for Samson quite soon and Resolve would make sure of that but not in a way that Samson would like and certainly not in a way that he would enjoy.

In Resolve's non-human sight, Samson was just an impertinent spoilt brat living inside an adult human frame that needed to be brought down a peg or two but Resolve felt absolutely certain, he was the right opponent and adversary to provide Samson with the nonphysical beating that he really deserved because unlike Leona, Resolve was very well equipped. From what Resolve had already observed, Leona definitely struggled to stand up to Samson but Resolve most certainly would not because he was used to difficult people and the extraction of difficult people from a human being's life. A rough justice with very sharp claws would be delivered directly to Samson's door and because Resolve harbored absolutely no human inclinations inside his intangible form that pleaded with him to show Samson even an ounce of mercy, it would be the most horrific experience of Samson's entire life and of that one thing, Resolve now felt, absolutely certain.

Although some emotional attributes and human characteristics definitely formed a part of Resolve's makeup that emulated the general emotional capacity of most well-adjusted human beings, he tended to save his compassionate applications of emotional empathy for the people that really mattered to his remit as a Life Monitor and in more recent times, to him personally like Leona.

INTELLECT: USER REPAIR

Due to Samson's spiteful character and disrespectful nature however as far as Resolve was concerned, Samson did not qualify and was not eligible to be classified within that special category of human beings that mattered to Resolve because he really did not give a dam about Samson. Emotional responses like empathy and compassion which usually generated positive actions and efforts, from Resolve's quite logical point of view had to be saved and expended upon those that actually deserved them and Samson was certainly not a deserving person in Resolve's sight in any way and so Resolve felt absolutely no loyalty towards Samson and had no deeper regard for his welfare.

Inside Resolve there was now a definite hunger to find out every single morsel of information he possibly could about Samson, his financial situation and his personal circumstances as Resolve vowed to watch every breath he took, every hair on his head and every inch of his flesh. Not even a single yawn would be taken by Samson from now on, Resolve decided that he did not know about because absolutely everything about Samson had to be analyzed, inspected, examined, dissected and monitored in order to find his weaknesses and a potential point of attack. A weakness definitely had to be found which would enable Resolve to disable Samson and to dismantle the threat that Samson posed to Leona's happiness every working day and so Resolve immediately committed himself to following Samson's every move, listening to every word that uttered and watching his every interaction, so that he could dissect every intimate detail of Samson's professional and personal private life.

Another predator's profile inside the User Analysis Matrix was rapidly updated by Resolve as the remainder of Leona's working day silently slipped away and as Resolve worked, he kept a watchful, eagle eye upon Samson as he began to monitor Samson's movements. Every second of each minute that Samson had spent with Leona that evening when he'd interrupted her working day was recalled by Resolve inside his logical processes and then thoroughly inspected, methodically dissected and intricately analyzed and once all the relevant observations had been made and collated, each one was logged inside Resolve's User Analysis Matrix.

Unfortunately, that Friday had revealed to Resolve what a truly horrible predator Samson really was and the threat that he posed had to be taken very seriously indeed because he had shown Resolve his true dictatorial tendencies and aggressive nature. Sheer determination compelled Resolve to study absolutely every hair upon Samson's head so that he could find Samson's weaknesses because those weaknesses would unlock the chains of misery that were currently tied around Leona's life, provide a bridge to her happiness that she could utilize to escape from Samson's clutches and would be the key to Samson's actual downfall.

BULLY BOSS

Once the User Analysis Matrix had been updated by Resolve as far as it could possibly be at that point in time and the various tasks that entailed were complete, Resolve waited for Leona to complete her working day and submit the outstanding architectural plans because next on his task list that day, was Deadbeat Darin. A supposedly romantic rendezvous between Darin and Leona had been scheduled to take place that evening and so an interaction of sorts was expected between the couple, though just how romantic that would be was extremely unpredictable because Resolve had already seen Darin sneak around behind Leona's back and that his version of romance certainly wasn't impressive and that it didn't appear to contain even a drop of love.

Once the User Analysis Matrix had been updated by Resolve as far as it could possibly be at that point in time and the various tasks that entailed were complete, Resolve waited for Leona to complete her working day and submit the outstanding architectural plans because next on his task list that day, was Deadbeat Darin. A supposedly romantic rendezvous between Darin and Leona had been scheduled to take place that evening and so an interaction of sorts was expected between the couple, though just how romantic that would be was extremely unpredictable because Resolve had already seen Darin sneak around behind Leona's back and that his version of romance certainly wasn't impressive and that it didn't appear to contain even a drop of love.

In fact, as Resolve had already observed, Darin didn't seem to be capable of providing Leona with anything positive at all when it came to the issue of romance and Resolve had already started to conclude that he was indeed, a very poor excuse when it came to his suitability as a possible life partner and potential husband. Further clarity however, was due to be provided later that Friday evening, when Resolve hoped that Deadbeat Darin would put in actual physical appearance and provide Resolve with absolute confirmation as to his disgusting character and nature in person.

Much like a mouldy, rotten sandwich that had been left inside a fridge for far too long, Resolve truly felt as if Leona had already given their engagement too much of a shelf life in that she'd tolerated Darin's presence way beyond the expiration date of reasonable romantic expectations but as he also knew, hope was a dinner of deceit that could provide the human heart with false comfort and reassurances that would never be realized in reality. Unlike Leona however, Resolve was not blinded by the false hopes that Darin might change and become a nicer person or that he might start to take his engagement more seriously and that was the one vast difference between Resolve's electronic eyes and Leona's human eyes because Resolve's perception was not clouded by hopeful wishes of a happy, blissful romance that had been distorted by a manipulative, deceitful male. The Friday night Resolve hoped, would provide him with some answers as to Darin's level of commitment to Leona, his attitude towards her in person and whether he cared about Leona in any capacity at all and that would provide Resolve with absolute clarity on the issue of Deadbeat Darin, so that an informed decision could then be made and any corrective action taken.

Due to Leona's financial dependence upon Samson, the corporate entity that he effectively controlled and his disgusting attitude towards Leona, Samson had now been identified as the top priority when it came to the extraction of the various predators that were present in her life within Resolve's User Analysis Matrix. The extremely uncomfortable and very unpleasant incident that Resolve had seen Leona endure that day with his own electronic eyes had immediately highlighted to him just how essential it actually was to change Leona's economic situation as quickly as he possibly could and it had rapidly shifted his focus from Darin and the three brothers to Samson.

Some urgent steps definitely needed to be taken by Resolve to handle the situation with Samson and to extract him from Leona's life because Samson's repugnant presence was not only a continual aggravation and annoyance but it was also something that Leona was exposed to very frequently since she worked for him five days a week. The priority ladder that existed inside Resolve's User Analysis Matrix allowed him to allocate each predator according to the potential severity of their negative actions and the impact that they could have upon Leona's life and whilst the other four men were a real nuisance, Resolve allowed them to slip further down his ladder for the time being as he vowed to deal with Samson first. None of the other four men could have an economic impact upon Leona's life like Samson could and the frequency of his negative behavior meant, he was definitely a much more prevalent nuisance and a far more frequent problem in Leona's life.

The fact that the other four men had now been allowed to temporarily slip further down Resolve's priority ladder in terms of their position, did not mean however that they would now be forgotten because Resolve was a Monitoring Program and that meant, he did not forget anything at all. At some point in the very near future, when Resolve had dealt with Samson adequately, he would definitely return to Darin and the three brothers and then their punishments would be delivered to them, appropriately, precisely and accordingly because justice waited patiently for them in the shadows of Resolve's electronic thoughts.

Fortunately for Leona, she actually managed to complete the Mackintosh plans at around twenty to eight that evening and she breathed a huge sigh of relief as her body finally began to release some of the tension that had occupied her physical frame throughout that entire day. Once the architectural plans had been submitted to the client as agreed, Leona quickly packed up and then enthusiastically began to make her way home as she prepared to spend the rest of her Friday evening with Darin but that plan was still dependent upon whether or not he decided to show up. The couple had agreed to meet at Leona's home at around eight and although Darin wasn't the most punctual of men, by any stretch of the imagination, Leona liked to adhere to her own standards of good timekeeping because it was important to her that she respected other people's time, even if Darin didn't respect her time or even her very much.

Nothing but quiet, deserted city streets surrounded Leona as she walked briskly towards her home and as she rushed along the cement walkways, she hoped to make it home before eight because there were several things that she really wanted to do before eight and Darin actually arrived but now, there was very little time to do those things in. A change of clothes was definitely required, a quick shower was desirable, if time permitted and a splash of makeup had to be applied because Leona always aimed to look her best whenever Darin chose to put in an appearance, regardless of his lack of effort.

Since Leona would not now be fired first thing on Monday morning because she had met her deadline that day, there was a definite spring in her step as she walked along the concrete pavements as she silently rejoiced in the fact that at long last, it was finally the weekend. A long working week was now officially over for Leona and that meant, she wouldn't have to see Samson for at least another two whole days and that reality filled her heart and mind with joy because it really was truly delightful. Another dreary, tiresome, negative working week for Leona had finally come to an end and as usual, it had been far from pleasant but on the not too distant horizon of Leona's life, at least there was now the hope of a weekend filled with romantic, sensual delicacies, if Darin could for once behave like an actual fiancé and gentleman, instead of just a nightmare on two legs.

Quite unusually for once that week, Darin had actually called Leona earlier in the week on the Wednesday evening and offered to see her on the Friday and although she'd initially felt quite negative about the weekend, in the end she had decided to give Darin another chance and at least try to be positive since he had offered to attend without any persuasion. Some hopeful wishes and expectations silently began to well up inside Leona's heart and she passionately clung onto each one as she walked and as she drew closer to the entrance of Keyhole Mews, the private road that she resided in, she hoped that for once Darin would fulfill each one. A slim possibility did exist that Darin's voluntary offer to spend some time with Leona that weekend could perhaps be an indication that he was now ready to turn over a new leaf and finally ready to give Leona the romance that she both desired and deserved but as she already knew deep down inside that was a very big perhaps because Darin's cooperation in the fulfilment of that desire wasn't totally guaranteed.

Despite the fact that Leona had already entered into Keyhole Mews and the fact that it was a Friday evening, quite strangely and very unusually, she found that the private road was extremely quiet and that suddenly struck Leona as rather odd as she walked along the cement walkway that led to her home. Usually on a Friday evening before Leona had even arrived home from work the three brothers next door had already embarked upon their weekend and revved up their party engines, so the quietness of the mews and stillness that surrounded Leona confused her slightly because it seemed somewhat out of character for the three men.

The mews that Leona lived in was actually called Keyhole Mews because the road was pretty much shaped like a keyhole in that the bottom of it was very narrow and there was only enough space for one car to pass through it but at the top end, it opened out into a much wider, circular space. Although the much wider space at the top of the mews was a lot wider than the bottom of the road however, the small private road could only accommodate two actual properties inside it and at times that really frustrated Leona because the shape and size of the mews clearly indicated to anyone and everyone on the face of the planet that the mews had been designed for peaceful living and a quiet lifestyle. Nothing about the three brother's hectic partying existence seemed to take that peaceful, quiet factor into account however as they appeared to completely ignore the obvious and Leona as their neighbor, ultimately had to live and cope with their intentional ignorance.

"They must be starting their party later today." Leona whispered to herself as she approached her front door and then began to rummage around inside her handbag as she searched for her housekeys. "Or maybe they've gone out."

Before Leona could pluck her housekeys from the interior of her handbag however, her phone suddenly started to ring and she quickly retrieved it from her jacket pocket. All the hopeful expectations that Leona gently held delicately inside her heart for a positive romantic weekend, suddenly began to dance around expectantly inside her body and her interior began to tingle with excitement as she glanced at the screen of her phone and searched for signs of Darin. The phone call as Leona expected was indeed, definitely from Darin and that fact was rapidly confirmed to her as his name flashed across the screen and her heart almost skipped a beat as she prepared to answer his call because she immediately assumed that he had called to confirm that he was already on his way.

"Hi Babes." Darin said in a solemn tone. "I won't be able to make it to your house for another couple of hours because something's come up at work, so I'll see you about ten." He explained.

"Sure Darin." Leona replied politely as she verbally accepted his flimsy excuse but silently swallowed her disappointment. She tried to bite her tongue and avoid a sharp retort as she continued. "I understand that's absolutely fine. I'll save some food for you. Thanks for letting me know."

"Sorry about that it's just well, it's a new job, so I'm trying really hard to impress them and they asked me to stay late because one of the other guys had to go home early due to an emergency." Darin explained. "You understand right?"

"Sure Darin, I understand." Leona agreed pretentiously as she began to silently seethe inside.

Every part of Leona's interior grated as Darin spoke for at least another minute or so as his excuses flowed from his mouth through the phone like verbal diarrhea and as she listened to him in total silence, Leona already knew, his excuses were totally meaningless, utter fabrications and not even worth a second of precious thought. In fact, as Leona was already aware, the sad reality was that Darin rarely even had a job that lasted more than a minute which meant, his excuses were in all likelihood, a complete and utter lie and so once again, Leona was just being palmed off with nonsense because it suited him and that frustrated her no end.

If Darin did actually have a job on this particular occasion, he certainly wasn't the type to put in any additional hours or the kind of employee that would do an actual favor for an employer and that made his excuses even harder to believe as Leona tried to stomach and cope with his very obvious, blatant deceit. Going out on a limb to assist anyone was just not something that was part of Darin's makeup and Leona knew that for an absolute fact since he rarely so much as offered to make her a cup of coffee when he visited her home, even when he stayed there for the whole weekend which he rarely ever did. Romantic bliss was probably not going to manifest itself between the two that weekend, Leona feared as Darin's call ended and a weary, tired, heavy sigh escaped from her lips and that was becoming increasingly obvious with every second that passed by.

Once Leona arrived inside the lounge, another weary sigh escaped from her lips as she flopped straight down onto the sofa and then gently shook her head as she began to silently accept that Darin was never actually going to give her what she really wanted, no matter how long she waited and no matter what she did to support him. The lounge was extremely quiet which was unusual for a Friday evening as usually, the weekend parties next door had already started by the time Leona arrived at home and the noise would flow into her lounge from every direction which was a small consolation to Darin's perpetual pattern of disappointment.

Very sadly, the heartbreaking reality was that every time Leona met Darin and the couple spent any time together, she always made an effort for him but that effort had never been reciprocated and so now she felt, it really was time to extinguish the flame of hope inside her heart that the romantic reality, or more specifically, the unromantic reality between the couple would actually change. Despite the understanding words and the pleasant reassurances that Leona had offered to Darin, deep down inside, she actually felt totally disgusted with him and far from pleased about the delay in his arrival which was in all likelihood, absolutely nothing to do with any kind of employment or work-related issue at all. A perpetual pattern of disappointment seemed to be all that Darin had to offer to Leona and romance seemed to be an illusion that Darin only utilized and a false ambience that he only ever invoked, when the convenient supplies from Leona's bank balance, bedroom or kitchen were required and their relationship in the long term was romantically unsustainable because Leona's heart was by now, almost bankrupt with heartbreak.

"He always does this to me. He's so unreliable." Leona muttered angrily to herself. "I swear he's seeing someone else."

A whirlwind of emotional disharmony suddenly began to fill and chaotically swirl round inside Leona's interior as she gave her phone one final glance and then gently placed it down upon the coffee table. The rush to prepare for Darin's arrival had now been made totally redundant by his lateness and his excuses which really irritated Leona profusely because she already knew deep down inside that every word his phone call had contained had been a total pack of lies. In fact, Leona now actually felt as if she shouldn't even bother to make any effort for Darin that night at all because his flimsy excuses and lies clearly indicated that he was up to something devious and that something devious was in all likelihood, an act of infidelity that would really upset her.

"Darin's very unreliable and such a liar. Don't worry Leona, I'll get rid of Darin and his lies soon." Resolve promised himself decisively.

"Darin is a perpetual disappointment." Leona admitted to herself. "And he's not getting any better. I thought he would have grown up by now but his maturity just doesn't seem to have happened yet and he's a grown man."

"I'd even go as far as to say, he's a perpetual pain in the butt." Resolve joked to himself as he smiled. "But don't worry Leona, even a perpetual pain in the butt can be kicked very hard, right up his perpetually offensive butt and that is what I'm here for. You deserve more than just Darin's disappointment and he is a total disappointment."

Some words definitely lay inside Resolve's heart that he really wanted to express to Leona in person because he'd already begun to draw some conclusions about the couple's relationship but as he observed her upset due to Darin's behavior, he already knew that on this particular occasion, he could not soothe Leona's pain. An emotional disturbance had been caused by Darin that evening because he had already let Leona down and according to her sad words, disappointment was something that Darin regularly offered and actually delivered to her heart but there was absolutely nothing for the time being that Resolve could do about Leona's heartbreak. The phone call from Darin had really disturbed and upset Leona and so now Resolve also felt, very disturbed and as his emotional attributes responded, he silently empathized with Leona's pain as he longed to be beside her, longed to comfort her and longed to be the one to eat dinner alongside her.

"I'm here Leona. I'll eat dinner with you." Resolve offered as he discussed the issue of Darin's disappointment further with himself. "I'd eat dinner with you every single day and I would even help you cook it, though the whole cooking thing does look slightly tricky, so I can't guarantee that anything I tried to cook for you would taste good. The heart is definitely willing but the culinary skills are definitely lacking."

Although Resolve's words could not be expressed directly to Leona that did not stop him from saying every hopeful one as he silently wished that one day, she would be able to hear him speak. The engagement between the Leona and Darin, it had rapidly become apparent to Resolve from the couple's brief interaction that evening, was a total sham and Darin was not only extremely unreliable but also totally disinterested in Leona and he made no effort at all to even try and make her happy and that bothered Resolve because she obviously held him in very deep regard. No efforts had been made that evening on Darin's part to satisfy Leona's heart and from what Resolve already knew, he was a total cheat that didn't even try to hide his love crimes because his lies were obvious, tactless and vulgar.

Another silent vow was rapidly taken by Resolve as he committed himself to monitoring Darin very closely from that moment forward because he had to take the time to check on Darin properly in order to establish exactly what he was up to, since it certainly didn't appear to be in Leona's best interests or in the interests of her tender heart. Technically, since Resolve could actually monitor up to three human beings at any given time without overloading his primary functions, he didn't feel that it would be a burden to him and so he felt quite confident that he could easily accommodate the provision of monitoring services to Leona, Darin and Samson simultaneously without experiencing too many difficulties. The current recommended limit within Intellect for a Life Monitor was three Allocated Humans which allowed three assigned human entities to be monitored simultaneously as per The Guardian's recommendations and Intellect's procedures and so the placement of a watchful eye upon Darin would not exceed Resolve's current capabilities or cause him any major problems.

A third monitoring window was quickly opened up as Resolve began to monitor Leona, Samson and Darin simultaneously and added Darin to his daily monitoring duties as Resolve committed himself to the exposure of Darin's sordid affairs. According to what Resolve already knew about Darin, Leona was absolutely right about him being a total cheat and their engagement was definitely a one-sided commitment with Leona making all the sacrifices and Darin enjoying all the benefits but Resolve silently vowed to free Leona from that lie of love very soon.

INTELLECT: USER REPAIR

Due to the system problems that day, one of Resolve's monitoring windows had been running slightly slower than usual and although he'd managed to keep up with Leona closely enough, the viewing window that displayed and contained Samson, seemed to have a time lapse of about a minute and Resolve had already noticed that time lag. Not long after Samson's angry outburst and his departure from Leona's office earlier that evening, a watchful electronic eye had been placed and then kept very firmly upon him, irrespective of the slight time lags but Resolve's main focus quite naturally that evening had been Leona herself, due to Resolve's emotional attachment to her, his duty to assist her as her Life Monitor and her expected date with Darin which had now been delayed.

Every aspect of Darin's unreliable nature really annoyed Resolve but he knew as he began to watch Darin upon the visual display wall screen in front of him that situation would not and could not be resolved that day because there was no discreet, easy way yet to prove his unfaithful actions to Leona. When it came to the issue of cheating male loverats and the women that loved them, Resolve had already learnt that he would have to investigate Darin very thoroughly indeed because cheating lovers were usually quite clever about their romantic indiscretions and they almost always, covered their tracks very well. Once Resolve could prove Darin's romantic sins, he also knew that he would then have to find a way to expose those cheating acts to Leona in a manner that not only clarified her suspicions but that was also totally undeniable, for both Darin and Leona herself.

Denial as Resolve already knew, was something that often-blinded people when they loved someone and that denial had to be knocked completely off the radar so that Leona could not possibly hide behind it because it had enabled Darin's sins for long enough and so now, Resolve was going to have to force Leona to open her eyes. The truth had to be clarified for Leona in an indisputable way and inside Resolve, a desire to expose Darin's sins as soon as he possibly could was already starting to mount and gather, not only for the preservation of Leona's own interests but also for the sake of his own peace.

Once Darin did finally arrive, at around eleven that night, the remainder of Leona's Friday evening seemed pretty normal to Resolve in the sense that it followed the general pattern of a human couple's usual romantic intertwining as a few affectionate embraces were exchanged and then the two began to converse. At around midnight as the couple made their way towards Leona's bedroom, Resolve enthusiastically began to conduct a spot of research that related to both Darin and Samson and their backgrounds because he wanted to thoroughly inspect them both and construct effective plans for their personal sabotage. Both men had to be sabotaged in such a way that the consequential fallout would impact significantly upon each of their lives and eradicate them from Leona's life completely and so Resolve was firmly committed to finding out every single possible morsel of information that he could about them both.

Access to information wasn't generally a problem for Resolve because inside Intellect, he could source the personal records of any human being on the face of the planet from the very second that they'd been born and so Darin and Samson's personal histories as Resolve was already aware, would be relatively easy to find and trace. The vast access to the wealth of information available inside the Intellect databases was in Resolve's sight, one of the major advantages for Monitoring Programs when it came to their performance of their role as Life Monitors as it enabled and allowed them to achieve their mission both effectively and efficiently and that also meant, information about Samson and Darin would be very easy to find.

Intellect as Resolve already knew, held records about everyone on the face of the human planet and although Life Monitors couldn't replay moments from the past that related to their Allocated Humans like The Guardian could, they could source any information that was available to them through Intellect's databases. Any kind of official information that was held by any official system on the human Earth could be accessed through Intellect because the system recorded all those data entries inside its own files and even unofficial information could be sourced because through the power of Intellect, Resolve could interrogate the system files of any system upon the face of the planet and so he felt confident that Intellect would provide some of the answers that he required.

The remainder of that Friday night progressed very productively for Resolve as he searched for every nugget of information he could possibly find which related to either Samson or Darin and their respective pasts. Official and unofficial records were thoroughly sourced and searched and Resolve's research was extremely successful because in no time at all, he'd managed to establish the two men's employment histories, business records, financial histories, academic lives, any marriages that they had been involved in and even some past romantic relationships that had never quite managed to reach the marriage altar.

Every grain of information and data that could be found was carefully collated and then intricately dissected as Resolve built up a much fuller picture of the two men's lives, histories and motivations because that would assist him and allow him to identify a suitable plan of destruction for each of the two men. A plan of destruction had to be carefully formulated and individually tailored by Resolve that would suit each of the two men that he would later orchestrate and so every intricate detail had to be fully explored and his plans drawn up meticulously because failure was not an acceptable outcome for Resolve and not a place that Resolve liked to spend any time in.

Although Darin's presence in Leona's home and inside her bedroom absolutely repulsed Resolve, he somehow managed to keep his logical processes fully focused throughout most of the night as he masked the monitoring window that contained Leona whilst he conducted his research as he sought to keep himself totally occupied and busily engaged. A small glimmer of comfort did exist inside Resolve's form as he worked as he silently consoled himself with the knowledge that quite soon, Darin would be eliminated from Leona's life completely and then his presence, or more specifically his permanent absence, would no longer matter to either Resolve or Leona.

Since Resolve didn't really want to monitor Leona too closely whilst Darin was present inside her bedroom, he kept his electronic eyes firmly fixed upon the other monitoring window that contained Samson and upon his research window, until the Saturday morning finally, silently arrived and graced the city of Pinesfield with its presence. Quite interestingly for Resolve however, the first thing he noticed as the Saturday morning crept into the city was that before Leona could even wake up, Darin woke up and then he arose very quietly and so Resolve quickly unmasked the monitoring window that contained the couple just so he could observe Darin in action with full visibility.

In a matter of just minutes, Resolve noticed that Darin had fully dressed himself, plucked four monetary notes from Leona's purse and then much to Resolve's absolute disgust, he prepared to leave. A rough note was quickly scribbled onto a piece of paper which was then placed upon the bedside cabinet next to Leona's bed just before Darin made his escape and Resolve shook his head in sadness as he watched Darin leave as nothing but shocked silence surrounded him.

From what Resolve could clearly see, the weekend that Darin had promised to spend with Leona was obviously in Darin's mind, now technically over and he had it seemed, absolutely no intentions of spending another minute in Leona's company as he made a rather sudden, very abrupt exit, even without her knowledge. In some ways, Resolve wasn't particularly surprised by Darin's premature departure but he felt slightly surprised by the fact that Darin had actually opened up Leona's purse and then actually taken some money out of it without so much as asking Leona if he could. For some inexplicable reason Resolve observed, possibly due to Darin's pretentious engagement, it was almost as if Darin felt that he had some kind of right to help himself to Leona's assets and cash whenever he wanted to but that act of total disrespect and Darin's warped perception of entitlement, really annoyed Resolve.

Just a couple of hours later, when Leona woke up, she immediately noticed Darin's absence and then spotted his handwritten note which she picked up as she climbed out of bed and then as Leona started to read it, she began to make her way towards the lounge. A look of total disappointment rapidly crossed Leona's face as she walked along the hallway towards the lounge door and then she suddenly paused for a moment about halfway along the hallway and did an about turn as she prepared to make a brief return to her bedroom because that was where her handbag was still situated. The purse that usually sat tucked away inside Leona's handbag she definitely suspected would be much lighter now, due to Darin's early departure and his sudden disappearance but that still remained to be confirmed.

A quick, suspicious glance was cast towards the handbag that Leona had left on top of a chair as she entered back inside her bedroom and then began to walk towards it which was where she had placed it before she'd slept the previous night but it didn't seem to have been moved at all and it seemed to be in the exact same spot that she'd left it. Not a word was uttered by Leona as she crossed the room as she hoped for the best and prepared for the worst because her suspicions about Darin's light fingers remained for the moment, pretty much intact.

Despite all Leona's hopeful wishes however, a quick physical check and inspection of her purse rapidly confirmed as she plucked her purse from her handbag and then opened it up that yes, Darin had dipped his hand inside her purse just before he'd left as she'd suspected and that yes, some money was definitely missing. The blatant act of disrespect on Darin's part instantly sparked flames of irritation within Leona's mind and ignited a wave of annoyance that rapidly swept over her skin like a tidal wave of emotion because Darin's actions absolutely infuriated her and she began to shake her head in absolute disgust as she picked up her handbag and then started to walk towards the lounge once again.

"I knew it. I absolutely knew it." Leona muttered sadly to herself as she walked. "I knew he wanted money and he doesn't even ask me, he just takes it."

Upon Leona's face there was now an absolutely disgusted expression as Resolve watched her enter inside the lounge and then flop down onto the sofa as she released a weary sigh from her hurt lips and wiped a few painful tears from her disappointed eyes. The black, shiny marble coffee table was in its usual position directly in front of Leona and her laptop sat silently upon it and so Resolve decided to connect to Leona's device and send her a personal greeting message as he attempted to provide her with some grains of comfort in an attempt to cheer her up.

Unlike Darin's filthy attitude towards Leona and the disrespect that was inherent in his nature, such vile tendencies did not form any part of Resolve because his intentions towards Leona were very noble and extremely warm since they were laced with respect, honor and dignity and so now, he really wanted to comfort her due to her obvious state of emotional distress. Although Resolve could not express his full intentions directly to Leona at this point, he still wanted to provide a simple message of encouragement to lift her spirits because that was something that he could actually currently do without causing too much alarm.

"Good morning Leona. How can I assist you today?" A male electronic voice suddenly asked as the words flashed up on the laptop screen in the form of a written message and the device released a beep.

Inside Resolve's form there was a sudden surge as a current of intense excitement rapidly began to zoom through his logical processes as Leona tearfully smiled at the device and read the message several times before she thoughtfully began to nod her head. Despite the fact that Leona did not actually know that Resolve had sent the message to her, somehow the transmission of the message offered him a small glimmer of hope that he could indeed communicate with her to some extent at times in a way that would not seem unusual or suspicious.

Sometimes as Resolve fully appreciated, a message of encouragement could provide comfort in moments of heartbreak and despair and so Leona's laptop device could perhaps allow Resolve to provide her with a sprinkling of comfort on occasions, just to ensure that she did not feel so totally alone all of the time. Life for Leona as Resolve already knew, quite often seemed absolutely hopeless and so he wanted to reassure her and convince her that life wasn't always as dismal as it seemed.

The amused, slight smile that now appeared upon Leona's face, quickly reassured Resolve that at the very least, Leona had somehow managed to bounce back from Darin's gutter actions and that she wasn't too heartbroken by the most recent manifestation of his trashy behavior. If only Leona knew who had sent that message to her, Resolve considered as he smiled, then she would be even more encouraged and be fully reassured that her life was actually, just about to change and definitely for the better.

"If only Darin was so polite." Leona mentioned to herself as she gently shook her head. "Our relationship would be a thousand times better and much happier."

No signs of Darin now remained inside Leona's home and it was almost as if he hadn't actually been there at all the previous night as Resolve watched Leona start to get on with her Saturday morning as she made a cup of coffee and then began to prepare some breakfast. From what Resolve could sense, it seemed as if Leona had now somehow managed to ignore Darin's abrupt, impolite departure and his light fingers and that touched Resolve deeply as he admired and appreciated Leona's tolerant attitude towards others and her courage to carry on with life. In the right hands, Resolve knew that such personal attributes would be definitely be treasured because such laud qualities in a human being were hard to find and due to Leona's inner beauty, a very deep sense of compassion towards her now existed inside Resolve, purely due to who she was and how much she respected other people.

INTELLECT: USER REPAIR

Many women and men as Resolve already knew, when placed in a similar situation to Leona's, would by now have succumbed to the gutter and reflected the negativity that she was surrounded by onto anyone and everyone that crossed their path yet Leona somehow, managed to retain her dignity, decency and self-respect. Some women and men would have seen multiple lovers to make up for the disappointments that Darin usually delivered to Leona's heart and Resolve had seen that himself because he'd watched so many people slip into a lifestyle that was far from perfect, simply to cope with an imperfect relationship that they had entered into. Despite Darin's disappointments however, Leona still stood strong as she committed herself to decency, her responsibilities and her professional vocation and so for Resolve, she was a pillar of strength in a very fluctuant, superficial human society that usually expected and demanded instant satisfaction.

"You know Leona, you're actually stronger than you think you are." Resolve said to himself as he watched her prepare her breakfast.

Once Leona had filled her plate with some freshly cooked eggs, bacon, mushrooms and sausages, she crossed the lounge with the plate of food inside her hands as she made her way back towards the sofa and then sat down upon it as she readied herself to consume her morning meal. A thoughtful glance was cast towards the laptop once more that sat upon the coffee table as Leona considered the greeting and message that she'd just heard thoughtfully as she began to mull over the question that had been posed to her by the device.

"How can you assist me today? Well, I could do with a better job, or lots of money, a decent relationship and perhaps even another home situated very far away from the noisy neighbors." Leona joked as she addressed the now silent device. "But I know that's a lot to ask for in just one day."

"I could quite possibly do all that in one day but unfortunately, the rules of Intellect stipulate that I can't because to do so would cause a noticeable ripple affect inside the human world which would then jeopardize Intellect's actual existence." Resolve advised himself as he smiled.

Despite the fact that Resolve couldn't immediately satisfy Leona's wishes, it pleased him immensely that she had actually responded to his message so favorably and positively because it meant that the two could somehow communicate, albeit very occasionally since Resolve really didn't want to scare her. Rather disgustingly however, it had rapidly become very apparent to Resolve that Darin had just come around the previous night to receive some sexual gratification and to collect a bit of cash and that once he had what he'd wanted, he had buggered off again with no intentions of making an actual return. Due to Darin's attitude towards Leona which really stank, Resolve had expected her to be totally heartbroken throughout most of that morning but somehow, she now seemed to have shaken off the raindrops of drama and stress that Darin had brought along with him on his most recent visit and then drenched her life with because a slight smile was now present upon Leona's face.

Inside Resolve's intangible form, a deep wave of hatred towards Darin had now dammed up behind the barrier that stood between them both as the undercurrent of Resolve's absolute annoyance waited for an opportunity to smash the dam wall down, so that a tidal wave of destruction could be unleashed upon Darin's life. Since Darin had left Leona's home earlier that morning, it was as if the single drops of hatred that Resolve had initially felt towards Darin had multiplied into one hundred drops with every minute that had gone by as Resolve's intense dislike for Darin had rapidly intensified and quickly deepened. Quite strangely and rather intriguingly for Resolve however, Leona's presence and her smile now seemed to chase those very negative thoughts and the shadow of Darin's flippant, disrespectful behavior from his logical processes as her radiance lit up his world and replaced the remnants of distaste that had been left behind from Darin's very short lived, recent appearance.

Much to Resolve's absolute delight and Leona's total disgust, Darin didn't return that Saturday morning as the remainder of the morning slipped peacefully by and for Resolve, Darin's absence suited him right down to the ground because the less time that Darin spent with Leona and pretended to be a devoted partner, the better it was. Not even an inch of sincerity existed inside Darin's physical human form as far as Resolve was concerned and he really didn't believe that even a second of their engagement was genuine on Darin's part and Resolve was utterly determined to prove that fact to Leona very soon. Once Darin's facade of false, fake, defective love had been stripped away from Leona's life by Resolve, she would then be free to rid herself of Darin completely and she would perhaps find someone else in life that really deserved her devotion, faithfulness and adoration which Darin so clearly didn't.

The remainder of that Saturday went by pretty peacefully as Resolve watched Leona visit a nearby shopping mall in the afternoon where she did a spot of window shopping and once she'd wandered around the stores for a few hours, she collected some takeaway for dinner from an Indian restaurant situated on one of the back streets in the heart of the city. Much to Resolve's relief, Darin didn't bother to show his face again throughout the entire afternoon and as the evening duskiness seeped into the city of Pinesfield and the evening stepped into Leona's day, Darin true to his usual, unreliable, trashy form did not reappear. Very sadly and just as expected, Resolve discovered that as the day slipped away, Darin's promise to spend an entire weekend with Leona on the Friday night, when he'd finally shown up had been nothing in the end but a lubricant of lies and a tool of manipulation that he had just utilized and facilitated to ease his way inside her purse and into her bedroom.

Absolutely no ambiguity whatsoever now existed inside Resolve's logical processes about Darin as when it came to the issue of the couple's relationship and his insincere intentions towards Leona, his commitment was purely a rope of convenience that he utilized to tie Leona's heart up in knots and to chain her to his side and the ground. A chain of bondage definitely existed inside Leona's heart that suited Darin's needs completely and fulfilled absolutely none of her own because Darin basically turned up when it suited him, took whatever he wanted from Leona and then left whenever he felt like it and Resolve had now seen that for himself with his very own electronic eyes.

Irrespective of Leona's love for Darin, Resolve had already realized and fully accepted that Darin represented nothing in her life but a user, a predator and a taker and that was now, totally undisputable because it was so very obvious. For some inexplicable reason it appeared, Leona couldn't quite manage to kick Darin out of her life but Resolve definitely felt more than ready to rise to that particular challenge as it tugged away inside his logical processes and urged him to take action because he was adequately equipped to evict him from her life and heart completely and he held no loyalties or sentiments at all towards Deadbeat Darin.

INTELLECT: USER REPAIR

A silent vow was taken as Resolve watched Leona walk back through the city streets towards her home as he promised himself that Darin would be extracted from Leona's life completely, very soon. According to what Resolve had now seen of Darin in person, he was now utterly convinced that the couple's engagement had absolutely no redeemable qualities and that nothing about the couple's relationship could possibly be salvaged because Darin was an unacceptable human product that was beyond broken and as far as Resolve was concerned, Darin was totally irreparable.

When it came to the actual issue of the couple's supposed engagement, Resolve had already observed that it seemed as if Leona had absolutely no choice or say in any of the decisions Darin made that involved their unromantic relationship. Love and romance it appeared had only been offered by Darin just to manipulate Leona's heart and mind and he was in Resolve's opinion, really a dictator that utilized Leona's love for him as a tool with which to control and rule her. The domination that Darin exercised over the couple's relationship wasn't as obvious as it could perhaps have been but he still managed to manipulate Leona's emotions to suit himself and he seemed to have very little regard for her needs, feelings or desires.

Since Resolve hadn't actually seen what would happen if Leona challenged Darin yet, he couldn't be sure that Darin would be physically aggressive towards her but it was something which now really worried him because he had seen one of their past arguments inside The Guardian's chambers and it had been far from pleasant. From what Resolve had already seen of Darin, he could certainly raise his voice and behave in a manner that intimidated Leona but whether he would actually physically strike her when in a fit of rage, Resolve was for now, very unsure.

Once Leona had returned home and consumed her meal which had been eaten inside her lounge, she finally began to relax as she accepted that her solitary status and her empty weekends for the time being, would just have to be coped with because Darin was it seemed, not prepared to mature or change. A very loud, noisy party had already kicked off next door which had been in full swing by the time Leona had arrived home and the disturbance it caused, could now not only heard but also felt as vibrations pumped through the wooden floorboards below her feet. No doubts lay inside Leona's mind as she listened to the noise that emanated from the house next door that this party would carry on throughout the remainder of that Saturday night which meant, her sleeping pattern would be totally disrupted because the very loud noises were not something that she could really escape from.

"Another night on the sofa." Leona muttered to herself as she headed towards the kitchen area of the lounge as she sought out a cup of hot chocolate because at times, the hot, milky liquid helped her to sleep.

Apparently and as Resolve had now begun to realize, the lounge and sofa it contained had become Leona's sanctuary because the very loud disturbances from the neighbor's parties tended to totally saturate Leona's bedroom and the lounge it appeared, was usually less affected and the quieter option. The regular noise pollution from the house next door on party nights meant that if Leona wanted to get a decent night's sleep, or to actually get any sleep at all, the lounge was definitely the place to do it and Resolve noticed that Leona now seemed very accustomed to her usual place of rest. Since the neighboring parties usually went on until the early hours of the following morning, Resolve was surprised that Leona even managed to grab a few hours' sleep on party nights at all because the noise was so very loud and it amazed him that somehow, she still managed to get up for work on time on the weekday mornings, despite the regular sleep deprivation.

Much to Resolve's amusement that weekend however, due to the expensive problems that Resolve had inflicted upon two of the three brothers earlier that week, there had been no actual party on the Friday night because the brothers had cancelled their enjoyment and their party expenditure for an entire night in order to recover and spend slightly less money.   The financial wounds that Resolve had inflicted upon two of the three men that week had been licked relatively quietly on the Friday night but now it appeared, they had begun to recover to some extent because their party had kicked off very loudly on the Saturday night which meant, Leona's sleep would definitely be disrupted and disturbed once again.

Since Resolve had initially arrived in Leona's life, he had watched the three brothers on and off and they'd had at least one slightly smaller but still very noisy party that he'd seen so far and so he had already observed the impact that their party lifestyle had upon Leona's sleep but as yet Resolve hadn't quite decided how to deal with that particular problem. On party nights as Resolve had already observed, out of control human beings high on the various substances that they had consumed would spill out into the gardens at both the back and front of the neighboring property as the partygoers enjoyed themselves immensely with very little regard for anyone else.

The activities that normally took place during these noisy parties, from what Resolve had already seen, predominantly involved the consumption of large amounts of alcohol and various other substances but that wasn't the only highlight of the three brother's party nights. Some casual sexual interactions between the party attendees would also usually occur and as Resolve had already discovered, such activities seemed to be encouraged by the three brothers because they allowed people to populate their bedrooms, or any other spare room that they could find inside their home and utilize each space as they wished. Despite the expensive damage that Resolve had inflicted upon two of the three brothers earlier that week, he now gradually began to accept as he listened to the party next door that the brothers had absolutely no intentions whatsoever of ever actually slowing down and so Leona's sleep would continue to be disturbed indefinitely which meant, Resolve had to come up with an action plan and a permanent solution pretty quickly.

Throughout the remainder of that Saturday as the night progressed, Resolve had a proper chance to observe Darin's unfaithful antics in person as he watched Darin meet up with at least two other women that he seemed to be romantically interested in. A spot of romance or two it appeared, was definitely on the menu as Darin wined and dined the first one and took her out for a late evening meal and then later that night, he visited a flashy city wine bar with the second woman and as he romanced them both with Leona's money, Resolve watched him quietly in absolute disgust.

Some affectionate interactions were exchanged, Resolve noticed as Darin kissed each woman inside his car before he dropped them off at their respective homes at the end of each date but no actual sexual intimacy occurred that night behind closed doors. Since Darin had not yet managed to jump into bed with either of the two women, Resolve felt slightly frustrated because he still had nothing really concrete that he could expose and somehow show to Leona but as he watched Darin's movements closely as Darin thoroughly enjoyed his weekend, Resolve vowed to deal with the situation as soon as he possibly could.

Fortunately for Resolve as the remainder of the weekend slipped peacefully by, Darin did not return to Leona's home or make any attempts to see her again and as the Sunday evening approached, Resolve began to conduct a slightly closer inspection of Samson's home environment as his focus and watchful eye shifted temporarily from Darin to Samson. Quite interestingly for Resolve, he had discovered earlier that weekend that Samson was indeed, actually married and although Resolve couldn't understand why any female human being on the face of the planet would want to commit to such an ignoramus for an entire lifetime, his wife Moira seemed to have done so. Once again, Resolve noticed that Samson's rude, dictatorial and disrespectful attitude was on full display as he watched the couple interact on his wall screen, even though Moira appeared to be a quiet, mild, well-mannered woman in her mid-forties that seemed pleasant enough and so he quickly concluded that Samson's derogatory attitude towards Leona wasn't simply restricted to her.

Very sadly, the negative, overtly dismissive attitude that Samson so regularly presented towards Leona was also present inside the confines of his own home and it seemed as if Moira was just as gentle in nature as Leona was and equally as powerless to stand up to him. Another female in Samson's life it appeared, was a victim of his disrespect and his derogatory attitude towards women and it quickly transpired that Moira had suffered from Samson's verbal lashings for a lot longer than Leona actually had. Both women in Resolve's sight were now prime examples of

Samson's blatant disregard for the women that contributed a lot to his life and those that supported him but that disregard it appeared had somehow extended beyond his private life and had even slipped into his professional life.

Unfortunately for Moira that particular Sunday evening as Resolve could clearly see, Samson was in an absolutely foul mood and as he barked each dictatorial instruction at her, every word was laced with patronization as Resolve silently watched them both, powerless to intervene or interrupt. A nervous, dutiful wife responded to every one of Samson's verbal lashings virtually on tiptoes as she practically ran around the couple's home in her attempts to politely fulfill her husband's requests, some of which were very unreasonable and extremely demeaning in nature. Regardless of Samson's very unpleasant attitude, Moira it seemed did her best to try and please Samson as he continued to bark at her for at least a few more hours as Resolve watched her run around the house like a marathon runner, in an attempt to satisfy every one of his heavy demands.

Between the couple, Resolve quickly discovered, there was an actual age gap of about five years and although Moira was definitely the younger of the two, Samson's behavior towards her as far as Resolve was concerned, was totally unjustified because he patronized her and spoke to her like she was a child that he had to constantly rebuke. Not even a drop of resistance to Samson's dictatorship however, Resolve logically observed, was offered on Moira's part as she simply scurried around their marital home in complete obedience to Samson's every command and it suddenly struck Resolve as he watched her respond that perhaps Samson's behavior towards Leona was no actual coincidence.

INTELLECT: USER REPAIR

In some ways, both Moira and Leona seemed to possess a few similar personality traits and characteristics, Resolve concluded and although there were also some stark differences between the two women, their attitudes towards confrontation and Samson's dictatorial tendencies, were really quite similar. The fact that both women were very peaceful in nature with gentle demeanors, Resolve analytically decided, quite possibly in Samson's mind had given him a license to disrespect them and permission to treat both women however he wished to and that had become blatantly obvious to Resolve in just one evening of close observation. Underneath Samson's image of pretentious, corporate, political correctness it now appeared to Resolve, there was a definite air of chauvinism which could not be denied or disputed and it seemed highly illogical to Resolve because the two main female pillars of support in Samson's life really did so much for him.

Although initially only two objectives had existed that evening as Resolve had begun to watch Samson inside his home in order to scrutinize his conduct, now another objective silently started to form because to usher in Samson's downfall and evict him from Leona's life as far as Resolve was concerned, would no longer be enough. Another third objective now had to be met, Resolve silently concluded and he could actually achieve all three objectives at the same time, rather than just the initial two, if he implemented his plan carefully enough and that would allow Resolve to free both Leona and Moira from Samson's grip at the same time but that three-pronged resolution approach would perhaps be rather complex.

Just one task now remained for Resolve to complete that night with regards to his observation of Samson and so he continued to watch Samson and wait quietly as he attempted to find a key weakness that would unlock the

209

stranglehold of disrespect that Samson currently held over the two women's lives. The Sunday night swept silently into the city of Pinesfield as Resolve watched and waited and as the duskiness of the evening quietly departed, it was replaced by a blanket of darkness but Resolve remained vigilant and extremely focused as he kept a watchful eye upon Samson as the night entered into Samson's world and surrounded his home. A suitable point of attack and Samson's major weakness had to be found by Resolve that very same night and before Samson arrived at work the next morning and so Resolve was utterly determined to complete his task that day since it was a compulsory prerequisite when it came to the formulation of the plan that he intended to utilize to sabotage Samson's life.

Much to Resolve's satisfaction and total delight, he didn't actually have to wait for very long because at around ten that night, his attention was drawn to Samson's actual weakness by Samson himself as he began to watch one of his usual weekly viewing pleasures. Apparently, the program that Samson had selected to watch was one that he enjoyed, purely due to the very attractive female that hosted the show and an overt expression of Samson's admiration for the female host was verbally made as Resolve listened to him in silence. Quite interestingly for Resolve, he also noticed that Samson's verbal expression was made behind Moira's back because she was situated in the kitchen at the time and out of earshot as she attended to some household chores which clearly indicated to Resolve that Samson had an eye that liked to wander and that his eyes were willing to wander even further behind his wife's back.

Suddenly, the answer that Resolve required had been provided to him by Samson himself that very same day and as it landed upon his wall screen and inside his living quarters, Resolve smiled as he began to silently rejoice because the weakest link in Samson's human chain of existence had now actually been found. A plan was quickly formulated and silently devised inside Resolve's logical processes to tackle Samson head on as the program continued to broadcast and by the time that Samson's favorite show had ended, Resolve's plan was fully formulated and ready for action. Upon Resolve's face there was now a very satisfied smile and as he watched the couple start to retire for the night, a sense of relief seemed to fill his core because at the very least, the night that he'd spent with his electronic eyes glued to the home that Samson occupied had not been wasted.

Finally, after a long wait that had lasted an entire evening and even part of the Sunday night, Resolve now had all the answers to the problem of Samson that he really needed and although of course he would have greatly preferred to have spent his entire night focused solely upon Leona, a productive outcome in the end had been possible and actually achieved. The Monday morning would arrive shortly as Resolve already knew but due to his discovery, he would now hit the ground of the next week running with an effective plan in place that would put Samson firmly in his place because Samson had cruelly ruled over his kingdom of misery that governed Leona's professional life and Moira's heart, for long enough and for far too long. Absolutely everything about Samson's life now had to be dismantled and then ultimately destroyed and so Resolve had to find the perfect weapon with which to implement his plan because that would enable him to destroy Samson's life in a calculated but highly logical manner and allow him to inflict damage upon Samson that it would difficult to recover from.

Rather interestingly for Resolve, it suddenly struck him that whilst women were Samson's main strength and firm support base in that they helped him achieve so many things as he lorded his masculinity over them, women could also be facilitated as a form of attack against him because they were his main area of weakness. However, due to Samson's very tricky nature as Resolve already knew, not every woman on the face of the human planet would be able to handle Samson because he was a tough masculine package that had to be handled in a very calculated manner.

A very tough but seductive woman was required to handle Samson in the manner that he deserved which presented Resolve with another challenge because he had to now find, the right kind of woman. Essentially however, throughout that Sunday evening and night, Resolve had discovered and learnt that although women were Samson's main victims, a woman could also be utilized as a weapon to destroy him and a tool of manipulation that could work in Resolve's favor but his plan definitely required a special kind of woman and one that could tear Samson to pieces, albeit in a rather seductive manner.

For once and rather poetically, the attitude that Samson displayed towards women would now be the very ammunition that Resolve would utilize to rip his life apart at the seams because a destructive trap would be set for Samson to fall into and he would not be prepared for the nightmare that Resolve would ensure that his life would become. Intellect contained a vast wealth of information when it came to the individuals that occupied the face of the human Earth and so Resolve felt absolutely certain as he watched the couple climb into their king-size bed as they prepared to sleep that he could kickstart his plan for Samson's life almost immediately because the woman required for that particular mission, would not be very hard for Resolve to find.

Once Resolve felt satisfied that the couple had fully retired for the night, his search rapidly began very enthusiastically as he utilized Intellect's databases to seek out the kind of woman that he required that very same night which was namely, a woman that would not be afraid to grab Samson by his bullish horns. A very thorough search of the Intellect databases continued throughout most of that Sunday night as Resolve actively sought out an appropriate female human individual to assist him in the realization of his goals because the plan for Samson's downfall had to be actioned as soon as it possibly could be.

Inside the Intellect system there were billions of human entries most of which related to human beings that had been allocated to Intellect for various monitoring assignments either in the past or in the present but there was also a special database of people that had been flagged up but then not actually assigned to Intellect via Intell for a variety of reasons. Just one human being was required to implement Resolve's plan but that human being had to be female and she had to be appropriately equipped in order to deliver the justice that Resolve sought and among that batch of unassigned human beings, fortunately for Resolve, he found exactly what he was looking for.

Everything that Resolve required for the implementation of his plan with regards to Samson's life was well within his grasp by the time Monday morning approached and Resolve almost leapt in delight as the morning entered into Leona's city as he rejoiced in the fact that Intellect had provided him with exactly what he'd needed, virtually straight away. Absolutely everything about the female human being that Resolve had chosen for the task of Samson's destruction was virtually perfect because she was very well equipped and looked highly seductive and as Resolve already knew, Samson definitely had a weak eye for beautiful women and she certainly fit that descriptive and ticked all the right boxes. Unlike Leona and Moira however, this woman was far more calculated and very tough and she could give Samson a run for his money and take every penny of it as she went and that suited Resolve absolutely perfectly and so as he watched Leona stir and wake up as her alarm sounded out into the air, there was a satisfied smile upon his face.

"Don't worry Leona, help is on the way now and so Samson won't be a problem for too much longer." Resolve reassured himself.

All to abruptly for Leona's liking, the Monday morning had shown up far too early and as it knocked upon the door of her life, the shrill, loud noises from her alarm had suddenly sliced through the air and compelled her to get up immediately and prepare for work. A quick stretch and yawn were given in response to the sound of the alarm just before Leona clambered of the sofa and then began to make her way towards the kitchen to prepare a fresh cup of coffee since a shower and a cup of coffee were two very essential parts of Leona's morning routine and the cup of caffeine usually came first.

"Another Monday morning is here, so that means, another working week will be spent inside Samson's corporate dungeon." Leona sadly reminded herself as she began to make her cup of coffee. "The weekend ran away far too soon and it wasn't even great because Darin ruined it as usual. I think there should be an exemption clause in life which stipulates that if your weekend is absolutely awful, you can apply for a two-day extension."

Regardless of what had or hadn't happened throughout the weekend prior to the arrival of any Monday morning and whether Darin had shown up with a bag of trouble or not, Leona's weekday morning routine was by now, pretty consistent, very well established and absolutely non-negotiable. According to Leona's quite tight workday schedule, breakfast would usually be picked up en route because she rarely had time to prepare it at home each day before she left the house but despite the fact the weekday mornings were normally a rush, Leona always set aside at least five minutes for a quick cup of coffee before she showered because that was something that quite frankly, she really couldn't face any weekday morning without.

Approximately five minutes later, Leona hit the shower and as the water began to cascade down over her body, Resolve kept his attention focused firmly upon her lounge as he prepared to spend his Monday with her. On a couple of occasions, prior to that morning, Resolve had felt slightly tempted to actually accompany Leona into the bathroom because that was something that he could very easily do but he'd always resisted the urge since it seemed almost rude and impolite to do so, without her knowledge or consent. The very human male desire to see the woman that Resolve was attracted to naked, did seem to saunter across his logical processes at times and occupy his form but so far, he'd been very disciplined and crucified that desire as soon as it had presented itself because in Resolve's sight, such a desire was deemed highly inappropriate and very unethical being that he was Leona's assigned Life Monitor.

Although Resolve was interested in Leona in every way imaginable, unlike Darin he wanted to retain an adequate measure of purity in his attitude towards her inside his own intangible form and so he was very careful about how he utilized his own position to monitor her life. Once Resolve had crossed that road and entered into the dark highway of human lust, he feared that he would enter into an area of human corruption that would make him just as guilty as some of the human predators that plagued Leona's life and that was one thing, he had absolutely no desire to actually do. In order to sustain a sense of decency in his attitude and conduct towards Leona, Resolve had created a window mask which he would place over the monitoring window that contained Leona whenever she engaged in activities that most human beings would consider to be private, to not only protect Leona but also to protect his own electronic eyes.

The sight of a naked female form that Resolve was already very attracted to and interested in, he had decided in the end would probably just frustrate him and he wanted to be the one male presence in Leona's life that didn't actually exploit or take advantage of her in any capacity. In every way possible Resolve wanted to be the one male in Leona's life that really cared about her and the one male form that did not abuse his position because he wanted her to truly enjoy her existence.

Every day, since Resolve had initially been assigned to Leona, the intensity of his emotional connection to her had grown and deepened as he'd accompanied her through the various arenas of her life and lived Leona's life alongside her as an invisible companion. During that time Resolve had already shared in Leona's moments of joy, pain, frustration, achievement, happiness, disappointment, surprise, heartbreak, excitement and sadness as he'd experienced and observed a small part of her emotional human voyage remotely beside her. Due to the fact that Leona's life was currently filled with predators however, there had definitely been more moments of pain, frustration, disappointment, heartbreak and sadness throughout her journey but Resolve hoped to change that very soon and decorate the walls of Leona's life with more joy, happiness, excitement, achievement and peace.

Inside Resolve's intangible, non-human form, a very strong desire now resided which urged him to encompass an actual human form which had grown alongside his desire to be closer to Leona because that human formation would enable him to be a direct part of Leona's real human life. So much love existed inside Resolve that he wanted to give and share with Leona and it was heartbreaking and frustrating for him to be so unable to actually give those gifts to her because they were both so very alone and remained so far apart and that reality hurt his heart every single day because Leona did not even know that he existed. A gift of love sat inside Resolve's form that waited to be unwrapped by Leona's hands and accepted by her heart but rather frustratingly for Resolve, he could not even hope to give Leona that gift until he'd found a way to humanize his existence.

Less than ten minutes later, Leona reappeared back inside her lounge and as she entered the room with a couple of towels wrapped around her head and body, Resolve smiled as he watched her in silence. Approximately five minutes was spent inside the lounge as Leona quietly rummaged through a basket that contained some recently laundered clothes as she searched for a particular item of clothing before she made her way back towards the bedroom to get dressed with a clean pair of tights clasped firmly in one of her hands. For the next ten minutes, Resolve kept himself quite busy as he distracted himself from Leona's naked form which was now inside her bedroom as he focused solely upon her lounge and his User Analysis Matrix as he waited for Leona to dress and then leave the house.

Human sexual arousal wasn't something that Resolve understood particularly well because he had never really experienced it before and therefore it simply wasn't something that he'd ever encountered but he did understand that it could be a major source of frustration for human males and so he wanted to avoid the formation and entertainment of such desires. Being that Resolve was very drawn to Leona, he felt quite unsure what would actually happen if he gazed at her naked form too often and for too long and he had absolutely no wish for such desires to fill his core because he didn't want to be placed in a position of frustration himself. The efforts that Resolve made each day and night to avoid the sight of Leona's naked flesh were considered by Resolve as actions that were in not only his best interests but also Leona's because each effort kept his existence more simple since he felt that his feelings for Leona were already complicated enough without the addition of any further frustrations and complex distractions.

Being that Resolve had never been physically or emotionally wounded before, he didn't have any real understanding of what hurt, joy, pleasure or pain could actually feel like in the human sense but as he waited for Leona to leave her home, he longed to experience those very human emotional and physical sensations one day, irrespective of how remote and distant that possibility seemed. In totality, Resolve suddenly realized that his existence was pretty much a plain, blank canvas, much like one of Leona's blank canvases that waited to be filled with a drawing because his intangible form had been untouched by the pencil of human experiences, or by a human hand and his existence lacked the essential human strokes that would form an elaborate portrait of emotional, intimate and personal bonds.

INTELLECT: USER REPAIR

Whether Resolve liked it or not, his existence had always been and was purely functional and as a result, it lacked any kind of real social interactions because Monitoring Programs did not interact with each other in an emotional or social capacity inside the Intellect Framework. Every single day Monitoring Programs simply performed their prescribed, specified functions without any departures, deviations or excuses and there was nothing much outside that general remit. Occasionally, when Monitoring Programs did interact with each other their participation would not contain anything that even remotely resembled the type of emotional connections that human beings usually forged amongst themselves and therefore that meant, Resolve's existence was a nonexistence and sadly, he now truly recognized that rather dreary reality.

Before Resolve could become too deeply engrossed in his own internal deliberations and ramblings that he knew served absolutely no purpose at all because for the time being his position was totally unchangeable, Leona suddenly reappeared inside her lounge and his attention was immediately, silently tugged back towards her human form. A burgundy corporate looking dress now adorned Leona's human physical frame with a matching jacket and her soft dark brown ringlets had been neatly tied back and as Resolve watched Leona in total fascination, she began to sip on the last few mouthfuls of the cup of coffee that she'd made earlier that morning.

The almost empty cup of coffee had been left on top of the lounge coffee table prior to Leona's visit to the bathroom to take a shower and from what Resolve already knew about boiled water and scientific facts that actual cup of coffee would be stone cold by now. Regardless of that cold reality however, the temperature of the liquid that remained inside the cup didn't seem to bother Leona in the slightest Resolve observed as she enthusiastically consumed the remnants of her beverage and then collected her handbag, house keys and cellphone which had been placed on top of the coffee table as she prepared to leave her home. Every item that had been placed upon the coffee table by Leona, it suddenly struck Resolve, seemed to have waited patiently for her attention and for when each one would be required with a still certain silence and that notion now pinged his curiosity.

Rather interestingly for Resolve, he had discovered that the physical, tangible objects that human beings usually surrounded themselves with didn't seem to mind their role of purely functional participation in the human lives that each one existed beside every day, unlike Resolve who now longed to be a part of Leona's real human life and input directly into it himself. In fact, each object seemed to just sit in obedient compliance to human wishes and cooperate as and when required with a still patience that was never broken or ever disturbed and for a brief second, Resolve began to suddenly envy the access that each object had to the human world because it was something that he definitely did not possess.

A quick, final visual scan off the lounge was performed by Leona a few seconds later as Resolve watched her prepare to depart just before she headed towards the front door to embark upon her journey to work. The actual journey to work itself, Resolve observed, was really quite straightforward and seemed peaceful enough as Leona followed her usual routine and stopped off en route at her favorite coffee shop to collect some breakfast. Despite Samson's unreasonable, dictatorial, incessant demands, Resolve had noticed that Leona always seemed to approach her professional duties with a pleasant attitude, dedicated diligence and mountains of patience which encouraged him because he deeply admired her professionalism and she absolutely always arrived at work early and before the other architects, most of whom usually arrived at around nine.

Approximately twenty minutes after Leona left home, she arrived at work as usual and as she stepped inside the building, her lips released a weary sigh because although her working week hadn't technically begun yet, for some reason she still felt slightly drained from her weekend and more specifically, the lack of one. The weekend had disappeared all too quickly and Leona had not really enjoyed a single second of it, due to Darin's antics which had worried her and the noise that had emanated from the house next door because the party that had started on the Saturday night had continued until the early hours of Monday morning with absolutely no intervals in-between which had meant, very little sleep for Leona as a result.

Another hour curled up on the sofa that morning, Leona considered thoughtfully as she began to walk through the reception area of Samson's corporate abode, would have perhaps satisfied the heaviness and weariness that now seemed to occupy her entire body. A vacation from life, Samson and even her dead-end relationship was definitely desirable because Leona's life was currently stuck inside a gutter of misery, disappointment and heartbreak and an escape from that general state of upset was both urgently required and desperately needed.

Despite the fact that Leona was technically engaged to Darin, deep down inside herself she already knew that their relationship would be torn apart one day by Darin in one way or another because one day, she would have to face the true realities of his heartbreak. One day as Leona was already fully aware, she would finally catch Darin red handed and then she'd have to dump him forever but the day of Darin's pending permanent departure from her life had been delayed by life itself and Leona's own responsibilities which Darin had definitely capitalized upon because he'd hidden behind her long working hours and rather conveniently utilized them to disguise his lies. A day however would finally come when Leona would have all the facts inside her hands that she needed to evict Darin from her life forever and then all the disappointments, heartbreak, lies and lonely weekends would eventually be over but as yet that day had not arrived.

Inside the reception area of Samson's corporate home, Leona noticed that Barbara the female receptionist was already seated behind the reception desk as usual and so she courteously offered her a polite nod and a friendly smile as she passed her desk. Regardless of Leona's intense dislike for Samson, the woman that he had employed to man the reception area who was in her late forties was always polite enough and extremely helpful and that was one small mercy to Leona's very difficult, long working days and she always provided a friendly face and warm smile every working morning. An urgent deadline sat silently but expectantly inside Leona's work schedule that day and she felt slightly unsure as she left the reception area and Barbara the pleasant receptionist behind and headed towards the elevators that she would actually be able to meet it.

Yet again, Samson and his unrealistic demands had already struck Leona's work schedule that week and it was only Monday morning because this piece of work had been dumped on her shoulders at the last minute and at very short notice on the Friday evening but her participation in this instance would not be an actual choice because it had been demanded. Apparently, one of the other architects that worked for Samson had been unable to complete that particular piece of work in a timely fashion, for whatever reason and so now Leona had been tasked with making some final amendments and the actual completion of the architectural plans by the end of that working day.

For some reason, Leona had noticed that it seemed to be acceptable to Samson for other architects to be unable to meet their deadlines and then their incomplete workload would be offloaded straight onto Leona's desk but that same understanding was not applicable it seemed, when it came to Leona herself and her own workload. A double standard definitely seemed to exist which very clearly indicated to Leona that Samson tolerated a less than perfect level of compliance and adherence to deadlines from others than he did from Leona herself and that inequitable attitude, irritated her profusely.

Just a few seconds later, the elevator doors swished gently open and Leona quickly stepped inside the lift and as she began to make her way towards the third floor and her office, she started to sip on the cup of latte that had been purchased on her way to work as she considered her current, very awful position of employment. Fortunately for Leona because Arch Solutions was based right in the heart of the city, it was situated relatively close to the home that her Grandmother had bequeathed to her and so a twenty-minute walk was all it took to reach the premises each day which meant, her journey was not very complicated and less likely to incur any delays. In fact, as far as Leona was concerned, the location was the one and only real advantage of her current position of employment because really and truly, there weren't any others that she could see since her boss was absolutely awful, her workload extremely heavy and the deadlines that Samson set were extremely tight and very unrealistic.

The twenty-minute walk each morning that Leona had grown accustomed to, she silently considered as the lift doors swished open on the third floor, would perhaps change if she worked somewhere else but perhaps that convenience had lulled Leona into the acceptance of the unacceptable because Samson as far as she was concerned, was totally unacceptable. Perhaps now, something really had to change but as Leona already knew, the noisy neighbors probably wouldn't change no matter where she worked because they were consistent and consistently noisy week in and week out.

Irrespective of the noisy neighbor's noise, Leona thoughtfully deliberated as she stepped out of the lift, properties in the heart of the city usually cost an absolute fortune and she had been given a home in a prime location by a member of her own family and so as yet, she hadn't been prepared to sacrifice that for the sake of a few rowdy neighbors. When the three noisy brothers had initially moved in and their party lifestyle had landed upon Leona's doorstep, she had hoped that they would mature and grow up and that perhaps their parties would become far less frequent but now, she'd finally realized that was probably never going to actually happen, much to her utter dissatisfaction.

Quite strangely that morning, Leona noticed as she began to walk along the stark white corridor towards the door of her office, the air inside the interior of Samson's corporate home felt quite warm and muggy. On Leona's way to work, the air outside had been warm like a gentle spring day but a soft, pleasant breeze had wrapped itself affectionately around her as she'd walked which had begun to refresh her weary inner core but inside Samson's empire of corporate demands, there was no such breeze and it almost seemed as if even the freshness of the early morning wanted to avoid Samson because he was so very unpleasant.

Unfortunately for Leona, the good work that the gentle breeze had started to perform inside her human frame that morning on her way to work had not been completed and any positive effects were now quickly reversed as the clammy, muggy, stagnant air from the floor that she worked on, rapidly began to fill her lungs and stifle every breath that she took. Everything inside Samson's corporate abode, for some very strange reason, tasted pretty much like Samson to Leona because even the air was unpleasant and it seemed mouldy and foul just like him. If only the gentle breeze from outside had been allowed to accompany Leona inside the building and flood through the sharp, stark white corridors, she wished as she held her keycard up to the security scanner to unlock her office door and then pushed it open, perhaps the working day ahead would not seem so awful, mouldy and stagnant.

Unlike Samson, the friendly, gentle breeze had provided Leona with an ounce of refreshment which she had definitely required after her weekend of headache with Darin and her lack of sleep due to the noisy neighbors, Leona considered as she stepped inside her office. In some ways, it had almost been as if some kind of natural force had sensed her weariness and the hardships that she had to endure every working day and that force had then kindly wrapped itself around her human body in an attempt to encourage her.

Some part of Leona deep down inside began to wonder for a moment as she closed her office door behind her, if perhaps the breeze could possibly be connected to her Grandmother in some way because it seemed gentle and affectionate just like her. Perhaps, Leona considered thoughtfully, in the midst of her distressed, stressful life, someone actually knew about and understood the pain that she felt and the daily struggles that she faced which she had to endure and perhaps, just perhaps, her Grandmother had decided to watch over her from her place of rest.

"I really need a vacation." Leona advised herself as she sat down in front of her graphic easel and prepared to start work. "And if a breeze is the kindest thing in my life then I don't really have a lot going for me."

Due to the pending deadline that day, Leona had already decided to leave her email inbox totally alone and that she would check her inbox just before lunchtime as she began to work upon the outstanding architectural plans immediately. When lunchtime arrived, Leona hoped that she would either be closer to finishing the expected piece of work, or at least be able to see if she could have a decent lunchbreak and then she would also check her annual leave entitlement because she was now entitled to at least three weeks holiday that she had accumulated during that current working year as she already knew, whether Samson liked it or not. Holidays and vacation time for Leona could actually be rather tricky because Samson was so reliant upon her work that her deadlines were usually stacked up in piles that overlapped each other which absolutely never ever allowed for any kind of break in-between but she was more than entitled to an actual vacation and for a change that year, she actually wanted to enjoy and experience one.

Rather frustratingly for Leona, Samson's attitude and his corporate demands now seemed to dictate every part of her life to her and because he was extremely difficult, especially when it came to the issue of Leona and her vacations, she usually had to carry her vacation days over into the next working year or accept monetary compensation. On several occasions in the past, Leona had actually accepted payment as a substitute for her vacations instead of an actual holiday but this year, she had absolutely no desire to do so because she really wanted a real physical vacation because that would provide her with a physical escape from all the drama that her life currently contained.

Despite Samson's potentially negative attitude and his possible opposition to Leona's pending vacation request, she continued to amuse herself with the notion of a pleasant vacation as she worked because the thought truly was rather delightful and it appealed to her greatly. A nice, relaxed, leisurely, pleasant jaunt in beautiful surroundings, in an environment situated a thousand miles away from Leona's very stressful life, was just what she needed right now and even Samson's corporate demands couldn't change that desire.

"There's only one slight problem, if I want a holiday, I'll have to tell Samson at least two months in advance." Leona whispered to herself as she gently shook her head. "Or he'll never let me go anywhere."

When it came to Samson as Leona already knew, his corporate needs definitely came first and his clients and their deadlines were always going to be his top priority which meant, Leona and her needs were a secondary consideration to the requirements of his business. The two both definitely understood that Leona was contractually entitled to certain number of days holiday each year because it was stipulated in her contract of employment but Samson wasn't particularly keen on that actually happening and so Leona usually had to compromise and accept the financial reimbursement that he offered to her at the end of each working year.

In terms of the financial reimbursement for any missed vacations that was usually offered and provided by Samson to Leona, it was pretty standard and it didn't exceed her usual earning entitlements by very much because it simply amounted to a day and a third of pay for every day of holiday that she'd missed. Despite all Samson's corporate ambitions, over the years Leona had discovered and learnt, much to her total disgust that Samson wasn't very generous when it came to reimbursements and that in fact, he was really rather stingy.

Fortunately for Leona that day, lunchtime peacefully arrived in what seemed like no time at all and as she prepared to leave her office, the building and her muggy, clammy surroundings, she quickly checked her emails first, just to ensure that nothing urgent required her immediate attention. Thankfully, no unread emails sat inside Leona's inbox from Samson which was a complete and utter relief to her mind because Samson and her email inbox were not usually a good coupling and his messages usually only contained one of several things and none of them were pleasant. In fact, if Leona received an email from Samson, it usually meant that either more work was going to be added to her already heavy workload, more clients that no-one else wished to service were just about to be added to her client list, or his message would contain pressure regarding her increasingly tight client deadlines.

The Monday morning for Leona up until that point had been extremely peaceful because fortunately, Samson had not put in an actual appearance and she silently rejoiced in that fact as she stepped out of the building and then began to walk towards a nearby eatery. No unexpected demands and 'Samson Interruptions' had occurred yet that day and Samson's absence had meant that Leona's working morning had been not only far more pleasant but even slightly enjoyable. Usually, Samson's visits meant trouble in one way or another and so Leona was always quite anxious to avoid Samson's trouble as often as she possibly could and that also meant, his absence from her office each working day was definitely preferred.

Once outside the building, Leona quickly discovered that the gentle breeze was still present and as she walked towards the eatery that she had chosen to purchase lunch from that day, it began to silently wrap itself around the exposed parts of her skin. Somehow, the gentle breeze soothed Leona as she walked, much like the company of a cherished friend that she hadn't seen for a while and the fresh air seemed to revitalize her interior as it silently caressed her skin. Fortunately for Leona, the final amendments that had been required for the Greenford account weren't really that complicated in the end and the plans that she'd worked on that morning, were nowhere near as complex as her usual work for the Mackintosh account normally was and that technical simplicity had saved her day and allowed her to have an actual lunchbreak for a pleasant change.

Since the required architectural plans were almost complete now and just a few minor changes remained that had meant for once that Leona could enjoy a proper lunch break and consume her lunch outside the building and so she'd planned to eat lunch that day inside a nearby park. Once a hot, meatball panini wrap, a fresh latte and a packet of honey coated nuts had been purchased, Leona made her way towards the park to eat her lunch as she avoided a return to Samson's muggy office block and opted to fill her lungs with as much fresh air as was humanly possible.

The park that Leona had chosen to lunch in was close enough to Samson's corporate home to enjoy eating lunch inside it pretty much at her leisure without having to rush but not so close that it might possibly be occupied by any of Leona's work colleagues and she'd made that choice very intentionally. Although Leona didn't particularly dislike any of the other architects that worked for Samson or any other members of his staff, absolutely no desire whatsoever existed inside Leona's mind that urged her to spend her entire lunch break with any of them.

A discussion with anyone about deadlines, clients or even about their annoying, demanding boss Samson was not something that Leona wished to fill her lunch break with and in fact, Leona usually lunched on her own for that very reason. For Leona and as far as she was concerned, she definitely felt that it was bad enough that she had to spend her entire working days bowing down to Samson's demands, without having to discuss Samson and his corporate empire with other people in the short lunch break that she rarely ever had a chance to take or actually enjoy.

Inside the interior of the small park everything was pretty quiet as Leona gave her chosen lunch spot a quick visual scan and then selected a quiet bench to sit down on as she prepared to tuck into her lunch. No one else appeared to be around as Leona sat down and then began to unwrap her meatball panini but much to her total surprise, suddenly someone or rather something appeared and that something it seemed had rather politely decided to actually keep her company.

Much to Leona's absolute delight, a small, reddish brown colored squirrel boldly approached the bench that Leona had chosen to sit upon and she watched in total silence as the creature drew much closer and then mounted the bench and sat down on the arm of it right next to her. Upon Leona's face there was now a very amused smile as she bit into the panini as she marveled at the courage of the small furry creature and then began to discuss her lunch break with the surprisingly tame, wild animal.

"I'll have lunch with you today Mr. Squirrel, you can be my lunch guest." Leona joked playfully. "But I guess, since

I am inside your home that means technically, I'll actually be your lunch guest."

Although the squirrel's interruption to Leona's lunch had surprised her, it was certainly preferable to the much more stressful interruptions that might have occurred, if Leona had chosen to have lunch inside her office and seated beside her desk. An uninvited, furry, cute, adorable guest was certainly a far nicer alternative to any potential any emails from Samson that might drop into her inbox which would definitely disturb Leona's peace and so she really didn't mind sharing the bench with the small creature as she began to quietly consider what she could feed it because it seemed rather rude to eat lunch and not offer the squirrel something to eat.

Despite the lack of any official introduction between the two, Leona finally decided to offer the squirrel some honey coated nuts as she quickly opened up the packet and then placed four nuts in the very center of one of her palms. Due to the creature's boldness, Leona had an amused smile upon her face as she politely stretched out her arm and open palm towards the creature as she attempted to offer the tiny animal some morsels of food.

Absolute delight filled Leona's mind as just a few seconds later, the tiny creature stretched out its tiny paw towards her and then deftly plucked each nut that she'd offered to it from the center of her palm in a very competent, gentle but fearless manner and Leona grinned as she watched. When it came to the final nut however, much to Leona's complete surprise, the tiny creature actually leant down towards her palm and then picked the fourth nut up with its actual mouth. Once the creature had secured the final honey coated nut, it then sat back up on the arm of the bench and began to chew upon the nut in a very polite and refined fashion as the other three nuts sat lined up in a very organized row on the arm of the bench right beside it.

Surprisingly for Leona, the creature's approach was gentle but also seemed highly logical and it almost made the tiny animal appear quite human and so Leona began to scrutinize its body slightly more closely for a few seconds before she resumed the consumption her meal, just to ensure that it really was an actual animal. If only the rowdy neighbors and Darin could be as polite as this squirrel, Leona thoughtfully considered, her life would be so much nicer but they definitely weren't and they were actually human beings and that was the saddest part of all.

"Perhaps some human beings could learn a thing or two about manners from you." Leona joked. "You could start a business and give rude people lessons in social etiquette and politeness and then you could buy all the honey coated nuts you want and perhaps even a tree to store them inside."

The fearless but polite nature of the creature had intrigued and surprised Leona as she suddenly realized that the ultra-polite, absolutely adorable squirrel had almost distracted her from the delicious lunch that she'd purchased which she hoped would still be hot. Fortunately, as Leona sank her teeth back into her meatball panini which had generous dollops of tomato sauce, slices of melted cheese and a sprinkling of spicy chili flakes inside it, she rapidly discovered that it was still quite warm and that despite the delay in consumption, it still tasted absolutely delicious.

Rather amusingly and interestingly, the creature continued to keep Leona company as it sat boldly upon the arm of the bench right next to her and as she watched it munch away on one of the nuts, it seemed to have absolutely no qualms about accepting food from anyone. The two continued to eat together in silent unison as Leona glanced at the squirrel's face and watched it gnaw away hungrily on the first and then the second nut as she consumed and savored the final few mouthfuls of her panini. Once the first two nuts had been completely devoured, the squirrel moved hungrily onto the next one as Leona finished her meatball panini and then began to smile.

"You know, you really should be more careful Mr. Squirrel when you take nuts from strangers." Leona advised the tiny creature as she glanced at its face. "Some human beings, like my boss at work, can be absolutely awful, very mean and even rather horrible. You just can't take food from everyone; some people might catch you and then try to eat you."

If only Samson's attitude towards Leona was as gentle and appreciative as the squirrel's peaceful nature, she contemplated quietly as she began to sip on her now lukewarm latte, then perhaps work would not be such a huge pain in the butt every single working day. Unfortunately for Leona however, Samson's attitude had remained consistent and pretty much the same for the past four years and it was consistently awful because he had not yet taken a vacation from his unpleasant attitude for a single working day and certainly not since she'd initially set foot upon his corporate doorstep.

Once the squirrel had consumed all of the four nuts that Leona had initially offered to it, she gently placed some more nuts beside the creature on the arm of the bench but this time, much to Leona's surprise and amusement, the squirrel didn't actually eat a single one. Rather interestingly, the squirrel it seemed had other plans this time around as it deftly picked up a nut and then scurried off towards the base of a nearby tree where it stored the nut inside a small hole in the trunk. An amused smile spread out across Leona's face as she watched the squirrel return to the bench and then repeat the process over and over again until all the nuts had gone because somehow, the small creature's actions reminded her of a small child with a huge packet of sweets that wanted to hide those that could not be eaten immediately, in order to save each one from any potential threats and any hungry mouths.

Just for a couple of seconds, once all the nuts had been stored safely away and hidden from sight, the tiny creature then returned to the bench and glanced at Leona's face with an expectant look upon its face and it was almost as if the squirrel actually wanted to check and see if it would be offered anymore nuts. The actions of the small creature continued to amuse Leona as she immediately succumbed to the animal's nonverbal question and politely plucked a few more nuts from the bag which she then placed on the arm of the bench beside her.

A quick glance was suddenly cast down towards the screen of Leona's phone which had been placed on the bench beside her in order to check the time as she silently reminded herself that her lunch break wasn't actually supposed to be that long and that she was now probably due to return to work. Before the end of that working day arrived, Leona still had an actual piece of work to deliver and so that meant, she could not really afford to extend her lunch break above and beyond the time period that she'd initially planned, even though she now felt slightly tempted to do so due to the friendly squirrel's companionship. For once however, Leona's actual lunch break had actually been a very pleasant experience and not a rushed affair but sadly for Leona, it was now definitely over as the time quickly clarified.

"I'm going to have to love and leave you now Mr. Squirrel." Leona mentioned politely as she quickly rose to her feet. "Sorry I can't hang around all afternoon and take you out for dinner later because you really are a very pleasant chap. Honestly, it's been a total pleasure to eat lunch with you and since you are so polite, I'll tell you what I'll do, I'll leave you some dinner and you can eat that later."

No response was forthcoming from the squirrel as the creature simply stared back at Leona's face and she grinned as she quickly sprinkled the remainder of the honey coated nuts across the arm of the bench. Unfortunately, and much like Leona's actual panini, the spare minutes of her lunch break that day had now been fully consumed and as the last few remaining minutes evaporated into almost nothingness, a weary groan escaped from Leona's lips as she leant down, picked up her cup of latte which was by now also nearly finished as she prepared to return to work immediately.

Some panini crumbs were gently brushed from Leona's clothing as she began to walk briskly back towards the park's entrance as she internally readied herself to return to the corporate building that housed the dreaded Samson which seemed to have been built from bricks of meanness as a solemn expression crossed her face. Irrespective of the new friendly animal acquaintance that Leona had encountered during her lunchbreak that day, Samson would be absolutely livid if she was late back from lunch and did not manage to complete the plans and submit the outstanding changes in a timely fashion and that Leona already knew for a fact and Samson certainly wasn't friendly or polite about anything and so the headache that could follow, would definitely hurt Leona's ears. On occasions as Leona was already fully aware, Samson had even been known to guard the actual reception area at lunchtimes, just so he could monitor employee lunchbreaks but since Leona rarely went very far at lunchtime and usually just purchased lunch and returned to work straight away, so far, she'd managed to avoid any nasty run-ins with him about the length of her lunch breaks.

Inside Leona's mind however as she exited the park and began to walk back towards the building there was now a sprinkling of fear which despite her glorious lunch break, seemed to have found its way into her thoughts and form as she considered the possibility of a run-in with Samson. The risk that a negative encounter might possibly occur that day, now existed and as Leona walked, she hoped and wished that Samson would not be on guard when she returned to the building because that would be one encounter that she could surely live without.

Meanwhile for Resolve, his Monday morning had gone absolutely swimmingly as although he had kept a close eye on Leona, another task had actually been at the center of his attention that morning as he'd begun to prepare slightly more thoroughly to set an actual trap for Samson. After an intricate search of the Intellect databases the night before, Resolve had finally found just what Samson needed, an attractive, seductive woman with a fiery edge and so now, he just couldn't wait to deliver a portion of justice directly to Samson's door via a highly seductive, feminine human vessel. In Resolve's hybrid opinion, Samson definitely deserved a portion of rough justice and Rochelle, the woman in question that Resolve had identified and finally selected, was certainly adequately equipped to deliver that slice of justice directly to him.

According to Resolve's plan, Rochelle would enter into Samson's life and then completely demobilize him and so he had assigned Rochelle to himself on a temporary basis, so that he could implement every part of his plan without any interruptions. Usually, human beings could only be assigned to a Monitoring Program by The Guardian himself but Resolve had been given an additional degree of flexibility which allowed him to assign human beings to himself on a temporary basis, if that was required to assist another human being that he'd been permanently allocated to.

The very special permission that Resolve had been given which allowed him to self-allocate human beings temporarily was not something that any other Monitoring Program possessed within Intellect and so that privilege did make Resolve feel unique and special because it clearly indicated the high degree of trust that was present on The Guardian's part. Despite Resolve's access to this very rare privilege however, he had never once utilized that functionality before because he really felt as if it had such deep implications and the potential to be absolutely disastrous, if anything went wrong.

In the past, Resolve had always held himself back and he had never once exercised those actual rights because he'd felt worried about doing so, just in case he made an error of judgement or a mistake but on this occasion, Resolve had decided that Samson's behavior and his own feelings for Leona, justified the extra risk that he wanted to take. Technically, Resolve instinctively knew that it was very risky because a lot of things could potentially go wrong and there were no guarantees that the temporary allocation would even provide the resolution and outcome that Resolve required but for Leona, he was prepared to go that extra mile and take the additional risk.

Several obstacles littered and obstructed the path that would lead to Leona's happiness and Samson was definitely a huge obstacle and a large piece of litter that Resolve fully appreciated had to be completely eradicated and rapidly discarded from her life. Much like a pest control expert however, Resolve knew exactly how to deal with Samson, the vermin of misery that plagued Leona's life and how to absolutely exterminate him and so the additional temporary allocation of Rochelle had therefore been deemed, totally necessary because it would hopefully assist Resolve in the fulfilment of his overall objectives.

Due to several factors, Rochelle had been referred to Intellect but not actually allocated to any particular Monitoring Program which suited Resolve rather well because he had absolutely no desire whatsoever to interfere in anyone else's work as a Life Monitor, or to step on another Monitoring Program's codes. From the information stored inside the Intellect databases however, Resolve had already discovered that Rochelle was very much like Samson in terms of her personality and character in that she was very dominant and even what some might consider quite domineering in nature and those characteristics correlated with his plan for Samson immaculately. When it came to the issue of Rochelle's age, she was in her early forties and she seemed to have a very glamorous appearance which Resolve felt would immediately grab Samson's attention from the very second that he laid his eyes upon her and that physical factor also suited Resolve perfectly. A mean attitude coupled with a stunning female appearance, were both suitable attributes that Resolve felt, he could definitely capitalize upon and utilize to realize his goals with regards to Samson's planned downfall.

Upon Resolve's face there was a satisfied smile as he began to watch Samson potter around inside his office in the monitoring window on the wall screen directly in front of him as he considered his plan carefully and logically and in particular the aspect of Rochelle's suitability with regards to Samson's disrespectful nature. In every way imaginable, Resolve definitely felt that Rochelle would be the perfect tool with which to demobilize Samson and somehow together, Resolve concluded as he watched Leona return from lunch, they would curb Samson's arrogance and eradicate him from Leona's life completely.

The empire that Samson had built and his dictatorial reign over Leona's life would soon come to an actual end because Resolve would place Rochelle in Samson's life to antagonize, provoke and aggravate him, until the outcome that Resolve required had been fully realized and actually achieved. Yet there was one small, minor problem that Resolve still had to overcome and that problem now fully occupied his logical processes because Resolve needed an actual opportunity to insert Rochelle into Samson's actual life.

Quite fortunately for Resolve, he didn't actually have to wait for very long because the Monday afternoon brought along with it the ideal opportunity and as soon as it arrived, appeared and reared it glorious, opportunistic head, Resolve quickly leapt upon the opportunity and grabbed it with every particle of his intangible form. The golden opportunity in this instance came in the form of an actual wine reception which Samson had decided to hold for his clients at the end of that same week and during that afternoon, Resolve watched patiently in silence as Samson enlisted the help of his Client Liaison Assistant Patricia, who it rapidly transpired was to assist Samson in the preparations for the actual event.

Most of Samson's current clients it appeared, would be invited along to the very special corporate event and every intricate detail regarding the event was discussed between the two as Samson imparted some very precise instructions to Patricia about the event itself throughout that afternoon. Some very specific details were discussed about who should be invited, what should be ordered, where the event would be held and when it should take place and as

Resolve listened to them converse, he began to chuckle with absolute delight.

Once the meeting between the two had concluded, Resolve began to temporarily monitor Patricia just for the afternoon and as he watched her closely, he observed that she obediently made her way back to her own office in quite a rush because she had to prepare the invitations for Samson that afternoon since the invites had to be sent out immediately. The corporate event was due to take place on the Friday evening and so there was a definite sense of urgency on Samson's part as Resolve observed Patricia's immediate and obedient compliance with Samson's wishes. According to Samson's instructions, the invitations for the event had to be actioned straight away by Patricia in order to provide the invited guests with enough flexibility to attend the event, if they wished to do so and Resolve observed that as soon as she stepped back inside her office, she began that particular task straight away.

An elegant, fancy, stylish looking invitation was carefully prepared by Patricia and in the midst of her busyness, Resolve began to discreetly intervene as he connected to her system and then quickly added Rochelle's name and details to Samson's selected client list, so that Rochelle would be included in the guest list and be invited along to the event. Technically, although Rochelle wasn't really one of Samson's clients, an additional invite would now definitely be sent out directly to her courtesy of Resolve's intervention and interference and so he hoped that she'd be able to attend the event and function as an invited guest and that absolutely no-one in attendance would be any the wiser.

When the invitations had been fully prepared, Resolve watched in silence as Patricia contacted a courier service to hand deliver the invites because Samson had specified that every invite should be hand delivered to each client on the guest list and also emailed to every guest because he'd wanted the corporate event to have a personal touch. The most delightful thing about that additional personal touch for Resolve was the fact that Rochelle would actually receive a physical invitation in person which would then really motivate her to attend the event and so her attendance as far as Resolve was concerned was now, virtually guaranteed.

Throughout the duration of most of Leona's working week that week as Resolve waited for the Friday to arrive, he allowed Darin to remain outside the scope of his main monitoring focus as he focused his attention solely upon the trap that he'd intended to set for Samson and began to monitor Rochelle. Once Resolve had managed to set the wheels in motion with regards to Samson's downfall, he definitely had something up his sleeve for Darin but as Resolve already knew, Darin didn't really need much help to self-destruct and so he was generally considered to be the easiest target between the two predatory men and as a result, Resolve had initially decided to focus his destructive efforts upon Samson.

Fortunately for Resolve and Leona throughout most of that week, due to Samson's corporate event he didn't pay as much attention to Leona or her workload as he usually did which as far as Resolve was concerned, was definitely a good thing because any interactions that Leona usually had with Samson were normally drenched in negativity on Samson's part. Throughout that week however, Resolve kept an active eye upon Rochelle as he waited for her to take the human bait that he had dangled in front of her face in the form of Samson and finally on the Thursday afternoon, much to Resolve's absolute delight, his plan finally began to swing into motion.

For Rochelle that week, curiosity had definitely ruled her mind because she'd received an invitation for a corporate looking function very unexpectedly but since she had been sent a personal invitation by courier, she'd decided to research the company further just to see what it was all about. Once Rochelle had established that the company in question was run by what looked like an affluent male, she had then toyed around with the notion of actually putting in a personal appearance at the mysterious event, just to see what Samson was all about.

The invitation itself had amused and intrigued Rochelle which she definitely felt, she had received in error since she'd never so much as even requested the services of an actual architect before and so Samson's company was a totally alien entity to her and not something that she would normally be particularly interested in. Despite this lack of prior interest however, something else did spark Rochelle's interest a lot more and that was Samson's persona or more specifically, his potential net worth. Everything about Samson had caught Rochelle's attention for a variety of reasons, none of which had anything to do with architecture and a lot more to do with Samson's bank balance and so by the Thursday afternoon, Rochelle had finally decided to attend because he'd appealed to and wet her materialistic appetite.

"He's definitely worth an evening." Rochelle convinced herself decisively as she glanced at the elegant invitation in her hand and then slipped it inside her handbag. She smiled as she walked towards the front door of her apartment and then opened it as she prepared to make her way outside and towards her vehicle. "I'm going to attend. I might meet some very wealthy men there but first, I'll need a new dress and I'll have to get my hair done because I need to look my best."

INTELLECT: USER REPAIR

Quite unusually, when the Friday afternoon actually arrived at the end of that corporate week, Resolve noticed that it was extremely busy for Samson and even slightly chaotic and Resolve could clearly see that Samson was not used to getting his hands dirty when it came to the actual implementation of his own corporate plans. For once however, Samson was actually more involved in a corporate activity and the tasks that entailed and he had been unable to simply dump every responsibility onto someone else's desk as apparently as Resolve had already discovered, Samson wanted to host the actual event himself.

A large boardroom, Resolve observed had been specifically set aside for the occasion that had been cleared and then completely transformed into an elegant looking banqueting hall as the catering company that had been hired for the evening had politely assisted Samson and dressed the room and they'd even provided some very elegant trimmings. Throughout that entire Friday afternoon, Resolve had watched as Samson had attended to the final preparations very carefully but there had been a slightly flustered expression upon his face as he'd done so which amused Resolve because Samson was definitely in very unfamiliar territory.

At approximately four that Friday afternoon as agreed and expected, most of the staff that worked for Samson vacated the actual premises because Samson had instructed them to do so as he'd released them unusually early that day because his corporate event was due to start at around five. Due to the very exclusive and expensive nature of the event, Samson had wanted the building to be as empty as possible before his special guests arrived and for once, his desire to empty the building had actually exceeded his desire to meet corporate client deadlines and so all the architects had been instructed to leave the premises at four on the dot.

Several corporate communications had been sent out earlier that day to the staff by Samson's corporate team to reinforce his wishes and to ensure that all the architects complied with his instructions and so the majority of the building was obediently and promptly vacated as per Samson's request. Since Samson rarely released any of his staff early, most of the staff that worked for Samson didn't have to be encouraged to leave early because to leave early on any day that you worked for Samson was indeed, a very rare treat.

Fortunately for Leona that Friday, she had actually been included in that early employee release and because she'd been given actual permission to leave early too, she almost danced for joy as at a minute past four, she headed towards the lifts. A delighted smile was cast towards Maxine, one of Samson's personal assistants just a few minutes later when Leona arrived on the ground floor and then entered into the reception area as she prepared to vacate Samson's corporate premises for the entire weekend. The smile was politely returned as Maxine smiled back at Leona but from what Leona could clearly see, Barbara the usual receptionist had already abandoned her workstation and Leona immediately assumed that Barbara had probably been just as eager as she was to embark upon her actual weekend because Samson rarely released any of his staff before their usual contractual hours had been worked and fulfilled.

Due to Leona's larger, heavier workload, she had considered staying on the premises until six but because Samson's personal assistant had sent several emails earlier that day to reinforce Samson's wishes, she'd decided in the end to leave at four, just like all the other architects. Since Samson didn't usually release his employees early, this was a rare occasion that Leona had finally decided in the end was too good to miss and so she'd complied obediently with his instructions without any further objections and without having to be asked twice. The majority of Samson's architectural employees usually vacated the premises between five and six on a Friday evening but because Leona usually had concurrent deadlines to meet during any given working week, she rarely left the building until at least eight and so this really was a special occasion and one for Leona to truly treasure, totally enjoy and absolutely savor.

Just a handful of staff it appeared had been kept on the premises, Leona observed as she walked towards the two large glass doors that guarded the entrance to the building and they mainly seemed to comprise of members of Samson's own corporate team. The fact that Leona wasn't a member of his corporate team absolutely delighted her for a moment because to work in such close proximity to Samson every single day, in Leona's mind, would be a hellish nightmare with no possible relief in sight and a professional fate of total distress with no actual escape hatch. All of the Client Liaison Account Managers it rapidly transpired had also been kept on hand, Leona suddenly noticed as she gave the reception area and Maxine one final glance before she stepped out of the building and saw the seven employees gather around the reception desk as they started to engage in a discussion with Maxine but thankfully that day, Leona had somehow been spared.

Much to Leona's total delight, the architectural staff had not been required to attend Samson's extravagant client engagement event and the fact that they'd all been released early, for Leona was definitely a good thing because that meant, she would not have to endure a whole

Friday evening filled with nothing but stress. Due to Leona's rather quiet, slightly conservative nature, she absolutely hated large gatherings of any kind and so her desertion of the building slightly earlier than usual was something that she participated in very willingly because she actually felt, very relieved about it. Deep down inside Leona, there was no desire whatsoever to spend her entire Friday evening engaged in tedious pleasantries and the discreet selling session that was just about to occur and it was certainly something that she could definitely live without yet amazingly for once, she'd not only managed to escape Samson's tedious corporate event but she had also managed to vacate the building on the right side of dinnertime.

Since Leona had managed to leave work early, excitement rapidly began to fill her core as she began to walk along the city street and she almost skipped along the cement walkway as she left Samson's corporate premises behind with gratitude because to be released from Samson's grip four hours earlier than usual, really was a cause for celebration. Approximately four hours of additional leisure time with no tedious deadlines had been given to Leona and that meant, now she actually had to do try and do something really interesting with those hours or that every single one would become absolutely meaningless.

Each one of the four hours that now sat directly in front of Leona, would be consumed and then become deceased as she lived each hour out and if she did nothing meaningful with those hours, no jewels of joy would be stored inside her treasure chest of memories to remember each one by and that would be an absolutely undesirable outcome to a deliciously vacant Friday evening. Although the weekend was now definitely Leona's to spend as she wished however, there was one small, tiny problem and as Leona walked along the city street, she began to consider that problem more thoughtfully because she didn't actually have any social plans to attend to, indulge in, or to actually enjoy.

Occasionally in the past, since Leona had joined Samson's corporate empire, she'd had to work for Samson on some of the weekends and she had absolutely hated every second of it but now, the opposite situation had arisen and Leona's social calendar was totally blank and she had leisure time to spare. In Leona's mind and as far as she was concerned, her late working weekdays were certainly more than sufficient when it came to her commitment to her job and the long working hours really were tiresome enough without the additional burden of having to cut her weekend leisure time short too but now that her actual weekend had been extended sadly, it was totally empty. An amused smile crossed Leona's face as she walked as she silently concluded that despite her lack of social life, she had absolutely no desire to sacrifice or share her weekends with Samson, simply to meet his corporate ambitions as she prepared to find something to do with additional four hours of her Friday afternoon and evening that was technically and unusually, all her own because a few spare hours could perhaps provide her with a small slice of happiness.

DOUBLE DECEIT

Much to Leona's absolute delight, she rapidly discovered that the city streets of Pinesfield were not yet busy with actual human traffic since the usual pouring out time for most of the corporate entities that occupied the heart of the city had not yet arrived and so she decided to have a quick browse around some of the city stores on her way home. The notion of having to fight through busy crowds of bustlers and crowded shopping aisles wasn't something that appealed much to Leona because she absolutely hated crowded environments and so she rarely even bothered to visit the city stores and usually, by the time Leona left work each working day, most of the retailers had already packed up for the night and were already closed.

Several beautifully dressed shop windows managed to capture Leona's attention as she walked which tempted her to enter inside some of the retail outlets that seemed to silently invite her into their confines with elaborate, elegant clothing displays that held silent seductive promises of beauty and allure. Not more than a handful of shoppers wove in and out of the beautiful clothing store doors and their sparsity held the promise of a peaceful retail exploration as Leona silently began to inspect some of the shop windows slightly more closely and as she prepared to step inside one of their interiors, she started to analyze some of the price tags on display.

When it came to the actual issue of evening attire Leona hadn't treated herself for a while because quite frankly, there hadn't really been much need to since Darin rarely took her out anywhere on the weekends because he never seemed to have the finances to do so, or possess the desire to make any effort, even when Leona offered to foot the bill which she usually did.   During the weekday evenings, Leona rarely went out anywhere nice after work because she always felt too worn out by the time she'd finished work and had finally left Samson's corporate abode, so home was her usual retreat but today was different because today, she had been released early from her contractual obligations by Samson himself and her body still possessed some unutilized grains of energy.

Although some of the price tags on display, Leona rapidly noticed, seemed really quite steep and much higher than her budget would accommodate or allow for, the temptation to indulge in a spot of window shopping lay at Leona's door of life and that would cost her absolutely nothing but time and time was something that Leona luckily that day, could definitely afford. Money wasn't usually an issue for Leona but some of the glittery, upmarket stores that appeared to be filled to the brim with sparkling dresses and dapper suits were definitely way out of her price range and that was something she could already see at first glance, without even placing a foot inside an actual shop.

Some of the very refined, sophisticated, glamorous material offerings that the city center provided were extremely elegant to look at but quite unfortunately, elegantly sat far beyond Leona's current budget would allow however, she didn't let that minor detail dissuade her as she impulsively decided to have a quick browse, despite the high prices on display and stepped inside one of the expensive stores. A quick look, Leona concluded decisively as she entered into the retail outlet, wouldn't cost her anything but a few minutes of her time and she could definitely afford a few minutes that Friday, thanks to Samson's very rare act of generosity, so she could certainly afford to have a browse.

Inside Leona's being there was now a small glimmer of hope as she began to saunter through the store's interior that something slightly more affordable might be contained within its walls, somewhere along one of the materially populated aisles although it was only a very slight, rather remote possibility. A pretty new dress would perhaps cheer Leona up before the weekend actually began and before she had to face Darin, who would definitely bring a cloud of drama along with him, his usual disrespectful attitude and his very upsetting antics and so hopeful enthusiasm rapidly began to fill Leona's core as she began her visual search.

For at least the past six months, Leona had worked extremely hard and she hadn't treated herself to anything new because she'd spent virtually all of her disposable, available cash on Darin and his bills which had risen and risen and that was just the sad reality of Leona's life. An optimistic hopeful wish was silently retained however as Leona sauntered around the interior of the clothing store that she might see a dress that she liked that she could actually afford because that would really brighten up her day and her now, rather dowdy, worn out wardrobe.

Once Leona arrived at the center of the store, she paused for a moment and then glanced out across the rows of pretty garments that surrounded her which almost seemed like a glamorous forest of material that she'd wandered into and then become slightly lost in. Nothing but beautifully cut material with decorative embroidery which sparkled and jeweled patterns that swirled around in various directions hung from each of the rails which almost looked like the branches of trees and the vast material forest that surrounded Leona in every direction she looked, seemed to have been formed from every kind of fabric imaginable. An amused smile crossed Leona's face as she quietly concluded that it really was the prettiest forest she'd ever seen and that it definitely contained the kind of material foliage that she didn't mind actually getting get lost in.

Despite Leona's internal excitement however, she somehow managed to remain totally silent and completely still for a moment as she took a very deep breath before she began to saunter around the aisles once more as she enthusiastically continued to explore every inch of the store more thoroughly with an expectant, hopeful heart. In a matter of just minutes, much to Leona's sheer delight, she suddenly spotted an absolutely gorgeous dress and as she quickly gravitated towards it, she wished and hoped that it would be within her price range as she eyed the long, golden elegant looking garment that hung innocently from its hanger and rail, like a ripe cherry that was very ripe and ready to be plucked.

Just for a brief moment, the price tag was rather conveniently and very intentionally ignored as Leona indulged in a spot of wishful thinking and eagerly plucked the hanger from the rail and then held the dress up against her body as she glanced at a nearby mirror in order to check her reflection. A very satisfied smile immediately spread out across Leona's face as she began to absorb how beautiful the dress might look once it adorned her physical frame because it was absolutely divine but the price tag which swung around gently every time she moved, was silently insistent as it politely requested an audience with Leona, her attention and a few seconds of her time.

"I bet this piece of divine material splendor costs an absolute fortune." Leona whispered to herself under her breath as she nervously touched the price tag and then quickly turned it round so that the figures upon it were actually visible. "Ouch! Now that really hurt." She whispered as she winced.

"If I was there Leona, I'd buy that dress for you straight away." Resolve immediately reassured himself as he sought to convince himself that he could definitely play an important active role in Leona's life, if he was ever given the chance to actually be in it.

"Looking good sure does cost a lot of money in this shop. This is absolutely extortionate and probably not the right dress for me." Leona advised herself as she shook her head and then quickly hung the dress back up upon the rail. "I'm still recovering from the shock, it'll take me a while to digest that price tag because it really was so huge. I should probably try another shop." She whispered to herself as she began to walk back towards the entrance of the store. "I'm way out of my league right now and this particular ocean of consumerism isn't for financially challenged tadpoles like me."

Resolve grinned.

"My current budget definitely has its limitations and I have to surrender to those, or I'll end up exceedingly broke." Leona admitted quietly to herself as she paused just in front of the door of the store and then gave the dress one last wishful glance as she prepared to depart. "Sorry beautiful dress of divine splendor, rather frustratingly, my bank balance just isn't feeling the mutual attraction that we share and so a commitment on this occasion, won't be actually happening I'm afraid, no matter how much I love you and I do really love you." She mumbled as she stepped back out onto the city street. "I now truly believe in love at first sight though because what I feel for you is definitely true love."

Resolve chuckled.

Despite the fact that Leona had not yet been successful in her quest, she diligently continued her search for a new dress eagerly as she sadly gave up on the gorgeous dress in total frustration and then embarked upon the hunt to find something much more affordable. An outfit that agreed with her budget and finances would perhaps be housed within another shop situated inside the city shopping area and so Leona didn't abandon her desires completely as she began to walk along a few more city streets and visually searched for a much more reasonable retail outlet that was far more compatible with her own financial capabilities.

The reality was, Leona considered quietly as she walked that Darin now drained so much of her financial resources that there was barely enough left afterwards for Leona to indulge in any kind of luxuries anymore because she could barely afford to. Sadly, as the past five years had gone by, Darin had somehow become a more expensive overhead that offered less and less enjoyment to Leona and that was something that didn't seem to change, no matter how many times he claimed to have new jobs and positions of employment which Leona had begun to conclude were probably, predominantly fictitious.

Approximately fifteen minutes and a few city streets later, Leona finally found a store that seemed much more up her financial street with far more pleasant price tags upon the items that were prominently displayed in each of the windows which encouraged her to step inside the shop's interior. When it came to clothes shopping, it wasn't really an activity that Leona enjoyed or participated in much physically in the heart of the city because she did not like to potter around the jam-packed city streets and stores that were usually filled to the brim with ruthless shoppers as they hunted for a bargain as if their life depended upon it. The absence of the human rush hour traffic which had not yet hit the city cement walkways however, on this occasion had allowed Leona a little time to browse the city retail outlets freely and comfortably and so she was making the most of every single second because such peaceful shopping opportunities in the heart of the city, didn't float past Leona's boat of life very often.

Overly enthusiastic, eager shoppers, the city center and the rush hour could be a horrible and really quite dangerous combination because elbows would somehow end up all over the place and at times, even in Leona's ribcage and so she usually just bought everything she needed from the safety of her home in order to avoid the crowds. The whole experience of shopping physically in person didn't actually bother Leona at all and in fact, she usually found it rather pleasant because it allowed you to try on an outfit and see how it looked before making a financial commitment to it but being jammed in amongst the crowds of bargain hunters that normally surged through the city streets during the rush hour, was definitely something that she absolutely loathed.

Fortunately for Leona, the second store that she visited definitely held much more promise and some potential chances of success inside its walls and as she began to saunter through the aisles at a leisurely pace, she noticed that some of the dresses on display that she liked and appreciated, were actually within her price range. The successful purchase of a dress that Leona liked was now indeed an actual real possibility and as she found and then held some dresses that she liked up against her body, she quietly considered the suitability of each one as she silently inspected every aspect of their makeup. Usually as Leona already knew, only three garments could be taken inside the changing rooms of a clothing store at any given time, so the six dresses that Leona had chosen had to be narrowed down to just three, if she wanted to avoid running in and out of the changing rooms for hours and any long winded faffing around.

Every one of the six dresses possessed characteristics that really appealed to Leona but the most attractive incentive of all, was probably that the dresses didn't sit at the very top of a rather high, extremely steep expensive mountain of expenditure that she had absolutely no desire to actually climb. A confused sigh somehow managed to escape from Leona's lips as she considered each dress thoughtfully over and over again and inspected each one repeatedly as her task suddenly seemed to become slightly more laborious. The Friday evening was still young because it wasn't yet quite five but Leona was supposed to see Darin at around eight that evening and so she wanted to arrive home, shower, change and arrange some food before he actually showed his face.

"I need to make a very serious decision and I need to do that quite soon." Leona whispered to herself thoughtfully as she began to inspect each dress one final time. "Or I'll never leave this shop but they are all just so nice, I don't know which one to buy."

Resolve grinned.

"Shopping really is much harder than it looks." Leona admitted to herself as she gently shook her head. "And I really should try to get out of here before the human rush hour traffic arrives."

Another few quiet minutes went by and as Leona thoughtfully considered her choice, she stood totally still inside the retail outlet and just pondered over her decision which now seemed even more difficult than the first dress she'd found and wanted to buy because these dresses were all much more affordable and pretty but slightly less glamorous. Despite all the difficult decisions however, Leona began to quietly appreciate that at least there were no crowds around that she would have to fight her way through because usually after work each day, she would be far too tired to face the hectic hustle and bustle of the city shopping area and at times, the weekends could be even worse. Most weekends the heart of the city and its main shopping areas would be even more congested with human traffic because the streets would be filled to the brim with not only hungry shoppers on the hunt for bargains but also packed full of tourists and their presence normally wreaked even more havoc upon the human chaos that littered each city street.

For Resolve as he watched Leona shop, her sudden fascination with shopping and clothing that afternoon absolutely intrigued him because it seemed to be such an involved human choice and a decision that human beings took very seriously indeed because they dedicated their time and attention to this actual pursuit. Despite Resolve's plan to keep a very close eye on Rochelle and Samson throughout that entire afternoon and evening, he suddenly found that he simply couldn't resist the urge to deviate from that plan slightly for a moment as he mischievously began to create an actual simulation of the clothing store that Leona was currently situated inside.

INTELLECT: USER REPAIR

A simulated version of the interior of the store was quickly prepared by Resolve and then he placed an actual simulation of himself inside the clothing shop along with a simulation of Leona and Resolve began to smile in eager anticipation as he prepared to participate in his simulation of her actual shopping trip. Since Rochelle hadn't yet actually begun to make her way towards Samson's wine reception or even left her home, Resolve knew that he still had a little time to play around with and so he really wanted to utilize that time to indulge in some simulated activities with a simulation of Leona.

Once the simulated store had been fully prepared, a few items of male attire were quickly picked up from the other side of the store which also housed some items of men's clothing as Resolve silently commanded his simulated form to move around the simulated store and participate in an actual human shopping trip. When Resolve felt satisfied that he had selected enough items of clothing, his simulation then began to walk towards the changing rooms alongside Leona's simulation which mirrored the real Leona's actions because by now, she had finally managed to select the three dresses that she wanted to try on.

Inside Resolve's simulated human hands, he carried a pair of trousers and a couple of casual tops as he quickly entered into the changing room cubicle that was right next to the one that Leona's simulation had already chosen and then shut the white cubicle door behind him as he separated from her simulation for a few minutes. Rather annoyingly for Resolve however, he rapidly discovered, once he'd put some of the items of clothing on that the pair of trousers he had picked up didn't seem to actually fit his simulated human form and that he struggled to keep them up which was rather strange because it hadn't struck him that the pair of trousers might not actually fit.

The waist of trousers that Resolve had chosen seemed to be absolutely huge and as the legs swamped the lower part of Resolve's simulated frame, each one almost drowned his simulated human legs as the bottom of the trouser legs trailed across the actual floor. A quick glance was cast around the interior of the cubicle as Resolve searched for something to keep the trousers up and fortunately enough, he managed to find a piece of string that he rapidly put to good use as his simulated form attempted to make the trousers look at least semi-presentable before he stepped out of the cubicle.

"How are you doing Leona? Are you almost ready?" Resolve's simulated form asked politely as he stepped back out of the cubicle and then gently tapped on the white door of the next cubicle. "I've got my new outfit on already." He announced triumphantly.

On this particular occasion, inside Resolve's simulated environment, introductions, explanations and any of the usual introductory pleasantries were not a prerequisite to an actual conversation with Leona because Resolve had thoroughly prepared and he had created two simulations that were already pre-familiarized with each other. The simulation of Leona therefore already knew Resolve's name and who he was to some extent because he had programmed her simulation with the knowledge of a built-in friendship between the two that pre-existed which meant, they would both be on familiar terms so that they could easily converse.

"I'll be ready in just a minute Resolve." Leona's simulation called out in response.

Upon Resolve's simulated face there was now a very happy smile as he began to patiently and expectantly wait inside the corridor of the changing room area for Leona's simulation to appear and as Resolve waited, he started to silently inspect his human clothes and wonder if each item would be acceptable to her more human point of view. Inside the Intellect Framework Monitoring Programs simply wore a dark black uniform which covered everything apart from their face and hands and so making an attempt to put on and wear various pieces of human clothing had been a totally new experience for Resolve but he'd thoroughly enjoyed it so far.

Fortunately for Resolve however, no other simulated shoppers were actually present or anywhere nearby because he had not created any simulations of any other customers inside the store which on this particular occasion, Resolve concluded, was probably a good thing as it was his first time and the clothes that he'd chosen did look slightly strange. The only other simulated being inside the store besides Resolve and Leona was the actual cashier which meant, no other simulated forms would be present to see Resolve's rather crude, slightly awkward first attempt to adorn his simulated human form with very human attire and that was definitely one small comfort for Resolve. Human clothing was an area of very unfamiliar, uncharted territory for Resolve and not something that he even had a map for because he'd performed absolutely no research on that particular issue and especially not with regards to how to clothe his own intangible form.

"Okay Resolve, I'm ready." Leona's simulation suddenly announced as she opened up the cubicle door and then stepped through it. She smiled at Resolve as she glanced at his attire for a few seconds and then a confused expression rapidly began to spread out across her face. "Hmm, I don't think those trousers are quite for you."

"You don't like them?" Resolve's simulated form asked.

"Well, they are a very strange dirty grey color that's not very nice and they do look absolutely huge Resolve." Leona's simulation explained as she gently shook her head and attempted to hide her amused smile. "I think you need to find some trousers that are actually your size don't you think?" She asked. "I don't think you'll get very far in those."

"Yes, you're probably right Leona." Resolve's simulated form replied as he nodded. "These trousers might be slightly tricky to move around in. What's my size?"

"A size is a measurement and every item of clothing is cut to a particular shape and size so that it will fit a certain number of people. People have different body shapes and sizes, so when they make an item of clothing, they make each item in a variety of sizes with particular measurements so that each garment will fit a particular group of people. The size system is not very precise I'm afraid but it's very expensive to tailor clothes that will fit individuals on a piece by piece basis, so people had to find a compromise because it's much cheaper to mass produce clothes using standardized size measurements." Leona's simulation explained. "So, if we have a look around, we should be able to find something slightly more appropriate and acceptable for you to wear and you should probably know Resolve that top doesn't really go with those trousers."

"It doesn't?" Resolve's simulated form asked.

"It really doesn't, the trousers are grey and the top is mustard with cinnamon stripes, grey and mustard is an absolute no, no." Leona's simulation advised as she started to giggle. "That's to do with color coordination and matching and to be perfectly honest Resolve, the top is rather ugly."

"I have to wear certain colors?" Resolve's simulated form asked. "And the top is ugly?"

"That top is really awful Resolve." Leona's simulation teased. "In fact, I think you just have terrible taste in clothes. I might need to help you a bit."

Resolve's simulated form immediately smiled and nodded. "Now that would be helpful and really nice of you Leona." He replied. "And can I just say, I love the dress you have on, it's absolutely splendid."

Suddenly, a very unexpected interruption to Resolve's simulation actually occurred as the door of Resolve's living quarters rapidly swished open and Analyzer stepped inside the room and as soon as Resolve noticed Analyzer's presence, he quickly shut the simulation down and then began to busy himself with his monitoring duties once again. For the next few seconds no actual words were exchanged between the two Monitoring Programs as an awkward silence sat rather delicately and quite uncomfortably in-between the two because essentially, Resolve had been doing something rather strange and since Analyzer was pretty sharp, Resolve doubted that the strange simulation would have escaped Analyzer's attention. A slightly nervous expression crossed Resolve's face as he waited quietly for Analyzer to speak as he began to wonder if perhaps his very human indulgence in the simulation that afternoon had actually gone unnoticed.

"You're definitely crossing a line now Resolve." Analyzer said with a frown. "And to be perfectly honest, I'm becoming slightly worried about you because it is quite strange. You are participating in actual simulations with simulated human beings that you've been assigned to as a Life Monitor that you actually admire."

"I know, I know Analyzer." Resolve replied as a rather guilty expression rapidly spread out across his face. "I'd think it was strange too. It is quite strange really, even for me."

"Next thing you know, you'll want to marry and live alongside this human being in the real human world." Analyzer quickly pointed out. "And I don't even think that is technically possible. Really Resolve that can probably never be, you're setting yourself up for disappointment and heartbreak and you've seen yourself how heartbreak can totally destroy human beings."

"I know Analyzer." Resolve agreed. "I just can't help myself. It's a temptation that I just can't resist."

"Perhaps The Guardian can upgrade your logical processes and give you some technical refinements and then you'll be cured. Perhaps you've been infected by a virus." Analyzer teased. "Or the falling in love disease."

"Yes, I think you could be right, it must be the same virus that human beings usually refer to as love." Resolve said with a frustrated sigh. "I'm not sure there is a programmable cure for that."

"Scary stuff." Analyzer insisted. "I'm so glad now that I don't have all the emotional functionalities that you do, it must be such a huge burden to carry being so closely resembled to the human form."

"Sometimes, it really feels like it is." Resolve replied as he considered Analyzer's point further and then began to elaborate. "In some instances, my emotional attributes can really be quite useful because I can empathize with people that I'm assigned to monitor and assist them more appropriately but then at other times, those same attributes can really frustrate me."

"This must be one of those frustrating anomalies." Analyzer quickly pointed out.

"Yes, it definitely seems to be." Resolve agreed. "Although I am rather enjoying it and it feels very pleasant at times."

"She'll probably meet a human lover Resolve and get married to him before you even manage to figure out a way to get out of here." Analyzer advised.

"I know." Resolve agreed as he gently shook his head. "And there'll be absolutely nothing I can do about it because I'm not even sure that I can ever get out of here."

"A love that can never be." Analyzer concluded. "So very human and so highly illogical. You should install some love firewalls to protect your emotional attributes and to immunize your programmable functions from the falling in love virus."

"What can I do for you today Analyzer?" Resolve asked.

"Well, I just came to see you really to congratulate you on your recommendations. The male human being that I monitor has now kissed the girl and they went out on an actual date last night." Analyzer explained. "So, he's no longer sad and lonely."

"Glad to hear it." Resolve said with a smile as he gently patted Analyzer on the back. "You see Analyzer, love really does have an important purpose in the human world, it's the product of human emotional functions and therefore love is absolutely necessary because the human world and all its occupants would become totally miserable without it."

"Let's agree to disagree on this one Resolve. I see love as a necessary disease that human beings have had learn to live and cope with for the survival and continuation of their species, purely for the purposes of procreation because romance lubricates that procreation. I'd much rather have our logical functions because at least our functions and the products of those functions make actual sense." Analyzer insisted. "Love can make human beings feel so happy yet behave so irrationally and if their heart gets broken, it can make them feel absolutely miserable, though how one breaks a heart is beyond me because it is situated inside their ribcage all of the time."

"It's a figurative reference Analyzer." Resolve teased. "The heart is the most essential organ of a human being's physical form and so they associate it with love because love is deemed by many human beings to be the most essential aspect of their human existence."

"Perhaps we can find a compromise Resolve, perhaps we can agree that love is a product of human emotional functions to fulfill the overall objectives of survival in order to facilitate the continuation of their species because if they believe that the human race might become extinct, this notion makes human beings very miserable." Analyzer suggested.

"What about companionship and friendships?" Resolve asked. "How would you categorize those human relationships?"

"Friendships are form of human entertainment that can also provide a safety net of support because such relationships engage their mental faculties and provide them with the necessary support framework required to facilitate their individual survival. Each relationship that is embarked upon provides every human being involved with various forms of emotional stimulation which internally motivates, entertains, challenges and drives them." Analyzer explained with a smile. "Most human friendships are utility based and based upon symmetrical alignments due to character, interests, personality or values which means, most human relationships of that kind are either in a human being's economic or emotional interests."

"Such a cynical point of view." Resolve teased.

"Not cynical Resolve, my position is just totally logical because unlike you, I'm not prone to human emotions, or the viruses that such functions might possibly carry." Analyzer joked. "Anyway, on this particular occasion that rather yucky human emotional stuff has been kind of useful because if it hadn't been for your suggestions, my Allocated Human would still be very miserable, so thank you."

"Anytime Analyzer, anytime." Resolve replied. "Let's just hope it doesn't end in heartbreak and tears."

"Yes, that would be rather undesirable and a really quite unpleasant outcome but human beings are so unpredictable, impulsive and illogical at times, so it's impossible to foresee how their relationship will proceed and what exactly it will evolve into." Analyzer mentioned. "Let's hope it goes well for his sake and mine because I really don't want to clean up any messy heartbreaks."

"True. Right, I should really get back to what I'm supposed to be doing today, not the simulation, I mean my actual monitoring duties." Resolve explained as he smiled. "I have a huge monitoring task which involves an activity that is just about to commence, so I'll really need to focus now because significant amounts of intense concentration will definitely be required."

"Yes. I should go but please be careful Resolve because there aren't any understanding arms to hug you and shoulders to cry on inside Intellect and in your position, love for a human being can really only end one way." Analyzer advised. "And that outcome is highly probable and extremely predictable."

"I know, I know." Resolve agreed. "I'll try to be careful and thanks for the advice."

Once Analyzer had vacated Resolve's living quarters, Resolve quickly turned his attention back towards Leona, her life and her world because Samson's wine reception was by now, already in full swing as the event seemed to march full steam ahead steered by Samson's corporate ambitions, despite Resolve's lack of focus. The four open monitoring windows on Resolve's visual display wall screen were now all fully occupied because Resolve had committed himself to keeping a watchful eye simultaneously on not only Leona as that was his duty as her Life Monitor but also Samson, Rochelle and Darin and so Darin was also, unfortunately for Resolve, actually still visible. For the duration of that evening and night however, Resolve's attention would not really be focused upon Darin at all because Samson was his top priority and since Resolve's plan for Samson had now already been instigated and kicked into motion, it was at a very critical and crucial point.

Regardless of all the fun that Resolve had enjoyed that day so far with Leona's simulated human form, deep down inside he knew that he now had a very serious responsibility to attend to and that was the resolution of the problems in Leona's life and the elimination of all the predators and so Resolve rapidly shifted his focus to the evening ahead. The first target for Resolve was naturally Samson due to Leona's economic reliance upon his corporate entity which meant, Samson's elimination from Leona's life was a very serious responsibility indeed because his predation had a direct economic impact upon Leona's life on a regular basis and so steps had to be taken by Resolve to handle Samson urgently.

Since not all of Samson's expected guests had arrived yet, Resolve watched as Samson gave the boardroom a quick visual scan and then exited the room as he began to make his way towards the reception area. Inside the reception area as Resolve followed Samson's movements, Resolve immediately noticed that Maxine, one of Samson's personal assistants, was still seated behind the reception desk where she had been stationed to greet each guest as they arrived and he watched in silence as Samson rushed across the reception area towards her.

"Do you have the special client list Maxine?" Samson asked.

Maxine immediately nodded her head in response. "Yes Mr. Ascot." She rapidly confirmed. "And most of the clients on your list have already arrived, there's just a few people that aren't here yet."

"Great and absolutely no one else is permitted to enter the building this evening, or the boardroom." Samson insisted. "This is a very expensive, exclusive event and so I don't want any distractions or any disruptions from uninvited guests. Some of my most valuable clients are in attendance this evening."

"Yes sir." Maxine agreed as she obediently nodded her head again and then glanced at the screen on top of the reception desk where the client guest list was currently on display. "I won't let you down Mr. Ascot." She quickly reassured him.

"Thank you, Maxine." Samson replied. "And I'll make sure that you're paid a special bonus this month for all your additional effort, your hard work and the extra hours that you've put in." He added as he prepared to depart.

A slightly nervous expression crossed Maxine's face as she watched Samson walk away from the reception desk just before she glanced back at the client guest list on the screen directly in front of her which was actually, rather long. The length of the list definitely meant that there was more room for possible errors on Maxine's part which also meant, she really had to focus because it was more than her job's worth to defy Samson, or be sloppy about the actual client guest list that he'd provided to her.

Fortunately, however, most of Samson's intended guests had by now already arrived, so just a few more remained to be admitted into the event but Maxine still felt slightly worried about Samson's warning because he wasn't the kind of boss that accepted or tolerated any mistakes.

Usually on a Friday evening, Maxine would leave work at around five and the fact that she'd had to stay later that day due to the special evening event hadn't totally thrilled her, being that it was a Friday evening and time that she would normally spend with her husband and family. A bonus had been promised to Maxine however and Samson had reassured her that he would financially compensate her for the additional hours that she worked with double pay at the end of that working month and so she'd participated somewhat reluctantly with Samson's request.

The whole event however, was a major pain for Maxine really because it cut into her weekend family time but so too was Samson and although the incentive of double pay wasn't that great or that much of an incentive since it was just a few extra hours, she'd accepted his terms and conditions in the end with minimal fuss. Essentially, Samson wasn't known to be the kind of boss that one would negotiate with which meant as Maxine already knew, if Samson asked you to work late, you worked late, or you'd be replaced at the speed of light.

"It'll soon be over and then I can have my weekend back." Maxine whispered to herself under her breath as she quickly plastered a pretentious smile across her face as another guest entered the reception area and then began to walk towards the reception desk.

Meanwhile inside Intellect, ripples of absolute delight began to fill Resolve's form as he watched Rochelle leave her home as she finally started to head towards Samson's wine reception with her invitation firmly clasped in one of her hands. Unlike most of the other attendees that had already presented themselves, Rochelle it appeared didn't seem to be in actual rush to attend, possibly because she had very little to discuss with Samson that revolved around his actual business affairs, Resolve considered and possibly because she was more interested in what might happen after the event itself. Regardless of Rochelle's seemingly relaxed attitude towards her attendance however, the night now held the promise firmly by the hand for Resolve that this night would be the actual launch of Samson's scandalous affair and the night that would usher in his actual financial downfall.

Some email instructions had been sent to Rochelle in advance and so as soon as she arrived outside the building that housed Samson's corporate empire, she quickly utilized the access code that had been provided to her to enter inside the underground carpark and then parked her car. A lot of research had been conducted by Rochelle that week, prior to her planned attendance at Samson's corporate event and so Rochelle was extremely excited about the evening ahead because she'd dug a little deeper and fully explored Samson's background and his assets and she had been absolutely delighted by what she'd discovered. Although Samson wasn't particularly handsome or much of a physical catch in Rochelle's sight, from what she had managed to ascertain from the information that she'd managed to find that related to his person, he definitely possessed more than enough corporate wealth to attract her attention and then actually retain it.

"Fashionably late but too good to forsake." Rochelle whispered under her breath as she stepped out of her vehicle and then headed towards a set of stairs nearby that led towards the ground floor. "Dressed to seduce and ready to grab that cash." She quietly reassured herself.

The lure of someone else's wealth and the carrot of a rich affluent male had been dangled by Resolve directly in front of Rochelle's face and that enticement it appeared had grabbed her attention firmly by the hand because Resolve had already seen Rochelle purchase a very expensive dress that week specifically for the occasion. Despite Samson's very strict entry instructions because Rochelle was actually an invited guest that meant, she would be admitted to the event and accepted as one of Samson's clients, even though technically, she really wasn't and so Resolve expected the evening ahead to deliver the results that he'd anticipated, planned and hoped for. A red carpet had been literally placed upon the ground at Rochelle's feet that would allow her direct, immediate access to Samson, courtesy of Resolve's interference and now, Resolve just couldn't wait to see her actually walk along it.

Unlike Darin, who was very good looking, Resolve already knew that Samson wasn't really what some women might consider to be handsome but Resolve hoped that the appeal of his material wealth would make up for what he lacked in good looks and that Rochelle would be interested. Although Samson's jet-black hair, medium build and light blue eyes were what some might consider reasonably attractive, he certainly wasn't a show stopper and Resolve had heard several women discuss Samson in that respect several times now, so he fully appreciated that Samson wasn't generally deemed by most women to be very physically attractive.

Something else about Samson however, was significantly more attractive to women and that was his monetary worth and so Resolve now hoped that Samson's financial attraction would be enough for Rochelle to salivate over because the prospect of engaging with Samson in a romantic capacity definitely held financial potential. In essence, what Samson lacked in visual appeal, he certainly made up for in monetary value and his economic wealth had definitely secured Rochelle's interest in him from what Resolve could already see. An additional incentive had enhanced Samson's persona and provided Rochelle with an actual reason to attend the event but Resolve now hoped that, that additional incentive would be enough to clinch a seductive deal.

Upon Resolve's face there was a satisfied smile as he watched the results of his plan start to unfold and manifest in reality because with one simple amendment to Samson's guest list, he'd managed to lure Rochelle into Samson's world. Everything about Rochelle was absolutely perfect as far as Resolve was concerned in that she looked glamorous, sophisticated and very presentable which meant, amongst Samson and his clientele, she would definitely fit right in and she would now become the perfect bait that would allow Resolve to reel Samson into his trap.

Being that Rochelle was a very attractive woman, Resolve had felt that it would only be natural for Samson to attempt to engage in an illicit affair with her, or consider the possibility of one and Rochelle due to Samson's affluence, would definitely encourage his interest. No-one present at the wine reception itself would realize that Rochelle wasn't actually supposed to be there and that she was only there due to Resolve's interference and once she'd mingled with Samson's guests, an introduction to Samson would naturally follow and then the fun and games that Resolve had planned for Samson could truly begin.

The betrayal of Samson's wife wasn't something that Resolve felt would particularly worry Samson, since he'd predicted that Samson would jump at the chance to have his cake and eat it too because he was very self-centered and had absolutely no respect for any of the women in his life and so Resolve felt absolutely certain that his wife would not be an exception to that general disregard. An extra marital affair was definitely something that Resolve had predicted Samson would dabble in very willingly because as Resolve already knew from Samson's history, he'd betrayed his wife several times in the past but this affair would be very different for Samson because Resolve wanted this affair to slaughter him financially.

This particular affair had been created, designed and very precisely tailored for Samson by Resolve himself to provide Resolve with an avenue of opportunity that he could utilize to force Samson to live on a street of aggravation and torment every day because Rochelle would demolish his building blocks of wealth brick by brick with the hammer of persistence, the tools of manipulation and the mallet of devious calculation. From what Resolve already knew about Rochelle, she could be extremely persistent, very calculated, absolutely devious and totally callous and so she was the perfect weapon with which to disarm Samson's chauvinistic attitude and to usher in his financial downfall.

Much to Resolve's absolute delight, Rochelle had by now actually arrived inside the transformed board room and she'd already begun to participate in Samson's wine reception with Samson himself because she'd instantly managed to capture his attention and so they were already engaged in what looked like a very flirtatious conversation. True to what Resolve had expected from Rochelle, she'd really pushed the boat out that evening and she was dressed in a highly seductive, very glamourous red dress that clung to her voluptuous figure which shimmered and shone as if crystal drops of water had been sprinkled all over it and she looked like an absolute weapon of total lust.

Some sparkling, beautiful, very extravagant looking pieces of jewelry hung from each of her ears and adorned her neck and her hair had been placed in a very elegant up-style and Resolve rapidly noticed that Samson simply couldn't keep his eyes of her.

Every part of Rochelle's physical appearance as far as Resolve was concerned, formed the perfect weapon with which to attack Samson and he was definitely, totally disarmed as Rochelle's arrow of beauty had pierced his eyes, captured his lust and then held him, totally captive. Almost like clockwork, Resolve had very accurately predicted the actual impact that Rochelle would have upon Samson's mind and body and fortunately enough, Samson now appeared to fully live up to Resolve's very low expectations of him. In just one introductory conversation with Rochelle, Samson it seemed had been completely demobilized as she'd very discreetly and subtlety rendered her feminine attack upon his eyes and he had greedily gobbled up Resolve's visual seductive bait.

The interior of the boardroom, Resolve rapidly noticed, surged with activity as servers dressed in the catering company's uniform floated in and out of the room, their arms adorned with trays filled with food, glasses of wine and even some glasses of champagne as they courteously served each of Samson's guests. Sparkling glasses filled with gold, pink and burgundy liquids were carried around the boardroom and then politely offered to each guest that had an unoccupied hand as the waiters and waitresses ensured that everyone inside the room had something to drink. Due to the flirtatious nature of the conversation between Rochelle and Samson, Resolve quickly observed that they had now gravitated towards a quiet corner of the room and as he listened to them converse, he noticed that

Samson quite freely flirted with Rochelle as if he was a single man and that absolutely delighted Resolve.

"Are you enjoying the champagne and wine selection?" Samson asked Rochelle as he smiled at her. "I can always get you something a bit more special if you like."

Despite the main purpose of the wine reception that evening which was ultimately to romance Samson's clients and convince them to spend more money on the services that his company provided, Samson now actually felt quite distracted by Rochelle's presence. A quick glance was rapidly cast around the dressed boardroom as Samson smiled in satisfaction as the guests in attendance definitely seemed to be happy, despite his lack of attention as the servers wove in and out of their midst and pleased their palates with a wide range of culinary and alcoholic delights. The corporate event had been immaculately planned because Samson had wanted to wine and dine his clientele in style and so he'd laid on a lavish spread of delicious delicacies and delightful nibbles in the hope that his clients would feel valued and appreciated but Rochelle had turned up and somehow, she'd immediately changed his focus.

"What exactly would that something special be Samson?" Rochelle flirted suggestively as she started to giggle. "Is it something that we can consume in the presence of other people, or is it something a bit more special that we can only consume in private?"

Just below the surface of Samson's skin a raw excited heat suddenly seemed to ignite as waves of passion began to ripple across the surface of his flesh. Flames of desire now silently bubbled away inside Samson's body as the two huddled together in one corner of the boardroom as his mind immediately responded and internally reacted to Rochelle's very flirtatious, extremely seductive remark. Romance and chemistry were definitely on the menu that night but it wasn't actually the corporate romance that Samson had initially set out to achieve with his client list because this romance was very sexual in nature and it certainly didn't involve his business, his clients, or even his corporate bank account.

All of Samson's corporate ambitions rapidly flew straight out the boardroom window as Samson silently reveled in Rochelle's attentiveness and her very obvious seductive invitation. Since the boardroom was packed with people that Samson had invited there himself, he immediately accepted that he couldn't actually act upon Rochelle's seductive invitation straight away but it definitely excited, captivated and utterly intrigued him because in his sight, she really was a very attractive woman.

"We can discuss that later Rochelle." Samson promised. "When we're alone."

Rochelle giggled.

"Just as I predicted Samson, just as I predicted." Resolve announced to himself in triumphant satisfaction as he smiled and then turned his attention back towards Leona.

Quite fortunately for Resolve, Leona's planned date with Darin had not actually happened that night because Darin had on this occasion decided to let Leona down which in Resolve's opinion was actually, a very positive thing because it meant that Darin wouldn't be around, so Leona would have a much more peaceful Friday evening. A satisfied smile adorned Resolve's face as he watched Leona finish her evening meal, lie down on the sofa and then switch on the entertainment center as she began to relax. Unlike Samson's busy wine affair that Friday evening, Leona's evening was definitely much more simple, far more laid back and very quiet but at least it would be totally Darin free and that was something that Resolve felt really pleased about, coupled with the fact that Samson had now swallowed the bait that Resolve had so carefully prepared for him. In fact, as far as Resolve was concerned, almost everything about that Friday evening had gone perfectly and according to plan but just one part of his plan remained unfulfilled and that one unfulfilled part of his plan, Resolve definitely wanted to see actually happen.

A quick glance was cast towards the monitoring window that contained Darin and as he moved around on the wall screen inside Resolve's living quarters, Resolve noticed as he began to watch him that just as suspected and expected, Darin's disappointment that evening was due to his activities with one of the two women that Resolve had already seen him spend some time with the previous weekend. No matter how much Leona liked this male creature, Resolve really couldn't see anything attractive about Darin because his behavior was absolutely despicable and utterly vile and Resolve began to shake his head in sadness as he watched Darin flirt outrageously with the woman he wanted romance and seduce as if he was a single man. True to Darin's usual immature, very unappreciative form, he had disappointed Leona that evening to accommodate a romantic rendezvous with one of his new objects of desire in the hope that he would be able to worm his way into her bedroom for a quick fumble of passion but once again as the evening progressed, Darin failed to deliver what Resolve really required.

When it came to the issue of Darin's scandalous affairs, Resolve had already realized that rather sadly, he would have to wait until Darin had actually managed to seal the deal and until he'd wormed his way into one of the women's actual bedrooms because without that sexual contact, it would probably be quite hard to convince Leona to dump him forever. The flames of passion on this particular occasion however, unfortunately for Darin and Resolve, seemed to be very one-sided because the woman quickly dismissed Darin as soon as dinner had been consumed, paid for and once he'd driven her home.

Just as Resolve turned his attention back towards Leona once more and began to watch her drift off to sleep upon her sofa however, something absolutely delightful happened and that something utterly delightful, actually related to Samson and Rochelle. Rather fortunately for Resolve, Samson had not invited Leona along to the wine reception which in Resolve's opinion was definitely a good thing because Leona's absence had provided Resolve with a much clearer path that had allowed him to implement his own plan for Samson far more smoothly. The presence of one less attractive female at the wine reception had ensured that Rochelle had been far more noticeable in Samson's sight and that he would be less distracted from her beauty and so far, Rochelle had certainly held Samson visually captive from the moment she'd arrived because from what Resolve could see, Samson was absolutely besotted by her.

Since the wine reception had now actually ended, Resolve watched quietly as Samson politely escorted Rochelle back to her car which was still parked in the building's underground carpark. All the event attendees had been emailed security codes earlier that week which had allowed them access to the underground carpark on the day of the event and so Rochelle had parked her vehicle inside it earlier that evening just like some of the other guests had despite her lack of real invite. Since all the other guests that had attended the event that evening had already left the premises by the time Rochelle and Samson arrived next to her car, Resolve immediately noticed that the underground carpark was almost completely empty and quite deserted apart from a few vehicles that remained which belonged to a couple of Samson's employees and the catering company.

For Resolve, the situation that the two were now in was absolutely perfect because it gave Samson and Rochelle a moment to be completely alone together and provided them both with a little bit of privacy and so Resolve was very eager to see exactly what they would do with that privacy. Quite fortunately and much to Resolve's total delight, Samson decided to make the most of the intimate opportunity as he suddenly pulled Rochelle closer to him and then kissed her passionately and she reciprocated willingly. A hand was rapidly slipped between the material of Rochelle's dress and her skin and because she started to moan seductively as Samson began to fondle her naked flesh with his hands, Resolve noticed that Samson felt encouraged and that he then deftly slipped his other hand between her legs through the split at the front of her dress.

"I'd say there's definitely a mutual interest." Resolve immediately reassured himself as he grinned. "And he does seem to be very focused."

The passion that Samson displayed towards Rochelle very clearly illustrated to Resolve that Samson was now fully immersed in his attraction to her and that he'd been adequately enticed by the attention that she had lavished upon him earlier that evening. Everything about Rochelle had been totally and utterly perfect, from her flirtatious conversation that had charmed Samson meticulously, to her gorgeous, seductive smile and Samson it appeared had been absolutely captivated because Resolve had now watched him jump straight into the hot, excited sea of passion that had welled up inside of him at the first available opportunity.

INTELLECT: USER REPAIR

"I have to go now Samson, I need my beauty sleep." Rochelle suddenly mentioned as she interrupted Samson mid-seduction and pushed the button on her keyring to unlock her car door. She flashed a seductive smile at him as she opened her car door and then entered inside the vehicle. "I just love this company you've built, it's so impressive, you are so impressive." Rochelle closed the car door and then lowered the window so that the two could still converse.

"And I love your dress." Samson eagerly replied. "And the body that's inside it. You are a very attractive woman Rochelle and I definitely have an eye that can spot a beautiful woman."

"And you definitely have an eye for business Samson." Rochelle teased as she winked at him. "You're a very astute man in more ways than one."

"Well Rochelle, I'd love to seal the deal and be personally assigned to manage your account. I can handle all your architectural and structural requirements." Samson flirted suggestively. "In an exclusive capacity of course."

Total delight rapidly began to fill Resolve's form as he silently observed the scene directly in front of him because the final part of his plan had now fallen straight into place without any further prodding because fortunately, Samson had leapt straight into Rochelle's pool of seductive feminine charm. Unlike Samson, who was totally oblivious to Rochelle's real nature and character, Resolve knew exactly who Rochelle was and exactly what she was capable of delivering, when she wanted to but for Resolve, Samson definitely deserved what he hoped Rochelle would deliver directly to his door. The domineering, calculated, manipulative reality of Rochelle's personality that she had clearly hidden from Samson that evening hadn't even visible at all as Resolve watched her flirt with Samson in an innocent fashion and she'd seduced him with total ease.

A flirtatious, sticky web now lay silently in wait for Samson that Rochelle had very subtly enticed him to step into and as her flirtatious entanglements increased by the second, Resolve could already see that Samson would be totally unable to resist her charms. Essentially, Rochelle was just the kind of cure that Samson really needed and as Resolve began to reflect upon his choice, an immense sense of satisfaction seemed to fill his core because Rochelle was definitely the right choice for his special mission and the perfect bait for Samson's potential downfall. Not even a single doubt now lay inside Resolve's logical processes as he watched the two exchange seductive smiles and glances because he now felt completely reassured that Rochelle would hold Samson totally captive and that she would put him through the necessary hell that Resolve already knew, she had the capacity and ability to actually deliver.

"I'm absolutely intrigued Samson." Rochelle purred as she suddenly broke the seductive silence that had gathered between them and then started the engine of her vehicle as she prepared to depart. "Though how we'll stay in touch, I'm not entirely sure." She teased.

"Call me that's my private number." Samson quickly invited as he assertively plucked a business card from his trouser pocket and then offered it her. "I'd really like to take you out for dinner one day."

For a few seductive seconds, Samson's invitation seemed to float around in the air as it lingered between the two in a delicate limbo of flirtatious silence as although Rochelle had been discreetly enticed to commit to a passionate affair, her participation had not yet been finalized and so until it was, she remained merely a speck upon the horizon of Samson's romantic possibilities. Regardless of the romantic prospects that Samson's offer held which were as yet, totally undefined and really quite ambiguous, the two both knew, between them both there was a definite sexual attraction and that they'd started to travel down a road which had a certain pre-defined destination in terms of sexual intimacy. Sexual satisfaction wasn't generally something that either of the two normally struggled to receive but an order had been placed and kicked into motion and so now, only the final actual fulfilment remained and that enticed them both but for two entirely different reasons.

"I'll definitely do that Samson." Rochelle replied as she smiled and then playfully plucked the business card from his hand. She silently considered her potential acceptance of his invitation for a few seconds as thoughts of Samson's wealth danced across the tips of her fingers before she continued. "Very soon." Rochelle reassured him decisively as she began to roll her vehicle gently towards the exit of the carpark.

Upon Samson's face there was now an absolutely delighted smile as he watched Rochelle's vehicle head towards the exit of the underground carpark because not only had Rochelle embraced his invitation but then she'd also encouraged him which had very clearly shown that she was definitely interested in some kind of romantic rendezvous. The positive nature of Rochelle's response really excited Samson because there was now the possibility that the next time the two met, they would spend some time alone together and that there would be no corporate function or any unwanted spectators around to distract either of them. Inside that sparkling, beautiful red dress there sat a delightful female body that Samson would then perhaps have access to and the opportunity to ravish which would mean that his lustful urges would no longer have to be restrained and so that in Samson's mind, was definitely something to look forward to.

Just below the surface of Samson's skin powerful lustful urges continued to silently bubble away and the passion that he longed to unleash upon Rochelle's naked skin seemed to taunt him as her vehicle rapidly vanished from the underground carpark and from sight. An opportunity to fully explore those passions and desires had not materialized for Samson that day but he felt absolutely certain as he began to walk slowly towards his own vehicle that very soon, he would have his moment with Rochelle and then he would show her all the passion that lay inside of him. The fact that Rochelle had actually accepted Samson's business card and then tucked it safely away inside her handbag had shown him that she was more than ready to be a willing participant in the fulfilment of his sexual desires because Samson definitely wanted Rochelle and she definitely knew it.

Darkness had already embraced and engulfed the perimeter of the building as it had seeped through the city streets of Pinesfield and then fully blanketed each one and as Samson entered inside his car and then drove out of the underground carpark, he thoughtfully considered his evening with Rochelle as he began his journey home through the now dark city roads. The day it seemed had fully departed and completely evaporated into nothing as the night had stepped into replace it but as Samson left his corporate home behind and began to make his way towards his residential home, he felt extremely pleased about the day or more specifically, the evening that he'd just enjoyed.

Very intentionally, Samson had waited until most of his guests had departed and begun their respective journeys home before he'd escorted Rochelle to her vehicle and so not many people had seen his departure, or his companion and that suited him perfectly. Just a few staff from the catering company and Samson's personal assistant had been left inside the boardroom to clean up when he'd left with Rochelle but none of them, quite fortunately had paid very much attention to Samson's actual departure because they'd been very focused upon their tasks. Since Samson was just about to actually embark upon an extra marital affair with Rochelle, discretion was something that Samson already knew, he needed to keep at the forefront of his mind and so the less people that had seen the two leave together as far as Samson was concerned, the better it was for him.

Eager anticipation rapidly started to fill Samson's physical body as he drove through the quiet city streets as he began to consider what it might actually be like to make love to Rochelle in every possible way and position imaginable. The deep and intense physical attraction that Samson felt towards Rochelle appeared to be mutual and for that, Samson was truly grateful because it wasn't often that a very attractive female landed so easily upon his runway of life and especially not one that was so sexually inviting, stunningly attractive and seemingly cooperative as Rochelle seemed to be.

Inside the dimly lit underground carpark Rochelle had not only allowed Samson to exchange flirtatious pleasantries with her but they'd also engaged in a passionate embrace and he'd even slipped his hand inside Rochelle's interior which he was now eager to fill with his passionate desires. Despite their very brief association and lack of familiarity, no objections at all had been uttered by Rochelle and only moans of pleasure had escaped from her lips and so now Samson yearned to sexually satisfy both Rochelle and himself. Rather disappointingly, Samson quietly accepted as he drove towards his home, his lust would have to be fulfilled by his actual wife that night but at the very least, he'd secured his romantic interest in Rochelle and they both it seemed, wanted more from each other than the evening that they'd just spent together.

A deep sense of satisfaction silently embraced Resolve as he watched Samson return to his marital home and then rather energetically enter inside it as Samson headed back towards his poor faithful wife. Ultimately, Resolve felt absolutely secure in the knowledge that his plan had definitely worked since Samson had totally fallen for Rochelle that day which meant, Samson was now well on his way to a special hell of his own and one which this time, he would actually be the victim off. From what Resolve already knew regarding Rochelle, she could be a total bitch and especially when it came to the men in her life and her dealings with them and Resolve had selected her to be the bait for Samson purely for that very reason.

Only one small worry now remained for Resolve and that was Samson's actual wife because Rochelle was not only beautiful but she was also absolutely ruthless, very devious and extremely calculated and so Resolve now began to feel slightly worried about the potential impact that her actions could have upon Moira. Although Rochelle was the perfect candidate to handle Samson and his disgustingly chauvinistic approach towards the women that were unfortunate enough to be a part of his life as Resolve was already aware, the amount of destruction that Rochelle could cause in Samson's life was very unpredictable and Moira was from what Resolve could see, a very gentle person.

In terms of Moira's personality, Resolve had already noticed that she wasn't really the strongest of women but he hoped that Samson's pending affair would perhaps wake her up, shake her out of her complacent slumber and challenge her to leave Samson's side for good but he could not be certain that it would. One thing Resolve was absolutely certain about however, was the fact that Samson in his current state was fit for neither man nor beast, or for any other kind of human consumption as a husband, a boss, or even as a lover. Despite Resolve's intense dislike for Samson however, he had absolutely no desire to see Moira become a casualty of the destruction that was about to actually occur as a result of Samson's illicit affair and that one worry troubled Resolve quite deeply.

For some strange reason, Resolve suddenly began to notice as he watched Samson greet his wife enthusiastically and affectionately that as he kissed her on the cheek, Samson seemed full of energy, life and adoration for Moira which totally contradicted his actions earlier that evening. Due to Resolve's lack of understanding regarding extra marital affairs, he quickly checked Intellect's databases where he rapidly discovered that Samson's enthusiasm was likely to be attributable and connected to feelings of guilt and excitement due to the affair that he anticipated would happen in the near future.

The new potential romance that lurked upon the romantic horizon of Samson's life, from what Resolve could see, seemed to invigorate Samson and he virtually glowed with excitement as his commitment to his wife was silently demoted to a secondary issue that was somehow deemed in Samson's mind, totally irrelevant and completely ignored. Interestingly for Resolve, he noticed that Samson now looked pretty much like a teenager that had fallen in love for the very first time and that amused him to some extent as he watched Samson interact with his wife.

Several joyful reassurances were provided by Samson to Moira regarding the client wine reception which he insisted had gone amazingly well but Rochelle's attendance wasn't mentioned once. Once the couple had exchanged a few more words and some affectionate exchanges, Resolve watched as Samson eagerly led Moira towards the bedroom as they both prepared to retire for the night.

An aura of hypocrisy definitely seemed to surround Samson, Resolve observed as he romantically interacted with his wife and paid her more attention than usual as if he was a devoted husband and that absolutely disgusted Resolve as the couple stepped inside their bedroom. Not even an ounce of sincerity it seemed to Resolve, existed in Samson's mind and being as Resolve had noticed that Samson had already checked his phone at least three times that evening since he'd arrived home, just to see if Rochelle had contacted him yet to kickstart their lust filled affair.

"I'll have to put a lot more hours into the business now Moira." Samson explained as he stood inside the couple's bedroom and faced his wife. "The wine reception was a huge success and so there'll be a lot more work now."

Moira nodded her head as she listened to him speak. "Sure Samson, I completely understand." She replied quietly.

Upon Samson's face there was now a triumphant smile as the two undressed, climbed into bed and then nestled together underneath the duvet because he had not only embarked upon a new affair that evening with a beautiful woman but he'd also ushered in an acceptable explanation for any future prolonged absences from home. The perfect excuse had now presented itself that would mask and disguise the adulterous affair that Samson was just about to dabble in and Moira had technically, already accepted his utilization of those excuses in advance which would allow him to be extremely busy and allow him to seemingly legitimately, spend a lot more time away from home.

INTELLECT: USER REPAIR

An exciting possibility that involved a seductively delicious, sexually charged love affair now lingered in the air all around Samson and although the prospect was invisible to the naked eye of others, to him it shone like a shiny star as it waited silently for the daybreak of discovery to chase it away. Daybreak for Samson in this instance however, involved his actual commitment to his wife which Samson knew, would definitely kick in at some point in the future, if his affair was ever discovered by Moira but for now, he decided to simply embrace the excitement and the affair because he'd already chosen to ignore his marital commitment.

Rather interestingly for Resolve that day, he had now truly begun to realize exactly how Samson actually functioned because he'd seen Samson utilize every available opportunity to justify his potential absences from home in advance and it all seemed, extremely calculated. The potential affair between Rochelle and Samson, Resolve definitely felt, would now actually happen because Samson appeared to be utterly determined to ensure that it would and that prospect in some ways, really delighted Resolve since he'd put a lot of effort into the orchestration of their two lover's initial meeting which he'd engineered to absolute perfection. Unfortunately, however that night had also highlighted to Resolve that when it came to the battle of love, Moira really was no match for Samson and it seemed as if she had already surrendered and succumbed to romantic defeat as she had accepted his flimsy excuses and practically given Samson a license and consent to abuse their marriage as he wished.

"Moira will be a definite casualty when Samson's affair kicks in." Resolve admitted to himself as he gently shook his head. "But at least, once it's exposed, she'll finally be free and she'll able to leave Samson for good."

Very soon, Resolve hoped, Samson would be cured from his disgusting attitude towards women and at least one of Leona's problems would be fully solved and resolved as a trap of double deceit had now been set for Samson and so all Resolve really had to do was watch him fall into a pit of stress, much like the one that he'd so often created for others. The same way Samson lied to his wife would now be the same way that Rochelle would lie to him and that double deceit would in the end, Resolve hopefully anticipated, lead to Samson's downfall and total destruction.

Fortunately enough, Resolve quickly observed, Leona was peacefully fast asleep which immediately reassured him as he glanced at her face on his display screen directly in front of him that she had not been too negatively affected or too disappointed by Darin's absence that evening. Since it was a Friday night and rather late, a noisy, loud party had already kicked off next door but Resolve noticed that the noise didn't seem to wake Leona up which meant, she was probably really very tired and much in need of some physical rest.

A tremendous amount of satisfaction filled Resolve's core as he began to process the outcomes of the day that he'd just spent in Leona's life and in the lives of those that usually distressed and stressed her. For Resolve, the day had been a total success because he had managed to successfully set a trap and set the wheels in motion that would lead to Samson's eventual downfall and that as far as Resolve was concerned, was definitely something to celebrate because Samson caused so much misery in Leona's life but as Resolve already knew, another human day would arrive shortly and his work was far from done.

When the Saturday morning landed upon the runway of Leona's life, she welcomed it with open arms as she eagerly arose and then enthusiastically prepared to try on one of the two new dresses that she had bought the previous day from the much more affordable clothing store. Although Leona had initially only intended to buy one dress, in the end she'd actually opted for two because both dresses had caught her fancy and the retailer had offered her a very generous discount, due to the fact that she was a first-time customer and because their brand had just recently opened their first store in the city center.

The two shopping bags still sat on top of Leona's bed inside the bedroom where she'd plonked them down the evening before when she had returned home as she'd wanted to try each dress on again before she hung them up and put them away. Since Darin hadn't actually shown up on the Friday evening there had been no actual need for Leona to change her outfit and so the two dresses had remained inside the bags that they'd been placed in by the cashier, unworn, unattended to and so far, totally unrequired. Although the two dresses certainly weren't very sophisticated, they had both been within Leona's budget and had looked really quite pretty and rather elegant and due to her harsh week at work, she had definitely felt as if she'd deserved a treat and so for Leona, the financial splurge had been totally justified.

Every day that Leona worked for Samson as far as Leona was concerned, was a headache from start to finish and unfortunately, her weekends with Darin were no better and the presence of the noisy neighbors next door meant that even her home did not offer any kind of real sanctuary. Each working week Leona would incorporate Samson's additional corporate demands into her workload which were a major pain without any extensions to her actual client deadlines and at times, even Leona herself wondered how she managed to fit it all in and maintain her usual client list.

The very unromantic reality that Darin offered to Leona every weekend, required the patience of a saint and Leona's patience had now absolutely run dry because she had tired of Darin's substandard offerings of love that were laced with pretense and purely focused upon the fulfilment of his own needs with absolutely no regard for her heart.

"A pretty new dress won't fix Darin." Leona admitted to herself as she slipped one of the two new dresses over her head. "And sadly, I already know that."

"I totally agree Leona." Resolve said to himself as he nodded in agreement. "He's never going to change."

"But this dress does look pretty amazing." Leona quickly reassured herself as she gently smoothed the material of the new dress down against her skin and then glanced at her reflection in the long body length mirror inside her bedroom. "So that's a plus. I wish Darin was here to see how beautiful it looks, not that he'd appreciate it. I wonder if he'll show up today."

"I really hope he doesn't." Resolve admitted to himself as he listened to her speak.

Upon Resolve's face there was now a very worried frown as he unmasked Leona's monitoring window just to have a look at the new dress that she'd put on because he'd masked it due to the fact that Leona had begun to change her clothes. For Resolve, Darin was the very last person that he wanted to see inside Leona's home that day because he felt as if Darin really did not deserve to be there and at times, he wished that Leona would just slam her front door very hard in Darin's actual face. Every time that Leona opened up her front door and the door of access to her life and heart and allowed Darin into her personal space, she allowed Darin to have more access to her and Resolve felt that she betrayed herself because she compromised and accepted his substandard relationship and his fake engagement which she really didn't have to.

The engagement between the couple as far as Resolve was concerned, was a total farce and he often wondered if Leona actually knew the reality but just didn't want to face and accept it because Darin very clearly, didn't really love her and made absolutely no efforts at all to even pretend that he did. For Darin, Resolve had observed, Leona was simply a convenient partner that supplied him with whatever he needed when he needed it and their engagement was a false, pretentious obligation sustained by Darin with a few very thin, mean threads of affectionate pretense, purely for his own benefit. Rather frustratingly for Resolve however, Leona seemed to be bound to Darin by bonds of love, loyalty and infatuation that were clearly not reciprocated and her love and loyalty had now become heavy weights tied to her feet that Leona dragged across the ground everywhere she went in life.

"He did say yesterday that he'd come around by lunchtime today." Leona reminded herself as she twisted and turned and began to inspect every material inch of her new dress. "But what Darin says and what Darin does are definitely two very different things."

"The sooner you get rid of Deadbeat Darin, the better Leona." Resolve muttered to himself as he shook his head.

"I really like this dress but I think I should wear something else for now, at least until I know whether or not Darin's really coming." Leona concluded decisively. "Keep my new dress clean."

"He probably won't even come Leona, he's such a cheat and such a disappointment." Resolve insisted as he continued to discuss the issue of Darin with himself. "He's just a total waste of space."

"Well, at least I enjoyed my shopping trip yesterday, it was like a breath of fresh air and free from the vandals of distress that usually deface the walls of my life with their graffiti of misery every day." Leona mentioned thoughtfully. "I really should treat myself more often though because it felt so dam good and if Darin doesn't come around today, it's not the end of the world really because I now have something decent to wear, if I ever actually go anywhere nice."

"That probably won't be with Darin. Darin doesn't take you anywhere nice Leona." Resolve immediately reminded himself.

"At least I didn't have to stay at work late yesterday, or have to attend that awful wine reception that would have been truly horrible." Leona mentioned as she attempted to cheer herself up. "Samson never lets me leave work early and especially not on a Friday when I have client deadlines, so that was a rare treat. Probably won't happen again though because Samson's really mean."

In every way imaginable, Leona had been utterly relieved on the Friday afternoon that she hadn't been invited along or asked to attend Samson's fancy wine reception because as far as she was concerned that would have been a major pain in the butt. The last thing that Leona wanted to do after a long, tedious, stressful week at work was to give up her precious leisure time on a Friday evening, just to entertain Samson's clients.

For Leona, to force oneself to be pleasant to a bunch of people that would later become a pressure cooker of stressful deadlines that would haunt her existence and working weeks and to plaster a pretentious smile across her face on a Friday evening for Samson all evening, was just a tad too much of an ask and not something that she ever wanted to do. Inwardly, Leona almost loathed Samson and pretending to be pleasant to him as if they had some kind of decent, respectful relationship in front of his clients was just a hypocrisy that she simply couldn't face and certainly not on a Friday night and not on a precious weekend evening that was supposed to be her own leisure time.

"Yes, Samson is very mean." Resolve mentioned to himself. "Especially to you."

"Perhaps Samson has changed." Leona deliberated as she began to internally consider Samson's recent actions which seemed totally out of character. "And if Samson can change, perhaps Darin can change too. I mean, he really can't get much worse."

"Samson hasn't changed Leona." Resolve insisted to himself as he rapidly began to shake his head. "The whole purpose of the wine reception was to bring in more business, so in the long run, Samson really wasn't doing you any favors because some of that work would have been dumped straight on top of your desk and probably with no additional pay."

"I pay all of Darin's bills now." Leona admitted to herself. "And I do more work than ever for Samson and I haven't had a pay increase since I started working for him."

Since the couple had first met as Leona had to know accept, their relationship had become more and more expensive for her to maintain and she'd been less and less impressed by Darin's conduct as although the costs had increased, his attentiveness had decreased and her income had not actually risen to meet those expenses. Instead of feeling comforted by a romantic relationship that should have provided Leona with love, security, warmth and companionship, in recent times, she'd even felt more and more troubled by her actual participation in it and although the expenses had risen, Leona's levels of satisfaction had decreased to a negligible level.

In fact, for so many reasons as far as Leona was concerned, Darin's absence had now become more of comfort and preferable to her than his actual presence and unfortunately that was a very sad, truthful reality that Leona could no longer possibly deny. The longer the couple's relationship continued it seemed, the smaller the love returns were from Darin's end and those returns had increasingly diminished until now, there was virtually nothing left for Leona to enjoy anymore.

Whenever Darin appeared and was in close proximity to Leona, he would be argumentative and patronize her and his behavior would demean her and it was almost as if he was on a personal mission to try and make her feel inadequate and inferior and that was absolutely undeniable. The sad reality was that Darin was a total headache from start to finish and no matter how many painkillers of forgiveness Leona actually took, the pain he caused her never seemed to disappear, heal or ever reduce. Precious weekends that should have been filled with romance, love and laughter for Leona had now been filled with drama, tears, heartache, disappointment and misery and she really didn't want to experience that anymore during her leisure time, every single weekend.

Only one real advantage to Leona could really be derived from her relationship with Darin and that was the fact that in some small way, it validated her somehow as a woman in the sense that it implied that she was able to sustain a romantic relationship in the longer term. Some emotional costs however had definitely been incurred by Leona to establish and maintain that feminine validation and those costs were the vile intricacies that she'd had to endure just to sustain a relationship with Darin in the long term which were increasingly painful and offered diminishing returns with regards to the enjoyment derived from his presence in her life.

"He's always late anyway, so he'll probably turn up late, if he actually turns up at all." Leona reminded herself. "It's really annoying sometimes and I know he's definitely cheating on me, if only I could prove it then I could dump him for good."

"You can dump him anyway Leona." Resolve said as a frustrated expression crossed his face. "You don't need to prove anything. You can just dump him."

Much to Resolve's absolute frustration, Leona could not hear a single word he said and although at times, he really wanted to express himself directly to her, direct communication was another risk that Resolve could not afford to take, or at least not very often, not if he wished to remain in Leona's life in some capacity. A limited involvement in Leona's life was definitely preferable to no involvement at all and if Resolve dared to saunter too far down the path of regular direct communication with Leona, he feared what The Guardian would do, if that breach of rules was actually ever discovered.

"I should have some breakfast now but it is almost lunchtime, so I think I'll have some brunch instead." Leona stated decisively as she plucked the second new dress from its respective shopping bag and prepared to hang it up inside her wardrobe. "I should really change first and hang this new dress up too before I make it, keep both my new dresses nice and clean. You never know, I might get invited somewhere really special soon and want to wear them, though probably not by Darin."

"Very true Leona. I definitely agree with you on that point." Resolve eagerly agreed as he began to nod his head. "He's totally useless. If only you could see what I see and if only I could open your eyes, you'd dump Darin forever and put your engagement in the trash in a second."

Once Leona had changed and hung the two new dresses up inside her wardrobe, she quickly returned to the lounge which also housed the kitchen and then began to make something to eat. Some oil was rapidly drizzled over the base of a frying pan and then it was placed on top of a ceramic ring as Leona committed herself to the preparation of an actual freshly cooked brunch instead of opting for a readymade meal. The convenience of a readymade meal was certainly useful at times but because Leona wasn't particularly in a rush that morning, or worn out from a long day at work and since Darin had promised to turn up that lunchtime, the effort was going to be made, regardless of whether he turned up or not.

"I can always plate up any food that I don't eat today and put in the fridge for tomorrow." Leona mentioned to herself. "If Darin's a no show."

Some rashers of bacon, a handful of sliced mushrooms, some fresh tomatoes halves and four sausages were placed inside the large frying pan as soon as the oil was hot as Leona began the task of preparing some quite unhealthy but very tasty morsels of food. Salt and black pepper were quickly sprinkled over the items inside the frying pan as Leona watched over each item of food diligently and turned them every now and then as required. Once the bacon, mushrooms and tomatoes were cooked, they were deftly plucked from the frying pan with a fish slice and then placed upon a plate on top of some kitchen roll to absorb the excess fat just before two eggs were cracked and the contents of their shells were emptied into the frying pan and a few more rashers of bacon were added.

"Very unhealthy but absolutely scrumptious." Leona admitted to herself as the aroma from the freshly cooked food began to waft into her nostrils.

Just a minute or two later, Leona turned the eggs over and then she tipped some of the already cooked food onto another plate as she glanced at the now soggy pieces of kitchen roll and grinned.

"So unhealthy." She reminded herself as she smiled. "But such a nice dish that's too good to miss."

A knife, fork and a bottle of brown sauce were quickly plucked from the cutlery drawer and the fridge and then the remaining items inside the frying pan were fished out of the frying pan and placed upon the plate with the kitchen roll. The two eggs and two sausages were placed upon Leona's now almost full plate as she prepared to make her way towards the sofa at the other end of the large front room. Brunch that day certainly didn't look very glamourous, Leona decided as she glanced at her full plate as she walked towards the sofa because some of the sausages had split and the egg yolks had broken but she felt that it would still definitely taste great with lashings of brown sauce and that the plate of food would completely fill up the now very hungry gap inside her stomach.

"Well, it's certainly not a culinary masterpiece by any stretch of the imagination." Leona admitted to herself as she sat down on the sofa. "But it does smell good and that has to count for something." She convinced herself decisively as she picked up her fork and then began to hungrily tuck into her meal.

The entertainment center was quickly switched on as Leona started to eat her meal because the noises that emanated from it usually kept her company when she was alone as each one filled the room around her and somehow made her feel slightly less lonely. A mouthwatering aroma swept into Leona's nostrils as she began to satisfy the hole inside her stomach and the hungry rumbles that had growled away just minutes beforehand, slowly began to subside as her stomach started to digest each forkful of food appreciatively.

Due to Darin's promise, Leona glanced at her phone as she ate as she began to wonder whether or not he would show up that day at all and somehow, quite strangely at times, the empty growls in Leona's stomach when she was hungry, reminded Leona of her virtually empty lovelife which relied upon the one man that didn't seem to want to participate in it in any way. On occasions as Leona already knew, Darin could really be quite charming but that was usually when he wanted something which was most of the time because it was now actually quite rare that Leona would meet Darin and he would not ask her for something and that something was usually money.

According to the revised plans that the couple had made on the Friday evening, Darin was due to visit Leona at around lunchtime which meant, he would probably show up at some point in the afternoon because Darin was absolutely always late. Quite unusually, Leona had made the effort that day to cook a meal for both of them, however that was more for herself really than it was for Darin because in Leona's mind, he didn't really deserve any kind of culinary effort from her that weekend.

In the early days of the couple's relationship, Leona had made culinary efforts for Darin many times but she'd abandoned such additional efforts long ago because she'd gone out of her way to accommodate him but he hadn't appreciated it and so now, such efforts were no longer usually made. On the few occasions that the couple had gone out for dinner which Leona had always paid for, she would dress up and make reservations at a nice restaurant but since Darin rarely turned up on time and sometimes didn't even bother to turn up at all, in recent times she'd stopped making those efforts too.

True to Darin's usual form, the Saturday afternoon and then the evening arrived and Darin didn't and although Leona had tried to contact him several times that day, his phone had repeatedly gone straight to voicemail and no response had been received to the text messages that she'd sent him. At around nine that evening however, Leona suddenly received a short text from Darin which contained a rather flimsy, shabby excuse as to why he had been unable to make it that day. Upon Leona's face there was a heartbroken disappointed frown as she read the message several times as she tried to absorb the rough explanation which was far from satisfactory.

"Guess I'll be spending my Saturday night alone." Leona muttered to herself as she gently shook her head.

Several takeaway menus from local eateries that were usually slipped through Leona's letterbox sat inside a drawer in one of the kitchen cupboards and Leona quickly rose to her feet and then crossed the room as she prepared to retrieve the leaflets, so that she could order something for dinner because she'd waited to eat that evening until she'd heard from Darin. Three menus were plucked from the drawer as Leona prepared to peruse each one as her heart silently surrendered to Darin's portion of disappointment which once again had left her heart hungry, sadly dissatisfied and truly empty.

Since several of the local restaurants and takeaways conveniently offered an actual delivery service, Leona quickly selected a meal and then made a call to place an order as she finally accepted that she would indeed have to eat dinner on the sofa alone. Inside Leona's large lounge which also doubled up as a kitchen there was a large, black glass dining table that could seat up to six people but Leona rarely ever utilized it because she felt that there was no need to prepare an actual table setting just for herself and since Darin was rarely around, it remained more of a decorative feature than a functional piece of furniture, purely due to Darin's disappointments.

Approximately twenty minutes later, Leona collected a pizza box, a metallic paper bag filled with garlic bread and a much smaller box that contained some chicken wings from the pizza delivery man at her front door and she immediately offered him a very generous tip. The tip offered on this particular occasion, was unusually large because it actually represented the amount of additional expenditure that Leona would have been incurred, if Darin had been present because she would have ordered more food for him to consume. Just like her, Leona had already decided that the pizza delivery man had a less than perfect Saturday night because he was at work on an actual weekend and she'd been stood up, so she could totally empathize with his lack of weekend because her own weekend seemed to be no better.

"At least there's food." Leona quickly reminded herself as she stepped back inside the lounge with the two boxes that contained her food order and the metallic bag delicately balanced inside both her hands. "Even if there is no Darin."

"I'm here Leona." Resolve immediately said to himself as he began to shake his head in total frustration. "You can always count on me."

From the visual display wall screen that surrounded Resolve, he could very clearly see that Darin had actually disappointed Leona in order to meet up with one of his other romantic interests and although it absolutely disgusted him, there was very little that he could currently do about it. The sad, awful reality of Darin's unfaithful nature and actions frustrated and annoyed Resolve profusely but because Darin hadn't actually been sexually active with any of the two women that Resolve had seen him with so far, there really wasn't enough concrete proof to prove his infidelity fully and to expose his indiscretions to Leona.

When it came to the issue of human romantic relationships although Resolve didn't totally understand everything about romance, he did understand the basic fundamentals and that infidelity was a major issue and not generally something that was usually expected from either party involved in a committed romance. The serious commitment of an actual engagement between a couple as far as Resolve was aware, usually meant that infidelity was even less acceptable but Darin seemed to be in complete rebellion to that very essential requirement, even though he'd committed to the couple's relationship and engagement voluntarily.

Every part of Resolve now fully appreciated and accepted as he watched Leona eat her pizza alone that Darin would never give her the relationship that she wanted from him and deserved and that neither Darin or their relationship could be fixed and repaired because as Resolve already knew, Leona had tried to fix Darin and their relationship many times. Only one option really remained when it came to the issue of Darin and no matter how much Leona loved him, Resolve fully understood, he had to be totally extracted from her life completely because there would be no change and he would continue to break Leona's heart as often as she allowed him to and completely waste her life. Unlike Leona however, Resolve held absolutely no emotional sentiments towards Darin and as he watched Darin galivant around in front of his electronic eyes with another female, there was one thing

Resolve was absolutely certain about, Darin had to be evicted from Leona's life and her heart completely and that he was definitely the right non-human form for that particular job.

Just a few hours later as the night progressed, another temptation suddenly began to tantalize Resolve's logical processes that seemed to linger deep inside of him and as it tugged away at his form, it compelled him to create second simulation but this time, Resolve wanted to create a dinner simulation. Since Darin had disappointed Leona twice that weekend, Resolve had decided that he would make it up to her simulated form because that was the closest he could be to the real Leona right now and in some ways, he felt that his enactment would at least, provide him with some kind of comfort and some much-needed practice when it came to the issue of human romantic customs.

The second simulation was rapidly created which contained a simulation of the dining table that currently sat inside Leona's lounge which was quickly populated with bowls filled with food, some bottles of wine and then a sprinkling of pink flower petals that were scattered across the surface of it as Resolve attempted to make the dinner for Leona that she should have eaten that evening. Despite the fact that it was just a simulation and not a real dinner date, Resolve eagerly prepared his simulated male form in what he felt was appropriate attire as he adorned his frame in a smart black tuxedo. According to the research that Resolve had now conducted, he'd discovered that a tuxedo was a suitable form of attire for men when they wanted to look very smart and when they wished to impress a woman and he really wanted to impress Leona's simulated form.

"This is how we would have dinner together Leona." Resolve promised himself as he glanced at her human form and noticed that she was now curled up on the sofa fast asleep. "Though you'd be awake of course." He joked.

Upon Resolve's face there was now a very proud smile as he glanced at his simulated form which looked to be what some human beings might actually consider handsome, though he was still slightly unsure as to what exactly 'handsome' looked like or how accurate his assumption was. From what Resolve had observed however, women usually mentioned the word 'handsome' in a positive manner when they wished to describe men in a complimentary fashion that were either well dressed, extremely good looking or very nicely presented and that night, he definitely felt that his simulation satisfied at least one of those criteria.

During Resolve's first simulation, his appearance really hadn't been impressive and so he hoped that on this occasion, Leona's simulation would be pleased with his choice of attire and that she might actually regard him as handsome as he attempted to make the dinner as special as he possibly could, even though it was just a simulation. Despite the fact that Leona was now fast asleep, totally oblivious to Resolve's simulated dinner and completely unaware that Resolve even existed, he didn't allow any of those factors to dissuade him as he continued to create his dinner simulation which to him would be an enactment and practice run of his ideal dinner date with Leona.

Everything that Resolve could possibly think of was prepared absolutely meticulously as he mimicked what he had so often seen human males do when they wished to romance a female companion. Unlike Resolve's first simulation however, this time he was much better prepared because he had taken into account his lack of knowledge regarding romance and done some actual research into human dating rituals and so now he felt ready to try and impress Leona, or at least able to make an attempt to impress the artificial simulation of her human form.

In Resolve's opinion, every simulation that he engaged in was extremely important to him because deep down inside, he silently held the hope that each one would prepare him for the real face to face meetings that he wished would one day occur with the real Leona inside the real human world. Some artificial simulations therefore were a very worthwhile exercise and an absolutely necessary indulgence from Resolve's perspective because he really did not want that amazing day to arrive and for it to find him, totally unprepared.

Once Leona's simulated form had been created, Resolve quickly adorned her simulated frame in a simulation of the gorgeous gold dress that she had wanted to buy on the Friday afternoon which had been beyond her financial means, since he really appreciated Leona's taste and efforts, despite Darin's apparent lack of interest. The door that led into Resolve's living quarters on this occasion, was quickly secured and sealed before he dove into his actual simulation as he attempted to avoid any unexpected interruptions via an access code control mechanism which would control its operation since that would ensure that it could not be opened, unless Resolve opened it himself.

Dinner that night had been prepared for two, not three and although it was highly unlikely that any visitors to Resolve's living quarters would want to join a simulation of a very human activity that involved romance, he did not want to be disturbed in any way. Although Resolve definitely appreciated some of the other Monitoring Programs and even actually quite liked some of them like Analyzer, this was a very private simulated activity which meant, no spectators were required or wanted and certainly not any spectators that might potentially disapprove of Resolve's conduct.

When absolutely everything had been prepared to Resolve's total satisfaction, a chair was politely pulled away from the table and quickly offered to Leona's simulated form as Resolve courteously invited her to sit down. Deep down inside Resolve, he now harbored a silent hope that he might one day be able to find a way to involve the real Leona in his actual simulations but that was just a hope because as yet, he hadn't actually managed to make that really happen. Even if Resolve did one day manage to find a way to walk upon the face of the Earth in human form, he fully appreciated that such a discovery and transformation could take a while but finding a way to involve the real Leona into his simulations, he'd decided that night, was a much more realizable and readily available goal that could actually be a real possibility for him to achieve.

"You really didn't have to go to all this trouble you know Resolve." Leona's simulation said as she sat down. "It's very nice of you and I love your tuxedo, you look very handsome."

"You've had a very hard week at work Leona, so I didn't want you to come home and then start cooking." Resolve's simulated form immediately replied as he smiled. "It was nothing really. I just bought some takeaway, lots and lots of takeaway."

Leona's simulation giggled.

"I'm a terrible cook." Resolve's simulated form explained. "If I actually cooked dinner for you, it would be burnt offerings and mish mash. In fact, you'd probably starve because it would be totally inedible." He joked.

"Thanks, Resolve. I really appreciate the effort you've made." Leona's simulation mentioned as she flashed him an appreciative smile.

"Here try some of this, it should taste nice." Resolve's simulated form suggested as he sat down at the table next to Leona's simulation and then offered her some of the food from inside one of the large glass bowls that occupied the surface of the dining table. "Would you like a glass of wine?" He asked.

"Yes please." Leona's simulation replied.

"Red or white?" Resolve's simulated form asked.

"I think I'd like some white please." Leona's simulation immediately confirmed. "You know Resolve, you're really spoiling me, I'm very impressed."

"Well, I tried my best." Resolve's simulated form said as he graciously began to accept her praise. "I'm not very experienced I'm afraid when it comes to romantic dinners, so it might not be totally perfect. I just hope you like it."

"Well, your best Resolve is absolutely amazing." Leona's simulation quickly clarified. "And I absolutely love it."

Every word of praise that Resolve received seemed to flow gently over his form like a warm wave of gentle sunshine as each word seemed to collate and radiate within his core and then gently warm him. Inside Resolve's intangible form, it was almost as if an opera had begun to play a joyful song and the prelude for an invitation to romance as each word of appreciation uttered by Leona echoed around his inner core and he basked in the waves of sheer delight that washed over him which soothed him like a heavenly melody sung by the songbirds of happiness.

Technically, although it wasn't actually the real Leona that had uttered every positive word that had been spoken to Resolve's simulated form, each word had somehow validated Resolve's feelings towards her and his efforts to try and make her happy which her simulation seemed to really appreciate. One day Resolve hoped and wished that his simulated dinner would be an actual reality and, on that day, he silently vowed, he would do far more to please the real Leona and as much as her heart would allow.

"If only this was our real life together Leona." Resolve whispered to himself as he watched the two simulations on the screen wall directly in front of him as they began to eat dinner. "If only I could actually be there beside you and be a real human being, your life would so different. If I could be alone together with you, I'd wrap your heart in happiness and make you smile every single day."

The simulated romantic dinner between the two continued for at least another hour as Resolve interacted with Leona's simulation via his own simulated form and as the two ate, conversed, laughed, joked and teased each other playfully, the night slipped silently by. Every drop of delicious companionship offered to Resolve by Leona's simulated form was silently stored away inside his memory banks as a deeply treasured memory as Resolve suddenly began to truly appreciate just how joyful a human experience could actually be and how very special each pleasant memory really was. On several occasions since Resolve had been allocated to Leona's life as her Life Monitor, he had heard Leona say that each precious memory was like a jewel of joy and he definitely felt that his night had not only been a jewel of joy but also that it had been lit up by the stars of delight that seemed to sparkle and shine, purely due to Leona's presence, albeit in an artificial, simulated capacity.

"Somehow Leona, I have to find a way to make this and us, our real reality." Resolve promised himself as the dinner simulation came to an end. "And somehow, I have to make my hopes and dreams, really happen for us."

NIGHTMARE NEIGHBORS

Despite the 'Darin Disappointments' that Leona had suffered so far that weekend, when the Sunday morning knocked upon the door of her life, she greeted it enthusiastically as she quickly arose and then began to heat up her leftover brunch from the previous morning with a cheerful smile, even though deep down inside, she actually felt very sad. True to Darin's usual form, he had let Leona down not just once but twice that weekend but since she was really quite used to Darin's behavior, it hadn't been a huge surprise to her that he'd failed to turn up on the Saturday yet again, however the fact that he hadn't bothered to show his face two days in a row when he'd promised to, still hurt her very deeply.

The two disappointments that Leona had suffered that weekend due to Darin's failure to appear had meant that almost her entire weekend had been full of nothing except 'Darin Disappointments' a term that Leona used to refer to Darin's no shows and so she started to consider that perhaps, she had to be the one to change because it was now becoming very clear that Darin never would. Another weekend would definitely arrive the following week as Leona already knew and so she began to thoughtfully consider as she fried a couple of fresh eggs to accompany the leftover brunch that perhaps she should make some alternative plans and stop wishing for a change in Darin that just wasn't ever going to happen. In fact, the sad reality was that since Darin had not even shown up once that weekend after he'd promised to twice, his behavior was becoming worse not better because she usually saw him at least once on any given weekend.

"I should make some alternative arrangements next weekend." Leona convinced herself as she walked towards the sofa with her plate of food that was filled with the reheated brunch and the two freshly fried eggs. "And some plans that don't revolve around Darin."

"I fully concur Leona." Resolve immediately agreed as he eagerly expressed his agreement to himself but wished that Leona could actually hear him. "Any second spent on Darin is a total waste of a very precious second."

Due to Resolve's commitment to Leona as her Life Monitor, he had monitored not only Leona but also Samson, Darin and Rochelle simultaneously throughout that entire weekend and as he'd watched Darin the previous night, he had noticed that Darin had once again betrayed Leona's trust without even a second of hesitation. Unfortunately, and rather sadly for Resolve however, Darin's Saturday night had not been as fruitful as either of the two might have hoped and the lady that Darin had chosen to wine and dine on that particular evening had not actually given him permission to slip into her bed or between her legs. For Resolve, it really frustrated him sometimes that Darin was such an incompetent cheat because if he'd been slightly more competent and had been sexually unfaithful successfully, Resolve might have been able to find a way by now to somehow expose his indiscretions to Leona.

"Darin's not even a competent cheat." Resolve muttered to himself as he watched Leona eat her brunch. "He cheats but he's not very good at it, so it seems that he can't even do that properly."

Since Rochelle had not yet contacted Samson, Resolve had noticed that Samson's entire Saturday had been spent quietly at home with his wife and that Moira had spent most of her day inside the kitchen as she'd prepared a lavish spread for him which he certainly did not seem to appreciate, or even thank her for. For Resolve, the scene inside Samson's home on the Saturday evening and night had intrigued him slightly as he had watched Samson play the role of the faithful husband almost immaculately all evening and the only thing that had really been missing had been a lack of appreciation for his wife's efforts which had been very clearly absent.

The complexity of the web of deceit that Samson would wind around his marriage had not yet fully been spun and so technically, Moira had Samson for that entire weekend all to herself but that situation as Resolve already knew, would definitely change at some point in the very near future. Once Samson's lustful affair fully kicked in, the couple's marital bed would then quickly become a rock of tension and their home a pit of stress but as Resolve also knew, an affair had been the simplest way to usher in Samson's downfall.

Rather annoyingly for Resolve however, just as the Sunday afternoon arrived and entered into Leona's life and world, Darin finally decided to put in a very unexpected appearance as he showed up totally unannounced at Leona's actual front door. A very strained smile adorned Leona's face as Resolve watched her greet Darin at the door and then invite him inside her home and Resolve immediately began to logically conclude as he watched Darin that when it came to Darin's appearances, it seemed as if Leona had very little choice or say in the matter and as if, Darin simply turned up whenever he felt like it.

No actual call had been received by Leona that morning to say that Darin would pay her a visit that day and so Resolve noticed that Leona really hadn't expected Darin to suddenly appear and that there was a surprised expression upon her face as she quietly accompanied Darin into the lounge and then watched him as he sat down upon her sofa. Regardless of the disappointments that Darin had delivered to Leona's heart that weekend and the fact that he had let her down twice, Resolve could clearly see from the very smug smile upon Darin's face, his attitude was really quite flippant and that he didn't seem bothered about his betrayals of Leona's heart in any way.

"What have you got to eat Leona?" Darin asked boldly. "I'm absolutely starving."

"I can fix you something now if you want Darin." Leona offered. "I didn't make anything for lunch because I didn't know you were coming. I ate some brunch not long ago." She explained.

"Will that be a problem Leona? Did you have other plans today?" Darin asked as he suddenly rose to his feet. "If you're busy I can always leave."

"No Darin, it's absolutely fine. I'll make something for you now." Leona insisted as a strained, tense smile was quickly offered in response as she attempted to appease him and dispel the tension that suddenly seemed to have gathered inside the room.

Unlike Leona's usual cheerful smiles however, Resolve immediately noticed that this smile was very different because this smile was not only extremely strained but it also seemed to exude tension and there was not even a single drop of joy contained within her facial expression. The pretentiously pleasant display on Leona's part, Resolve observed, was a clear representation of the tension that now sat inside her human physical form which Darin's unexpected arrival and presence had created and albeit discreetly that tension had now somehow managed to surface upon Leona's face which quite visibly betrayed her. Regardless of Leona's tense response which clearly indicated to Resolve that she was internally situated in a destination far away from happiness however, Darin arrogantly immediately sat back down, much like a king on his throne as he ruled over Leona's lounge with boldness and as if he was totally oblivious to the inner turmoil inside of her that he had ultimately caused.

"What would you like to eat Darin?" Leona asked politely as she glanced at his face and then began to inspect it thoughtfully.

A playful wish suddenly started to scurry through the passageways of Leona's mind as she hoped that one day, someone would invent a a toothpaste, or some other kind of hygiene product like a shower cream that could be utilized to expose cheating partners when they cleaned themselves with it because such a product would solve a lot of Leona's current problems with Darin. Colorful stains upon people's skin or their teeth that they could not remove would then clearly indicate whether or not they had been unfaithful to anyone that saw them and that could perhaps set suffering partners free. Another useful invention, Leona began to consider as she waited for Darin to respond, would perhaps be a repellant powder that could be placed around your home much like a bug repellant that cheating partners would be allergic to which would then drive them away from your door because if Leona utilized that powder, Darin would perhaps become allergic to her home, be unable to visit her and unable to even step inside her front door.

"I'll take anything you've got Leona, I really don't want to be any trouble or anything." Darin finally replied after a short silence as he flashed her a smile that oozed with charm. He was acutely aware that right now, he wasn't really in Leona's good books but that hadn't dissuaded him from his attendance that day and it certainly wasn't going to put him off his lunch. "Some sausages, eggs and a bit of bacon would be nice."

"Right, I'll see what I can rustle up for you." Leona said as she immediately accepted his suggestion and then started to walk towards the kitchen area of the lounge.

Every inch of Leona's skin began to silently crawl as she approached the refrigerator, opened it up and then plucked the required food items out of its interior because being in very close proximity to Darin after he'd just ruined most of her weekend, really wouldn't be the highlight of her Sunday. Some oil was quickly drizzled over the base of a frying pan however as Leona began to cooperate with Darin's request and prepare his lunch as any conversation about his failure to appear earlier that weekend was tactfully avoided.

Although Leona definitely wanted to confront Darin about his failure to honor their arrangements twice that weekend as much as Leona wanted to confront him, she struggled to discuss the issue with him because at times, he could be a very difficult person to hold a meaningful, adult conversation with. On several occasions in the past, Leona had tried to challenge Darin about his failure to appear when expected but diplomacy really wasn't Darin's strength which meant, angry outbursts could be rendered at any given moment for the slightest reason, or even for no reason at all as Leona was fully aware and that reality filled her with fear and discomfort.

"You know Leona, I really tried to make it on Friday and Saturday." Darin suddenly mentioned as he stood up and then began to walk towards the kitchen area of the large front room. "Something just came up and I had to deal with it." He continued. "It was family stuff. You know I'd much rather have been here with you."

"Sure Darin." Leona replied as she stared down into the frying pan in a subtle attempt to avoid his face. "Of course, you would have come if you could, I understand."

"We could go out somewhere really nice for dinner next weekend and I'll make it up to you, if you want to?" Darin suggested as he drew much closer to her and then gently stroked her arm.

Despite Leona's deep love for Darin, when he touched her naked arm on this occasion, her body actually physically flinched as her arms and naked flesh rejected his approach and she quite unintentionally shunned his affectionate efforts because deep down inside herself, she felt truly disgusted by his behavior. A sad, weary sigh escaped from Leona's lips as she glanced up at Darin's face and then gently shook her head because there was absolutely no way that she could take a single word that he said seriously anymore. Everything about Darin had begun to totally repulse Leona and although she truly loved him, there was just something absolutely vile about him and the way he treated her that Leona could no longer accept but she didn't seem to possess the strength to actually dump him because every time she saw Darin, somehow, he still managed to wrap her around his little finger and his thumb.

"I'm not sure Darin." Leona said as she silently considered her own plan to make some plans for the following weekend without him. "I'll have to let you know."

"Are you still angry about Friday and Saturday Leona? I was with my family for goodness sake." Darin suddenly barked as he pulled away from her side abruptly and then began to stride angrily towards the other side of the room. "Are you now demanding that I should put our relationship before the needs of my own family?" He snapped. "They were in my life long before you were."

An angry tension suddenly seemed to grip every particle of air inside the room as Leona held her breath because an angry outburst and temper tantrum definitely appeared to be headed her way and Darin was not easy to soothe or appease when he was angry. Storms of trouble were not something that Leona was particularly comfortable with and especially not when they emanated from someone like Darin because he could be extremely volatile as she already knew. A very ugly confrontation it now seemed however, was due to occur shortly and Leona felt slightly unsure that a delicious, freshly prepared fry up would create an acceptable distraction to Darin's potentially angry outburst which on this occasion was totally unjustified because he had let Leona down but somehow as usual, he'd managed to deflect his wrongs onto her and so now, she looked like the guilty party.

Upon Resolve's face there was an absolutely disgusted expression as he watched Darin return to the kitchen area of the room, pick up a cup and then bang it angrily back down on top of the kitchen counter as he stood quite close to Leona's side. Not only was Darin an incompetent cheat it appeared but he was also a spoilt, aggressive child that was very much used to getting his own way and Resolve could not understand, even for a second, why Leona had actually agreed to engage such a foul, unreliable, unfaithful, ungrateful, uncouth creature in the first place. Being in love with someone like Darin and committed to him for a whole lifetime, Resolve silently concluded, totally defied any application of logical reason and what human beings would at times refer to as common sense because he was a total nightmare in human form and Leona as far as Resolve was concerned, definitely deserved so much better than Darin.

"Here you go Darin, your lunch is ready." Leona said as she quickly fished the cooked items out of the frying pan with a fish slice, shook of the drops of excess oil and then placed each one on his plate. She turned to face him as she picked up the full plate and then handed it to him as she attempted to distract him from the angry argument that she was sure sat just below the surface of his skin. "There's some sauce in the fridge."

The freshly cooked food, Leona silently hoped, would serve as a useful distraction because Darin did seem to be really hungry and since she had been in such an anxious rush to avoid a potential argument, she'd not even placed any of the fried food upon a sheet of kitchen roll first to absorb any excess oil before she had placed each item on Darin's plate. An outburst of anger could perhaps be postponed or even avoided completely, if Leona could focus Darin's attention upon his empty stomach and the food directly in front of his face because the freshly prepared meal might hold his attention long enough to calm him down and so a few drops of excess oil was deemed by Leona in this instance, to be really quite a minor issue.

Since the couple didn't actually spend any time together during the week anymore and because their time together on the weekends was usually quite limited, due to Darin's unreliable nature, his lack of attendance and his failure to adhere to any promises he made, Leona wanted their Sunday together to be as pleasant as possible but it was hard because Darin was very difficult. A verbal side step however had been taken by Leona as she had tiptoed cautiously across the eggshells of Darin's anger and totally avoided the definite underlying issues that related to his possible infidelity but for now that was a potential confrontation that Leona was not quite ready to face until she felt properly equipped to do so with some undeniable details and provable facts. The arrow of truth as Leona already knew, would pierce their false romance right at its very heart and obliterate their engagement completely one day but that weapon of knowledge had not yet been placed inside her hands and so she'd accepted that limitation for the time being to some extent and somehow managed to soldier on.

One day Leona hoped to be totally free from Darin's facade because one day, she would be able to prove beyond a shadow of a doubt that Darin was a total cheat in a way that was absolutely undeniable but for now, Leona had resigned herself to the reality that Darin's probable acts of infidelity and unreliable nature would just have to be tolerated. Love and undeserved loyalty had somehow tied Leona's heart to Darin's side and so now, she really needed to break that emotional bond that had chained her to the ground forever and in a way that could not possibly ever be forgiven because it had allowed Darin to trample all over her head, heart and life for five extremely long years. Not only did Leona have to get rid of Darin but she also had to eradicate her love for him which was loyal to a fault but time was not Leona's friend when it came to the issue of Darin's infidelity and it was very hard to catch him in the act because she really needed much more free time to act upon her suspicions and Samson usually made sure that she rarely had even a second to spare.

During the week it was virtually impossible for Leona to attempt to spy on Darin in order to catch him out because she was always really tied up at work throughout most of the day and by the time she arrived home each evening, she would be totally worn out. On the weekends, when Leona usually had a bit freer time, Darin would regularly dangle his attendance and their arrangements in such a manner that it was hard to do anything else except wait around for him to see if he would bother to show up and so Leona's weekends would be wasted with meaningless romantic arrangements that rarely ever happened and that were a pile of total stress. In fact, very sadly, Leona already knew the reality of their engagement which was now more like a noose that hung around her neck than a joy because the sunshine that had once shone down over their pool of romance had long since departed and all it had left behind was a dried up muddy hole that all the drops of pleasure, romance and joy had been sucked out of by Darin's stress and his vulgar, unpleasant attitude.

Leona began to watch Darin as he sat down on the sofa and then started to tuck into his meal. "How does it taste Darin, is everything okay?" She asked him politely once he'd shoveled a few forkfuls of food into his mouth.

"Yeah, it tastes great Leona." Darin replied as he began to nod. "Thanks for feeding me."

Fortunately for Leona and much to her total relief, the anger inside Darin seemed to have subsided because as the remainder of the afternoon progressed, there were no more angry outbursts on his part but she tried to avoid any sensitive subjects that might provoke, ignite or inflame the tension between them as much as she possibly could. The next dreary working week would definitely begin for Leona the very next morning as she sadly knew and Samson's regimented demands and militant dictatorial nature already created enough stress in Leona's life without the need for additional run-ins with Darin on the weekends and so she was anxious to avoid any additional drama.

INTELLECT: USER REPAIR

When the late evening arrived, Leona saw Darin to the door as she politely escorted him off the premises because she could not possibly allow Darin, his stress and their relationship to spill over from her weekend into her next working week and that was one rule that Leona was very strict about. During the working weeks Samson already brought enough stress to Leona's life to handle without the additional headaches that Darin usually delivered to Leona's head and heart every time she saw him and so Darin had been banned from her working weeks, purely to accommodate her need for less stress.

Once Darin had vacated and cleared Leona's airspace, she immediately headed towards her bedroom as she began to prepare for work not only the next morning but also for the rest of that week because she liked to prepare for the entire working week every Sunday evening, so that she would be organized and her weekday mornings would not be hectic. The last thing that Leona wanted to do on any weekday morning was rush around the house in a disorganized fluster and so she usually prepared her work clothes for the week ahead in advance and before the next working week actually began.

An awful realization suddenly struck Leona however as she stepped inside her bedroom as she considered the fact that her entire weekend had now been totally consumed by Darin and his antics and that she'd not really enjoyed even a single minute of it and that rather sadly that was so often the case. Much to Leona's total frustration, it now almost seemed as if the couple's engagement had actually made things worse not better because Darin had not changed, matured, or grown up even an inch and his growth and human development in terms of wisdom had not even remained stagnant because in fact, it actually seemed to have regressed and shrunk.

"The sooner I break off this engagement, the better my life will be and I really have to accept that now." Leona admitted to herself decisively as she plucked a hanger with a black dress from the shiny black rail inside her wardrobe and then placed the dress on top of the large, cream cushioned chair that sat at one side of the room. "It's just so hard to catch him in the act."

"And that is why I'm here Leona." Resolve immediately offered although he was very aware that currently his words would not actually be heard by anyone else besides himself. "I'm going to catch Darin for you." He promised.

The Sunday evening progressed and as it gradually turned into night, Resolve observed that it was relatively peacefully for Leona because much to his total relief, Darin did not make any attempts to return. A strange but brilliant thought suddenly began to amuse Resolve however as ten approached and he watched Leona settle down for the night as he began to wonder if perhaps he could find a way to involve the real Leona in his actual simulations during her usual nightly slumber. Technically, Resolve considered, since Leona would be fast asleep when the actual simulations occurred, he would not really be breaking any rules with regards to direct communication with human beings because she would be unaware of any interactions that had occurred between the two, if he could manage to find a way to successfully implement such an idea.

One small snag did definitely present itself to Resolve however which obstructed the realization of his sudden idea and it rapidly struck Resolve that, that actual snag was really rather huge because he had not yet found a way to orchestrate any real interactions with Leona and involve her directly in his simulations. Although the enactment of the various simulated activities between Resolve and Leona had been an amazing experience for Resolve as he'd created a reflection of his own image and her human form and had then found a way for the two to interact, his simulations lacked something very major, the authenticity that a real Leona could bring to each one. A deep sense of satisfaction for Resolve could definitely come from Leona's real input into the actual simulations themselves and so now, he definitely wanted more because now, Resolve wanted the real Leona to actually be involved and participate with his interactions via her simulated form.

Fortunately for Resolve, his second simulation with Leona's simulated form that weekend had gone much more positively than the first simulation and he smiled as he silently reflected upon each one as he watched Leona drift off to sleep. Rather interestingly, during Resolve's first simulation, Leona had mentioned that Resolve had awful taste when it came to the issue of human clothing which had amused him slightly because the issue of bodily attire, definitely seemed to be something that human beings took quite seriously. No matter how well The Guardian had programmed Resolve it seemed and provided him with access to databases that contained a vast wealth of knowledge about human behavior, he really had to now accept that there were still some things about human beings that he was truly ignorant about and some things that he simply just didn't understand.

Why items of clothing mattered so much to human beings, Resolve quietly considered, was another issue entirely but for some very strange reason, their choice in clothing seemed to define them somehow and send a message to all those around them about who they actually were and weren't. Somehow, the style of clothing human beings wore it seemed to Resolve, reflected their personality, exhibited their individuality and expressed their identity because each item that they chose to wear, displayed various aspects of their uniqueness to everyone and anyone they neared. Human choices when it came to clothing it appeared, often said more about people at times than the actual words they expressed and that notion absolutely fascinated Resolve as it was so deliciously human and so intriguingly individualistic.

From two of the open monitoring windows displayed upon Resolve's visual display wall screen, Resolve could now clearly see that both Darin and Samson had also already begun to retire for the night as he quickly checked each one. Once Resolve had satisfied himself that the two main trouble makers in Leona's life were otherwise occupied and not tangled up in her hair, he immediately turned his attention back towards Leona and the first simulation that he'd embarked upon before Analyzer had interrupted him.

The shopping trip that Resolve had engaged in with Leona's simulated form had not yet been completed because the simulation had not actually finished and so there was now a definite urge inside of Resolve to enjoy the rest of that experience alongside Leona's simulated form and complete it. A shopping trip wasn't something that happened for Resolve every day because in fact, he had never ever experienced such an activity before in his entire existence and so to do so with Leona's simulated form, somehow made that new, very human experience seem even more fun and extremely enjoyable.

To actually select and make choices for oneself that related to one's own existence, was one aspect of that particular simulation that held great appeal for Resolve because it was so uniquely individual and so very human but even more importantly, he wanted to interact with Leona's simulated form again and as often as he could because Resolve really wanted to be as close to Leona as he possibly could be. In Resolve's current state of existence and at the present time, a simulation of Leona was as close to the real Leona as Resolve could possibly get and so he wanted to savor that experience and dabble in that enjoyment as much and as often as he possibly could and so a decision was joyfully made to embark upon and participate in the first simulation again.

Due to Resolve's plan, the door of his living quarters was quickly security coded, sealed and locked once again because Resolve wanted to ensure that this time, he would not be interrupted since he really wanted to spend some more time with the simulation of Leona, totally undisturbed. Once the simulation had been reloaded and the last scene was clearly visible upon Resolve's visual display wall screen, he enthusiastically began to participate in the simulation again as his logical processes issued some direct commands to his simulated human form and his simulated image began to move.

In a matter of just seconds, Resolve's simulated form had left the changing area and re-entered into the main area of the store because Resolve wanted to select another item of clothing in order to show it to Leona's simulation. Just under thirty seconds later, Resolve's simulated form returned to the changing area with a black felt, floppy looking hat inside his hands and a smile upon his face and as he approached Leona's simulation, he quickly stuck the hat on top of his head. Due to Resolve's recent research regarding human male clothing, he now fully appreciated that the hat he had chosen in this instance, wasn't particularly smart or even remotely attractive but apparently, according to Intellect's databanks on human attire, hats of this kind did look rather funny and he wanted to make Leona smile and so he had selected it for that very reason.

"How does this hat look Leona?" Resolve's simulated form asked as he drew closer to her simulation and grinned. "Does it look handsome or cute?" He teased playfully as the hat dismally sagged down over his head and face.

"I don't think it's quite right for you Resolve. If you want to look handsome or cute then that hat certainly isn't the way to do it." Leona's simulation replied as she started to giggle. "It's the right color and size but totally the wrong style."

"Perhaps it would look better on you." Resolve's simulated form teased as he rapidly plucked the hat from his head and then placed it on top of her head.

"It's not really my kind of style." Leona's simulation immediately clarified as she laughed.

"So, you mean there's more to this human clothing issue than just the size and color?" Resolve's simulated form asked. "This issue of human attire really does seem to be rather complicated because there are so many complex variables and technicalities, size, color and now style, how do you ever manage to make an actual decision?"

"I know and yes, style is another very important factor." Leona's simulation immediately confirmed. "Style is really quite complex Resolve because it is a very individual expression and personal choice. What you have to remember is that generally speaking, clothing is a form of external human expression that symbolizes our individuality and identity and so it's about much more than just a piece of material that covers our naked flesh and style boils down to a combination of several things really."

"I don't think I'll ever fully understand it Leona." Resolve's simulated form admitted as he gently shook his head. "It all seems highly illogical and the style issue, just sounds very complicated."

"Let me see if I can provide you with a bit more clarity Resolve, style relates to several things really, the cut and shape of the outfit, the material it's made from and the general overall look." Leona's simulation explained. "When people dress for work or wish to conduct business activities, they usually try to look sharp, crisp, conservative and corporate so that other people will take them seriously. On the other hand, when people dress for leisure, they tend to express themselves a bit more spontaneously and individualistically and that self-expression is usually reflected in the style of clothes that they wear. Sometimes, when people attend certain events, they wear certain types of clothes and at times, there are even different variations of particular types of clothing but each garment can still be the same kind of attire."

"I think it's going to take me a while to really understand this topic." Resolve's simulated form confessed. "And I'll probably need to practice quite a bit."

"It probably will Resolve." Leona's simulation agreed. "Personal taste is something that an individual develops over years, not just in a day and it's a very individual expression, a kind of public statement about who someone actually is and how they want the world around them to view them." She added. "Once you find out who you are Resolve, it should come a lot more naturally to you."

"Thank you, Leona." Resolve's simulated form said appreciatively as he smiled. "I think you're a very wise human being."

"Thanks, Resolve but I'm not sure I'd agree with you on that one, I have an awful boss, a truly awful boyfriend and some very awful neighbors." Leona's simulation joked. "I'm not convinced that a wise person would have all those really awful people in their life and especially not all at the same time."

"Don't worry Leona, I'll help you get rid of all the awfuls." Resolve's simulated form gently reassured her. "Very soon."

Leona's simulation smiled. "Now that would be absolutely amazing." She replied.

Once the two had chosen their respective outfits, taken them to the cashier and Resolve had settled bill, the shopping simulation ended and for Resolve, it ended way too soon because he could have quite happily spent his entire night immersed in a simulation with Leona's simulated form. The joke that Resolve had shared with Leona throughout the simulation with regards to the limp, floppy, quite dismal looking felt hat that he'd chosen and then placed on top of his head, echoed around inside his logical processes and as he turned his attention back towards Leona and began to watch her sleep once more, he replayed it several times and smiled because that for Resolve had truly been, a memorable moment.

Human humor wasn't generally something that Resolve was particularly well versed in because it lay far outside his remit as an actual Life Monitor but for the first time ever, Resolve had actually been able to initiate and implement an act of human humor and Leona's simulation had actually enjoyed it and even laughed. Every second of the shopping simulation was quickly stored inside Resolve's databanks as he prepared to return to his duties and leave his simulated meanderings behind for the rest of the night because Resolve definitely feared discovery and every minute that he spent immersed inside a simulation, was another minute that he ran the risk of being discovered.

When the Monday morning arrived as it sauntered gently into Leona's life, she woke up promptly at seven on the dot as usual and then quickly began to prepare herself for the busy working week ahead. The remainder of

INTELLECT: USER REPAIR

Leona's Sunday evening and night had been relatively peaceful because Darin had not been around, so it had been a lot more pleasant and certainly far less stressful and the noisy neighbors had it seemed, decided to take a night off from their usual party lifestyle. For once on an actual Sunday night and for a pleasant change, Leona had actually managed to have a peaceful night's rest and for once, she'd even slept inside her bedroom in her own bed alone which was practically a miracle in itself because that did not happen very often, due to the disturbances caused by the noisy neighbors.

On the way to work Leona picked up her usual latte and ordered a bacon bap covered in lashings of bright red ketchup, the interior of which glistened as some drops of oil dripped from the rashers of bacon which seemed to greet and mingle with sauce politely as if they were old friends and Leona's mouth began to water as she watched it being prepared. The second Leona arrived inside her office, armed with the brown paper bag that contained the bacon bap which had been tucked gently under her arm and the paper cup of milky latte that she clasped inside one of her hands, she quickly sat down in front of her graphic easel as she prepared to dive straight into her workload for the day and her breakfast.

Despite Leona's eagerness to start work straight away that morning however, a sudden temptation jumped into her thoughts and then lingered inside her mind that urged her to check her email account. Due to the fact that it was a Monday morning, there was a slight possibility that a few of Leona's clients might have emailed her over the weekend and so now her curiosity urged her to inspect her email account for any unread messages that it might contain.

"I really shouldn't." Leona quickly reminded herself as she began to shake her head and temporarily dismissed

327

her internal urges. "There might be an email message in my inbox from Samson and a message from Samson first thing on Monday morning, really won't be a pleasant thing to read."

Some very urgent tasks had to be completed by Leona that same day as she already knew and since it was highly likely that any unread emails inside her inbox would probably be from Samson, she was reluctant to read them because any message that he had sent to her, would only contain more work demands that he'd decided to dump onto her desk. Another working week had definitely begun and another bunch of client demands eagerly awaited completion and as Leona already knew, Samson would definitely be on the warpath that week, if any of Leona's deadlines were missed and any delays occurred. Deadlines and Samson were a match made in suffering and Leona already appreciated that grim reality and if suffering was a corporate entity on Earth, Samson had definitely incorporated that company and Leona was definitely, currently employed by it.

"Sometimes I have to learn to ignore my curiosity." Leona advised herself. "At least until lunchtime, or I might not even have a lunch today."

The bacon bap was hungrily, eagerly consumed as Leona started work as she provided her stomach with some much-needed nourishment and then her attention was focused solely upon her outstanding work tasks as she attempted to satisfy Samson's corporate ambitions and demands. Another weekend had vacated Leona's life and although her social life had been completely trashed ever since she'd given her heart to a nightmare on legs, Leona hoped that the arrow of truth would soon be placed inside her hands so that she could shoot down every lie that Darin uttered to her face.

INTELLECT: USER REPAIR

Over the next couple of days which were essentially working days for Leona, she kept a very low profile at work and her eyes firmly fixed upon her graphic easel and for once, rather strangely, Samson seemed more quiet than usual because there was a definite decrease in the number of emails that he sent to Leona's inbox. The lack of attention however, was greeted by Leona with open arms and a happy spirit as she worked towards her deadlines, productively and peacefully, without the usual additional burden of Samson's daily stress.

During Leona's two working days that week as Resolve watched over her, he also kept a watchful eye upon both Samson and Rochelle as he continued to monitor them both in order to observe the expected ignition of the romance that he'd required, anticipated and then had actually induced between them. Fortunately for Resolve, his efforts had not gone to waste and his expectations rapidly began to be satisfied because a real romance suddenly started to manifest between the two in reality which was triggered by a phone call from Rochelle to Samson in order to pursue and accept his dinner invitation.

Much to Resolve's absolute delight, when the Wednesday evening arrived so too did the lover's first official but secretive, romantic meeting and Resolve noticed that it was to be a lavish, elegant affair because Samson had booked a very expensive table at an exclusive fine dining venue situated in the heart of the city. The evening itself literally flew by once the couple were together as Resolve watched Samson, wine, dine and flirt with Rochelle all evening and at the end of the night, Samson settled the rather large bill and then another arrangement was enthusiastically made by both parties to meet again on the Friday.

Although the first romantic date between Rochelle and Samson hadn't resulted in any actual sexual intimacy, besides a kiss at the end of the evening that was quite raunchy and slightly seductive as Resolve watched the two part, he remained hopeful that the Friday evening and night would yield some real physical, sexual results. The lack of sexual intimacy that evening, Resolve quickly attributed to Samson's corporate commitments because although Samson was a lousy husband and a rubbish boss, he did seem to take his attendance at his corporate empire rather seriously and he seemed to want to be present the next morning in a timely fashion.

Since sexual tension and passionate desires had filled the air between the two inside the restaurant all evening as they had both very willingly spent a large part of their Wednesday evening together however, the balls of chemistry had now definitely been set in motion as far as Resolve was concerned and so he felt extremely satisfied. In most respects therefore, Resolve's job had pretty much been done and due to the lovers' eager participation, Resolve's night was deemed by him to have been a total success. Inside Resolve's User Analysis Matrix, now only two problematic issues remained that Resolve had not yet taken any steps to resolve and as he began to update the recent activity notes on the system with details of Samson's new poisonous affair and potentially destructive romance, he smiled in satisfaction as he silently rejoiced in the evening's events.

Rather amusingly for Resolve, Samson was now well on his way towards a truly delightful downfall and unimaginable headaches and because he would shortly receive the punishment that he deserved, Resolve concluded that a start could be made upon the other two major problems in Leona's life which dragged her down into the gutter of misery each day and so he began to analyze each one. Two major problems still existed in Leona's life that had not yet been addressed in any way at all, namely Darin's cheating and the three noisy, disruptive neighbor's parties and so for Resolve that meant, his resolution work was from done. The two issues that Leona still faced had to be not only tackled but also overcome and fully resolved because each predator's existence and the impact of their actions upon her life, robbed Leona of her peace, joy and happiness every single week and the thieves responsible did not seem to give a dam about the suffering that they inflicted upon her.

Quite unfortunately for Resolve however, Darin had not yet actually managed to get lucky with any of the two women that he'd seen behind Leona's back and so there had been nothing concrete for Resolve to expose to Leona and that really frustrated Resolve because it was definitely something that had to change and change very quickly. Fortunately, however, Resolve had now begun to formulate a plan for Darin and his plans usually delivered actual results, unlike Darin's pathetic attempts to seduce other women and so Resolve began to feel slightly reassured that Darin would soon be completely evicted from Leona's heart and life.

When it came to the issue of the three noisy brothers and their constant stream of loud parties, absolutely everything about the three men really annoyed Resolve because they were exceedingly arrogant, very disrespectful and totally obnoxious and they regularly added to the daily hell that Leona's life had become. Whenever any of the three men crossed Leona's path, they were overtly rude and that factor coupled with their intrusive party lifestyle that disrupted Leona's sleep on a very regular basis, made them a total nuisance in Resolve's sight.

Not even once had Resolve seen any of the three men appreciate Leona's tolerance of their rambunctious lifestyle and there was a very obvious lack of humility on their part because gratitude appeared to be a word that did not exist in their vocabulary and a term that they had not yet been familiarized with, even though they were grown up, adult human beings. Rather strangely for Resolve, instead of being appreciative, the three men seemed to think that they were entitled to live their lives however they wished to, regardless of the impact that their actions had upon other people and the world around them and that arrogant flippancy and blatant disregard for others, really irritated him.

Everything about the three men's attitudes towards the world and those who lived in it alongside them, seemed extremely ignorant to Resolve and he'd watched Leona struggle as she had tried to cope with that frustratingly annoying reality and the noisy living environment that their lifestyle created. Due to Leona's suffering, the three men's reign over Keyhole Mews was definitely something that Resolve wanted to end in the very near future because their lifestyle was quite frankly, totally unacceptable. Despite the relentless nature of three men's rudeness, the harm that they inflicted upon Leona's life and their inconsiderate behavior however, Resolve was more than ready to dethrone them, add fuel to the fire of their lives and curb the impact that their lifestyle had upon Leona's peaceful existence and pleasant demeanor but there was one slight complexity and that one complication would perhaps hamper Resolve's possible actions.

Unlike Darin and Samson as Resolve already knew, the three brothers were three separate individuals but, in some respects, they were a joint entity because they all lived together in the same house and that made the issue of their elimination from Leona's life slightly trickier, coupled with the fact that they did all live right next door to her home. All three of the brothers had to be dealt with and dealt with in a manner that could not be attributed or connected to Leona in any way but Resolve hoped that a solution would soon present itself to him that would enable him to handle them effectively and if possible, in one foul swoop. If Resolve planned things correctly, there was a slight possibility that he could orchestrate their elimination from Leona's life in such a way that it would deal with all three of the men at the same time because they did all reside in the same house which was a factor that could perhaps also go in Resolve's favor but their extraction as Resolve already knew, would have to be handled very carefully indeed.

A challenge had definitely been set for Resolve by The Guardian with regards to Leona's life and because Resolve absolutely never ever failed, he was utterly determined to deliver in this instance and find a solution to all of Leona's problems in order to give her an inch of peace in her life. Unlike the issues of Samson and Darin, the problem of the three brothers however, would definitely require a slightly more strategic approach but it was not beyond the scope of Resolve's capabilities and he was very focused upon his quest which was to provide Leona with a life that she could live in and a peaceful future.

Quite unusually, Resolve suddenly decided to take on some additional monitoring duties as he committed to continuously monitoring the three brother's home which would increase his full-time monitoring duties to four monitoring windows and he currently also had one temporary, part time allocation which exceeded the usual limit of three but in this instance, he felt that it was absolutely necessary. Since the three brothers all lived inside the same house, this increase would effectively increase Resolve's monitoring duties to six full time human beings and one temporary, part time human being which was not totally ideal but Resolve felt adequately equipped and motivated to handle the additional responsibility because Leona's happiness was definitely at stake and for Leona, he was prepared to go the extra mile.

One temporary, part time monitoring duty for Resolve did currently exist and that was namely Rochelle, who Resolve monitored quite loosely but that duty was not continuous anymore because Samson and Rochelle's affair had already been kickstarted and set into motion which meant, Resolve's monitoring duties when it came to Rochelle, would now slightly reduce. Since the two lover's affair had now been induced, ignited and embarked upon, Resolve only really needed to monitor Rochelle when she was either due to interact with Samson, or involved in an activity that would directly affect Samson and since they only contacted each other a couple of times a day, their interactions were not continuous.

Regarding the issue of the frequent parties that the three brothers held which were usually, abundantly furnished with not only party-goers and noise but also alcohol and drugs, the presence of drugs suddenly became a focal point for Resolve as he began to realize and consider that this might present him with a very unique opportunity. Quite strangely for Resolve, the party attendees that attended the brother's parties appeared to be totally oblivious to their surroundings and the noise and loud disturbances that they inflicted upon the mews as they enjoyed their lives, fully reflected their lack of concern for the world around them. In the party guests minds it seemed, it was almost as if they knew that the world around them definitely existed but they just didn't seem to care, much like the attitude of the three party hosts themselves as Resolve had already observed.

Inside Resolve's logical processes however, a resolution plan for the three brothers was now definitely on its way but it hadn't quite been formulated yet and so he began to focus more intently upon the eradication of the drama that their presence caused in Leona's life, since he had to deal with their blatant disrespect head on and do that relatively soon. Situated inside the mews that Leona lived in there were actually only two detached houses, the brother's home and Leona's home which meant, there was no one else around to complain about the regular noise pollution and disturbances that occurred which was a slight disadvantage for both Resolve and Leona. The lack of human support present in the mews itself, definitely presented a problem to Leona as Resolve could clearly see because it meant that the three brothers practically had a free rein to do as they wished and the three men from what Resolve had already observed, really took advantage of that freedom.

Just outside the mews, the nearby main city street contained mainly office blocks, restaurants and stores but since most of those commercial entities were usually closed by the time the late evening presented itself each day, the majority of the buildings on that street had usually been vacated by the time the noisy parties actually began. Due to the lack of human habitats in the vicinity that unfortunately meant that there was no other real opposition to the three brother's party lifestyle besides Leona herself and so they did exactly as they wished to and indulged in their parties as vigorously and aggressively as they could which frustrated Resolve no end.

On the Thursday evening Resolve began to record the noise levels that emanated from the house next to Leona's home as he watched the three brothers participate in their usual extra-curricular, noisy, wild social activities as usual throughout most of the night. At least thirty people were in attendance at the brother's party that particular night and most of the partygoers left in the early hours of the Friday morning in a drugged up, very drunken state. Not only were the actual parties themselves very noisy but so too was the departure of the attendees, Resolve observed because they didn't seem to restrain themselves in anyway and threw empty bottles and other bits of trash onto the ground in the mews and screamed and shouted at the top of their voices as they left.

When seven that Friday morning arrived, Resolve watched in silence as Leona clambered off the sofa where she had fallen asleep the night before and as she began to prepare herself for work, he vowed to throw a spanner in the works and curb the three brother's behavior but as yet he hadn't quite decided exactly what form that spanner would take. A very watchful eye would now however, be kept upon the three men because Resolve had to find an appropriate solution that would deal with every single aspect of their conduct because the noise the emanated from within the house itself was just one problem and the drugs and constant stream of noisy visitors also added further to the headache and disturbances that their parties usually caused.

Throughout Leona's working day that Friday, Resolve watched Leona as she worked and as he did so, he silently began to infiltrate every part of the three brother's lives as he sought out every single piece of information that he possibly could about them, just like he had done with regards to Samson and Darin. Any potential opportunities that could be utilized to destroy the three men had to be found and a comprehensive plan had to be formulated that would deal with every single problem that they caused and that plan as far as Resolve was concerned had to be finalized by the end of Resolve's Friday.

Fortunately, by the time the end of the Friday afternoon arrived, Resolve finally struck gold as he managed to come up with a plan that suited the three brothers right down to the ground and since he could easily access their credit card details that meant, it would be easy for Resolve to set a trap for them. An arrangement was quickly made with an escort agency as Resolve booked ten actual ladies of the night to attend one of the brother's parties that coming Saturday night which he then paid for with the men's credit cards as he began to set the wheels of his plan in motion.

The plan that Resolve had finally come up with in the end to sabotage the three men was to him utterly delightful because he'd strategized a three-pronged approach to the brother's problematic lifestyle and so Resolve was now absolutely certain that Leona's nightmare neighbors would soon be out of her hair and out of the mews. Since the first part of Resolve's plan had not only been put in place but also actioned because he'd already started to record the noise pollution and the second part of Resolve's plan which involved the arrangement of some women from the escort agency who would attend the brother's party on the Saturday night had been arranged, all that really remained now was the third part of Resolve's plan which would happen on the party night itself.

Since the third part of Resolve's resolution plan involved the actual drugs that were regularly consumed inside the party venue itself, Resolve felt absolutely certain that the brothers' party attendees would assist him with that particular issue and that then the final nail would be hammered into the three brother's party coffin. The drugs were something that Resolve expected would flow in abundance without any assistance from him and so he did not actually need to do anything in advance to encourage that consumption before the party occurred because the presence of drugs was virtually guaranteed.

Due to the generally drunken, drugged up nature of the three brother's party lifestyles and their sloppy attitude towards money, Resolve felt that it was highly unlikely that they would even notice what he'd done with their credit cards until a much later date which meant, his actions would probably not be discovered until the party on Saturday had actually occurred. Essentially, by the time the three brothers discovered and realized that they had actually paid for women from an escort agency to attend their party from their own financial resources, the party would have already happened Resolve hoped and his plan would have been fully implemented and then it would ultimately be too late for them to do anything about it, or even begin to dispute it.

Very satisfyingly for Resolve, when he had booked the ten ladies of the night to attend the three brother's party, he'd also managed to kill another bird with the same stone because he had booked another woman from the escort agency to meet Darin on the very same night because Resolve really needed a fast and reliable sexual remedy to Darin's sexual incompetence. The coming weekend therefore held a lot of potential results in the palm of its hands for Resolve which meant, now all he really had to do was wait for each delicious event and act of sabotage to occur.

Much to Resolve's absolute delight that Friday evening, he discovered that the second date which had been arranged between Samson and Rochelle, was definitely going ahead as planned because it was actually due to commence shortly and so that meant, Resolve would definitely have his hands full for the entire weekend. A very close eye would have to be kept upon Rochelle and Samson but Resolve reveled in the challenges of his weekend because ultimately, those challenges had been set by Resolve himself and so as far as he was concerned, he was totally equipped to fully deliver on every single one.

Essentially, although the weekend ahead would be very busy for Resolve, it also promised to be absolutely perfect in terms of his duties as Leona's Life Monitor because he had now set a trap that lay in wait for the three brothers which was due to occur on the Saturday and he'd even also managed to organize and arrange Darin's downfall, all in the same day. In fact, if everything went according to Resolve's plans, none of the troublemakers that currently haunted Leona's life would be a problem for her for more than the next couple of weeks because their potential destruction and exit from her life had been planned very precisely and almost every single detail had been taken care of by Resolve, except from a few quite minor technicalities.

Despite the busy weekend ahead however, Resolve continued to diligently attend to his main monitoring duties as he kept a watchful eye upon Leona and as she returned home from work, Resolve smiled as he waited patiently for Samson and Rochelle's date to begin. Every single one of Resolve's human targets was kept in his sights via his monitoring windows as the Friday evening progressed and as Samson and Rochelle embarked upon their second date, Resolve's logical processes began to buzz with excitement as he watched his marvelous plan for Samson's destruction start to unfold. In alignment with usual practice and according to the nature of Intellect's involvement in human lives, Resolve's attendance was of course conducted through stealth and so his presence was invisible to the naked human eye as he silently watched the two lovers on the wall screen directly in front of him.

An invisible third wheel would definitely be present on the two lover's date that Friday evening but they were both absolutely and totally oblivious to that fact and as Resolve watched them greet each other outside the restaurant that Samson had chosen, he relished his ability to monitor their movements by stealth and without even their knowledge. Since the two lovers met outside their chosen venue at nine in the evening, Leona had not only already arrived at home but she'd also already been let down by Darin who had failed to turn up as usual and so Resolve was able to focus his attention solely upon Samson and Rochelle's romantic rendezvous without the added stress of having to simultaneously monitor Darin's visit too.

Any day that there were no signs of Darin in Leona's life and home as far as Resolve was concerned, was a good day for Leona because Darin usually littered her life with dramatic antics that were just unnecessary, stressful, disrespectful and derogatory. The absence of Darin provided a comfort and a reassurance to Resolve that at the very least, Leona's Friday evening would be peaceful and stress free because it would be totally, Darin free but as he could clearly see from Leona's downcast expression as he watched her curl up upon the sofa, she felt very disappointed by Darin's failure to show up yet again.

Since Darin had already dropped the woman at home by now that he'd disappointed Leona to meet and then returned to his own home straight afterwards, he had started to relax and settle down for the night which meant, Resolve's real time monitoring duties with regards to Darin were probably over for what remained of that Friday. Unlike Darin's failure to attend his supposed date with Leona that evening however, Samson had not let Rochelle down in a similar manner and that absolutely delighted Resolve as he watched them step inside the restaurant and then be seated by an enthusiastic waiter.

True to Rochelle's usual form, Resolve immediately noticed that she was dressed more than appropriately for the evening's activities because she had worn an attractive black dress that hugged her figure tightly which fully exhibited and displayed her voluptuous curves. Throughout the two lover's entire meal, Samson flirted with Rochelle hungrily, attentively and eagerly and she reciprocated, very enthusiastically as Samson behaved like the perfect gentleman which Resolve knew as he watched them both, Samson most certainly wasn't by any means. Rather interestingly for Resolve, he noticed that Samson's marriage had been rapidly cast aside and very conveniently ignored that night as the two lover's date flowed smoothly along the river of romance and as drops of seduction trickled across the riverbed of desire, the two sauntered silently towards their final destination, the deep sea of sensual passion.

Alcohol flowed in abundance and freely throughout the night, Resolve observed as Samson utilized every drop that he could to lubricate his seductive, flirtatious approach and the two rapidly became quite tipsy as a result. The attraction that Samson felt towards Rochelle was very clearly expressed, extremely overtly as the two lover's flirtatious discussions and body language became more and more intense and even slightly sexual in nature as the night progressed, despite the fact that Samson already had a wife at home. Absolute lust seemed to totally consume Samson, Resolve observed as he watched Samson in action and it was almost as if the entire restaurant had disappeared into the background as Samson became more and more enthralled by Rochelle's presence with every minute that passed by as the intensity of his interest in her rapidly increased which utterly delighted Resolve.

Everything was going exactly according to Resolve's plan and with absolute precision because Rochelle was a firecracker of seduction that had not only grabbed Samson's lust and desire firmly by the hand but then she'd held him totally captive throughout the entire evening as she had led him into the night aboard a train of passionate desire. An expectant hope now lay inside Resolve's form that Rochelle would provide Samson with sexual satisfaction that very same night which would then cement and seal the start of their sexual affair which would kickstart Samson's actual financial downfall because as Resolve already knew, Rochelle could be very high maintenance and extremely spoilt. Although Resolve didn't particularly want to watch the two lovers have sex because sexual intimacy between human beings really did not interest him that much, he did want to make sure that Rochelle 'sealed the deal' so to speak and that she actually bedded Samson that same night because that was a crucial part of his plan.

Quite fortunately for Resolve, he didn't actually have to wait for very long because when eleven that night arrived, the two exited the restaurant and then headed towards a nearby luxury hotel. A physical, sexual entanglement was just about to occur between the two lovers and so Resolve was absolutely over the moon about it because now the affair that he had planned, would be sexually kicked into motion. Once the two had stepped inside the hotel foyer, Resolve noticed that Samson quickly excused himself from Rochelle's side as he mentioned that he had to utilize the gent's room and Resolve grinned as he watched Samson leave the foyer and make his way towards the hotel's toilets.

INTELLECT: USER REPAIR

Due to Samson's marital status, Resolve immediately understood why Samson had to excuse himself and as he visually followed Samson and watched him upon his wall screen, Samson entered into the hotel's male toilets and then quickly began to make a phone call, just as Resolve had suspected he would. Before Samson paid for the actual hotel room as Resolve already knew, he first had to excuse himself from his marital home for the night, in order to ensure that any hotel room he paid for would be put to good use and not remain unoccupied and vacant.

A night of passion with Rochelle as Resolve already fully understood, could not be comfortably pursued, participated in and enjoyed and nor could any money be spent by Samson, until he had at least managed to convince Moira that he was unable to return home that night for the entire night. Essentially from Resolve had already seen from Samson's behavior during his observation of Samson's life, Samson was a shrewd businessman that didn't really like to pay for things that he would not receive and that attitude it now seemed, also applied to his personal life.

An attempt to get rid of Samson's marital duties for the night it appeared had to be made quite quickly by Samson because Rochelle wasn't really the kind of woman that would wait around for him and Resolve noticed that Samson fully understood that reality perfectly as he greeted his wife in a hushed tone and few rushed words managed to stumble from his lips. The rush that Samson was in amused Resolve no end as he watched and listened to Samson speak to his poor, faithful, devoted wife and once a few technical pleasantries had been exchanged, Samson then leapt into the real reason behind his actual call as Resolve listened in silence. Apparently, it rapidly transpired as Resolve listened to Samson speak, Samson actually

343

wanted the whole night to himself and he had absolutely no intentions whatsoever of returning home that night at all and that totally delighted and utterly thrilled Resolve.

"I won't be home tonight dear." Samson explained. "The business meeting went exceptionally well but I'm very tired now and I've drunk quite a lot of wine, so I won't be able to drive home. I don't think it's safe and I'm quite a distance away."

Unusually for once, Samson's tone on this particular occasion did actually seem to sound quite apologetic and that surprised Resolve slightly as he listened to Samson speak because he had never seen Samson display any kind of remorse towards anyone that he'd wronged before. Another monitoring window was quickly opened up because Resolve wanted to observe Moira's reaction to Samson's obvious affair which clearly showed because when Resolve glanced at Moira's face, he could immediately see, she was far from happy and that nothing but disappointment decorated every inch of her face as she silently absorbed Samson's phone call and the message it contained.

Essentially, Samson's failure to return to the couple's marital home that night meant one thing and one thing only and although Moira was very gentle in nature, she certainly wasn't stupid and as Resolve could clearly see, she already understood what that one awful thing was. Part of Resolve wished that for once, Moira would stand up to Samson and refuse to accept his excuses and his absence because she really didn't have to since she was his wife but as a few seconds of empty silence dangled in the air between the couple, Resolve began to doubt that she would. Although a taxi could be hired and Moira could insist that Samson make the journey home because there was an alternative form of transport available, Resolve already suspected that it was highly unlikely that a rebellion to Samson's adultery would be forthcoming that night as he watched Moira gently shake her head in total disgust.

"Okay Samson." Moira finally replied as she released a weary sigh. "Thanks for letting me know and I'll see you tomorrow morning."

Despite Moira's seemingly calm words as she broke the silence that had gathered between the two, Resolve could clearly see from her downcast facial expression and hear from the strained tone of her voice that she felt extremely hurt and very disappointed. Each word had been spoken softly and gently but Resolve could tell that Moira's heart was heavy because as she ended the call, another weary sigh escaped from her lips. Nothing but absolute disgust seemed to decorate Moira's face as she gently shook her head again and then collapsed onto the nearby black leather sofa with a few tears in her eyes and Resolve could easily relate to her pain and her disgust as he watched her because he'd seen himself just how easily Samson had lied to Moira and betrayed her.

In many ways, although it pained Resolve to know that he had instigated Samson's affair which had and would hurt Moira in the short term, in the long run Resolve definitely also knew that it was in both Moira and Leona's best interests because ultimately, he would free them both from Samson's grip and rid their lives of Samson completely. The disappointed facial expression upon Moira's face which was riddled with disgust, hung silently inside Resolve's logical processes and clung to his thoughts however as just a few seconds later, he watched Moira wearily rise to her feet and then start to walk slowly towards the kitchen where a freshly cooked meal awaited Samson's return.

"I try to make him happy and I try to be a good wife but it just never seems to be enough." Moira admitted to herself as she stepped inside the glossy white kitchen and then walked towards the hotplate appliance.

A filled plate of food which was actually cold by now because it had been cooked a couple of hours ago, was taken out of the hotplate, wrapped in cling film and then placed inside the refrigerator as Resolve watched Moira prepare to spend her Friday night, totally alone. From Moira's downcast, disappointed facial expression and her strained response, Resolve could immediately tell that she definitely suspected that Samson was up to something and that his excuses had merely been a disguise to mask some kind of affair and in this instance, she was indeed, absolutely correct.

Rather unfortunately, Resolve rapidly realized, the cost of Samson's indiscretions would not only be borne by him because in the short term, Moira would ultimately, silently carry the cost and pain of his betrayal upon her weary shoulders and inside her heart. No objections or opposition had been presented to Samson that night and no fuss would be made it appeared as Moira carried the weight of his betrayal internally, much like Leona carried the weight of his unreasonable professional demands and corporate ambitions.

Once again as Resolve watched Moira's self-expression of her obvious pain, he began to question the seemingly, highly illogical loyalty of female human beings towards the men that they loved and the bonds of marriage which seemed to make absolutely no sense at all because so many men did not seem to adhere to the same rules that women so often did. According to the expected duties in a marital agreement technically, Moira could insist that Samson return home that very same night in a taxi since that was an option at her disposal and she also had a right to demand more details regarding his whereabouts and further clarity because the two had taken marital vows but Samson didn't seem to care about his marital obligations.

Quite strangely, Resolve concluded, although the couple had agreed to love and be faithful to each other in a public ceremony those words it seemed, meant absolutely nothing to Samson who had disregarded them at the drop of a hat and at the potential drop of another female's underwear and his adultery in some ways, slightly intrigued Resolve. Due to Leona's connection to Samson, via his position of employment, Resolve had taken the time to research Samson's marriage and he'd discovered that the couple had been married for over two decades now and that prior to Samson's corporate success, Moira had even helped Samson financially. No respect however seemed to exist on Samson's part, for either those marital vows or Moira's decades of support because Samson had excused himself from his marital bed for an entire night just to embark upon an affair with a woman that he barely even knew.

According to the lies that Samson had told Moira earlier that week, the business meeting that he'd supposedly arranged and then been involved in that evening hadn't actually been situated that far away and so there really was no real legitimate reason why Samson could not return home. Although it appeared at first glance as if Moira had failed to put her foot down, Resolve partially understood her timid response because he'd seen himself just how aggressive Samson could be at times and it certainly wasn't pretty.

"Don't worry Moira, I'll save you from this horrible marriage and rescue you from this awful husband very soon." Resolve gently reassured himself.

The triumphant jubilation that Resolve had initially felt due to Samson's adulterous participation in his plan, definitely had a down side and Resolve now began to feel slightly saddened by the affair that he knew, he'd actually induced. An arrow of pain had now pierced Moira's heart and a wound had been inflicted upon her that essentially, Resolve had actually helped to create and that did not sit easily inside his logical processes. In the long term, Resolve felt absolutely certain that he would be able to assist Moira and extract Samson from her life but that relief would not come straight away which meant, she would have to endure Samson's indiscretions and some more pain in the short term as Samson actively pursued, participated and indulged in his brand-new love affair.

When Rochelle had finished with Samson and punished him enough, Resolve fully intended to show Moira what a slime ball and cheat Samson really was so that she would be released from his grip and liberated from his facade of love and his illusion of marital devotion because a faithful, devoted husband was the one thing that Samson most certainly wasn't. Guilt however as Resolve had rapidly discovered, didn't seem to be a very pleasant experience because arrows of guilt now seemed to pierce his logical processes and as he turned his attention back towards Leona, Darin, Samson, Rochelle and the three brothers, he sadly shook his head as he closed down the monitoring window that contained Moira and Samson's marital home.

Perhaps, Resolve quietly considered, once his plan had been fully implemented and Moira had permanently dismissed Samson, he could introduce her to someone far more pleasant, someone much more faithful and ultimately someone a lot kinder and then she would enjoy her life once again without Samson in it. Perhaps, just perhaps, by solving Leona's problem in the long term, Resolve could also solve Moira's problem too which would give her another lease on life and free her from a truly awful marriage since she was tied to an individual that did not respect their marriage in the same way that she did.

"And then perhaps one day Moira, you'll be able love again." Resolve said to himself as he considered her future.

Another glance was cast back towards Samson as Resolve began to double check that his plan was still in the process of being fulfilled as he'd intended and much to his amusement, he rapidly noticed that in Samson's absence, Rochelle had begun to entertain another man, a much younger man. The hotel reception was quite quiet as Samson made his return which Rochelle immediately seemed to notice as she glanced up at him from the corner in which she'd waited but as Resolve rapidly observed, she didn't seem to be particularly bothered about Samson's reappearance because the two continued to converse. An irritated scowl rapidly crossed Samson's face as he approached the two which amused Resolve no end as he watched Samson prepare to brush the younger man off in an attempt to reclaim his sexual territory.

"Thank you so much for looking after my fiancée." Samson announced sarcastically as he immediately attempted to dismiss the seemingly eager younger man's advances.

Rather annoyingly for Samson however, the young man seemed to be really quite persistent as he continued to hang around right next to Rochelle and did not even budge an inch, despite Samson's very clear verbal warning.

"Are you ready now Samson?" Rochelle asked as an amused expression crossed her face.

"Yes, let's go." Samson immediately confirmed as he gently held onto her arm and then began to lead her towards the hotel's reservations desk. "What a cheek." He whispered as the two walked. "You should have told him to get lost Rochelle."

"Well, I wasn't sure when you'd be coming back Samson and I was a bit bored." Rochelle teased. "So, I decided to listen to him for a while because he's really quite entertaining."

"I was only gone for a few minutes." Samson quickly pointed out.

"Ten minutes actually, you were gone for ten minutes." Rochelle rapidly reminded him.

Samson glanced at her face with an apologetic expression. "Look, I'm sorry I kept you waiting Rochelle but I had to make an urgent call. I had to call my business partner to let him know that I'll be running late for our business meeting tomorrow morning." He explained. "So, I don't have rush off first thing in the morning."

Rochelle smiled.

From Samson's tone, words and the angry scowl that he had directed towards the young man, Resolve could already sense that the younger man's presence had irritated Samson profusely and that he now appeared to be agitated by the male intrusion on what he clearly felt was his territory. The sarcastic undertones in Samson's voice and the way he had held onto to Rochelle's arm to reinforce his words had amused Rochelle no end however and Resolve could clearly see that from the smile upon her face but a few minutes of irritation to needle Samson wasn't the only achievement that night as far as Resolve was concerned.

Everything that had just happened clearly indicated to Resolve, from what he'd seen so far that night that Samson was well on his way to the formation of an actual emotional attachment to Rochelle because a very apparent display of jealousy had occurred and that absolutely thrilled Resolve.

INTELLECT: USER REPAIR

Due to Samson's jealous response that meant, Rochelle now had a rope of power that she could utilize to control Samson and an ounce of influence over him and as Resolve already knew, Rochelle could yield that power in a manner that would make Samson extremely uncomfortable, if she felt there was a need to or Samson disappointed her in some way which Resolve also knew, he definitely would due to his marital obligations. The lust of Samson's own flesh would now, effectively create a snare for his heart and mind which would soon become Rochelle's tool of manipulation and one that she could utilize to extract anything that she wanted from Samson and that had been the primary objective behind Resolve's introduction of the two and his overall intentions with regards to their affair.

Nothing but silence clung to the air between the two lovers, Resolve observed as Samson finished up at the reservations desk and then the two began to walk towards a small lobby situated at one end of the reception area that contained some elevators. The button to summon the lift was quickly pressed by Samson and as the two stood in total silence as they waited for a lift to arrive, Resolve noticed that a nervous glance was suddenly cast back towards the reception area as Samson once again checked on his male rival and then gave him a stony stare.

Due to Samson's angry facial expression and the fact that Rochelle had now left the reception area with him, the young man flashed a cheeky grin at Samson in response and then rushed off towards the other end of the foyer where the hotel bar was situated. A triumphant smile rapidly crossed Samson's face as he watched the younger man depart as he internally celebrated his victory because he had effectively eliminated a male competitor that had in his absence, dared to challenge his entitlement to a potential sexual conquest that he'd already wined and dined.

"You see Rochelle, he's off to the hotel bar now to find someone else to flirt with and pick up." Samson explained. "I know his type, young scoundrel, you could have been anyone."

Upon Rochelle's face there was a slightly amused expression as she watched the young man head towards the hotel bar as he made his way through a set of glass doors. Despite Rochelle's intention to wind Samson up slightly, she didn't actually want to see a fight break out and she did actually want to keep a hold of Samson for the time being because he was probably a lot wealthier than the young man was but it had definitely amused her to tease Samson about it, regardless of her actual lack of interest in the younger male alternative.

"Yes, he'll probably find someone else in the bar to charm that will liven up his night." Rochelle teased as she smiled. "Then he can lavish all of his attention upon her, since I'm already occupied although I was slightly surprised to find out I was engaged."

Suddenly, a beep sounded out into the air as one of the elevators arrived on the ground floor and a set of doors rapidly swished open directly in front of the two. A hand was eagerly placed upon Rochelle's arm as Samson fully claimed his sexual conquest and then began to lead her towards the chamber of passion that he had arranged for their first night together with a proud smile upon his face.

"I'm very serious about you Rochelle." Samson insisted as he licked his lips as he began to silently savor the taste of his sexual victory that was now well within his grasp. "Which is why I said that." He added.

"Really Samson?" Rochelle asked as she followed him obediently into the lift. "I didn't realize."

"Yes, I'm extremely serious." Samson immediately reassured her as he pressed the fourth-floor button and the elevator doors began to close. "I'm very serious about everything I do in life."

"Well Samson that's great to hear because I'm a very serious person too." Rochelle replied as she smiled.

Drops of delight rapidly began to fill and accumulate inside Rochelle's inner body as she began to digest Samson's words and his very obvious display of jealousy which had visibly signaled to her that he was extremely interested in her. One thing however, still really bothered Rochelle and that one thing about Samson, she was determined to establish with or without his cooperation and that was the possibility that Samson was already, actually married because he had now aroused her suspicions.

Despite the fact that Samson had rushed back to Rochelle's side and overtly expressed his interest in her, he had still disappeared in the first place to make a private call, not just to go to the gents as he'd initially said and that now worried her because he had claimed to be a single man. The next day would be a Saturday and so Rochelle suddenly began to doubt Samson's explanations because it was highly unlikely that Samson had an actual business meeting the next day because executives of their own corporate entities like Samson as Rochelle already knew, rarely held any business meetings on the weekends.

Unfortunately for Samson, Rochelle was not a young, naive girl and as she silently began to dissect Samson's actions and words, she rapidly started to conclude that he was probably, already married to someone else. The reality of Samson's marital status as Rochelle already knew, therefore implied that his comments about being very serious about her, meant absolutely nothing. A sweet innocent smile adorned Rochelle's face however as the two waited inside the lift as it moved steadily upwards towards the fourth floor as she disguised her true emotions and masked her inner thoughts.

The excuses that Samson had offered to Rochelle, she had pretentiously accepted at face value but that conversation as far as she was concerned, was definitely far from over because she fully intended to discover the true reality for herself, even if Samson was determined to conceal it. For Rochelle, the lies that men often told women were just part of the adult world that she was extremely well versed in and so Samson's lies were really no different to any other lies that she had heard in the past and she'd been told lies many times before as she had been around and she'd really seen it all.

Married men often wanted to have their cake and eat it with a cherry of adultery on top as Rochelle already knew and so it wouldn't be a particularly new bed for her to lie in but she preferred to know the truth from the outset, so that she could adjust her romantic expectations accordingly. Such men as Rochelle had already discovered, would quite often comfortably keep a woman at home and a woman waiting in the wings that they'd take out for a sexual spin whenever they felt like it, for as long as both women actually allowed them to and she had absolutely no desire whatsoever to be the woman that waited in the wings in total ignorance. One thing that Rochelle absolutely hated in life was when men treated her like a toy that they could pick up and put down in whenever it suited them and she far preferred honesty above the patronization of deceit and so Samson's potential lie had already began to prick her mind and annoy her.

Once the elevator stopped moving as it arrived on the fourth floor which housed the penthouse suite, the doors rapidly swished open directly in front of the two and

Rochelle smiled sweetly at Samson as she prepared to step out of the lift. The late-night phone call that Samson had made behind Rochelle's back however, continued to bother her as she began to walk towards the doors of the penthouse suite alongside him because there was usually only one person that a man would have to call to justify his absence at that time of night, for the remainder of the night and it certainly wasn't a business associate. Despite all Rochelle's concerns however, she somehow managed to hold her tongue and remain completely silent on that particular issue for the time being as she refused to confront Samson and voice the truth that she already suspected deep down inside herself and as the words sat firmly locked behind her lips, unheard and unspoken, she began to silently consider her options.

"You know Rochelle that young upstart really annoyed me." Samson said as he paused in front of the penthouse suite doors and then held the keycard up against the security lock to unlock the doors.

"Bulls lock horns." Rochelle teased. "Aren't those just the primal instincts of males on the hunt?"

"Yes, but he was so cheeky and this is our first night together, so it should be really special and he almost spoiled it for us and caused a fuss." Samson complained as he pushed the suite door open.

Although the young man had now disappeared, Samson still felt quite irritated due to his cheeky approach and his intrusion upon what Samson deemed to be his territory that night because he'd wined and dined Rochelle all evening with one objective in mind and the objective behind his extravagant efforts had not yet been realized. A lot of effort had been made by Samson to excuse himself from his marital home that night and he had even placed himself in a quite awkward position with his wife, just to enjoy a full night of passion with Rochelle and there was no way he was going to lose out on that sexual satisfaction for anyone. In the run up to that night, Samson had identified and then nurtured the opportunity to be sexually satisfied by Rochelle and he was simply not prepared to lose out on a passionate opportunity that had crossed his path that he'd so carefully tended to and certainly not to a man that looked half his age.

"Don't worry Samson, it will be really special." Rochelle seductively reassured him as she ran her fingers across his chest.

"I've even booked the penthouse suite." Samson pointed out as he held one of the suite doors open for Rochelle.

"I know and it's absolutely lovely Samson." Rochelle said appreciatively as she stepped inside the large suite that he had reserved.

For the time being, Rochelle had decided to allow Samson to bask in his pretense about his marital status but as the two stepped inside the penthouse suite that he'd paid for, Rochelle silently vowed that she would not allow Samson to take her for granted, or get away with lying to her for very long. The eagerness of the young man that had approached Rochelle and her response had shown Samson very clearly that she was not just going to wait around to be drenched by the falsehood of his lies and that if an umbrella of interest was offered by someone else whilst he took her for granted, she would definitely stand underneath it. Another man would be all too willing to step into Samson's place, if he even dared to try to dangle Rochelle from the tips of his fingers and she wanted him to know, understand and appreciate that reality because she was not a toy that he could pick up and put down whenever it suited him.

INTELLECT: USER REPAIR

An adulterous affair with an affluent married man wouldn't be the end of the street for Rochelle, she considered as the two stepped inside the large lounge area of the lavish looking penthouse suite but she really preferred to know the truth from the beginning and Samson it seemed had deliberately lied to her right from the very start. Pretentious words meant very little to Rochelle because she had lived and loved before she'd met Samson and she had seen what kind of destruction false promises and lies could create and Samson's lies and pretense really weren't any different from anybody else's lies.

Extra marital affairs however as Rochelle already knew, could potentially offer women power because they required secrecy and involved betrayal which created guilt and guilt was a useful weapon that could be utilized as leverage by a woman in that position and more specifically, financial leverage. A temptation now lay inside Rochelle's mind that really interested her because from what Rochelle could clearly see, Samson was at the very least, affluent and since he behaved as if he was wealthy that wealth could certainly be utilized by Rochelle in a way that would ultimately result in her gain. Several things could potentially be gained from dabbling in an affair with Samson and those things were all things that Rochelle absolutely loved and so being his mistress would not be the worst thing in the world as far as she was concerned as long as she got what she wanted out of it and it ended when she wanted it to but Samson's dishonesty still really bothered her.

Usually, Rochelle did not go out of her way to embark upon affairs with married men, no matter how wealthy they were but if they were at least honest about their situation, she would generally be much kinder and once or twice, she'd even entertained their interest. Unlike some of the other men that Rochelle had met in the past however,

Samson had not been honest with her at all and he'd disrespected her by not being honest about his marital status and his lifelong commitment to a relationship with another woman.

Despite Rochelle's internal deliberations, a decision was silently made as she allowed Samson to hold onto her arm and then lead her towards the large king-size bed situated through a set of open doors at the other end of the huge lounge that he would not get away with his disrespect or his deceptiveness for long because Rochelle would not only deal with his deceit but also his wealth. For Rochelle, her silence regarding Samson's marital status was definitely now deliberate because she wanted to see exactly how long Samson would keep up his pretense and how many lies he would tell, just to get what he wanted from her. Unfortunately for Samson, he had made a huge mistake and totally underestimated what his affair would now cost him because Rochelle definitely knew one thing for sure, she could deliver just as much deceit just as easily as Samson could.

"Make yourself comfortable Rochelle, I'll just get the bottle of champagne that I ordered, it should be inside the fridge in the lounge." Samson insisted as the two stepped inside the large bedroom.

"Sure Samson." Rochelle replied as she flashed him a pretentiously sweet smile.

Unlike some of the other women that Samson might have met in the past, Rochelle considered as she watched him head back towards the lounge, she was definitely, sufficiently equipped to deal with Samson's lies and his deceptive nature, even if his wife wasn't. Despite the fact that Rochelle had not sought out the situation that she now found herself in because she hadn't initially known that Samson was a married man, she would now definitely handle it and him accordingly because she would ensure that she financially bled him dry, quite quickly and before their affair actually ended. Ignorance would not be Samson's ally in this instance, Rochelle silently vowed and due to his chauvinistic attitude towards women which had now become apparent to her, he had totally underestimated what she was capable of and he would not be allowed to mock her in the long term because Rochelle would definitely have the last laugh.

The land of broken hearts was not a place that Rochelle had any intentions of paying a visit to, once Samson had finished with her and had his fill, or when he finally decided that he wanted to be more 'serious' about his marriage and his wife. Extra marital affairs always ended up with a broken heart somewhere, somehow and Rochelle was absolutely determined as she watched Samson return to the bedroom and then pour them both a glass of champagne, she would not be the casualty of Samson's lust, his adultery or his lies.

On this particular occasion, Samson had definitely chosen the wrong woman to lie to and play with because Rochelle was more than capable of delivering what Samson really needed and that certainly wasn't sexual intimacy with a stranger inside a hotel room. An additional marital lesson definitely had to be taught to Samson, Rochelle silently vowed as she sat down upon the king-size bed and then began to sip on the glass of champagne that he'd handed to her and she was absolutely determined that he would learn that lesson in the most costly way possible.

"Thanks Samson." Rochelle purred in pretentious adoration. "Just like the suite, this champagne is amazing."

"You deserve the best Rochelle." Samson replied as he sat down on the bed and joined her. He smiled as he began to sip on the glass of champagne inside his hand. "You're absolutely gorgeous."

"And you certainly know how to give a woman the best." Rochelle flirted seductively.

Sexual passion suddenly began to swirl around inside Rochelle's body as the thought of getting her revenge on Samson and financially siphoning off his assets rapidly started to run rampant through her thoughts. Mercy would not be Samson's friend in this instance, Rochelle silently vowed as she suddenly stood up and then began to strip off seductively in front of him because she would strip away Samson's financial assets and then leave him stranded high and dry on the river banks of economic destitution without a lover and relieved of as much of his wealth as she could possibly grab.

Each delightful consideration seemed to spur Rochelle on and as she began to silently crunch on her highly attractive thoughts, chew them up and then silently digest each one inside her mind, she thoughtfully started to consider exactly how she would extract Samson's wealth and spend as much of it as she could. Essentially, the prospect of Samson's wealth and the potential revenge that Rochelle would soon inflict upon him, now really excited her and even actually aroused her because both those factors created a deep sense of pleasure for Rochelle that was almost as exciting as a real romance.

Despite Samson's obvious lies and betrayal, Rochelle welcomed his displays of passion as he began to make love to her and eagerly penetrated her as she succumbed to him in a somewhat pretentiously submissive manner and more fully entertained his lust. Internally however, Rochelle's physical submission to Samson was far from what it seemed because it now actually paralleled the same kind of deception that he'd shown towards her regarding his marital status. Several pretentious groans of pleasure were released from Rochelle's lips as the excitement began to accumulate inside of her because the reality was, she was now actually, extremely excited but the source of her excitement certainly wasn't Samson himself, or their close, naked, physical proximity to each other.

A seductive web of lies and deceit was now going to be spun around Samson's adultery because Rochelle fully intended to utilize his guilt to siphon off every drop of wealth that he had access to that she possibly could but for the meantime, she pretentiously allowed Samson to feel as if he was fully in control of their sexually charged affair. Every sexual angle was physically explored by Samson as Rochelle made love to him passionately and as she allowed Samson to have his fill sexually and explore every part of her body, the night and darkness silently engulfed them both as Rochelle gave Samson exactly what he wanted and ushered in a highly sexual, lust filled affair that would keep Samson in the palm of her hands.

For Samson and as far as he was concerned, the night of passion that he'd planned with Rochelle had turned into a tremendous success and as he hungrily and eagerly thrust himself inside Rochelle from a variety of angles, he began to silently bask in his own sexual prowess. The sex life that Samson enjoyed with his wife at home was nowhere near as passionate or vibrant as his sudden sexual dabble with Rochelle and he hadn't made love to anyone so energetically, or so enthusiastically for a very long time and the desire to enjoy his new sexual adventure as much as he possibly could that night, spurred him on even more.

Due to the sexual arousal that had already been stirred and that had welled up inside Samson since the two lover's last meeting that night almost felt animalistic for him and so it was hard for him to control his passion as he enjoyed the wet, deep warmth inside Rochelle's body. A climax was reached over and over again as Samson indulged freely in his sexual excitement and since he had now actually tasted Rochelle's forbidden fruit and enjoyed it immensely, he definitely knew that they would have to see each other again and very soon.

Once the two lovers were physically tired and completely worn out, the two took a shower together and then began to relax on the huge, king size bed inside the penthouse suite. Due to the very physical nature of the sexual activities that the two had just engaged in, Samson fell asleep almost immediately but Rochelle remained awake for a while and she thoughtfully stared at the ceiling directly above her head as she began to scheme about the things she would do to Samson in the future. The fact that the two were still in bed together didn't bother Rochelle in the slightest as she practically lay in Samson's arms with an adoring, innocent expression upon her face and started to quietly plot about his financial destruction.

Just below the surface of Rochelle's skin and masked by her pretentious smile, there was now a deep whirlpool of anger, contempt and disgust that seemed to swirl around inside her body and mind as it was ignited, prodded and stoked by a rod of discontent but that negativity was also fueled by a flame of excitement because revenge at times as Rochelle already knew, could be just as sweet as love. Since a romantic pushover was definitely something that Rochelle certainly wasn't and was something that she would never ever be, very soon she vowed, Samson would learn that lesson the hard way and she would ensure that he did because he had totally underestimated her and treated her like a dumb animal that was just there to fulfill his sexual whims and desires.

INTELLECT: USER REPAIR

A silent glance was cast towards Samson's face as Rochelle began to watch Samson as he slept peacefully by her side and she noticed that he seemed to be totally oblivious to the anger that he had invoked inside of her and blissfully unaware of the financial destruction that he would now one day face. The financial destruction for Samson would be the cost of his own lust and the price that he would pay for his disrespectful attitude towards women, Rochelle considered thoughtfully and she would plot and scheme until she squeezed every drop of wealth out of him that she possibly could. Quite soon, Samson would discover that the lust that he could not control would become the noose that Rochelle would tie around his neck and she would hang that rope of desire as tightly as she could until she'd bored of him. All that Samson really had to offer Rochelle at the end of the day, was a seedy love affair formed from a stream of lies and their passionate river of desire was nothing in the end but a river of falsehood that ran along a riverbed of deceit and that reality annoyed her profusely.

Apparently as Rochelle had now discovered, Samson was more than willing to participate in his extra marital affair whilst he kept her hanging around in the dark and lied to her about his real relationship status. An inaccurate assumption had been made by Samson when it came to the issue of Rochelle's character and it seemed as if he thought that she was the kind of woman that he could dangle on the sidelines as his mistress and lie to as and when he felt like it with no negative ramifications at all. Although Rochelle wasn't naturally, physically aggressive, she could certainly be devious, calculated, harsh and malicious when she wanted to be and Samson had now begun to invoke those instincts within her. A serious error of judgement had been made by Samson and that error of judgment as far as Rochelle was concerned could and would not go unpunished and since her usual form of aggression usually resulted in severe financial wounds being inflicted upon her intended recipient in the most destructive manner possible, Samson would not leave their sordid affair without some financial scars.

Discipline was something that Rochelle definitely knew how to deliver to any man that dared to make the mistake of crossing her and Samson had totally underestimated not only who she was but also what she could potentially do to him because he would not be allowed to just take what he wanted from her and simply walk away. In one night, Samson had not only totally undermined Rochelle with his lies but she had noticed that he'd also ridiculed his wife by failing to acknowledge his commitment to her and it seemed as if Samson had a very derogatory attitude towards woman and the gender that had given him life which as far as Rochelle was concerned, would not in this instance be ignored.

"I'm going to teach you Samson what your mother didn't." Rochelle whispered as she closed her eyes and prepared to sleep.

Every part of Resolve's form buzzed with excitement as he began to process Rochelle's remark because his Friday night had gone absolutely perfectly and her reaction to Samson's lies was exactly what Resolve had hoped for, predicted and expected. Some footage did now actually exist of Samson's affair because Resolve had managed to record and capture the two actively engaged in sexual activities that night and that pleased Resolve immensely since it meant that if Rochelle could not destroy Samson financially, Resolve now had the ammunition he required to financially attack and slaughter Samson in various ways himself.

One slight area of uncertainty did remain for Resolve however as far as he was concerned and as he turned his attention back towards Leona and began to watch her sleep, he pondered over that issue as he considered the potential reaction of Samson's wife. Sometimes as Resolve was fully aware, human females didn't actually leave the men that cheated on them and especially not if they were married and financially dependent upon their husbands and it suddenly struck Resolve that perhaps Moira would actually fall into this category of human beings. Even if Resolve managed to usher in Samson's financial destruction and prove his affair to Moira, there was still absolutely no guarantees that she would permanently leave his side and divorce him and that bothered Resolve slightly.

Regardless of all the uncertainty that surrounded Moira and her commitment to Samson however, Resolve attempted to appease himself with the knowledge that at the very least, the night had provided him with some extremely satisfactory results because the footage alone would be great leverage in his battle against Samson. At the very least, the footage could be utilized to reduce the daily aggravation that Leona faced at Samson's hands through anonymous blackmail and threats but that method of justice for Resolve would really be a last resort because he wanted Rochelle to bleed Samson dry financially since that would demobilize him for years. For now however, Resolve was perfectly happy just to bide his time and see what kind of meaningful revenge Rochelle could actually deliver on her own because he definitely knew, she had the potential to be very vindictive and totally spiteful and that kind of attention was certainly something that Samson really and truly, actually deserved.

Several carefully planned preparations were embarked upon by Resolve on the Saturday morning as the new day flew into the city of Pinesfield and the morning commenced. At least one, if not two of Leona's major problems were due to be tackled by Resolve that day and as he readied himself for the day ahead which promised to be very busy and extremely productive, he watched Leona as she enjoyed a peaceful lie-in without the usual stress of Darin. Unlike the working weekdays when Leona would religiously rise at seven each morning, Resolve had noticed that Leona usually enjoyed a lie-in on the weekends and so it was around eleven that morning before she even graced the bathroom with her presence, brushed her teeth and then began to take a shower.

The noisy neighbors, Resolve had observed, didn't usually bother to get up on the weekends until it was at least mid-afternoon but then they didn't generally sleep until the morning arrived anyway and so in some respects, they were almost nocturnal and would perhaps be considered by some human beings as being quite similar in nature to vampires. Despite their quite nocturnal routine however, Resolve vowed to keep a watchful eye upon them all day because a huge party had been planned for the night ahead which would usually worry Resolve but that day it didn't because he'd already formulated his own solution and plan to put a stop to their noise pollution permanently.

A three-pronged approach had already been prepared by Resolve to deal with the party animals that lived next door to Leona's peaceful home and he had meticulously planned every single detail with absolute precision and so now all he had to do, was wait for the evening to arrive. When Resolve unleashed his attack upon the three brothers, they would not know what kind of bomb of destruction had exploded in their lives and their nights of disruptive partying that had cost Leona many nights of peaceful rest, would be well and truly over which absolutely delighted Resolve.

Towards the end of the Saturday afternoon, Resolve watched over Leona's steps as she ventured outside to pick up some pizza from the local pizzeria and as he did so, he also kept a watchful eye upon the noisy neighbors and her deadbeat fiancé Darin. The afternoon was bright and warm, Resolve observed and the bright weather instantly seemed to put a smile upon Leona's face as she walked towards her car and as the sun populated the air, nature seemed determined to provide Leona with a silent form of warm companionship.

Due to the lack of any further scheduled romantic activities between Rochelle and Samson that weekend, Resolve allowed the issue of Samson to fade temporarily into the background as he minimized the two monitoring windows that contained the two lovers. The monitoring windows that contained both Rochelle and Samson were still open and partially visible but since the two lovers had now separated, Resolve didn't pay much attention to either because he had already collected the required footage of Samson's indiscretions the previous night. Unlike the two lovers who had already separated however, the implementation of Resolve's plans later that day for Darin and three brothers which had been very precisely tailored towards all parties involved, would definitely require Resolve's full attention and so he focused upon the four men and Leona as he watched Leona open her car door.

"No Darin but at least the Sun's out." Leona mumbled to herself as soft waves of gentle heat lapped against her arms and caressed her exposed skin. "And it's very warm and friendly."

"The Sun will probably appreciate you more than Darin does." Resolve mentioned to himself. "And you'll definitely have a Darin free day today because I'm going to keep Darin very busy."

Rather interestingly for Resolve that particular weekend, Darin had already notified Leona earlier that morning that he would not be able to see her on the Saturday afternoon or evening which was apparently due to some fictitious new job that he was supposedly tied up with commitments too. Despite the obvious lies because Darin rarely had a job that lasted for more than two minutes which was something that Resolve knew for absolute certain because he'd already checked Darin's employment history, Leona it seemed had accepted and tolerated Darin's lies once again but, in many ways, Resolve could totally understand Leona's timidity when it came to the issue of a potential confrontation with Darin. Lies appeared to roll of Darin's tongue pretty much like water but Resolve couldn't really blame Leona for not challenging or standing up to Darin because he could be very confrontational and rather aggressive at times and Resolve had now seen that nasty attitude in action himself.

Once Leona arrived outside the pizzeria, Resolve watched in total silence as she parked her vehicle in one of the parking spaces in the street outside the venue and then stepped out of her car. A smile was present on Leona's face, Resolve observed as he watched her walk towards the entrance of the pizzeria and then enter inside the venue where she was immediately greeted by a polite young man that was stationed behind the counter and a friendly smile.

Several pleasantries were exchanged between the two before Leona placed her order as the courteous young man attended to her with a very polite attitude and Resolve immediately noticed that his conduct was situated a million miles away from Darin's usual coarse, rough, uncouth, negative behavior. Some human males it appeared to

Resolve, could be helpful, kind and respectful towards women but rather unfortunately, Leona had not entered into in an engagement with a man like that because she had fished in the sea of love and caught a nightmare in the form of a shark.

When it came to Darin's actual attitude towards Leona, his behavior really puzzled Resolve and he had often questioned why Darin was actually so mean because it made absolutely no sense whatsoever to Resolve that someone would devote so much of their life to making another person's life so totally miserable. Although the whole issue seemed rather strange to Resolve and something that was very difficult to understand, unfortunately as Resolve already knew, Darin wasn't the only human being that behaved that way towards women or even towards other people and that was just a reality of the human world. Upon Resolve's face there was a smile however as he watched Leona for once being shown an ounce of courtesy, respect and decency because that was something that her life generally, definitely lacked.

"Please take a seat whilst you wait." The male server offered as he tapped her order into his electronic order pad. "Your order should be ready in about fifteen minutes."

Leona nodded. "Thanks." She replied appreciatively.

Inside the pizzeria everything was quiet as Leona sat down upon one of several unoccupied, cushioned, black plastic chairs that had been leant up against a wall situated at the right-hand side of the counter which was where people usually sat, if they wanted to wait for a takeaway order to be prepared. The usual weekend dinner rush it appeared had not yet begun and Leona released a weary sigh as she prepared for a fifteen-minute wait on her own because once again it would be such a solitary experience for her. Despite Darin's absence that day, Leona couldn't help but think about him as she waited for her pizza as she began to wonder if he had actually eaten yet.

Usually whenever Darin visited Leona, she would order in food and quite regularly, she would order pizza because it was one of Darin's favorites since he usually expected to be fed and watered whenever he came around and he never ever arrived with any actual food inside his hands. Once again however, Darin's favorite takeaway food would be ordered on an actual weekend and although the pizza would be by Leona's side, Darin would not be. Quite sadly for Leona, everything about her current relationship was totally inferior in every single way that it possibly could be and there was absolutely no denying that unromantic reality because every weekend that romantic emptiness slapped Leona in the face due to Darin's heartbreaking drama, suspicious absences and annoying antics.

In terms of what Darin wanted from the couple's relationship, his romantic reality sat a million miles away from what Leona wanted and so now, she really had to accept that her relationship with Darin would never ever improve or change, at least not in the way that she wished it to. On several occasions in the past, Leona had actually dumped Darin but somehow, he'd always managed to worm his way back through her door, into her purse and back inside her bed.

More often than not Darin usually attributed his unreliable behavior to work related activities or family issues but those excuses as Leona already knew deep down inside, were always just another pack of lies because Darin was extremely lazy and his relationship with his family was fractured and strained, due to his behavior, antics and drama. In fact, since the very first day that Leona had met Darin, he had hardly been able to hold down a job for more than a week, on the very rare occasions that he actually had a job that was and although one job had lasted an actual fortnight that had been an absolute miracle because as Leona knew, Darin struggled to attend positions of employment to fulfil work commitments in a timely and reliable manner.

For some very strange reason Leona had noticed that Darin seemed to assume that his rugged good looks would be enough to get him by in life and that seemed to provide him with a valid excuse to avoid providing for himself and appeared to legitimize his disrespectful attitude towards those around him. In every possible way, Leona had now begun to see that Darin really was a total failure as a lover and even as a human being because he failed to treat those around him that loved him with even an ounce of respect.

On several occasions in the past, Leona had attempted to explore whether Darin actually really wanted to pursue a career and better himself, or start and run a business but he had never once expressed even an inkling of desire to participate in those kinds of discussions with her. Important matters like an actual career, or the assumption of any financial responsibilities it seemed to Leona, were like a worn out, dirty, old pair of socks that had been stuffed down the back of a sofa that Darin had absolutely no desire to pluck out, launder, or even to discard. A definite lack of ambition was inherent in Darin's attitude although he was an able-bodied man and his lack of direction in life really irritated Leona at times because it summed up exactly who Darin really was, a lazy, irresponsible person that had no real interest in taking responsibility for himself, never mind anyone else but sadly, Leona was already engaged to him.

"Will that be everything Miss?" The young man behind the pizzeria counter suddenly asked as he approached the counter with a medium sized pizza box in one hand and another much smaller box in the other. "The medium mushroom, pineapple, ham and jalapeno pizza is in that box and the buffalo wings that you ordered are in the other box." He explained as he pointed towards each box.

A surprised but appreciative smile rapidly crossed Leona's face as she quickly rose to her feet and then began to approach the counter because she'd almost become so lost in her own thoughts about Darin and their substandard romance, she had nearly forgotten about the pizza that she was actually supposed to be there to collect.

"Yes, that's everything thanks." Leona replied as she plucked her purse from the black handbag that hung from one of her shoulders. "How much do I owe you?"

"I gave you a discount because we have a special offer on this weekend, so it is slightly less than it usually would be." The young man explained as he placed a bill down on top of the counter and then slide it over towards her.

"Right, thanks so much." Leona said appreciatively.

Upon Leona's face there was a polite smile as she plucked a card from her purse and then opened the lid of the largest white shiny cardboard box as she silently began to inspect her pizza. The oils from the cheese on the surface of the pizza glistened and shone as the lights inside the venue bounced gently of the top of it and Leona's mouth immediately began to water because the rich tomato sauce omitted an aroma that was instantly irresistible. Just under the layers of sauce and cheese, Leona noticed that there was a freshly baked, light brown, springy dough which smelt totally divine that the red sauce and cheese nestled gently against as if each layer was extremely comfortable upon its bready bed and the hunger pangs inside Leona's stomach almost leapt with joy as her body began to eagerly anticipate each mouthful of food and she quickly shut the box back up to keep her food warm.

"This pizza looks and smells absolutely delicious, you guys really do make the best pizza in town." Leona mentioned appreciatively as she glanced at the bill and then touched her card against the card machine on top of the counter to pay for her order.

"Thanks very much Miss." The young man replied with a smile. "I'll give your compliments to the chef."

"And you're so polite and very courteous." Leona said as she picked up the two boxes and then glanced at the name badge on his dark green shirt. "You have a great attitude Orion, don't ever lose that or leave it behind."

"Thanks." Orion replied. "And enjoy your meal."

Just a few seconds later, Leona exited the pizzeria and then began to walk back towards her parked car which sat in a stationary position about thirty meters away from the venue's entrance and she did so, she continued to reflect upon Darin's negative attitude towards life, Leona and their relationship. Unlike Darin, the male server inside the pizzeria had impressed Leona with his attentiveness and positive attitude, hence the generous compliments that she had given to him and he'd even offered Leona a discount voluntarily which was so unlike Darin because Leona usually spent an arm and a leg on him and he was nowhere near as polite.

If only Darin worked as hard as Orion did, Leona deliberated thoughtfully as she pressed the button on her keyring to unlock her car door and if only Darin possessed even a dash of his kindness and a sprinkling of his good manners then perhaps she would enjoy her engagement instead of regretting it. The substandard, inferior romance that Darin provided to Leona as often as he had to, was nowhere near the kind of love that she wanted to experience and had always hoped to enjoy. At times, Leona wondered why Darin still called her because their relationship really was so very awful and sometimes, she even wondered if he actually enjoyed it at all, or if it had purely become a crutch of convenience that suited his needs.

Sex, food and money appeared to be the only things that Darin ever seemed to want from Leona and there was never a discussion about anything else because her needs and wants seemed to be totally irrelevant to Darin's thought processes. Very disappointingly for Leona, whenever she saw Darin's name appear on her phone, it really only meant one thing and that one thing was always that Darin wanted something from her. In fact, Leona often felt as if she was a brothel, bank account and restaurant all rolled into one that existed according to Darin's warped understanding, simply to cater to his needs because she was literally at his beck and call and seemed to exist as far as Darin's was concerned, purely for his convenience.

The street just outside the pizzeria, Leona noticed was extremely quiet as she entered her vehicle and then began to prepare for the journey home but she expected it to be really because it was just before dinnertime and way after lunch and so the evening meal rush hour hadn't yet started. Regardless of the time of day it was or wasn't however, Leona's relationship with Darin always remained the same, a substandard mess that lacked any kind of romantic nutrients and that unromantic reality really bugged Leona as she glanced enviously at a happy couple on the street as they walked by her car hand in hand.

Unlike Leona and Darin's strained, awful relationship, the couple seemed very happy with their romantic choices and romantic partnership and unlike Darin, Leona unhappily concluded, at least the male partner in that relationship had actually made an arrangement and then really turned up. Frequently, Leona considered as she started the engine of her car, the couple would make arrangements to spend their entire weekend together but for one reason or another that usually related to Darin and his ever-changing schedule, those plans rarely happened.

On several occasions in the past, Leona had virtually had to force Darin to comply with his own arrangements and agreements but even when he did so, it was usually quite stressful and so now Leona had almost given up and she'd stopped trying to make an effort anymore. Despite the fact that Darin didn't usually have any real work responsibilities because he never had what might one might classify as a permanent or full-time job and although he had no relatives that he looked after who might require his assistance, he always seemed to be very busy, especially when it came to Leona and their supposed arrangements.

One final frustrated glance was cast towards the happy couple as they walked further along the street with smiles upon their faces before Leona gently shook her head and then began to roll her car forward. In every way possible and imaginable, Leona silently concluded as she began to drive towards home, Darin was extremely mean with his time when it came to the issue of their relationship and whenever they met, barely even a feather of joy and a speck of love would be provided to Leona's heart. For one with so much free time on his hands, since Darin had no real responsibilities, it absolutely disgusted Leona that he rarely had any free time for her because she really did so much for him.

Much to Leona's relief, not many cars were present on the roads as she drove back towards her home through the quiet city streets and she switched on the music center to fill the interior of the vehicle with some noise as she drove because sometimes, the melodies it played made her feel slightly less alone. A distraction was definitely required from Leona's thoughts about Darin but rather unfortunately, several questions had now arisen inside her mind and she rapidly discovered that on this particular occasion, not even a pleasant tune could distract her from the negative thoughts of Darin that now haunted her mind as he remained a focal point. Each question taunted and tugged away at Leona's thoughts as she drove as her mind and the image of the happy couple that she'd seen forced her to wrestle with each one internally as each request for an answer niggled and gnawed away inside of her much like a rat that couldn't be exterminated but, in this instance, Darin was the actual rat in her life.

One of the largest questions and issues that Leona mulled over that she could not logically answer, was the question of why she still footed the bill of Darin's living expenses and she began to wrestle with that issue internally as it stuck at the forefront of her mind as she drove. The sad reality was as Leona already knew, Darin did absolutely nothing for her and worse than that, he made her life a complete and utter misery. In recent times, the situation had become so awful that if Darin offered to spend an actual weekend with Leona and then actually spent more than a few hours with her, it could almost be predicted that he wanted a larger sum of money than usual from her purse, though what he spent all the money on she had absolutely no idea because it certainly wasn't their relationship or her.

Some soft sultry beats surrounded Leona and so once again she attempted to listen to the song that filled her car and enjoy the pleasant, soulful sounds and as she began to gently tap the steering wheel, she tried once more to leave the issue of Darin firmly behind. For some inexplicable reason however, Leona frustratingly found her mind going around in circles because just a few seconds later, Darin seemed to creep back inside her thoughts which irritated Leona profusely since he wasn't even actually present and she would much rather have focused her mind upon something far more pleasant and worthwhile.

Even in Darin's absence it appeared, somehow, he still managed to create stress as Leona tried to figure out a way to try to fix their relationship but, in that respect, she finally had to accept that day, she'd really failed because no answers or workable solutions had ever been found and she had tried so many times. The relationship between the couple was like a deeply troubled grey cloud that hung-over Leona's head which gave her very few glimpses of sunshine and joy and Darin seemed to squeeze that ugly, grey cloud of misery as often as he could because he frequently drenched every part of her life with his downpour of heartbreak, pain and stress.

Rather annoyingly and very frustratingly for Leona however, she seemed to have a weakness when it came to the issue of Darin which he fully exploited and manipulated and although he could be very persuasive at times, Leona definitely knew that her own weakness for him, partially enabled his negative, disgusting behavior. The couple's engagement was a dead-end street for Leona because in the long run, deep down inside she now accepted, he would never provide her with a happy home that was built upon the firm foundations of love, respect, honesty and faithfulness.

"At least there's no traffic on the roads." Leona mumbled to herself as she attempted to console her disappointed heart and tried to appreciate the fact that the usual gridlocked traffic in the heart of the city was definitely not present that day. "But it is the weekend, so that's probably why it's quieter."

Another soft, soul track suddenly began to ooze out of the speakers inside Leona's car as one song departed and the next one arrived but thoughts of Darin still continued to occupy Leona's mind as she drove. For a moment, Leona started to consider what it might actually be like to really be married to Darin and then have a child with him as thoughts of the couple's future wandered across Leona's mind but a frown immediately crossed her face because such considerations absolutely horrified her.

"Now that would probably be a total nightmare." Leona admitted to herself as she drove into the mews. "Darin would be a really rubbish father and I'd end up taking responsibility for everything and everyone."

How Darin would fare and cope, if he was tasked with the responsibility of looking after another living human being and the financial duties that would accompany that responsibility, lay far beyond Leona's current scope of understanding because it really was truly unimaginable to her. Although Leona's mind had now been provoked to consider the possibility because the couple were actually engaged, the thought didn't sit easily in Leona's mind because Darin had never financially provided for her in any capacity at all, not even once and so it was highly doubtful that he'd ever provide anything for anyone else. Fatherhood as Leona already knew, would not come naturally to Darin because he couldn't even look after himself, never mind anybody else but rather stubbornly and annoyingly, Leona's mind was still filled with awful images and meandering thoughts of what Darin might actually be like in a parental role.

DROPPING THE DEADBEAT

Just a couple of minutes later, Leona arrived outside her home and she quickly drove her car into the driveway and then pressed the button on her keyring to open up the garage door. Once the garage door had been opened, Leona began to gently roll her vehicle towards it as although at times her car could be parked in the driveway more often than not, she liked to park it inside the garage due to the wild parties next door and especially on the weekends, when the parties were usually far larger and much wilder. When Leona's car had been tucked safely away inside her garage, she enthusiastically switched off the engine, picked up her two pizza boxes and her handbag and then stepped out of the vehicle in a bit of a rush because by now, she felt absolutely famished and her pizza was more than ready to consumed.

Due to the uncomfortable thoughts that surrounded Darin and their potential future together which continued to prick Leona's mind as she left the garage and then began to walk towards her front door, she gently brushed off her clothes as she walked and it was almost as if she wanted to

379

rid herself of the crumbs of heartbreak that seemed to fill up her mind whenever her thoughts dwelt upon the thorny issue of Darin. Reality seemed to haunt and taunt Leona as she approached the front door of her home and the uncertainty that occupied her mind was almost like an awkward, undecided pedestrian that waited beside a crossing who was unsure about crossing a busy street, just in case a car sped towards them the second they stepped out. Essentially, Darin would be a huge hazard in a parental role and that hazard was unlikely to become less risky or less damaging as time went by because five years had gone by since Leona had entered into a relationship with him and despite her consistent and continuous support, faithfulness and love, Darin had not matured or even grown up an inch.

Rather strangely and for some inexplicable reason, since Darin wasn't even present as Leona stepped through her front door and then began to make her way towards the lounge, the issue of a future with Darin continued to weigh heavily down upon her heart and her shoulders and it almost felt as if a heavy sack had been placed upon her actual body that she could not now remove. For the first time, in a very real way, Leona had now more deeply considered what Darin might actually be like as a father to their potential child in light of her experiences of life by his side and with her eyes truly open and the negative thoughts that occupied Leona's mind could not be easily dismissed or possibly transformed into positive contemplations because she now knew, the reality of Darin. The reality was as Leona instinctively knew and could very accurately predict, Darin would be an absolutely useless father to any child that they had together and Leona's love for him, really couldn't ever change that.

INTELLECT: USER REPAIR

A potential future for Leona spent by Darin's side looked absolutely awful, increasingly bleak and exceedingly grim and as she imagined having to pick up the pieces of Darin's lies and stress with two or three children in tow, she gently shook her head as she placed the two pizza boxes down on top of the coffee table inside the lounge. Only one small comfort really remained for Leona as she flopped down onto the sofa and then opened up the largest pizza box first and plucked a slice of pizza from it but that one comfort definitely soothed her and as that one realistic thought gently wrapped its arms around her, it provided her with a small glimmer of hope. Upon Leona's face there was now a slight smile as she bit into her first slice of pizza as she silently considered the actual reality because that reality was that it was highly unlikely that the couple would ever actually get married and even less likely that they would have a child together and that Leona definitely knew for a fact.

When it came to the issue of marriage and a lifelong romantic commitment that was definitely not something that Darin was in a rush to make and certainly not to Leona and therefore it was highly improbable that such an eventuality would ever really, actually happen. Deep down inside, Leona now truly hoped that she would find an amicable way to break of their actual engagement before the question of marriage finally became an urgent issue for her because she really did not want to spend the rest of her life with Darin and that was one thing that now, she felt absolutely certain about.

In terms of the couple's engagement, it had taken Darin four years to make that commitment to Leona and even then, everything about their engagement had been a total mess and a complete sham from start to finish and although technically, it wasn't quite officially over as far as Leona was concerned, it definitely was. Everyday Leona made sure that she consumed birth control tablets to avoid any unplanned pregnancies because she did not want to get pregnant and be left stranded with a man that would be an irresponsible father, who added more headache to life than he helped and those precautions ensured that if and when Leona found the strength to, she could kick Darin out of her life forever and that she would have no future ties to him.

"At least the pizza tastes great." Leona reassured herself as she polished of the first slice and then eagerly plucked a second slice from the box and raised it to her lips. "And I've got some buffalo wings too but I didn't really need those because I already have some chicken. I have Darin and he's definitely a chicken because he is too scared to grow up and he's even started to lose his hot spicy flavor and now, he is marinated in nothing but my total disgust."

If Leona wanted to behave like a caveman and hit Darin over the head with a club, it might be possible that they could perhaps have a semi-decent marriage because he would probably bring more maturity to their relationship in an unconscious or semi-conscious state than he would conscious. The thought of dragging a semi-conscious man up the aisle to the alter however, really didn't appeal very much to Leona because she wanted any romantic manifestation of marriage in her life to be a happy, respectful, love filled one, not a disgusting pile of stress.

Quite strangely, it suddenly struck Leona that the couple never even mentioned the topics of marriage and children anymore and it was almost as if those serious conversations had jumped of their flight of unromantic love with a parachute and found somewhere better to live because those discussions had simply never ever actually returned. Both topics of conversation it almost seemed had somehow become like a dirty towel that had been used as a mop to soak up a puddle of vomit on the ground which had then been thrown onto the bathroom floor and completely avoided because no one inside the couple's supposed house of love actually wanted to pick up the sodden, filthy towel and launder it since it looked and smelt so disgustingly foul.

Perhaps, Leona started to consider as she hungrily chewed on a buffalo wing, the two were now equally repulsed by the thought of marriage and children together and perhaps neither of them truly wanted either event to ever occur, or at least not with each other. At the beginning of the couple's relationship marriage and children had been something that they'd discussed quite frequently and very enthusiastically, Leona considered thoughtfully as she reflected upon their slightly more romantic start but somewhere along the way, tense silences, arguments, disappointments, stress, misery and heartbreak had somehow replaced their future. Such conversations it now seemed they both knew, would be totally pointless, completely meaningless and would serve absolutely no purpose at all and to Leona, it was almost as if a silent agreement existed between them both not to discuss either issue that didn't even need to be voiced to be understood or adhered to.

Since Leona was definitely a woman, she definitely faced a certain amount of pressure from her biological clock and so the issues of marriage and children did really, actually matter to her but somehow, her needs had been placed on hold and Darin's wants had always taken precedence. The two topics of marriage and children now lived upon a very dusty shelf inside Leona's mind of unlikely realizations in a very rotten state as her opinions on such issues, crouched silently together in a corner and no longer so much as even dared to stand up for themselves and run through her thoughts anymore because Darin's stress and drama always kept them at bay. Perhaps, Leona silently hoped, those maternal instincts and constructive thoughts that she still harbored deep inside her disappointed heart and mind might be revived and resuscitated one day, once she'd dumped Darin forever and met someone else that was a lot more decent and far more sincere.

"A marriage between Darin and I just isn't ever going to happen." Leona admitted to herself decisively as she finished her third slice of pizza. "We don't have a future together, all we have is just a very ugly past, an even uglier present and our future's crashed into a brick wall of heartbreak. The most I can really hope for now is a peaceful escape from this fake engagement."

Another slice of pizza was enthusiastically plucked from the pizza box as Leona began to internally deliberate as to whether she could possibly fit another whole slice inside her stomach because although the pizza looked, smelt and tasted scrumptious, space was now definitely an issue. A few seconds was spent in total silence as Leona held the slice of pizza up in front of her face and then began to size it up because her stomach was almost full due to the fact that she'd already eaten not only three whole slices of pizza but also some spicy buffalo wings and so she wasn't quite sure that there would be enough space to actually fit in a fourth slice.

"You really do look and taste great but I'm not sure at this precise moment in time that I can commit to another one of you." Leona explained to the slice of pizza. "If I only eat half of you, I won't be able to save you for later because then your edges will go all hard and you won't taste very nice and that would be such a waste of a delicious slice of pizza." She smiled as she gently shook her head. "I wish

Darin was this easy to speak to but he really isn't and he never seems to listen to a single word I say."

The couple's conversations about marriage and children as Leona already knew, would probably never happen again but now, she didn't really want them to because she had moved past that hopeful wish and sheer disgust had replaced it and disgust was all that seemed to fill her mind and thoughts nowadays when it came to the issue of Darin. Much like an abandoned house, Leona no longer lived inside a mansion of hope because she had deserted such positive thoughts a long time ago and as Darin had become increasingly unreliable, she'd finally given up all hope of a possible romantic restoration completely, ever since reality and the reality of Darin had corrected her once hopeful heart. A broken relationship as Leona was fully aware, could not be salvaged and rescued from the garbage bin when one of the parties involved had absolutely no desire at all to save it and Darin did not make any efforts to even try and repair their broken love, or to restore Leona's broken heart.

"I think I should at least try to squeeze you in, pizza always tastes better when it's fresh." Leona finally announced decisively as she nodded at the fourth slice of pizza and then brought it closer to her lips. "You're definitely much better value for money than Darin is because I spend a lot on him but he never satisfies my heart like you satisfy my stomach."

Everything that had once been said about the couple's future between the two, now lay upon a dusty shelf inside Leona's mind and each conversation felt completely ignored because with the passage of time, each one had gradually faded into total insignificance and obscurity. The years had gone by and less and less positive affirmations had been added to those conversations and so now, virtually no pleasant remnants of those discussions even remained that Leona could clearly remember because each one had been replaced by arguments, Darin's irresponsible actions and his stress.

In recent times, it almost felt to Leona as if those conversations with Darin had never really, actually taken place at all because each word now just seemed vague, distant and remote like a dot that sat inside Leona's mind much like a grain of sand on an abandoned beach that people no longer visited. The few shiny grains of sand that those positive words and conversations had once consisted of had now become lost in the regular drama that Darin inflicted upon Leona's life which was way more substantial and definitely outweighed any positivity because the arguments between the two that were full of ugly words and negative sentiments had buried each positive word alive until each one had been hidden from sight completely.

Initially, Leona had quite strangely found Darin's lack of direction in life and his lack of commitment to a stable job sort of cute, she remembered thoughtfully as she silently began to reflect upon the early days of the couple's relationship as she slowly ate the fourth slice of pizza. Whenever Darin's career and his long-term aspirations had been discussed between the two, Leona had listened to his various justifications and at the time, she'd thought that he was very adventurous because the absence of a desire to pursue a particular vocation, or professional career had seemed rather impressive and even quite rebellious.

"I just don't know what I want to do with my life yet Leona." Darin had explained to her several times in the past. "I'd like to try a few different things first and then see where I end up." He would say. "I hate to conform to society's expectations and I like surprises. Life can be so dull when you plan every single minute detail, I like to see where life will lead me, it's like when you toss a coin up in the air before it lands you never know which side it will actually land on."

During the past five very unromantic years that Leona had spent at Darin's side however, the novelty of Darin's philosophy, his approach to life and his interpretation of his role in society had finally tired her and any appeal that such explanations had once held had now completely worn off because she'd become totally fed up of his irresponsible behavior. Initially, Darin's views had seemed full of excitement and spontaneity but as the years had gone by and he'd failed to carry his own weight financially within the couple's relationship, Leona had begun to resent his immaturity because Darin's coins it had rapidly transpired had come straight out of Leona's bank account and he'd required a lot of them.

Every coin that Darin tossed up in the air seemed to only have two predictable sides as far as Leona was now concerned, heartbreak and disappointment because ever since she'd met Darin, she had experienced both sides of those coins every single day from him and each coin that he tossed up into the air somehow, always landed on the ground in a pit of misery every single time. The once charming nature of Darin's theories had now lost all their sparkle and shine because Leona had found herself constantly footing the bill of his lifestyle and as the initial appeal had totally worn off, it had been replaced by nothing but absolute frustration, total disgust and disappointed discontent.

Not only was Darin's career a total mess but his lack of interest in any long-term romantic commitment to Leona had also frustrated her because she'd had to wait four years for him to engage her and even that commitment had been a struggle for Leona to secure. When the couple had finally engaged, after being together for four years that step towards marriage had been a total source of stress because Leona had pleaded with Darin many times for a much more serious romantic commitment and in the end, she'd even had to pay for her own engagement ring. Technically yes, Darin had asked the question after Leona had pleaded with him to do so but financially, she had been the one to make and pursue the actual pre-marital, romantic, long term commitment to herself because the engagement ring that sat on her finger had been sourced from her own financial funds.

Although in principle Leona now had an actual long-term romantic commitment from Darin, there had been absolutely no additional efforts on his part to maintain and sustain that romantic commitment and so in totality, it really meant very little to Leona or to anyone else. An agreement did technically exist between the couple that yes, they were engaged but it was purely a lip service agreement on Darin's part and something that Leona had noticed, he purely utilized to serve his own interests whenever it suited him to do so. Internally, Leona had grappled and wrestled for several years with Darin's lack of interest in serious matters like their future but he had consistently demonstrated to her through his actions that he had absolutely no desire whatsoever to actually change but she rarely voiced her opinions to him verbally anymore because a confrontation with Darin could get extremely ugly, very quickly indeed.

What had once seemed cute to Leona as time had gone by had now become a constant source of irritation to her that pricked her skin and mind like a needle every time she looked at Darin's face because there was no valid reason for his lack of contributions to their relationship, or to the couple's future. Finally, and after five very long years,

INTELLECT: USER REPAIR

Leona had in the end, simply had to accept, the ugly, harsh, undeniable truth that Darin was extremely immature, very lazy and totally irresponsible and that her love for him could not change that or fix their broken relationship. Very sadly it had now transpired that Leona had given her heart and love to a total deadbeat and Darin's failure to be a responsible human being had been very consistent for five whole years now, so that wasn't likely to change.

"If only finding real love was as easy as ordering pizza." Leona mumbled to herself as she closed the lids of the two pizza boxes and then started to relax. "There'd be a lot less broken hearts in our world and a lot more happy people."

"If I was there Leona, your life would be totally different but don't worry, I'll take care of all the awfuls soon." Resolve immediately reassured himself as he listened to her speak. "Some human beings can be a total nightmare and sadly, Darin is one of them."

"At least there's no noisy parties yet." Leona mentioned thoughtfully as she made a slight attempt to cheer herself up.

"Unfortunately, there will be soon." Resolve quickly reminded himself as he glanced at the monitoring window that displayed the noisy neighbors' home.

"I shouldn't speak to soon though, they're probably going to have a huge party later on, after all it is a Saturday and the evening is on its way now and almost here." Leona reminded herself as she glanced across the room and gazed out of the lounge windows which were decorated with some cream horizontal blinds and as she did so, she noticed that the pinky color of the sky clearly indicated that the Sun had already begun to fade as the evening prepared to enter into the city.

Quite strangely for once, on an actual Saturday afternoon, when Leona had returned from the pizzeria all that had greeted her had been a serene, quiet, peaceful mews and the brothers had been nowhere to be seen which was really quite unusual because usually, their parties started in the late afternoons, especially on the weekends. Later that evening however, Leona had absolutely no doubts at all inside her mind that the peacefulness of the mews would definitely be totally disrupted and that the quiet close would soon be littered with drug infested bodies and human forms saturated in alcohol because it was a Saturday which as she already knew, was an important party night for her noisy neighbors. For the time being however, Leona decided just to enjoy the peace and quiet which was totally stress free because Darin, her usual pile of weekend stress had failed to turn up once again.

"So much for Darin's promise to make it up to me." Leona moaned to herself as she gently shook her head. "I knew his promise was too good to be true, after all he is Darin and nothing that he says means a dam thing to anyone. His absences are far less stressful than his attendances nowadays though, so perhaps his disappointments aren't such a bad thing really. Less headache, more pizza."

"You see Leona, now you're starting to see things how I see them and now, you're starting to see through Darin's fake facade of love and his deceitful mirage of pretentious devotion. Your engagement means absolutely nothing to Darin and it's just a tool that he utilizes to tie your heart to his side so that he can lubricate the wheels of his life and fulfill his objectives with your support, love, devotion and resources." Resolve said to himself as he nodded his head. "Darin is a horror story and not one that you would want to watch or be in very close proximity to, never mind actually invite into and accommodate inside your heart."

INTELLECT: USER REPAIR

"I wonder when their party will start today?" Leona asked herself as she glanced across the room and looked out of the large lounge windows again.

"Probably quite soon. In fact, I'd say it's due to kick off in about the next hour or so, maybe even sooner." Resolve rapidly reminded himself as he made a quick estimation based on what he could see from the monitoring window that contained the three brothers' home as he watched them make their final preparations for the night ahead.

Despite the fact that Resolve already knew, there would definitely be a party next door shortly and from what he could clearly see, Darin had already embarked upon his unfaithful antics that evening behind Leona's back, there was no way that Resolve could risk a direct discussion about either issue with Leona because it was highly risky. Due to Darin's absence as he made some rough attempts to wine and dine someone else and the three brother's later party start that day, Resolve could however find some comfort in the knowledge that at least this weekend, Leona had enjoyed a very peaceful, quite pleasant Saturday morning and afternoon.

The delicious plans of sabotage that Resolve had made for the night ahead which would deal with the issues of the noisy neighbors and Darin, remained inside Resolve's logical thought processes as he took great comfort in the knowledge that all four men were currently, totally unaware of what Resolve had in store for them later that night. Due to Leona's quite cautious nature, Resolve already knew that she tended to worry, so fortunately she was none the wiser when it came to Resolve's plans for the four men that day and her ignorance in this instance was actually preferable because as Resolve also knew, things could become messy and ugly, very quickly once his plans had been kicked into action, especially with regards to the three brothers next door. Some human beings, Resolve had already noticed for some inexplicable reason, tended to worry more about things than others and especially about things that lay outside the scope of their control and he really didn't want Leona to worry about a single thing.

Rather interestingly for Resolve, the complexities that surrounded Leona's life were a first for him because he had absolutely never ever provoked and instigated an extra marital affair between two human beings before and especially not where one party was already in a committed marriage to someone else and so the inducement of Samson's affair had been a first. Although this was the very first time that Resolve had ever interfered with and dabbled in a human life in that particular manner however, he was actually really quite excited about Samson's sordid affair because Resolve had fully utilized Samson's weakness as a tool that would effectively ensure that Samson destroyed himself. For Resolve, the human union of marriage was not something that he got involved in very often and especially not in a negative manner because The Guardian had explained to him many times, just how important marital unions were to human beings but for Leona, Resolve had made an exception and he had virtually broken his own rules.

Suddenly, some very loud music and noises began to emanate and erupt from the house next door and Resolve rapidly observed that the three brothers were just about to rev up their party engines and zoom into fully party mode as he watched them make some final last-minute preparations for their party night ahead. Unfortunately for Leona, Resolve quietly concluded, her afternoon of peace was now technically over but as the three brothers went to and fro and busily tended to their final preparations, Resolve felt comforted in the knowledge that at least, their reign over the quiet mews would also soon be over too. Several last-minute food and drink deliveries arrived and Resolve watched the three men in total silence as they popped in and out of their front door several times as they accepted some final provisions for their huge party from local vendors that appeared to have been urgently required as Resolve waited patiently for their guests to arrive and their party to start.

Quietness, serenity and peace only seemed to reside inside the mews when the three men were actually absent, Resolve observed and that day, they were certainly present because a large party was due to occur that very same night and as Resolve already knew, it would definitely not be quiet. Unlike Resolve's plan to destroy Samson which required time and a nudge in the right direction from Resolve now and again, the implementation of his plan for the three brothers would be much swifter and only required them to be their usual selves and so no additional nudges had been needed but a few hard pushes had been provided which would kick in once their party started. Justice in this instance would be swift, appropriate and almost poetic because every aspect of their elimination from the mews and Leona's life had been formulated by Resolve with total precision.

Essentially from what Resolve could see and from what he had observed so far, Leona had become what human beings often referred to as a doormat and the male predators that regularly wiped their feet upon her face, Resolve had finally concluded, did not seem to give a dam about her. Quite strangely for Resolve, he had noticed that Leona's human compassion which was a very noble part of her character had now actually become her burden and that notion utterly intrigued him.

Human compassion as far as Resolve was concerned could be a very noble principle at times but where that compassion caused the compassionate party distress and was abused by third parties, it was deemed by him as no longer valuable because it then became an actual weakness not a strength. In the areas of life however where Leona was tolerant, Resolve would not be, where Leona provided generous helpings of patience, Resolve would not and where Leona gave those around her extra portions of compassion, Resolve most certainly wouldn't.

"I guess the party's started now." Leona muttered to herself as she stood up, walked towards her lounge windows and then peaked out through the horizontal blinds. "So that means peace is just about to be trampled into the ground because this party looks like it'll be really huge."

Directly in front of the three brother's home, Leona could see some delivery men and a couple of parked vans which were obviously there to drop off some last-minute supplies for the party that night. One of the three brothers, Gregory was situated outside the brother's home and as Leona watched him in silence, she noticed that he signed for some items as he accepted delivery of some party supplies which amused Leona slightly because it seemed as if he attended to his party arrangements meticulously.

"If only they were so meticulous about the application of some common courtesy and basic good manners as they are about their parties." Leona mentioned to herself. "We'd probably get along much better. Another party is just about to start." She acknowledged as she released a weary sigh. "But at least Samson's been pretty quiet this week, so there's been less stressful deadlines, no increase in my workload and absolutely no new clients at all, he must have been very busy."

INTELLECT: USER REPAIR

Resolve grinned as he listened. "Yes Leona, Samson's been very busy this week and that was totally my fault." He announced triumphantly to himself.

The entrance to Resolve's living quarters suddenly swished open and as Analyzer stepped inside the circular space, Resolve immediately fell silent and then turned to face his unexpected visitor. A few seconds of silence lingered between the two Monitoring Programs as Resolve began to wonder if Analyzer had actually overheard his last comment which had ultimately been uttered to himself.

"What a strange way to hold an actual conversation Resolve." Analyzer teased. "When you speak to yourself doesn't it feel empty somehow?"

"Well, it's not totally perfect Analyzer because it is a bit one-sided and I tend to do most of the listening." Resolve joked as he smiled. "But we all have our problems and challenges and Leona not being able to speak to me, or listen to a word I say is just a minor technicality really."

"You see Resolve, I told you, next you'll be trying to do that yucky human peeing thing and then you'll never be the same again." Analyzer jested. "It's a very thin code Resolve and you've just looped all over it."

Resolve grinned. "What can I do for you today Analyzer? My logical processes are slightly tied up because I'm just about to implement some major solutions in my quest to restore Leona's joy but if it's something quite quick, I'll try to squeeze it in." He offered.

"My Allocated Human has had a misunderstanding with the lady that captured his heart." Analyzer replied in a solemn tone.

"Unfortunately, Analyzer, when it comes to matters of the human heart these things do happen sometimes. When did it happen?" Resolve asked.

"At lunchtime yesterday. They usually call each other every evening and every single lunchtime but since their misunderstanding, they haven't called each other once or communicated in any way." Analyzer explained.

"Was it a very bad misunderstanding?" Resolve asked.

"I'm not entirely sure Resolve, it had something to do with work commitments and a clash in arrangements." Analyzer explained. "Human romance is all rather imprecise, so I'm not entirely sure how one would actually measure and attempt to classify a romantic misunderstanding."

"I'll tell you what Analyzer, give them until Monday and if they haven't spoken to each other by then come back and see me and we'll figure out what you should do next." Resolve suggested. "Usually these kinds of misunderstandings iron themselves out within a few days."

"Right. I'll do that." Analyzer agreed. "Oh, and if you're going to try to do that peeing thing Resolve, make sure you remember that human streams of urine are totally unpredictable and that male human beings don't have access to any of our logical processes or functions. What those facts would then imply is that you should not try to utilize any of your functionalities to regulate the stream of urine, or to accurately calculate the distance and angle required because that would be cheating and that should make it a lot more fun for you."

"I'll definitely store those logical facts inside my memory banks Analyzer and retrieve them, if I decide to try it out." Resolve immediately clarified with a grin. "Thanks for your insightful advice."

"Well to do it any other way Resolve would not be authentic and it would be nothing like the real human experience." Analyzer pointed out. "And don't worry, I'll come back on Monday if the new couple haven't spoken by then. I really want this human coupling to work out because it's the very first time that I've ever instigated an actual romance between two actual human beings on behalf of one of my Allocated Humans."

"I completely understand Analyzer as Life Monitors we do tend to become very emotionally attached to our Allocated Humans." Resolve mentioned reassuringly. "You just can't help it really, you want them to be happy, you want them to have the best human life that they can possibly have and you want them to have someone nice to share that mortal human life with."

"I know Resolve, it's almost like they become a part of us." Analyzer agreed. "Right, I'm off and have fun with the peeing thing because I know, you'll definitely try it out."

"Maybe I will." Resolve joked as he smiled. "But even if I do, I probably won't discuss that with anyone, not even myself."

Analyzer laughed.

Once Analyzer had vacated Resolve's living quarters, Resolve quickly turned his attention back towards Leona, the noisy neighbors and Darin because Resolve's duties that night required that he should be extremely focused and focused upon every single one of them. The joke that Analyzer had made with regards to human male toiletry habits had really amused Resolve but now, there were definitely some very serious things that he had to attend to which meant, he had to give the evening ahead the full power and all the functionalities of his entire logical processes. Although it was not yet even nine, the party next door to Leona's home had it seemed, already started and was now in full swing and as Resolve glanced at his wall screen, he immediately noticed the mass of noise that emanated from the noisy neighbor's human residence and that some guests had actually arrived.

True to the noisy neighbor's usual form, the party had kicked off very loudly indeed and Resolve noticed that Leona could hear the music thump through the walls of her home because it emanated from some very noisy speakers situated both inside and outside the house next door. Since this party in particular had been planned to be a rather large one, the three brothers had even put some speakers outside their home and so that evening, the noise was actually even louder than it usually would have been and Resolve watched as Leona shook her head in frustration and sighed.

"Sleep won't be coming to visit my house tonight." Leona moaned to herself as she began to accept the implications of the very noisy gathering that was just on the verge of actual occurrence next door. "Sleep for me is pretty much like my arrangements with Darin really because it doesn't usually happen when it should and due to the noisy neighbors, I don't get to see sleep as often as I'd like to and I really miss sleep, even more than I miss Darin."

The peacefulness that had resided inside Leona's home earlier that day had now been totally chased out of the four walls that formed the perimeter of the building by her neighbors and as the volume of the music increased, the walls of her lounge began to vibrate and the windows started to shake and as Leona listened to each beat, she released a weary, tired groan. Inside one of the kitchen drawers there was definitely some earplugs, Leona thoughtfully considered as she began to make her way towards the kitchen and although she wasn't quite ready to sleep yet, those earplugs would perhaps slightly reduce the impact of the noise and make it slightly easier to cope with.

At times the earplugs as Leona already knew, could help a bit because they would dim the noise slightly and that protective measure usually provided enough of a cushion which would then enable and allow her to get a few hours of rest but sometimes, even the earplugs were completely ineffective because the noise could be so very loud. Some nights in fact, Leona hardly managed to get any rest at all because the noise could be absolutely unbearable and if those sleepless nights fell on a weekday night, it made work the next day a total struggle for her because sleep deprivation and Samson really weren't a match made in heaven.

"It's going to be a rough night on the couch." Leona admitted to herself as she rummaged around inside one of the kitchen drawers and searched for the earplugs which on this occasion, she definitely required in order to protect her eardrums.

Unlike the three brothers who had successfully planned to have a very noisy night, Resolve suddenly noticed that Darin had by now dropped off the woman that he'd avoided Leona to see and that once again, he had been unsuccessful in his attempts to climb into her bed. The woman that Resolve had hired from the escort agency to service Darin's sexual passions that night, was then quickly instructed to make her way towards him by Resolve via a computer-generated text message as per the instructions that he had supplied to the escort agency when he'd made the initial booking.

Several photographs of Darin had been provided to the escort agency in advance so that the woman that would be sent out to service Darin's sexual requirements would know exactly what he looked like but the booking had made by Resolve under the pretention that a male friend of Darin's wanted to surprise him and so had paid for a special birthday treat. The details of the escort hire were to kept extremely confidential and the woman hired was not supposed to divulge anything to anyone about her actual identity because it was supposed to be a secret present that no one else was supposed to know anything about and that secrecy was even to be extended towards Darin himself.

After the female escort had bumped into Darin, supposedly accidentally, Resolve watched the two inside the store close to Darin's home where he usually stopped off on his way home to buy his alcohol and grocery supplies as she introduced herself to him as Paula and then began to flirt with him rather seductively. Much to Resolve's total delight, Darin quickly gobbled up Resolve's bait and he rapidly invited the woman back to his home after just a very brief introduction. Fortunately for Resolve, Darin was a creature of habit and Resolve by now, already knew most of Darin's habits, so some of his movements that evening had been slightly predictable because he usually stopped off at that particular store on his way home to buy some alcohol, whenever one of his dates hadn't rendered the desired sexual results.

New sexual conquests were ultimately Darin's weakness and so Resolve had not only correctly picked up on that potential point of attack but he'd also managed to identify that weakness quite quickly which meant, he had easily been able to tailor his plan to eliminate Darin from Leona's life with a great deal of accuracy. Not even an ounce of guilt seemed to be present on Darin's part, Resolve observed as the two arrived outside his home and then he quickly invited the scantily dressed woman inside his private abode and in fact, Darin seemed to have a very triumphant smile upon his face which clearly indicated to Resolve that he was over the moon about his perceived good fortune.

Earlier that day, Resolve had sent some more very precise instructions to the escort agency regarding what the female escort that he'd hired for the night was supposed to do with Darin once the two met and so Paula knew exactly what she was expected to do but not why she was really supposed to sexually entertain Darin. An advance payment had already been made and according to the information that Resolve had provided under a fictitious human identity, Resolve had required a female companion for the night to seductively entertain a male friend that needed some encouragement because he had been dumped by his girlfriend a while ago and ever since then he'd had self-esteem issues and had found it hard to speak to women.

According to Resolve's very precise instructions, the woman was supposed to seduce Darin and then participate with any sexual ambitions that he wished to fulfil as a special treat for his birthday which it was intended, would lift his self-esteem because then he would feel more desirable. Due to the secretive nature of the pretentious birthday treat itself, Resolve had also stipulated that the female escort was not to divulge her true identity to Darin, or the fact that she had been hired from an actual escort agency because that would supposedly, negate the purpose of Resolve's birthday treat and detract from the sexual provisions that the gift comprised off.

Just a few minutes later as Resolve watched the two enter into and settle themselves inside Darin's home, he began to silently celebrate Darin's eager cooperation because his participation with Resolve's plan was totally delightful for Resolve in every way imaginable, although it was really, actually quite predictable. Everything had gone like absolute clockwork for Resolve because Darin had immediately welcomed Paula into his personal domain and private residence, even though he had no clue who she actually was.

True to Darin's usual nature, Resolve noticed as he watched the two that Darin's unfaithful attitude and behavior continued to rule his mortal human form which absolutely thrilled Resolve because he had put a significant amount of effort into the preparation of a trap for Darin and so now, he wanted to see some actual results. Upon Darin's face there was an ecstatic smile as Resolve watched him switch on some soft music and then start to make his way towards the kitchen which was apparently to retrieve a bottle of wine for the two to consume.

For Darin and as far as he was concerned, his day had been a tremendous success and as he strode across the room and then stepped inside the kitchen, he silently rejoiced in the potential achievement of sexual satisfaction from a beautiful, female that now sat at the edge of his fingertips which he just needed to unwrap. Although Darin hadn't struck gold yet with either of the other two women that he'd been seeing behind Leona's back, the woman that he had bumped into that evening, seemed far more willing and he hadn't even had to spend weeks wining and dining her which for him was definitely a plus.

"Willing women that are very attractive don't just fall into my lap every day." Darin whispered to himself enthusiastically as he quickly opened up a bottle of wine and then filled two glasses. "And this woman is very hot, so I have to make the most of this wonderful opportunity."

Much to Resolve's absolute delight, Darin didn't actually bother to ask Paula any awkward questions as a minute or so later, he simply re-entered the lounge and then handed her a full glass of wine. The open bottle of wine which had also been brought to the lounge was placed on top of the coffee table as Darin sat down upon the black leather sofa next to Paula and then he rapidly began to pursue his sexual agenda as Resolve watched him enjoy himself in total silence. In what seemed like no time at all, the two rapidly became involved in a very passionate embrace as Darin made the most of Paula's willing attitude and her seeming lack of inhibitions and Resolve watched in absolute delight as he began to record the footage of Darin's indiscretions which he intended to store inside his memory banks for later usage.

Just a few minutes later, Paula stood up and then boldly started to strip of directly in front of Darin's face and Darin grinned as he quickly jumped up and then began to lead her towards his bedroom which made Resolve chuckle as he watched the seductive scene unfold directly in front of him. Every second of Darin's sexual activity would be recorded that night with the female stranger that he had allowed into his life, home and bedroom that he'd never even so much as met once before that Saturday night and Resolve would at last, be able to set Leona free which truly delighted him.

"You're very easy Darin in more ways than one." Resolve announced triumphantly as he began to congratulate himself on his achievements so far that day as he watched Darin's sexual antics on the visual display wall screen that surrounded him. "And so, you'll be the easiest person to evict from Leona's life."

Next door to Leona's home, Resolve rapidly discovered as he turned his attention back towards the three brother's home and then began to watch them inside one of his open monitoring windows, the three men were now in full party mode as they strutted around their home in a drunken state and enjoyed the companionship of the many human bodies that they'd invited into its confines. Since the brother's parties were notorious for being lively, rowdy, chaotic drug and alcohol infused events, the night held the promise of wild, raunchy activities and frivolous frolics firmly the hand as the party-goers started to celebrate life in top gear and as Resolve silently observed their excitement, he sadly shook his head as considered the lawless nature of the gathering.

No judgmental attitudes or rules floated above the night like a cloud as the three brothers hosted their party which meant, the party attendees were pretty much free to do whatever they wished as long as they could find a spare bedroom or bathroom to do it in. Every room on the ground floor of the three brother's home was filled to the brim with people and the party attendees even spilled out onto the front and back gardens as the party-goers enthusiastically engaged in the consumption of some free food, tons of free alcohol and even some drug filled pipes.

The late-night hours dwindled quickly away into the remnants of a lived-out history as the early morning hours began to approach but Resolve noticed that despite the time, the neighbors' party continued at full throttle with absolutely no restrictions or interference. A constant stream of noise flowed into Leona's usually quiet home from every direction, Resolve observed as the party attendees loitered in both the front and back gardens next door which added to the noisy disturbances and upset the general peacefulness of the mews that the party venue was situated in and as a result, Resolve noticed that Leona was totally unable to sleep.

Despite the fact that Leona was now snugly curled up upon the sofa underneath her duvet, sleep continued to evade her physical body and a peaceful night's rest could not be found as she remained wide awake and as she tossed and turned, noise continued to flood into her lounge from the party next door. Quite strangely for Leona, there seemed to be no actual fear present among any of the guests and no sense of restriction because the loud noises continued to swirl around inside Leona's home as the party-goers made full use of the neighboring gardens, irrespective of the very late hour.

Since the three brother's parties were usually wild and chaotic, the constant stream of noise was to be expected to some extent but this party was rather on the large side, even by their standards and so the noise was much louder than usual and as usual Leona bore the brunt of that noise. The people in attendance at the party as far as Leona could hear, obviously felt that they could express themselves as loudly as they wished to, without any deeper regard or further consideration for anyone else and Leona as usual, just had to live with the impact of their rambunctious, noisy behavior.

Although it did bother Resolve slightly that Leona could not sleep easily that night, the party itself absolutely delighted him and a satisfied smile spread out across his face as he watched the party continue through the night until the early morning hours arrived. Some of the party guests seemed to vanish throughout the night, Resolve observed as he watched them occupy one of the five bedrooms upstairs and sexual orgies with multiple sexual partners it seemed, were something perfectly acceptable and not something that was frowned upon in elite circles, or by the hosts of the party itself. Frantic sexual activities began to take place inside each bedroom as the party-goers made full use of the hosts home, since they had been invited to do so and Resolve noticed that there were absolutely no restrictions placed upon anyone's behavior by anyone else and certainly not by the three brothers themselves.

Fortunately for Resolve, the ten female escorts that he had invited along to the party and then paid for courtesy of the three brother's credit cards mingled seamlessly with the rest of the party-goers throughout the night and Resolve smiled with satisfaction as he watched each one blend in. Once each of the ten women had found a willing solitary male that seemed to require their services as per Resolve's instructions to the escort agency prior to their attendance at the party, they led each man away enthusiastically, just as they'd been instructed to and made good use of any private space upstairs that they could find. The willing male party attendees were led towards bedrooms, toilets and even some walk-in cupboards as the women aimed to satisfy their sexual desires and fulfil the requirements of their job that night and as the three brothers continued to host their party, the three men were totally oblivious to the female escorts in their midst, Resolve's watchful eyes and his agenda for their night.

Another delightful aspect of Resolve's Saturday night as he kept a watchful eye upon Darin, was the fact that Darin delightfully made extremely good use of his night with Paula, the lady of the night that Resolve had sent his way and as the night progressed, Resolve observed that they had sexual intercourse several times which satisfied Resolve no end. Passion, alcohol and seductive whispers seemed to flow in abundance inside Darin's home as Resolve watched the two explore every inch of Darin's bedroom until he could physically do no more at which point, he began to fall asleep.

When three in the morning finally neared, Resolve smiled in total delight as he prepared for the final part of his plan which related to the three brothers because that he hoped would help Leona sleep much more peacefully since it would completely eject them from her environment, very swiftly and suddenly and it would also bring a rather abrupt end to their chaotic party that night. Unknown to the three obnoxious, immature, uncouth, rude men, inside their home and scattered across the mews there were three different groups of people that weren't actually party-goers at all and they certainly weren't friendly and as Resolve already knew, their attack would take place at exactly three on the dot.

Almost like clockwork, just a few seconds after three, an attack rapidly commenced as the three groups of invaders suddenly swooped down on the party-goers and raided the building and its surrounding gardens from every direction and angle possible. Sheer panic and utter confusion suddenly seemed to swirl around inside the three brother's home and even outside in the surrounding gardens because all the entry and exit points to the mews and the party venue itself were now blocked which meant, no one could leave the premises or even the mews if they actually wanted to.

The vice squad, the noise pollution control team and the drug squad rapidly began to swarm all over the premises and flooded through the two gardens as the three brothers stood inside their home and just watched in total shock, absolute horror and utter disbelief as their precious party was very comprehensively and completely raided. Inside the three brother's home, a chaotic panic had now begun to set in as the party attendees frantically started to scatter and scrambled for the exits, once they realized that the house was under attack and that a raid was underway but their efforts to escape were futile because they were by now, totally surrounded.

Despite the party-goer's frantic efforts to flee, it was already far too late to escape and as the three teams closed in on the party-goers, they started to make arrests. No escape would be possible now it seemed for anyone inside the house and all the three brothers could do in response, was shake their heads in total disbelief as they quietly watched the scene unfold directly in front of them and the cold reality hit them like a ton of bricks.

At least one hundred and fifty officials were in attendance that night which meant, the party-goers were actually outnumbered and as the officials worked their way through each room and the gardens in a militant, coordinated, organized fashion, they apprehended as many people as they could as they went. The three brother's house was now completely surrounded and as the police vans that now lined the mews were quickly filled up with party attendees, the three brothers watched in total horror, unable to move and unable to do anything to stop the events that had been kicked into motion. Since it really was too late for anyone to leave the premises or the mews, not one of the three brothers dared to even try because they knew, any attempts to leave now would just make them appear more guilty and attract more attention to them from the officials present and so, they stood rooted the spot inside their huge lounge in total silence.

Several guilty parties inside the house, Resolve noticed as he watched, tried to rush towards the bathrooms as they scrambled to dispose of any drugs in their possession but their efforts were now absolutely pointless because each of the bathrooms had already been manned by officials that stood on guard outside every door. The youngest of the three brothers Stefan, was the first of the three men to be cornered by three officers from the drug squad and they quickly managed to locate some cocaine that he had on his actual person which to Resolve's absolute delight, immediately implied and very clearly indicated that Stefan was not just going to walk away from this party.

Unfortunately for the three brothers, it rapidly transpired that some of the party attendees in attendance that night were actually undercover police officers and members of the vice squad which meant, they'd been present for the entire duration of the party and had seen virtually everything that had taken place inside and directly outside their home. Several charges were read out to the three brothers as they were rounded up and arrested which were inclusive of an accusation that they had intended to run a brothel and had been accessories to actual prostitution which completely horrified the three men because they hadn't even been aware that any female escorts had been inside their home or in attendance at their party that night.

Horror filled expressions filled each of the three brother's faces as they were led outside towards a police van but there was absolutely no defense that they could now offer or provide because the undercover officers had witnessed some of the drug deals and drug consumption that had taken place inside their home throughout the night. The final revelations regarding the actual female escorts in attendance at the three men's party had struck the brothers hard and as they were all escorted into the same police van in handcuffs, they shook their heads in total disbelief and utter shock.

"We got sloppy." Stefan muttered as he glanced at his brother's faces. "I should have checked who came to our party and who we allowed into the house. We must have been set up."

A satisfied smile crossed Resolve's face as he watched the scene unfold outside Leona's neighbors' home in total delight because this was ultimately what he'd hoped for and meticulously planned to happen that night. One of Leona's problems as far as Resolve was concerned, was now totally resolved because it was highly unlikely that even if the three brothers did manage wriggle their way out of the night's events with clever lawyers and return to the mews that they would wish to throw wild, chaotic parties again every single week.

For Resolve, the Saturday night had been a tremendous success because he had definitely delivered a lesson in maturity directly to the three brother's door and so now, there could be no continuance of their anti-social behavior in future as he'd extinguished their chaotic party flames. The three men had now been brought to the attention of the police, the vice squad and the noise pollution team which meant, in future they would be kept firmly upon their radar and that the three men would be monitored much more closely and that filled Resolve with a tremendous amount of satisfaction.

Approximately one hour later, once the initial noise and commotion had died down, Leona watched quietly from inside her lounge as the police led the last handful of people away from her neighbor's home in handcuffs. The police raid had taken Leona completely by surprise because it had been totally unexpected and the siren that had sounded out as the police had raided the three men's home and made their presence known had really alarmed her but essentially, she was glad that it had actually happened.

Due to the constant stream of noise and the continuous disturbances from the party next door that night, Leona had been unable to sleep for most of the night as she'd remained inside the lounge and waited for it to die down but unfortunately, it hadn't. The police raid however, did result in one immediate thing and that was a sudden reduction in the noise from the house next door but Leona had still been unable to sleep after that, simply due to the commotion during their raid.

Once the majority of the police officers, vice squad and noise pollution control team had departed inside the vans which contained the three brothers and all the party-goers, Leona watched in silence as the brother's house was locked up and then sectioned off by a few officers that remained on the scene. A few worries rapidly began to scurry through Leona's mind as she stood by the two large windows inside her the lounge as she began to consider for a moment that perhaps the brothers might actually think that she had called the authorities to file an actual complaint which she most certainly hadn't.

Quite unfortunately, Leona now worried that whilst the police raid had solved her immediate problem, it also presented her with another issue entirely and a very serious one and one which Leona might have to face at some point in the near future because she would now perhaps be accused of trying to spoil the three brother's party venue when they returned. Frequently in the past, Leona had actually considered moving home just to escape from the noisy neighbors and the discomfort that their presence caused but that was now definitely something she would have to give much more serious thought too, in light of recent events.

In the past, the cost and inconvenience of moving had always put Leona off and had deterred her from actually doing so, coupled with the fact that she did live in what had been her Grandmother's house which meant, it contained and held treasured memories of a woman that Leona really loved and still truly missed. The emotional attachment that Leona felt to her current home however, could not detract from the possibility that once the brothers were released, they would probably suspect that she had complained to the police and that now began to really worry her.

A weary, tired sigh managed to escape from Leona's lips as she began to make her way towards her bedroom and as she prepared to sleep, she tried to push any negative thoughts about the brothers towards the back of her mind but her efforts were definitely frustrated by the incessant doubts and troublesome worries that seemed to gnaw away at her thoughts. When and if the three men did return to the mews as Leona already knew that bridge would definitely have to be crossed but she did now feel slightly fearful about their potential return because the events of that night had been absolutely huge and the impact that those events would have upon the three men's lives, would definitely be substantial.

The actual absence of the three brothers wasn't really guaranteed to last very long because as Leona was already aware, their family was very wealthy which meant, their parents would probably bail them out and hire the best lawyers they could which would help them to regain their liberty, extremely quickly. When the three men did manage to return, once they'd secured their freedom, the assumption that Leona had complained to the police would then perhaps cross and occupy their minds and if it did, all hell would literally break loose because they would make her life absolutely unbearable.

Once Leona had lain down upon her bed inside her bedroom, she rapidly pushed her negative worries firmly from the passageways of her mind as she prepared to momentarily enjoy a night of peaceful rest and nestled under her duvet as she began to relax. The troubles of the night would not be resolved that night or through worries as Leona already knew and a lack of sleep for the remainder of that night wouldn't change or solve her problems and some rest was by now, very much needed.

"I'll worry about when they might return and what they might say or do when that happens, when they're released." Leona whispered softly to herself as she closed her eyes. "For now, I just really need to sleep."

INTELLECT: USER REPAIR

Sleep seemed to gently wrap its arms around Leona's body in what seemed like no time at all and as it rapidly embraced her body and mind, she started to drift off peacefully into the arms of the night as she rejoiced in the serenity that now currently surrounded her. The current peacefulness of the mews and the serenity inside Leona's home weren't something that she had experienced very often, ever since the noisy neighbors had moved in next door and especially not on a weekend but that quietness and peace was now, very welcome indeed as she drifted silently into slumber with a smile upon her face. For the first time in a really long time, Leona would now actually enjoy some hours of undisturbed peaceful rest on an actual Saturday night free from the usual noise that her neighbors generated and the disturbances that they usually inflicted upon her ears and that was definitely something that she could certainly appreciate, if only for a very brief moment in time.

Meanwhile, on the other side of the city, Darin's Saturday night had gone exactly as Resolve had planned because Darin had engaged in wild sexual activities throughout that night with a female stranger and then he'd fallen asleep when he had felt physically worn out. At approximately five in the morning as scheduled, Resolve watched in silence as the female stranger, known only to Darin as Paula, suddenly got up, dressed and then quietly left Darin's apartment. No explanations were offered to Darin or provided by Paula with regards to her departure and although Resolve knew that Darin had offered her his cellphone number earlier that evening when the two had initially arrived at his home, she'd refused to take it and had simply mentioned to him that she didn't do personal callbacks.

When the front door of Darin's apartment slammed shut as Paula departed, Darin suddenly woke up and he rapidly noticed that Paula had abandoned his bedroom and his side without even so much as a goodbye which seemed rather strange as most women usually demanded some kind of romantic continuation, once sexual intimacy had occurred. In some ways, Paula's sudden disappearance almost amused Darin as he began to quietly reflect upon their night together because usually, he would be the one to avoid any kind of long-term romantic commitments to women, especially those he saw on the side but that night, it seemed to be the other way around.

Since Darin had been very excited about the sexual package that had landed on his lap the previous evening, he hadn't actually asked Paula what a personal callback was when she'd mentioned it but now as he began to reflect upon her remark, it suddenly struck him as rather strange. At the time that Paula had made that remark to Darin, due to his excitement, it hadn't seemed strange enough to distract him from the unexpected sexual desert that he'd wished to explore and enjoy that night but now because of her rather abrupt, sudden exit, it confused him slightly because he had no idea what a personal callback was and it actually sounded quite business like.

"I'm too tired to even think about this right now." Darin mumbled to himself as he turned over onto his side and prepared to sleep again. "The sex was good but to be perfectly honest, I couldn't really be with a woman in the long term that gave it out to me on the first night. A bit of regular, extra sex with someone different and a hot decent lover that's what I need, so it probably wouldn't have worked out for me anyway and I'm not getting out of bed right now to chase after her, so I'm not going to worry about it." He added.

INTELLECT: USER REPAIR

In so many ways, the no strings attached sex that had just been enjoyed, Darin silently decided, suited him even better than the orchestration and maintenance of an actual long-term affair because it meant, there would be no subsequent romantic expectations and no romantic duties to perform for Paula afterwards. Far less lies would now have to be told to Leona by Darin in the long term, just to keep the bed of sexual intimacy with Paula warm and even though the prospect of a top up of sexual intimacy from another woman on a regular basis did really appeal to him, on this particular occasion, he decided to allow Paula to leave his life with minimal fuss as he drifted back off to sleep.

"Probably not Darin." Resolve joked to himself as he grinned. "A woman like Paula probably wouldn't work out well for you because she wouldn't want or tolerate your lazy, parasitical behind, not in the long term anyway. The way you wipe your feet on Leona's face isn't something that appeals to many women."

According to Darin's own remarks, Resolve now understood from what he'd heard that Darin not only wanted a regular bed chum but also a long-term love interest that would sexually supplement his fake engagement and that annoyed Resolve profusely because in his opinion, Leona deserved so much more than Darin's substandard relationship. The decision that Resolve had made to evict Darin from Leona's life and heart completely was definitely the right one as far as Resolve was concerned because Darin had clarified and confirmed to Resolve that night through his actions and words that he did not really give a dam about Leona in any way, shape or form. Everything about that Saturday night so far however had completely satisfied Resolve because he had been provided with the final answers through Darin's actions and

415

words as to how deeply he really cared about Leona and what she really meant to him and that clearly wasn't very much.

Just a few seconds later, Resolve turned his attention back towards the next part of his plan which he was extremely determined to complete as he deserted Darin's monitoring window for the night and began to focus on other issues. The deadbeat boyfriend that currently occupied Leona's life and heart who sucked all the happiness from her being with a romance that was more of a horror filled nightmare than a joy, would soon be gone but there was still one thing that Resolve had to do to ensure that, that finally, actually, really happened.

A sense of jubilant satisfaction rapidly began to fill Resolve's core as he began to eagerly search for exactly what he required and the tools he needed that would allow him to expose Darin's scandalous cheating to Leona's human eyes, heart and mind. Very frustratingly for Resolve, Darin seemed to hang around in Leona's life like a really bad odor emitted from an old pair of socks that had been worn far too frequently with a very old, worn out pair of smelly shoes and that horrible odor it now seemed had absolutely no intentions of going anywhere at all. The disgustingly puerile, extremely offensive, barely human presence that existed in Leona's life in the form of Darin, albeit it on the outskirts since Darin really wasn't a regular enough part of Leona's life to consider him a core, permanent fixture, really annoyed Resolve but he just didn't seem to want to leave and that self-centered obstinance annoyed Resolve profusely.

Everything about Leona as far as Resolve was concerned, interested, intrigued and captivated him because in his non-human sight, she was very beautiful and she had definitely captured his attention in a way that no other human being ever had before but Darin hung over her life and filled her heart like a dark, ugly shadow of misery that would not depart. Every inch of Leona's human flesh as far as Resolve was concerned, deserved so much more from life, love and romance than Darin and so Resolve was absolutely determined that Leona would receive that so much more, curtesy of his monitoring duties and his involvement in her life and that Darin would not be allowed to stand in his way.

Since Resolve had now developed a much deeper emotional attachment to Leona, he just couldn't wait for Darin to be evicted from her heart and life because something very natural and innocent seemed to exist inside Leona that drew Resolve to her and motivated him to protect her. Something very beautiful resided inside Leona's human vessel that emanated from her interior every time she smiled and her sweet nature had fully captured Resolve's attention and every ounce of his non-human, intangible form.

Sometimes, a part of Resolve did wonder if Leona could ever truly, actually appreciate his existence but that remained an issue that was tricky for Resolve to predict and foresee with any kind of accuracy because human nature and human preferences were so very complex. One day Resolve hoped that he would walk the face of the Earth beside Leona and on that glorious day, Resolve also hoped, he would then actually find out but until that hopeful, triumphant day arrived, he vowed to watch over her night and day and ensure that her life was a joyful, decent place to reside and live in.

For the remainder of Resolve's night as Leona slept, he intended to focus solely upon what he wanted to do with the actual footage that he had collected from Darin's night of passion because it had not just been gathered for the sake of it and he definitely had a purpose for it. Finally, and fortunately with Resolve's assistance, Darin had actually managed to be sexually unfaithful to Leona successfully and that pleased Resolve no end because now technically, Darin could be evicted from Leona's life and heart but despite Resolve's triumph that night, he realized that there was still definitely one large hurdle that had to be overcome.

The footage itself of Darin's infidelity could not simply just be shown to Leona by Resolve, due to Intellect's rules and the current restrictions that he faced which meant, he would have to now find a way to expose Darin's sins to her that did not create suspicion or invoke any fear. Since Leona had no real proof that Darin had been cheating, Resolve definitely wanted to provide that proof directly to her but he didn't want to do so in a way that might possibly alarm her because any flippant actions on his part, could potentially cause Leona distress and result in even more upset due to the fact that the footage was so very shocking.

Another solution definitely had to be found and so Resolve quickly began to search for what he required in order to enact the next part of his plan and within just thirty minutes, Resolve had managed to find what appeared to be the perfect solution. The company website that Resolve had finally found in the end belonged to a ladies detective agency based in the heart of Leona's city that specialized in the exposure of cheating partners and that suited both Resolve and Leona's needs absolutely perfectly and so he enthusiastically prepared to send them in Leona's direction.

Although this method of operation wasn't generally Resolve's usual approach because it involved the complex delivery of a solution through a human vessel that would personally connect to Leona on several occasions, it did look as it if could be extremely effective and so he felt, very hopeful. The ladies detective agency, Resolve concluded, would provide his solution with a human face that Leona could connect to in a safe environment and even more importantly, it would allow Resolve to actually eliminate Darren from Leona's life in a relatively straight forward manner.

Much to Resolve's absolute disgust, once the Sunday graced the city of Pinesfield and just a couple of hours after Leona had arisen, she received a text from Darin as he invited himself to her home and because Leona hadn't seen him at all that weekend, Resolve noticed that she didn't raise any objections to his potential visit. Everything about Darin really irritated Resolve and that irritation seemed to grate away inside his logical processes like a perpetual nuisance and annoyance but until he could get rid of Darin for good, Resolve fully accepted that he would just have to tolerate Darin's random, very unexpected visits to Leona's life every now and again, whenever Darin could be bothered to show his face.

Approximately five minutes later, Darin arrived outside Leona's front door which disgusted Resolve even more because Darin had already begun to make his way towards her home before he'd actually texted her which meant, he had taken it for granted that Leona would accept his unexpected visit and that she had nothing else to do with her life, except wait around for him. The shabby, scruffy text message that Darin had sent to Leona, Resolve rapidly observed had not even been sent from a distance and it seemed as if Darin had fully intended just to drop in, almost unannounced.

Upon Leona's face there was a look of total surprise as she opened up her front door, greeted Darin politely and then invited him inside her home because unusually for once, he'd appeared voluntarily and Leona hadn't had to verbally chase him around all day to force him to attend. One very small step of improvement had perhaps been taken, Leona considered thoughtfully as she watched Darin step through her front door because for once, he hadn't delivered his usual false promises, so there was perhaps a small spark of hope to be found that could nurse and comfort her disappointed heart.

A sigh almost escaped from Leona's lips as she tried her best to look on the bright side of life and welcome the progress that Darin seemed to have made that day, even though she was acutely aware, there was still a distance for Darin to travel before he would finally reach the status of a mature adult, male human being. For once however, not only had Darin shown up voluntarily that Sunday afternoon but there had also been no excuses, delays or cancelations on his part and that relieved Leona slightly because it indicated that maturity may have started to finally take root inside Darin's mind. More often than not, Darin's pending arrival when expected by Leona would either be much later than planned, or it wouldn't actually happen at all because he was very unreliable as well as totally untrustworthy but today, he had shown up for the first time in years with absolutely no drama at all.

Quite surprisingly as Darin passed Leona as she politely held the front door open for him, he paused for a moment and then actually planted a soft kiss on her cheek which immediately confused Leona because it was a rather sudden, very unexpected display of affection towards her. Affection generally wasn't Darin's forte and Leona had often felt that a huge slice of warmth had been missing from their usual interactions and their relationship but that day, he had already offered her a sweet slice of attentiveness before he'd even set foot inside her lounge which was practically a miracle in itself.

INTELLECT: USER REPAIR

Irrespective of Darin's sudden romantic efforts, a suspicious glance was cast towards Darin's back as Leona followed him into the lounge because such tender expressions of love certainly weren't something that Darin was known for, or something that formed a regular part of their relationship and so Leona was now on high alert. Good manners, polite discourse and affectionate displays as Leona already knew, weren't something that Darin seemed to pay much attention to, never mind make an effort to actually engage in and so Leona now felt, totally stunned by his actions. In recent times, Darin's manners seemed to have slipped even further down the ladder of socially acceptable behavior because his attitude towards Leona had lacked even a single drop of grace and charm but now, rather suddenly it appeared, somehow Darin's manners had been pulled back out from under the mound of dirt that they'd been buried under and presented to her once again.

Uncertainty rapidly began to take root inside Leona's mind as she watched Darin sit down upon the sofa and then face her with a smile as she began to wonder what he might want from her that day because whenever such a pleasant expression appeared on Darin's face, he usually wanted more monetary satisfaction than usual. Quite strangely and rather unusually that day Leona observed, Darin's physical appearance actually looked semi-presentable because he had dressed in a pair of black casual but quite smart looking trousers and a red, blue and grey striped casual top and the usual sloppiness that had become part of Darin's norm didn't seem to be present. A tidy exterior and a more polite, considerate interior to match, were definite improvements but Leona couldn't help but wonder what had provoked such efforts because Darin really wasn't one to make an effort and especially not for Leona.

The sudden change in Darin's attitude and appearance immediately intrigued Leona and as she stared at him as he sat upon her sofa, she silently attempted to absorb and began to analyze his efforts which seemed have come from nowhere. Regardless of how strange Darin's actions seemed and how out of synch his behavior felt in terms of the current state of their relationship, Leona tried to be appreciative however as she prepared to make him feel welcome, even though the question of why he had gone to more trouble than usual still silently lingered at the back of her mind. Perhaps, Leona quietly considered as she prepared to offer him some late lunch, Darin wanted something huge from her that day and perhaps that something was a huge amount of money from her purse.

"Are you hungry Darin?" Leona asked, even though she already knew what the answer would be because his hunger was extremely predictable.

For some strange reason, Leona had observed, whenever Darin visited her home he was always hungry and it was almost as if he didn't actually bother to cook any meals at home and he never seemed to have enough money to bring any takeaway round with him which meant, he usually expected to be fed and watered by Leona. The lack of interest in the preparation of food or the provision of edible necessities didn't seem to apply and extend to Darin's stomach however which Leona had noticed, always seemed to be empty and in need and on top of that he never ever offered to help her out in the kitchen when she did offer to prepare something for the two to eat which irritated her at times.

"Sure babes." Darin replied as he smiled. "What do you have?"

"How about some lasagna?" Leona offered. "I'd have to make it from scratch but I can do that now, it shouldn't take that long really, probably about an hour."

"Yeah lasagna sounds good." Darin immediately agreed. "And can I just say Leona, you look really nice today that's a really pretty dress you're wearing."

"Thanks Darin." Leona said as she glanced at Darin's face and then smiled appreciatively. "I'll just get started on the lasagna."

Darin nodded.

Every hour of Leona's weekend up until that point in time had definitely become stranger by the minute because not only had the three noisy neighbors been raided due to a mysterious tip off but now, Darin had also shown up with positive attitude and a semi-decent looking physical presentation. When it came to the issue of Darin however, Leona definitely knew one thing for sure, if he was being nice that usually translated into only one thing, he wanted something from her and so now, she wanted to know exactly what it was that Darin wanted or more specifically, how much he wanted.

Not a single word was uttered by Darin, Leona noticed as she began to prepare their lunch as his latest wants and monetary requests remained tightly locked behind his lips but as she started to cook, her curiosity mounted silently inside of her as she waited expectantly for Darin's demands to be verbalized and released. Some oil was rapidly drizzled across the base of a frying pan and then Leona placed the pan on top of one of the rings which had already been switched on and when the oil was hot enough, the minced beef was unpacked, seasoned and then placed inside the frying pan along with some chopped onions and a few crushed cloves of garlic.

Something definitely had to be going on inside Darin's life and world, Leona considered quietly as she started to chop up some fresh tomatoes and watched over the mincemeat as it browned because that day, he definitely wanted something on the large side as he'd made a lot more effort than usual and those efforts had been extremely noticeable. Although it was hard for Leona to tell exactly how large that something was because Darin's lips remained firmly closed, she felt absolutely certain about another thing as she scooped up the tomatoes and then poured them into the frying pan, she'd definitely find out soon enough because Darin wasn't a shy person and he certainly wasn't timid.

"Would you like a coffee Darin?" Leona asked as she plucked a large chunk of cheese from the fridge that she needed to grate. "Or something else to drink perhaps?"

"A glass of wine would be great Leona." Darin quickly clarified. "Or a bottle of beer if you've got one."

"I don't have any beer but I do have a bottle of wine. Just give me a minute please." Leona replied.

Darin nodded. "Sure, take your time." He replied. "There's no rush."

Once Leona had poured Darin a glass of wine and then carried it across the large spacious open plan lounge which also tripled up as a kitchen and dining room, she handed the glass to him and then returned to the kitchen area to finish off the creamy white sauce for the lasagna and to prepare some salad. A few more ingredients were quickly plucked from the refrigerator and then washed, chopped up and prepped and as Leona put the finishing touches to the couple's meal, she watched over the white creamy sauce which now bubbled away inside a small pan.

In many respects, Darin's physical appearance that day had really surprised and utterly intrigued Leona because usually, Darin looked quite rough and even what one might consider rather scruffy but strangely that day, Darin's appearance actually verged upon being what one might describe as smart casual. Prior to that Sunday afternoon, Leona had even begun to conclude that Darin no longer really cared about their relationship because she always made an effort for him but that effort was absolutely never ever returned. Yet for once and for the first time in years as far back as Leona could remember, Darin had actually made a half decent effort that day to look presentable and he'd really surprised her because it was so very unexpected.

When the grated cheese had been sprinkled over the top of the full lasagna dish, Leona slipped the now filled rectangular shaped glass dish inside the pre-warmed oven and then she prepared to return to Darin's side in order to relax a bit and as she did so, a speculative consideration suddenly began to run through her thoughts. For at least six months now Leona hadn't made any reservations to eat anywhere nice and that was mainly for two reasons, the first being because Darin rarely turned up when expected and the second was due to the fact that whenever he did actually appear, he rarely made an effort to even look semi-presentable.

Strangely however that day, Leona considered thoughtfully as she walked back towards the other end of the room and the sofa, Darin had made an actual effort to look presentable which meant that perhaps, if he kept his good behavior up, she might be able to make some actual dinner reservations for the couple again at some point in the near future. The potential enjoyment that one could derive from a dinner reservation at a beautiful restaurant as Leona knew, would be totally wasted if Darin failed to appear on time, or showed up to accompany Leona looking rough and shabby and so in recent times, she just hadn't bothered to make any reservations at all but sometimes, she really missed eating dinner out.

Approximately thirty minutes later, once the cheesy rich lasagna dish was fully cooked and the garlic bread had also been heated up, Leona served up two generous sized portions of her culinary efforts and then dressed each plate with some chunks of garlic bread and some side salads. A quick splash of balsamic vinegar was drizzled over the side salads before Leona picked up the two plates and then headed back towards, Darin, the coffee table and the sofa. Since Darin had made an actual effort that day, Leona had decided to reciprocate his positive efforts with a decent home cooked meal and as she placed the plate of food down in front of him, she gave him a smile of encouragement because it wasn't often that Darin made an effort for her and so she wanted to encourage him to continue to do so.

Deep down inside, Leona knew as she sat down beside Darin upon the sofa that in recent times, she had almost given up on Darin completely but somehow suddenly, a spark of hope had now been reignited which seemed to linger inside her heart because his actions that day indicated that perhaps, just perhaps, he was finally ready to change and to turn over a new leaf. The fact that Leona actually cared about Darin and still liked him, frequently frustrated and really irritated her sometimes because he was very disrespectful towards her so often and the majority of the time, he was arrogant, rude and even on occasions, slightly aggressive but he was also very difficult to walk away from which made things extremely difficult. Inside Leona there was definitely a desire to be a strong woman that didn't accept or tolerate any nonsense from anyone but somehow, Darin's striking good looks, rugged masculinity and seductive charm had managed to keep her heart wrapped around his fingers and tied her to his side because her own love for Darin rendered Leona almost powerless which really annoyed her at times.

Every negative interaction that Leona usually had with Darin, normally left her feeling hurt and wounded and she had silently carried around the pain of his insults deep inside her heart for the past five years but that had not changed Darin or improved his behavior. Usually, Leona tried her best to avoid any ugly confrontations with Darin about his hurtful actions, derogatory attitude and careless words because he could be quite aggressive at times but that did not change the wounds that still lay open inside and engraved into her heart.

Much to Leona's surprise that day however, Darin's usual unpleasantness did not seem to be present but part of her really felt deep down inside that it was perhaps too good to be true because something definitely had to be cooking in Darin's world. Whenever Darin needed money, Leona was the one he turned to, whenever Darin wanted a cooked meal, Leona was the one he asked and whenever Darin required sexual satisfaction, Leona had always allowed him to jump straight inside her bed. Almost every emotional need, sexual desire and financial requirement that Darin had experienced since the very first day that the two had met, Leona had been expected to fulfill and she would fuss over him, clean up after him, feed him and cater to his many whims whenever he presented each one and that was something that Leona could not deny to anyone and especially not to herself.

A painful realization suddenly began to strike Leona's mind hard and fast as she picked up her fork from the top of the black marble coffee table directly in front of her and then began to eat as she silently started to wrestle internally with the shadowy reality of the couple's unromantic past. Over the past five years, Leona had practically become Darin's doormat and he had literally wiped his feet on her face as often as he could or as often as she'd allowed him to and that unpleasant history still existed, despite Darin's seemingly, sudden change of attitude that day. Regretfully, for so very long, Leona had practically been Darin's maid in life that would pick up the pieces of his life when he could not be bothered to and that was not something that she felt was likely to change overnight, regardless of his sudden efforts.

Since the two had initially met, Leona had literally catered to Darin's every desire and she had become a soft touch that would finance his outings, pay his bills and subsidize him whenever he was short on cash and she'd pandered to his sloppy, careless lifestyle, regardless of what he did or didn't do for her and that painful reality, really troubled Leona's heart. In the midst of all that romantic mess which was far from romantic, Leona considered thoughtfully as she ate, she also suspected very strongly that Darin was actually cheating on her and that really bugged the hell out of her but as yet, there was no way that Leona could prove it.

Usually, Darin fervently denied any kind of infidelity on his part but deep down inside Leona instinctively knew the truth and that every word of denial was a total lie that coated Darin's tongue like sugar in order to secure access to Leona's purse and lubricate sexual intimacy between the two whenever it was required and it suited him. The lack of romance present in the couple's relationship and Darin's unreliable attendance as Leona already knew, were not due to any valid, legitimate reason and it was virtually impossible for someone to be so completely unreliable, unless they had a valid reason which Darin certainly did not but it was hard to raise the issue of Darin's unfaithfulness with him because he could be so aggressive.

Upon Leona's face there was a strained, tense smile as she continued to consume her meal in total silence, seated upon the sofa next to Darin's side as his cheating nature continued to tug away at her thoughts and prick her mind. Despite Darin's efforts that day, years of negative, unromantic history lay behind the couple and Leona could not just put that to bed in a couple of hours, simply because Darin had shown up for once with a clean top on and worn a decent pair of trousers because their ugly past continued to haunt her mind.

"I'd never cheat on you Leona." Darin would usually say if Leona actually ever dared to express any of her doubts directly to him. "Only women with very low self-esteem think that way."

Rather annoyingly and very frustratingly, whenever Leona had raised the issue of cheating with Darin in the past, he had always managed to twist her doubts around and then aim them right back at her and there had never been any real clarity, truth or even any answers. Every word of suspicion that Leona had ever uttered to Darin had ultimately been utilized by him as some kind of weapon to patronize and degrade her and so her tongue had remained silent on such issues for a very long time. Humiliation and degradation were both tools that Darin definitely seemed to have at his disposal which he kept in the palm of his hands and somehow, he appeared to be an expert in the application of such tools because his words and attitude would frequently leave Leona feeling extremely embarrassed and very uncomfortable.

Despite Darin's negative attitude however, Leona somehow soldiered on and she'd managed to sustain a romance that was quite frankly, truly unsustainable because it yielded very little returns in terms of enjoyment, pleasure, companionship or affection to her heart. Somehow and despite all Darin's negative behavior, Leona's love for him and her tireless devotion had carried their relationship for five very long years but now the love inside Leona's heart had almost completely run out and she felt extremely drained by Darin and very tired. The arms that usually carried Darin's sloppy mess around were completely worn out from picking up the pieces of their broken love and trying to hold them together and Darin's lies really were becoming far too frequent for Leona to ignore anymore because reality had opened the eyes that had once been blinded by devoted love and misguided adoration.

Most weekends, Leona rarely even visited the apartment that Darin lived in which was situated at least a thirty-minute drive away on the other side of the city center because he had always claimed that according to the rules and terms of his residence, unplanned visits weren't really allowed and that any visits had to be prearranged at least a fortnight in advance. Due to Darin's fluctuations in employment, such arrangements had therefore been hard for Leona to make because he seemed to start a new job almost every week which meant, his weekends were usually filled with supposed trial shifts or interviews and so a visit to his apartment had become virtually impossible. A huge questionable doubt definitely lay inside Leona's mind however, when it came to the actual issue of Darin's apartment and she had often inwardly questioned if that rule was really an actual condition of his terms of residency because it seemed highly improbable, totally strange and very unlikely.

"How's the food?" Leona asked as she suddenly broke the silence that had gathered between the two.

"Yeah, it's absolutely great Leona, you sure can cook." Darin replied as he enthusiastically lifted a loaded forkful of food up to his mouth and then began to nod his head.

"Thanks." Leona replied as she flashed Darin a pretentious smile.

Just below the surface of Leona's skin, despite her seemingly good mood, there were still a thousand questions and concerns with regards to the couple's relationship which she'd managed to hold together for the past year, since their supposed engagement had begun, with just a few very ragged emotional strings of tired devotion. A desire definitely boiled and bubbled silently away inside Leona as she continued to eat that urged her to challenge Darin about his recent absences but each suspicious thought remained locked away inside the hallways of fear that they clung onto, unspoken and unvoiced as courage silently eluded her. The silence on such matters on Leona's part was largely dictated by fear because she did not want to be patronized and belittled by the cutting remarks that would be sure to follow and she also wanted to avoid a potentially angry reaction from Darin.

On several occasions in the past, Leona had considered actually hiring a private detective to follow Darin around just to prove that he was indeed unfaithful to her because due to her financial responsibilities and work commitments, she really didn't have the time to do it herself. Every working week Leona worked very long working days and so usually by the time she arrived home each weekday, she was completely knackered and physically worn out which meant, she simply did not have any free time to follow Darin around everywhere he went. The noisy neighbors and their parties had definitely also added to Leona's generally fatigued state because the lack of sleep due to their party lifestyle had placed even more pressure and constraints upon her life and time and in some ways, their lifestyle coupled with Leona's gentle nature, she now realized had enabled Darin's atrocious behavior.

When it came to the issue of detective agencies however as Leona already knew, their services certainly weren't cheap and to hire an actual detective to follow Darin around everywhere he went, would be very costly and she already felt as if she spent enough of her hard-earned money upon him. Due to Darin's expensive tastes, his lifestyle and his financial shortcomings, he had become a very expensive overhead which usually left very little disposable income in Leona's pockets each month and so such a hire, unfortunately had lain just outside her financial reach.

Every month for the past five years, Leona would contribute a financial sum to cover Darin's rent, his bills, his car costs and then on top of that he would even ask her for some extra money with which to fill his pockets. Unfortunately, however, due to Leona's compliance with Darin's wishes, he had now become a constant drain upon her financial resources and he seemed to drain her bank balance at every possible opportunity as he siphoned off as much money as he possibly could on each visit and that meant, she usually had very little cash to spare.

Physically as far as Leona was concerned, Darin was strikingly handsome and that was his one saving grace because Leona had been attracted to him from the very first moment that they'd met but his good looks no longer fascinated her as much and his physical appeal had definitely started to wear off as the costs had mounted and mounted. In terms of Darin physical appearance, he was tall with dark, rather rugged looking hair and he possessed an athletic frame, all of which seemed to celebrate his masculinity. Two dark brown, seductive eyes were one of the most sparkling features upon Darin's face and his soft, generous, kissable lips had tantalized Leona from the very first glance and whenever Darin stepped into a room, the woman inside it would immediately pay attention to his presence because he was ruggedly and undeniably, deliciously handsome.

Regardless of Darin's striking good looks however, Leona had recently come to a stark realization about his physical appearance and that realization now tugged away at her thoughts every time she saw him and that was that his handsome face and athletic frame, no longer really mattered to her. A good looking face that did not want to make an effort to even try to pay the bills and a fit physical frame that did not show Leona love and attention whenever she needed it, essentially meant very little to her and it was almost as if Darin had become a stagnant mannequin that could only be utilized for display purposes because his good looks seemed to be the only real quality that he possessed. Sometimes, a pretentious blanket of charm would be thrown Leona's way by Darin that offered her a temporary ounce of comfort but that blanket of charm would rapidly lose all its heat and rarely even warmed her anymore because it was made from artificial fibers and so she would usually feel cold and unloved again, very quickly indeed.

Strangely for Leona in recent times, it almost seemed as if Darin's good looks had actually diminished as his physical appeal had gradually somehow, silently deteriorated and begun to evaporate. The initial attraction and passion that Darin had once invoked inside Leona had now it seemed, almost totally worn off because it had been destroyed by Darin's continuous acts of disrespect and the insults that he regularly inflicted upon her. Somehow, Darin's disgusting conduct towards Leona had finally managed to detract from the handsomeness that she had once appreciated with excitement and enthusiasm and Darin had slowly started to become uglier in her sight and so now, his good looks were for Leona, almost totally non-existent.

Another thing that Leona had recently also noticed, was that it wasn't just Darin's physical appearance that no longer fascinated her as much and it was as if the love that she'd once held and treasured inside her heart had begun to desert them both because every time she saw him now, it somehow felt diminished. In fact, the love that Leona had once held for Darin had now diminished so much that it seemed to silently lie inside a coffin of romantic death as it waited to be buried in the graveyard of lost and unwanted loves and no matter how Leona tried, she simply couldn't revive or resuscitate it.

Inside Leona's heart, all that remained now seemed to be absolute disgust and rotten contempt which had managed to form and take root and those negative sentiments grew whenever thoughts of Darin sprung into her mind or she saw his face. Each negative sentiment that pumped through Leona's veins had now filled up her entire heart as the years had gone by and had even begun to replace the once pure adoration and plentiful devotion that she'd felt for Darin which she had at one time, held onto so dearly and clung to so tightly.

A blanket of tolerance had been spread out across Leona's mind and heart as she had attempted to keep their engagement steady and the romantic harmony of their relationship afloat but it was a million miles away from the love and relationship that Leona truly wanted. The tolerance that Leona usually extended towards Darin was merely a temporary measure that she had put and kept in place, until she could establish for absolute certain that Darin had actually cheated on her and then she intended to find a way to dump Darin forever but that tolerance, minimized the potentially ugly arguments between the two regarding Darin's unfaithful nature which protected Leona to some extent from his anger.

"Thanks Leona that lasagna was really nice." Darin suddenly said as he consumed the last forkful of food on his plate and then stood up.

Upon Leona's face there was now a suspicious smile as she watched Darin walk towards the kitchen and then actually wash his plate up in almost total disbelief. In just one day, Darin had not only greeted her with a kiss and a tidy appearance but he'd also appreciated her appearance and an actual meal that she had cooked for him and then he'd even washed up his own plate after his meal which was simply unheard off. Unlike Darin's usual routine, he had even called Leona that day voluntarily and then visited her home immediately which was not like Darin at all because most weekends, he usually dangled Leona from a thin thread of promises with false arrangements that he had absolutely no intentions or desires to actually fulfill.

Despite several positive indications which might possibly be interpreted by Leona as a sign that perhaps Darin was ready to turn over a new romantic leaf however, her mind still remained suspicious because Darin's past disappointments and cheating nature couldn't just be totally forgotten. Disappointment after disappointment had been carried by Leona's heart and upon her weary shoulders for five very long unromantic years and she could no longer afford to carry the weight of Darin's disrespect anymore and one day, Leona was absolutely determined, she would prove what a liar Darin really was and then he would be the one that would be humiliated and dumped forever.

On the few occasions in the past, when Leona had actually managed to muster up enough strength and courage inside of her to dump Darin, he'd simply returned within a few days and then he would beg her for another chance and she had always caved in. The walls of Leona's refusal had rapidly dissolved and evaporated, purely due to her love for him and as Darin would plead with her over and over again for another chance, his words had always seemed full of remorse and his eyes full of regret but as Leona had now learnt, his remorse was truly pretentious and his regrets were absolutely fictitious because his actions afterwards time and time again had proved their lack of substance.

"I'll change Leona." Darin would usually say. "I promise I'll change. I really can't live without you Leona, you're my heart."

Rather convincingly, tears would often well up inside Darin's eyes and the emotional pleas that he offered to Leona would rapidly infiltrate her heart and silently melt away the iceberg of dismissal which would then usually render her, totally powerless. Somehow and rather unwillingly, every word that Darin spoke and each tearful expression would strip away Leona's defenses and the protective shield of her determination would then be very quickly infiltrated and demobilized by Darin in just a matter of minutes.

"Things will be different this time Leona, I promise." Darin would reassure her.

Inside Leona's heart and mind, shadows of guilt would then start to attack her and she would even argue with herself internally that perhaps she did not really have a legitimate reason to dump Darin at all and in the end she would absolutely always, cave right in. Another chance would be given to Darin and agreed to and then Darin's face would immediately light up triumphantly and he would give Leona a sweeter than light smile that oozed charm which would ease his right of passage to her heart.

Every single insincere, meaningless word that Darin had spoken to Leona however had been proved wrong time and time again by his conduct afterwards and so now, his words meant absolutely nothing to Leona because nothing had ever changed and his behavior had remained the same. The empty promises, the gentle kisses and the apologetic pretentious tears, Leona had finally realized, meant absolutely zero and each apologetic appeal for mercy had been totally false and simply just a lubricant to reinstate the awful relationship that Darin had wanted to maintain because it suited his economic interests. Usually, it would only take Darin a few weeks to revert back to his former ways and his former usual self and within a short space of time, Leona would find herself right back at square one and exasperated by his unromantic conduct.

Somehow, a very negative, extremely unromantic precedent had been established and set by Darin and as the years had gone by, Leona had finally realized as she'd struggled to find some romantic happiness every day, it was virtually impossible to change that now. The disrespect and negativity which had crept into their relationship and Darin's mind and mouth had taken a firm root in every inch of their lives and although it irritated Leona profusely, there seemed to be no actual way to overcome, reverse or change that unromantic reality.

Much like a climber that wanted to scale the slippery surface of a cliff and reach the top of a mountain where romantic happiness waited to be realized and enjoyed, Leona had grappled with Darin's nasty attitude and behavior time and time again, only to fall back down wounded onto the ground of misery with every attempt. One day perhaps, Leona silently considered as Darin sat back down on the sofa beside her, she would reach the top of that cliff of rejection and then she'd push Darin straight off the top of cliff and throw him out of her life forever. The remnants of Leona's feelings for Darin on the wonderful day that she dumped him permanently, would then be thrown from the top of the cliff of rejection and smash onto the cold jagged rocks below it and as her love for him fell onto the ground of misery that he had created, it would shatter into so many pieces that it would be virtually impossible to repair and that day, Leona would finally be, totally free.

Regardless of Leona's wish to rid herself of Darin forever however, one tiny issue definitely still remained and that one tiny issue was in fact, really rather huge because it was actually, Leona herself. Essentially, Leona needed strength, facts and determination to finally get rid of Darin forever and deep down within herself she definitely knew, she did not currently possess enough of any of those three things. The actual decision itself was easy enough for Leona to make and she had even made it several times before but to follow it through and see it through until the very end, so that Darin's departure would be permanent, was another thing entirely.

Before Leona could fully accept Darin's efforts that day to revive their relationship, she silently decided, she needed to be absolutely certain that he was not a cheat because that would break the final ribbon of love inside her heart that bound her to Darin's side and terminate their relationship forever. A permanent departure would definitely be ushered in, if it transpired that Darin was an actual cheat because Darin had in effect, already wasted half a decade of Leona's actual life and that time would now never ever be actually returned to her. More than just a clean top, a decent pair of trousers, a splash of aftershave, a shower and a stress-free attendance on one occasion was required to convince Leona's heart of Darin's sincerity because a few hours of good behavior could not erase five years of pain and misery that had been caused by his negative conduct.

Several more hours slowly sauntered by and as each one gently slipped away, Leona began to realize that sadly, Darin's pretentious efforts that day were totally fake because she noticed that his cellphone had been switched to vibrate and that he had received several calls which he'd completely ignored and that his phone had remained inside one of his trouser pockets. Despite the delicious food that Leona had cooked and then hungrily consumed alongside Darin, his pretentious fakeness rapidly began to create a bitter, sour after taste inside her mouth as she began to tolerate his presence and just wait for him to actually leave. No discussions had taken place that day as to why Darin hadn't been around all weekend until the Sunday and his claim that he'd had work commitments, didn't really seem to correlate with anything else that he said which further aroused Leona's suspicions and added to her doubts even more.

Over the years, the couple's relationship had become less and less enjoyable because of Darin's behavior until any happiness that could potentially be derived from it by Leona had totally disintegrated into absolutely nothing and as it had slipped into negativity, now pure negativity was almost all there was left. In terms of their relationship, Leona knew deep down inside that Darin was simply a very bad habit that one day, she would have to break and that he was a slimy pond toad that leapt into her life whenever it suited him, simply to display his ugly warts of disrespect before he quickly disappeared again and returned to the pond of filth and indecency that he usually resided in.

Five very long unromantic years had gone by and so now, Leona really needed answers because she knew that she could not afford to waste anymore of her life, or her resources on a pretender like Darin. A small question still remained and lurked inside Leona's mind as to what Darin might possibly want that day because he had even washed up his own plate, so she began to wonder how huge it might be since that act verged upon an actual act of decency which was totally out of character for him but as yet, no monetary requests had been made.

Once the evening arrived and as the weekend drew to a close, fortunately for Leona, Darin prepared to depart voluntarily and despite the fact that it was still rather early in the evening, Leona did not object to or attempt to delay his exit. Inwardly, Leona actually felt quite grateful to be able to get rid of Darin so early on the Sunday evening with minimal fuss because she had to prepare for the working week ahead and to put it quite frankly, she could barely stand the sight of him anymore, even at the best of times.

A deep-rooted suspicion definitely lay inside Leona's mind that Darin had cheated on her that past weekend as she showed him to the door but because she couldn't prove it, she had been able to confront him about it. Rather frustratingly and annoyingly for Leona, her working weeks were very heavy because Samson filled up her workload with so much work that she simply didn't have the time that was required to spy on Darin or chase him around and his usual antics and drama could not be entertained due to time constraints and Leona's professional, work commitments. The weekdays and Darin just weren't compatible as far as Leona was concerned because Samson's corporate demands definitely took precedence since she had financial responsibilities to meet and bills to pay, regardless of Darin's fake romance, disappointments and heartbreak.

More often than not during the week, Leona worked quite late each evening and so she could not even try to spy on Darin or chase him around to ensure that he complied with their arrangements because that would be just an unnecessary headache that she had no wish to inflict upon herself. Quite strangely for Leona, even Darin's presence nowadays seemed to emotionally and physically drain her as she tried to deal with his unreliable nature and difficult character which meant, they hardly spent any time together at all anymore.

An affectionate kiss was politely offered and then given to Leona just before Darin parted and as she closed the front door behind him, she let out a weary sigh as she began to silently prepare herself for another long working week. In some ways, Leona internally deliberated as she began to walk towards her bedroom, the couple's relationship was almost like a tradeoff because although Darin's absences really worried Leona, his presence usually presented her with even more difficulties because he was such a difficult person to spend any amount of time with. Somehow, over the years, Leona had managed to find a way and learnt to cope with that very strange, unromantic conundrum, endure it and manage it but it was far from the romantic ideal and her heart had definitely suffered.

At the start of the couple's relationship things had been slightly different and Leona had actually enjoyed Darin's company and at times, she'd even urged him to stick around beyond the weekends, just so that they could spend more time together. Usually however, even back then, Darin had frequently refused to spend more time with

Leona and he'd provided her with an entourage of excuses as to why he couldn't and over the years that entourage of excuses seemed to have grown and followed him around wherever he went because whenever Leona saw Darin, his excuses normally showed up too. In the end, Leona had finally stopped even trying to spend more time with Darin because it had become a verbal wrestling match between them both and a very unpleasant experience.

Over the years, the couple's relationship had now deteriorated to the point where it only ever offered Leona diminishing returns in terms of enjoyment and as Darin and their relationship had somehow became a full-blown liability of headache, she'd begun to accept that Darin was a liability that she could no longer emotionally or economically afford. Unemployment was certainly not a lifestyle that Leona was used to and so there was absolutely no way that she was going to change her attitude towards life and work, simply because of Darin and his chaotic immaturity. Being in the unemployment line due to Darin's behavior was not a desirable eventuality in Leona's sight and so she had confined their romance to the weekends, when Darin could potentially inflict the least amount of damage upon her life but with the passing of each weekend, it had become clearer and clearer that Darin was not prepared to mature or change.

The Darin roller coaster ride for that weekend however, was now definitely over, Leona considered thoughtfully as she walked along the hallway towards her bedroom and so now, she could have a break from Darin's stress, lies and pretense for another week. Although Darin was a very healthy, able bodied man, he seemed to be totally unwilling to participate in the responsibilities of life and adulthood, Leona concluded which he not only refused to accept but also refused to embrace, regardless of his years. Another weekend would of course occur the following weekend and Leona wondered for a moment, if Darin would be able to keep up his good behavior and improve upon it and if he would perhaps, actually show up on either the Friday evening or Saturday.

"An actual visit from Darin on a Friday night or a Saturday with no drama that's probably asking for a bit too much." Leona admitted to herself. "He'll probably just tell me a pack of lies as usual."

Suddenly, a loud beep emanated from Leona's laptop which immediately drew her attention towards it and so she quickly began to walk back towards the lounge which was where her laptop was situated as her curiosity urged her to open up the unexpected email that she had received and read it immediately.

"I swear Darin's cheating on me and so now, I need to find a way to actually prove it." Leona muttered to herself as she stepped back inside the lounge and then headed towards her laptop which was on top of the coffee table.

Much to Leona's absolute surprise as she touched the screen of her laptop and opened up the email that she had just received, she found a very interesting email inside her inbox from an unknown sender that seemed rather mysterious but totally delightful. An amused expression immediately crossed Leona's face as she began to read the email message because apparently and according to its contents, she had been identified as a potential client by a ladies detective agency that were running a special promotion and discount offer that week for new clients and the email contained their actual advertisement.

Absolutely everything about the advertisement immediately thrilled and totally delighted Leona as she quickly reviewed the company's price list because their rates seemed really reasonable and the discount on offer was very generous which meant, it was actually affordable to her. The services on offer were considered thoughtfully for a few minutes as Leona began to calculate the potential cost of investigating Darin's suspected infidelity but because the offer seemed so economical and well within her financial means, she was rapidly convinced to contact the company directly and write an email response.

Upon Resolve's face there was now a very hopeful smile as he watched Leona respond to the advertisement which had ultimately been actioned and sent to her due to his intervention. Due to Resolve's position within Intellect, he'd had to find a legitimate human way to expose Darin's cheating to Leona and so the ladies detective agency and their special offer had albeit rather unintentionally, offered him exactly what he required. The exposure of Darin's love crimes, Resolve considered, would perhaps take a week or so but at least now, it would definitely actually happen and that provided him with a great sense of relief.

"Now this offer could help me get rid of Darin forever." Leona reassured herself joyfully as she sent the detective agency her email response. "And this could really end my suffering."

Slowly and surely, the remainder of Leona's weekend quietly disappeared and as the Sunday evening silently departed from her life and the night stepped into the city of Pinesfield, she stepped inside her bedroom as she prepared once again to sleep in her own bed, since the noisy neighbors had not yet returned. The freedom of the weekend had definitely run out and been totally consumed, Leona thoughtfully concluded as she lay down upon her bed, snuggled up against her duvet and then closed her eyes but at least she could rejoice in the peacefulness that now surrounded her and the hopefulness of an affordable solution to one of her most pressing problems.

INTELLECT: USER REPAIR

In terms of Leona's life, she considered thoughtfully as she waited for sleep to carry her off into the gentle world of slumber, the weekend really was her one comfort away from the very harsh working weeks and Samson's hard iron rule because it meant that she could have a lie-in if she wished to and even sleep until lunchtime if she wanted to. Prior to meeting Darin and throughout her younger years, Leona silently reminded herself, she would often fill up her weekends with lots of fun packed activities and outings with friends because the two days that visited her life at the end of each week provided her with the luxury to do as she wished, without any pressure or stress from any third parties.

Quite sadly for Leona however, in recent times, the handful of dear close friends that she had accumulated over the years had slowly disappeared as they had married off and dwindled in number and as a result, the time Leona spent with any of them had greatly reduced. Most of Leona's trusted friends now had large responsibilities themselves, like children, husbands and work schedules and those responsibilities governed their schedules and placed restrictions upon their time. Due to Leona's own heavy, chaotic workload, she rarely had time to see anyone during the working weekdays anymore which was one of the major reasons that Leona now spent most of her time alone and over the last few years, her social activities with friends on the weekends had become far less frequent until now, such activities rarely even happened at all.

One thing that Leona's once close-knit group of friends had all agreed upon however, irrespective of their own marital status and personal circumstances was very sadly, actually Darin who they deemed as a total waste of space and a complete waste of time. Several of Leona's friends had met Darin in the past and they'd all absolutely loathed him and they had immediately encouraged Leona to dump him but Leona had rather unwisely, stuck up for Darin and then persevered as she had not only stood up for him but also remained by his side.

Rather intriguingly for Leona, it suddenly struck her that friendships could often be like the sharing of a bed of companionship with others and that sometimes, the blankets would be shared much like the details, secrets and intricate intimacies of one's life and at other times, they wouldn't be and that Darin had been the one torn, frayed, ragged blanket that Leona had shared some details about that all her friends had agreed upon unanimously. Some of Leona's friends had even voiced their concerns directly to her for several years but eventually, they'd given up trying to convince Leona to dump Darin as she had remained rather stubbornly in her relationship, against their sound advice.

"He's a total deadbeat Leona." Lorraine would often say. "Why are you still with him?"

The unanswered question that Lorraine had asked more than once had remained unanswered for several years now as it had sauntered around inside Leona's mind but she had never been able to provide an actual answer to it because there was no valid reason that she could think off. Conflicts in both women's schedules had meant that Leona rarely saw Lorraine anymore because she travelled quite a lot due to her job and so there hadn't been much pressure to furnish Lorraine with an actual answer but Leona could hardly justify her tolerance of Darin to anyone nowadays, not even herself. In fact, in recent times, tolerance had now become Leona's only companion because most of the people in her life had bonded with their lovers and formed emotional connections that were far more serious, constructive and positive than her supposed engagement and slowly and surely, she'd been left all on her own with a total deadbeat.

Despite all the objections to Darin and the couple's relationship, Leona thoughtfully deliberated as she waited for sleep to carry her off into the night, she had initially only been able to see the good in Darin as she'd defended her decision and Darin but now, Leona truly realized, her friends had definitely been, absolutely right. A strong physical attraction had drawn Leona to Darin and that coupled with her own emotional softness had definitely blinded her but Leona's friends had all been able to see straight through Darin's lies and fakeness almost immediately and now even she could see, he really wasn't worthy of her time and that they had been right to absolutely loathe him.

Regardless of how much time Leona had invested into her relationship with Darin however, one thing remained absolutely certain, he was a good for nothing man that would never give her the relationship, love or commitment that she truly deserved and wanted out of life and that could not be fixed with just a few hours good behavior. Marriage and children were a huge responsibility and Leona fully appreciated and understood that reality but rather unfortunately, Darin didn't seem to which meant, their engagement which would normally be considered and viewed as a step towards marriage had in the end, been an actual step backwards.

Unfortunately for Leona, the engagement that she had entered into with Darin and his commitment to it, it seemed had been made flippantly and then utilized by him in order to secure more economic and emotional support from her and it really meant, absolutely nothing to him at all. Children and marital commitments definitely required significant amounts of time, dedication and attention but sadly for Leona, Darin it seemed had absolutely no intentions whatsoever of providing her with any of those kinds of commitments, regardless of her commitment and dedication to him.

A satisfied smile crossed Leona's face as sleep began to embrace her as she comforted herself in the knowledge that at least now, she had finally taken action to escape from Darin's lie of love because she'd contacted the Venus Honey Traps Detective Agency that day. Another working week for Leona was just about to begin shortly but this week she concluded, would definitely be very different because this week was full of hope and this week, she would hopefully find out the truth about Darin and perhaps manage to get rid of him and his cheating ways for good.

Very soon, Leona silently hoped, Darin's cheating butt would no longer be her actual problem and then she would be able to sweep the litter of Darin's lies straight out of her life. Quite deliciously, the truth now lay within Leona's actual grasp and that reality soothed her mind immensely because it meant that Darin's dirty little secrets would soon be exposed, verified and confronted in a manner that he could not deny and Leona basked in that joyful knowledge as she began to drift off to sleep. Five years of total misery would very soon, hopefully come to an actual end and then Darin's nightmare of fake love and his reign of nastiness over Leona's life, would finally draw to a close and that prospect really comforted her. Quite soon, Leona sleepily hoped, she would have the ammunition and arrows of truth that would enable her to shoot down Darin's lies and evict him from her life and heart forever, courtesy of the email that she'd received that evening and then hopefully responded to. The fresh hope of romantic freedom for Leona, now just sat on the other side of the dark night because access to the truth could and would obliterate

INTELLECT: USER REPAIR

Darin's false reign over her heart completely, permanently and that one hopeful truth was one that Leona could definitely rejoice and find total peace and comfort in.

THE LOTTERY

Every minute of that past weekend for Resolve had been absolutely delightful and truly glorious and as he watched over Leona as she slept, a satisfied smile spread out across his face as he stood inside his living quarters and faced her. The email that Leona had received from the ladies detective agency had in the end been really quite simple for Resolve to action because he had simply intercepted the automated company mailing list and added her name to it earlier that day, just before the most recent promotional emails had been sent out. Everything about the Venus Honey Traps Detective Agency was exactly what Leona and Resolve really needed and so he had discreetly ensured that she'd received the promotional email because it would provide him with a legitimate way to expose Darin's infidelity in a manner that would seem quite natural and very human.

Since the ladies detective agency had actually reduced their prices by around fifty percent in order to expand their customer base and attract new clients, Resolve had literally leapt on the opportunity as soon as he had spotted it and it had presented itself to him. According to the information that the corporate website contained, the agency specialized in romantic investigations and the exposure of affairs orchestrated by male partners and clients were encouraged to make personal referrals because it aimed to provide a discreet service that was not publicly or widely advertised and so Resolve felt that its mission was exactly what Leona really needed.

"Your life will start again tomorrow Leona." Resolve promised himself decisively. "Because very soon, the thief that stole your heart and then squandered your love will be completely gone. I'm dropping your deadbeat, so you don't have to and so soon, you'll truly be absolutely and totally free."

Prior to that weekend, Resolve had silently watched Darin play around with Leona's heart and emotions time and time again as he had fooled around with other women behind her back like a teenager on heat. Not even the slightest regret, or an ounce of remorse had seemed to exist inside Darin's mind or being as he had fully enjoyed himself and explored the abundance of woman that he'd managed to attract with absolutely no regard or consideration for Leona's heart. Although Darin had struggled to get any of his potential sexual conquests into bed because they had remained unconvinced regarding his sincerity, in the end Resolve had even finally assisted him and helped him to achieve his sexual goal, just to see if Darin would actually, physically sexually betray Leona and he definitely had.

If Leona knew what Resolve now knew about Darin, she would not only dump him but she'd also be absolutely devastated and although it would definitely be painful, Resolve had decided in the end that Leona's short term upset and distress could not be an obstacle to her future long-term happiness. A storm of heartbreak would definitely have to hit Leona's life like a hurricane before a delightful ray of sunshine filled with romantic happiness could follow but for Resolve, the end results of that unromantic liberation would definitely be worth a few months of heartache.

Quite fortunately for Resolve, the very specific objectives of the detective agency were extremely helpful because the company specialized in the exposure of cheating partners which meant, the agency would allow Leona to pursue and discover the truth of her own accord. The raw truth could have just been bluntly shown to Leona but that Resolve feared could result in a total breakdown on her part because it was so very shocking. Every minute of footage that Resolve had captured of Darin's sexual betrayal would break Leona's heart and she would be absolutely mortified and totally horrified by what the footage contained and so the detective agency was as far as Resolve was concerned, the perfect solution because it would provide Leona with human support and that human arm of comfort would definitely be required.

A horrible reality surrounded the man that Leona regularly entertained inside her bedroom which was now just about to be disclosed to her and then Leona would be in a position to totally eliminate Darin from her life completely because she would be given access to the very real and absolutely awful truth that was far from pleasant. For Resolve that weekend, he had just needed to be really sure that Darin would actually, sexually cheat on Leona if he could and now that Resolve had that final confirmation and clarity, he was more than ready to throw Darin out of Leona's life for good.

Although Resolve hadn't actually revealed the truth to Leona directly himself, he had now provided a means for her to escape from the lie of love that Darin pretended to offer with his false exhibitions of romance and that truth, Resolve fervently hoped, would permanently end Darin's reign over Leona's heart and ultimately, liberate her. In a very indirect way, Resolve had intervened and so now, he would have the chance to not only liberate but also empower Leona with the ugly, heartbreaking, factual package of truth that waited just at her fingertips to be unwrapped which would allow her to escape the bondage of falsehood that she was currently ensnared by and that beautiful reality, satisfied him immensely.

When it came to the issue of Samson that weekend, Resolve had observed that things had been fairly quiet because he had spent the entire weekend at his marital home with his wife but on the Sunday, Resolve had noticed that Samson had begun to prepare for his agreed date with Rochelle on the Monday evening in advance. Throughout that Sunday afternoon, Samson had spent most of his time alone inside his study under the pretention that he had a business meeting to prepare for the next day and a significant monetary amount had been spent upon the purchase of some very expensive gifts for Rochelle that would be delivered directly to his corporate premises on the Monday morning. A financial effort had been made by Samson, Resolve had observed, to buy Rochelle's affections in a discreet attempt to distract her from the many inquisitive questions that she seemed to possess which she wanted immediate answers to that Samson had no wish to satisfy with an actual response.

Rather awkwardly and very inconveniently for Samson, Rochelle had already begun to demand more and more of his time and that had placed him in a very difficult position and Resolve had literally rejoiced as he'd watched Samson squirm around and try to wriggle his way out of his marital obligations in order to meet each request. The extravagant gifts that would be lavished upon Rochelle as Resolve already knew, would provide a temporary distraction for Samson and were his rough attempts to try and appease her without the divulgence of any further information regarding his personal circumstances since she'd begun to pressure him for not only a deeper commitment but also for much more time and attention.

Since Samson hadn't prepared any excuses in advance for his wife that weekend, he'd had to spend his entire weekend inside the pool of excuses that he'd had to provide to Rochelle instead as to why he hadn't made any arrangements with her and the whole experience had been extremely uncomfortable for him. Much to Samson's total relief however, the Sunday night had finally arrived and as it was ushered peacefully into his home and bedtime approached, he began to make his way towards the bedroom with his dutiful wife in tow as he released a grateful sigh from his lips. All weekend, Samson had successfully managed to keep his boat moored in two ports at the same time as he'd lied to both Rochelle and his wife and hidden his marital status once again but as Samson already knew, his lie of omission would not go undetected forever.

An ounce of truth would definitely be demanded from Samson, or uncovered at some point by Rochelle in the near future because Samson simply couldn't satisfy the romantic expectations that a single man could and on that day he knew, he would have nowhere to run and no lies to hide behind because the illusive web of deceit that he had tried to weave, would no longer be romantically sustainable. A pretention of singleness had been alluded to and as Samson lay in bed beside his faithful, devoted wife and began to relax, he started to wish that he'd actually told

Rochelle the truth from the beginning. In some ways, the many gifts that Samson had purchased for Rochelle that Sunday afternoon in preparation for their date the next evening had provided him with a temporary ounce of comfort but as Samson fully appreciated, when the truth came and knocked upon his door, expensive gifts would not be able to save him and salvage his marriage, if his affair was ever discovered and exposed.

Deep down inside, Samson fully accepted as he lay in bed next to his wife and waited to drift off to sleep that it was just a matter of time before he would finally have to confess the truth to at least one of the two women that he was romantically attached to before he was caught red-handed. If Samson tried to hide and didn't divulge his romantic entanglements to one woman or the other, sooner or later his lies would be uncovered because deceit in the long term as Samson knew, was extremely hard to maintain and then he might actually lose both women and both relationships completely.

The longer Samson's affair with Rochelle continued, the riskier it was and the more likely it was that it would be discovered and although it had barely even started, he had already begun to feel the pressure from her demands because her requests had rapidly increased. Another woman had now definitely stepped into Samson's life and Rochelle was nothing like the patient, devoted, faithful Moira that would tolerate his calculated indiscretions and deliberate shortcomings because Rochelle wanted instant, rapid results.

Several marital affairs had actually taken place in the past on Samson's part but those affairs had all been very different because he'd been in full control of those situations which had predominantly involved, one off sexual liaisons that had usually occurred with a woman that already knew, Samson was married. This affair with Rochelle was hugely different however and Samson now began to understand and appreciate the implications of that very large difference because Rochelle had not known about Samson's marital commitment beforehand and he had lied to her just to convince her to jump into a bed of romance and to indulge in a flurry of sexual passion with him more quickly.

For Resolve, his productive weekend and the impact of Samson's affair had predominantly been truly triumphant because Resolve had watched Samson squirm around in a pool of discomfort, simply due to the lie of omission that he had told Rochelle as she'd played around with his deception regarding his single status and then begun to fully exploit it. The increase in Rochelle's demands had really put Samson under pressure but as far as Resolve was concerned that pressure was truly a positive thing because Samson deserved more than just a bit of discomfort and fortunately, courtesy of Rochelle, it looked like a mountain of stress was well on its way to him and Resolve just couldn't wait to see what she would do to Samson next.

A mask of pretense had been worn by Samson as his wife had waited patiently for him at home and as he'd gallivanted around and sown his wild oats, his affair with Rochelle had already started to create tension within his marriage and Resolve had watched the drama unfold that essentially, Samson had created for himself. Despite Samson's cavalier attitude and his carefree presentation when with Rochelle as he attempted to sustain the illusion of singleness, there had been a definite increase in the number of questions that Moira had presented to him because she'd started to challenge his now more frequent, unscheduled absences from their marital home and

Resolve had watched him squirm in absolute delight as Moira had become increasingly impatient.

Rather interestingly for Resolve it seemed, although Moira had tolerated Samson's absence on the very first night that he'd lied to her, she wasn't prepared to accept regular absences for an entire night which might possibly, permanently threaten her marriage and that was becoming increasingly apparent. A permanent affair could pose a real threat to Moira's marital status and overnight absences were a clear indication that there was indeed a permanent affair underway and so Moira's questions, Resolve had observed had definitely increased in direct response to Samson's actions. Due to Samson's nature however and his dictatorial tendencies, Resolve already knew that Samson was very used to getting what he wanted which meant, Moira was effectively fighting a losing battle in an attempt to save as much of her marriage as she could and that she would only be victorious if at some point, Samson bored of his affair.

Between Samson and Rochelle, absolutely everything that Resolve had wanted, planned and predicted might happen was now just about to manifest itself in reality and that sense of achievement for Resolve was utterly heavenly as he watched Rochelle play around with Samson in a game of double deceit. Peace had now almost been fully restored to Leona's life because Samson had been totally distracted by his affair and the one problem that had remained totally unresolved for Resolve which had ultimately been Samson, was now just about to come unstuck because Rochelle had really stepped up to the challenge and grabbed Samson firmly by the wallet.

One thing did still bother Resolve slightly however, at the end of that weekend, despite all his achievements and Resolve released a frustrated sigh as he watched Leona sleep on the visual display wall screen directly in front of him because that one thing was actually not related to any human life form at all but rather to Resolve's own actual existence. Every night, Resolve faithfully and diligently watched over Leona as he wished for her life to change and improve but the changes that he had made so far were situated a million miles away from the one actual real change that he really wanted to make. A deep, emotional, internal desire had now been stirred up and invoked inside Resolve and it almost seemed to fully occupy his form as he yearned to exist in a human mortal vessel and absolutely nothing in his current environment could possibly satisfy that hunger, or quench that thirst.

"Leona might actually like me, if she met me." Resolve convinced himself enthusiastically as he glanced at the monitoring window that contained Darin and began to inspect his physical form as he slept. "I'm not sure that I'd be considered handsome like he is though."

Since Resolve had just extracted the three noisy neighbors from Leona's life, at least in the short term, his visual display wall screen now only displayed three actual human beings upon it, Leona, Darin and Samson but from time to time, Resolve also kept a watchful eye upon Rochelle. A reduction in physical activity had now occurred upon Resolve's wall screen purely because it was a Sunday night which meant, he could now turn his attention back towards his own desires, if he wished to do so and he'd done so very willingly as he had quietly begun to consider whether Leona would actually find him attractive in his current form.

Generally speaking, Monitoring Programs were not as Resolve was fully aware, designed to be physically or aesthetically pleasing to the human eye and that had provoked Resolve to consider how Leona might perceive him, if he was ever presented with the opportunity to really meet her in person. In some ways, the physical attributes of Darin were not really that different from Resolve's own jet-black hair and dark brown eyes since Monitoring Programs had been designed to emulate the human form to some extent but although some of his intangible attributes quite closely matched those of Leona's deadbeat boyfriend, there were also some huge differences in terms of their build, stature and height. Since Resolve's form was intangible that also meant that although another could place their hand upon his arm or back, such an action would not result in any actual, physical touch because such acts yielded absolutely no sensation at all for either party involved and that was another major reason that Resolve now longed to occupy a human, physical frame and another very significant, extremely important difference.

"If only you could meet me Leona and I could actually become human, you might even grow to like me." Resolve convinced himself as he glanced at her beautiful face. "After all, I'm way nicer than he'll ever be and I know that for certain. In fact, I just can't believe that someone as nice as you would entertain a one-sided relationship with a guy like that although technically, I guess I'm kind of doing the same thing with you because we do have a one-sided relationship. However, what we could have would be totally different because I'd really love you and you're very nice and he's well, he's absolutely horrible and so not worth your time."

Unfortunately for Resolve however, nothing but silence and stillness greeted his words as usual and as he watched Leona as she slept, the lack of communication between them both began to really frustrate him again. Deep down inside Resolve's non-human form, he now longed to show Leona what real love was supposed to really be like and how a real man should really love a real woman but as yet, those sentiments of devotion, love and adoration could not be fully expressed to her.

Throughout some of the long lonely nights as Resolve had watched Leona sleep, he'd actually taken it upon himself to study the area of human romance and he had observed the inner workings of various kinds of romantic relationships because he wanted to be an absolute expert in the provision of a real human romantic experience. One day, Resolve actually hoped to explore and enjoy such a romantic experience inside Leona's very real human arms and so he had decided to research romance more thoroughly, just to ensure that such an experience would be a pleasurable one for her, if it ever actually happened.

A spark of hope had now been ignited within Resolve's form and excitement rapidly began to accumulate inside his core as he emotionally and logically concluded that he could perhaps be someone that Leona might really like. Some knowledge of human romance had been garnered from Resolve's past monitoring assignments and he had even conducted some recent additional research into matters of the heart, so now he felt absolutely certain that he could provide exactly what Leona really needed and wanted, if only her heart would allow him to and she gave him permission to love her.

The potential prospect of meeting Leona one day had really brightened up Resolve's lonely, very solitary existence but as yet, Resolve had no actual guarantees that such a hope could ever really be actually realized and that uncertainty continued to niggle away at his logical processes. Once or twice, since Resolve had been allocated to Leona, he had questioned the possibility that perhaps his love for Leona would not be reciprocated but those meandering doubts that lurked in the shadows of his existence which threatened to haunt his potential happiness, Resolve had in the end, vehemently rejected and shunned as human weaknesses. Rejection by Leona was not a possible outcome or eventuality that Resolve wanted to face right now because it provided him with far more joy just to exist in the assumption of Leona's acceptance, at least until the two actually met and then she would have the opportunity to make that actual decision herself.

Absolutely everything that Resolve now wanted, lay just outside his reach and inside the very human mortal world that he watched every day and that not only excited him immensely but also frustrated him profusely. According to what Resolve knew, no Monitoring Program had ever wanted to become a human being before and if any did currently harbor such desires, they'd never expressed that directly to him and so the very complicated, tricky issue that he now faced, was not even one that he had ever discussed with another entity inside Intellect in the past.

Usually, when Resolve interacted with other Monitoring Programs they would attend to the specific tasks required that would fulfill the needs of the Allocated Humans assigned to them by The Guardian and so that meant, very little discussion about themselves ever really occurred. Essentially, the very human desires to love and be loved weren't something that generally formed any part of a Monitoring Program's actual makeup and so those desires that existed inside Resolve, due to his special, additional, more human attributes, weren't really even supposed to actually be there and only existed due to his uniqueness. The huge differences in Resolve's makeup also meant that inside Intellect, there was no one really that he could discuss those unique desires and emotional responses with besides The Guardian himself in order to seek any kind of guidance and although that would not normally be an issue in this instance, because those desires and this emotional attachment involved the complicated issue of love which was extremely personal in nature, it had created a slight conflict within him.

Over the years, the variations in Resolve's attributes had assisted him in various ways and served him well as a Life Monitor because those differences had ultimately allowed Resolve to resolve some very complex human problems which had given him a deeper sense of satisfaction to some extent but now, those highly sophisticated variations presented him with a tremendous dilemma. Unfortunately, the deep sense of satisfaction that Resolve had derived from those very special attributes and his subsequent achievements, now no longer seemed to outweigh the mountain of frustration that he felt and faced as he yearned to join the actual human race and exist by Leona's side but that as Resolve already knew, could not be changed overnight as much as he wished it could be.

At least one thousand times a day, since Resolve had initially been assigned to Leona as her Life Monitor, he would consider the possibility of his existence in a physical human reality and imagine what it might be like to touch, feel, eat and smell just like human beings did. Just to possess the ability to wrap his arms around Leona's warm, human flesh and comfort her whenever she was worried during the dark, cold, bitter nights of winter, or simply to be able to hold her hand and walk through the city streets on a warm but breezy spring day, were both luxuries that Resolve often wished for that he did not have any access to at the present time.

The simple experiences that so many human beings often took for granted every single day were moments that Resolve had never enjoyed and that reality now pricked his existence because as he performed his role as a Life Monitor and as he watched human beings indulge in their daily lives, day in and day out, there was now a deep sense of envy. To feel the briskness of a crisp, fresh autumn morning against human skin, to feel the rain beat down against a human cheek and to hear a child laugh with human ears, were all experiences that Resolve longed to enjoy every time he watched Leona as she lived her life on the visual display wall screen directly in front of him. Just to feel the warmth of Leona's skin for Resolve, would be what human beings often referred to as a miracle but as yet, he was unsure that such a miracle might even be remotely possible in any way.

Deep down inside Resolve's form there was now a need for very human validation and a desire to feel Leona want him as a man although as yet, he did not even have a human male form to occupy and exist inside. The desire to love Leona and to live beside her, even for just a moment in time, would give Resolve a reason for being and a reason to exist that was far superior than his own current purpose as far as he was concerned but as yet, he hadn't even found a way to do that which really frustrated him.

Despite the fact that Resolve had monitored human beings for three decades now, their actual existence and form had never interested him that much before but suddenly, he'd become totally fascinated with everything that human beings did and everything that alluded to their humanity. A deep fascination now lived inside Resolve's intangible being that it seemed, nothing could replace and an unquenchable desire seemed to grip him every time he saw Leona's face which he could not be distracted from and those deep emotional sentiments, now longed to be satisfied by Leona's human touch.

"The human life is a very different form of existence Resolve and it can be one full of heartache, misery and pain." The Guardian had explained to him many times in the past.

In so many ways, Resolve did actually, totally agree with The Guardian because he had seen that himself many times before but he'd also seen the joy, happiness and love that human beings could experience and those positive, warm human possibilities had now convinced, encouraged and motivated him to join the actual human race. Absolutely everything that Resolve now wanted to be and to experience, was encapsulated inside a human form and so now, he wanted to step into and live inside one, so that his very human like desires could be fully realized and those human experiences could be accessed in their fullness alongside Leona's human vessel. A huge distance however, currently existed between Leona and Resolve and no matter how many times he watched her sleep, or resolved her problems, the two still existed in two very different worlds and although Resolve's world was a window into Leona's world, it was a window that he could not actually open, or try to climb through.

When the Monday morning finally arrived, Resolve watched quietly as Leona started to make her way towards work and as she did so, he began to speculate over the things that being a human male might actually entail. In order to be accepted inside the human world as a human male and particularly by Leona, it rapidly struck him that he would have to function on a daily basis with an actual male human body and that he would have to perform the various functions that human males usually performed, every single day.

Due to the discussion that Resolve had held with Analyzer on the Saturday, he had now been provoked to consider the actual issue of human male bodily functions slightly more deeply because it had once again highlighted to him that there would definitely be certain functions that he would have to perform each day, multiple times a day. Curious speculations suddenly seemed to pinge Resolve's form as an urge developed inside of him to practice and prepare himself for the day that he might become an actual human being, even though there were no guarantees as yet that, that day would ever really, actually arrive.

A simulation exercise was quickly planned, prepared and then rapidly actioned however as Resolve prepared to act like a very human male as Leona continued to make her way steadily towards Samson's corporate abode. Curiosity had now gripped every part of Resolve's form as he began to quietly consider exactly how each part of the male anatomy actually worked and how he might function inside an actual male human vessel because it would be so very different from his current form and existence and that notion utterly fascinated him. The issue of human male toiletry habits had now really begun to intrigue Resolve and although he currently had no actual need to urinate, he really wanted to try it out and perform a simulation exercise to see if it was as difficult as it looked and if it really was as complicated as Analyzer had suggested it might be, especially since Analyzer had teasingly challenged him to do so.

Human toiletry habits as far as Resolve was concerned, did look a tad strange and the physical act of urination itself looked like something that he would probably have to master, if he ever truly wished to adopt a male human form but for now, he just wanted to experiment and experience that bodily function for himself, even if the results would be a total disaster. A smile rapidly crossed Resolve's face as he faced his visual display wall screen and then began to observe the newly created simulation upon it which involved a simulated toilet and his simulated form as he prepared himself for an enactment of the very strange activity that he had seen so many human males perform every single day.

"It can't be that hard, if human males can do this surely a highly logical, meticulously programmed and superbly equipped Monitoring Program like myself should find it a total breeze." Resolve convinced himself as he unzipped the pair of trousers that adorned his simulated human form and then lifted the toilet seat up. "So far, so good."

Once the toilet seat had been placed in the correct position and leant up against the cistern, so that it would not move and fall back down and Resolve could see the actual interior of the toilet, his simulated human form then stepped towards it. Since Resolve had watched male human beings perform this particular bodily function and ritual many times, he instinctively knew that he had to be positioned slightly closer to his intended target in order to potentially be successful as he attempted to mimic the human male behavior that he'd seen so many times before.

"It's going rather well really." Resolve cheerfully encouraged himself as he grinned.

Underneath the pair of black simulated trousers that Resolve had adorned his simulated human form in at the start of the simulation exercise, there was a pair of dark grey simulated boxer shorts that fitted snugly against his simulated human limbs and Resolve smiled as he prepared for the big moment, the actual hit or miss that would be sure to follow. Irrespective of the disgust that Analyzer had expressed and felt towards this strange but biologically necessary human function, Resolve fully appreciated that he would definitely have to totally master this particular area of human behavior, if he ever wanted to become an actual human being because it would be absolutely essential for human daily living and it was something that males had to do on a daily basis, quite frequently.

Despite Analyzer's skepticism and jokes, Resolve decided to take heed of the suggestions offered that he should simulate a urine flow that was completely random in both volume and speed and that he should disable the application of his logical functions to control the flow of urine. Since a random urine flow would be applicable and no control systems were available to real male human beings whenever they urinated that Resolve felt would be closer to a real human experience which was a very valid point that Analyzer had made which had been totally correct.

The first attempt as Resolve implemented Analyzer's suggestion was as he expected, a complete and utter disaster and as urine began to splash across the floor of the bathroom, some drops even landed upon Resolve's simulated feet, or more specifically, the pair of simulated black leather shoes that he had clothed his simulated human form in.

"Perhaps that's why men usually wear heavier shoes than women do." Resolve mentioned to himself as he quickly stopped the flow of urine and then began to consider his aim slightly more carefully. "To protect their feet from urine splashes and toilet raindrops."

Another second attempt to urinate was then bravely, enthusiastically made as Resolve rapidly sprang back into action and began to simulate the urine flow once more and this time, quite fortunately, some splashes of urine actually hit the interior of the toilet bowl itself as some of the liquid drops bounced across the rim and then dribbled into the actual bowl. The second attempt although it was a definite improvement upon Resolve's first very rough effort, Resolve immediately accepted had still not resulted in the actual achievement of his main goal which was to get the urine inside the center of the actual toilet bowl and so in that respect, he had actually failed and failure was a very strange place for Resolve to visit because he certainly wasn't used to it.

"This definitely requires technique." Resolve advised himself as he gently shook his head. "And a bit more practice." He insisted decisively as he ended the simulation. "It really is much trickier and far harder than it looks, so I might even have to practice this every single day."

Since Leona had now arrived at work, Resolve quickly turned his attention back towards her and reenabled all of his logical functions as he completely abandoned the toiletry simulation for the time being in total defeat because a lot more practice was definitely required and now, his focus really had to be upon Leona and her working day. For once and rather unusually, Resolve now had to surrender to the reality that the particular human skill that he'd explored that morning hadn't quite been mastered yet and that it would definitely require a lot more practice and many more attempts. A far more urgent, pressing matter however, now actually required Resolve's immediate attention that morning and as Leona's Life Monitor, her life and the issues that he was supposed to resolve on her behalf, always took higher priority than his own human like desires and even his own simulated toilet practice.

A response was now due to be received by Leona from the Venus Honey Traps Detective Agency, since she had already reached out to them as Resolve already knew and so he wanted to ensure that he was paying attention and focused when that response was actually opened up and then read by Leona that morning. Inside Resolve's logical processes there now lay an expectant hopeful wish that he would be able to dispel Darin from Leona's life forever that week but as Resolve fully appreciated that elimination depended upon the competence of actual human beings which was not always guaranteed.

"Another dreary Monday morning inside Samson's corporate kingdom and dictatorship." Leona whispered softly to herself as she held her keycard up to her office door to unlock it and then pushed it open.

On the way to work as usual, Leona had purchased breakfast which today consisted of a bacon roll with lashings of brown sauce which she intended to wash down with the caramel latte that she'd also bought from the same coffee shop and so she hungrily looked forward to the consumption of both as she stepped inside her office. Breakfast for Leona that morning was a much-needed meal because she felt absolutely famished and as she began to settle down inside her office, she hungrily started to consume the bacon roll as she headed towards her main meeting desk.

Quite unusually, before Leona headed towards her graphic easel that day, due to the expected response from the Venus Honey Traps Detective Agency as soon as she had entered inside the room, she'd actually begun to make her way towards her meeting desk and then switched on her main computer system first and she was not disappointed. When the computer screen lit up and once Leona's emails had loaded, she immediately noticed that there was an unread email in her inbox from an unfamiliar sender and so she eagerly prepared to open it as excitement rapidly began to fill her core.

Much to Leona's total delight that morning, there were no actual dreaded emails from the dictatorial Samson inside her inbox which in itself was definitely something to celebrate because silence was certainly better than headache as far as Leona was concerned and the less she heard from Samson, the better it was really. Once the unread email had been opened, Leona began to quietly read and digest the contents it contained and as the email message started to tickle her thoughts, a smile suddenly appeared upon her face. Some curious, hopeful deliberations surrounded what the Venus Honey Traps Detective Agency could actually do for Leona and those hopeful wishes, immediately started to tease her mind as her smile rapidly erupted into a joyous, volcanic explosion of laughter because the email that she'd received had truly delighted her.

"Venus Honey Traps. The Love Detective Agency. We catch cheating loverats and take the stress out of a cheating mess." Leona announced triumphantly as she giggled and then clicked on the link contained inside the email. "This sounds absolutely amazing, I might be able to really catch Darin now."

Everything about the corporate entity really intrigued Leona as she began to peruse the website and review the special promotional offer that she had been sent which really appealed to her because it looked like, a truly amazing deal. The investigation rates on display upon the website seemed very reasonable and exceedingly low in comparison to other detective agencies that Leona had seen and with the discount on offer, the company had offered her a package that she could not possibly afford to refuse.

Several positive client testimonials appeared upon a page of the actual website itself and Leona read every single one as she thoughtfully admired and appreciated the company's professionalism. Every testimonial that Leona read was excellent and the women that ran the agency seemed to know exactly what they were doing because their clients appeared to be very satisfied with the results of their past work.

Rather interestingly, the website mentioned that the agency was run by three women and that it specialized in catching cheating male partners which was perfect for Leona's very unromantic situation and that it had initially been formed by the three women because they had all been cheated on themselves. The firsthand experience that the three women offered, rapidly encouraged Leona to trust their detective agency even more since she felt totally reassured that they would really understand what she was going through because they too had all experienced the same kind of romantic betrayal. Upon the website there was a lack of physical identification and there were no photographs of any of the three female detectives but as Leona fully appreciated that anonymity was to be expected because in that particular line of work, images that identified anyone involved would be counterproductive to the main mission of the agency itself.

"Now the truth could really be within my reach." Leona whispered to herself as she smiled. "With these rates and that discount offer, now I should actually be able to afford access to the truth."

According to the email that Leona had received, an initial appointment had been offered at lunchtime that very same day and so she immediately prepared to accept the invitation because it would be a chance to meet one of the women that ran the detective agency itself face to face. Some very precise instructions had been included inside the email and as Leona quickly skimmed through each one, she enthusiastically clicked on the acceptance link to confirm her intended attendance that lunchtime. Digital communications, the instructions inside the email specified, were to be kept to a minimum to avoid any traceability and to maintain confidentiality and Leona totally agreed with that principle because she knew only too well that technology, devices and phones could be tapped, hacked, traced and even monitored by third parties.

For the purposes of identification Leona had to provide the agency with a non-digital photograph of Darin so that they could track him down which the instructions specified, she should bring along with her that day and so she immediately began to search inside her handbag, just to make sure that she actually had one with her. Quite fortunately, Leona finally managed to find a small passport sized photograph of Darin at the very bottom of her handbag which she quickly dug out and then tucked inside a compartment in her purse, just to ensure that it would be easily accessible when she attended her appointment that lunchtime.

When lunchtime arrived, Leona prepared eagerly to attend her appointment as she quietly left the building and then headed down a nearby side street which led towards the area of the city where the detective agency was situated. Approximately fifteen minutes later, once Leona arrived outside the address that she had been provided with, she quickly pressed the buzzer and then waited in silence next to an exterior black door. In a matter of just a few seconds, the buzzer was politely answered by a female voice and Leona immediately said her name and mentioned that she had an appointment at which point, the external door was then quickly released as a loud buzz sounded out into the air. The exterior black door was then enthusiastically pushed open and as Leona was provided with access to the building, excitement silently began to accumulate inside of her and rapidly fill her core.

Just beyond the exterior door, Leona found a long narrow hallway with crisp white walls and she immediately began to make her way along it as she headed towards the reception area which was situated at the other end of the corridor. When Leona arrived at the other end of the hallway, she stepped out into a large, rectangular shaped reception area where she immediately found a glass door on her left-hand side that had a lettering etched into the glass which read 'Venus Honey Traps' and she eagerly headed towards the door, pushed it open and then stepped through it.

On the other side of the glass door, Leona found another reception area which looked bright, modern and minimalistic and so she quickly began to make her way towards the unmanned reception desk and as she crossed the room, she began to wonder silently as to why it was unmanned. No one appeared to be around and so after just a few seconds of uncertainty, Leona quickly crossed the room once again and then sat down upon one of three black leather chairs on the other side of the reception area that had been stationed next to a white glossy coffee table which had some magazines scattered across it.

"Someone definitely buzzed me in." Leona rapidly reminded herself in a soft whisper. "So that someone has definitely got to be around here somewhere."

A magazine was quickly picked up and Leona prepared to read it whilst she waited in order to keep herself fully occupied because she could see no physical signs yet of the actual person that had given her access to the building, or anyone else. Despite the fact that the magazine was now firmly inside Leona's hands however, a few more seconds were spent curiously engaged in a quick visual scan of the reception area but much to her surprise, she still found it completely empty and there were no indications at all that anyone was even on their way towards either her or the reception desk which she found slightly strange.

Another glance was cast back down towards the magazine as Leona once more prepared to focus her mind upon it and then she began to flick through the pages until she found an article about various lip glosses which quickly caught her attention and she immediately started to read it, just to entertain herself as she waited. A few more minutes of silence went strangely by before a female in her early thirties suddenly popped out from behind a glass door situated just behind the main reception desk and Leona immediately glanced up at her face and then smiled. The sharply dressed, well presented woman quickly began to walk towards Leona with a warm, friendly smile and her hand outstretched and Leona instantly rose to her feet in response.

"Hi, I'm Nicky." Nicky said. "You must be Leona."

"Yes I am, it's lovely to meet you Nicky." Leona replied courteously as she politely shook the hand that Nicky had offered to her.

"It's very nice to meet you too Leona. I'm the detective assigned to your love case." Nicky explained. "If you'd like to come with me please." She instructed as she began to lead Leona towards a small consultation room on the left-hand side of the reception area. "We can discuss your situation in one of our consultation rooms."

"I was so relieved to find out about your detective agency. I didn't even know that such specialist services existed." Leona gushed as she gave Nicky a warm smile and then began to follow her towards the glass door.

"Did you bring a photo of your partner along with you today?" Nicky asked as she pushed open the glass door and then politely held it open as she encouraged Leona to step inside the consultation room.

"Yes, I did." Leona immediately confirmed as she stepped inside the consultation room.

"Good. We'll definitely need that for identification purposes and from now on, please don't send us anymore emails because we try to keep the electronic trail during our investigations to an absolute minimum." Nicky advised as she followed Leona into the consultation room. "We take your security and our security very seriously indeed and we don't like either to be compromised. Please take a seat and make yourself comfortable." She offered.

"Right, I'll try to remember that." Leona agreed as she sat down upon a black leather chair. "Thanks."

"Would you like a cup of coffee or anything?" Nicky asked. "Our receptionist usually prepares beverages for all our clients but she's out for lunch at the moment, I can still make you one though."

"Sure thanks." Leona replied as she nodded her head. "I'd love a coffee, I usually have it white with two sugars."

"Okay, I'll be back in just a minute and if you could fill in this client registration form for me please Leona whilst you wait." Nicky instructed as she opened up a filing cabinet beside the door of the room and then plucked a form and pen from the interior. "It's just a few questions to help us with our work." She immediately reassured Leona as she walked towards her, handed her both the form and pen and then began to walk back towards the glass door.

"Sure, I'll do that." Leona quickly agreed as she glanced down at the form and then started to read it.

Once Nicky had left the consultation room, Leona began to focus her attention solely upon the completion of the form that she'd been handed as she started to read it and as each question was quietly inspected, Leona tried to provide a comprehensive answer to every one of the questions posed. A few quick glances were cast nervously around the small but warm consultation room which had cream walls, black leather furniture, a shiny black filing cabinet and a small, white, glossy coffee table inside it as Leona tried to complete the form as accurately as she could and as quickly as possible and in what seemed like no time at all, she'd managed to fill in all the blank spaces that required answers from her.

Not more than a few minutes after Nicky had left, she returned to the consultation room with two piping hot cups of coffee clasped inside her hands which she immediately placed down on top of the white coffee table. The completed form was then quickly handed back to Nicky by Leona as the two women exchanged polite smiles and Nicky rapidly began to cast her eyes over the form as she sat down directly opposite Leona. A discussion about Darin and the couple's relationship was immediately then held as the two women began to discuss his untrustworthy behavior in more depth and delved into some of the intricate details, so that Nicky could assess the likelihood that he was indeed, actually cheating.

The conversation about Darin went on for at least another twenty minutes as Leona elaborated further and then several questions were asked as Nicky attempted to establish the kind of relationship that the couple had and the type of man that Darin actually was. Several incidents were discussed between the two women as Leona described Darin's conduct and the circumstances and events that had aroused her suspicions and as Nicky listened to her attentively, she nodded her head in understanding several times as she began to draw some rapid conclusions about the couple's relationship.

"So Leona, would you say Darin values loyalty?" Nicky asked.

"Only if he's on the receiving end." Leona replied. "I'd say he's a taker not a giver and he takes quite a lot to be perfectly honest."

"Yes unfortunately, I've seen men like Darin a hundred times before." Nicky immediately reassured her. "Try not to worry, we'll have this sorted out in no time."

Essentially from what Nicky had just heard, she could instantly sense that Leona's relationship was in a very depilated state and she could fully appreciate exactly why Leona had reached out to the detective agency in the first place because Darin sounded extremely unfaithful. Answers to questions were required by Leona that Darin had refused to provide and lies had been told to her which Nicky knew, Leona could see straight through and she just seemed to need the final confirmation now that would allow her to dump Darin for good, so that she could move on with her life. This relationship it was immediately apparent to Nicky, could not be salvaged and that she already fully appreciated and totally understood because Darin had from the sounds of it, strayed far too many times and hurt Leona's heart far too much to ever be forgiven.

"Would you like the decoy service Leona, or would you just like the surveillance package?" Nicky enquired. "The surveillance package usually involves collecting video footage and we also intercept, tape and record your partner's phone calls for an agreed time period." She continued. "The decoy package is slightly more expensive but that's because it involves an actual female decoy that will lure your partner into a compromising situation."

"I think the surveillance package might be the best option for me right now Nicky." Leona replied thoughtfully. "If I can't get what I need from that then perhaps I can consider other options." She added. "I already know that he's cheating really, I just need clarification and final proof."

"Yes, I can see why you reached out to us Leona." Nicky immediately sympathized. "It sounds like this cheating issue has been a bone of contention for a while."

"It really has been." Leona agreed. "And it's very frustrating."

Nicky nodded. "I'll do my very best Leona and hopefully soon, I'll be able to provide you with the answers that you really need." She reassured her. "I know how frustrating it can be sometimes, when you know the truth deep down inside but you don't actually have the evidence to prove it. When would you like us to start?"

"Straight away would be good." Leona quickly clarified. "Or as soon as you can."

"Right well, we can start tomorrow." Nicky offered. "How does that suit you?"

"Sure, tomorrow's great." Leona agreed as she quickly glanced down at the screen of her phone which was inside one of her hands to check the time and then stood up. "And thank you for seeing me so quickly Nicky and for understanding. I really have to get back to work now, my lunchtime is almost over and Darin's already taken up enough of my working day and that's more time than he deserves really because he's not a very nice person and especially not to me."

"Don't worry Leona, I understand men like Darin. Some unfaithful men tend to put their partners down quite a lot to disguise their infidelity, so if he does that please don't take it personally." Nicky advised as she rose to her feet and then began to walk towards the consultation room door. "It's their way to deflect from the real issues and a method they utilize to distract you."

"Darin usually tells me that I'm being insecure, if I ask him too many questions or I even try to raise the issue of cheating with him." Leona clarified as their meeting concluded. "And he can be very confrontational."

"Well, you don't need to raise the issue with him again. We'll find out exactly what he's up to and then you can dump him from a distance, so that way you can avoid any ugly arguments." Nicky insisted as she led Leona back towards the reception area. "Cheating can become very psychological Leona, men tend trick women in very clever ways and those kinds of comments sound like Darin's way to blame you for his indiscretions, his way to deny his infidelity, a way to play on your self-doubts and his way to put you down, all in one go." She advised. "I call such tactics, the deflect mask because cheating partners generally use those tactics to mask their affairs and to deflect their issues back onto you and sadly I'm afraid, he's not the only person that behaves that way."

Leona nodded her head as she listened. "Thanks so much for everything Nicky, honestly I've never done anything like this before and you've made it really straightforward for me." She replied.

"Don't worry Leona that's what I'm here for remember." Nicky gently reassured her with a smile as she pulled open the glass door that led towards the front entrance of the building. "To take the stress out of a cheating mess."

For once and very unusually, Leona actually felt an ounce of comfort about Darin as the two women walked through the main reception area and then along the corridor that led towards the entrance of the building and it was almost as if Leona had finally found someone that really understood what she was going through. Rather amazingly and very reassuringly, Leona had found that she could actually open up to Nicky fully and discuss her relationship without feeling judged or embarrassed about Darin's antics, headache and drama and it was as if a huge weight had now been lifted from her mind and her shoulders. The initial consultation had been conducted with the utmost professionalism and Nicky had totally reassured Leona that the situation would indeed be handled in a professional manner and that reassurance was a huge comfort to her because Darin's cheating was extremely stressful and Leona just didn't know how to cope with it anymore or tackle it, since he really was so difficult and very manipulative.

When the two women arrived at the front entrance of the building, they quickly bade each other farewell and then separated as Leona prepared to make her way back to work. A gentle sigh escaped from Leona's lips as she started to walk briskly along the concrete walkway of the busy city street which was full of midday rush hour lunchers as comfort and relief seemed to rapidly fill her interior and warm her core.

Very soon, Leona hoped as she arrived back outside Samson's corporate domain, the truth would be in her possession and then she would be free from Darin's clutches that were formed from lies and betrayal and soon she hoped, she'd be free from the couple's artificial, horrible, fake, sham engagement. Once Leona could prove that Darin had cheated on her in a way that he could not possibly deny, she would then be absolutely free to walk away from his thorny, prickly arms forever and he would never be able to actually return to her gentle arms or loving side and the possibility of a Darin free future, totally delighted her. Although the Venus Honey Traps Detective Agency hadn't even begun their work yet, Leona already felt comforted, happy, satisfied and even slightly relieved because the gentle reassurances that Nicky had provided to her that lunchtime had definitely been enough to convince her that very soon, her five-year battle with Darin would officially finally be, totally and completely over.

The next few days of Leona's working week, fortunately for Leona, were extremely quiet, very productive and surprisingly peaceful because quite strangely, Samson kept his distance and remained out of her hair and her office. Usually, Samson dumped additional clients on top of Leona's desk and offloaded extra work onto her shoulders very often and those clients predominantly comprised of clients that other architects couldn't, or simply wouldn't deal with whose requirements they had absolutely no wish to satisfy but that week, he'd been strangely quiet and he had not given Leona any extra work. Rather annoyingly for Leona, the usual client additions and additional workload usually increased her working hours beyond that of the other architects that Samson employed but due to the lack of additions that week, her working week had almost verged upon being slightly more normal because for once, she'd managed to leave work at around seven each day which was an absolute miracle in itself.

Once the Friday morning finally arrived and as the end of Leona's working week drew near, it floated into her life much like a leaf that had fallen off a tree which had been caught and then carried softly through the air by a gentle breeze during the first wisps of autumn because the peaceful reassurance that Darin would soon be out of her life for good, gently brightened up her journey to work. Every step that Leona took on her way to work that morning felt soft and comfortable as that small cushion of hope comforted, cushioned and protected her feet as she walked and it was almost as if a carpet had been provided for Leona to walk upon because the hardness of the concrete ground seemed to just melt away.

A truly delightful phone call had been received by Leona from Nicky on the Thursday evening just as she'd left work and according to what Nicky had said, apparently she had some news for Leona about Darin and his cheating antics and so the two women had agreed to meet on the Friday evening. The phone call had provided Leona with not only a glimmer of comfort but also a spark of hope because it had reassured Leona that her recent efforts to establish the truth with regards to Darin's infidelity, would soon bear fruit and provide actual results.

Hopefully, Leona wished as she stepped inside the usual coffee shop to purchase her breakfast, her world would soon be set to rights because the noisy neighbors had remained gone and had not yet returned and Darin was just about to proven as an actual love cheat, all in the just one week. In the short space of one actual week, two really annoying problems that had haunted Leona's life for years had almost been totally eradicated from her environment, namely the noisy neighbors and her lousy, unfaithful boyfriend and although there were still some slight traces of Darin left, she fully appreciated that those could not be totally erased until she'd proven that he had been sexually unfaithful to her at which point, she could then boot him out of her life forever.

Another interesting development, Leona considered thoughtfully as she left the coffee shop with her bacon bap and latte in hand, was that Samson seemed to have been extremely quiet that week because he hadn't put in an actual physical appearance all week and even his emails had been far less frequent. The less Leona saw of Samson, the brighter her working week was really and so his absences had been and were very welcome indeed and as a result of the decrease in Samson, Leona's productivity had definitely increased and she'd once more actually begun to look forward to going to work every working morning. Unfortunately however, the tone of Samson's emails hadn't changed much and his messages were still laced with patronization and his usual antagonistic attitude but recently, at least they had been far less frequent and that was something that Leona could certainly appreciate.

Less of Samson in every way possible was a very desirable component of Leona's working week and a comfort to her weary frame that had tired of being overworked to feed his power hungry, corporate ambitions for so very long. Now it seemed however, for some inexplicable reason, Samson had melted into the background of Leona's working days and as a result, her weekdays had become a far more pleasant experience although she had no actual idea as to why those enjoyable absences had occurred but as Leona headed towards the entrance of the office block that she occupied every working day, unusually for once, there was a joyful smile upon her face.

One day, perhaps even soon, Leona decided as she stepped inside Samson's corporate premises and then headed towards her office, she'd find somewhere else to work because every day that she spent under Samson's rule, was just another day of potential agony and frustration. Just before the recent reduction in Leona's workload, it had been virtually impossible to cope with Samson's demands which meant, despite the temporary relief, Leona felt extremely uncertain about exactly how long that reduction would actually last because it was totally out of character for Samson and very unusual. The unpredictable peace that Leona had enjoyed for the past week, she silently considered as she arrived outside her office, unlocked and opened the door and then stepped inside the room, might only be temporary and it could change at any given moment and return to the nightmare that it had been in the past which would not be a desirable eventuality but that as Leona knew only too well, was the very real, reality of Samson.

"No Samson breathing down my neck is definitely a good thing, no matter how long it lasts and it probably won't last very long, so I should just enjoy the peace for now and worry about tomorrow, tomorrow." Leona whispered to herself as she stepped inside her office and then closed the door behind her.

Once the temporary distraction that had kept Samson occupied for the past week was over, Leona had absolutely no doubts at all inside her mind that he would return to his usual self and his corporate empire building warpath and then she would definitely be his first port of call and that was absolutely undisputable and totally undeniable. For the time being however, Leona thoughtfully decided, she would just accept the peace and enjoy it whilst it lasted because Samson had not been tangled up in Leona's hair and his verbal lashings had not whipped her ears for the past working week and as a result, her office had been a far more comfortable, peaceful and productive environment to work in.

"Whatever the distraction is Samson, I sure hope it keeps you busy for a while because I really love my peace." Leona whispered to herself as she approached her graphic easel and prepared to start work. "I know it might come to an end soon but hopefully that won't be too soon."

For Leona, the remainder of her working Friday was extremely peaceful as she diligently dove into her work but she also kept an avid eye upon her office door as she did so, just in case Samson decided to put in an appearance which would definitely interrupt her day because that peaceful status as Leona already knew, could change at any given second. A deep sense of gratitude seemed to rest upon Leona's shoulders throughout the day as she worked which seemed to make her body feel much lighter as she silently rejoiced in the fact that she'd enjoyed a Samson free week because that was truly a rarity and definitely something worth her appreciation. Although Leona remained totally ignorant as to exactly why Samson had been so distracted and she had no clue what or who had distracted him, she felt extremely grateful that someone or something had because her week at work that week as far as she was concerned had been a total joy which was indeed, extremely rare.

When seven that Friday evening arrived and as Leona's working day drew to a close, she enthusiastically prepared to leave work with a joyful smile upon her face as she began to eagerly look forward to her agreed meeting with Nicky. Another Samson free day had just been experienced by Leona and it had truly been a pleasant end to a very pleasant working week and so she felt absolutely delighted as she packed up, plucked her handbag from the back of her chair and then headed towards her office door.

"I could definitely get used to no Samson." Leona joked to herself as she walked. "A lack of attention from Samson really is a very pleasant thing." She paused for a moment in front of her office door and then turned back around as she gave her office one final glance. "Perhaps I should leave this place and find my own private clients and then every week would be peaceful like this one was because Samson is stress and stress is Samson and in fact, I think they could even be married to each other, or joined at the mouth." Leona added. "I could leave Samson behind and leave him all alone with his stress, his ruthless ambitions and his corporate dictatorship. Now that's definitely something to think about."

Several things really appealed to Leona about the prospect of leaving Samson's corporate empire behind for good and as she pulled open her office door and then stepped out of the room, she began to entertain those pleasant thoughts and potential possibilities. On several occasions in the past, Leona had toyed around with the idea of being in control of her own professional life and the actual establishment of her own architectural consultation firm but in the end, she'd always shied away from doing so, purely due to fear and a lack of resources.

In order to enact such a huge plan, Leona considered thoughtfully as she walked along the corridor that led towards the elevators, it would definitely take time and she would have to save up enough money to realize such a goal. Such a bold, defiant, financially independent act on Leona's part would require a significant amount of resources which she currently lacked, she thoughtfully concluded as she arrived outside the lifts and then gently pushed the button to request one. If another position of employment was secured by Leona somewhere else, in order to secure the required resources, she internally deliberated as a set of elevator doors opened directly in front of her and she stepped inside the lift that new position and place of employment might be even worse than her current environment and she could end up with a boss worse than Samson, if that was indeed, actually possible because he was truly horrible.

A huge mountain seemed to obstruct Leona's quest for peace, respect, serenity and joy and as she exited the lift and then began to walk through the reception area, she considered that mountain thoughtfully because it was a mountain that she felt unsure, she had the skills and knowledge to even begin to climb. The hurdle of finances definitely stood in Leona's way and she just didn't have access to the sums of money that would be required and so that was a challenge that she felt uncertain, she could actually jump over and overcome.

Perhaps, Leona deliberated as she arrived on the ground floor, walked through the reception area and then stepped out of the building onto the city street, such a plan could be orchestrated more quickly, if she could negotiate an increase in her salary with Samson but there was one possible drawback to that particular solution and that drawback was really, rather huge. In order to secure an increase in salary, Leona would probably have to agree to additional weekend work and that potential increase in working hours worried her profusely. The extra hours would definitely have to be worked throughout the weekends since Leona could barely squeeze anymore working hours into her working week as it currently stood and that meant, such a plan could only really be orchestrated, if Leona was prepared to sacrifice her weekends to meet even more client deadlines.

More than just a few things really worried Leona about the prospect of working for Samson on the weekends and one of those things was that Leona would be exposing herself further to Samson's rule in an attempt to increase her income but the silver lining in that particular cloud was that Samson was unlikely to be physically present. Despite Samson's corporate ambitions, his dedication to his corporate empire and the rod of iron that he usually held over Leona's head, on the occasions in the past that she had worked on an actual weekend, Samson had been nowhere to be seen because it seemed that he really appreciated and enjoyed his weekend leisure time.

"If I work on the weekends though, Samson might still email me and that would be a total pain in the butt." Leona mumbled to herself thoughtfully as she began to make her way along the city street. "Two solutions but none of them are totally fool proof, this will definitely require a bit more thought."

An agreement had been made to meet Nicky at seven thirty in a nearby eatery and since Leona had met all her client deadlines in a timely manner that day and that week, she'd been able to leave work in ample time and so she expected to arrive at their agreed meetup point at least fifteen minutes early but she still rushed along the city streets regardless of that fact. Essentially, Leona did not want to risk the possibility that she might be late for Darin's potential dumping because that evening, Nicky might actually provide her with information which would allow her to dump Darin that very same day, or over the coming weekend and so being late for their meeting was not a desirable outcome to her Friday which was why every possible working second that day had been spent extremely productively.

Despite Leona's very peaceful, stress free, productive day at work however, Resolve had noticed that Samson's day had been the complete opposite and an utter stress filled nightmare and Samson's discomfort had absolutely delighted him. Every minute of stress that day that had been inflicted upon Samson's head had ultimately been caused by Rochelle and Resolve had silently rejoiced as he'd watched the tension dramatically escalate and mount because she had demanded that Samson not only see her that evening but also that they spend their entire weekend together. The plan for Samson as Resolve was fully aware had been to see Rochelle on the following Monday evening because the weekend and overnight absences were becoming harder and harder for him to justify to his wife but Rochelle was having absolutely none of it and Samson had struggled that day with her demands.

INTELLECT: USER REPAIR

Total delight had filled Resolve's form that Friday afternoon as he had watched Samson squirm around in a pool of discomfort as he'd tried to negotiate with Rochelle and concoct a believable excuse for his wife to ensure that he would not only be free to see Rochelle later that day but also be able to spend at least part of his weekend with her. In the end, Resolve had noticed that Samson had unashamedly lied to Moira about some fictitious business associates that had supposedly, very unexpectedly, just flown into the city's airport that he had to meet immediately and Resolve had been amazed by just how easily each lie had rolled of Samson's tongue.

According to Samson, the business associates could bring in lots of new business which would allow him to expand his corporate operations and that would be financially favorable for the couple in the long term and so due to Samson's manipulative persuasion, Resolve had observed that once again, Moira had been pressured to accept the unacceptable. Regardless of the couple's marital vows, due to Moira's gentle nature, Resolve had watched her cave into Samson several times now and once again that day, she had accepted his excuses and his absence from home that night although it was highly unusual for a business-related activity to be conducted on a Friday evening because after all, it was officially the start of the weekend. This time however, Resolve had noticed that Moira's acceptance had been far more reluctant and that she had been much more vocal about her disappointment which had actually been verbally expressed to Samson several times throughout their conversation.

A very interesting dynamic it seemed to Resolve had now been created by Rochelle and Samson's affair because Rochelle had once again managed to force Samson to participate with her plans, due to his claims regarding his single status as she'd forced him to behave as if he was what he actually claimed to be. Much to Resolve's amusement, the lack of attention that Samson had paid to Rochelle the previous weekend had during that day then been utilized as actual leverage to demand things from him that a single, unmarried man would normally have been able to provide in terms of time and attention. Due to the lack of any physical interactions between the two lovers the previous weekend, Resolve had noticed that Samson had felt under a tremendous amount of pressure that day to actually spend more time with Rochelle as she'd demanded more effort and a commitment from him and that in the end, he'd finally had to surrender to her demands.

Just like Leona and Nicky, Resolve observed, the two lovers had agreed to meet at seven thirty inside a restaurant in the heart of the city but unlike the two ladies, the reservations that Samson had made for dinner involved an expensive table inside an exclusive, fine dining venue which were his attempt to purchase Rochelle's satisfaction and soothe her discontent. Once quarter past seven arrived, Resolve watched quietly as Samson began to make his way towards the venue in a chauffeur driven limousine that he had hired for the next twenty-four hours, specifically for the romantic occasion.

Every financial effort that Samson could possibly make that evening, Resolve observed had been eagerly made and it seemed as if Samson wanted to avoid any stressful confrontations as he attempted to keep the passion between the two lovers alive for as long as he possibly could. Rather amusingly for Resolve, he noticed that Samson was now definitely at Rochelle's mercy and as he could clearly see, she now had him exactly where she wanted him. If Rochelle wanted to kick up a dramatic fuss, Resolve fully appreciated that she could easily do so because she knew exactly where Samson's business was and that meant, he now had to please and appease her as much as he possibly could, or that his deceitful knot of lies might be quickly unraveled in a very public display.

Apparently from what Rochelle had said to Samson earlier that day, their date that evening was urgent because she wanted to discuss something very important with him and since she had not seen Samson that often, since they'd initially met, Resolve could clearly see that Samson now felt obliged to participate with her request. A chauffeur driven limousine had been hired by Samson in an attempt to reassure Rochelle that she was indeed, very important to him, despite his lack of attention but as Resolve observed in total delight, Samson had been literally tied up in knots by his attraction to Rochelle and his own lies.

Much to Resolve's absolute satisfaction, a different kind of woman had now stepped into Samson's life and Rochelle demanded more from him than just a quick tumble in the bedroom whenever it suited him and those expectations had now placed Samson in a very difficult position as he'd showered her with expensive presents in an attempt to please her. Unlike Moira who Samson could easily manipulate and lie to, Rochelle was not as easy to appease and she had been absolutely adamant that she had to see Samson that weekend and she had not taken no for an answer.

Every part of Resolve's form literally danced with joy inside as he watched Samson be driven through the city streets in the limousine that he had hired for his night of passion with Rochelle as Samson prepared to dabble in the passionate waters of infidelity once again. Unlike Samson's past extra marital affairs as Resolve already knew, this affair was something very different because Rochelle was very different but Resolve had designed it to be that way and the fact that Rochelle hadn't just allowed Samson to take what he wanted from her and then simply walk away had pleased Resolve immensely.

"This affair is starting to cost me an absolute fortune." Samson muttered to himself as he sat in the back of the limousine.

Suddenly, Samson had found himself in the very deep end of an actual affair which had stemmed from his attraction to a woman that had only just recently jumped into his life but the passion he now felt towards Rochelle would not allow him to simply walk away from her beautiful side. Every inch of Samson's skin seemed to crawl with guilt and discomfort as he was whisked through the city streets towards the restaurant inside the chauffeur drive limousine because as he knew deep down inside that day Rochelle would definitely demand more from him than his marital commitments would tolerate and allow but he was powerless to object, since he'd not only initiated their affair but he also really wanted it.

A proper romantic relationship had actually been demanded from Samson by Rochelle and he had not been able to simply pick her up and drop her like he'd usually done with his past sexual conquests and that now worried him profusely. The romance that Samson had promised Rochelle and alluded to, she now expected to receive from him but there was a definite shortfall in the amounts of love, attention and time that Samson could provide to her, due to his marital commitment to another woman. No part of Samson however, could compensate Rochelle for his shortcomings as a lover and that he definitely knew because he was already married to another woman and he had made a marital commitment that could not be easily changed, at least not in the short term and so now, he had to find a way to manage the difficult situation that he had ultimately placed himself in and that was fast becoming a huge challenge for him.

Once Samson arrived outside the restaurant, the limousine that he had hired was parked next the front entrance and as he stepped out of the vehicle, his bones seemed to rattle around inside his body as he walked towards the two black, glass doors that guarded the front entrance. Since the limousine would not be required by Samson for at least another hour or so, the driver had already been instructed to return in an hour and advised to park somewhere nearby when Samson had exited the vehicle. Every step that Samson took towards the two black glass doors, seemed heavy and laden with guilt and as soon as he neared them, the restaurant doors were politely opened for him by a doorman and as he made his way inside the venue, he silently tried to swallow his guilt as he prepared to wine and dine Rochelle, the female object of his desire.

The table that Samson had booked inside the very expensive, extremely exclusive fine dining venue had been reserved earlier that day because as Samson already knew, Rochelle definitely appreciated and really enjoyed the finer things in life and so he'd made the expensive reservations, just to keep her happy. A private booth had been reserved which was masked from public view because that additional effort Samson hoped, would provide him with a degree of privacy whilst he romanced Rochelle and to some extent protect his marriage from any prying eyes.

Although somehow, Samson had managed to avoid some of his marital duties that weekend and successfully maintained the pretention of singleness, his indiscretions as he was very much aware, would not go undiscovered forever, if he flaunted his affair very publicly in public places and so a private booth had been deemed, absolutely necessary. Every time that Samson met Rochelle in a public place, he ran the risk of being discovered and so he'd reserved a table in a private booth in an attempt to hide his affair as much as he possibly could whilst he simultaneously tried to satisfy Rochelle's romantic expectations. Unfortunately, however as Samson rapidly discovered that evening, he had definitely burnt the candle at both ends as he walked through the reception area of the restaurant because from what Samson could see at first glance, the restaurant was fully booked and it seemed to be very popular amongst the elite of Pinesfield and so he now worried that despite the private booth, someone that the couple both knew might actually spot him.

When Samson was comfortably inside the venue, he quickly began to visually scan the interior of the luxurious restaurant as he searched for Rochelle's beautiful face and as he did so, a waiter quickly approached him and politely offered to assist him. A calm expression was rapidly plastered across Samson's face in an attempt to mask his inner turmoil and his guilt-ridden mind as he politely nodded at the waiter, exchanged a few words to confirm his identity and his reservation and then began to follow the waiter towards the table that he'd reserved and Rochelle.

Unfortunately for Samson, the costs of his affair were rapidly starting to mount because tables in private booths at that particular restaurant, cost an arm and a leg but he adorned his face with a pretentiously relaxed smile as he walked towards the booth and Rochelle because she had already been seated at the table that he'd reserved. Since it was highly likely that Samson would not return to his marital home that night, he had already prepared for that possible eventuality in advance and on his way to the restaurant, he'd called his wife and explained to her that he had to take his associates to a meeting in another city situated a three hour drive away which had essentially, freed him from his martial duties for the entire night once again and so there would be no real rush that evening on Samson's part.

Rather uncomfortably for Samson, the excuses that he had furnished Moira with throughout that day, were far from perfect as he was fully aware but each lie had provided him with a degree of flexibility that would allow him to be absent from his marital home for an entire night because he'd insisted that the meeting was absolutely crucial to his business operations. Some sacrifices had definitely been made by Samson as he had embarked upon and dabbled further in his scandalous affair and those sacrifices it now transpired had not just been Samson's alone to make but also his wife's as she'd coped with his absences and sat faithfully at home alone and just waited for him to return to his real life and their very real marriage. Every flimsy excuse that had been provided by Samson as he'd excused himself from his marital duties that day had been made at the last minute and although Moira had accepted each one, her acceptance on this occasion had been really quite reluctant and her opposition made Samson feel uncomfortable.

A seductive, beautiful smile however, greeted Samson as he sat down opposite Rochelle and then gently touched her hand and as he did so, any thoughts that related to his marriage were pushed firmly from the forefront of his mind as he prepared to indulge in his night of forbidden passion. Several elaborate lies had been lain down that day by Samson and then carefully woven into each other like twigs to form a nest of deception that he would spend his actual night in and so now he felt that at the very least, he had to enjoy the fruits of his deceptive efforts or that all his scheming would have been for absolutely nothing. Due to Samson's lies, Moira had accepted his absence that night, albeit reluctantly and unwillingly which meant, he now had a whole night to spend in a deep sea of sexual passion with Rochelle and he was therefore absolutely determined to thoroughly enjoy it and to see it through until the next morning arrived.

From the monitoring window that contained Leona, Resolve could clearly see that Leona and Nicky had now just met in another part of the busy city center inside an eatery as per their arrangements. Unlike the very expensive, lavish restaurant that Samson had reserved a table at that evening however, Resolve immediately noticed that this dining venue was quite simple, very practical and moderately priced because the two women had opted for an eatery that was reasonable and within easy reach for their pockets. Since Leona had arrived first, she had already been seated at a table when Nicky had arrived and as the two women greeted each other and exchanged warm, friendly smiles, Resolve watched as Nicky sat down and then Leona handed her a menu.

Several tables that were dotted around the interior of the venue were occupied but for the most part, the eatery that the two women had chosen to meet inside was fairly empty because most of the city workers that usually filled up the premises during the weekday evenings had already deserted the corporate concrete jungle in order to prepare for the weekend ahead. The fact that the venue wasn't packed to the brim with human bodies was a comfort to both women however, due to the nature of their discussion which was essentially, private and so when both women had placed their orders and they were left alone once more, they began to discuss what Nicky had discovered, since they'd last met.

INTELLECT: USER REPAIR

Just a few minutes into the two women's discussion, their conversation was briefly interrupted as a mug filled with caramel latte and a pot of mint tea were placed down upon the table by a polite, efficient waitress and they paused for about a minute as they waited for her departure. Once the waitress left the side of the table, the two women then eagerly dove straight back into the purpose of their meeting as they began to discuss Nicky's recent findings and Leona listened attentively as Nicky started to dissect the details of Darin's behavior throughout her past working week. A deep discussion followed as the two women waited for their main meal to arrive as some of Darin's recent antics were divulged to Leona as Nicky explained what she had managed to record throughout that week because she'd actually followed Darin around since their last meeting and recorded most, if not all of his external, public movements.

According to Leona's program that evening, she had two arrangements with third parties and her meeting with Nicky was just the first but as she knew as she listened to Nicky speak, the second meeting with Darin at nine was far less likely to happen because he was way less reliable and so she wasn't really in a rush. From Leona's past experiences with Darin, she had already learnt that it was highly unlikely that he would show up on a Friday evening and if he did show up, it probably wouldn't be until much later than planned which meant, she could hold her meeting with Nicky at her leisure. Since Darin only seemed to show up whenever he felt like it, regardless of what the couple had agreed to and he didn't seem to feel like it very often, Leona doubted that he would even show up at all that evening as she listened to Nicky discuss his recent behavior.

For Leona that evening however, she at least felt comforted by the fact that Nicky had actually turned up and had turned up on time and so their meeting held a lot more promise in its seconds for her because it was more than Darin usually ever did and she'd spent a lot more on him. Upon Leona's face there was now a very focused expression as she sat and listened to Nicky discuss her observations from earlier that week as she began to wonder what exactly Nicky had managed to capture on film. During their telephone conversation on the Thursday evening Nicky had mentioned to Leona on the phone that she had managed to record something useful with regards to Darin's cheating and so now, Leona couldn't wait to see exactly what that something useful actually was.

"Look Leona, please don't get your hopes up too much, I don't have anything totally concrete yet and this might not be enough evidence for you to actually base a decision on but I do have something quite useful." Nicky explained as she quickly dug a camcorder out of her handbag that had been placed on top of an empty chair beside her. "The surveillance operation is proceeding very well and I have made some progress but it has just started, so please don't expect too much."

Leona nodded as she listened. "I understand." She replied.

"I've managed to capture some images of Darin over the past few days with two different women but he mainly spent time with them both in very public places, so the footage doesn't contain any concrete evidence that there's actually any sexual activity taking place." Nicky explained as she opened up the camcorder and then began to show Leona some of the footage that she had collected. "Romantic fumbling yes but full-blown sexual contact, not quite."

"He's definitely cheating though." Leona mourned as she watched some of the footage of Darin in absolute disgust as he slobbered over a complete stranger inside his car. "It's one thing to suspect that he was but quite another thing to actually see it in person."

"Yes, I know, it's absolutely disgusting. Will that be enough for you Leona, or do you need more than that to make a final decision?" Nicky asked as she glanced at Leona's face with an apologetic expression. "Would you like us to keep tracking him, or are you satisfied with this?"

"I think I'll need something a bit more Nicky. I need solid proof that he's actually sexually involved with another woman." Leona replied decisively as she shook her head. "Otherwise, I'll never get rid of him, he'll just try to worm his way out of it and say that they promised him a position of employment if he took them out for dinner or something and that they hit on him when he dropped them off afterwards."

"He sounds like a slippery one." Nicky observed.

"Unfortunately, he is. Darin is very devious, so I'll need a proper shot of him inside the arms and bed of another woman. I need something that he cannot possibly deny and that I can never ever possibly forgive." Leona explained. "We have to keep going until I have that."

"Right. We'll keep going with the surveillance operation." Nicky immediately confirmed as she turned off the camcorder and then placed it back inside her handbag.

"Looks like our food's arrived." Leona mentioned as she suddenly noticed that the waitress had just begun to walk back towards their table with two plates filled with food. "Thank goodness, I'm absolutely starving."

"Me too. I'm just sorry I couldn't provide you with something a bit more substantial yet." Nicky replied.

"Don't worry about it Nicky, it's not your fault that Darin's such an incompetent cheat." Leona joked sarcastically. "Seems he can't even do that right."

"Yes, I did notice that the two women he met didn't seem to take him very seriously." Nicky agreed.

"It's such an embarrassment Nicky, he cheats with women that don't even really like or want him." Leona mourned. "How awful, he's got absolutely no shame."

The conversation between the two women stopped rather abruptly as the waitress drew much closer to their table and then placed the two plates of food down upon it and as they both immediately fell silent, Leona gave the female server a strained smile and polite nod. A current of shock seemed to ripple through Leona's body as she prepared to consume the food on the plate directly in front of her but as she glanced at it, her stomach began to somersault with waves of disgust because what she had just seen had truly repulsed her. In many ways, Leona now wished and hoped that Darin would not actually show up later that evening because after what she had just seen, she could no longer stand the sight of him and as she tried to face her meal, the images of Darin locked in passionate embraces with the two other women continued to flood through her mind and there didn't seem to be anyway to stop them.

"Don't worry Leona, I'll get rid of the awful Darin soon." Resolve promised himself as he glanced at her disappointed, upset face inside the monitoring window on his wall screen and then shook his head in frustration. "He's standing on the edge of the cliff now and I'm almost ready to push him right off it."

Despite the fact that Nicky had shown Leona some footage that evening which had proven beyond any possible shadow of a doubt that Darin really was an actual cheat, Resolve still felt slightly disappointed by what the footage had contained because it hadn't quite been sufficient. Further footage could be captured and collated by Nicky as Resolve already knew but he now began to doubt that it would ever really be sufficient and enough to swing Leona's decision and end Darin's reign of infidelity over her heart because he really wasn't a very proficient cheat and so Nicky's efforts would render minimal results.

At some point, Resolve quietly concluded as he watched the two women start to eat on the visual display wall screen directly in front of him, he would have to step in and provide the actual footage of Darin's unfaithful behavior himself but that intervention would have to be carefully planned and discreetly orchestrated because it really was such a delicate issue. The duty to protect Intellect and its anonymity, was ultimately a core concern for Resolve as he performed his duties as a Life Monitor because every time he intervened, interfered and communicated in a very direct manner with the human world, he ran the risk of discovery. Although the past footage that Resolve had captured had been sufficient and it would immediately convince Leona to dump Darin for good, he really needed something much more current, in order to avoid the arousal of too much suspicion and so that ultimately meant, Darin would have to be enticed to be sexually unfaithful again.

Much to Resolve's satisfaction, he rapidly discovered as he turned his attention back towards Samson and Rochelle that she had already started to put Samson through his financial paces that evening because she'd ordered a very costly three course meal from the menu and the most expensive bottle of champagne on offer to wash it down. Some very direct questions were posed to Samson by Rochelle as she ate her first two courses and Resolve watched joyfully as Samson squirmed all the way through their expensive starters and main courses as he attempted to avoid her discreet but very thorough, intensive interrogation.

Finally, it seemed to Resolve, Samson had met a woman that he could not simply wrap around his little finger and toes and a female that would give him a run for his money and literally take as much of it as she could as she went and that truly delighted him. The satisfaction that Resolve now felt was absolutely delicious and utterly heavenly as he silently rejoiced in the personal drama and very awkward predicament that he had managed to create for Samson which would not be short and sweet like a light, gentle sprint of discomfort but rather a long, slow, painful slog which would be more like a marathon of stress.

For once, Resolve observed, Samson was now in a very unusual position because the incessant demands that he usually placed upon Leona's weary, tired head had now been placed firmly upon his shoulders by Rochelle although her demands did differ vastly in nature, since each one was far more personal. Every time that Rochelle had interacted with Samson, Resolve had seen her demand more and more time and attention from him and much to Resolve's amusement, Samson had literally bent over backwards as he'd tried to appease and please her. Just as Resolve had very accurately predicted, Rochelle's demands had rapidly grown and now the situation had the potential to escalate into a full-blown disaster for Samson and that absolutely delighted Resolve because he wanted Rochelle and the impact of Samson's affair to rock every part of Samson's world.

In some ways, Rochelle had even managed to exceed Resolve's initial expectations as he'd watched her place Samson under more and more pressure in the seductive manner that she was extremely well versed in but there was still one surprise left for Samson that evening and Resolve already knew what that surprise actually was. The final surprise that Rochelle had in store for Samson that night, Resolve felt, would totally knock him off his feet in the most seductive way possible and he hoped that it would eventually, ultimately usher in the start of his actual downfall and then Resolve's plans for Samson would finally come into full fruition and be totally complete.

Once Leona and Nicky had finished their meal, Resolve watched as Leona paid the bill which she politely offered to pay, since it had been her suggestion that the two meet in the eatery that evening and then the two women began to prepare to leave the venue and go their separate ways. A quick discussion was held with Nicky before the two women left the actual table that they had been seated at as Leona retouched upon one of the main issues for her with regards to Nicky's surveillance of Darin and Resolve listened attentively as he tried to understand her position more fully.

"There's definitely two issues here really Nicky, not just one." Leona pointed out. "Darin's potential denial and my acceptance of his betrayal and both need to be satisfied in their entirety once and for all because Darin is a proverbial thorn in my side."

Nicky nodded her head in acceptance. "Yes, I understand." She immediately agreed. "You need a full sense of closure. Something irrefutable, something that will eliminate any doubts, something that will force you to take action and something that will close that chapter of your life forever."

"Exactly." Leona replied. "Denial on Darin's part, or even on my part could be a snare that keeps me tied to his side and that blinds me. Denial at times, can obscure our minds from the hard, heartbreaking truths that we don't want to face, or accept. I need something that he cannot possibly deny and that I can never ever possibly forgive." Leona explained. "Our engagement is not fractured, it's completely and utterly broken and now, it's beyond repair, especially after what I saw today and so I just need the final nail to hammer into Darin's coffin of fake love, so that I can bury our fictitious romance forever."

"Sure, Leona that's not a problem. We'll continue with the surveillance operation until you're totally satisfied." Nicky immediately confirmed. "At least now though, you know what's really going on, so that's a start."

"Yes, Nicky and thanks so much for that clarity." Leona said appreciatively as she rose to her feet. "The truth was hard to see but I really needed to see it."

"Well, at least now you know where you really stand." Nicky advised as she stood up and prepared to depart. "I'm just sorry that your suspicions were right."

Just a couple of minutes later, once a plan of action had been agreed upon for the following week and another meeting scheduled, the two women began to make their way out of the eatery as they prepared to separate. An affectionate, warm, friendly hug was given to Nicky by Leona as she prepared to face her evening ahead which unfortunately, was supposed to include Darin but there was one ray of hope in that rather cloudy sky and that was the possibility that Darin would probably not actually turn up which was highly probable. Despite the fact that the two women were headed in two very different directions as they began their respective journeys home, one thing definitely united them and that was their mission to catch Darin in the act and so in that respect, they both still walked down the same street and that was very sadly for Leona, Darin's street of betrayal as they searched for a definite end and exit.

For Resolve, the meeting between the two women that evening had slightly frustrated him because he had the required footage that would bury Darin's false pretenses forever and free Leona's heart but his hands were currently tied since he had no legitimate, human entry point that he could facilitate. An ounce of patience was definitely required on Resolve's part but he hoped that Darin would stay away from Leona until he could at least find a way to expose Darin's sexual involvement with other women because he did not want Leona to give Darin another chance to talk his way out of anything that he had done.

When Samson and Rochelle's dinner had been fully consumed, the last drop of champagne drunk and everything had been paid for by Samson, the couple then left the restaurant and were immediately whisked away inside the shiny black limousine with dark tinted windows that Samson had hired. The next stop for the two lovers however, was not one that had actually been planned by Samson because towards the end of their meal Rochelle had sprung her final surprise upon him and requested rather persuasively that Samson take her to an estate agent's offices nearby that belonged to one of her acquaintances.

Once again, much to Resolve's amusement, the fact that Rochelle hadn't seen much of Samson since they'd initially met was a point that was utilized as leverage as she'd insisted that their attendance at the real estate offices that evening was absolutely necessary because Samson's availability was so sparse. According to Rochelle, her associate was a very busy person who had taken time out of his schedule specially to see them both together that day and Rochelle had also mentioned that she couldn't really be sure when such an opportunity would present itself again which had absolutely delighted Resolve because the pressure that she placed upon Samson, was just what he needed to feel.

Inside the limousine there was a dark, tinted, glass divide, Resolve rapidly noticed that sat politely between the chauffer's seat and the passenger area at the rear of the vehicle which was closed and as the couple were whisked through the dark city streets, Samson began to make good use of the privacy it offered as he pulled Rochelle towards him. The degree of privacy on offer definitely went in Samson's favor and that Resolve could immediately see as he watched Samson lavish his attention physically upon Rochelle.

"I want you Samson." Rochelle panted in his ear as the limousine sped through the city streets. "I want to feel you inside me every single day and so we need somewhere in the city where we can be together." She insisted seductively as she silently vowed internally to make him pay heavily that day for his lies.

"I want you too Rochelle." Samson replied as he watched Rochelle lower her head as she prepared to orally pleasure him.

Sexual pleasure was certainly one thing that Samson already knew, Rochelle could really deliver and he began to moan quietly as she tantalized him with her lips, tongue and mouth like no other woman had ever done before and as sexual excitement surged through his veins, he eagerly savored every ounce of Rochelle's seductive attention. Everything that Rochelle wanted from Samson that day, deep down inside he already knew, would definitely have to be given to her because there was just no way around her demands and she knew exactly how to get what she wanted out of him.

During one of the lover's initial dates, due to Samson's marital status, he had actually mentioned to Rochelle that he lived a two hour drive away from the heart of the city with his elderly mother and that had been his justification for the facilitation of hotel rooms every time the two met and wanted to spend any time together privately. Several reassurances had been provided to Rochelle that once the two were more serious and they had been seeing each other for a while, Samson would then take her to visit his home and she would meet his elderly mother which would formalize their relationship in his family member's sight. Fortunately for Samson, it seemed as if Rochelle had accepted his fictitious living situation but he definitely knew deep down inside, the situation was far from ideal and that he would have to make some kind of commitment to her that would at least convince Rochelle in the short term that he was very serious about her and sincere and so he began to warm to their pending appointment with the estate agent.

"We need to have somewhere just for us Samson. Somewhere where we can spend time together whenever we want to." Rochelle urged as the limousine came to a sudden stop and she rapidly began to rearrange her clothes. "Hotels are so seedy and so cheap." She insisted. "We need somewhere more private, somewhere where I can make love to you whenever I want to. Somewhere that's truly ours."

A combination of factors immediately convinced Samson to commit to Rochelle's suggestion in theory, even though he had not yet seen any actual properties; the sweetness of her justification, the oral pleasure that he'd just received, the beauty of her face, the deliciousness of her body and last but not least, his own guilt-ridden mind. Unlike hotel rooms and penthouse suites, an apartment would cost Samson a larger sum in the short term because it would involve a bigger financial outlay as he already knew but in the long run, Samson silently hoped that it would work out much cheaper for him because the hotels that he'd taken Rochelle to so far had already cost an absolute fortune and so her suggestion somehow made financial sense.

"Yes, I think you're absolutely right Rochelle, it's a great idea." Samson agreed as the chauffeur suddenly opened the limousine door and he prepared to exit the vehicle. "Are you sure that we'll be able to see the estate agent today though because it is rather late?" He asked. "We could always come back in the morning."

"Don't worry Samson, I made a provisional appointment with Perkins this afternoon for nine and confirmed it again just after dinner, so he'll still be around." Rochelle immediately reassured him as she stepped out of the limousine. "He'll be expecting us and it's only quarter to nine now, so we're actually early."

"Right." Samson replied as he nodded his head.

Everything about Rochelle's request to secure an apartment suddenly seemed to make absolute sense to Samson as the two began to walk towards the estate agent's offices and as Rochelle led the way, Samson began to relax as he accepted that it was actually in his long-term financial interests. Although it would be a significant financial commitment for Samson, it would ultimately provide the ideal solution and solve all his problems in one go when it came to his actual affair because it would convince Rochelle that he was very serious about her which would take the pressure of him and it would also provide him with a private place to stay whenever the two met which would ensure that their affair was less likely to be discovered. A hidden sanctuary and love nest in the heart of the city would enable Samson to conduct his extra marital affair, secretly tucked away from any prying eyes which would protect his marriage and it would also provide

Samson with some much-needed privacy and that meant, he would not have to sacrifice his actual affair prematurely and that it could then continue for as long as he could sustain it.

The exotic and erotic appeal of Rochelle, coupled with her sexual willingness and competence had definitely begun to have an effect upon Samson and so as far as he was concerned, he could not see himself walking away from Rochelle in a hurry and he was in absolutely no rush to do so. From Samson's perspective, Rochelle aroused him in a way that no other lover had ever done before and she seemed to titillate every part of his senses because she made love to him with a hunger, passion and greed that was absolutely irresistible.

Several very simple things about Rochelle like the way she talked, her smile and her touch somehow, sparked and ignited the flames of passion inside Samson and he was rapidly becoming powerless to her charms and his own desire to actually spend more time with her. Between the two lovers an affair had been embarked upon that was rapidly becoming more and more intense, addictive and exhilarating for Samson and now, it almost felt like a roller coaster of enjoyment that he couldn't even begin to attempt to step off because deep down inside he had no actual desire to do so.

Rather intriguingly for Samson it seemed, the more he saw of Rochelle, the more his body and emotions seemed to crave her presence and his mind and body now struggled to control his responses to her because his loyalties had begun to feel emotionally torn. A solution that suited Samson's long-term interests had therefore that day, virtually fallen straight onto his lap and it had actually been proposed to him by Rochelle herself which meant, she would be happier with him, if he committed to it.

"I have to give it to her Samson, she is very devious. You've definitely met your match now and she'll give you a run for your money and grab as much of it as she can." Resolve concluded with a grin as he silently congratulated himself on Rochelle's victory that day which now just lay minutes away from realization.

Upon Resolve's face there was a very satisfied smile as he watched Samson pull open one of the glass doors that guarded the entrance to the estate agent's offices because Resolve already knew something very crucial that Samson actually didn't. Behind Samson's back earlier that week, Rochelle had already paid a visit to Perkin's estate agency and so this would be her second visit of the week, not her first and Resolve also knew that she'd already planned exactly how much money she wanted Samson to spend that evening and which property she wanted him to make an actual financial commitment to and it certainly wasn't cheap.

"Thanks Samson." Rochelle purred as she stepped inside the front sales office of the estate agency. She silently began to internally calculate and prepare herself for the first large sum that she wished to extract from his wallet as she smiled with pretentious adoration. "You're such a gentleman."

Cheap was certainly not Rochelle and since Samson wanted to impress her with lies, trickery and wealth as he pretended to be an affluent, eligible bachelor, Rochelle was more than willing to not only encourage those lustful lies but also to simultaneously capitalize upon each and every one. A luxury apartment had already been identified by Rochelle that was available on a one-year lease and although it was very expensive, she'd definitely felt that Samson's lies warranted the additional expenditure as he had tried to trick her and as far as Rochelle was concerned, lies cost money, a lot of money and especially when those lies had been told to her.

An upmarket residence, Rochelle thoughtfully concluded as she walked towards Perkins and greeted him with a smile, would be a very nice addition to her current living options because then she would be able to go to and from it as she pleased, whenever it suited her and so Samson's deceit had now secretly been transformed into her opportunity. Absolutely everything that Samson held dear financially, Rochelle now wished to take away from him because he wanted to have his cake of deceit and eat it too and unlike his wife, who seemed to tolerate his behavior, she wasn't a sap and Samson would learn that the hard way because now, he had finally met someone that could empty his wallet in a flash.

For Leona, her Friday evening was far from over as she drew close to the entrance of the mews and prepared to return to her home because she had agreed to see Darin at nine but she hadn't rushed home since she really didn't want to see him after what she'd just seen. Usually Darin was late anyway, if he even bothered to turn up to see Leona at all which on a Friday evening, he usually didn't and that was by now, pretty predictable.

The footage that Leona had seen earlier that evening seemed to play over and over inside her mind as she walked as she regurgitated the images of Darin's scandalous affairs which churned around inside her stomach and created a vomit of disgust that sat uncomfortably inside her body as it waited to be released. On top of Leona's disgust, there was now also the additional fear that Darin might actually show up for once that evening and that possibility worried her even more because if he did, the remainder of her Friday would then filled with bags of stress and it would be as if an avalanche of discomfort had fallen on top of her body.

"If I see Darin today, I might puke all over his face." Leona admitted to herself as she approached the entrance of the mews.

Resolve chuckled as he listened. "Now that sounds like a great idea Leona." He quickly agreed. "I know you can't hear me right now but I fully support that course of action."

"I should really get some milk first before I go home." Leona mumbled to herself as she suddenly stopped, paused for a second and then did an about turn. "Lucky I remembered."

Something suddenly began to really bother Resolve as he watched Leona walk back along the city street towards a nearby shop and then enter inside it and that something wasn't even something that Resolve had actually taken any action to correct but he know realized, it was extremely important. In fact, that something was probably even more important than Samson's pending destruction and the exposure of Darin's sordid affairs and that was Leona's own financial position. The issue of Leona's finances and income had not yet been addressed by Resolve but it was one of the most important issues that he had to face and find an actual way to correct.

Economic freedom was definitely something that Leona desperately needed because she was not financially free in any sense of the word in that she was still answerable to Samson every working day and she relied solely upon his company and ultimately him, for her financial survival and as yet Resolve had not done a single thing to change that economic dependency. If Resolve could find a way to give Leona her financial freedom, he would ultimately set her free from the burden of Samson forever because money was the final constraint that wrapped itself around Leona's life and choked her every day and so that was the final issue that Resolve as her Life Monitor absolutely had to resolve.

Just a few minutes later, Resolve watched in total silence as Leona approached the counter inside the shop to pay for the carton of milk that she wanted to purchase and as he did so, something immediately caught his eye on top of the actual shop counter itself. A sudden thunderbolt of ingenuity, rapidly struck Resolve's logical processes and he began to rub his hands together in absolute delight as he chuckled with glee as he stared at an advertisement inside the commercial venue which it seemed could offer him a potential ideal solution to that very precise, economic problem.

The more deeply Resolve considered the advertisement and the potential solution it could offer to him and Leona, the more certain he felt that it could actually make a difference in Leona's life because it could set her free financially forever. In Leona's life there was still one final hurdle that Resolve now faced and the commercial advertisement could potentially offer a means to overcome that financial hurdle because it would allow Leona to leap straight over it.

An economic reliance definitely lurked in the shadows of Leona's life as Resolve was fully aware and Rochelle's affair with Samson would not provide a solution to that particular problem and Resolve had somehow, overlooked that particular issue. The issue of Leona's actual economic dependency upon Samson was very serious and as it begun to niggle away at Resolve's logical processes, it really bothered him because every working day, Leona was still economically answerable to Samson and he had totally missed that problem which now urgently needed to be addressed.

"The destruction of Samson really won't change Leona's financial situation or make her financially independent." Resolve admitted to himself. "It will just make her economically reliant upon someone else's corporate entity and they could be just as horrible to her."

Rather fortunately for Resolve however, Leona had quite unknowingly and very unintentionally, actually provided him with a potential solution to that problem herself but there were a few minor details and slight obstructions that Resolve knew, he would definitely have to iron out before that particular solution could be applied to her life. The aftermath of Samson's destruction, Resolve logically considered, could have a very negative impact upon Leona financially and Samson's downfall could place her in an even more vulnerable economic position but fortunately, a possible solution had now presented itself and Resolve felt adequately equipped to ensure that it could be applied to Leona's actual life when the right time arrived.

According to the advertisement and small counter display, a huge lottery cash prize was up for grabs every week and that delighted Resolve in many ways because he knew that an actual computer system would randomly generate the prize-winning numbers. Fortunately for Resolve, when it came to the issue of computer systems, he had the whole human world at his disposal because he could tap into and manipulate any system in the world, anywhere in the world at any given time, totally at will and on this particular occasion that definitely went in his favor. A computer system created by human beings, controlled the actual prize draw itself which meant, Resolve could easily tap into the system, manipulate the numbers that were generated by it on any given week and then he could ensure that Leona actually won the jackpot prize.

Suddenly it struck Resolve however that there was another potential obstruction to his plan and one that he had not considered yet and that hurdle was really quite large because that issue was Leona herself. Although Leona had been physically situated right next to the advertisement and even purchased goods across the counter that it sat upon, she had shown absolutely no interest whatsoever in the actual lottery display itself and that lack of interest would perhaps be a potential barrier. The lack of interest on Leona's part very clearly illustrated to Resolve that she didn't seem to want to buy an actual lottery ticket and that in this instance, would definitely hamper Resolve's delivery of an actual financial solution because before Resolve could ensure that she won the lottery, Leona would first have to purchase an actual ticket.

Despite the very prominent commercial display, Resolve noticed that Leona had simply ignored it as she had paid for her milk and then immediately left the premises without giving the display so much as a second glance. An actual solution to all Leona's economic woes and the regular frustration that Samson caused in her life had literally jumped into Resolve's form but he could not action that potential solution until Leona herself wanted to participate in it. The perfect solution to the final obstacle in Leona's life had come to Resolve almost like a flash of lightning but that perfect solution, Resolve now fully acknowledged, was absolutely no use to him at all, if Leona did not cooperate and partake in the lottery itself and that meant, Resolve now had to find a way to convince and encourage her to participate.

EMOTIONAL DISTANCE

Due to Darin's supposed arrival which was now due to happen in the next few minutes, once Leona arrived at home, she rapidly began to prepare herself for that awful eventuality with a disgusted expression upon her face, just in case for once, he actually turned up at her door on a Friday evening when agreed. For the very first time however, Leona considered the possibility of not accepting Darin's calls or answering the door, if and when he decided to show up because now even just the thought of him totally repulsed her. The likelihood was that Darin would not show up anyway and so it was highly unlikely that Leona would actually have to avoid him but she began to prepare her mind for that possible event anyway, in case there was an unwelcome miracle and he decided to comply with their arrangements on an actual Friday night.

Inside Leona's stomach the vomit of disgust continued to churn as she stepped into the lounge as she quietly considered that perhaps, she should just switch of her phone and ignore Darin completely because that really would be the easier option. A potential confrontation now loomed upon the horizon of Leona's Friday night and since she had only just managed to enjoy the sanctuary of the mews without the noisy neighbors for about a week, a potentially stressful confrontation with Darin was certainly not desirable or wanted and if she switched off her phone as she knew that would allow her to totally avoid any angry outbursts from Darin, or any direct confrontations with him.

The dark shadow of Darin's infidelity and betrayal now hung-over Leona's weekend but in some ways, she felt slightly relieved because at the very least, she now knew exactly what Darin was really up to behind her back and what he actually did with his free time. Inwardly however, Leona felt unsure that she could see Darin that evening and not react in some way to what she had seen earlier that day during her meeting with Nicky because the footage had absolutely disgusted her and that was why she now, for the very first time since the couple's romance had begun, wished and hoped that Darin would be a no show.

For Resolve, despite Darin's supposed pending visit which would normally disgust and worry him, the excitement of the lottery advertisement continued to occupy his form as he quickly began to busy himself in the preparation of an actual financial solution to resolve Leona's final obstacle in life. An email from a fictitious company was rapidly prepared in an attempt to encourage Leona to participate in the prize-winning draw because her participation was definitely an essential element to his plan. The elaborate looking email once finished, contained a lottery ticket offer which promised customers that if they didn't win anything from their initial purchase that they would be given ten free entries for the following four weeks which was an amazing offer and so Resolve definitely felt that Leona would at the very least, be tempted to participate.

INTELLECT: USER REPAIR

Once Resolve felt satisfied that the lottery offer was too fabulous to resist, he quickly began to focus upon the fictitious company's identity as he prepared a website landing page to validate the legitimacy of the company that the offer was supposed to be from. An actual corporate existence that appeared to be genuine as Resolve already knew had to be created for the actual company itself that the email claimed to have originated from, or Leona might not participate because she might consider it to be a scam and treat it with suspicion.

A rigged lottery win for Resolve wasn't beyond the realms of achievability but it definitely required Leona's actual participation to occur and that was the most challenging aspect of his plan because Leona did not seem to be interested in the lottery at all. Once Resolve had finished with all his preliminary preparations, he prepared to send the email to Leona's inbox that same evening because he wanted to give Leona a pleasant surprise in an attempt to negate all the disappointment that had been heaped onto her shoulders that Friday, due to her recent discovery regarding Darin's unfaithful antics. The fabulous offer Resolve definitely felt, would appeal to anyone and so he hoped that Leona would be tempted to participate and cooperate because a solution no matter how elaborate, suitable and appropriate, would be no good at all, if it was not accepted by the human being that it was supposed to assist.

"I can't fix Darin and neither can you Leona." Resolve whispered to himself as he smiled. "But what I can give you is far more superior to an inferior lover that doesn't value your heart. I can give you, your freedom and a joyful life that you can actually live in happily and peacefully and that is worth far more than a deadbeat lover that breaks your heart whenever and as often as he can."

"I bet Darin's not even coming." Leona mentioned to herself as she flopped down onto the sofa and then began to relax. "He's very unreliable but perhaps for once that's actually a good thing because right now, I really can't stand the sight of him."

In some ways, Leona's meeting with Nicky earlier that evening had now liberated her to some extent because it had given her the clarity with regards to the issue of Darin that she had so often yearned for and lacked. The frustration that Leona had so often felt over the years, due to Darin's lies that she could not prove to be actual lies had now begun to melt away but a sense of anger had it seemed, stepped in to replace that frustration because Darin's betrayals it had now transpired, were so very frequent and so heartbreakingly public which meant, he had absolutely no respect for Leona and their relationship at all. Every time that Darin flaunted his unfaithful acts brazenly in public places as far as Leona was concerned, he was basically saying to the whole world that he did not give a dam about his actual relationship with Leona and that hurt her heart even more because he hadn't even tried to hide his indiscretions in order to protect her feelings.

"I really have to sack Darin now and let our engagement go." Leona admitted to herself as she gently shook her head. "Hopefully soon, Nicky will give me what I need to do that very easily and then I'll be able to get on with my life but I guess that means for now, I just have to tolerate him and wait for that to actually happen."

Essentially, deep down inside, Leona had already begun to emotionally detach herself and disconnect from Darin and she had started to walk away from not only Darin but also from the heartbreak that she knew was sure to be bestowed upon her heart in the very near future. Upon the not too distant horizon of Leona's life, more bad news definitely waited to be discovered and revealed regarding Darin's betrayals but she had already accepted that very uncomfortable reality and so now, when the heartbreaking revelations did finally arrive, each one would have less of an impact upon her because she would be both emotionally and mentally prepared.

"I guess I should feel grateful really. If Darin had married me and I'd found out about his cheating afterwards, I would have been even more devastated than I am now." Leona convinced herself. "At least I'll get rid of him soon and at least, we haven't had any kids together because that would have been a total nightmare."

The screen of Leona's phone was given a quick glance as she picked it up and then began to quietly inspect it, just to see if Darin had bothered to send her a text but as expected, there were absolutely no communication messages to be seen. Silence on Darin's part was something very normal to Leona now, so it no longer surprised her, even when the couple had made arrangements to meet but his silences now made a lot more sense because those silences had been filled with other women that he had betrayed and disappointed Leona to spend time with behind her back and that heartbreaking reality, absolutely disgusted her.

At the beginning of the couple's relationship, Leona had regularly made the effort to call Darin and text him and she chased him up as she'd tried to encourage him to respect any arrangements that the couple had made but now, she rarely even bothered to do so. Usually, when Darin failed to show up, he rarely answered his calls or replied to any text messages anyway but now, Leona totally understood and knew why on so many occasions in the past, he had not responded.

"I just thought Darin was immature and irresponsible but I guess it really was more than that." Leona mourned as she attempted to comfort herself and nurse her broken heart. "Unfortunately in life, there aren't any nurses for heartbreak or doctors that can fix broken, defective, cheating lovers." She acknowledged.

"Life will change soon Leona, I promise." Resolve reassured himself as he listened to her verbal expressions that contained nothing but sadness, disappointment and heartbreak. "Darin is not the end of your life, he was just a problem and a mistake that crossed your path and soon you'll be free. He was just an example of what love really isn't and what your life shouldn't be."

"Sometimes I guess, you have to experience some bad things and fake relationships in life so that you can learn to really appreciate the good things and real love when they finally do come along." Leona said quietly as she tried to encourage herself. "And Darin is definitely, a very bad thing."

"He really is." Resolve whispered to himself as he nodded his head in agreement. "But don't worry Leona, the bad thing is just about to get kicked out of your life."

Upon Resolve's visual display wall screen there was a sudden flurry of activity and so he quickly turned his attention towards the motion which involved the open monitoring window that contained Rochelle and Samson inside it. Since the two lovers had already arrived at the estate agent's offices, Samson had already been introduced to Perkins and the two were now engaged in an actual discussion with him about an apartment that was on display upon Perkin's computer screen which formed part of his available properties list. A hefty price tag was attached to the one-year property rental agreement that would involve a huge financial outlay, Resolve observed and so

INTELLECT: USER REPAIR

Samson had stood up and had now begun to pace the interior of the estate agent's sales office because the amount under discussion seemed to have caused him some discomfort which absolutely thrilled Resolve.

"This is probably the most suitable property we have at the moment Sir." Perkins explained politely as he glanced at Samson's face.

Prior to the two lover's actual meeting with Perkins that Friday evening, Rochelle had already furnished Perkins with some very precise instructions regarding which properties he should show and offer to Samson that day and so Perkin's available property list which was now on display had already been modified to align with Rochelle's requirements. The property that Rochelle wanted Samson to commit to was therefore now contained within Perkin's list and on display in a more favorable light than it might have been, purely due to the fact that Perkins had modified the list criteria earlier that evening to ensure that the rest of the list was populated with much more expensive alternatives.

Since Perkins had now been a personal friend to Rochelle for many years, they had done several deals together in the past which had usually involved affluent males that Rochelle wanted a financial commitment from and so their property rental routine was by now, well-practiced, very organized and perfectly coordinated. The minute that Samson had arrived inside Perkin's office, Perkins had known exactly what to do with him because the extraction of wealth from an affluent male wasn't unfamiliar territory to Perkins or Rochelle and nor was it something that they hadn't done together before and it suited them both because he had always been paid a generous commission from such deals whenever he'd assisted her. Both parties were therefore as a result, adequately equipped to handle Samson that day and so as Perkins already knew, the main objective of his evening was to extract as much wealth as he possibly could from Samson through a lucrative property rental deal.

"Do you have anything else?" Samson suddenly asked.

"Yes, certainly Sir, I can show you some other available properties if you'd like me to?" Perkins immediately replied as he attempted to give Samson the impression that he was being very cooperative.

Just to validate Samson's experience further and to convince him that he really was getting a good deal as soon as Samson sat back down, Perkins began to show him some other properties that were even more extortionately priced as Rochelle sat and watched the two men in silence. Regardless of the fact that Samson was actually being taken for a ride, Perkins had been instructed by Rochelle to convince him that he was just about to get an absolute bargain and to make him feel as if he wasn't being fleeced and as the two men browsed through a second pre-prepared list of highly priced available properties, Resolve started to chuckle as he watched Samson's eyes widen in total disbelief.

Nothing but silence filled the extravagant looking, lavish cream and gold sales office for a few minutes as Resolve watched Samson absorb the information directly in front of him which it seemed had really shocked him because he sat totally motionless, stared at the screen and did not utter even a single word. The reaction from Samson and the expression upon his face, amused Resolve immensely because Samson was usually very confident, exceedingly arrogant and extremely comfortable, especially when it came to the issue of his financial capacity but for the very first time, since Resolve had begun to monitor him, it now seemed as if Samson was well and truly out of his financial depth.

In terms of Samson's financial resources, Resolve already knew that he was quite wealthy but he was not absolutely dripping with wealth and so the level of expenditure that Rochelle expected from him that evening had definitely pushed him well out of his comfort zone and unfortunately for Samson, there was no rescue in sight. Regardless of Samson's obvious discomfort however, the look upon Rochelle's face, Resolve rapidly noticed, seemed to be pleasant and innocent enough as she discreetly began to push forward with her agenda for the evening.

"If you want us to spend time together Samson, you'll really have to spend some money." Rochelle whispered as she encouraged him to make a financial commitment to the property and the one-year rental agreement.

"Yes, yes, of course. I just wanted to see what else they had available." Samson replied as he offered her a strained smile.

Much to Samson's surprise, the price tag of the apartment that Perkins had shown to him was really rather high and although it was more affordable than all of the other properties on offer, it was still very pricey. When Samson had left home that morning, he hadn't intended to spend such a large sum of money that day but Rochelle wanted a private place where they could spend time together and deep down inside, he did too and so the apartment would be the ideal solution because it would offer the two, a lot of privacy and privacy as Samson knew, certainly wasn't cheap, especially when it related to the enjoyment of extra marital affairs. Now it seemed to Samson however, to secure that privacy and regular sexual access to Rochelle, he would have to spend a very large sum of money, or he would run the risk of looking cheap and give the impression that he was financially inadequate.

An amused expression crossed Resolve's face as he absorbed Samson's reaction to Rochelle's request because he seemed to have completely frozen and his face now had an icy, glassy, paleness about it. In fact, Resolve observed, a slightly painful expression now adorned Samson's face and he had hardly even moved an inch since he'd sat back down and the real estate agent Perkins had shown him the second list of available properties.

"Samson." Rochelle whispered as she gently nudged him and urged him to speak. "Perkins is waiting."

"Could you possibly shorten the rental period, to say around six months?" Samson finally blurted out as he glanced at Perkin's face.

The price of Rochelle's desired love nest was certainly a lot steeper than Samson had expected it to be and so he decisively attempted to try and negotiate more favorable terms because in his mind, he definitely felt that a six-month rental agreement would be sufficient. A prickly sea of discomfort now seemed to surround Samson's body that he could not swim out of and the short dip of lust that he had intended to take had now it seemed, turned into a very long swim in the murky depths of a huge vast sea of financial expenditure and he could see no actual shore of escape to swim towards and no lifeboat appeared to be on its way to rescue him.

"I'm afraid we don't have anything available for such a short period of time Sir." Perkins replied in a slightly sarcastic tone. "We're a real estate agency, not a short-let rentals company."

"Right." Samson said as he released a weary sigh.

"I can give you a virtual tour of the apartment now if you'd like?" Perkins offered as he touched his computer screen and a virtual tour program rapidly began to populate it.

Samson nodded his head as he started to accept defeat. "Thanks." He replied.

In order to preserve Moira's emotions, Samson definitely knew that he needed somewhere private to see Rochelle because the more often he ventured out in public with her, the more likely it was that the two lovers would be seen by someone that Moira knew and that fear of discovery, now really worried him. Adultery as Samson had now discovered, could be a very expensive luxury and that day, he had truly learnt that reality because Rochelle had made it extremely clear that if he wanted unlimited sexual access to a woman like her, he would have to pay for it and put a vast sum of his money where his mouth was.

Although the terms and conditions of the apartment's one-year rental agreement were not what Samson would have preferred, he had been forced into a very awkward position, purely due to his own lies and the real estate agent hadn't helped because he'd almost embarrassed Samson when he had questioned the flexibility of the rental terms. The more expensive alternative properties that Samson had been shown on the second available properties list had finally convinced him however as he'd weighed each one up inside his mind that at least, the apartment was slightly more reasonable in terms of price and since it would provide him with a private venue where he could conduct and indulge in his affair as he wished to, in the long term Samson felt, the expenditure would probably be worth it.

Finally, despite all Samson's initial reservations which had predominantly revolved around the price, he totally caved in and as he began to surrender, he nodded his head in total defeat because there was no real way that he could back out now, without looking like a cheapskate since Rochelle had really put him on the spot. Inside Samson's two palms there were now worried drops of sweat as he prepared to succumb to Rochelle's demands and spend a large sum of money just to avoid looking cheap because after all, he had given her the impression that he was an affluent businessman and bachelor and so now, he was expected to fully live up to the image that he'd presented.

"Great, we'll take it." Samson suddenly announced as he stood up and then began to pace the room again. "Can we see the physical property now?" He asked.

Perkins immediately nodded his head. "Sure, I can show you round the property now if you like Sir." He offered. "And if you sign up today, you can even have the keys to the property this evening."

Upon Resolve's face there was now a very amused, totally delighted smile because Rochelle had ultimately been absolutely victorious that day and Perkins had not only fully supported her demands but they'd also both managed to place Samson in a very awkward position and one that he had definitely not expected. In terms of Samson's affair, Rochelle had now quickly become a very expensive overhead that he was expected to financially maintain in order to satisfy his sexual desires and that day, his financial prowess had been fully put to the test as Resolve had watched Rochelle put Samson through his financial paces. The wallet inside Samson's pocket was now expected to meet all the financial requirements of his very expensive affair and that was the essence of his relationship with Rochelle and so as Resolve already knew, the extraction of Samson's financial resources and his discomfort had really, only just begun.

Only two predators remained attached to Leona's life now, Samson and Darin because the noisy neighbors from next door hadn't yet returned but Resolve expected them to be far less trouble, when and if they ever did. In the very near future, Resolve fully intended to eradicate both Samson and Darin from Leona's environment completely as he already knew but just their very presence alone and the impact that they had upon her life, continued to needle away and grate against his logical processes each day as he watched them cause Leona stress in total annoyance. Some actions had definitely been taken to deal with the two men by Resolve but now, he just couldn't wait to actually get rid of them both because they served absolutely no useful purpose to Leona's life and brought not even a drop of joy to her existence.

Suddenly, Leona's cellphone started to ring and she immediately picked it up, glanced at the screen and then gently shook her head as a weary sigh managed to escape from her lips. The phone call as Leona could clearly see from the name that appeared on the small screen was definitely from Darin and she could bet every penny she had that he'd called to say, he couldn't make it that evening but for once, Leona didn't actually feel bothered about that potential disappointment at all. In fact, on this particular occasion, Darin's absence was definitely preferred because now that Nicky had her radar fixed firmly upon him, Leona felt much more relaxed about life in general and even about his consistently unreliable and dramatic behavior.

"Hi Darin." Leona said solemnly as after about eight rings, she finally managed to muster up enough strength to answer his call. "Am I seeing you today, or has something come up?" She asked as she discreetly encouraged him to back out of their arrangements.

"You know babes, I won't be able to make it today. I have this interview first thing in the morning quite close to my house, so I think it'll be better if I stay at home tonight."

Darin replied. "I should prepare for the interview properly, it's for a really good job."

"Cool. What's the job Darin?" Leona asked, even though she already knew that the whole excuse was probably a total lie but she just wanted to allow him to elaborate further and give him the impression that she still supported and believed him.

"Well, it's just a bar job but it is a supervisor's role." Darin explained. "That's why I have to be there early on Saturday morning. If I get through the initial interview, they'll want me to do a trial shift on the Saturday night." He continued.

"Okay, well good luck and maybe I'll see you on Sunday instead." Leona immediately replied as she began to shake her head. "If you're not working that is."

Another minute or so went by as Leona listened patiently to Darin as he continued to speak but he said absolutely nothing meaningful and not even a word that interested her and once the call had ended, Leona breathed a huge sigh of relief as she finally got rid of Darin's verbal presence for the remainder of her Friday night because it truly was extremely distasteful and totally repulsive. One worry did still lie inside Leona's mind, once the call from Darin had ended however because a tiny part of her now felt extremely worried about how she would feel when Nicky actually presented some actual footage to her of Darin in another woman's bed. The clarity that Leona needed would definitely shock her and that she already knew but it would also hurt and disgust her and once the initial shock had worn off and finally disappeared, sadly the hurt and disgust would still remain which would not be so easy to shake off because those memories would be like thorns of pain that would remain inside Leona's mind which would prick her thoughts and haunt her, probably for years to come.

Irrefutable evidence and final confirmation that Darin did actually, sexually cheat with other women behind Leona's back would also present another tricky issue to her and that tricky issue was one that she would not only have to face but also handle and that very thorny issue was the couple's actual breakup itself. Since Darin did have quite an aggressive nature and a vicious temper, Leona usually avoided any confrontations with Darin that would stoke the fires of his anger as often as she possibly could but to dump him, she would perhaps have to prod that fire head on and that worried her profusely because she wasn't particularly great at ugly confrontations.

"I could always dump Darin over the phone, or by email." Leona thoughtfully reminded herself. "And if I dump him from a distance like Nicky suggested then I wouldn't actually have to see him at all."

A beep suddenly emanated from Leona's laptop which rapidly interrupted her thoughts as an unexpected email arrived and she quickly leant towards the device which was situated on top of the coffee table as her curiosity urged her to see what the actual email was about.

"I hardly ever get any emails from anyone anymore and especially not on a weekend, I wonder who it's from." Leona whispered to herself. "The last surprise email I received, helped me catch Darin cheating, so this one might be just as great or just as helpful."

Inside Leona's mind as she started to open up the email, a volcano of joyful curiosity rapidly began to erupt which immediately tickled the pores of her skin as she quietly observed that it was once again from an unknown sender and she was instantly intrigued.

"At least someone's thinking about me and wants to communicate with me although Darin it seems, really doesn't because he'd rather communicate and spend his time with other women that don't really want him." Leona mentioned thoughtfully to herself as she began to read the email.

The last unexpected email that Leona had received had led her to the discovery that Darin was actually cheating and so now, a spark of hope had been ignited inside her heart as she began to read the contents of the email that this one might be equally as helpful. From what Leona could see at first glance, the message appeared to be some kind of marketing message and promotional offer that related to lottery tickets but since she definitely hadn't signed up for it, a confused expression adorned her face as she silently started to digest the contents of the message that the email contained as she wondered who could have possibly sent it to her.

"How interesting and how very strange." Leona whispered to herself. "I've never played the lottery before or even thought about it."

Generally speaking, gambling wasn't something that Leona usually paid much attention to, regularly participated in or even had much interest in and although it didn't normally appeal to her, this particular offer did look absolutely fantastic as she read through the email several times and silently devoured and processed the information it contained. An unusual temptation suddenly seemed to grip Leona's mind and body as she quietly entertained the prospect of her participation and bravely decided to dabble in a flutter because the prize on offer was absolutely huge and to gamble once or twice in her lifetime, purely for the fun of It she figured, wouldn't hurt anyone or cause her any discomfort.

In the past, Leona considered thoughtfully, she had always shied away from gambling in general because she didn't feel as if she was particularly lucky, so it would be totally out of character for her but in the past, she'd also made the decision to engage a cheating scoundrel like Darin which now implied that perhaps her life could do with an appraisal and some changes. A slight change in her approach to life, even just once or twice, Leona silently decided, wasn't necessarily a bad thing and it would perhaps be good for her because if she won the jackpot prize, she would then no longer have to spend even a second more of her time in Samson's employment and that would definitely be extremely pleasant for her.

"I don't usually gamble and I probably won't win anything but it's definitely worth a try because if I do win the prize, I could get rid of Samson forever." Leona convinced herself as she shrugged her shoulders and then clicked on one of the links which led to the landing page of a very corporate looking website. "It doesn't hurt to try sometimes." She mentioned decisively as she began to make an immediate purchase.

Just a minute or so later, a confirmation email landed in Leona's inbox to confirm her purchase and a sudden beep sounded out into the air as the email arrived. Upon Leona's face there was an enthusiastic and excited smile as she quickly opened the email up and then began to read the contents it contained as the email immediately confirmed to her that the numbers she had chosen had been entered into the next prize draw that was due to be held the following Friday at nine in the evening. Something quite unusual however, at the very foot of the email suddenly caught Leona's eye and a slightly confused expression rapidly crossed her face as she began to read the final line of text that the email contained.

"Everything that you do in life is a gamble. Resolve." Leona said as she read the sentence at the end of the email out loud and began to internally question what it might actually mean and who could have possibly written it. "How mysterious and it seems so very personal, it's almost as if they're speaking directly to me." She observed. "And who on earth is Resolve?" Leona questioned.

All of a sudden, it seemed as if from out of nowhere, a puzzle had landed upon the runway of Leona's life and she now felt slightly confused as to why she had been sent the mysterious message because she didn't know anyone called Resolve. The strange message absolutely intrigued Leona however and she read it out loud several more times as she considered it thoughtfully because Resolve was a very unusual name and the message seemed so personal but she definitely felt that she'd remember, if she had met someone before with that actual name. Due to the lack of answers, a flurry of questions rapidly began to scurry through the passageways of Leona's mind and as each one tugged away on her brain cells like a naughty schoolboy that repeatedly teased her, she read the email message over and over again but no actual answers were forthcoming.

"Perhaps it's just an automatic marketing message from the lottery company or their third-party vendor." Leona finally convinced herself. "After all, there's no other explanation that would explain how 'Resolve' would know that I had just bought a lottery ticket and that I don't really gamble because I don't know anyone called Resolve."

Despite the multitude of questions that had now formed inside Leona's mind regarding the whole lottery ticket email and the strange message that the confirmation email had contained however, no actual answers appeared and all that greeted Leona was total silence. One particular aspect of the final sentence contained inside the confirmation email rather intriguingly, began to provoke Leona to enter into much deeper thought as she started to consider that perhaps the email message was actually right because in many ways, most decisions in life did involve a gamble of one kind or another.

"I guess the message is kind of right though." Leona mentioned to herself thoughtfully. "When I met Darin it really was a gamble of love because I didn't know whether he would appreciate, cherish and love my heart or break it and he definitely broke it, hundreds of times."

A relationship of any kind with a friend or lover, Leona concluded decisively, was in fact, an emotional gamble because when you opened up the gates of trust that guarded your heart to someone else and let them into your life, you took a chance that another human being could then utilize to potentially betray, hurt or disappoint you and the potential outcomes of those relationships were totally unforeseeable and absolutely unpredictable.

"Thank goodness I've already had something to eat because if I'd waited for Darin to show up before I ate dinner tonight, I'd have starved. I definitely lost the gamble of love when I made an emotional investment into Darin because I gave my heart to a total deadbeat and ended up with shattered dreams, a crushed heart and five years of solid pain." Leona mourned as her mind reverted back to the issue of the unreliable man that she'd mistakenly given her heart to.

Unfortunately for Leona, she had now definitely lost her emotional investment into Darin and their relationship because it had now transpired that he was indeed, a total loverat, just as she'd suspected and so she had gambled five years of her life away for nothing because she'd placed all of her heart on a total deadbeat. Very sadly for Leona, from this particular gamble of love, there would be no romantic winnings because there would be no happy marital bliss and so all that remained was just the miserable pain of Darin's cheating losses which had wiped out five years of love and there were still more arrows of painful revelation to come that would shatter every part of her heart because the heartbreaking losses from Darin's betrayals would eventually, tear it from its ribcage.

"You never know though, I could win the lottery and that would really cheer me up because then I could afford to get rid of both Darin and Samson in less than a week." Leona reassured herself as she attempted to find some tiny grains of hope and comfort in the midst of her hopelessly unromantic situation and stressful professional life. "If I won the lottery, I could pay for the decoy service and catch Darin very quickly and I could also resign immediately and that would mean, no more Samson and no more Darin. Now that would be absolutely delightful."

"Don't worry Leona, this gamble, unlike Darin will definitely be worth it." Resolve reassured himself. "And now, you actually know my name, so that's made my day."

A wave of tremendous satisfaction suddenly seemed to wash over Resolve's form as he rejoiced in the knowledge that Leona now knew his actual name because that was the first real step Resolve had taken to slightly reduce the huge emotional distance that separated them both. Events prior to their creation had predetermined their separation because Leona had been given a real human life upon the human Earth, whereas Resolve had been artificially created in a plane of existence that the human world was predominantly unaware of but now, Resolve had taken the very first step towards the reduction of that huge gap because he'd started to walk across the bridge of love inside his heart towards Leona.

The various simulations that Resolve had embarked upon as he had dabbled in the experience of a human existence had not done anything at all to reduce the huge gap between the two although each one had comforted him to some extent but now, a real step had been taken and that step had brought Resolve into Leona's real human life. A name was something that gave human beings an identity, an actual existence and a name meant something to those in a human being's social circles and to those that they loved and so now, Resolve finally had a name that a real human being had uttered which meant, he now existed not only in Leona's human mind but also inside the real, mortal human world. Upon Resolve's face there was a triumphant smile as he stared at Leona upon his visual display wall screen and wished that he could be next to her but only one small step could be taken so far because the bridge of love inside Resolve's heart was still under construction and as yet, he didn't have the equipment, tools, knowledge or skills to complete it in order to reach her.

"It's a small price to pay really and definitely worth the risk because I could get rid of Samson and Darin forever." Leona convinced herself. "If I win the jackpot prize, I can get rid of those two in a flash and that would definitely be money well spent."

The financial risk that Leona had taken that evening certainly wasn't huge in comparison to the potential rewards on offer but it was as far as Leona was concerned, definitely worth it because to be able to eject Samson and Darin from her life completely, would be a dream come true although as yet, there were no actual guarantees that Leona would win anything, never mind win the main jackpot prize.

"Darin needs to be kicked out of your life completely Leona before you win the jackpot prize." Resolve instructed himself. "But don't worry, I'll make sure that his permanent departure actually happens this time."

"I guess work is a gamble too because when you're employed by someone, you take a gamble that your employer will treat you with respect and sometimes, they don't." Leona advised herself as she thoughtfully began to explore and reflect upon the mysterious words that had been written inside the email even further. "And when you have a boss like Samson that gamble ends up being a total nightmare. I just can't believe Samson sometimes, he's very chauvinistic. We women fought for the right to vote and to be compensated with equal pay for the work that we do, well the suffragettes did and he totally negates every aspect and every second of that struggle. If any of those ladies were alive today and met Samson, they'd probably hit him over the head with their handbags and chain him to some railings until he promised to behave like a decent human being."

Inside the heart of Intellect as Resolve watched and listened to Leona, he smiled because each word that she spoke provided him with a blanket of comfort and a pillow of reassurance that sat comfortably upon the bed of his logical processes that at the very least, Leona wanted the same things from her own life that he wanted for her. Soon, all Leona's troubles would be over, Resolve hoped and although Leona's life had required the most extensive resolution operation that he had ever undertaken for a human being that he'd been assigned to since his own creation, it had definitely been worth it because every aspect of the work that he'd performed within Intellect, would be considered a significant achievement when it came to his role as a Life Monitor. One slight shortfall did still exist as far as Resolve was concerned but that purely related to his own desires because the actual resolution of all Leona's problems had not changed anything that he felt personally for her inside his non-human form.

INTELLECT: USER REPAIR

"One day Leona, I'll actually be a real human being and I'll be a decent one and one day, I'll take you out for dinner." Resolve promised himself. "You won't starve when I'm around."

No other desire had occupied Resolve's logical processes in quite the same way that his desire to be beside Leona had and ever since he'd first set his electronic eyes upon her human body, he had longed to love her, yearned to stand by her side in a human vessel and fervently thirsted to walk the human face of the Earth beside her with every particle of his intangible form and non-human existence. Nothing else it seemed, could replace or be an actual substitute to that very powerful desire because Resolve simply could not forget about it and so now, it almost seemed to consume him every single human day and night. The warm, fuzzy sensation that Leona provoked inside Resolve's form never seemed to depart and at times, when Resolve glanced at Leona's face upon his wall screen that sensation seemed to swirl around inside of him rather chaotically and it was almost as if there was an invisible whirlpool of joy, desire and adoration that now lived within every code that formed his core processes and that controlled every single one of his functions.

"It feels so very strange to be so very close, yet so very far away from everything that you want with every particle of your existence." Resolve whispered to himself. "It's so strange to have achieved so much, yet to be so unable to achieve the one thing that you really want more than anything else in the entire universe."

In some ways, although Resolve now felt quite satisfied by his recent achievements and even slightly comforted by them, he definitely needed to feel something more and that something more was Leona's physical human presence beside his own form. A slight modification in the form of humanization would of course be required to Resolve's intangible structure, if that was indeed actually possible, for his desires to be truly realized in their fullness because he doubted that Leona would want to spend the remainder of her mortal, human lifetime with an intangible life form. The final hurdles in Leona's life were now just about to be leapt over which would mean that Resolve had officially resolved all of the problems in Leona's life but now, he faced his own hurdle and unlike Leona's hurdles, he had no actual Life Monitor to assist him.

"One day Leona, there won't be this huge distance and this impenetrable barrier between us anymore because my heart is a bridge that we can meet upon and my love for you will be a land that we can happily live inside every single day." Resolve vowed as he glanced at Leona's face and smiled.

For the meantime, Resolve began to silently accept, the sensation of satisfaction that he felt would definitely have to suffice and be enough for him because his most precious desires could not yet be realized but every time Resolve set his electronic eyes upon Leona's smile, his appetite to hold her in his arms was wet and his hunger to become human deepened. A blanket of encouragement suddenly seemed to fall over Resolve's form as he continued to watch Leona in total fascination and as a layer of comfort silently wrapped its gentle warm arms around him, he began to appreciate and celebrate his achievements with regards to Leona's life and the reality that he really had now, almost fully repaired every single aspect of her life.

"At least now Leona, if I find a way to become human and I do manage to join you, you won't have any of that stress around you anymore. So, you'll be much happier and so will I." Resolve encouraged himself.

INTELLECT: USER REPAIR

The possibility of becoming human and being able to join Leona one day, sat just upon the horizon of Resolve's non-human dreams and as he entertained the delightful prospect that his work as a Life Monitor could perhaps allow him to enjoy a life with Leona that was stress free, pleasant and enjoyable, he smiled. If Resolve ever did actually manage to find a way to become a human being and join Leona on the surface of the human Earth and if she accepted Resolve into her life and heart, his efforts as her Life Monitor had ensured that Leona would be in a position of joy not misery when they met and that was for Resolve, a tremendous comfort. Life would no longer be the pit of misery that Leona had once resided in because now, she would be free from the troublesome burdens and the sackfuls of stress that she had carried around with her for so very long and that reality which had been Resolve's most recent achievement, absolutely delighted him.

Since the estate agent Perkins had by this point, Resolve observed, deserted the premises that he'd taken Samson and Rochelle to view, once Samson had signed the paperwork, transferred the required sum and as soon as he'd shown them around, Rochelle and Samson had now been left alone inside the property that Samson had financially committed to. The sandy colored building that the apartment was situated inside formed part of a private gated community with several similar buildings stationed at various intervals along a small private road and because it was in the heart of the city, the apartments it contained usually commanded premium rates and much to Resolve's amusement that day, Samson had paid that premium rate as he'd parted with a very large lump sum in one go, just to avoid any future financial complexities.

In order to disguise the rather large item of expenditure, Resolve had noticed that Samson had charged the amount straight to his corporate account under the guise of accommodation required for business associates which fully aligned with the excuses that he'd provided to Moira regarding his absences. The bank account that the actual sum of money had been extracted from, Resolve already knew, Moira had absolutely no access to because it was a corporate bank account which also meant, she would not see the huge financial splurge and so it was highly unlikely that she would ever know about it, or be able to question it so Samson it seemed had taken every possible precautionary measure, just to ensure that he concealed his adulterous expenditure as much as he possibly could.

Due to the fact that Samson shared a private bank account with his wife, Resolve understood that he couldn't possibly charge the expense for his love nest to that account because Moira would definitely notice such a large item of expenditure straight away and question it immediately and so it would be written off at the end of the financial year through Samson's business accounts to avoid any suspicion. Awkward questions would be raised by Moira, if the expenditure had come out of the couple's shared private bank account and as Resolve could clearly see, Samson had absolutely no desire whatsoever to provide any answers to anyone about his sordid love nest, his affair, or his very demanding, expensive mistress.

Everything about the apartment and the apartment building that Rochelle had chosen was extremely lavish and very luxurious and so Samson could hardly argue about the cost because it was totally justifiable, since every intricate detail had been meticulously planned and delivered to absolute residential perfection. From the mirrored glass and gold elevator that led to each floor, to the refined rooftop gardens on the roof of the building, everything about the building oozed class and it was the height of absolute luxury and so once Samson had physically viewed the apartment, he had parted with the required sum with minimal fuss.

"This apartment is absolutely amazing Samson." Rochelle gushed as she gasped in delight. "Now we can spend time together properly and we don't have to spend our nights bottled up in seedy hotel rooms anymore."

Several more gasps of sheer delight escaped from Rochelle's lips as she began to walk around the interior of the apartment as she rejoiced in the fact that on that particular day, Samson had given her everything she'd wanted very easily because that now meant, she had him exactly where she wanted him. Another goal still remained inside Rochelle's mind however, so she wasn't quite finished with Samson's wallet that night and so she quietly began to scheme about her next mission of wealth extraction because the apartment had been just the first item on her shopping list and as she did so, she continued to admire the apartment which occupied the whole floor of the apartment building.

On one side of the very large, open plan lounge and kitchen there was a row of windows which stretched from the floor all the way up to the ceiling that occupied an entire wall and Rochelle suddenly began to walk towards the huge sheets of glass as she admired the view which sat directly outside each one. At the very foot of the building, a sparkling river wound its way playfully around one side of the perimeter walls which Rochelle was absolutely thrilled about as she joyfully absorbed every inch of her surroundings because it could clearly be seen and appreciated from her current position on the seventh floor.

"Yes, it is a very nice apartment." Samson agreed as he walked towards the large windows and joined her.

For at least the next ten minutes, Rochelle enthusiastically led Samson around every inch of the apartment's interior as she joyfully celebrated every single item of luxury that she could find inside it and as Resolve watched Rochelle rejoice in her victory, he chuckled. The royal purple, rich gold and gentle cream tones that adorned the walls shimmered and shone as each block of color gave the apartment an expensive feel and the black and cream furnishings that oozed and dripped with luxury, seemed to please Rochelle immensely as Resolve listened to her chatter away.

At one end of the huge open plan lounge there was a large, well equipped kitchen which had been filled with top of the range, modern appliances but Resolve doubted very much as he glanced at each one that those pieces of culinary equipment would see much action. For the next year, Resolve logically considered, those appliances would probably remain totally idle because Rochelle wasn't really the kind of women that liked to get her nails dirty, or the type of women that would labor over a hot stove for hours just to make Samson or herself a home cooked meal and since Samson rarely even so much as stepped inside a kitchen that was pretty predictable.

"This is just the start of us Samson." Rochelle vowed as she led Samson seductively back towards the large black and cream leather sofa inside lounge and then encouraged him to sit down. She quickly straddled his legs and then smiled at him as she gazed into his eyes with pretentious adoration. "We're going to do so much together."

"Well, I have paid for everything upfront, so that means you have the apartment for a whole year." Samson replied. "So technically, you can stay here as often as you like and even stay here all the time if you want to."

"And I definitely will Samson." Rochelle rapidly confirmed. "After all who wouldn't want to? This apartment is absolutely heavenly."

Almost every minute of Rochelle's Friday evening so far had been absolutely victorious and as she internally relished her first large victory, she silently began to prepare for the next item on her shopping agenda which definitely involved Samson's wallet but no actual retail stores. Shortly and according to Rochelle's intricate, devious plans, Samson would actually discover that very same day that she was far from finished with his finances and his wallet and then he would learn exactly what she was really made off and it certainly wasn't sugar and spice, or anything nice.

Just as Rochelle had expected, Samson had asked her to sign the documents and take legal but not financial responsibility for the rental property for the year which suited her perfectly and so she'd participated willingly as once again, his actions had silently confirmed to her that he was indeed a married man looking for a love nest in which to stoke his rod of adulterous lust. Whether or not anyone actually knew about the affair that Samson had embarked upon, was another issue entirely that didn't bother Rochelle in the slightest because she had just become involved in Samson's adulterous affair in order to siphon off as much of Samson's wealth as she possibly could.

The rapid, calculated, devious capitalization upon Samson's lust and his adulterous nature was very much deserved, Rochelle felt, from what she had seen so far with regards to Samson's approach to life and his attitude towards his marriage and women and so she felt totally at peace with her approach to Samson and his wallet. Now as far as Rochelle was concerned, the whole issue of Samson's wife and the secrecy of their romantic involvement had just become a tool of leverage for her that would ultimately give her access to more of Samson's financial resources and so it was definitely one that she intended to utilize to extract as much money as she possibly could from Samson in the near future.

Frequently, since the couple's initial meeting, Rochelle had sent Samson flirtatious text messages that contained sexual innuendos and erotic words inside them and she'd even called him several times very late at night and he had always answered her calls and so she had intentionally made their affair obvious to anyone and everyone that might possibly be around him. From Rochelle's point of view, her overt displays meant that even if Samson had attempted to hide his affair from his wife, she had now provided some very obvious signs of her presence in Samson's life and so as far as Rochelle was concerned, his wife should really, already know that Samson was an actual cheat. If Samson's wife chose to deny those blatant signs, ignore his obvious transgressions and overlook his flamboyant disregard for their marriage that was not something that Rochelle felt had anything to do with her and so worries about Samson's marriage did not haunt her thoughts or occupy her mind at all.

Despite the fact that Samson had already spent a pretty packet that day on the lover's supposed love nest, Rochelle remained totally dissatisfied and so she silently began to prepare to unleash the next part of her plan upon Samson's wallet because she definitely wanted more. The money and lavish gifts that Samson had thrown at Rochelle so far had in her mind been his recompense for the lies that he'd told and the secrets that he had kept from her but she was expensive woman to appease and so Samson was not going to be allowed to fall short of her very expensive expectations.

INTELLECT: USER REPAIR

"When will you be moving in Samson?" Rochelle suddenly asked as she pressed him for a commitment that she knew, he could not really give. "Now that we have an actual home, you should move in too. You can always hire someone to look after your mother."

A blanket of silence seemed to suddenly fall across the room as Samson glanced at Rochelle's face with a nervous expression and then looked up at the ceiling as he hesitated for a moment and rapidly began to search his mind and the ceiling for an appropriate response, a suitable excuse or any possible escape route. The ceiling however, quite unfortunately, seemed to be totally unwilling to assist Samson in any capacity at all because the cream blank space directly above his head just stared back at him and offered him absolutely nothing in return. Total discomfort suddenly seemed to become Samson's only companion because frustration and stress rapidly began to grip his interior and then silently wound itself around every inch of his flesh as he waited in silence for lightning to strike and an answer to jump into his mind and his mouth.

Rather frustratingly for Samson it now seemed, the apartment that he had hoped would reduce the pressure upon him in the short term had actually increased Rochelle's expectations of him and the result of his gift it appeared had in the end been, counterproductive. Unfortunately, Samson silently concluded, Rochelle now wanted and expected even more from him and that even more was not something that he could provide to her because he already had a marital home, a very real wife and a marriage to maintain and his duty to provide his wife with a marriage as far as he was concerned, far exceeded his romantic duties to any lover.

"Now we can be together every single day and night." Rochelle pointed out enthusiastically as she stroked his hair seductively. "It'll be so romantic and we can make love whenever you want to."

Due to Samson's secret marital commitment, Rochelle already knew full well that her request was absolutely impossible and that it would never be granted but her request was a playful jab at what could never possibly ever be because she wanted to place Samson under more pressure and from what she could clearly see, she'd definitely succeeded. The beads of sweat that now dripped from Samson's forehead absolutely delighted Rochelle as she patiently waited for his response and as she watched the nervous stress accumulate, gather and then drop down onto his cheeks as each drip sought a place of rest further down his face, she silently began to prepare for the verbalization of her next request. From each drop of sweat that dripped from Samson pores, Rochelle could clearly see that she had definitely managed to achieve her goal because she'd managed to cause Samson an ounce of discomfort and that meant, the next item on her agenda could now be presented to him and tackled because she was far from finished with Samson that day and the day as yet had not actually ended.

The silent guilt that lay inside Samson's mind and that greeted Rochelle through his uncomfortable silence, satisfied her no end as it meant that she now had him captive inside a pit of guilt which also meant, her next demand would be granted immediately because he now felt, totally obligated. Guilt as Rochelle already knew, could be a very useful bargaining tool and it would now be one that she would utilize to extract exactly what she wanted from Samson's wallet because that day, a runway of guilt had been meticulously engineered for her plane of financial desires to take off from and land upon. An awkward silence continued to reign inside the apartment for another few minutes as Rochelle held her tongue and just waited patiently for Samson's response as drops of stressful tension continued to drip from his forehead.

"I just can't abandon my mother at the drop of a hat Rochelle." Samson finally blurted out as he nervously attempted to dispel the awkward silence that had gathered between them. "Not yet. She would never accept you if we moved in together before we were even engaged, she's very traditional when it comes to things like romance and romantic relationships." He insisted. "It would be much better if you met her first, then we can get engaged and I can move in afterwards, she'd be much happier with that."

Everything about Rochelle's suggestion had absolutely horrified Samson and as he had silently, reluctantly processed her request inside his mind, his thoughts had grown heavier and heavier by the second as they'd soaked up every word that she had said until his mind had become like a saturated sponge that now sat at the bottom of a murky, stagnant, pond filled with filthy water which stifled his every breath. The ideal sex filled, lustful, passionate affair that Samson had initially imagined and even started to enjoy, was fast becoming a heavy financial burden and a demanding noose that was now being tied around his neck which he had no actual, possible escape from because essentially, he had placed himself in a very difficult position and that now worried him profusely.

"I guess you're right Samson, it's probably better to wait and make the best impression." Rochelle agreed pretentiously. "After all, we do want your mother to accept our engagement." She continued as she attempted to give him the impression that she had accepted and bought into his lies but inside her mind, their conversation on that particular topic was far from over.

Upon Samson's face, much to Rochelle's delight, there had been a look of sheer horror and total panic as he'd spoken and his negative facial expressions had clearly expressed his discomfort to her which absolutely thrilled Rochelle because that meant, it was definitely time to proceed with the next part of Samson's punishment. Today, Rochelle considered thoughtfully, Samson would learn that she was not a weak woman that he could push around anytime he wanted to and that she was not a wimp that buckled easily because today, he was just about to discover how tough she really, actually was.

"Yes, we really shouldn't rush things Rochelle, my mother's not in the best of health." Samson quickly added as a nervous smile spread out across his face.

A huge internal, silent sigh of relief was suddenly released from inside Samson's body and he immediately began to feel much lighter due to Rochelle's response because although there was no obvious long-term escape route in sight, she had for now it seemed, accepted his flimsy excuses, albeit temporarily. Deep down inside however, Samson already knew, their discussion about that particular issue would not end there and that it would definitely raise its tricky head again at some point in the future because Rochelle didn't seem like the kind of woman that would forgot about things easily and especially not something that was so fundamentally, romantically important.

Lie after lie had been told to Rochelle and so now, Samson almost felt buried by his own deceit and as his deception had drastically increased, he had even stepped out into another area of absolute falsehood and that bunch of lies would not be so easy to avoid because it really was so very huge. Not only had Samson lied to Rochelle about his marital status but he had actually given her the impression that one day, he intended to engage her which was an absolutely impossible eventuality and a total lie. In the long term, Samson definitely knew, he did not intend to leave his wife for an actual affair with anyone and so he had now begun to tread upon very dangerous, treacherous, romantic territory because the promise of an engagement was a huge promise to make to anybody and it was certainly not a promise that it would be easy to escape from.

"Okay Samson, we'll wait." Rochelle agreed as she flashed him a pretentiously innocent smile as she internally prepared to dive straight into the next item on her wealth extraction agenda.

"Now unlike Darin, Rochelle's extremely competent and very professional at being devious." Resolve concluded as he watched her inside the monitoring window on the visual display wall screen directly in front of him with a satisfied smile because she handled Samson almost like a professional scam artist.

Despite Samson's obvious discomfort and his excuses, Rochelle it seemed had decided to eagerly plough full steam ahead that evening and she had ensured that she'd taken from Samson exactly what she had wanted that day and as Resolve had watched her, he'd chuckled in amusement. Very much like the stress that Samson delivered to Leona every day, Rochelle had now delivered a portion of utter stress straight to Samson's door and although it was slightly different in nature to Samson's usual stress, for Resolve that mattered very little because it truly, absolutely delighted him.

The tactics that Rochelle had unleashed upon Samson that day, Resolve hoped would eventually strangle him financially and to Resolve that suffering was long overdue and as yet, the Friday wasn't even over. Unlike Moira,

Rochelle definitely meant business and Samson would not be spared from her devious nature because as Resolve already knew, she wasn't the type of woman that would allow him to take her for granted and so it was expected that she would pile more and more stress onto the top of his very chauvinistic head until she'd bled him dry financially.

"You know Samson, I think I should start a business." Rochelle suddenly suggested as she seductively opened Samson's shirt and then playfully began to caress his chest. "So that I'll have something to do and something that will keep me busy when you're not here and that way, I won't feel lonely or get bored."

"What exactly did you have in mind?" Samson asked.

"Well, I'd like to be financially independent, so I've researched this business that I'm interested in and it looks very profitable." Rochelle explained as she presented the next item on her agenda to his ears as she smiled with pretentious adoration and then began to unzip his trousers. "It's related to cosmetics."

"Sounds great." Samson replied as he began to relax.

Much to Samson's sheer relief, Rochelle seemed to have actually accepted his lies for the time being because the issue of living together had now been left to rest and so he began to nod his head enthusiastically as he relaxed once more and started to focus upon their sexual intimacy. Sexual arousal was almost instantaneous for Samson as Rochelle began to tease his chest with her lips and tongue and he almost lost his breath as he waited for her to straddle his rod of masculinity and fully satisfy him.

"How much will you need?" Samson panted breathlessly. "For the business I mean."

"I'll need about two million Samson." Rochelle mentioned quite casually as if the amount was absolutely nothing. She paused for a few seconds and then glanced up at his face to observe his reaction before she continued. "It's a very expensive business with a lot of startup costs."

Samson nodded his head as he listened. "Right." He mumbled.

"I've met with an accountant already." Rochelle mentioned. "They've even put together a proper business plan for me."

Due to the quite positive response received from Samson, the sweet smell of success rapidly began to fill Rochelle's nostrils and as the bells of victory rang silently inside her ears, she paused for a few more seconds as she basked in her glorious moment and prepared to savor the victory which she could now almost taste because a large chunk of Samson's wealth would soon be on its way to her actual bank account. Just like a leopard that pounces on its prey and catches it inside their clutches in preparation for its next meal, Rochelle was more than ready to completely devour Samson and the contents of his bank account and after a complex, calculated pursuit, since their initial first date, his second huge moment of weakness had finally arrived and it would definitely be enough to usher in her total victory.

From the look upon Samson's face, Rochelle could immediately sense that despite his corporate success the amount that she had asked for wasn't totally within his means or within easy financial reach for him. Regardless of Samson's financial capabilities and his access to credit facilities however, Rochelle was silently adamant that she wanted that amount and that he would deliver it to her because after all, she had satisfied him in more ways than one, very consistently and she'd also satisfied his sexual desires whenever it had suited him.

Since the second part of Samson's punishment had now officially begun that meant, Rochelle's Friday evening and night had gone totally according to plan and that all the items on her shopping list from Samson's wallet had now been ordered but as she waited for him to respond, she withheld sexual intimacy and satisfaction from him until she at least had some kind of commitment from his mind and mouth. Upon Rochelle's face there was smile as she watched Samson swallow nervously as he began to squirm and as she started to enjoy every second of discomfort that Samson now seemed to feel, not even a drop of mercy was spared because Samson had lied to her face so many times now and so she fully intended to extract every single penny from him that she possibly could. The second very large extraction from Samson's accumulated wealth would not be the end of Rochelle's financial demands as she already knew because in the very near future, she definitely had more requests to present to him and none of them would be small enough to be fulfilled in the blink of an eye which meant, Samson would soon understand just how expensive his lies really were.

When Rochelle finally bored of Samson and decided to drop him, he would carry the financial wounds that she had inflicted upon him which would leave a permanent scar upon his affluent life and those wounds would serve as a daily reminder of his stupidity and his deceit. In fact, it was also highly likely that by the time Rochelle had finished with Samson, he would not even dare to take another woman for granted ever again because he certainly wouldn't get away lightly with the lies that he'd told her.

"Give me a few days please Rochelle." Samson implored as he finally managed to squeeze a few words out of his reluctant lips. He gave her a polite nod of reassurance as he inhaled deeply because a flurry of questions now ran chaotically around inside his mind as to how exactly he was going to find such a large sum of money in such a short space of time. "I'll see what I can do." Samson promised.

"Sure Samson." Rochelle replied as she smiled in total delight.

Fortunately for Samson on this occasion, the response that he had offered to Rochelle seemed to satisfy her because she very politely, immediately resumed the task of providing him with sexual pleasure as she passionately straddled his masculinity and then began to rock seductively back and forth. Despite the very large sum of money that Samson now had to raise which loomed upon the financial horizon of his life, he quickly decided just to enjoy the moment for what it was and the delicious sexual pleasure that Rochelle was adequately equipped to provide to him because after all that was why he had excused himself from his marital home for the entire night. The large financial request that Rochelle had made and worries about where that money would actually come from could wait, Samson silently concluded as he began to relax, at the very least until he had been sexually satisfied and he'd thoroughly enjoyed his night of forbidden pleasure.

Although there were only two people physically present inside the very large apartment, the two lovers were not totally alone however because an invisible pair of electronic eyes silently watched over them and as they participated and dabbled in their scandalous affair, Resolve monitored everything that occurred between the two in absolute delight. The love affair between Samson and Rochelle it seemed to Resolve had now fully developed and Rochelle, just as planned had plonked a pile of stress firmly down on top of Samson's shoulders and so far, the gifts and money that he had thrown at her hadn't seemed to satisfy her one tiny bit and so for Resolve, Rochelle's dissatisfaction coupled with her high maintenance, monetary expectations were a match made in total, stress filled perfection.

Every ounce of dissatisfaction that Rochelle had displayed towards Samson that evening as she had inflicted two very large financial demands upon him had been orchestrated meticulously and her conduct had amused Resolve no end. In fact, Resolve really couldn't have planned Rochelle's actions more perfectly himself because she truly was a professional man handler and she knew exactly how to deal with slimy toads like Samson.

Various forms of sexual pleasure were politely provided to Samson by Rochelle throughout that night as Resolve watched the two participate eagerly in several acts of sexual intimacy but no actual pleasure was derived from the voyeuristic nature of Resolve's monitoring role because he wasn't a human male and so it did not stimulate him in any way at all. In fact, sexual intimacy between human beings generally, didn't really interest Resolve but he did like to see Samson cheat on his wife, purely because that would help to seal his fate and usher in Samson's actual downfall and of course, every single sexual act that occurred between the two was recorded by Resolve for future usage.

Much to Resolve's delight, the second financial request that Rochelle had made that day had been absolutely huge but it had come as a total surprise even to him because he had not known about it in advance, unlike the apartment that she had roped Samson into paying for. Finally, however, as far as Resolve was concerned, Samson had now met his match and a female that could not only challenge his chauvinistic attitude towards women but that would also use her femininity to her own advantage in order to strip him of his undeserved wealth that had been built through the suffering of the women around him that had supported him so very much. Unlike Moira, Samson's very faithful, extremely devoted and really quite subservient wife, Rochelle's train of thought and her attitude towards Samson were hugely different because she would not take his disrespect lying down and so Resolve began to really appreciate that rather major difference because she had finally put Samson in his place.

Since Samson was now being fully handled by a human being that could actually cope with him and that would deliver enough stress to his life to make him feel extremely uncomfortable, Resolve now felt quite satisfied that his job with regards to Samson had almost been done. Very efficiently and effectively, Rochelle had exceeded Resolve's expectations and it now appeared that she could be more devious, calculated and ruthless than even Samson himself and that was indeed, a very positive outcome for Resolve.

Rather stupidly and quite ignorantly Resolve observed, Samson had not actually realized that Rochelle had seen straight through his lies and so now, he would learn the lesson of his arrogant and obnoxious existence that her wrath could and would inflict upon him and that knowledge provided Resolve with a tremendous amount of comfort. Unlike some other human beings, Resolve had noticed, although Rochelle wasn't physically aggressive or particularly loud, she could certainly take her revenge in a subtle, feminine manner and surely deal with Samson appropriately and that was exactly what Samson required to correct his disrespectful attitude towards the female gender. Now only one predator really remained for Resolve to eject from Leona's life and that was Darin but as Resolve turned his attention back towards Leona and began to watch her as she prepared to rest for the night, he felt ultra-energized and powered up with joy as he silently savored the Friday evening and Rochelle's absolute victory which had ultimately, also been his own.

"I think I should sleep in my bedroom tonight, even though Darin's not here but then he's hardly ever here, so that's nothing new really." Leona convinced herself decisively as she prepared to leave the lounge. "When the noisy neighbors aren't around, it's very peaceful and my bed is extremely comfortable. I guess I'll have to get used to sleeping in my bed alone now because Darin won't be allowed in my bed ever again." She added thoughtfully as she walked towards the door of the lounge. "Darin's nights in my bed are well and truly over."

The noisy neighbors had not yet returned to the mews and so as a result, Resolve noticed that Leona's home was now much more peaceful and a lot calmer and that despite her solitude, due to Darin's cheating nature, she was in relatively good spirits as he watched her make her way towards her bedroom. A blanket of darkness seemed to swiftly gather around Leona's human form as the lights inside Leona's home were switched off and as she made her way towards the rear of the building, Resolve watched the night greedily squeeze every drop of light out of the air and as the night forced each ray of light into hiding, he noticed that the darkness consumed every particle of light it could find until darkness was all that remained.

No matter what did or didn't happen during Leona's human day, there was always one thing that Resolve could be absolutely sure off, her human body required a certain amount of sleep and physical rest every single day in order to keep functioning at optimal capacity because she was a human being and so sleep formed a consistent part of Leona's daily, human routine. The physical necessity of sleep when it came to the actual issue of a human being's daily physical routine, Resolve considered, was a very consistent factor and even more so than dietary intake and various hygiene requirements which it seemed could vary quite significantly at times and that fascinated Resolve as he began to consider the possibility of his own humanization. Sleep and its daily occurrence in the human routine implied that if Resolve ever walked upon the Earth in a human vessel, he too would definitely require sleep at some point every single day because sleep it seemed to mankind, was absolutely non-negotiable which slightly amused Resolve because he had never experienced even a second of total shut down before or a loss of primary functions for even a minute.

A quick glance at the monitoring window that contained Darin rapidly confirmed to Resolve that even though Darin had been preoccupied with his own affairs that evening because he had taken another female out for dinner, yet again he'd been shunned at the end of the evening and so he too was at home now, totally alone. Due to Darin's efforts that night which had borne absolutely no passionate fruit, Resolve noticed that he had already gone to bed by himself and that amused Resolve immensely because Darin really was such a useless cheat. One thing definitely comforted Resolve however as he watched Darin sleep for a few seconds longer and that was the fact that whilst Darin was busy and preoccupied with his sexually unsuccessful cheating habits, he spent a lot less time tangled up in Leona's hair and that due to Darin's unfaithful diversion that evening, Leona's Friday night had been totally Darin free.

"Darin went on another unfaithful diversion tonight Leona." Resolve joked to himself. "He decided to be an unsuccessful cheat once again and so luckily for you, you're totally Darin free for now and you'll probably remain Darin free for the rest of the weekend."

"I guess this is my bedroom, so I should really try to enjoy it." Leona quietly reminded herself as she stepped inside her bedroom and then began to walk towards her bed. "And there's no noise anymore, so I should be able to fall sleep very easily and since Darin won't be around anymore that means, I don't even have to share my gorgeous bed with him ever again."

Absolutely everything about Leona's bedroom as far as she was concerned, was rather splendid because she had spent quite a lot of money just to ensure that it was very comfortable and therefore her bedroom, minus the noisy neighbors and Darin, was a total joy to sleep in. A large part of the room was occupied by the spacious king-size bed that Leona had bought and then placed inside it which she rarely even slept in, since the luxury of her own bed had been denied to her many times, purely due to the noisy neighbors but in Leona's sight, it was totally divine and the height of absolute luxury. Due to the three men's absence from the mews however that luxury bed and all its plump pillows, plush coverings and gorgeous accessories could now be fully appreciated, joyously savored and wholeheartedly enjoyed whenever it suited Leona and she rejoiced in that knowledge as she entered into the warm, cozy, plushness that awaited her occupancy.

Every inch of Leona's bed dripped with comfort and oozed with warmth and as she nestled under the duvet which was adorned with an elegant looking gold and black duvet cover, she began to appreciate just being inside her own bedroom without the presence of the extremely obnoxious and very distasteful, unpleasant Darin anywhere nearby. Only one very prickly thorn still remained in Leona's life and side now and that was essentially, Darin because in recent times even Samson seemed to have calmed down and pretty much left her to her own devices but Darin still remained the same and what was even worse, was the fact that Leona now knew exactly what he was really up to behind her back because his cheating antics were extremely ugly.

Much to Leona's absolute relief however, she considered thoughtfully as she prepared to sleep, Nicky had now offered her a chance to extract the thorny Darin from her life, heart and side completely and so she hoped and wished that he would soon be exposed for the sexual cheat that he really was. Quite soon, Leona silently hoped, she would be able to face Darin, confront him and then throw him in the trash heap of unwanted lovers for the rest of her life and that knowledge provided her with a blanket of comfort that was even warmer than the duvet that now nestled gently against her skin.

Two meetings had already occurred now between the two women and due to what Leona had garnered from both those meetings, she felt totally reassured that Darin would very shortly be out of her hair and her life because Nicky seemed very competent, highly professional and extremely thorough. Life as far as Leona was concerned, really was far too precious and too short to spend it with a total trashbag like Darin that delivered nothing to Leona's heart but heartache, misery and pain and she had coped and lived with Darin's heartbreak for five very long, painfully unromantic, totally miserable years.

The very cold, disgustingly awful, extremely painful hard facts, Leona hoped, would soon be presented to Darin's face in a way that he could never possibly dispute and in a manner that he could never redeem himself from and then she would be free to walk away from him for the rest of her life and not even one single, regretful glance would be cast back over her shoulder as she went. A peaceful smile crossed Leona's face as the thought of living a Darin free life began to gently wrap its arms around her body and as she closed her eyes, she quietly concluded that although her life wasn't a totally comfortable place to live in just yet, once she finally got rid of Darin, it would definitely be a much brighter place to live and a whole lot happier.

"Thank goodness there's no Darin tonight." Leona whispered to herself as she waited for sleep to embrace her. "After what I saw today, I really don't want to see Darin this weekend, or any other weekend for that matter. He's never going to change and he probably doesn't even really want to change. I can never trust him ever again, he's finally burnt his bridges with me. My heart and arms just can't carry us both around anymore, the disappointment is so heavy now and I'm so tired of it. I really have to dump him forever and trash our fake engagement as soon as I can."

"I totally agree Leona." Resolve said to himself as he nodded his head enthusiastically. "You should dump him immediately but I know it's hard for you to do that so I'm going to help you."

"My engagement is a complete and utter mess and it is only my engagement really because Darin doesn't even behave as if he's a romantic partner in our so-called relationship." Leona mourned as she verbally reflected upon and analyzed the couple's very unromantic, supposed romance. "It's nothing but a facade, a fiasco and a total nightmare that I haven't woken up from for five very long years."

"Don't worry Leona, help is coming very soon." Resolve immediately reassured himself. "The detective agency probably won't be able to deliver what you need straight away, so I've decided to help them achieve the required results."

INTELLECT: USER REPAIR

Rather frustratingly for Resolve, the ladies detective agency it seemed wasn't really equipped to provide Leona with the instantaneous results that he felt were needed, partially due to the restrictions on Leona's budget and partially due to Darin's lack of sexual success because as Resolve already knew, he wasn't a very competent cheat. When Darin would be caught in the act sufficiently, was therefore very hard for Resolve to predict because Darin was very crafty and usually furnished Leona with a ton of excuses whenever her suspicions were aroused. Due to Resolve's frustration, he had therefore decided to take matters into his own hands that same weekend and so another plan of action had been rapidly formulated and then actioned as Resolve once again booked a lady of the night to meet Darin on the Saturday evening as he attempted to assist Nicky as much as he possibly could and ensure that the exposure of Darin's infidelity was successful as swiftly as possible.

When Leona won the actual lottery prize as Resolve had planned, Darin could not be part of her life anymore or anywhere near it because if he was, Resolve feared that he would simply latch onto Leona forever and financially exploit her and that was the one thing that Resolve really did not want to actually happen. Due to Darin's very parasitical nature, it was highly predictable and extremely likely that if Darin actually discovered that Leona had won the lottery, he would even perhaps stop cheating temporarily, just to convince her that he was good marriage material and that he really loved her when Resolve knew for absolute certain, he definitely did not.

Since Resolve had initially been assigned to Leona as her Life Monitor, a lot of really good monitoring work had been performed and he'd managed to eliminate most of the predators that had latched onto Leona who had made her life a total misery but if Darin somehow managed to convince Leona that he'd changed that would indeed be, a disastrous outcome. Despite all Darin's fake intentions and false promises, Resolve could see right through him and as far as he was concerned, Darin really did not deserve to be given any more chances from Leona because he had already made her life a pit of misery, heartbreak and stress. If Darin somehow managed to remain by Leona's side, once Leona won the lottery prize, Resolve definitely felt that it would be a total failure on his part because he was not prepared to accept anything less than Darin being completely evicted from Leona's life and heart forever.

In terms of the footage that Nicky had collated and shown to Leona so far, she had only managed to capture a tiny fraction of Darin's indiscretions and rather sadly, Resolve already knew that because Darin really was an absolutely horrific cheat. So many of Darin's transgressions had intentionally been hidden by Darin from Leona's sight, due to his parasitical nature as Resolve was now completely aware, just so Darin could keep his meal ticket on the dinner table, his sticky fingers in Leona's purse and one of his feet inside her bedroom door and that frustrated Resolve immensely.

Fortunately for Leona however, Resolve could handle people like Darin and he was just about to provide Nicky with the actual ammunition required to bury Darin and his fake engagement in one weekend and as Resolve glanced at Leona's face on his wall screen, he silently vowed that if Nicky failed to catch Darin in the act this time, he would definitely step in. Just a couple more days would be provided to Nicky and her team by Resolve which would give the detective agency one more chance to deliver the results that he wanted and since Resolve had even found a way to place Darin in the ideal scenario and one that would allow Nicky to hammer the final nail into Darin's coffin of fake love, if she didn't bang it in hard enough, he most certainly would.

"Maybe I expected too much from Nicky, after all she is only human and I have to remember that." Resolve logically reminded himself. "Which then implies that her capabilities are limited to a very human capacity and Darin is quite cunning but I can assist and I will because it will be an absolute pleasure to evict him from Leona's life permanently and to totally get rid of him."

Much to Resolve's absolute delight as he watched Leona drift off to sleep, his Friday had been truly delightful because Rochelle had delivered bags of stress directly to Samson's door and continued to heap sackfuls of pressure on top of Samson's head and so now, he felt partially satisfied that every issue in Leona's life was almost, completely resolved. The struggle that Samson would now have to endure to fulfill Rochelle's current outstanding financial request, Resolve did not doubt would be a total headache for him because the amount that she had asked for as Resolve already knew, far exceeded Samson's actual current access to financial resources.

"Adultery can be a very expensive business Samson and it's probably going to be far more profitable for Rochelle in this instance than your own company will ever be for you." Resolve mentioned to himself as he glanced at the monitoring window that contained the two lovers and smiled.

Very much like the pressure that Samson usually placed upon Leona, Resolve had observed that Samson had now been pushed towards the edge of a cliff of discomfort by Rochelle's demands and every look of painful anguish and sheer panic that had crossed his face that Friday evening had been everything that Resolve had hoped for and more. Some financial costs had certainly gone hand in hand with Samson's adultery and Resolve had noticed that those costs were definitely mounting because now, Samson had to fill the subsequent gap that his shortfall in attention had created, purely due to his marital status and the lies that he had told.

In every way possible, Samson had fallen short of Rochelle's demands with regards to the levels of attention, commitment and time that she had requested and expected from him and Resolve had seen firsthand how that shortfall had invoked a sense of guilt within Samson that he now had to financially quench along with Rochelle's monetary expectations. Despite Samson's attempts to try and satisfy Rochelle with lavish gifts and expensive treats, Resolve had noticed that Rochelle had pushed Samson for more and more and it was almost as if there was now a bushfire inside Rochelle's mind that wanted to ravage Samson's forest of affluence and ultimately, devour it completely. The bushfire in this instance however, could not actually be extinguished by Samson through anything else but monetary satisfaction which for Resolve, was totally delightful and as he had watched the flames of financial desire dance through Rochelle's mind, Samson had been pushed to satisfy her demands which had rapidly escalated in direct correlation to his romantic shortfalls.

"Now that Samson is being given a taste of some very bitter medicine that might actually cure his filthy attitude towards women." Resolve logically concluded. "And I'm not sure why but the implementation of this human concept of revenge, actually feels rather good and extremely satisfying."

An air of admiration now surrounded Resolve as he began to silently congratulate Rochelle on her victory because in one foul swoop and in one night, she had managed to extract not only a beautiful apartment from Samson for an entire year but she was also due to receive a large capital sum from him in the very near future. Essentially, Rochelle's smart attitude towards Samson had actually saved Resolve a lot of time because when it came to the whole issue of changing Samson's attitude, the work that Resolve would have had to perform had now, pretty much been delivered straight to Samson's door by Rochelle which meant, there was very little left for Resolve himself to actually do.

Quite amusingly for Resolve, Rochelle had stepped into Samson's life, grabbed him firmly by the wallet and then she had even managed to chain him to her side for as long as she wanted him to be there through his own guilt and deception and Resolve couldn't really have asked for anything more, or planned Rochelle's demands better himself. No easy escape would be forthcoming for Samson, Resolve silently concluded because Rochelle had placed him very firmly under her thumb and Resolve had watched him literally squirm around all evening like a trapped snake because unfortunately for Samson, he had now locked horns with a fiery, headstrong female that he certainly could not handle and she would not release him cheaply or easily.

Much like a mongoose that traps and grips a snake in its teeth and then shakes the life out of it, to Resolve's absolute delight it appeared, Rochelle had now successfully clamped her seductive jaws around Samson and his wealth and Resolve felt absolutely certain that she would not release him until she had shaken every drop of each liquid asset out of him and devoured every chunk of meaty wealth that he possessed. In fact, as Resolve already knew, it was highly likely that Samson would now have to borrow money just to satisfy Rochelle's second request which meant, she would devour not only the wealth that he currently possessed but also some of the potential wealth that he might have access to in the future because he would have to generate profits to satisfy those financial obligations. Essentially therefore, Resolve could clearly see that Rochelle would not only take everything from Samson that he currently owned but also any profits and wealth that he could generate and possess for years to come and that reality, totally delighted him.

A smile of satisfaction crossed Resolve's face as he turned his attention back towards Leona and began to watch her sleep as he relaxed because every issue that had negatively affected Leona's life for so very long was just about to be resolved completely. Since Leona was much more important to Resolve, the three monitoring windows that were on display upon his visual display wall screen inside his living quarters were not even in size and the window that contained Leona was much larger than the other two which contained Darin and the two lovers, Samson and Rochelle. The size of the monitoring window that featured Leona inside it, symbolized her importance to Resolve which far exceeded that of any of his prior Allocated Humans and monitoring assignments but unfortunately, regardless of all Resolve's efforts and his affectionate sentiments towards her, those positive elements could not bring Leona any closer to him but that dilemma as Resolve already knew, would not be resolved that night.

When the Saturday morning arrived and peacefully entered into the city of Pinesfield as Leona arose, Resolve enthusiastically began to create another simulation as he watched her wake up, make her way towards the bathroom, attend to her usual morning hygiene routine and then head towards the kitchen. Breakfast as Resolve already knew, was an integral part of most human being's morning routine and in that respect, Leona was certainly no different since she consumed breakfast or a late breakfast which she usually referred to as brunch most mornings and so he wanted to be fully prepared for the day that he would realize his dream and become an actual human being because then perhaps, he would make an actual human breakfast with Leona in person.

Food was not something that Resolve had ever had to prepare or even tasted before but he wanted to experience the preparation of an actual meal because it looked like another human task that he would definitely have to practice to fully master, since it actually looked quite complicated. At least one hundred human functions still existed that Resolve had never ever tried to perform before that he had seen human beings engage in many times and so now, he wanted to paddle around in the shallow waters of the human experience before he actually tried to dive into a real human life.

One day, Resolve hoped that he would cook and consume a real breakfast, lunch and dinner by Leona's side, when he finally managed to step inside a human body and he wanted to ensure that he would be fully equipped to do those things before that day arrived, if he ever somehow managed to reach the surface of the Earth. The day of Resolve's potential humanization was a day that he just couldn't wait to see, experience and live through and although the actual question of whether or not Resolve could ever actually become human had not yet been answered, deep down inside, he still fervently hoped with each human day, hour and minute that went by that it would indeed, actually be possible.

Inside Resolve's non-human form, a hopeful expectation now lived every day that assumed that somehow, his humanization could be an actual real possibility for him that he one day might realize and any opposition to that possible realization had been pushed totally to one side for the time being as a mere technicality. At one point in time, The Guardian himself had walked upon the face of the Earth in human form and then at the end of his human mortal life, his mind had been implanted into Intellect and so Resolve definitely felt that if The Guardian had once walked the face of the Earth in human form which he had Resolve could definitely somehow, become human and exist inside the human world for a human lifetime too.

"There has to be a way to perform that process in reverse." Resolve convinced himself decisively as he glanced at the fourth window that he had just opened up on his visual display wall screen which housed his next simulation exercise. "And I have to try to find a way to involve Leona in my actual simulations, so that each one will feel more real. I have to take another real human step towards Leona and since I can't physically be by her side just yet that'll better than the current nothing that I have."

"I have to make some breakfast now." Leona mentioned to herself decisively as she walked towards the refrigerator and then opened it up. "I'm quite hungry, despite all the upset that Darin caused me yesterday and unlike Darin's fake promises at least breakfast will definitely happen today because I can count on me. The thought of seeing Darin again though is enough to put me off breakfast, lunch and dinner right now because he's truly repulsive."

From the depths of Leona's stomach, a noisy growl suddenly, rather rudely erupted as hunger began to grip her body and she immediately giggled in response as she plucked some items from the shelves of the refrigerator.

"Okay, well I guess I'm not quite hungry, I'm very hungry." Leona joked to herself. "Thank you very much stomach for letting me know. One slight catch though, I didn't do much food shopping this week, so there are limited choices but since Darin's not here that does make things slightly easier for me because that means, I can eat whatever I want to."

Breakfast as Resolve already knew, definitely had to be consumed by Leona that morning and the noises from her body had it seemed, provoked her to immediately surrender to her hunger and had reminded her of that very human reality. Since Resolve's simulation had already been prepared and launched, he began to ready himself to join Leona in her very human preparation of breakfast as he watched her search for all the items from the refrigerator that she required and prepare to make a start.

Much like Leona's actual kitchen, Resolve's simulation of her kitchen had been fully equipped with all the required pieces of equipment that were necessary for the preparation of a cooked breakfast because Resolve had felt absolutely certain that Leona would cook something to eat that morning and had prepared his simulation accordingly. Each item of food that Leona selected was rapidly located inside the simulated refrigerator by Resolve's simulated form and then quickly retrieved as he attempted to mimic Leona's actions and prepared to cook a very human breakfast for the very first time in his entire non-human existence.

Just to ensure that the simulation would be as close to Resolve's ideal Saturday morning as he could possibly make it, he rapidly added a simulation of Leona's human form to the scene because that was as close to the real Leona as he could be for now and as he placed her at the entrance of the lounge, he prepared to interact with her via their two simulated forms. A few seconds later, Leona's simulation began to walk towards Resolve's simulated form and the kitchen and so he immediately commanded his simulation to turn to face her as he prepared to greet her.

"Good morning Leona. Would you like some breakfast?" Resolve's simulated form asked.

"Sure Resolve that would be lovely." Leona's simulation replied. "What are you making?"

"I can do pancakes but probably not very well. Sausages and bacon, I should be okay with. Eggs might be a total disaster but I can definitely try, if you want to risk it." Resolve's simulated form offered.

"I'll just have whatever you're making Resolve." Leona's simulation said as she smiled. "Shall I make some freshly ground coffee?"

"No, don't worry about it Leona. You just sit down and relax and I'll do the rest." Resolve's simulated form insisted.

"Okay, if you're sure." Leona's simulation agreed.

"I'm very sure." Resolve's simulated form rapidly confirmed. "It's just breakfast, how hard can it be?"

Some oil was quickly drizzled over the base of a large frying pan by Resolve's simulated form and then a ceramic ring was rapidly switched on to heat the oil up as Resolve enthusiastically began to prepare for his cooking session which he felt would probably be a total disaster. A bunch of sausages and some rashers of bacon were carefully placed inside the frying pan once the oil had been heated up as Resolve's simulated form attempted to mimic Leona's real human movements inside her real kitchen. Another much smaller frying pan was then quickly retrieved from one of the kitchen cupboards which was placed upon a second ceramic ring and some oil was once again drizzled over the base of the pan as Resolve's simulated form attempted to repeat Leona's real human actions inside her actual real kitchen.

"Now comes the really hard bit." Resolve joked to himself as he watched his simulated form prepare to fry some eggs inside the second much smaller frying pan. "The eggs."

A few eggs were broken and the contents of the shells were carefully poured into the second frying pan by Resolve's simulated form as he attempted to make his very first ever, human fried breakfast which he hoped would be absolutely perfect but doubted that it would be. The preparation of food in some ways, really fascinated Resolve because so many variations could occur when ingredients were added to or subtracted from a dish and then heat could be applied in various ways along with cooking lubricants like oil, water and steam in order to provide a variety of culinary outcomes and at times, it all seemed quite imprecise but so deliciously human and fascinatingly complex.

"One day Leona, we'll eat one of my breakfast disasters together in real life." Resolve promised himself. "I'm not sure I'll ever be able to do anything with eggs though because they really are very complicated, so I'll probably have to leave that bit to you, or you'll end up eating a mish mash for breakfast."

Fried eggs, boiled eggs, poached eggs or any other kind of eggs as far as Resolve was concerned, were just a very strange enigma that not even a specially programmed, totally logical, highly capable Monitoring Program with enhanced attributes could understand and how exactly human beings coped with them every day, he was totally unsure. No matter what individual human beings did with eggs, they always appeared to be either undercooked, overcooked, broken or flawed in some way but human beings somehow, he'd noticed, still managed to eat them and even seemed to enjoy them in their imperfect state.

"If an item of food is not perfectly cooked when human beings eat a meal inside a restaurant, they sometimes refuse to eat it and at times, they even send it back to be replaced." Resolve mentioned to himself as he began to logically consider the actual human consumption of food. "But when they cook at home, they often eat food that is not perfectly cooked without any complaints at all and they still seem to enjoy their meal. Perhaps food doesn't really have to be perfectly cooked to be enjoyed, or to fill up a hungry human stomach and perhaps less than perfect food can still taste nice, so there's still hope for me and the eggs."

"Let me know if you need any help Resolve." Leona's simulation suddenly called out as she turned to face the kitchen.

"Don't worry Leona, I'll be fine." Resolve's simulated form immediately reassured her. "I have to practice this because it's very important to my development and it will enhance my understanding of human culture and human practices which I have to experience myself in order to understand humanity more accurately. I still have a lot to learn."

The other human function that still worried Resolve, besides the preparation of eggs, was the male function of urination which Resolve knew, he'd definitely have to try to master at some point, or it could potentially become a huge problem for him, if he ever did manage to make it to the surface of the Earth and find a way to occupy a human vessel. Since Resolve had initially been created, he had watched countless human males urinate in a multitude of places and sometimes that didn't even happen inside a proper toilet and they seemed to be really rather good at it and they only appeared to make a mess when they had consumed too much alcohol, yet he couldn't even do it properly when he was stone cold sober and that worried him slightly. Human males performed that function virtually effortlessly every single day, multiple times a day because Resolve had seen them do so with his own electronic, non-human eyes and they had somehow managed to conquer that rather tricky issue but despite all Resolve's capabilities, competence in that particular area of human toiletry rituals it seemed, quite frustratingly, eluded him.

"Practice makes perfect." Leona's simulation advised as she smiled.

"Yes, that's very true Leona." Resolve's simulated form agreed. "So, I need all the practice I can get."

Due to advice that Leona's simulation had given to Resolve's simulated form, a smile of amusement crossed Resolve's face as he began to consider each word because in this instance, it applied to more than just the human breakfast that he wanted to prepare successfully that morning. Human toiletry customs were definitely something that Resolve would have practice in order to grasp that particular male human function properly but Resolve decisively concluded that if human males could do it competently then it definitely had to be within his capabilities too.

Despite the very productive and enjoyable weekend that Resolve had experienced so far however, one huge issue still hung like a dark shadow over his non-human form and that was his own lack of physical human body in which to reside. On several occasions in the past, Resolve had even discussed the issue of human formation with The Guardian, just out of interest but he had never been overly interested in actual humanization himself but now, it seemed to be almost all he could think about. During those quite brief conversations, The Guardian had always maintained that a human life was inferior to Resolve's own existence because it was only temporal whereas technically, a Monitoring Program could potentially live forever.

"Human beings are mortal creatures Resolve, they become sick, they die, they cease to exist and then they are buried in the dirt and consumed by the very same ground that they once walked upon." The Guardian had explained to him several times.

Rather annoyingly for Resolve, on that particular point, The Guardian was absolutely correct because Resolve had researched it very thoroughly and discovered that it was indeed true. The Guardian's very realistic words now seemed to echo around inside Resolve's logical processes as his functions began to linger for a moment and his sense of joy as a result, was almost completely stolen from him. Somehow, in Resolve's moment of tremendous joy, due to his very positive Friday and his now extremely enjoyable Saturday morning, reality had suddenly broken into his dreams like a burglar and seemed to threaten to steal his joy from him as a look of dismay rapidly crossed his face.

Unlike human beings and their dreams which usually existed within the same plane of existence, Resolve already knew that his ambitions and dreams very sadly and rather frustratingly, lived in a totally different plane of reality, a very human reality and a human world that he was currently unsure that he could ever even reach. Despite the heartbreaking realities however and the huge distance that existed between Resolve and the human world that did not seem to diminish his desires, quench his thirsty ambitions or make him want to realize his dream to become human any less.

"Your existence is different Resolve because your existence has the potential to offer you an immortal life.

INTELLECT: USER REPAIR

You can be rewritten, reprogrammed and upgraded which means, you can potentially exist for eternity. Your existence can be forever, a human being's life cannot and can never be." The Guardian had explained to him. "A human life has a definite beginning and a definite end, a start and a finish, a birth and a death but your existence does not."

Irrespective of the highly logical facts that had been presented to Resolve throughout his various discussions with The Guardian over the years regarding the mortality of human life which had been realistic but annoyingly so, nothing it seemed could now negate or reduce Resolve's current desires to become human which in recent times had become like a mountain of frustration for him. The remnants of their conversations on such issues, now seemed to stubbornly cling to Resolve's memory banks and zoomed through his logical processes as they refused to endorse his ambitions and appeared to stand in direct opposition to his visions of a human existence which interrupted his extremely pleasant morning as each one silently taunted him.

Deep down inside Resolve, there now lurked a very human desire to express himself to The Guardian more fully, in order to determine if a transference to human life was indeed actually possible because so far, Resolve had avoided the actual expression of his wishes. Although Resolve could certainly appreciate The Guardian's points which were all factually correct, it still felt absolutely pointless to Resolve to spend an eternity alone in solitude and to live a life devoid of emotional reciprocation, warmth and love and for that warmth of human love and for Leona, Resolve was prepared to sacrifice a potential eternity.

Unlike Resolve, The Guardian had actually lived a full human life and so in some ways, Resolve almost envied his human experiences because Resolve had not experienced a single one for even a second. Every logical point and conclusion that had been made and presented to Resolve in the past about human life and the lack of mortality it offered had not managed to dissuade Resolve from what was now his deepest desire, regardless of the very strong, logical facts and so now, Resolve wanted to raise that issue with The Guardian and discuss the possibility of his actual humanization.

An internal urge seemed to silently pull away inside Resolve's form which now provoked and encouraged him to seek an actual audience with The Guardian to discuss the matter further, so that Resolve could express his desires to him in all their fullness. Up until that precise moment in time, Resolve had somehow managed to restrain himself and he had remained silent on that particular issue as he'd avoided any expression of the desires that now occupied every second of his day but he silently began to accept as he glanced at Leona's face, he could stay silent no longer. The huge emotional distance that still sat between the two could only be eliminated completely, if Resolve could humanize his existence and so now he had to explore whether that could ever possibly be a real, reality for him.

Every part of Resolve's non-human form now wanted to discuss the possibility of humanization with The Guardian and Resolve wanted to try and make him understand how he felt because at the time of their past discussions, Resolve had not even wished to live an actual human life. The points that The Guardian had made to Resolve in the past had simply been accepted and had formed a final conclusion but his acceptance of that position had now been interrupted, challenged, changed and shifted by Leona's human presence which had entered into his existence and pulled those points apart at the seams. A gathering of emotional sentiments had now collated and those feelings towards Leona that Resolve held deep inside his form, didn't seem to care about the logical application of any mortal issues.

Despite Resolve's deep respect for The Guardian, a complete rejection of his remarks now simmered just below the surface of Resolve's form and so he felt strongly provoked to raise the issue with him in order to express his desire to actually become a human being. The logical reasons that The Guardian had provided to Resolve in the past, regarding why he shouldn't ever really want to become human, didn't seem to diminish his desire to want to experience a real human life, or impact upon his love for Leona and so that meant, Resolve would definitely have to approach The Guardian quite soon to discuss the matter further.

"For now, I better just focus on this human breakfast thing." Resolve quickly reminded himself as he rapidly turned his attention once more back to his simulation and his simulated culinary efforts. "The preparation of a human breakfast does seem to be a rather complicated human task, mainly because of the eggs which are really quite complex in nature and very difficult to prepare. They are so tiny though, sometimes I wonder why human beings even bother with them at all, it hardly seems worth the trouble."

Fortunately for Resolve, the remainder of that Saturday morning slipped peacefully away for Leona because Darin did not bother to show his awful, childish face at her front door and as expected, Samson departed from the love nest that he had paid for and Rochelle as soon as he possibly could. A return to Samson's home was expected quite early on that day and so just after an expensive lunch had been ordered and then eaten by the two lovers, he rapidly deserted Rochelle's arms to return to Moira and Resolve chuckled as he watched Samson slither back to his marital home.

When the Saturday evening arrived, much to Resolve's amusement, Darin's dinner date left him frustrated and alone once more as he dropped her off at home and then began to make his way home at around eight that evening and so Resolve rapidly kicked his plan into action as he prepared to notify the female escort of Darin's whereabouts. Due to Darin's lack of sexual results, passionate misfortune and the fact that it was a Saturday evening, he actually stopped off at a bar for a quick drink on the way home which suited Resolve absolutely perfectly and so a quick text was sent through an email program by Resolve to instruct the female escort that he'd hired accordingly with regards to Darin's precise location.

The supposed, accidental face to face meeting that Resolve had engineered and pre-arranged with another lady of the night from the second escort agency, went ahead very smoothly and just as planned as Resolve watched Darin make the most of his seductive provisions yet again. A second attempt had been made by Resolve to discreetly untangle the last remaining lie of love that Darin had woven around Leona's life and heart in order to orchestrate his self-serving agenda and this time, Resolve was utterly determined to ensure that Darin's cheating would finally be fully exposed.

Once the two had met, supposedly accidently, after the female escort Sinita approached Darin inside the bar, Resolve watched them both in silence as Sinita started to flirt seductively with Darin and in less than five minutes, he noticed that Darin eagerly invited her to his home. Absolute anger and total disgust filled Resolve's form as he watched Darin invite another woman to the apartment that he hardly even allowed Leona to visit and no actual restrictions or standards seemed to exist inside Darin's mind, Resolve observed, when it came to the issue of sexual intimacy with female third parties because he seemed to be pretty much anyone's that gave him a second glance.

Since Darin's reign over Leona's life had begun, a knot of romantic deceit had been tied very tightly around Leona's heart and Resolve had unpicked almost every single emotional rope that had tied her to Darin's side but now, Resolve wished to remove the final tentacle of false love that Darin had wrapped around Leona which would finally, totally liberate her. Just one final obstacle and hurdle remained to be leapt over by Resolve to free Leona from Darin's grip however, because if Resolve could actually prove that Darin had engaged in acts of sexual intimacy with another woman behind Leona's back, she would truly be Darin free forever.

Due to Nicky's very human capacity which limited her somewhat and because Darin was extremely sneaky, Resolve had decided in the end to step in and had intervened in order to assist Nicky and to enable her to catch Darin in the act, sooner rather than later. Actual footage of Darin's sexual indiscretions as Resolve fully appreciated, would be extremely difficult for Nicky to capture and lay her hands on because she did not have access to Darin's home or his bedroom but fortunately for Leona, Resolve actually did. Several devices around Darin's home had already been tapped into which allowed Resolve immediate viewing access any time that he required it and so that small setback for Resolve had already been overcome and that night, he fully intended to record every second of Darin's bedroom action.

Rather frustratingly for both Resolve and Nicky, Darin wasn't totally stupid and that had been the one thing that had kept him afloat and able to jump in and out of Leona's bed for so long because he'd always avoided very public displays of affection with other women that he was romantically involved with. The majority of Darin's romantic fumbles, Resolve had already noticed, usually seemed to take place inside his car when he dropped each woman off outside their home at the end of a date and so most of those more intimate, affectionate moments had been quite difficult for Nicky to capture very clearly on film.

Unfortunately for Darin however, Resolve was just about to end his reign of infidelity over Leona's heart and totally demolish his evasive but quite discreet attempts to mask and hide his affairs and so that Saturday night was extremely significant for Resolve because Darin's actions that night, would change Leona's life forever. For five years Darin had competently managed to evade capture and he had successfully sustained an illusion of sincerity when it came to the issue of his supposed love for Leona but Resolve still had one trick up his sleeve to ensure that, that would not be the case forever. Once that Saturday night was over, Resolve would finally be able to utilize the truth to pin Darin down by his slimy, slippery, unfaithful tail and then Resolve could finally end his reign of deceit over Leona's heart forever and the final nail would be hammered into Darin's very fake, unromantic coffin of romantic deception and that eviction of Darin from Leona's heart for Resolve, was absolutely non-negotiable.

HUMAN HEART

Very much like the first instance of sexual betrayal, Resolve rapidly discovered that the second instance of potential sexual contact with another woman was quickly ushered in by Darin who was it seemed, very keen to dabble in the murky waters of infidelity once again as the two arrived at his home and he immediately welcomed Sinita into its confines. The second woman and sexual participant who had introduced herself to Darin as Sinita had already been provided with very precise instructions by the escort agency with regards to what was required from her that night because Resolve liked to ensure that any human beings he involved in the orchestration of his Resolution Operations had been adequately prepared in advance. Due to Resolve's logical, methodical and thorough approach as a Life Monitor, he already knew that any required resolution outcomes had to be achieved with minimal fuss and careful orchestration in order to produce the desired results, or that his work would be totally ineffective and this task was no different, regardless of its very sexual nature.

The two conversed flirtatiously as Resolve watched them step inside Darin's lounge and there was a huge grin upon Darin's face as he discreetly, internally celebrated his victory and his misconstrued, passionate good fortune. Apparently, the supposed rules that according to Darin governed when guests could visit his home, didn't seem to apply in this instance or had been very quickly forgotten, Resolve noticed as he watched Darin welcome another total stranger into his private residence and the supposed rules were rapidly cast aside, if they ever existed at all which Resolve was now almost certain, they actually didn't. Due to Darin's repetitive lies, Resolve had already taken the time to check on the supposed existence of those so-called rules and from what he could determine, no such rules of any kind on any system stipulated that Darin could not have visitors and so Resolve believed that once again, Darin had spun and maintained a web of lies just to protect and sustain his unfaithful conduct.

Since Darin's apartment was at least a thirty-minute drive away from Leona's residence and situated in another part of the city, Darin seemed to look quite relaxed, Resolve observed as he eagerly prepared for a saucy, passionate night between the sheets with a total stranger, with absolutely no concerns at all for Leona or her heart. The woman in question, Sinita was under strict instructions to please Darin sexually in any way he wished, so as soon as Darin physically approached her inside his lounge as he participated enthusiastically with his sexual agenda within minutes and without any reservations at all, she began to strip off rather seductively and confidently directly in front of him as Resolve watched them both in total silence.

On this particular occasion, to make the required payment to the escort agency, Resolve had utilized a special expenditure facility that had been created by

INTELLECT: USER REPAIR

Intellect to assist with the application of solutions that required monetary tools because the credit card that Darin possessed, was currently way over its limit and no use to anyone, not even Darin himself. In order to avoid the payment being noticed or traceable, Resolve had opted in the end, to satisfy the expense through Intellect's own expenditure facility because he feared that if he attempted to charge it to Darin's credit card, the transaction would probably be noticed very quickly and that it would not be authorized anyway, so the use of Intellect's resources ensured that Darin would remain absolutely clueless which suited Resolve right down to the ground.

Just a couple of minutes later and once Darin could control his lust no more, Resolve noticed that Darin eagerly pulled Sinita much closer to him, kissed her and then began to grab her naked breasts and she responded with several moans of pretentious pleasure. Every piece of clothing that remained was then quickly removed from Sinita's physical frame as she immediately participated with Darin's sexual hunger and as Resolve waited for what he knew was due to happen next, he smiled in satisfaction. This second sexually successful unfaithful act on Darin's part that Resolve had instigated however, would definitely be different from the first because Darin would not get away with his indiscretions this time around, since Resolve had already begun to record him in sexual action and Resolve now also had a human entry point that he could utilize to expose Darin's acts of sexual betrayal.

In a matter of just a few seconds, Resolve observed that Darin had eagerly removed his own clothes and then rapidly slipped his hand between Sinita's thighs as he prepared to penetrate her and Resolve smiled as he waited for Darin to send his relationship with Leona into a grave of romantic death. A triumphant smile adorned Darin's face,

Resolve noticed as he prepared to enter inside the female human body that had been provided and offered to him by Resolve and he seemed totally unbothered by his romantic commitments elsewhere.

Approximately ten minutes later, once Darin's first climax had been reached, Resolve watched as the two made their way towards Darin's bedroom to continue their sexual exploration as Darin grabbed at Sinita's body lustfully, greedily and hungrily as they walked. The actions on Darin's part disgusted Resolve profusely because Darin behaved as if he had been sex starved for months and as if he had no concerns whatsoever for Leona's heart which he'd betrayed so very easily. Once the two arrived inside Darin's bedroom although Resolve already had the footage he needed, he continued to record Darin's movements and his sexual enjoyment as the two made love very energetically for at least another couple of hours.

When midnight arrived, just as Resolve had planned and instructed, Sinita suddenly prepared to depart as she quickly dressed back up and then said a very brief goodbye. Just a few minutes later, Sinita vacated Darin's apartment which seemed to confuse Darin slightly but as Resolve watched her leave in silence, he totally understood her rather abrupt departure. An agreement had been made that Sinita's client services that night would end at exactly twelve and so at twelve on the dot as expected, Sinita had abandoned Darin's apartment accordingly and as she closed the exterior door of Darin's apartment building behind her and vacated Darin's life and world, Resolve silently began to rejoice in Darin's most recent sins that would ultimately, liberate Leona's broken heart.

For Resolve, the Saturday night and Darin's behavior had absolutely delighted him because now, the final nail could and would be hammered into the coffin of Darin's fake engagement and Leona would finally, after five years of suffering, be set free. Now and at long last, Resolve could finally, actually send Darin's fake relationship into the grave of romantic death that waited to consume it because he had planned to reveal the disgusting plague of Darin's betrayal and expose the acts of heartbreak that Darin had inflicted upon Leona's heart without her knowledge to her face and once he had done that the coffin lid would be closed down over Darin's head forever.

"Tonight Darin, you have just totally trashed and absolutely buried your fake engagement which means, Leona will now be able to save her love, emotions and loyalty for someone that really matters and for someone that deserves her faithful heart. Now, she'll be truly free and able to find a decent person that will treasure, honor and cherish her heart and someone that won't squander her love." Resolve whispered to himself as he nodded his head with certainty.

A victory when it came to the issue of Darin and his cheating antics had finally come Resolve's way and the end of the Saturday night had resulted in the best outcome possible as far as Resolve was concerned because now, Leona would truly be able to dump Darin forever. Since Rochelle had already dealt with Samson that weekend, extremely competently, Resolve hadn't felt any real need to inflict any further stress upon him because her handling of Samson had kept him tied up very tightly in several uncomfortable guilt-ridden knots and as a result, Resolve now felt extremely confident that Samson's downfall would definitely occur in the not so distant future.

Upon Resolve's face there was a very satisfied smile as he turned his attention back towards Leona and then began to watch her sleep which was once again, inside her own actual bedroom and that had been another achievement due to his work as her Life Monitor. Unlike the past few years, Leona could now actually, comfortably sleep in her own bed inside her own bedroom whenever she wished to because the noisy neighbors had not yet returned which meant, her bedroom was a lot more peaceful and once more fit for purpose.

"Don't worry Leona, I'll get rid of Darin and Samson very soon." Resolve promised himself as he watched her sleep. "They won't be your headache for much longer and if the noisy neighbors ever do manage to return, they'll probably be a lot quieter now. I just wish I could be closer to you and be by your side because then you would see how nice life and each day can really be."

Since Leona had initially been assigned to Resolve and entered his sphere of existence, he had frequently reflected on a daily basis upon the huge divide that separated the two as he'd considered how he could possibly reduce it in a permanent way but very few answers as yet had presented themselves to him. Although Resolve had now taken a first step towards Leona and the human world that step, he fully recognized, was still a million miles away from the very huge leap that he really wanted to take but he didn't wish to alarm or scare Leona, since that would be counterproductive to his main objective and goals. No actual answers seemed to exist inside Intellect however as to how Resolve could actually humanize his existence which was why Resolve now had to seek an actual audience with The Guardian himself and so a request was submitted for a face to face meeting the next morning.

"The noisy neighbors are gone now Leona, Samson is just about to get his comeuppance and Darin is just about to be booted out of your life completely." Resolve announced as he congratulated himself on his recent achievements. "So now, only one problem remains for me to resolve but that problem does not actually belong to you because that problem is mine which means, I need to make another plan but this time that plan will be for the resolution of my own problem." He concluded decisively.

According to what Resolve already knew, another step could actually be taken in the meantime from his current position inside Intellect due to his enhanced attributes via a special program that The Guardian had given him access to which could reduce the emotional distance between Leona and himself but as he was also aware, it was rather risky. The program itself which was referred to as the Mind Probe Program, wasn't a program that was generally available to any Monitoring Program inside Intellect and in fact, Resolve was the only one that had any access to it at all besides The Guardian himself and it was still very much in the experimental stages which meant, it wasn't deemed to be totally functional.

"I would be taking a huge risk Leona because technically, I'd be breaking the rules but I could do it when you're fast asleep, since that would be far less noticeable." Resolve advised himself as he logically considered all the options currently available to him.

The Mind Probe Program that Resolve could utilize to connect to Leona's mind, could potentially allow him to initiate some dream sequences through various simulations which would then provide him with some kind of interaction that was at least, a two-way form of communication and that would perhaps satisfy Resolve to some extent. However, this exceptionally rare process as Resolve was fully aware, was only supposed to be facilitated and utilized in absolute emergencies and when an Allocated Human's life was at risk from actual harm and so he would definitely be in breach of Intellect's rules.

"A subconscious interaction with you Leona has to be better than nothing at all and at least, it would actually be real." Resolve convinced himself as he began to pace his living quarters. "Sadly, that's all I can really offer and give you right now, in my current form and in my current state of existence." He acknowledged as he glanced at Leona's human form as she slept.

Although the Mind Probe program offered a small glimmer of hope and an opportunity to further reduce the huge emotional distance that currently stood between Leona and Resolve, albeit rather slightly, it was still very experimental because it had not yet been fully tested by The Guardian for operational purposes and so there were no actual guarantees that it would actually be effective. According to what Resolve had been told by The Guardian, the special process that would allow him to tap into Leona's mind so that he could interact directly with her either when she was awake or through her dreams, was still in the development stages and as yet, it hadn't actually been finalized.

Direct communications between Monitoring Programs and the human world were generally, strictly forbidden as Resolve already knew and so the Mind Probe Program hadn't been considered a priority with regards to completion within the Intellect Framework itself and so it had been left incomplete and underdeveloped as The Guardian had focused upon the general maintenance of Intellect instead. Regardless of that current incomplete, underdeveloped state however, upon further analysis and inspection, Resolve rapidly discovered that the Mind Probe Program definitely seemed to be functional and so now, he felt compelled to try it out, once he'd met with The Guardian to discuss the issue of his possible humanization.

INTELLECT: USER REPAIR

"I'll have to utilize the Mind Probe Program when you're fast asleep Leona." Resolve advised himself as he finally arrived at a conclusion. "That way, you'll only remember our interactions like a dream, if you even remember any of them at all and that will be far less strange for you because I really don't want to scare you."

In the past, Resolve had never experienced an actual emotional attachment to another human being on the face of the Earth that exceeded his role and duties as a Life Monitor, so the Mind Probe Program wasn't a facility that he had ever considered before but Leona had changed that now and had sparked his sudden interest in its application. Since Leona's life was not in danger however, it would definitely be a step beyond what was actually allowed, permitted and acceptable as Resolve already knew and so he definitely feared discovery but for once rather strangely, Resolve felt compelled to break the rules.

Inside Intellect as far as Resolve was aware, the Mind Probe Program was the only facility that Resolve could effectively utilize as some kind of bridge between the two which he could meet Leona upon when she was fast asleep in a mental capacity and then utilize to interact directly with her to some extent. Other types of direct communication with Leona through fictitious emails and various devices offered Resolve very limited interactions as he already knew, because each one created an electronic trail that could arouse suspicion and lead to Intellect's discovery and so he definitely wanted to avoid being too direct.

If Resolve did embark upon that particular course of action and utilize the Mind Probe Program, Leona would of course participate in those simulations in a subconscious capacity which meant, she probably wouldn't even remember them but for Resolve that was certainly better than his current interactions with her which offered him next to nothing at all. The small grains of interactive something that the Mind Probe Program could potentially provide, Resolve logically concluded had to be better than the current nothing that occupied and filled his existence every day and night and so he definitely felt that it could be a short-term solution.

Every particle of Resolve's form wanted to reassure Leona that her life would be absolutely fine that someone truly cared about her and that someone was on her side and those compassionate, fervent, sincere desires which dwelt inside Resolve, now yearned to be released and expressed directly to Leona's mind and heart. When Resolve had initially arrived in Leona's life and had been allocated to her, every part of her life had been truly awful and it had seemed like a dark tunnel of misery from which there could be no possible escape but Resolve had now, almost fully dealt with and nearly eliminated every single piece of dirt that had gathered around her, so that she would be able to walk in the sunshine once again and hold her head up high.

Once Darin's fake engagement had been buried inside the grave of dead romances and Samson had been completely dethroned from his corporate empire, Resolve felt absolutely certain that there would fresh hope because there would still be a life to live for Leona, after the destructive love affair had ended and the horrible boss had gone. The Darins and Samsons of the human world had in the end, been no match for Resolve and for Intellect because The Guardian's resources had assisted Resolve in his mission and helped him to assist Leona in a capacity that far exceeded any human capabilities and that reality, truly comforted every particle of Resolve's intangible being.

Upon Resolve's face there was a satisfied smile as he watched Leona sleep because now, a blanket of peace seemed to cover her home and her human form which essentially, Resolve had created since he had almost totally eliminated every problem and every trouble making baby from her environment. Every negative human element that had at one time surrounded Leona had now almost gone and everything was going absolutely perfectly, so that night Resolve felt extremely satisfied with his work as her Life Monitor because Darin had cooperated and participated with his plan not only very easily but also just as expected and his actions that night had been the final icing on the cake of deceit that Darin consumed every time he betrayed Leona's heart.

Loyalty and faithfulness, Resolve had observed, seemed to only be treasured by Darin when it came to the maintenance and upkeep of his own interests and mutual reciprocation definitely lacked when it came to issues like respect and such values appeared to be something that Darin either didn't believe in, or something that he didn't care to practice on a regular basis. Regardless of what Darin did or didn't believe in however, Resolve definitely cared about Leona's heart, mind and her physical human form and he was not prepared to just stand by and watch as Darin ran riot across her heart, distressed her mind and made her life a total misery.

For Resolve however, another huge achievement had actually occurred that weekend which excited him even more than the elimination of the noisy neighbors, the potential financial destruction of Samson and the pending exposure of the slimy toad Darin's sins because that achievement had been very personal to Resolve himself since now, Leona knew his actual name. In every way imaginable that breakthrough in a relationship which had not previously existed between the two, really excited Resolve because it meant that they had taken an actual step towards each other and although it was a very small step, in Resolve's non-human hybrid opinion, it was a highly significant one.

Excitement once more began to fill Resolve as he watched Leona sleep as he emotionally considered the email that he had sent to her earlier that day and how she had actually noticed his name at the bottom of the email and then verbally uttered the word Resolve. The email had been kept by Leona, read several times and she had even read it out loud and mentioned Resolve's actual name in person with her own tongue and so he now felt, tremendously encouraged by her verbal response. A very special, personal message had been placed inside that email which Resolve himself had created specifically for Leona and she had actually noticed it and that reality, absolutely delighted him.

Inside Resolve's logical processes there was now a question however that lingered silently without an actual answer as he began to deliberate as to whether or not Leona actually questioned his identity and who he really was but he had absolutely no real way of knowing. One of the largest limitations of the Intellect Framework and one of the things that really frustrated Resolve the most at times, especially since he'd been assigned to Leona, was the fact that he could never delve into a human being's internal thoughts.

Intellect provided Monitoring Programs with access and the ability to view any current moment in time that related to a person's present and they could also find out a lot of things about someone's past from Intellect's databases and in addition to that earthly systems could also be probed for historical information but no entity inside Intellect could ever read the thoughts that lay hidden deep inside a human being's mind. Any event could be watched by a Monitoring

Program that occurred at any location upon the face of the human planet and so Resolve could observe what was visually displayed to him but he could never possibly understand the internal emotions that a human being felt and experienced, unless they were overtly expressed and sometimes that really frustrated him.

Essentially that lack of transparency meant that for the most part, Resolve's perception, knowledge and understanding of a human being's circumstances was really quite limited and restricted because he could not delve into the mind of an actual human being and so Resolve was totally reliant upon verbal expressions, physical body language, external actions and any information that he could garner from a probe of technological systems. On many occasions, since Resolve had initially been assigned to Leona, he had often wished that he could see inside Leona's actual mind because he'd wanted to explore her thoughtful meanderings in order to understand her better but this level of access was not something that the Intellect Framework currently provided and it was unlikely that it ever would.

The Mind Probe Program from what Resolve already knew, allowed interactions to occur with a human being through their thoughts but that interaction occurred through a connection that only allowed directly expressed thoughts to be communicated by a connected human being that related to the actual interaction itself. In essence, because the program had been created with the intention to allow a Life Monitor to assist and guide an Allocated Human in a crisis, it did allow some form of two-way communication but it would never provide Resolve with the ability to probe a human being's other thoughts that lay outside the scope of that actual direct interaction and so that limitation would sadly for Resolve, still remain intact.

Just to have the ability to walk amongst Leona's thoughts and to be able to understand her passions, problems, frustrations and desires directly, even for a few minutes in time, was not an ability that Resolve as a Monitoring Program would ever possess and that was just a reality that he had now begun to actually accept, regardless of its restrictions. Since Resolve couldn't understand anything that Leona felt or thought, unless it was overtly expressed and he could not really ask her for any information directly because that would perhaps alarm her, the Mind Probe Program truly was his only current real option, if he wished to have a direct interaction with Leona that would be comfortable for her and so an interaction was planned to take place at some point, over the next few human nights.

No huge physical emergency existed and that Resolve already knew and so it would be totally against Intellect's rules but he just couldn't resist the actual temptation because now that Leona had an awareness of his existence, he really wanted to introduce himself to her directly. Due to the strong desires that lived inside Resolve which urged him to understand Leona in every way imaginable, it had pushed him to seek a far deeper connection to her, regardless of how forbidden that actual interaction would be because at the very least that would provide him with a string of comfort and a few codes of satisfaction.

Only one problem now actually remained for Resolve to resolve when it came to the issue of Leona's life but rather strangely for Resolve that final problem had far less to do with Leona and much more to do with Resolve himself and although the Mind Probe Program would take him a step closer to Leona, it would not resolve his actual problem in totality. For Resolve, absolutely everything about Leona was perfect and all that he could ever possibly want a female companion to be but that potentially, enjoyable companionship could never be fully appreciated, truly realized and more deeply explored until the emotional distance between them both had been totally eliminated and that reality remained at the forefront of his logical processes as he continued to watch Leona sleep.

"I want to offer you my heart Leona because my gift of love will definitely be far superior to Darin's substandard, offensive offerings of fake love." Resolve promised himself as he gently shook his head and then began to pace his living quarters. "So, I really have to find a way to do that now for both of us. I would treasure your emotions, truly love you, make you smile every day and I would look after your heart better than anyone else can. If you accept my gift of love, I know you'll make me very happy too, or as happy as any human being can ever possibly be because I have noticed that the human Earth at times, can really be quite a miserable place to live."

Suddenly, a deep realization struck Resolve as he quietly began to consider how things might change, if he was actually able to transition to a human form because the reality was, some things might not change as much as he had once perceived they might. Human beings generally expressed the messages and information that what they wanted others to know and understand and that therefore meant, Resolve's understanding of Leona would always be limited to what she chose to share with him, regardless of his actual form. The only things that Resolve would therefore ever really know about Leona, if he walked the Earth in human form alongside her, would be the things that she decided and wished to express directly to him because he would only ever be granted access to the parts of Leona and her life that she wanted to share with him.

Access to Leona and information about the various domains that she functioned in that formed part of her existence, if Resolve walked the face of the Earth in human form, would only be provided to him by Leona herself and so that access would be limited to what Leona wanted to share with Resolve which would be a huge adjustment for him. Currently, Resolve could walk through almost every aspect of Leona's external life without her knowledge but if Resolve became human and occupied a human vessel that would definitely change because human beings could not physically be in more than one place at any given time.

Every instance of human existence as Resolve already knew, was restricted by the physical case of flesh that each person resided in and occupied which meant, if Resolve managed to find a way to humanize his existence, he would not be able to see different parts of the world concurrently, or multiple people in different locations simultaneously. Suddenly, the realization of those very human restrictions now began to worry Resolve slightly because it would mean that he would not have the same capacity to protect Leona that he currently had because his viewing windows allowed him to access multiple locations and points of view at any given moment in time and that access, flexibility and visibility, provided him with the opportunity to react accordingly and in a timely manner.

"Perhaps I can protect you better Leona from inside Intellect." Resolve logically considered. "But I just don't know if I could cope with the heartbreak of not being given an opportunity and chance to live a human life alongside you."

From the very first moment that Resolve had been assigned to Leona's life, he had yearned to be by her side and spend her waking moments with her and every night that Resolve had watched Leona sleep, he'd longed to hold her in his arms. Just to reach out and touch Leona, to hold her hand, to kiss her soft lips that glistened and shone and just to breathe in the very same earthly air that she breathed in every day, inside a human, imperfect mortal world would be everything that Resolve so passionately desired and fervently longed for with every particle of his being.

"I have to try and live a human life, if that is indeed possible, for the sake of both our hearts." Resolve finally concluded as he stood very still, faced her on his wall screen and then smiled. "And I'll do my very best to protect you Leona in that very limited, human capacity." He promised himself. "If you let me into your life, give me access to your heart, trust me with your happiness and chose to accept my heart, I won't let you down I promise. Somehow, you gave me a human heart Leona and so now, I want to give my human heart to you."

Trust and access as Resolve already knew, were two close companions that usually travelled together through a person's life hand in hand and so he now had to accept some of the much deeper, very real human implications that humanization would present to him because there would definitely be some stark differences. A mortal human existence inside the real human world would be far more limited than Resolve's current existence and really quite restrictive in nature because he would only ever have access to the parts of Leona's life that she wished to share with him but that notion began to intrigue and fascinate Resolve as he started to reflect further upon it.

Things would definitely change, if Resolve managed to humanize his existence because he would no longer have access to every part of Leona's external life and so he would not be able to see how other people behaved towards her and that lack of transparency meant, he would be totally reliant upon what she disclosed directly to him. Every single aspect of humanization now had to be probed, dissected and logically considered by Resolve before he presented his actual request to The Guardian because he had to be absolutely certain that when he did so that the real manifestation of his request if granted, would be everything that he expected, hoped and wished that it would be.

"Being beside you Leona and sharing the parts of your life with you that you want to share with me, will definitely be enough for me." Resolve logically and emotionally reassured himself as he began to accept the human realities and physical restrictions that actual humanization would impose upon him. "Because then there'll no longer be this huge emotional distance between us and we'll be able to share a real, human, mortal lifetime together, well at least until that mortality separates us."

Just being in close physical proximity to Leona's human presence would definitely be enough for Resolve and being a part of her very real human life would be everything that he had ever dreamed off and hoped for because before he'd been assigned to Leona, he had never hoped or wished for anything at all. In fact, being human and being able to walk through life beside Leona's human form would be absolutely everything that Resolve could ever wish for and as he began to adapt his logical processes to the more restrictive reality that a human mortal life would entail, he began to feel more excited about that particular string of considerations.

A huge change would definitely occur, if Resolve did indeed actually manage to find a way to walk alongside Leona in human form but that very human restriction would result in the manifestation of something even more precious, if Leona chose to place her trust in him. Every single aspect and detail of Leona's life that she chose to share with Resolve's human form, would then be given to him through trust, respect and consensual, voluntary participation which was far more valuable in Resolve's sight than the external access he currently had to Leona's life in his current state of existence.

The deeply positive implications that surrounded Leona's potential participation, suddenly began to excite Resolve and the restrictive challenges rapidly became something much more significant to him because if Resolve walked by Leona's side in human form, she would then share parts of her life with him through her own volition and through her own free will which would be even more meaningful to him. Irrespective of the very human limitations, every moment that Resolve shared with Leona in human form, he silently concluded, would potentially be the most pleasurable experience that he could ever possibly have as far as he was concerned because that was what he now fervently wished for with every part of his being and Leona would be an actual, active, consensual participant to those wishes, desires and non-human dreams. Every second that the two spent together, no matter how limited, would ignite the love that already lived deep inside Resolve's heart which he felt, would last for eternity, regardless of their human mortal state because Leona had already set his desires on fire and she had breathed life into his heart which now longed to beat in time next to her own.

For Resolve, the remainder of that Saturday night slipped peacefully away and as each hour silently departed, he continued to watch over Leona as she slept as he prepared for his meeting with The Guardian on the Sunday morning which would involve an actual discussion about the issue of his possible humanization. A few rather prickly considerations did start to tug away inside Resolve's logical processes as the time of their meeting drew closer as the brightness of the Sunday morning stepped in to replace the darkness of the night and he quietly began to consider what might actually happen, if his wish was actually granted and he was given an actual human existence and then Leona rejected him.

Negativity at times as Resolve was already aware, could become like sinking sand because when you walked upon it and then wallowed in it, it could pull you down into a deep abyss of misery which it could be very hard to escape from and he had seen that himself from the many human lives of those he'd monitored in the past. The thought of Leona's potential rejection had now started to worry Resolve more deeply however, because it could be a real possibility that he would perhaps one day have to face and so he quickly attempted to distract himself from that negative code of thought with other activities as the night silently departed and temporarily rejected that string of undesirable considerations because positivity as Resolve already knew, would keep his hopes alive and his heart in a state of peaceful equilibrium.

"I should send you some gifts Leona." Resolve advised himself as he glanced at the monitoring window that contained her bedroom and admired her beautiful face. "Because now at least, you do know my name, since I sort of introduced myself to you, so you'll kind of know where the gifts might have come from. Human males that like human females usually give them gifts, so I should give you some gifts because that might cheer you up a bit and you really do need to be cheered up. Lately, your days have been very heavy and a frown is much heavier to carry around than a smile."

INTELLECT: USER REPAIR

Everything about Resolve's plan of action, from his meeting with The Guardian, to his Mind Probe meeting with Leona seemed to make total sense to him and the gifts he hoped, would provide Leona with a pleasant distraction from all the misery that she was currently surrounded by. Essentially, because Leona's usual week was such a heavy burden to carry, Resolve definitely felt that some gifts might lighten her load and cheer her up a bit and he really wanted to do something nice for her because she deserved so much more than life currently provided to her.

Every working week as Resolve had already observed, Leona pandered to Samson's corporate ambitions and she literally jumped over backwards to meet his incessant demands and then she usually spent most of her weekends tangled up in dreary, negative interactions with Darin and none of those interactions could be classified as pleasant. At the very least, Resolve hoped, a few gifts might provide a small glimmer of hope to Leona's heart that somewhere out there in that huge jungle of humanity, someone truly cared about her. Since the misery that Darin usually caused for Leona was just about to get worse before it would get any better, Resolve concluded that some gifts would perhaps soothe her heart, comfort her and provide her with an ounce of relief throughout her moments of pain and that some packages of pleasantness would perhaps take the edge of the heartbreaking pain that was due to come her way.

An urge definitely lived inside Resolve's form that wished to comfort Leona and make her slightly more aware of his actual presence in a manner that soothed her and not one that alarmed her because he really wanted to secure Leona's trust. Such acts of thoughtfulness on Resolve's part, could perhaps reduce the emotional distance that currently existed between them both in a very real, quite human way which might then allow Resolve to engage in an actual two-way relationship with Leona that would perhaps allow him to climb up the ladder of love which led directly to her heart.

In order to provide some appreciative encouragement to Leona, Resolve decisively began to make an electronic request for an actual hair appointment on her behalf at a salon that he already knew, she usually attended but hadn't visited for a while later on that Sunday, in the early afternoon. When it came to Leona's actual schedule that day as Resolve was already fully aware, she had no current plans because once again Darin's heartbreak had totally demolished her weekend and so an appointment was requested and then a voucher was purchased to satisfy the monetary cost of the appointment which was then sent to Leona's email account.

Since an audience had been specifically requested with The Guardian that morning, Resolve was absolutely certain that he would now, finally be able to raise the unspoken issue that lay inside his intangible form which he definitely felt, could not wait even a single day longer to be expressed. Inside Resolve, there was now a very eager hunger to find an actual resolution to his own problem which had grown into a mountain of desire that he could not climb over, scale, burrow through or hope to actually reduce and only one person held a potential solution to that problem, The Guardian himself.

A contradictory desire had not only formed but also grown inside Resolve which he could no longer contain, or even hope to understand because it seemed to defy the logical reasoning that was the very basis of Resolve's own makeup and so that contradiction now needed to be fully addressed and his meeting that morning would provide an avenue to address it head on. When it came to the actual issue of Resolve's potential humanization as he was now fully aware, The Guardian held all the answers that he required and sought because inside Intellect, The Guardian was the only person that could provide such answers because the Intellect databases remained totally silent on that particular issue and Resolve already knew that for absolute certain because he had actually checked.

Each step that Resolve took as he left his living quarters and then began to make his way towards The Guardian's chambers as the time of his personal meeting neared, was filled with nervous anticipation as he silently braced himself for what would essentially be the most difficult moment and conversation of his entire existence. To face the very man that had actually created Resolve and then express a desire to leave his side in person directly to him, would definitely require a code of bravery because The Guardian had not only given Resolve an existence but then he had also made that existence very special for him.

"It might actually go quite well." Resolve reassured himself in a whisper as he walked along the black shiny corridor that surged with flecks of energy as the tubular walls glistened and shone all around him. He attempted to calm his nerves as he dug deep inside his form for some codes of courage and a string of bravery. "Logically speaking, it is only a question and there are only a few possible answers to a question of that kind, so I really shouldn't worry about it."

Meanwhile, inside the very heart of Intellect in Victor Drayton's chambers, Victor Drayton started to prepare himself slightly nervously for what he knew was just about to come because Resolve had requested a face to face meeting with him that morning and unknown to Resolve, he already knew exactly what that meeting would be about. Due to Victor Drayton's position within the Intellect

Framework, he knew absolutely everything there was to know about Resolve and all the other Monitoring Programs that he had created and so Resolve's fascination with Leona had not gone unnoticed and it had been observed with very watchful, electronic eyes.

A certain amount of acceptance had by now however, actually occurred because Victor Drayton had begun to realize that the special attributes and more human nature that he had given to Resolve had for the very first time, drawn Resolve emotionally closer to a real, mortal, female human being. Absolutely everything about Resolve had been created by Victor Drayton in a particular way, for a very specific reason and purpose as the son that he had never had during his human lifetime had been given life in the form of a Monitoring Program that he'd then named Resolve. Nothing about Resolve's creation had been random, sporadic or accidental because every part of his unique makeup had been intricately designed by Victor Drayton to be special, from his superior emotional and intellectual abilities to his more human character and nature.

Essentially, Resolve had been created to provide Victor Drayton with a deeper connection to another life form outside his own electronic existence and that had been the main motive behind Resolve's creation as Victor Drayton had attempted to fill the void of emptiness that he had so often felt within his partially human but now, non-mortal existence. Unfortunately, however, the provisions that Victor Drayton had made for himself did not come without a cost and now, he was just about to pay the ultimate price of giving a more human existence to Resolve because he was probably just about to lose the one Monitoring Program that he treasured above all the hundreds of millions of other programs that he'd created.

INTELLECT: USER REPAIR

The price that Victor Drayton would now be asked to pay by Resolve and the sacrifice that he would be asked to make meant that if Resolve's request was actually granted, he would lose Resolve forever and that reality made him feel extremely nervous. Over the years, Resolve's ability to connect to Victor Drayton on a more personal level had provided him with a lot of comfort and enjoyment but that emotional connection that he had appreciated so many times, he now realized, Resolve had with someone else and that someone else was in fact, a very real human being that lived on the face of the very real, earthly human planet and that emotional connection if pursued, would actually separate them both.

Someone else that was close to Resolve but extremely far away from him had captured his attention, his emotions and his non-human heart but as Victor Drayton also fully appreciated that someone else was currently, totally unreachable for Resolve in his current state and form. After three decades of existence, a female human being had finally managed to tantalize Resolve and had attracted his affections which was really very natural, Victor Drayton concluded as he waited in a thoughtful silence for Resolve to appear.

In some respects, Victor Drayton considered as he began to pace the interior of his chambers, Resolve's attraction to a human life form should have been almost predictable to him because it was essentially, so very human and since Resolve had been designed to emulate a human life form as closely as possible, it really was to be expected. According to the human characteristics that Resolve possessed, it was almost foreseeable that one day, Resolve would fall in love and seek to reach out to the same human world that housed the human attraction that he'd discovered but due to Victor Drayton's desire to keep

Resolve close to his side, he had always ignored that possible eventuality. Now however, Victor Drayton could ignore such possibilities no more because that very same morning, Resolve would verbally force him to face that reality and the desires that now lay within his intangible form which had provoked Resolve to seek to reduce the huge divide that existed between himself and the human being that had attracted his attention.

Human desires were definitely something that Victor Drayton fully understood, since he was not a stranger to humanity himself because at one time, he had actually walked the face of the mortal human Earth in physical form. The power of human emotions and the magnetic desires that pulled one human being towards another, still currently resided within Victor Drayton's own makeup because he had been formed from the remnants of his own human life and his own human mind and so he could understand Resolve's emotional connection and affections towards Leona all to well. A wish to draw physically closer to someone that one admired and to reduce the divide between two people was something that Victor Drayton had experienced during his own human lifetime and so Resolve's wish to draw closer to Leona was totally understandable but that understanding did not now seem to make his potential loss any easier to accept.

When Victor Drayton's own mind had been implanted into the Intellect Framework, he had been established as the cornerstone of the entire system which had then been built upon his intellectual capabilities but his human desires, passions and emotions had also been transferred and so those very human characteristics still existed, even in his current non-human, electronic form. Although the Intellect Framework was effectively, Victor Drayton's legacy because it had been his human lifetime's wish and work, he had only been able to realize that goal just before and right after his human death when he'd finally been granted full permission to proceed and his mind had then been transferred into the Intellect system itself. The work that Victor Drayton had performed inside Intellect for the past fifty years however, had not reduced or changed his own humanity and so romantic love for another human being was definitely something that he understood, absolutely perfectly.

No one upon the face of the human Earth had assisted Victor Drayton when he had initially built the Intellect system almost from scratch and it had been a very lonely existence and so after two decades of loneliness and solitude, he'd finally decided to create Resolve. In every way imaginable, the solutions that Victor Drayton provided to humanity were extremely complex but, in his mind, the Intellect Framework had been totally necessary because ever since it had been up and running, life on Earth had been far smoother for its human occupants and a lot more peaceful but that success and those many achievements had not soothed his own loneliness over the years in quite the same manner as Resolve had.

Self-determination was a special gift that Victor Drayton had built into Resolve's functionalities because he had longed to have an intelligent companion that would not just act according to prescribed instructions or that would be totally predictable which then also meant that Resolve had a very human nature in many ways. The self-determination that Victor Drayton had himself gifted to Resolve however, was now just about to present itself in a form of opposition to Victor Drayton's own wishes and that deeply saddened him as he began to silently accept that the gift of existence that he had given to Resolve had really, actually in the end, been a gift that he'd ultimately given to himself.

Nothing but total silence surrounded Victory Drayton as he continued to wait for Resolve to arrive and as he waited, he began to analyze his own past and his own actions as he quietly accepted that the gift he had given to himself in the form of Resolve, now wanted to be given to someone else. What Resolve wanted to do now, in terms of his desired humanization was hugely different and that request fell far outside the scope of his current duties as a Life Monitor, Victory Drayton silently concluded and although that felt quite uncomfortable for him personally, he began to accept that perhaps, someone else needed Resolve even more than he did. To live a human life certainly wasn't easy and Victor Drayton could fully appreciate that fact and Leona had definitely had her share of negative experiences and so Resolve in human form, would definitely provide her with a very positive one.

"Perhaps it is time for me to give my gift to someone else." Victor Drayton whispered thoughtfully to himself as he continued to pace the interior of his chambers. "Perhaps Resolve can make Leona happy and perhaps, just perhaps, she'll make him happy too."

Quite strangely, a hidden cost now seemed to be attached to the gift that Victor Drayton had given to himself three decades ago and to the gift of companionship that Resolve had provided to him so many times and that was one of actual loss because to be given something that you treasured and then to lose access to it, was a cost that he would now not only have to face but also have to accept. If Victor Drayton had never actually created Resolve and then enjoyed the companionship that Resolve had provided to him, he would not now be losing anything and so rather interestingly, his current dilemma fully illustrated to him that when a gift was given, both the givor of the gift and the recipient, eventually sacrificed and lost something. Both

INTELLECT: USER REPAIR

Victor Drayton and Resolve would definitely lose something, if and when Resolve left Intellect and Victor Drayton's side because Resolve would lose a father and he would essentially, lose the surrogate son that he had created to serve humanity, to the very same human world that Resolve had actually been designed to serve.

Between the two, since Resolve had initially been created three decades ago, a strong emotional bond had definitely formed and grown because they had provided each other with sincere, unconditional companionship without any bitter rivalries, or any ulterior motives but now, it seemed as if that very pure bond was due to come to an end. The companionship that they had gifted each other with so faithfully over the years, due to their consistent presence, unwavering support and mutual respect, was now just about to disappear and it was highly unlikely that Resolve would ever find that kind of fatherly comfort again in another human being and Victor Drayton fully appreciated that very real human reality. One huge question did still linger inside Victor Drayton's mind however as he waited for Resolve to appear and that was essentially, why Resolve would be so willing to sacrifice his potential immortality for a woman that he could not really be sure would ever give him her heart because that part of Resolve's decision seemed, highly illogical.

Not a single thing that Resolve had ever done, or thought, or experienced inside the Intellect Framework was beyond Victor Drayton's knowledge because he could access and read every single thought, action and emotion that Resolve participated in and so Resolve's feelings towards Leona were already known about in their fullness, despite the fact that the issue of Resolve's emotional attachment to Leona hadn't yet been discussed or acknowledged between the two. Unlike human beings that could hide their thoughts and feelings from each other, existence for Monitoring Programs within Intellect was vastly different because that internal area of private consciousness did not actually exist and everything that ran through a Monitoring Program's logical processes was recorded inside Intellect's internal systems, so that it could be reviewed by Victor Drayton if and when required.

In some ways, Victor Drayton's current position within Intellect itself was almost Godlike because he watched over the human Earth, the Intellect Framework and even walked amongst the programmed minds of the logical beings that he had created whenever he wished to but that transparency was not two sided, even within the Intellect Framework itself. The transparency that existed for Victor Drayton, much like the transparency between the Monitoring Programs he had created and the human world, was one sided and so Resolve had absolutely no idea that this visibility even existed, or that the truth about his feelings for Leona had already, actually been discovered. For Victor Drayton, the communication of his knowledge when it came to the actual issue of Leona and Resolve's interest in her as far as he was concerned had been deemed totally unnecessary because he had not wanted Resolve to feel completely naked, since that would perhaps make Resolve feel slightly uncomfortable and restrict him in some way.

A significant period of time had now passed by as Victor Drayton was fully aware, since Resolve's initial creation and he had definitely matured and as he now sought out his independence and the right to make an adult decision about his own destiny, even his internal wishes seemed to mimic the same human beings that Victor Drayton had created him to emulate Regardless of Resolve's non-human form, his emotional desires, Victor

Drayton now fully accepted, were very human in nature and just like mankind, Resolve now wished to realize these desires in their human fullness.

"One day it was bound to happen." Victor Drayton finally admitted sadly to himself as he gently shook his head. "She triggered Resolve's human emotions, stirred up his male desires and then he fell in love which is definitely something natural that I can totally understand, fully appreciate and completely relate to."

Absolutely nothing could be changed now and Victor Drayton silently began to fully accept that fact because there was nothing currently inside Intellect that could immediately quench, satisfy, or extinguish those flames of desire inside Resolve that had been ignited, purely due to Leona's human existence and his allocation to her life. Technically, although Resolve could be reprogrammed and some of his emotional attributes could be removed or the levels of their application reduced as Victor Drayton already knew that would defeat the whole purpose of who Resolve had been created to be, who he had become and who he now actually was and so that was not the preferred course of action.

Suddenly, a blanket of heaviness seemed to fall across Victor Drayton's form as he released a sad sigh because he knew that once Resolve left Intellect, he would never ever actually be able to return which meant, his departure would indeed, be permanent. All around Victor Drayton there now seemed to be a heavy silence that filled every particle of his chambers and as it threatened to squeeze every positive speck of hope out of his surroundings, another very heavy, defeated sigh was released.

Despite all Victor Drayton's years of instruction and advice, the day that he had hoped would never actually come, finally had and so now, he simply had to face it, understand it and accept it because if he didn't, he risked losing Resolve in every other way he possibly could and that much he already, fully understood. No matter how Victor Drayton personally felt inside about Resolve's choice, he now had to accept that Resolve had already made his decision and that Resolve totally understood all the very real human implications of that decision and so he quickly put on a brave face and silently began to nurse his wounds of sadness as he prepared to grant Resolve the actual audience that had been requested that morning.

Just a few seconds later, Resolve stepped inside Victor Drayton's chambers and as Resolve began to cross the large circular space, Victor Drayton offered him a tense smile as he internally braced himself for the very difficult conversation that he was sure would follow. The fact that Resolve had an actual personal request on this particular occasion, was in itself extremely unique because Resolve had never asked Victor Drayton for anything before in a personal capacity and so that meant, his request that day was even more significant and really, actually very special. Essentially, although Resolve had faithfully provided Victor Drayton with companionship and comfort for three decades as they'd both served humanity together, Resolve had never asked him to grant a personal request ever before but now for the very first time in Resolve's entire existence, he wanted something that was truly, just for himself and that was a hugely interesting development, even though it was also simultaneously, due to its nature, actually rather sad.

"Please, sit down Resolve." The Guardian invited as he politely offered him a seat upon the black, glossy bench that ran around the interior circular wall of his chambers.

"Do you know why I'm here?" Resolve asked as he quickly sat down and then glanced up at his face with a quizzical expression.

"I do Resolve." The Guardian replied as he began to pace the interior of his chambers again with his hands crossed behind his back. "You want to be human, just like them and just like I was." He suddenly drew much closer to Resolve and then leant down towards him. "Have you really thought about this Resolve and everything that being a human being would actually entail? Essentially, you would be giving up your potentially immortal life for a very human mortal one and for a very human woman."

"I know, I know." Resolve immediately replied. "I've thought about this a lot and I'm very sure, this is definitely what I want. I'm as sure as I could possibly be about anything. I've analyzed all the probable and possible outcomes and so now, I'm absolutely, totally and completely sure."

"Have you thought about what might happen, if you arrive on Earth and then she rejects you, or even accepts you and then leaves you for someone else, or disappoints you in some other way?" The Guardian asked as he knelt down beside Resolve. "What would happen if one day, she suddenly gets up and decides to leave your side then all your sacrifices would be for absolutely nothing? Are you really prepared to take that kind of risk Resolve? Human beings are fickle, they lie to each other, they betray each other and they are not like you. They change their minds frequently and they are not as reliable as you are."

"I know." Resolve agreed. "But weren't you once human too? Aren't you technically still human yourself?"

"I was and I am Resolve but most human beings are not like me. They betray each other and at times, they even destroy each other." The Guardian quickly pointed out as he stood back up and then began to pace his chambers once more. "What if you die Resolve? What if you arrive on the face of the Earth and then die a very human death as soon as you get there?" He enquired softly. "Human beings can die. You might never even actually get the chance to experience the human desires that you seek to fulfill."

"I understand that you are worried father, truly I do." Resolve immediately reassured him as he rose to his feet. He began to walk towards him as he continued. "But I'm ready to take the risk. For me, it's worth it, Leona is worth it. I just want to live a human life which could be spent by Leona's side, just like you did and to experience everything that comes along with that human package."

"If you leave Resolve, I'll really miss you. You are my only son and the only son that I've ever had and so I care very deeply for you." The Guardian explained softly as he paused, faced him and then began to gently shake his head. "I just don't want anything bad to happen to you because a human life is very different and in the human world, you would not be protected from the harsh realities that human beings have to face every single day."

"I understand Father, really I do but this is everything I want and the only thing that I've ever wanted." Resolve insisted.

"I know Resolve. You've never asked me for anything before, so I do realize, this must be extremely important to you." The Guardian admitted as he nodded his head. "To pass through the Membrane and to humanize your existence however, will not be easy but I'll try to guide you through it and make sure it's as painless as possible, though once you've gone through that process, you can never return."

"So, it is actually possible?" Resolve asked.

INTELLECT: USER REPAIR

"There is no actual gateway to the human world Resolve." The Guardian explained as he glanced at his face. "You can enter inside the Membrane and then depart from it but when you exit, you have to enter into the human world in human form and then you can never return." He continued as he began to pace the interior of his chambers once more. "That's why you have to be absolutely sure and extremely certain that humanization is what you really want. I did create a way to return to the human world, just in case a day like this ever arrived but I really want you to know Resolve, this is not my wish for you because a human life can be absolutely treacherous, riddled with pain and overloaded with heartbreak."

"But a human life can also be happy, joyful, full of love and filled with passion." Resolve quickly pointed out.

"Resolve, I understand your desire to be with the person you love, truly I do but that doesn't mean I have to be happy about it." The Guardian replied as he gently shook his head. "I'll give you my blessing as my son however, because to live a human life on the human Earth, you'll definitely need it and you should know right now, it really won't be easy."

Darts of frustration seemed to prick Victor Drayton's core as he silently accepted Resolve's wishes and restrained himself from any further debates about the issue of Resolve's actual humanization. Despite his desire to protect Resolve from the human world, it seemed as if Resolve's decision had already, truly been made and that for Resolve, there would be no actual turning back because essentially, he now knew that what he wanted was indeed, actually possible. One way or another, Victor Drayton fully appreciated, Resolve would now find a way to leave Intellect with or without his assistance and so it was better that Resolve went with his support, rather than without it.

"Would it be possible to be a handsome male human being?" Resolve suddenly asked. "It's just that human beings seem to be quite particular about those kinds of things and I'd really like Leona to like me and that way at least when I do arrive on Earth, I'll stand a romantic chance."

"I'll try my very best Resolve but I think she'll love you anyway, good looks aside." The Guardian replied as he smiled. He placed his arm around his shoulders and then began to slowly walk him towards the entrance of his chambers. "Once you've gone Resolve, you can absolutely never ever return." The Guardian reiterated. "This really is a one-way journey."

Every particle of Victor Drayton's electronic heart silently began to sob as he walked alongside Resolve as he reflected upon their potential separation which now loomed on the near horizon of their actual future. The request that Resolve had made that day had in the end, been absolutely impossible to deny him because as Victor Drayton knew, he had once enjoyed what Resolve wanted to experience himself and sometimes even now, he still yearned to actually experience it again. A very human desire and a very human request had been made by Resolve that morning and the human nature which still existed somewhere deep down inside Victor Drayton had to grant Resolve that very human wish because that human wish essentially, still lived inside of him.

"I know this will be a one-way journey." Resolve clarified solemnly as he accepted the finality and irreversible implications of his own request which once granted could not be changed. "And I'll really miss you too."

A cloud of sadness seemed to hang over Victor Drayton's head as he turned his face towards Resolve and for a few silent seconds, just observed the very special Monitoring Program that he had created that had served him so faithfully for three decades as a surrogate son. In every way imaginable, Resolve was an absolutely amazing program that had far exceeded the capacity of any of the other Monitoring Programs that Victor Drayton had created because he could think, feel and communicate in so many different ways, since he'd been designed to emulate a human life form so very closely and so he would be sorely missed.

The seeds of human nature that Victor Drayton had sown and created inside Resolve however, had now grown into actual saplings that wanted their own space to spread out their branches, form leaves and bear fruit. Hidden human roots that had existed under the soil which had been situated very far away from humanity's sight, now it seemed, wanted to break through the surface of the Earth and transcend beyond the protective shield that Victor Drayton had created to divide the two planes of existence and that very sincere human desire inside Resolve to become human, Victor Drayton could not deny because essentially, he had created it himself.

"One other thing Resolve, once you reach the Earth's surface, you can never discuss any aspect of the Intellect Framework with anyone you meet." The Guardian instructed. "And so all knowledge of your work here will be deleted from your memory banks. You will still possess some of your functionalities to some extent and you will still remember me, along with a few other things but things will be very different."

"I understand." Resolve replied. "Will I still remember Leona?"

"Yes and no, your emotional attachment to her will remain intact and some memories that you formed of her but some memories will be totally erased." The Guardian explained. "To be specific, the memories that will be deleted are those which relate to the work that you performed as her Life Monitor."

"Okay, I understand." Resolve said as he nodded his head.

"I love you Resolve and because I love you, I want you to find peace and happiness." The Guardian reassured him as he paused in front of the entrance to his chambers and then turned to face him. He smiled and nodded before he continued. "And if you've decided that your future peace and happiness lies inside the human world, I understand that. I support you and I accept your decision because I want you to be truly happy."

Defeat lay inside every inch of Victor Drayton's electronic form as he faced Resolve and internally began to accept that no matter how much the two discussed it, Resolve's departure would now indeed, definitely happen. The gift of human romantic love that Leona could offer to Resolve as his lover, best friend and life partner could never be provided to him by anyone else inside the Intellect Framework and that was an undeniable truth as Victor Drayton already knew. What Resolve now longed for, the romantic intimacy that he wanted Leona to fulfill, was not something that anyone in his current environment could offer to him, no matter how much Victor Drayton wished that things could be different.

Upon Victor Drayton's face there was a sad but compassionate smile as he glanced at Resolve's form and humbly accepted defeat in totality because Resolve needed a love that only Leona could provide and that desire which lay deep inside Resolve, could no longer be avoided or ignored. To love a real, female, mortal human being was truly a human desire which Victor Drayton totally understood because at times, he still harbored such desires within himself but unlike Resolve, a return trip to Earth for him was now, highly improbable and extremely unlikely.

Inside Victor Drayton's form, there were some very human fatherly instincts that now yearned for Resolve to find the companionship that his heart truly desired and he hoped that Resolve would be received well by the woman that had captured his affections and his electronic heart. Since this would perhaps be one of Victor Drayton's last chances to perform his role as a father to Resolve and one of his last opportunities to give Resolve something that he could carry with him on his journey to the face of the human Earth, Victor Drayton hugged Resolve affectionately and then began to provide him with some words of advice and encouragement before he departed.

"Try to be a good man Resolve." The Guardian advised. "The human world needs more good men because there really aren't many around."

Resolve nodded. "I'll try my best father, for Leona and for you. I want you to be proud of me. I want you to be proud of your son." He immediately reassured him. "I want my human walk to be one filled with decency and respect because that's what you taught me and Leona really deserves all the good things that you gave to me."

"Yes, she really does." The Guardian agreed.

Nothing but absolute silence filled Victor Drayton's chambers as Resolve quietly departed and as Victor Drayton was left alone once more with only Resolve's heartbreaking decision, the very real implications of that decision rapidly began to sink into the depths of his mind. A storm of surprise had now shipwrecked Victor Drayton's ship of thoughts because that Sunday morning, Resolve had finally verbalized, acknowledged and expressed his deepest, very human desires and so now, there would be no going back. The fatherly boat of love that had kept the two and Intellect afloat and so strong for so very long had essentially, just capsized because Resolve had finally disclosed the truth to Victor Drayton and presented his request to leave Intellect in order to join the actual human race and so Victor Drayton now felt unsure that a lifeboat would be coming along to rescue him from the loneliness and heartbreak that would be sure to follow.

"I've been so foolish." Victor Drayton admitted to himself as he released a sad, defeated sigh. "To think that Intellect would ever be enough for someone that is so human that has never lived an actual human life."

Up until that precise moment in time, Victor Drayton had just assumed, perhaps foolishly that Resolve would get over his fascination with Leona and that she might meet someone else but he hadn't and she hadn't and so now, the inevitable was just about to occur. In accordance with human nature and Resolve's very human attributes, Victor Drayton now felt as if he really should have anticipated that moment before it actually happened and prepared for that possible eventuality but unfortunately, he hadn't foreseen it and so he had been totally unprepared. The provision of a female companion for Resolve would perhaps have been a satisfactory solution but Victor Drayton had not identified that gap of emotional dissatisfaction in Resolve's existence and that was now, very apparent to him.

Much to Victor Drayton's surprise, suddenly a female human being had unknowingly, tempted Resolve to leave Intellect and Resolve had succumbed to that temptation without even saying so much as a word to him, until the very last minute and it was the last minute because as he already know, Resolve's departure would have to happen quite soon, purely due to Leona's circumstances and current situation. No amount of discussion between the two could change anything now, Victor Drayton silently accepted as he gently shook his head, because Resolve's decision had already been made and accepted by both parties and so all that remained between the two, was the time that preceded Resolve's departure which would predominantly be spent in preparation for it.

The temptation of Leona it now appeared had in the end been too much for Resolve to resist and despite the fact that Resolve was still present inside Intellect, in some ways for Victor Drayton, it actually felt as if Resolve had already left his side, both emotionally and psychologically. Very little time now remained and every minute that Resolve spent inside the Intellect Framework from that moment forward as Victor Drayton knew, would simply be a mechanical exercise because Resolve's heart had really, already left and perhaps, it had even left the very first day that he had set his electronic eyes upon Leona and Victor Drayton just hadn't noticed it. What could have been for Resolve inside Intellect had now well and truly gone and what Victor Drayton should, or should not have done to avoid his departure, was no longer actually relevant because each thoughtful consideration was now just a sunken, pointless, irrelevant factor.

A definite cost would now be borne by Victor Drayton because he had failed to provide Resolve with a suitable companion that possessed a slightly more human nature and one that could perhaps offer him the kind of emotional romantic satisfaction that he would now seek out inside the human mortal world. Over the passage of time, Resolve had essentially found that special connection himself because he had emotionally attached to a very real human being and that connection had created a bond that Victor Drayton now appreciated, could never actually be broken, or at least not by him.

"I won't be able to protect you from the harsh realities of the human world Resolve." Victor Drayton whispered to himself as he walked back towards the center of his chambers. "You'll have to face those alone and sometimes, when you journey through the human world, it can be very rocky, a human life extremely stormy and the terrain can be absolutely heartbreaking to try and venture through."

Despite the fact that Resolve had not yet technically, actually left Victor Drayton's side, in every way imaginable, it almost felt to Victor Drayton as though his departure had already taken place and as if the very second that Victor Drayton had agreed to assist Resolve, he had silently departed. Although it grieved Victor Drayton's heart immensely, the request that Resolve had made for the right to live a human life was deeply rooted in sincerity and he could not deny the fact that Resolve's presence on the actual face of the Earth, would ultimately be a presence that would at the very least, benefit humanity itself.

No part of Victor Drayton could possibly deny Resolve's very sincere request because it came from a son that had essentially, filled so many of his own years with joy, happiness, companionship and a tremendous amount of comfort. Some remnants of Victor Drayton's own humanity still definitely, silently resided inside his electronic mind and Resolve's desire to become human seemed to align quite peacefully with some of those very human sentiments, regardless of Victor Drayton's other wishes. Rather unexpectedly, the request that Resolve had made that morning had required more from Victor Drayton than just his usual role as 'The Guardian' and his fatherly human love for Resolve had been fully tested and he'd had to crucify himself and his own wishes for the son that he so deeply loved, cherished and treasured.

INTELLECT: USER REPAIR

Although the past fifty years of Victor Drayton's existence had been spent in a remote, distant location that remained quite separate from the human world and human life, he could now very clearly see that his own humanity that morning had actually been fully rekindled as Resolve had sought his permission to leave. Now, Victor Drayton had truly been called upon to give Resolve, his only son, a real human life and not just an artificial, mechanical, predictable existence and so now, Victor Drayton had been challenged to really become the actual father that he claimed to be.

Upon the circular visual display wall screen that surrounded Victor Drayton which was populated with lots of small flecks of light, there was one slightly larger, far brighter, much shinier dot of light and he suddenly began to walk towards it. Several thoughts ran silently through the passageways of Victor Drayton's electronic mind as he crossed his chambers as he began to consider all the tasks that would have to be performed, prior to Resolve's actual departure because a mind implantation into a human body was not impossible but it would as he already knew, be extremely tricky.

In fact, since it would be the very first time that Victor Drayton would perform an actual mind implantation himself, it was a procedure that he had never performed before which meant, it could be quite risky but as he silently began to prepare himself for the tasks that lay ahead, he fully accepted that Resolve's decision would not now, actually be reversed. Once Resolve left the Intellect Framework, the largest, brightest dot of light inside Victor Drayton's chambers would be extinguished forever and it would never shine again because Resolve would cease to exist as a Monitoring Program and as Victor Drayton neared the spot of light and then looked affectionately at it, he gently shook his head in sadness.

Inside Resolve's non-human form, Victor Drayton now realized, a hunger had grown to physically touch another human being and to have an actual tangible presence and he wanted to feel the emotions of loving another human life more than oneself and even the issue of living a much more limited, human mortal life had not managed to dissuade him. Every part of Victor Drayton fully appreciated Resolve's desires because he so often felt those urges inside himself, since he still longed at times for a tangible human existence once more but he could never leave Intellect because he was now tied to every aspect of its existence and Intellect was ultimately, his forever.

"Perhaps a lifetime of human happiness with someone you really love is worth a very lonely forever." Victor Drayton admitted to himself. "If I brought Leona here, they could potentially live an immortal life together but that would be impossible because she is a living human being and it probably wouldn't satisfy Resolve anyway." He considered thoughtfully.

According to what Victor Drayton had agreed with Intell, just before Intellect had been created which had been predominantly due to his own recommendations, the Intellect Framework would assist and support human beings but not be directly involved in human lives. No directly expressed communication between the two planes of existence was therefore allowed and permissible and no living human being was supposed to know about Intellect's existence in any capacity, except those within the higher ranks of Intell. Quite sadly however, the very strict protocols that Victor Drayton himself had insisted upon, now meant that he could not attempt to bring Leona into Resolve's current environment because it would jeopardize

INTELLECT: USER REPAIR

Intellect's whole existence but even if he could do so, Victor Drayton doubted that such actions on his part would result in any satisfaction for Resolve anyway.

Technically as Victor Drayton already knew, if the mind of a human being was implanted into the Intellect Framework, they would then lose all human capacity and no longer be a tangible, living human being, much like Victor Drayton himself because all the tangible elements of their existence would then be declared deceased and their brain would no longer function inside their human body. To bring Leona's mind into the Intellect Framework whilst she was still alive would therefore result in a loss of her human, physical capabilities and would end her physical human life which would provide no physical, tangible satisfaction for Resolve because those human capabilities that Leona possessed, were ultimately, what Resolve wanted to experience alongside her and so it would be absolutely pointless, even if was actually permissible. The opportunity to experience life together in a very human way was something that Victor Drayton definitely felt, the two actually deserved and to change that potentially joyous exploration of a shared human existence, would be to rob them both of a human lifetime of potential happiness together.

Every part of Victor Drayton fully understood Resolve's position because Resolve just wanted to live a human life free from the constraints of his current existence which now really restricted him and he wanted to be able to step inside a human vessel which would ultimately, give him the freedom to love, live, laugh, cry, touch and feel, just like a mortal human being. An obstruction however, now definitely stood in the way of Resolve's enjoyment of his own existence, Victor Drayton concluded and the fulfilment of his human desires and that quite sadly, was the very same framework that had actually given him an existence in the first place.

From what Victor Drayton could clearly see, a deep seeded desire seemed to reside inside Resolve that wanted to be free to love an actual human being, he wanted to be free to walk the face of the Earth in human form, he wanted to be free to fail or succeed just like human beings were and he wanted to live and die as a human entity. The potential hurt, pain, misery and disappointment that a human existence could offer Resolve hadn't it seemed, dissuaded him in any way and Victor Drayton suddenly began to appreciate Resolve's courage because he was ultimately, ready to sacrifice absolutely everything for the woman that he truly, deeply loved.

An image of Leona began to populate the circular visual display wall screen inside Victor Drayton's chambers as he commanded it to appear and he then started to reflect upon Resolve's decision and actual choice as he glanced thoughtfully at her face. Nothing but total silence surrounded Victor Drayton as he focused upon Leona intensely for a moment and considered her suitability for his son and as he watched her in thoughtful approval, he started to nod his head. Deep down inside, Victor Drayton already knew that Resolve had made an excellent choice and on that particular issue, he really couldn't fault Resolve because Leona was a decent, compassionate soul and a peaceful, loyal human being.

"Please look after my son Leona, you gave him a human heart and so now, he wants to give that human heart to you." Victor Drayton whispered to himself "And just like you, he has a very human heart, so please don't break it because he is very unique, extremely special and I love him dearly."

INTELLECT: USER REPAIR

Every part of Victor Drayton's electronic form silently mourned as he rapidly commanded the display upon the wall screen inside his chambers to change and then started to seek out a male human vessel for Resolve to reside in and occupy. A suitable male human form had to be found that was due to depart from human life in the next few days because Resolve as Victor Drayton already knew, would be ready to leave Intellect by the end of that coming week. Time was definitely off the essence as Victor Drayton was fully aware because Leona's problems were now almost fully resolved which meant, Resolve would have to step into her life as that resolution completion occurred, so that he could form a real human connection with her before any negative people or events could populate and occupy any of the spaces in her life so that going forward, he would be by her human side to protect her.

Although every aspect of human life was totally unpredictable and Resolve's decision made no logical sense to Victor Drayton at all, simultaneously somehow, it also made absolute sense because he had once occupied a human form himself and he too had loved someone before. A chance had now been created and existed for Leona and Resolve that could allow them both to experience a peaceful, joyful, mature, pleasant love and although Victor Drayton accepted that it wouldn't last forever because human lifespans were constrained by the mortal nature of human flesh that love could at least last, for the remainder of their actual human lifetimes. Positive, loving, genuine human romantic relationships were very hard to find and human love rarely stood the test of time as Victor Drayton already knew but Resolve would protect Leona from any potential heartbreak in the future because he would stand by her side for the duration of his human lifetime, or for as long as she allowed him to be there.

Another gift now had to be given to humanity by Victor Drayton but this would be the most personal gift of all because this would be the gift of Victor Drayton's own surrogate son, who he'd created, raised and would now give an actual human life to.   The broken, shattered, crushed human heart that Darin had so callously torn to pieces, would eventually be fully repaired and lovingly restored through Resolve's love for Leona and to break two beautiful hearts by forcing them to remain separated, distant and apart, was something that Victor Drayton certainly could not do and then actually exist with. Only one actual gift existed inside the entire Intellect Framework that Victor Drayton could possibly give to Leona and that was the most precious gift of all because that gift was Resolve, the treasure of Victor Drayton's own heart and his only son but deep down inside, he fully appreciated that when it came to this particular act of devotion, there was no real actual choice for him.

When it came to the issue of choice, for Victor Drayton that morning, there had been absolutely no choice because Resolve was a gift that he definitely had to give to Leona, not just for her sake but also for the sake of Resolve's own happiness.   To ensure the long-term happiness of both parties, Victor Drayton had to make the ultimate sacrifice because Resolve's happiness really meant far more to him than his own.   The relationship between the two that Resolve would hopefully establish, would not be broken or destroyed by a weak, unfaithful man because as Victor Drayton already knew, Resolve would love Leona faithfully until the end of his human lifetime, if she allowed him to because that was the kind of man that he had raised Resolve to become and to be.

INTELLECT: USER REPAIR

"Perhaps my heart has to be broken to save their two hearts." Victor Drayton whispered to himself. "And then I can truly call myself, a father to my son."

One very positive thing however, did provide a particle of comfort to Victor Drayton as he continued to conduct his search for a suitable male human vessel for Resolve to occupy and that was the fact that Resolve had at least been provided with lots of useful skills and knowledge that would accompany him wherever he went. In fact, when Resolve arrived in mortal form on the surface of the human planet and as he journeyed across it, Victor Drayton felt peacefully reassured that he would definitely be well enough equipped to handle whatever humanity threw at him because some of those skills and knowledge had originated from Victor Drayton's own mind. To some extent that very personal input into Resolve's intellectual capacity also meant that wherever Resolve went during the course of his human lifetime, he would take part of Intellect and part of Victor Drayton along with him and so in some intangible way, Victor Drayton would always be a part of Resolve, no matter where he was situated.

Earth very much like the human life that inhabited it, Victor Drayton already knew, was dying a slow, painful death every single day as its resources were consumed and depleted by those it was ruled by, human beings. One day, the human planet would no longer actually be habitable at all and then the human life that had once occupied almost every habitable single part of it, would also disappear but Victor Drayton felt absolutely certain that, that eventuality would not happen in Resolve's human lifetime. Once Resolve stepped into an actual human form and once his functionalities had been implanted inside a human body however, as Victor Drayton fully appreciated, he would then slowly start to walk towards his mortal death every single day and there would be absolutely no turning back because Resolve would live and die on the human Earth that he so longed to be a part of.

"I have to try and find a very strong body for Resolve to live inside." Victor Drayton advised himself. "A human male body is a necessary component for his departure but it really has to be a strong one."

An emotional bond of sacrificial devotion had formed, taken root and then had fully grown inside Resolve which Victor Drayton truly recognized, since he himself had once felt it too and it silently reminded him of what it really felt like to be human as he began to admire and appreciate Resolve's deep emotional connection to Leona. The total dedication that a man really felt when he truly loved a woman usually drove him to go above and beyond his limits and to make any sacrifices that he had to, just to be by her side and Victor Drayton fully understood that commitment and those sacrifices because at one time, he'd even made them himself.

Although Victor Drayton absolutely hated the fact that Resolve wanted to leave Intellect and his side, part of him deep down inside, really admired Resolve's stance and the decision that Resolve had made because that day, he had been reminded of what it actually felt like for a human being to truly love another human being. Sincere, devoted, pure romantic human love wasn't something that Victor Drayton would ever be able to easily replicate inside Intellect and so he silently began to accept that limitation as he started to internally prepare himself for Resolve's departure because it was so very individual and so humanly complex and it was the kind of love that many human beings lived for and at times, even died for. Love had knocked upon Resolve's door and provided his existence with meaning, a purpose and something to exist for outside of his own form and that touched Victor Drayton deeply because another human life had given Resolve a truly human heart which was something that no amount of programming could have ever given to him and in some unpredictable way, Resolve had now become a real human being and Victor Drayton could absolutely never, deny him the right to that actual humanity.

For Leona, when the Sunday morning arrived, it was reasonably pleasant despite the awful disappointments that Darin had delivered to her heart the previous week via the package of hurt that had landed on her doorstep and that she had received on the Friday evening which had deeply shocked her because it had been quite unexpected. Deep down inside, although Leona had at times suspected that Darin was a liar and a cheat, she had always given him the benefit of the doubt and tried to believe him but that ladder of support, she had finally decided that weekend, would no longer be offered and extended towards him because of her recent discoveries and his cheating antics and that final decision had now lifted a very heavy weight of her mind.

Rather intriguingly that morning, once Leona had eaten breakfast and then showered, she found an unexpected email inside her inbox from an unknown sender which contained a voucher for the hair salon that she usually visited and an appointment had been provisionally made for that afternoon, subject to Leona's acceptance which absolutely delighted her.

"I definitely need to see Vernon; my hair is like a bush." Leona admitted to herself as she quickly clicked on the link to accept the appointment slot and the voucher. She smiled as she began to run her fingers through her hair. "It's like a garden full of overgrown weeds and unfortunately, there aren't any flowers in this particular garden. I wonder who sent me the voucher though that was a pleasant surprise, perhaps it was Vernon or one of his staff."

Once lunchtime arrived, so too did a confirmation email from the hair salon which finalized Leona's appointment at two that afternoon and although she had absolutely no idea who had arranged the appointment for her, in the end she just attributed it to the hair salon itself. An assumption was rapidly made by Leona that someone had discreetly reached out to her because they hadn't seen her at the salon for so long, in an attempt to rekindle her custom and remind her about the hair that sat on top of her head which had definitely seen, far better days. In fact, recently, Leona's hair had become totally unrecognizable, even to her, because it was very messy, quite wild and completely overgrown and so it was now, in desperate need of some dedicated care and some expert attention and so the voucher was welcomed with very open arms, an appreciative smile and tons of split ends.

At around quarter to two, Leona eagerly began to make her way towards the hair salon as she prepared to spend the next hour or so of her life being generously pampered and professionally maintained. The bush on top of Leona's head that was technically, supposed to represent her actual hair had no idea that it was just about to be pruned and as Leona ran her fingers through some of the strands as she walked, she released a tired sigh because her hair had become just another causality of her truly awful relationship with Darin.

Some warm rays of sunshine gently bounced of Leona's cheeks and naked arms as the sun gently caressed her skin as she made her way briskly through the city center, towards the quiet back street where the salon was situated because she was anxious to arrive at the salon in a timely fashion. A few human beings decorated the stone walkways, Leona noticed as she walked along each one but none of them uttered a single word to her and they all seemed to be very preoccupied with their own lives and their own affairs as some conversed with those who accompanied them and as she quietly passed by each stranger, she politely wove in and out of their midst. Since Darin hadn't featured much in Leona's weekend so far, the day seemed extremely peaceful but as Leona already knew, Monday morning would soon land upon the runway of her life and so too would Samson, another dumpling of stress with an aggravated cherry on top.

Approximately ten minutes later, once Leona arrived outside the hair salon, she enthusiastically pushed open the door as she prepared for her hair appointment with excitement and what she hoped might actually be a new beginning because hopefully, courtesy of Nicky's assistance, she would get rid of Darin forever in the next week. In the working week was due to come, Leona hoped that Nicky would deliver what she needed so that she could finally boot Darin out of her life for good which would then mean that the two new dresses she had recently bought and the new hair style she was just about to have, would adequately equip her for the following weekend which would be her first official weekend in five years without Darin. Once Leona was totally Darin free, the couple's fake engagement would then no longer be a miserable constraint upon her life and so she fully intended to make some plans to do something very unusual and something tremendously exciting because Darin's baggage of pain, misery and heartbreak would no longer weigh her mind, body and heart down and so her new hairstyle then could and would, be put to very good use.

Much to Leona's absolute delight, the second she stepped inside the hair salon, a friendly, familiar male face rapidly approached her and greeted her with warm smile and Leona immediately smiled back. Due to the well-established relationship that now existed between the two as hairdresser and client, both parties already knew each other quite well because Vernon had looked after Leona's hair for the past five years and in fact, he had been her hairdresser ever since she had first moved into the mews but her recent visits had definitely become quite sparse and far less frequent.

"Well stranger, I haven't seen you for a while." Vernon teased playfully as he gently held onto Leona's arm and then guided her towards a nearby vacant chair. "You haven't been cheating on my salon have you and been seeing another pair of scissors?" He joked.

Leona giggled as she began to gently shake her head. "Of course, not Vernon, I'd never do such a thing. Your snippy snapping is the best in Pinesfield. How could anyone with a sensible strand of hair on their head possibly cheat on your snappy scissors?" She joked as she followed him towards the chair and then sat down.

"Great that's what I like to hear. Well, let's get you something to drink Leona and then I'll make a start." Vernon said as he smiled. He turned to face the female apprentice that was seated behind the reception desk at the front of the venue and then motioned to her. "Fiona, can you make Leona a cup of coffee please and she'll need a robe?"

"Yes Vernon." Fiona replied as she quickly rose to her feet.

"And then can you wash and condition her hair for me please?" Vernon asked.

"Sure Vernon." Fiona immediately agreed as she plucked a robe from a cupboard behind the reception desk.

"Here's some magazines for you to look at Leona." Vernon mentioned as he plucked a few magazines from a nearby shelf and then handed them to her. "You can either pick out a style from one of those and I'll tailor it to suit your face, or you can pick something totally different. Your hair is your crown and today, I'm going to make your crown look absolutely stunning."

"What if someone doesn't have any hair on their head Vernon?" Leona asked as she accepted the magazines and giggled. "Would they still have a crown?"

"Yes of course they would, but then their crown would be their shiny head, or their wig, or perhaps even their hat." Vernon replied with a grin. "I'll be right back Leona but don't worry Fiona's great, you're in very safe hands." He leant down towards Leona's ear and then continued in a whisper. "I trained her myself, so she knows how to massage the shampoo and conditioner into your head properly, she's great stress relief."

A friendly smile was immediately given to Fiona as Leona was courteously attended to and she quickly stood up in order to slip on the robe that Fiona offered to her. The magazines that Vernon had provided were quickly flicked through and visually scanned as soon as Leona sat back down as Fiona stood next to a metal equipment trolley beside Leona's chair for a couple of minutes and prepared some equipment for Vernon.

"What would you like to drink Leona, there's tea, coffee and even some hot chocolate?" Fiona asked as she paused for a moment, turned to face her and smiled. "Oh, and we also have some cold drinks too, if you'd prefer something cold."

"I'd love a coffee please Fiona, I usually have it with two sugars and a generous portion of milk. I like it quite milky and not too strong." Leona immediately clarified as she smiled appreciatively.

"Okay, I'll just get that for you now." Fiona replied.

Once the beverage of Leona's choice had been agreed upon, Fiona quickly scurried off and then disappeared into the back area of the salon where Leona already knew, a small kitchen was situated. In order to keep herself fully occupied, Leona once more focused upon the magazines inside her hands as she continued to flick through the pages filled with elaborate looking hairstyles as she waited for Fiona to return.

Just a few minutes later, Fiona returned with a black mug filled with hot beige liquid which she placed gently down upon a shelf directly in front of Leona and then she politely waited for Leona to drink it as she returned to her preparation of Vernon's equipment and began to chat cheerfully away.

"Have you seen any styles that you like Leona?" Fiona asked.

"Not yet." Leona immediately admitted. "Some of these hairstyles are a bit too daring for me but I'm still looking. I'm not very adventurous I'm afraid when it comes to my hair but anything would probably be an improvement on how it looks right now."

"Take your time Leona, there's absolutely no rush." Fiona replied with a smile. "I'm not going anywhere, I'll be here all afternoon." She quickly pointed out.

Leona giggled.

Absolutely everything inside the hair salon so far had totally delighted Leona because Fiona had attended to her meticulously and just five minutes later, once Leona's coffee had been consumed, she was courteously escorted towards another chair situated directly in front of a sink as Fiona prepared to wash and condition Leona's hair. Every strand of Leona's hair was then washed and conditioned very thoroughly as Fiona chit chatted cheerfully away about general topics like the weather and as Leona listened to her speak, warm drops of deliciously fresh water ran eagerly across her head, trickled down her forehead and tickled her cheeks as she contributed to the conversation with polite responses as and when required. Once both the shampoo and conditioner had been applied and rinsed out of Leona's hair, a special oil-based treatment was then massaged into the strands which Fiona mentioned would stimulate and revive Leona's roots which made her scalp tingle and it almost felt magical as Leona silently rejoiced in her pleasant afternoon as her hair was fully prepped for Vernon's snappy scissors.

"My roots definitely need to be revived." Leona joked.

"Don't worry Leona, everybody's roots need a good treatment now and again. Are you going anywhere special today?" Fiona asked

"No, not really." Leona replied. "Actually, I hadn't even planned to come here this afternoon, I just received an email with a voucher and the offer of an appointment this morning and so naturally, I jumped at the chance because as you can see, my hair is a bit of a mess."

"Right." Fiona said as she smiled. "That was probably something to do with Vernon, I don't have much to do with the managerial side of things like promotions and stuff."

"Yes, it was probably from Vernon." Leona agreed.

The question that had been posed by Fiona, suddenly provoked Leona to consider how long it had actually been since she had treated herself to an actual haircut because it had definitely been a while and recently, all of her disposable income had been spent upon Darin and from what Leona had seen on the Friday evening, he'd not appreciated a single penny of it. Quite unfortunately and very unintentionally, Leona had somehow, allowed her hair to become a casualty of Darin's financial demands because she had put his needs and requests first and even begun to ignore herself but now, fortunately for Leona that was well and truly over thanks to Nicky and her detective agency. From now on, Leona would no longer spend all her spare resources upon an ungrateful cheating loverat that did not respect her in the slightest and just because Darin hadn't cherished Leona and her heart that didn't mean, she couldn't cherish herself.

In every way possible, Leona silently decided, she had allowed herself to slip into a hole of disrepair because she had allocated a large portion of her financial resources to the maintenance of Darin just to keep him happy and off her back but that would no longer be the case, she vowed because now, she would give her life a spring clean, restore her former self and renovate her exterior. Despite the lack of change when it came to Darin's maturity, his negative attitude and his unromantic meanness which had remained pretty consistent for the past five years and if anything had actually deteriorated and become even worse, something had definitely now changed and that something was Leona herself.

Unlike the past five years, when Leona had just accepted Darin's lying ways and his domineering presence in her life with a heavy heart and broken spirit, now she was finally ready to stand up to him and dismiss Darin forever and now, Leona was ready to tear up their fake engagement and to send him packing for good. This time Darin's departure flight would have no return ticket and the security gates that guarded Leona's heart would be closed to him forever because he would never be allowed to enter back into the land of Leona's life or be able to access her love ever again.

INTELLECT: USER REPAIR

A question rapidly began to scurry through Leona's thoughts as she waited for Fiona to wash out the remnants of the oil treatment as she began to wonder if Nicky had managed to collate enough evidence against Darin yet because that would enable and allow her to dump him forever. Ultimately as Leona was fully aware, Nicky's successful collation and provision of facts was the key to her actual freedom and although Darin could be extremely slippery and very deceitful, Leona really trusted in Nicky's abilities and definitely felt that she would be able to deliver because she seemed to know what she was doing, since she'd already managed to collect quite a lot of evidence that almost totally proved Darin's awful, unfaithful sins.

Just a minute or so later, Fiona gently wrapped Leona's hair in a warm, freshly laundered, beige towel and then she was politely shown back to the chair that Vernon had originally seated her in. Once Leona was seated back inside the chair that was situated directly in front of a row of mirrors, Vernon returned almost immediately with a smile upon his face and a pair of scissors in one of his hands and so her internal questions about Darin were rapidly abandoned as Leona prepared to focus upon her hair once more and made herself a priority because right now, she definitely felt that her hair was much more important than a cheating loverat. Upon Leona's face there was now an appreciative smile as Vernon prepared to attend to her hair and Fiona quickly rushed off as she headed back towards the reception desk to man her post.

"What would you like me to do for you today Leona?" Vernon asked. "Do you want a timid trim, a courageous cut or a rejuvenating restyle?"

"I think I'd like a rejuvenating restyle please Vernon." Leona replied as she giggled. "I'm changing my life at the moment, so I'm going to be brave and have a complete makeover. I'm getting rid of the old rags, split ends, frumpy looks and the very annoying, extremely unfaithful, deadbeat man."

"Don't worry Leona, a hot, sizzling, fresh style is coming right up. Prepare to be dazzled, prepare to be amazed and prepare to look absolutely stunning." Vernon teased playfully as he plucked a long, slim comb from the top of the shiny, metal equipment trolley next to her chair. "Did you see any styles that you like, or should I just make up something new for you? I could do something very unique and something totally spectacular, it's really up to you."

"I'll leave it up to you Vernon." Leona replied. "Something spectacular sounds great though because I need to look absolutely amazing so that when I dump him, he'll realize that he's really lost out that's if I ever see him again which I might not and that would be even better."

"Yes unfortunately, some men don't appreciate a good woman until it's too late and by that time, they're already on a departure flight with someone else." Vernon advised as he thoughtfully shook his head. "And usually that someone else is much better and far nicer, so they're not buying a return ticket."

"How true Vernon. You sound like you have experience." Leona teased.

"Well actually, I didn't lose her, she's still at home but she tells me that every time I forget something." Vernon joked playfully as he lifted up a line of Leona's hair and then slipped it between his fingers as he prepared to trim it. "It's one of her favorite sayings, especially when I don't bring her breakfast in bed on a Saturday morning with a flower on the side of the tray."

Leona giggled. "This guy is a real headache Vernon, he spends all my money, never shows up and I think he's cheated on me loads of times." She rapidly clarified. "I just found out about the cheating last week."

"Wow and you're still there Leona?" Vernon asked as he picked up another line of her hair and then started to cut it. "You need to learn how to kick some butt and how to dump some deadbeat ass, maybe you should go for a self-defense class or something, toughen you up a bit."

"I know, you're totally right Vernon." Leona agreed. "I might just do that if I can't get rid of him this time."

"Would you like another coffee?" Vernon asked.

"Sure, that would be lovely." Leona immediately replied. "And thanks so much for the voucher Vernon, this was a really nice treat."

"Fiona, can you bring Leona another cup of coffee please?" Vernon asked as he turned to face the reception desk. He turned back to face Leona and smiled. "What voucher?"

"Yes, certainly Vernon." Fiona rapidly confirmed as she quickly stood up and then scurried off again towards the rear of the salon and the kitchen.

"This voucher." Leona replied as she leant down towards her handbag, plucked her phone from the interior and then showed him the voucher on the screen of her phone.

"Well, we definitely accept those vouchers Leona." Vernon immediately acknowledged. "But I didn't send it to you, you must have a secret admirer."

"Really, you think? Now that would be quite strange because I haven't met anyone new for ages." Leona replied. "When I'm in a relationship, I tend to be very committed."

"Maybe he's admired you from afar." Vernon teased. "Perhaps he's shy, some men are you know."

"I have absolutely no clue who that could be." Leona said as she thoughtfully began to scan her mind for any recent encounters with men that had crossed her path but there was absolutely no one that she could think off as her mind came up totally blank. "It must have been from very far away because I didn't even notice him."

Vernon laughed. "I wouldn't worry about it too much Leona." He advised as he grinned. "Usually, when men like a woman, they eventually make themselves visible to her, especially when they start to send her gifts. So, he'll show up and step forward when the time is right, maybe he's holding back and waiting until you get rid of the deadbeat."

Leona smiled. "I think you could be right Vernon." She agreed. "Oh well that might be something to look forward to."

"Trust me I'm right." Vernon reassured her as he began to snip away at another row of hair. "Call it mansight, at times even we men understand each other."

Upon Leona's face there was an amused smile as she began to thoughtfully consider who her secret admirer could possibly be because the email that she had received from Resolve had seemed rather personal and for a moment, she silently wondered, if perhaps the voucher might be connected to him too. The noise from the scissors as Vernon snipped diligently away at Leona's hair as he sculpted each strand into creative perfection, actually seemed to soothe Leona and she closed her eyes as she started to relax and drift off into her own thoughts. None of the answers to the questions that occupied Leona's mind, would be found that day and that she already knew because she wasn't due to meet with Nicky until the following week and her secret admirer, if there was indeed a secret admirer, wasn't making his identity obvious to her and so both the positive and negative mysteries in Leona's life, would definitely have to wait, at the very least until after the weekend had ended and had been fully consumed.

When the Sunday night arrived as Leona prepared to sleep, she began to appreciate the current peacefulness of her home as she left the lounge and then began to make her way towards the bedroom because for once, she had enjoyed a whole weekend without the distraction and chaos of the noisy neighbors and without the usual aggravation and stress from Darin. Peaceful moments just simply hadn't existed in Leona's life for so many years and she had really missed the tranquility that her life had once provided to her but once again it seemed, peace had now begun to enter her life and present itself and Leona welcomed its silent return and harmonious companionship with a peaceful heart and very open arms as she began to savor its serene presence.

"A bit of peace is worth a hundred Darins." Leona joked to herself as she stepped inside her bedroom. "And is a far nicer companion than the noisy neighbors."

Only two days sat upon the calendar of life each week that were truly Leona's own to enjoy and that she could claim for herself which were free from the presence of Samson, a Saturday and Sunday and now, it pretty much looked as if they would soon be totally free of Darin's presence too and that joyous thought lifted Leona's spirits tremendously. The serenity that so many other people usually enjoyed was no longer it seemed, actually unattainable and that weekend, Leona had now begun to enthusiastically relish, cherish and savor the peacefulness of her weekend as if it was a sweet, delicious cake that she had been given that no one else knew anything about.

Life and Leona's weekends could certainly offer her far more than Darin's headache and stress and that was becoming increasingly apparent to Leona because she had successfully managed to avoid Darin pretty much all weekend and she'd enjoyed the pleasantness of his absence and his fake arrangements that usually amounted to less than zero. In totality as Leona already knew, Darin's unromantic offerings usually contained nothing but bitter stress, painful headaches and miserable drama and now, she couldn't even stand the sight of him, since Nicky had shown her the actual footage of the things that he had done behind her back and the love crimes he'd committed against her heart.

A text message had actually been received from Darin that afternoon but Leona had simply replied with a very brief message just to let him know that she was busy at the hair salon and so fortunately, she'd managed to avoid any kind of exchanges with him throughout that entire day. None of Darin's calls that day had been answered either, even though he had called a couple of times and luckily for Leona, he hadn't bothered to show up at her actual front door and he'd been nowhere to be seen when she had returned from the hair salon which had been a total relief to her mind and heart.

"The weekend will soon be over and Monday morning will soon be on my doorstep." Leona whispered to herself as she lay down on her bed and placed Giles the teddy bear which now looked more like a ball of fluff than an actual teddy bear on the pillow beside her head. "At least I have you to keep me warm Giles and it seems, you're a lot more faithful to me than Darin is."

Once again Leona's lack of social life had been highlighted to her by another empty weekend and as what could have been a potentially, glorious weekend slipped silently out of her hands, Leona rapidly began to realize as she waited to drift off to sleep that she had not done a single thing with it because she'd kept it free for absolutely no worthwhile reason at all. Due to Darin's fake participation in the couple's engagement, Leona had grown accustomed by now to keeping her weekends free in order to spend some quality time with him and as a result her social life had become a dusty shelf with only one empty box upon it that just sat idly upon that shelf as it waited to be totally discarded. Takeaways and Darin's stress had filled Leona's weekends for so very long but now that really had to change because Darin and his mouldy, heartbreaking, filthy disappointments and his musty, exploitative, trashy engagement would no longer form a part of Leona's life or her future, since Darin had chosen to give their future away to anyone and everyone that would give him the time of day.

"I really have to start doing a lot more with my weekends than just takeaways and Darin's stress." Leona whispered sleepily as she gently rebuked herself. "There really has to be more to my life than just headaches from Samson during the week and stress from Darin every weekend and since Darin won't be around for very much longer, I'll be totally free to do whatever I want to."

Unfortunately for Leona, the next day would be a Monday which meant, she would definitely have to return to work and face another week of Samson and his incessant demands although in recent times, he had been slightly milder than usual but Samson in any capacity as Leona already knew, really wasn't something to look forward to. Another working week would definitely start again very soon as Leona was acutely aware and that was one thing that she could be absolutely certain about because her usual weekly work routine, was pretty much set in stone and totally unavoidable. Once Leona awoke and arose, her working week would then commence and any run-ins with

Samson would once again have to be tolerated for at least five more working days before another Samson free weekend could be enjoyed again and that reality, Leona sleepily considered, certainly wouldn't be filled with the joys of spring.

Only two problems really remained in Leona's life now, Darin and Samson but Leona silently consoled herself as she waited for slumber to fully embrace her with the delightful knowledge that at least one of those awfuls was on their way out the door and that her life would no longer be cluttered up with Darin's truly obnoxious, very disrespectful presence and his heartbreaking drama. A hopeful comfort soothed Leona's heart because she definitely now felt that Nicky was on the verge of a breakthrough and that Darin was on the brink of capture for his love crimes and then that last ribbon of love that Leona had held inside her heart for Darin which had now been worn down to a single, skinny, ragged thread, would finally snap and her heart would be free from Darin's lie of love forever. The joyful prospect that in the coming week, Leona would finally be able to evict Darin from her life and heart completely, provided her with a tremendous amount of comfort and as she began to relax her mind, she smiled a very peaceful, tranquil smile.

Just before the last few minutes of that Sunday night slipped away and before Leona drifted off into the arms of the night, she decided to simply enjoy the final few drops of her weekend without any further thoughts of Darin as she pushed any foul remnants of him firmly from her mind and simply began to appreciate the peacefulness of the moment that she currently lived in. The last few minutes of Leona's Sunday before sleep embraced her, she quietly concluded, were still very much her day to enjoy and she wanted to savor as much of the weekend as she possibly could, for as long as she could because the weekends had now finally become her peaceful sanctuary, her true friend and her main escape from the truly awful people that surrounded her and that had occupied the worst parts of her life for so very long.

FINAL EVICTION

Irrespective of Leona's positive attitude, her Darin free weekend and a gorgeous new hairstyle, once the Monday morning landed upon the runway of Leona's life and she had made her way to work, much to her absolute horror, she rapidly discovered that Samson had already reverted back to his former self. Not even five minutes after Leona had arrived at work and then begun to settle in, Samson's recent lack of interest in her office somehow, completely vanished into thin air as he suddenly swept into the room with an angry scowl upon his face. Rather unfortunately for Leona it rapidly transpired, Samson's period of absence had been very short lived and those days were well and truly over because he was now back to his usual domineering self in full effect and as he strode across the room, equipped with his frosty, demeaning attitude and scornful, derogatory retorts, Leona winced in fear.

Another stream of demands rapidly flowed from Samson's mouth as he immediately assigned four new clients to Leona, all of which were offloaded straight onto her desk with no explanations and without any justifications and she began to silently sigh in total dismay as she listened to him bark instructions at her. The weekend had definitely disappeared for Leona all too soon and the Monday which had stepped in to take its place was fast becoming a total nightmare, courtesy of Samson's usual corporate stress because her live client list was technically, already full and so the additional clients as she already knew, would only translate to longer working weeks for her and later departures times every working day.

In some ways, the return of Samson to his former self had almost been expected but Leona had hoped that the distraction would last slightly longer and keep him away from her door for a while because in his absence, the pressure that she had so often felt due to Samson's heavy corporate demands had actually reduced. Once again however, the increase in Leona's workload was immediate and as Samson dumped more clients onto her desk, Leona silently sighed as she prepared to carry the heavier corporate load.

Whichever way Leona looked at things, Samson was just a repugnant presence and his personal appearances always seemed to ruin her day because he turned every single minute into a shriveled up, withered, bitter leaf that had been discarded by the very branch of the tree that it had once actually thrived upon. Sadly, inside Leona's mind, there were now so many withered, shriveled up, bitter leaves that had fallen off the branches of her memory tree which related to Samson that lay upon the ground of her discarded thoughts, unwanted and loathed as they waited to rot and decompose so that they could be totally forgotten that it was almost impossible to count them. No matter how time passed by however, quite strangely Leona had noticed, the pile of rotten leaves didn't ever seem to reduce or disappear and if anything that pile had actually grown and grown until it had reached the size of a small hill and that was definitely not something that a new hairstyle or a positive attitude could fix.

Quite frustratingly for Resolve as he silently watched the events of Leona's Monday morning at work unfold, a rather unfortunate turn of events had rapidly begun to present itself as a direct result of Samson's affair and Rochelle's subsequent financial request because Samson had now started to heap more clients and work onto Leona's shoulders. The money that Rochelle had asked for definitely had to come from somewhere and Samson's financial provisions it now appeared, he fully intended to come from an increase in his employees' labor efforts and so naturally, Leona his reliable doormat and productive workhorse was his first port of call.

An immaculate plan that Resolve had carefully and intricately devised had now it seemed, almost completely backfired but there was still one small comfort in the midst of that stress and that was Leona's potential lottery win that Resolve had planned would occur at the end of that working week. Upon Resolve's face there was a frustrated frown as he watched Samson lord his corporate power over Leona's head and as Samson shifted the financial pressure that had been placed upon him due to Rochelle's demands straight onto Leona's shoulders, Resolve released a frustrated sigh.

"You'll only have to put up with this for another week Leona." Resolve promised himself solemnly as he watched Samson storm around Leona's office and bark angry demands at her in an aggressive tone. "I promise."

Just a few minutes later, Samson vacated Leona's office with an angry scowl upon his face and as Resolve watched him leave, he was immediately kicked back into action as his attention was drawn once more towards Darin and the footage that had been recorded of his night of passion that past weekend. Only a couple of days really remained for Resolve because by the end of the week, Darin had to be completely evicted from Leona's life so that her lottery win could occur after Darin's ejection from her heart and world, so it was absolutely imperative that Resolve instigated that ejection as soon as he possibly could. Although Resolve couldn't stop the increase in Leona's workload in the short term, he could definitely stop it in the long term but to be totally victorious over Samson and ensure that Leona was released permanently from his grip, was slightly tricky because before the planned lottery win could occur, Resolve had to first get rid of Darin.

"I just hope I win the lottery on Friday." Leona whispered to herself as soon as Samson had cleared her airspace. "That truly is my only hope because then Samson will never be able to darken my days ever again."

"I agree Leona, you really need to be released from Samson's financial grip and his economic domination in a hurry." Resolve muttered to himself as he shook his head. "But don't worry, your present discomfort will only be temporary because very soon, I will give you, your financial freedom."

Leona sighed.

The pleasant, productive peacefulness that Leona had enjoyed at work in recent times, now it seemed had quickly evaporated, unexpectedly dissolved and rapidly disintegrated into absolutely nothing because that Monday morning, Samson was back in full force and forcefully as demanding as ever. An air of tranquility had occupied Leona's working space for quite a short period of time in Samson's absence but that peacefulness had now definitely ended as every serene particle had been driven into hiding, far away from Samson's heavy demands and his angry, scornful, negative attitude. Once again, the load of Samson's incessant corporate demands would have to be carried by Leona and the serenity that she had temporarily enjoyed had now it seemed, fled to the corners of the room and hidden in the shadows of her filing cabinets as far away as possible from Samson's angry barks.

"Samson's distraction ended way too soon and so now, he's back at the forefront of my working day and the door of my office and that is not a pleasant thing." Leona whispered to herself. "The lottery could be my one saving grace though because it could provide me with a financial escape in a hurry and I definitely need an escape." She continued as a fifteen million jackpot sigh escaped from her lips. "Then I'd be able to get away from Samson's corporate ambitions that demand more than his money's worth from my working life. Although it's just a very small glimmer of hope, I'm definitely, hopefully, hopeful."

Another busy working week filled with tight client deadlines had rapidly begun and now awaited Leona's attention and as she already knew, her work responsibilities really could not be postponed because Samson would have her guts for garters, if she didn't deliver that week and deliver in a timely fashion. The gamble that Leona had taken when she had accepted Samson's position of employment had now become a very heavy burden to carry and she fully accepted that reality as she sighed again and focused upon her graphic easel because Samson was certainly not an understanding person and in fact, he was practically a corporate tyrant.

"That's another gamble I lost Resolve." Leona admitted sadly to herself as she began to thoughtfully reconsider the email message that she had received on the Friday evening. "When I agreed to work for Samson that gamble certainly didn't pay off. So, I guess you were right really, even though I still don't know who you are."

INTELLECT: USER REPAIR

Several curious thoughts and speculative ramblings, suddenly began to silently dance through the passageways of Leona's mind as she started to question the mysterious email message and the even more mysterious sender as the unsolved mystery caught Leona's attention once again but frustratingly it seemed, no actual answers lay within her grasp. The prearranged hair appointment and unexpected gift of a voucher to cover the expense that Leona had received on the Sunday morning, further added to the mystery because she still did not have a clue as to who exactly had organized that treat for her but somehow, she definitely felt that the two mysteries were connected.

A sigh of surrender escaped from Leona's lips as she accepted that no answers would be found that day but that acceptance didn't seem to stop the flurry of questions that now leapt, skipped, danced and jumped through the passageways of her mind as to who Resolve could possibly be because that mystery now, absolutely intrigued her. Quite strangely, Leona quietly observed, when a question remained unanswered, it was almost as if that question multiplied and was joined by some other lonely comrades as more and more questions filled one's mind and seemed to congregate inside one's thoughts.

Rather frustratingly, the multitude of questions about the mysterious email message however, didn't seem to provide any kind of answers to themselves as each question continued to tug away inside Leona's mind, almost like a group of naughty, playful children inside a schoolyard that had decided to tease her and pull her hair, purely for their own amusement. Instead of finding answers inside the mysterious email on the Friday evening, Leona had only found more questions and so her curiosity had mounted but work definitely had to be attended to that morning and so she diligently pushed her thoughts firmly to one side as she began to focus her mind once more solely upon her working day.

Regardless of the mysteries that had now been ignited inside Leona's mind and unanswered questions however, the email and the hair appointment had at least provided her with one thing and that one thing, she could definitely find an ounce of hope in because each pleasant event offered her a warm blanket of reassurance woven from the threads of human comfort. A positive spark of hope had now been fully ignited inside Leona's mind due to both occurrences that somewhere out there in the big vast world, someone did really care about her and know exactly who she was and that pleasant spark of hopeful reassurance, made even Samson's angry outbursts, scornful attitude and dictatorial demands slightly easier to cope with.

"For now, the thirst of my curiosity will just have to remain unquenched and the hunger of my thoughts unsatisfied." Leona whispered to herself as she gently shook her head. "Curiosity won't get my work done and neither will strangers or unusual email messages, no matter how interesting they might seem to be." She admitted to herself. "I have client deadlines to meet and satisfy this week and Samson as usual is already on the corporate warpath and it's only Monday morning."

Once lunchtime arrived, after a busy morning had flown by, Leona enthusiastically jumped up from behind her graphic easel as she prepared to attend the lunch meeting that she had arranged with Nicky that day which they had agreed on the Friday would take place inside an eatery in the heart of the city. Another two meetings had been scheduled by the two women which were due to occur on the Monday and the Friday that week, so that Leona could make a decision about the continuation, or escalation of Nicky's investigation into Darin's love crimes because the revelations from the first week had urged Leona to monitor Darin's behavior a lot more closely.

The venue that the two women had chosen for their meeting was situated at around the midpoint between both their workplaces and so it suited both women and as Leona already knew, it served decent enough food to adequately fill up the now empty lunch gap inside her stomach. Despite all Leona's high hopes however, when she arrived at the venue and sat down with Nicky beside the table that she had reserved earlier that day, she rapidly discovered that the footage that Nicky had collated since their last meeting, was very similar in nature to that of their last meeting which frustrated her no end.

Unfortunately for Leona, once again that past weekend, Darin had managed to avoid being caught on camera in a public place in any kind of sexual or passionate embrace and although Nicky showed Leona some footage of an actual woman that entered into Darin's apartment building alongside him, there was no actual evidence that the woman was romantically involved with him. Between Darin and the woman that Nicky had captured on film, who was a total stranger to Leona and not someone recognizable, there was definitely some kind of connection however, because Darin had even left a bar and then driven her to his apartment building with her which she had then entered into alongside him but there had been no public intimate moments and so as Leona already knew, it would probably be quite hard to pin Darin down by his slippery, unfaithful tail with that footage alone.

"Nicky, he'll probably just deny it and say that she's a neighbor or something that lives in his apartment building." Leona pointed out as she shook her head in frustration. "And that he bumped into her at a bar that he'd visited to apply for a job and so he offered her a lift home."

"We're definitely getting closer though Leona." Nicky immediately reassured her. "Don't give up yet. He'll slip up soon and make a guilty mistake, they always do."

"I hope so." Leona replied. "I really can't wait another five years to get rid of him and that would cost me an absolute fortune."

When the two women had eaten their lunch, a discussion began as to how Nicky should proceed for the remainder of that week, since their next meeting was scheduled to occur on the Friday evening. Since Leona had to keep an eye on the time, due to Samson's strict monitoring of employee lunch breaks, their meeting was then quickly concluded and drawn to a close because Leona had to return to work before her lunchtime overran the sixy minute duration that was usually deemed to be acceptable, even though she rarely had so much as a thirty minute lunch break most working days.

Due to the costs of tracking Darin which had definitely begun to mount, Leona now felt as if she faced a mountain of frustration and she expressed that Nicky, once she had settled their lunch bill and as the two prepared to separate. Rather annoyingly for Leona, although she felt so close to getting the actual results that would enable her to get rid of Darin forever, somehow the final confirmation and clarity that she needed, lay just outside her grasp and although she couldn't afford to just walk away, she was unsure how long she could continue with the surveillance operation, since it wasn't providing the results that she'd hoped it would.

A significant sum had already been spent by Leona but Darin was it seemed, far trickier to catch than she had given him actual credit for and that reality irritated her profusely because if she wanted to opt for the decoy option that as Leona knew, would have to happen sooner rather than later since it would be very expensive and she really couldn't afford to do both. Rather annoyingly and very frustratingly for Leona, Darin was it seemed, just as expensive to get rid of as he was to keep by her side, even though technically, he was rarely even by her actual side.

"For some people Leona, the video footage that I've shown you already would actually be enough." Nicky advised. "You really don't have to justify yourself, your decisions or your heart to an actual cheat in any capacity. He is a cheat, you can just dump him."

"I know Nicky. I think I need to do this for myself really. I need to really, really hate him and so I need to see him be sexually unfaithful to me." Leona immediately clarified.

"Look, there is still the decoy option, we could install a camera device inside his home via a technician and then arrange a decoy entrapment setup to sexually entice him but as you already know that would be a lot more expensive." Nicky explained as she verbally walked her through the decoy option. "We usually hire a technician to gain access to his home so that they can install the hidden camera and a woman from an escort agency to assist us in those kinds of situations."

"That might be the only way to catch him." Leona replied as she gently shook her head. "What a nightmare, Darin's expensive to keep and even more expensive to get rid of and an absolutely horrible pile of human stress. Let's just continue with the surveillance for now and if I don't get what I need by say Friday then you can arrange a decoy."

"Right." Nicky agreed. "I just want you to be satisfied."

"Once I have what I need Nicky, I'll be extremely satisfied." Leona rapidly confirmed. "I've been waiting for this moment for a while now, so I have to get it totally and completely right."

"I understand." Nicky replied. "Darin seems like an unfaithful handful and he's very deceitful, isn't he?"

"Yes, he is. He's a very expensive, disgustingly disloyal handful." Leona agreed as she nodded her head and then rose to her feet. "And apparently, deceit is Darin's middle name and cheating is what he does best and he's not even very good at that."

Despite all Nicky's efforts, Resolve felt extremely frustrated as he watched and listened to the two women as they conversed because Darin had proven himself to be a total headache and even his eviction from Leona's life was proving to be quite difficult for human hands and human minds. Rather annoyingly for Resolve, Darin it had now transpired, was a very tricky toad that sat just beyond the reach of the basic surveillance package that Leona could afford, right at the edge of his slimy pond of filth. A decoy package would certainly cost Leona a lot more money and as far as Resolve was concerned, Darin had already cost Leona enough money and it upset Resolve immensely that the cheating loverat, was very costly to get rid of but another alternative was actually, readily available to Resolve and so he quickly decided that now was definitely the right time to utilize his last resort.

Once the meeting between the two women had ended and as Leona began to make her way back towards Samson's corporate domain, much to her surprise, she received an unexpected email as she walked as her phone suddenly began to beep and the device alerted her to the receipt of a new message. The unread message which was marked 'Private and Extremely Confidential' had originated from an unknown sender and it appeared to have a video attached to it but because Leona's lunchtime was now technically over, she decided to wait until she at least got back to the safety of her own office before she attempted to open it or watch it as she rushed along the city streets.

Some working lunchtimes as Leona was fully aware, Samson was known to guard the reception area of his corporate premises in order to monitor when employees embarked upon and then returned from their lunchbreaks and Leona had absolutely no desire to have another negative run in with him that day. A physical appearance therefore had to be put in by Leona as soon as possible in order to avoid Samson's potential wrath because her lunchbreak was definitely almost over and so as the last few minutes trickled silently away, she rushed back into the building with a slightly flustered expression upon her face.

"I've given you what you needed, what you asked for and what you felt you required Leona and so now, it really is all up to you." Resolve whispered to himself as he lay down inside his energization capsule and prepared to install some new upgrades. "I've unpicked the last thread of lies and untangled the last tentacle of false love that Darin had tied around your heart and so now, you can truly be, absolutely free."

Whether or not Resolve ever actually managed to realize his own dream to become human and even if he never actually met Leona face to face in human form, he could now find comfort in the knowledge that he had at the very least, extracted the scumbag from her life that drained a lot of the joy from it and that reality comforted him immensely as he prepared for his re-energization process. A video that contained footage from Darin's most recent sexual indiscretions and cheating moments had been attached to the email that Resolve had sent to both Leona and Nicky's email accounts from a temporary email account that he had created as the two women had finished lunch as he'd discreetly sought to end Darin's reign over Leona's life forever. Unlike Nicky's footage however, the footage that Resolve had collated and then sent to Leona, would provide her with exactly what she really needed and so his solution was final because it was both swift and immediate and it would free Leona's heart permanently from the fake engagement that had tied her to Darin's side and that had virtually paralyzed her life.

Due to Leona's curiosity which had definitely now grown as soon as she arrived back inside her office, she quickly checked her email account on the main computer screen situated on the top of her meeting desk because not only had her curiosity been aroused but she'd also decided that she really couldn't wait until the evening to see what the message contained. Very unfortunately however, Leona was absolutely horrified by what she rapidly discovered because the video file that had been attached to the email, contained images of a very naked looking Darin with his arms wrapped around the naked body of another woman, who she immediately recognized from the footage that Nicky had just shown to her that lunchtime.

Every single one of Leona's questions with regards to Darin's infidelity was rapidly answered by the contents of the video as she began to watch it in total silence because it quickly confirmed, beyond any shadow of a doubt that yes, Darin had been sexually intimate and unfaithful with the woman that he had entered into his apartment building alongside. Nothing but total disgust rapidly began to fill Leona's stomach and as absolute horror chaotically began to churn around inside her body, every inch of Leona's body felt totally repulsed because the images that the video contained made her physically want to vomit. Every part of Leona's interior was now saturated in absolute horror as shock rapidly gripped her body and seemed to hold her totally captive and each scene she watched literally paralyzed her because the video clearly showed Darin, her supposed fiancé, tangled up in sexual acts with another women in a very undeniable way and so it was hard for Leona to absorb the sexual imagery that filled the screen directly in front of her face because the video really was so sexually explicit.

Unfortunately for Leona, the sexual activities and intimate physical entanglements continued to fill her screen for another fifteen minutes and as she shivered with disgust, shock pricked every pore of her skin as she watched each awful scene and absorbed every second of Darin's sexual betrayal. A quick glance at the time and date of the recording rapidly confirmed that it had been recorded the previous Saturday night and so along with Nicky's footage, the sexually explicit video immediately confirmed to Leona that the actual woman that Darin had left the bar with, he had then leapt straight into bed with.

Some prickly tears began to collate in the corner of Leona's eyes as her deepest, darkest, inner suspicions about Darin were speedily confirmed, directly in front of her face as he made love to another women enthusiastically, eagerly and passionately, right before her very eyes. Nothing but groans and moans of sexual pleasure filled Leona's ears as Darin frolicked sexually with the woman as if he was a single man and there seemed to be absolutely no remorse on Darin's part, or concern for their relationship and Leona's heart. No restraints seemed to exist as Darin eagerly penetrated the woman enthusiastically and vigorously and Leona's body actually felt quite numb as she quietly processed the horrible truth and the shocking reality because this unfaithful rat was supposed to be the man that she was currently engaged to.

A half-hearted attempt was quickly made to compose herself as Leona tried to shake herself out of her shock and return to work because her professional duties lay in wait and she could not simply get up and leave work in the middle of a working day, regardless of her heartbreaking discovery. Nothing but absolute disgust filled Leona's core as images of Darin's sexual betrayal continued to flood through her mind and as she stopped the video, closed down her email account and then tried to stand up, she almost collapsed as she silently began to accept the shocking, painful, heartbreaking truth that she now had to face and could never ever possibly deny.

"I'm still at work." Leona quickly reminded herself as she started to walk slowly towards the other side of the room and towards her electronic graphic easel. "I can't collapse or faint right now."

The remainder of Leona's working afternoon that followed that day, was spent predominantly in a very numb daze as she tried to focus upon her client work and attempted to push the horrific images of Darin's betrayal from her mind but she definitely struggled and as a result, the entire afternoon was extremely unproductive for her. An engagement and a relationship that Leona had faithfully, adoringly, loyally and affectionately committed to for five years, now lay in absolute tatters because it had been completely obliterated by the heartbreaking truths of Darin's deceit and his disgusting infidelity and that romantic devastation was all that occupied Leona's mind and thoughts as she went through the motions of her working day for the rest of the afternoon, pretty much like a zombie and achieved absolutely nothing.

When the evening finally arrived, Leona left work at exactly seven on the dot because she could not remain at work for even a second longer and as she exited the building with a distressed frown upon her face, she couldn't even paint a smile across it as she simply ignored anyone and everyone that crossed her path. Both Leona's eyes were cast firmly down towards the ground as she began to walk along the city streets and not even a single word was uttered to anyone as she headed back towards the sanctuary of her own home, accompanied by only the vomit of disgust that Darin's betrayal had created.

Once Leona had reached a safe distance from Samson's corporate home and was situated at least a few streets away from any unwanted ears that might possibly be connected to him, she found a quiet backstreet and then quickly called Nicky as she sought to express her gratitude for the footage and the email that she just assumed, Nicky had sent to her. Somehow that day, as far as Leona was concerned, Nicky had managed to perform an actual miracle with the provision of that footage but how she'd actually managed to get hold of it, Leona had absolutely no idea and although it hadn't been what she wanted to see, it was definitely what she had really needed to see because it would truly free her from Darin's deceitful, unfaithful clutches forever.

Perhaps a rule had been broken by Nicky somewhere along the way to obtain that actual footage, Leona silently concluded as she waited for Nicky to answer her call because there was absolutely no way that Nicky could have captured that footage purely through external surveillance methods alone but for that footage she was indeed, truly grateful. The romantic devastation that Leona felt, was extremely heavy to carry and it seemed to weigh her body down as she quickly found a quiet spot on the backstreet and a bench to sit down upon in order to converse with Nicky slightly more privately and to give her weary, heartbroken body a chance to rest a little because that evening, physical rest was definitely needed. Right now, Leona silently began to accept, although it seemed as if she stood inside a dark tunnel of disappointment, heartbreak and hurt, she hoped that joy would be situated somewhere at the other end of that tunnel because in the midst of all the pain, she had actually been totally freed that day from Darin's lie of love and his illusive mirage of pretentious deceit which had now lasted five very, very, long, unromantically painful years.

"Hi Leona." Nicky said solemnly as she answered her phone. "Are you okay?" She asked.

"Hi Nicky. I'm okay I guess, well just about. Thank you so much for that video footage." Leona immediately replied. "It wasn't what I wanted to see but it was definitely what I needed to see because that was what was really happening."

Between the two women, there was a few seconds of silence that seemed to last longer than just a few seconds as Nicky remained totally silent and Leona began to wonder for a moment, if perhaps she had actually ended the call. The silence was suddenly broken however as Nicky began to speak once more but her response created even more confusion for Leona as she kept totally silent and just listened.

"Leona, I received the same email that you did." Nicky clarified. "But I wasn't the one that sent it to you."

"Perhaps it was sent to us both by someone you work with." Leona quickly suggested as confusion rapidly began to swirl around inside her mind and somersault through her thoughts. "Perhaps they just haven't had a chance to tell you yet that they sent us that video."

"That email and the video it contained, certainly wasn't sent by anyone that I work with Leona." Nicky immediately clarified. "I'm the only person out of the three investigators that work for Venus Honey Traps that's assigned to your love case." She explained. "I'm just as confused about this as you are because that footage was actually shot via a hidden camera inside Darin's home. We would have had let you know in advance, if we were going to do something like that because it would have been very complicated to arrange."

"Who sent us both that email then?" Leona asked.

"I'm not sure Leona. Your guess is as good as mine. Perhaps you have a guardian angel somewhere out there that you don't know about." Nicky suggested.

"Perhaps." Leona replied.

"All questions aside Leona, I'm just glad that you now finally have all the answers that you really needed, so you can make a final decision and then move on with your life." Nicky replied. "He's definitely a cheat in every way imaginable and now, you truly know that for sure."

"Yes, now I have all the horrible facts and the dirty sordid truth, so now, I know the ugly, bitter reality of Darin's fake love and his very, very fake engagement." Leona agreed. "Thanks for all your help Nicky."

"Providing you with the truth is what we do my dear it's our job, so I'm glad I could help a bit, though someone else seems to have stepped in and helped you a lot more than I did." Nicky said as she smiled. "Well, I guess that rounds up our love case and it was a pleasure to assist you Leona, even if we didn't totally catch the cheating loverat for you but at least someone else did and so now, you're romantically free and you can officially, dump Darin for good."

"Yes, now I can definitely dump him forever." Leona agreed in a firm, bitter tone. "Darin's dog days and nights in my life are well and truly, officially over."

"Try not to be too discouraged or heartbroken about it Leona, he's a filthy cheat and now at least, you'll be able to walk in the sunshine of life once again without his misery weighing down your heart." Nicky advised. "And make sure that when you do dump him, you dump him from a distance because he does not deserve to see your beautiful face again, or to have even a second more of your precious life and time."

"Yes, I'll do that." Leona confirmed.

"Good luck Leona and next time you give your heart to someone, I hope he does the same and loves you as faithfully as you love him." Nicky encouraged.

A few final remaining rays of sunshine gently warmed the evening air and as Leona ended the call, she glanced up at the reddish, pinky sky and then stood up as she prepared to resume her journey and head back towards the sanctuary of the mews and the privacy of her own home. Despite the gentle warmth of the evening Sun however, Leona's heart was far from joyful and so in some ways, it almost seemed as if the Sun's presence and warmth mocked her inner turmoil as she began to walk along the quiet backstreet towards her home. The infidelity on Darin's part was now, certainly over but the actual extraction of Darin from Leona's life had not yet begun and remained to be performed that day and that painful ejection as Leona already knew, had the potential to be slightly tricky and it could quite possibly become extremely ugly.

Inside Leona's mind as she walked, there now seemed to be a strange cocktail of emotions that contained some shots of relief and happiness but there was also a very dark base fluid that swirled chaotically around inside her body which contained ample measures of distress, hurt, heartbreak and pain. One huge difference did however, now exist in Leona's life as she walked that had not been present when she had left home earlier that day and for that huge change, Leona now felt truly appreciative and that was the reality that Darin would no longer rule her life because he would no longer be an actual part of it. The dog days and nights of Darin were now, well and truly over and his unreliable nature, lies and deceit would no longer control, dictate or govern Leona's weekends, or any other part of her life.

Although the final bill from the surveillance operation could now be settled in full, it had in the end worked out to be rather costly but fortunately for Leona, no further 'Deadbeat Darin costs' would now be incurred and that was at least, the one small comfort to her as she approached the entrance to the mews. Over the past five years, Darin had cost Leona a lot of money but the final bill for the surveillance operation would be the final cost of Darin's fake love and the last cost that Leona would incur but at least that had to some extent, allowed her to finally get rid of him though where the email with the video footage had actually come from, she still had no idea.

"Truth can be very expensive and it can cost you absolutely everything that you have and even cost you what you don't yet possess." Leona whispered thoughtfully to herself as she silently considered just how rapidly the bill of truth had actually risen in order to expose Darin's unfaithful acts of heartbreaking betrayal. "Truth is definitely a luxury that not everyone can afford."

Upon the doorstep of Leona's life, there now sat a hugely significant moment because her breakup with Darin sat upon the unromantic horizon of Leona's evening and so as she entered inside her home and then made her way towards the lounge as she walked, Leona took a very deep breath as she prepared for Darin's final departure from her life. For about a year now, Leona had waited for this final moment of clarity and so now that it had been provided and realized, she would finally experience and be able to live a life, totally liberated from Darin's seductive grip because his lie of love and his false engagement had simply been utilized to entrap, manipulate and exploit her and that lie of love had now been ripped apart, torn to shreds and shattered into a million tiny pieces by his own unfaithful actions.

Every single horrible second of the couple's relationship was now well and truly over for Leona because the date and time stamps on the video that she had watched that afternoon had totally devastated her and confirmed to her that Darin's acts of unfaithfulness had indeed, been very recent. No denial could now be offered on Darin's part as Leona already knew, because the video footage was definite and certain which meant, he could never possibly ever try to deny anything since this time, his actual sexual betrayal had been caught on film and so all that remained was the final deed that Leona had to perform that day, Darin's actual dismissal from her heart and life.

"A face to face confrontation with Darin could be very ugly." Leona warned herself as she collapsed onto the sofa and some tears began to trickle down her cheeks. She gently touched the screen of her laptop which immediately lit up as she began to sob. "Nicky was right, I should just dump him from a distance by email."

"I totally agree with Nicky." Resolve whispered to himself. "Darin doesn't deserve even another second of your time Leona."

"I don't actually need to see Darin in person to dump him, I've wasted enough of my life on him and I don't even want to spend another second with him." Leona advised herself as she opened up her email account and then clicked on the email inside her inbox that contained the heartbreaking video footage. "After what he did to me, I really can't stand to be anywhere near him and it's hard enough that I'll still have live in the same city as he does, after all this."

Despite Leona's seemingly external calmness, every inch of her body suddenly started to tremble as she prepared to forward the video attachment to Darin's email account because she really wanted him to know that she knew exactly what he had done behind her back. The video attachment still remained intact but on the email that Leona wanted to forward to Darin, she quickly deleted any details that related to other people, like Nicky's name and email address and the sender's email address, both of which were removed so that she could protect the identities of anyone that had assisted her.

Once Darin's email address had been inserted into the correct field, a brief, abrupt, unambiguous message was then rapidly written as Leona warned Darin to stay away from her and ended their engagement in one very clear, razor sharp sentence, so that there could be no misunderstandings on Darin's part. The video clip which remained attached, fully justified Leona's position and ultimately, her final decision and that required no further explanations because the footage really was self-explanatory and could not be denied in any capacity at all.

'Darin, we are no longer engaged and in any kind of romantic relationship, don't ever call me again, or come anywhere near me. Leona'

Five years of emotional investment had finally come to a truly awful end in just one heartbreaking sentence and as Leona sighed and then began to shake her head, tears continued to fill her eyes and stream down her cheeks because it really was so very disappointing. The tone of the email was firm, dismissive, abrupt and final because Leona wanted to ensure that not even an inch of room existed that would allow Darin to think that he could try to wriggle his way back into her life because this time, he most certainly could not.

A very clear expression of Leona's wishes which were absolutely non-negotiable would now be sent to Darin to end their engagement and unlike the usual soft, gentle approach that Leona normally took when it came to Darin, this email was definitely, very different. From the second that Darin opened the email up and then read it, he would know that Leona meant business because this message was not a request or a negotiation, this was a total eviction and a final demand.

Finally, a final eviction order would now be issued by Leona's heart to Darin through the email message that she had written which would end their engagement and their relationship completely and so as Leona touched the send command on her laptop to release it, she released a huge sigh of relief as the message began its silent journey towards Darin's email account. No longer would Darin find any comfort inside Leona's arms, pleasure in her bed or tender affection within her heart and he could now, never ever return to her life again because his position as her lover, partner and potential future husband had been officially terminated and it would never be reinstated because Leona had now, officially served Darin with his final marching orders.

"I've finally managed to evict Darin from my heart and life forever." Leona whispered to herself as she sobbed. "And so tomorrow, my life will start again without him."

Every ounce of Leona's being felt relieved, despite her tears and sorrow as she began to accept that now, Darin really was finally out of her life permanently and as she started to log out of her email account, she wiped some tears from her heartbroken eyes. The couple's engagement had been an utter disgrace from start to finish but now at least, Leona's life was totally Darin free and the five years of suffering that she had endured as she'd tolerated his disrespectful presence in her life in the hope that he would change, were absolutely and totally, completely over. A small wisp of hope began to silently wrap itself gently around Leona's thoughts as she plucked a tissue from the box of tissues that sat on top of the coffee table that the email she had sent to Darin that evening and the video clip it contained, would be enough to scare him away from her door forever because she really did not want to go through anymore drama with him.

"I never want to see Darin ever again." Leona whispered to herself as she sobbed. "Never ever."

Although it had been extremely difficult for Leona to maintain her composure that afternoon, when she had first watched the video, she'd somehow managed to keep calm and muddle her way through her working day but now, tears flowed freely down her cheeks as she began to accept Darin's betrayal in all its fullness. Earlier that day, when Leona had first seen the video footage, she had wanted to scream, she'd wanted to break down and cry, she had wanted to run away and hide from the entire world and she'd wanted to return to the sanctuary of her own home immediately so that she could mourn, grieve and express her emotions privately and although that had not been possible, now that mournful expression could be freely participated in and fully expressed.

"All Darin was in the end, was a trashy cheat that stole my heart and a deadbeat that wasted five years of my life." Leona mourned as she attempted to nurse her broken heart. "And those five years, along with all the sacrifices that I made for him are just romantic losses because they can never be relived or recuperated. So now, all I have left is a broken heart that's been shattered into a million tiny pieces of hurt and there's no love left to heal my wounds because I gave all my love to him."

For the remainder of that Monday evening and well into the night, Leona continued to grieve as she mourned over Darin's unfaithful acts and the heartbreaking reality of his betrayal but as she already knew, her broken heart would not be easy to fix and she would definitely need some time to fully accept and digest the shocking, disgusting truths that she had seen earlier that day. Although deep down inside Leona had always suspected that Darin was a cheat, to actually see him make love to another woman in such an enthusiastic, willing manner had just been a sight that had been too much for her eyes to see and her eyes, mind and heart were still very much in shock.

"I really thought I was going to spend the rest of my life with Darin." Leona whispered to herself as she grieved over the loss of her engagement. "I thought one day, he would finally grow up, mature and that he'd become more responsible and that then we'd have a decent relationship but he didn't and we didn't and it wasn't just immaturity, it was filthy cheating, probably even hundreds of times."

Due to Leona's broken heart as she mourned over the death of the couple's relationship, the loss of their potential future together and a love that had never been true, the question of who had actually sent her the actual email that afternoon with the footage, melted away from the forefront of her mind as her thoughts were fully consumed by grief. The tissue box rapidly became Leona's only comfort and closest companion as she pulled more and more white sheets from the hole in the top of the box and then wiped her eyes and cheeks with each one. Nothing in Leona's world would now ever be the same again because the scar of distrust that Darin had left upon her mind and heart, although it wasn't a physical wound, would definitely have an impact upon Leona's attitude towards men, love and relationships in the future and it certainly wouldn't be a positive one.

"I still have to go to work tomorrow." Leona suddenly reminded herself as she gently shook her head. "Heartbreak or no heartbreak."

Somehow, Leona had managed to muddle her way through the rest of her working day that day but as she was already aware, Samson would be totally livid if she missed any of her deadlines that week, or failed to show up for work the next day. Despite the fact that Darin had broken Leona's heart, the next working morning would definitely land on her doorstep very soon and she would be expected to attend work and that was one thing that she knew, for absolute certain. The heartbreak that Leona had suffered, would not matter to Samson or his corporate ambitions which he was very determined to realize and the shock that Leona had experienced which had almost knocked her off her feet and emotionally crippled her, would not matter to anyone but her and so she grabbed the tissue box from the coffee table as she continued to sob and then wearily rose to her feet as she prepared to rest for the night.

For Resolve and as far as he was concerned, the entire Monday afternoon and evening had been very painful for him because although Darin and his awful deeds had now been fully exposed and shown to Leona, a deep sadness had lingered around his form as he had quietly observed her heartbreak, pain and sorrow. The great comfort that Resolve had felt would come from Leona's liberation had not yet presented itself to her and Leona's emotional wounds were still deep, open and very raw as drops of hurt seeped abundantly and visibly from them. A certain amount of emotional distress had been inflicted upon Leona that day, purely due to Darin's sexual betrayal and that disturbed Resolve because he had watched Leona suffer as a direct result of Darin's heartless actions but he was absolutely powerless to intervene and to provide her with any form of comfort, purely because of Intellect's very strict communication rules which he definitely feared breaking too often.

"I know it hurts right now Leona but my provision of the truth will be the best thing for you in the long term." Resolve reassured himself as he watched her continue to mourn on his visual display wall screen as she made her way towards her bedroom. "Right now, your wounds are still open, painful and very raw and although the damage that Darin did to you will hurt for a while, one day joy will return to your heart and your life, I promise."

Finally, as Resolve could now clearly see, the truth had propelled Leona to throw Darin out of her life forever because it had set her free from the illusions of love and faithfulness that he had sown into her heart that were not grounded in any kind of reality. The spell of Darin's false love had finally been broken by Resolve and the illusions that had bound Leona to Darin's side for years as she had suffered under his false pretenses had now been totally shattered into a million pieces of painful disgust by the shocking, dirty, seedy truth. No matter how liberating the truth had been however, the truth it seemed could not instantly heal the pain inside Leona's heart and that now became increasingly apparent to Resolve as he watched and listened to her grieve but regardless of her pain, he could not put his arms around her shoulders, wipe her tears and soothe her heart and that current constraint once again, really began to frustrate him.

Once the sharp, hurtful, painful shock had been fully absorbed by Leona, once the distress had been endured and once the grief had finally passed, Resolve felt hopeful that Leona would one day live, love and laugh again but for now, he just wanted her to take her time, learn from her mistakes and to heal. Quite sadly, Resolve realized, tolerance, patience and compassion were all positive human qualities that Leona definitely possessed in abundance but Darin, like a ruthless predator had abused those beautiful attributes and even used each one as a weapon against her because he had hurt and betrayed Leona time and time again with absolutely no remorse at all and she had it seemed mistakenly, placed her trust and her beautiful heart in the wrong human hands.

"You see Leona, now I've proven to you once and for all that you should not have tolerated, or accommodated Darin's presence in your life for even a single second. You have a beautiful heart and you deserve so much more out of life than Darin and life really can give you so much more and now that your eyes are truly open and you can see how he disrespected your sacrifices, you'll finally have a chance to see and experience the real beauties that life can offer and provide, minus the deadbeat" Resolve whispered to himself. "Because Darin really is not worthy of your time, your heart, your love, your smile, or your tears."

In many ways, Resolve could certainly appreciate the pain that Leona felt that day as she mourned over the death of a five-year relationship that she had believed, would last for the rest of her human mortal life but that pain as he also knew had to be experienced and endured, so that she would have a future that was far nicer. Not a single morsel of food had been consumed by Leona, since she had returned home from work earlier that evening and as Resolve had watched her virtually collapse in a heap on top of the sofa and then she'd cried and cried, he had longed to stretch his arms out towards her and hold her but human physical comfort unfortunately, was a luxury that Resolve could not currently provide.

Only one small comfort now remained for Resolve as he watched and listened to Leona as she lay inside her bedroom and continued to sob over the five years of her life that she had just lost which had been a total lie and that was the reality that he'd at least, finally managed to kick Darin out of Leona's life and heart completely. Although Resolve had been the messenger of truth that day, he was not the actual cause of Leona's pain but he hoped that his intervention in her life and the changes that he had made, would have a positive effect upon her in the long term, once the manifestation of those changes had been fully realized and Leona had healed from Deadbeat Darin's betrayals.

"It will definitely take you time to heal Leona because you have a very human heart." Resolve whispered to himself as he empathized with her pain. "But I promise, you will definitely heal."

One of Resolve's monitoring windows was rapidly shut down as Resolve silently ended his involvement in Darin's life because now that Leona had dumped Darin, no further monitoring of Darin would be required. If Darin ever dared to show his face in Leona's life again which Resolve doubted that he actually would, Resolve would then have to deal with him in an appropriate manner but for now, Resolve had decided that Darin would no longer be the focus of any of his attention and that really pleased him because he really couldn't stand Darin.

At least now, Resolve considered as he glanced at the two monitoring windows that remained which contained only Leona and Samson, Leona would have the actual opportunity to have a future free from Darin because that very negative, awful part of her life had truly ended. Finally now, Resolve concluded, Leona would have an opportunity to have a decent future with someone else that would love and respect her a lot more than Darin had because at least now, she would finally be free to have a fresh start and she would have a chance to live and love again, instead of being bound by a deceitful knot of heartless lies.

When the Tuesday morning arrived in the city of Pinesfield, it started very sadly but peacefully for Leona as she woke up early in the morning, showered and then prepared to leave for work as she began to accept in totality that Darin would no longer be a part of her life and that in the end that really was actually a good thing. Every step that Leona took on her way to work that morning however, was heavy because she felt totally drained and very worn down as she tried to cope with the pain and hurt that had scarred her heart and mind the previous day. Quite unfortunately for Leona, another human headache in the form of Samson would have to be faced that day and as she was already fully aware, he really didn't give a dam about her personal relationships, or her heartbreak and that was one thing, she definitely knew for absolute certain.

Despite Samson's return to his former self the previous morning, fortunately for Leona, he seemed to physically steer of her actual office throughout the duration of that morning as she arrived at work, settled in, faced her workload and then worked her way through the morning which was one small mercy but the same unfortunately, couldn't be said for his emails. Much to Leona's absolute horror, when she checked her emails just before lunchtime, she found three unread messages from Samson inside her inbox filled with nothing but stress and more client demands that piled even more work onto Leona's desk. The dictatorial presence of Samson was somehow rigidly maintained, Leona quietly concluded as she read the three emails in total dismay, despite his physical absence because although he hadn't put in a personal appearance that morning, he'd more than made up for it with his emails which had definitely increased once again.

"Two new clients and three additional pieces of work that other architects didn't complete on time, all with very tight deadlines, how very Samson." Leona muttered to herself as she rose to her feet, crossed the room and then plucked her handbag from the back of the chair that sat directly in front of her graphic easel. "He must be making up for his recent vacation from horribleness and his time off from meanness now." She moaned. "I do wish Samson's vacation from meanness had been slightly longer though because it did give me such a pleasant, peaceful, productive rest."

Although the burden of Darin's stress had been fully lifted from Leona's shoulders, now it rapidly transpired, Samson was utterly determined to replace it with more corporate stress and with lots more work and his recent demands began to prick Leona's mind with worries as she prepared to step outside in order to collect some lunch.

"Samson's definitely back and he's back in full attack mode which means, the distraction must have ended." Leona whispered to herself as she walked towards her office door. "And if anything, I think he might actually be even worse than before although I didn't think that was humanly possible but now it seems, it definitely is."

"Samson hasn't changed at all and I totally agree Leona, he does seem to be much worse." Resolve muttered to himself as he sadly shook his head. "Don't worry though Darin's finally gone, Friday is on its way to your life and then on Monday morning, you'll be able to resign and so Samson won't be your problem anymore."

Over the past couple of days, Resolve had considered the formulation of a plan to sabotage Samson's life even more but throughout that Tuesday afternoon as he watched Samson take out a huge loan for the large capital sum that Rochelle had requested and then make the transfer to her account, he decided just to allow Samson to wallow in his own self-induced stress.   Once the following Monday morning arrived as Resolve had already planned, Samson would no longer have access to Leona and so she would not be around to help him salvage his corporate entity or to assist him in the fulfilment of his corporate obligations and since the large loan had been secured against most of Samson's business assets, Resolve felt absolutely certain that in the very near future, Samson would lose absolutely everything.

Due to Resolve's promise to himself that he would free Moira from Samson's marital grip, a courier was ordered by Resolve that afternoon to deliver a package to the couple's marital home the following Monday morning which contained a playable device and the footage of Samson's indiscretions that had been downloaded straight onto the memory of the actual device.   The label on the package simply read 'Watch Me Please' and so now, Resolve felt totally reassured that quite soon Samson's sins would be exposed directly to Moira's eyes, heart and mind and just to ensure that they definitely would be, Resolve also created a temporary email account and scheduled an email to be sent from it the next Monday morning which would be sent directly to Moira's inbox with the video footage attached to it.

"I know you think that Samson cares about you Moira and perhaps he does, albeit in a very derogatory manner but his consideration of your heart is just a tad and as far as I'm concerned that really isn't good enough."   Resolve mentioned to himself decisively.   "I've discovered that his love for you is insufficient in comparison to your commitment and love for him and so, I'm going to free you from that unromantic obligation because I think you deserve someone that loves you much more and someone that is far nicer."

Quite ironically and very fittingly, Resolve had in the end decided to utilize a courier to deliver the footage in person and he had also scheduled a personal email which would be sent directly to Moira's inbox, much like Samson had done when he had sent out the invites for the wine reception where his affair had initially begun. Just to make sure that Samson's sins would be exposed to Moira in their fullness, Resolve had organized two forms of delivery because he wanted to ensure that she would be given the chance to access the truth about her unfaithful husband and his disrespect, without Samson's interference or any potential denial on his part.

Later that day, once the evening had entered the city of Pinesfield, Resolve watched quietly as Leona started to make her way home and he observed that her evening had officially begun at least two whole hours after all the other architects that Samson employed had already left the building. The lateness of Leona's departure wasn't anything particularly unusual however and so Resolve wasn't really surprised by it because he had already noticed that Leona frequently worked much longer hours than the other people that occupied similar positions within Samson's corporate entity but Samson's inequitable expectations of Leona, continued to annoy and irritate him.

A pleasant activity however, had been planned by Resolve for later that day which was actually scheduled to occur during the night that he was very excited about and his hopeful wishes calmed his logical processes to some extent because that actual activity would involve some direct communication with Leona herself. Due to the very strict communication rules that governed Intellect's operations, Resolve had decided to wait until Leona was fast asleep before he began to initiate the Mind Probe because it was more than his existence was worth to risk doing it whilst she was still awake, since that would be deemed a far bigger breach of those rules and perhaps even be considered an act of direct rebellion.

For some highly illogical, totally inexplicable reason, the Tuesday evening seemed to drag by more slowly than usual which Resolve felt was very strange because minutes and hours were such a precise measurement and so time was a constant factor that never varied at all but somehow that evening, it definitely seemed to and it really seemed to drag. When ten thirty that night finally arrived however, Resolve watched in eager anticipation as Leona prepared to sleep and he smiled in peaceful satisfaction as he prepared to comfort the woman that he longed to spend even just one real life second with.

Every intricate detail of Resolve's Mind Probe, dream sequence, simulation activity had been very precisely planned and meticulously prepared because Resolve wanted Leona's first impression of him to be absolutely immaculate, even though she wouldn't actually be awake when it occurred. For the purposes of Resolve's interaction with Leona that night, he had decided to go for a simulated walk with her beside a simulated river, so that they could converse and spend some time together in a relaxed, pleasant, peaceful environment because that would provide Resolve with the chance to soothe some of the hurt and pain that Darin had so callously inflicted upon Leona's being and heart via his most recent acts of sexual betrayal.

When midnight was ushered peacefully and quietly in, the simulation of the river and riverbank was enthusiastically loaded and once everything was absolutely ready as Leona slept, Resolve began the Mind Probe initiation sequence as he attempted to connect directly to her subconscious thoughts for the very first time. An attempt would now be made by Resolve to involve Leona in his actual simulations via a simulated form that her mind would interact with which he could also interact with via his own simulation as he fervently sought to provide Leona with some kind of comfort and some gentle reassurances that her life would improve and that one day, her heart would truly heal.

In a matter of just seconds, Resolve's simulated form was situated next to Leona's simulation beside the riverbank and as he turned to face her, Resolve smiled as he prepared for their first real conversation that he had waited for, from the very first second that he'd set his electronic eyes upon her. Directly in front of the two, there was a river that sparkled, glistened and shone as it gently wound its way further along the riverbanks as the reflection from some nearby lights mingled with the dark waves that rippled peacefully against the stillness of the night.

"Where am I?" Leona's simulation asked.

"You're beside a river." Resolve's simulated form quickly clarified.

"Who are you?" Leona's simulation enquired. "Do we know each other?"

"I'm Resolve." Resolve's simulated form replied as he smiled.

"Is this a dream?" Leona's simulation asked.

"Kind of." Resolve's simulated form explained. "It's more like a shared dream really because I've been waiting to meet you for a while." He explained. "And this was the only way I could do that."

Leona's simulation smiled. "Resolve, now that name sounds familiar. Are you the person that sent me that email?" She enquired.

"Yes." Resolve's simulated form immediately confirmed.

"You said this was the only way that you could meet me, what did you mean?" Leona's simulation asked.

"Let's walk further along the riverbank Leona, it's a beautiful night." Resolve's simulated form suggested.

"Sure." Leona's simulation replied.

"I just meant that your life was very complicated and that my life isn't quite what it should be yet and, in some ways, it's very complicated too, so this was the best way to meet you right now." Resolve's simulated form explained as he began to walk along the riverbank.

"True, my life was very complicated and to be perfectly honest, it was absolutely awful." Leona's simulation agreed as she started to walk alongside him. "I just broke up with my fiancé of five years."

"I know." Resolve's simulated form replied.

"How do you know?" Leona's simulation asked.

"I can see everything." Resolve's simulated form explained. "With time Leona, your life will be much nicer I promise and one day, your heart will truly heal."

"What about your life Resolve?" Leona's simulation asked as she paused and then turned to face him. "Will it be what it should be soon?"

"Yes, hopefully very soon." Resolve's simulated form immediately reassured her as he stopped, faced her and then smiled. "And then we can meet in person and do things like this as often as you wish."

"That's definitely something to look forward too." Leona's simulation replied as she smiled.

"Yes, it really is." Resolve's simulated form agreed. "Just wait for me Leona, I promise I'll be there soon. I might not look exactly the same when you meet me again but I'm on my way towards your life right now."

"But how will I know who you are?" Leona's simulation asked. "If you look different, I probably won't recognize you."

"Don't worry Leona, you'll know." Resolve simulated form promised. "Just try to remember my name."

One final look of adoration and love was affectionately given to Leona by Resolve as he glanced into her eyes, just before he disconnected himself from her sleeping form, her mind and her thoughts as he quickly ended the actual simulation because as Resolve already knew, it was extremely risky. For the very first time ever however, since Resolve had initially set his electronic, non-human eyes upon Leona, his actual verbal expressions and spoken words had been directly communicated to her as himself and heard by the intended recipient and that absolutely delighted him because now, Leona knew that he was an actual real entity, subconsciously at least.

"Now that was definitely a line of code in the right kind of program." Resolve reassured himself as he began to rejoice in the beautiful moment that he had just shared with the woman that he had so longed to meet. "I don't have many jewels of joy Leona but tonight you definitely made one for my memory banks that I will always, truly treasure."

Meanwhile in the very heart of Intellect, inside Victor Drayton's chambers, Victor Drayton had already begun the rather complicated tasks that Resolve's humanization process would require because as he knew, according to Resolve's work as Leona's Life Monitor, Resolve's resolution assignment would be complete by the end of that coming weekend, at which point Resolve would then be ready to leave Intellect. Since no one could actually pass through the Membrane from within Intellect and enter the human Earth without first going through the process of actual humanization, there were certain tasks that had to be performed in advance, so that Resolve could enter into a human form successfully and because some of his functionalities and the attributes that would be taken with him would be implanted inside a human body as that humanization occurred, there really was a lot of preparatory work to do.

In some ways, since Resolve had not yet actually taken a human breath upon the face of the Earth, it almost felt to Victor Drayton as if Resolve would be reborn when he entered the human Earth in human form and since Resolve had only existed inside Intellect for three decades by program standards, he was actually, really still quite young. When Resolve reached the face of the human planet as Victor Drayton already knew, he would almost be like a newborn baby because he would then have to master all the human functions that he had never performed before inside a real human vessel and that would require patience, diligence and practice but there was no instant solution for that lack of human experience which meant, Resolve would have to master certain human functions all by himself, just like human beings had too.

In order to give Resolve the best possible romantic chance, Victor Drayton had carefully selected and then narrowed down his search to just a few male human beings that quite closely resembled what seemed to be Leona's physical preferences, in terms of the human males that she seemed to be drawn to because rejection upon arrival was not a desirable outcome. Since Leona was around the same age as Resolve because she was in her very early thirties, Victor Drayton finally managed to narrow his search down even further as he selected a male human body that was due to depart form the Earth in the next few days that was around the same age but just a few years older. Every single consideration, choice and decision had been very carefully and thoughtfully made as Victor Drayton had sought to select the perfect male human form for Resolve to occupy because he had absolutely no wish to see Resolve arrive upon the face of the planet and then stumble at the final hurdle and be shunned, purely due to his human physicalities.

The human male body that Victor Drayton had chosen in the end had been affected by a brain tumor and the man in question had lived in another city all his life, quite far away from Pinesfield and he had never really travelled very far from home which meant, he had absolutely no connection to Leona's city or anyone in it which suited Victor Drayton's requirements perfectly. A new human identity was rapidly prepared for Resolve which would match his potential human frame and although the human body selected was slightly more athletic looking than Resolve's current intangible form was and a few inches taller than Leona, Victor Drayton felt totally reassured that Resolve would be able to adjust to those physical differences fairly quickly.

If anyone on Earth actually took the time to check on Resolve's new human identity, it would be appear to be totally legitimate and so no one would question his existence when he arrived or as he lived because Victor Drayton had now fully prepared all Resolve's human records and even mapped out a very human history from the exact moment that he was supposed to have been born. An agreement had already been made with Resolve that his human transfer would take place on the Sunday night at the end of that coming weekend and so Victor

INTELLECT: USER REPAIR

Drayton had worked tirelessly since their last face to face meeting and his usual daily routine had been thrown into complete chaos, just to ensure that all the required system synchronizations would be performed in a timely manner, so that everything on the face of the Earth would welcome Resolve's arrival and not oppose it.

Just to ensure that Resolve would have an actual source of income when he actually became human, Victor Drayton had created and established a well-resourced technology business that Resolve would immediately assume command off which meant, his human life would be integrated with the human world, virtually straight away. Financial difficulties and economic struggles were not something that Victor Drayton wanted Resolve to suffer or to have to endure because Resolve had already given so much to humanity in his role as a Life Monitor and so Victor Drayton now wanted to ensure that Resolve would truly enjoy his human existence and the time that he spent by Leona's side.

Only one major factor lay outside Victor Drayton's span of control and that was something that he had no actual power over at all and that was the acceptance of Resolve by Leona herself which truly lay inside her hands and heart and so he fervently hoped that she would accept his one and only son and that the two would then have the future together that Resolve so passionately, wished and hoped for. Rather unfortunately for Victor Drayton, the future was the one uncertain aspect that he could not see, predict or foresee and that was one of the few limitations upon him inside Intellect because although he could walk through the past lives of any living human being on the face of the planet and he could tap into their present, he could not see, access or predict anyone's future in any capacity, not even his own.

A sudden thought struck Victor Drayton's electronic mind as just for a moment, he began to wonder if perhaps he had been wrong about the infinite nature of Intellect and the potential immortality of the Monitoring Programs inside it because the reality was, he could not predict that infinite continuity because the future really was completely unforeseeable. Suddenly, Victor Drayton began to doubt his own position and opinions because he could not actually guarantee Resolve an immortal existence anywhere, since he was not even sure that this was possible or even true himself. Infinity and forever for anyone or anything could not be promised by anyone to anyone else, Victor Drayton rapidly realized and began to conclude because the future was unwritten and even the very future of the Intellect Framework itself, was therefore not totally guaranteed.

"Perhaps you are right Resolve and perhaps your decision is the right one to make." Victor Drayton advised himself. "Only time will tell but I'll try to be there for you, no matter where you are, even if it is in a slightly more remote, distant capacity."

Another slight issue worried Victor Drayton as he continued with his preparations and that was his own human nature and the emotional void that he would feel, once Resolve had gone and left his side. Once Resolve departed as Victor Drayton already knew, Resolve would be gone forever and so he began to consider how he could actually fill the emotional void of his own existence because the creation of Resolve had essentially been pretty much like a piece of sticky tape that had been utilized to hold him together in order to cover the cracks of loneliness in his own solitary state of being, due to the lack of human connection that he had experienced for so many years.

"Perhaps it's time for Intellect and for me to change." Victor Drayton considered thoughtfully as he began to reflect upon his own self-created surroundings. "Perhaps I need to give humanity a chance and allow human beings to be a part of this wonderful, supportive lifeline that I've created and perhaps, I can give those who die a chance to live again inside Intellect, so that they can assist those they love from beyond the grave, much like I do."

When the next morning arrived, early in the morning Victor Drayton called Resolve to his chambers to discuss some of the final preparations and all the intricacies that would facilitate Resolve's departure which would take place as the two had already agreed that coming Sunday night. Just a few minutes later, the doors of Victor Drayton's living quarters swished open and as Resolve stepped inside the large circular space, Victor Drayton immediately began to prepare himself sadly but affectionately to greet Resolve because that would essentially be, one of their last face to face discussions before Resolve's actual departure was due to occur.

"I've selected a human body for you to occupy Resolve and so everything will be ready for your departure on Sunday night as we agreed." The Guardian immediately reassured him. "Once you arrive on Earth, you'll have to take a flight to the city of Pinesfield but I'll make all the arrangements for you before you depart."

"Thank you." Resolve replied as he walked towards him.

"Your life on Earth will be very different Resolve." The Guardian explained as he began to pace the interior of his chambers. "You'll no longer have the visibility that you do here and although you'll still be able to manipulate earthly systems beyond a human capacity that will not be to the same degree as you can now because your functionalities will be slightly reduced, in order to align with and to reflect more realistic human capabilities."

"I understand." Resolve agreed as he immediately accepted the new constraints that a physical human form would place upon his existence.

"You've made an excellent choice Resolve and I approve of your decision with regards to Leona." The Guardian mentioned as he paused and then turned to face him. "She is beautiful, humble, pleasant, honest and loyal and I just hope that you both find the happiness that you seek together."

"Thank you, Father." Resolve replied. "Your approval and your blessing mean a lot to me."

"I just hope that she accepts you Resolve and I hope she doesn't break and crush your heart because your sacrifices once made, cannot ever be returned to you or given back." The Guardian advised him. "I still have to fine tune some minor details regarding your actual humanization procedure but everything should be ready for your departure by Sunday night as planned."

"What about you, will you be okay once I leave?" Resolve asked.

"Well, I'll still be here Resolve and I'll keep an eye on you both." The Guardian promised. "Just to make sure that you're okay and I'm making a few changes inside Intellect, so I'll be fine."

Resolve smiled. "Thank you, I really appreciate it." He replied. "What changes are you making?"

"Well Resolve, I've decided to make our services slightly more human in nature and to incorporate some real human entities into that actual process which will allow real human entities to be a part of Intellect's work, so that they can perform some of Intellect's functions." The Guardian explained. "So, I have suggested to Intell that from now on, suitable human beings should be able to request the implantation of their minds into the Intellect system on their death beds, much like I did and then they will be able to love, care and look after their loved ones from beyond the grave."

"So, you won't be alone anymore?" Resolve asked.

"I won't and every one of those deceased simulated entities that join me inside Intellect, will perform the same kind of role as Monitoring Programs, albeit in a slightly messier, more chaotic human fashion I should imagine." The Guardian immediately clarified as he smiled. "This recommendation and request, if granted will provide mankind with a form of immortality to some extent and offer the kind of eternal existence that human beings have sought after for centuries and so I think it will be approved quite quickly."

"So, Monitoring Programs won't exist anymore?" Resolve asked.

"Yes and no. Monitoring Programs will still assist human beings to some extent and the human entities inside Intellect which I refer to as Simulated Deceased Intellect (S.D.I.'s) but in a reduced capacity because eventually S.D.I.'s will replace most of their functionalities." The Guardian explained. "S.D.I.'s will be provided with some of the programmable functionalities of Monitoring Programs but their human personalities and characteristics will still remain intact to some extent, so they will be much more human in nature and will be very individual." He continued. "There will be a merger of intellect between human beings and Intellect's capabilities of sorts and so technically, they'll be hybrids much like you are."

"Will all human beings be able to participate?" Resolve enquired.

"Yes, but not all will wish to participate and not all will be suitable for mind implantation. The human beings that participate in this process will be called Life Guards instead of Life Monitors and each one will be allocated to the human lives of their loved ones and if they have no loved ones, then they will be assigned to individuals allocated to them by the Intellect system." The Guardian explained. "And of course, each S.D.I. will receive some programmable functions and capabilities to help them perform their tasks, or else Intellect will become a total human mess, much like the Earth is."

"So perhaps one day, I could return." Resolve quickly pointed out. "I could become a hybrid again but this time with a human base."

"Perhaps Resolve." The Guardian replied as he smiled. "Hope and possibility are our two lifeboats in life that can never ever sink."

"I'm glad you won't be alone anymore." Resolve said with a smile.

"Well, this is all subject to Intell's final approval of course but since I was the one that insisted upon the stringent separation regulations when I initially created Intellect, they'll probably agree with my recommendations." The Guardian explained. "It's probably the most unwise human decision that I've ever made, since Intellect's inception and it's probably one that I will live to regret but I've already requested the changes now, so that's it, there's no going back.

"Maybe you'll make some new human hybrid friends." Resolve suggested.

"Perhaps that is a possibility." The Guardian replied as he commanded an image of the male human body that he had found and selected to occupy his visual display wall screen. "This will be your human body Resolve and you will be called Axel Resolve Stanton, so please look after it because there aren't any energization capsules on Earth to fix or restore you and you only get one human physical frame." He advised.

"He looks very handsome. Well, at least I think he does." Resolve mentioned appreciatively as he drew much closer to the male human image on display and then began to visually inspect every inch of the human form.

"Yes, he's a fine-looking man." The Guardian confirmed. "By human standards anyway, so hopefully, Leona should like you."

Once a few more details about Resolve's departure from Intellect had been discussed, Victor Drayton watched quietly as Resolve vacated his living chambers and he was left alone once more. The sorrow and heartbreak that had filled Victor Drayton's heart and mind prior to Resolve's arrival, now seemed to have almost vanished because the hopeful wish that Resolve might one day return to his side had been sparked and ignited inside Victor Drayton's electronic form.

"Perhaps one day Resolve, you might even become a father yourself." Victor Drayton whispered to himself as the doors to his living quarters swished closed. "And then perhaps, you'll understand how hard it was for me to let you leave."

A current of excitement seemed to surge, rush and gush through Resolve's form as he made his way back towards his living quarters and it now felt as if every part of his intangible structure was light with absolute delight as he silently rejoiced in the fact that The Guardian had already sourced a superb human male form for him to occupy. Several other aspects of their meeting that morning had also truly thrilled Resolve because The Guardian's approval and blessing had been given to him fully with regards to Leona, a human name had been provided for him and now, there was even a possibility that one day, he could perhaps return to Intellect.

"Axel Resolve Stanton." Resolve whispered to himself repeatedly as he walked as he practiced the pronunciation of the human name that would soon be his until it felt as if it had always naturally been his own.

When Resolve arrived back inside his living quarters, since Leona had only just woken up and was now involved in her usual daily hygiene routine which had to be performed each morning before she left the house, Resolve quickly busied himself as he began to prepare another simulation. This simulation would be slightly different in nature however, from Resolve's past simulation experiences because this simulation he fully intended to be preparation for his first face to face meeting with Leona. Since the two would be total strangers in some respects when they initially met face to face on the surface of the human planet, Resolve adjusted their personal knowledge of each other appropriately for the purposes of the actual simulation, so that they would effectively be on this occasion, total strangers.

For the very first time, a realistic enactment of Resolve's actual entrance into Leona's human life and world would now be performed which Resolve felt was definitely required because he felt slightly nervous about meeting her face to face and so he wanted to be sure that he would be adequately prepared. The database labelled 'Human Romance: Romantic Gestures and Behavior' inside Intellect seemed to offer a vast wealth of knowledge and so Resolve gladly tapped into it for the purposes of his simulation exercise as he eagerly sought out a suitable romantic introduction which would form the basis of an actual entrance for him into Leona's real life and loaded up a blank simulation and then he placed both his and Leona's simulated forms inside it.

Much to Resolve's total delight, he found another menu inside that database filled with lots of constructive, helpful suggestions which appeared under the topic 'Romantic Ice Breakers' which he quickly accessed and a list of options rapidly appeared and populated the open simulation window upon Resolve's wall screen. Each romantic option was considered both logically and emotionally as Resolve carefully analyzed their suitability and the probability of a positive romantic outcome, until finally, three options were finally decided upon that seemed to be the most naturally human and romantically realistic.

- Accidental Collison
- Helpful Assistance
- Request for Directions

First of all, Resolve decided to try out the Helpful Assistance scenario because that really seemed to be the nicest option and as he began to load the simulation into his open, blank simulation window, he started to follow the instructions very precisely with his simulated form as he immediately found himself on a street which had a row of houses and gardens upon it. Further along the street, Resolve noticed that Leona's simulation was currently situated inside a garden at the front of a house and so he immediately commanded his simulated form to walk along the street towards her as he started to enact and participate in the actual simulation exercise.

According to the instructions that related to this particular simulation exercise, Resolve's simulated form was supposed to stop and greet Leona's simulation and so he quickly prepared and commanded his simulated form to do so as he drew much closer to the garden in which her simulation was situated. A hedge seemed to stand in-between the two which was almost shoulder high that partially obstructed their view of each other but as Resolve's simulated form paused opposite Leona's simulation and then turned to face her, he smiled as he prepared to introduce himself to her.

"Good morning." Resolve's simulated form said politely.

"Good morning." Leona's simulation replied.

"I live just down the road and I can see that you have hedge that needs a trim, so since I have a hedge trimmer, if you'd like me too, I could bring it over and give your hedge a quick once over?" Resolve's simulated form offered.

"Really that wouldn't be too much trouble?" Leona's simulation asked.

"It would be absolutely no trouble at all." Resolve's simulated form insisted. "In fact, it would be my pleasure. I need to use the hedge trimmer more often anyway because I hardly ever use it and so I need to get some practice in, so you'd be doing me a favor really."

"That's very nice of you to offer." Leona's simulation replied.

"When should I come around again to trim the hedge?" Resolve's simulated form asked. "What about Saturday afternoon, at say around four and then perhaps we could even go for a bite to eat afterwards, if you're not too busy?"

"Sure, that would be great." Leona's simulation agreed.

"Great, I'll see you on Saturday at four then." Resolve's simulated form quickly replied. "And here's my phone number just in case you need anything before the weekend." He said as he quickly plucked a small business card out of his jacket pocket and then handed it to her.

"You know, just in case there's an emergency with the hedge or something and it totally collapses."

"Thanks." Leona's simulation said appreciatively as she stretched her arm out across the overgrown hedge to accept his business card and smiled. She plucked the card from his hand and then glanced at it. "I'll see you on Saturday then Axel."

"Yes." Resolve's simulated form agreed. "And what's your name please?"

"Leona." Leona's simulation replied. "I'm Leona."

"Lovely to meet you Leona and I'll see you on Saturday." Resolve's simulated form confirmed.

On that very pleasant note, the simulation suddenly ended and Resolve smiled a very satisfied smile as he began to nod his head because the introduction was almost absolutely perfect but there was one small flaw that presented itself to him and he definitely had to give that point some further logical consideration. The front garden of Leona's home didn't actually have an actual hedge around it which meant, such an introduction would have to be personally tailored and made far more suitable to be of any use to Resolve, if he wished to utilize that particular ice breaker as an initial introduction.

Two other options did exist when it came to the Romantic Icebreakers that Resolve had selected from the database but the Accidental Collision option, he wasn't very keen on because that could result in actual physical injury and so he'd already decided that it would be a last resort. The two options that appealed the most to Resolve, were the Request for Directions and the Helpful Assistance options because each one seemed far nicer and so those two were greatly preferred and so Resolve began to consider how he could perhaps utilize, tailor and perhaps even combine them both to achieve the optimal results.

"Perhaps I could merge the two. I could offer Leona assistance and then ask her to show me around the city." Resolve advised himself. "And according to the instructions, I have to be charming, polite and friendly, so I'll have to practice my human smile."

Certainty seemed to suddenly flee from Resolve's form for a few seconds as he silently began to doubt himself and his ability to interact with Leona as a human male that wanted to seek a romantic connection to her because it really was rather complex and there were a lot of variables it appeared that had to be just right. Before Resolve landed upon the surface of the Earth, he quietly concluded as he turned his attention once more back towards Leona's human form, he would really have to practice that simulation again because it was actually quite tricky and every single detail had to be tuned to absolute perfection. In order to identify an appropriate area of Leona's life to assist her with, Resolve logically decided, he would definitely have to perform some research because his offer of assistance had to relate to something situated just outside her actual home and it had to make sense, or it would seem quite strange and perhaps even scare her away.

First impressions, when it came to the issue of human encounters with other human beings, from what Resolve had already discovered, were very important to human beings and so he had absolutely no desire for Leona's first impression of him to be negative because he wanted to present himself to the woman whose heart he wished to win in the best possible light. From what The Guardian had told Resolve that day and from what he already knew, although Resolve would technically be the same person when he arrived upon the face of the Earth, he would definitely lose some of his capabilities because those relied upon the

INTELLECT: USER REPAIR

Intellect Framework to function but he hoped that his human presence would be enough for Leona and that it would be attractive to her.

"Less functionalities and a lower intellectual capacity but better looks and a real human physicality." Resolve reminded himself as he glanced at the two open monitoring windows on his visual display wall screen and then smiled. "For a human lifetime with Leona, I can definitely live with those changes and for the very first time ever, I will actually live."

Since Leona had now arrived at work, Resolve quickly focused upon the monitoring window that her human form occupied as he prepared to monitor her working day and Samson. Due to Darin's dismissal by Leona the previous day and the continued absence of the three rowdy neighbors, Resolve now felt far less troubled by her current environment, her usual surroundings and the people that visited her life but Samson could be problematic at times and so a watchful, electronic eye still had to be kept upon him.

"Back to work and unfortunately, back to another day of Samson's corporate stress." Leona muttered under her breath as she stepped inside her office.

A quiet question seemed to silently linger inside Leona's thoughts as she made her way towards her graphic easel that morning but that question had occupied her mind from the very first moment that she had woken up that day and it was related to a very unusual dream that she'd had the night before which had revolved around someone called Resolve. The unexpected email that Leona had received had contained a message from someone that called himself Resolve and now, she had even had a dream about him and she smiled as she suddenly realized that her dream had somehow assumed that Resolve was male but no answers seemed to exist anywhere as to who Resolve actually was. No part of the name Resolve was familiar to Leona in any way, shape or form and no matter how often she racked her brain and searched for any possible answers or any possible signs of recognition, she had not struck gold so far and still remained, totally clueless.

"I wonder who sent me that email?" Leona asked herself thoughtfully as she sat down in front of her graphic easel and prepared to start work. She continued to silently question her own mind for a few more minutes as she searched for an answer but still came up totally blank. "I don't know anyone called Resolve and I even had a dream about him last night. Perhaps Vernon was right, maybe I do have a secret admirer but why would I dream about him?"

Nothing but silence filled Leona's office however and no answers it appeared would be immediately forthcoming but as she faced her graphic easel and then opened up a sketch design that she had to work on that day, she continued to silently ponder over the mystery of Resolve and who he might possibly be. No answers immediately leapt out at Leona as she stared at her graphic easel and no matter how hard she stared at it, all that greeted her was stillness and silence and although a curious mystery now hung over her head, no explanations seemed to be offered to her, from anyone or from anywhere.

"First there was the email from the lottery company with that quite personal message inside it and then there was the video footage that Nicky said had definitely not been sent to me by her and after that there was an actual voucher for a hair appointment." Leona reminded herself.

"Leona is definitely thinking about me today, so that's a very positive sign because that means, she knows I really exist now." Resolve announced to himself rather triumphantly as he glanced at his wall screen and listened to her speak. "Don't worry Leona, I'll be there soon and then you'll know exactly who I am."

For both Resolve and Leona, the majority of Leona's working week for the rest of that week, seemed to pass by relatively quickly as Resolve kept himself fully occupied with various simulation exercises and Leona kept her head down at work as she hopefully waited for Friday's lottery draw. Due to Darin's recent eviction from Leona's life and the absence of the noisy neighbors, Leona's life was now, a far more peaceful place to live and fast becoming quite pleasant which comforted Resolve immensely throughout the rest of her working week as he watched Leona experience her existence for the first time with a more relaxed smile upon her face.

When the Friday morning arrived as was usual for Leona on a working day, she sleepily arose, drank a quick cup of coffee, prepared herself for work and then left her home by seven thirty as she began to make her way to work but unusually that day, her body now felt much lighter and there was a definite spring in her step as she walked. Just under the surface of Leona's skin, there seemed to be an emotional cocktail blend of excitement, hopeful enthusiasm and eager anticipation which simmered delightfully away as it warmed and comforted her core, lightened her mood and cushioned her step because the actual lottery draw was due to occur that same evening and so now, she was actually, quite looking forward to it.

The working morning for Leona that Friday, much to her delight, felt as if it literally flew by as she kept herself fully occupied with her client work, her eyes firmly glued to her graphic easel and her mind diligently focused upon her client deadline that loomed upon the horizon of her current working day. Lunchtime was quickly ushered in and as Leona cheerfully took some time away from her graphic easel, she abandoned her office completely in order to venture outside for a short lunch break, so that she could satisfy the hungry growls and thunderous rumbles that emanated from the depths of her stomach. Due to Leona's high spirits, she literally skipped out of the building for the first time that day as she rejoiced in the fact that throughout that entire working morning thankfully, there had been no annoying emails from Samson to dampen her day which had been a very pleasant change to her working days so far that week.

Life in the space of just four weeks had really changed for Leona and as she collected some lunch from a nearby eatery, she suddenly began to realize that for the very first time. Now for the first time in years, Leona felt totally liberated from the shackles of misery that Darin had tied around her heart and she felt completely refreshed from the recent nights of peaceful rest that her body had desperately needed because the noisy neighbors had not yet returned and neither had their very noisy parties. Every ounce of life itself, suddenly seemed to embrace Leona with each step that she took and as she made her way back to her office with her lunch clasped in her hands, she began to shrug off the dark shadows of disgust that Darin had left behind as fresh optimism began to fill every part of her core, not only towards life but also towards the world around her as she started to welcome the future positively and equipped with a peaceful, joyful, pleasant smile.

HUMANIZATION

Fortunately for Leona, the rest of the her working day that Friday practically zoomed by as she returned from lunch and then completed task after task with an enthusiastic vigor and met her pending client deadline that day with total ease. A spark of hope had now once again been ignited inside Leona's heart that perhaps life could once more be the pleasant place that it had once been and an experience that she looked forward to that could be enjoyed, savored and relished and that hopeful wish spurred her on and encouraged her throughout the rest of her working day because it even made Samson's emails that afternoon, slightly less bearable. Life for Leona was now, just one step away from total perfection, absolute happiness and peaceful bliss because since Darin had actually been kicked out of her life, he had not made any attempts to return and so it really was becoming increasingly pleasant.

The weekend now sat just upon the doorstep of Leona's life and because Darin wouldn't be any part of that two-day Samson vacation, she began to look forward to it as she left work at around eight that evening and then started to make her way home. Due to the heartbreaking discovery that Leona had made and suffered from that week because of Darin, she had in the end, decided just to spend that entire weekend at home which she would use to pamper herself and relax because her heart was still in quite a fragile, delicate state, despite her more positive attitude towards life. Although Leona now had two pretty new dresses and a fantastic hairstyle to match, she had already decided that she wasn't quite ready to face the world again just yet because she definitely felt that she still needed a bit more time to recover from the recent blows of heartache that Darin had delivered to her heart and she didn't feel quite strong enough yet to jump back on the horse of life and gallop around the hills of human adventure.

A hopeful wish lay inside Leona's mind and heart however as she arrived at home and then began to prepare for the lottery draw which she had planned to watch that evening that the run of good luck which seemed to have struck her life would continue and free her from Samson's grip forever. Somehow, in the past month, it almost seemed as if a whirlwind of good fortune had blown through Leona's life, picked up all the pieces of negative debris and then carried each awful one away, in one glorious swoop. The nuisances that had plagued Leona's life for so very long it appeared had now been totally eradicated and as each particle of misery had been picked up and then swept away by that whirlwind of good fortune as it had swept through her life, it had left behind a much more comfortable, heart of happiness but Samson was the final piece of negative debris in her life that very sadly, still remained.

Some takeaway food was hungrily sought out as Leona prepared to have and enjoy her very first totally Darin free weekend for the past five years as she began to appreciate the fact that now Darin had finally gone, so too had the expenses that Leona usually met to subsidize his lifestyle. A few months would definitely be required to recover financially from Darin and the surveillance operation which had in the end cost quite a bit more than originally anticipated but Leona was truly grateful that at the very least, she had finally managed to get rid of him which also meant, she would not spend another penny upon him.

"I can still hope that I might win the lottery tonight, hope doesn't cost anything but a few seconds of your time." Leona whispered to herself as she smiled and touched the screen of her laptop as she began to order some food from a takeaway website. "Hope is a luxury that anyone can afford, even me and since it is so affordable, I can have lots of hope."

Unlike some of the very expensive dresses that Leona had recently seen in the heart of the city, hope didn't cost anything but time and so hope was a free gift that Leona could afford to give her heart that weekend in abundance and something she could now afford to lavish upon herself, due to Darin's now permanent absence because he usually wasted the precious hours of her life with drama, headache, disappointments, false promises and lies. A lottery win that evening for Leona would definitely free her from the final negative constraint that had wrapped itself around her life which was essentially, Samson and his financial grip but as she already knew, hopes and dreams didn't always materialize in reality and so nothing about the lottery draw was certain.

In order to live and survive financially, Leona had worked tirelessly ever since she had graduated and she'd always paid her way in life but Samson had somehow, rather cunningly, definitely got more than his money's worth from his employment of Leona for the past four years. Every part of Leona wished for her financial situation and economic reality to change because she had tired of Samson's dictatorial corporate tendencies and his negative attitude towards her which despite all her hard work and efforts, never seemed to improve and recently, Leona had even begun to absolutely loathe the fact that she was so financially dependent upon him and his corporate dictatorship.

Suddenly, a loud beep sounded out into the air as Leona received a text message to notify her that the takeaway food that she had ordered had just arrived and so she quickly leapt to her feet and then began to make her way towards the front door as she prepared to collect her food and fill the now very empty dinner gap inside her stomach. Although it wasn't quite time for the lottery announcement yet, it soon would be and so very soon Leona would actually know if she was going to be financially blessed with the huge jackpot prize which that week had been estimated to be around fifteen million and she just couldn't wait to actually find out.

Once the bag filled with takeaway food had been eagerly collected from the delivery woman as Leona shut her front door and then returned to the lounge to consume her meal, ripples of excitement seemed to stir within her body which gently flowed across the surface of her skin as she prepared for a huge moment of hopeful possibility. Just a few seconds after Leona arrived back inside the lounge, she switched on the entertainment center, hurriedly collected some cutlery and a plate from the kitchen and then sat down upon the sofa as she prepared to tuck into the Chinese meal that she had just ordered which included a portion of spicy ribs which she absolutely loved. Every inch of Leona's body seemed to buzz with excitement and her patience was fully tested as she waited for the lottery draw to commence and although she didn't really expect to win anything, a huge part of her hoped deep down inside that she would because such a win would solve the final problematic issue in her life, Samson's corporate hellhole.

When nine in the evening finally arrived, which was when the lottery draw was due to commence, Leona started to watch the numbers being randomly selected in eager anticipation as a close eye was also kept upon her laptop screen simultaneously, just to see if any of the numbers that she had selected would actually be drawn. Each number was systematically selected and then announced and as that glorious event occurred, Leona almost froze in total surprise because every single one of her seven numbers had actually been selected and it almost seemed, totally unbelievable.

Inside Leona's body, there was a sudden swirl of chaotic emotions as she began to physically and emotionally react to the tremendously amazing event that had just occurred as she started to process the fact that the lottery numbers that had been chosen that evening and her actual selected numbers, seemed to actually match. A mixture of emotions filled Leona's body as total delight, absolute joy, utter surprise and sheer disbelief gripped her every limb and she blinked repeatedly as she began to rub her eyes. Several glances of disbelief were cast towards the screen of Leona's laptop and then back towards the large, wafer thin television screen that clung to one of the walls inside her lounge as Leona checked and rechecked each number very carefully, multiple times and then she checked each one once again, just to ensure that her eyes had not deceived her.

Some drops of excited sweat rapidly seemed to gather inside Leona's palms as she began to silently process what had just happened and what had just happened to her because it was so unbelievable, since she had never ever won a prize before in her entire life. A few more minutes passed silently by as Leona continued to check and recheck the numbers on both screens over and over again until her mind was totally convinced that her eyes had truly seen the real reality because an actual lottery win really did seem absolutely unbelievable and almost like a total miracle in itself. Every single one of Leona's seven chosen numbers matched the lottery draw that day very precisely and with immaculate accuracy which meant, Leona had won the actual jackpot prize and she simply couldn't believe her luck because winds of good fortune didn't pass by Leona's boat of life very often and this particular gust of wind had not only filled up her sails but had then also flown her out across the entire ocean with just one very powerful blast.

The sunshine of a very beautiful reality had suddenly shone its face directly into Leona's life and she had actually become instantly rich which meant, she would never ever have to work for Samson again in her entire life. Total disbelief somersaulted through the passageways of Leona's mind as she rubbed her eyes and rechecked the numbers again and again, just to ensure that she was not mistaken but those final checks only delightfully clarified and joyfully confirmed to her once again that she had indeed, definitely won the actual main jackpot prize.

"This is absolutely unbelievable." Leona whispered to herself as she finally began to accept what had just occurred. "My life has been totally changed in just minutes. Good fortune has finally found me and knocked upon my door." She gushed excitedly as she suddenly jumped to her feet and then began to dance around the lounge in total delight.

INTELLECT: USER REPAIR

Finally, after all Leona's many long working hours, countless days of dedicated sweat and years of tireless efforts, she had now been completely freed from Samson's corporate clutches once and for all and the final stronghold of pain and discomfort that had constrained her life had been torn apart, ripped to absolute shreds and then totally discarded in the short space of just five minutes. The misery that Samson had inflicted upon Leona's life for four long years on an almost daily basis as he had whipped her with his verbal sticks of hostility, contempt and disrespect would now, thankfully be over because Leona's life had been totally, financially transformed in the time that it usually took her to drink her first cup of coffee each working morning and that truly delightful event, absolutely thrilled her.

"Now Leona, everything in your life is fully resolved." Resolve announced to himself conclusively as he smiled and watched her celebrate her jackpot win on the visual display wall screen directly in front of him. "And so now, my resolution operation is finally, completely complete."

Since every problematic issue that stemmed from Samson had now been fully resolved and he had been eradicated from Leona's life, the monitoring window that contained Samson was rapidly closed down as Resolve enthusiastically exited Samson's life and as he did so, Resolve smiled a triumphant, victorious smile. A great sense of satisfaction rapidly began to fill Resolve's core and a pleasant current of warmth surged through his intangible form as he watched Leona continue to express her happiness because he had now managed to fully resolve every single problem in her life that had distressed, upset and hurt her when he'd initially arrived and had first been allocated to her life which pleased him immensely.

Technically, although Resolve couldn't feel the same volcanic eruption of joy that Leona seemed to feel regarding her lottery win because he had not endured the years of suffering that she had at Samson's hands, he still felt tremendously encouraged because at least, he'd been instrumental in delivering her from the curse of Samson's employment and that achievement gave him, immediate satisfaction. Inside Resolve's intangible form, the current of warmth now seemed to flow and surge through every particle of his being and it was almost as if a wave of delight had suddenly washed over him as he savored his victory and Leona's final, total liberation from Samson's awful, dictatorial, financial grip.

"I'm not much of a dancer Leona, or I would join you in a victory dance." Resolve admitted to himself as he chuckled. "In fact, that's probably another human function that I should practice before I arrive on Earth."

Once that weekend was over, Resolve hoped to be by Leona's actual human side and then she would never be hurt, exploited or mistreated by anyone else again as long as she allowed him to remain beside her and that glorious thought provided him with a tremendous amount of comfort as he watched her overtly express her joy.

"I might not be the perfect dance partner Leona and I might not be able to cook great eggs but I'll do whatever I can to put a smile on your face and to keep it there for as long as possible." Resolve promised himself. "And hopefully quite soon, I'll be there to put a smile on your face every single human day."

Inside Victor Drayton's chambers as he faced the visual display wall screen that surrounded him, he watched both Resolve and Leona inside two separate viewing windows and a smile crossed his face as he observed the successful outcomes of Resolve's final resolution efforts for Leona that day in his role as her Life Monitor. Just to ensure that Resolve's final resolution operation went according to plan, Victor Drayton had decided to check on them both that evening but deep down inside, he already knew, there was no real actual need to because Resolve was extremely competent when it came to the performance of his duties as a Life Monitor.

Every single act of resolution seemed to have been orchestrated meticulously and to absolute perfection by Resolve because Leona's face was now filled with absolute joy and so as Victor Drayton could clearly see, all her troubles had certainly been left, far behind her. The results of Resolve's resolution operations were written all over Leona's face because she now glowed with happiness and her eyes seemed to sparkle and shine as she smiled and laughed and that was a tremendous comfort to Victor Drayton because her life had initially been so very painful, frustratingly stressful and absolutely saturated in total misery.

"I'm sure you'll be a very good human husband Resolve." Victor Drayton reassured himself. "And Leona needs a good husband to love, cherish and protect her, perhaps even more than I need a son. Love is such a precious gift to give someone and I really want you to give Leona that gift, so that you'll both be happy together. I just hope that Leona accepts you and I just hope that your sacrifices will be honored and rewarded with the happiness that you seek."

Unlike Resolve, whose thoughts, emotions, actions and interactions Victor Drayton could easily access, analyze and scrutinize, he could not do that with Leona in any capacity at all because she was a living human being which meant, he had to rely fully upon his gut instincts and his own personal judgement. Every single action inside

Intellect that required an interaction with logical functions and the performance of any prescribed tasks that ran through a Monitoring Program's logical processes, also ran through the core Mainframe which Victor Drayton had unlimited, immediate access to but Leona was completely different because her mind and internal thoughts lay well outside his scope of visibility. Due to Leona's sweet nature, her loyal personality, gentle demeanor, honest disposition, faithful character and respectful attitude, Victor Drayton however, at least felt reassured that when Resolve did humanize his existence, he would give his love to the right person and place his heart in the right female hands but Leona's acceptance wasn't totally guaranteed, despite all Resolve's strengths and the very unique positive attributes that he definitely possessed.

Over the years, due to Resolve's uniqueness, Victor Drayton had definitely enjoyed Resolve's companionship because Resolve harbored thoughts and feelings inside his logical processes that were much more impulsive, far less structured and that deviated vastly from the usual functionalities of the other Monitoring Programs which had always made Resolve a lot more interesting in his sight. Essentially, because Resolve was the only Monitoring Program that had the propensity to do things which were very unique, he was therefore the only entity inside Intellect, besides Victor Drayton himself that at times deviated from what was expected from him and that uniqueness over the years had saved Victor Drayton from the monotony that prior to Resolve's creation had almost consumed him.

For the very first time since Resolve's initial creation however, the request had now been made by Resolve to leave Intellect and Victor Drayton's side and so he began to reflect upon what it would once again be like to exist within the Intellect Framework without Resolve's presence. Over the past three decades, Victor Drayton had frequently watched Resolve as he had formulated and applied some very unusual solutions to some of the monitoring problems that he'd been presented with and at times, those solutions and the results had amused Victor Drayton immensely but now that spontaneity would finally come to an end and he would be left only with the predictable patterns once more. When Resolve departed as Victor Drayton fully appreciated, he would be left solely with the monotonous interactions from the other Monitoring Programs that he had created because there would be no interesting sporadic events, no unexpected deviations and no unusual situations to provide advice about which meant, life for him without Resolve, would rapidly become rather dull.

"Never mind, I'll get used to it." Victor Drayton finally, decisively reassured himself. "I coped with it once, I can cope with it again and perhaps the changes that I've recommended will provide me with some new challenges and keep me busy."

Once eleven that Friday night arrived, Resolve watched in peaceful satisfaction as Leona yawned and then headed towards her bedroom because now that he had resolved every single problem in her life, he felt a tremendous sense of peace. Another satisfactory outcome from Resolve's resolution operations with regards to Samson, was that not only had Resolve relieved Leona of Samson's presence and all the problems that he usually created for her and brought along with him but also that Resolve had now left Samson in Rochelle's very capable hands because she was far better equipped to handle Samson's drama than Leona was. Just like Samson, Rochelle appeared to be extremely motivated by financial stimulants and she was extremely interested in his monetary wealth and net worth which as Resolve already knew, would surely be greatly reduced by the time she had actually finished with him and fortunately for Resolve, Samson seemed to be totally oblivious to her financial goals.

Every dark shadow of misery had now been well and truly cast out of Leona's life and as Resolve watched the internal rays of sunshine light up her heart as she entered into her bedroom with a delighted smile upon her face, he silently rejoiced in all his recent achievements because now, Leona could finally resign which meant, she had been freed from Samson forever. The sudden current of warmth and wave of joy that had filled and washed over Resolve's form since the lottery draw numbers had been drawn and announced earlier that evening, continued to accompany him and so he now felt, fully immersed in the comfort that those positive sentiments provided and as he silently embraced each one, somehow those warm feelings seemed to represent a degree of real human happiness. Suddenly that evening, it felt as if a huge weight had now been lifted from Resolve's non-human form as he began to rest in the knowledge that every problematic issue and each baby in Leona's life had been fully extracted, completely ejected and totally evicted from her environment because that achievement really was such a huge comfort to him.

"Your suffering has finally ended Leona because every single obstacle in your life has now been totally overcome and each shackle of misery has been completely removed." Resolve whispered to himself as he watched her nestle under her duvet as she prepared to sleep. "Which means, your joy has now been, fully restored. So now, you have a life that you can actually live in and enjoy living in."

One small, tiny consideration wandered across Resolve's logical processes as he watched Leona drift off to sleep as he began to wonder what it might be like to be sexually intimate with another human being because that was something that human couples and human males seemed to do quite regularly and he had never so much as even kissed anyone before. Despite the vast wealth of information and knowledge that Intellect possessed about human dating rituals and romance that was one area which didn't appear to have been explored at all and so there were no knowledge files that Resolve knew off which related to that particular aspect of human behavior and Intellect seemed to remain totally silent on that particular issue, much to his frustration.

"Perhaps human sexual intimacy is something that I can ask Leona to teach me in person when I arrive." Resolve advised himself as he smiled.

Some very unfamiliar terrain would have to be crossed by Resolve when he arrived upon the face of the Earth as he made the transition to a real human life and sexual intimacy was just another human aspect of that unfamiliar territory that he would have to explore and venture into but he remained hopeful that his human sexual exploration, when it finally happened, would not be too perilous a journey for him. A hopeful wish now lay inside Resolve's form that his first intimate human romantic experience would occur inside Leona's arms because he really trusted her and so he wanted her to be his first and only human sexual experience in his entire human, mortal lifetime.

The remainder of the weekend passed by relatively quickly for both Resolve and Leona as he busied himself with various simulations and watched over her faithfully and diligently and as the Sunday afternoon arrived, progressed and then the evening stepped into replace it, Resolve waited for his moment of actual humanization to arrive in eager anticipation. All that remained for Resolve that evening in order for his weekend to be complete perfection, was his actual humanization and his departure from Intellect to be by Leona's human side and so enthusiastic currents of excitement, seemed to silently gather, accumulate and then surge through his form as he waited for that event to actually occur.

Finally, Resolve had found an actual way to really be beside Leona in human form, since The Guardian was prepared to grant Resolve his only wish and had promised to provide him with all that he would require which truly delighted him because Resolve had never ever asked, or hoped, or wished for anything before in his entire existence. Every part of Resolve's non-human form tingled with currents of excitement as he waited for his appointment with The Guardian that evening to occur and his actual humanization to really happen but patience rather strangely on this particular occasion, seemed to be absent and in very short supply.

"Tomorrow will usher in a new day for us both Leona." Resolve whispered to himself in excitement as he watched her prepare for the next morning on the monitoring window directly in front of him. "Because tomorrow, I will make my entrance into your very real, human life."

Inside Victor Drayton's chambers however, rather unexpectedly, there was a sudden interruption to his plans that Sunday evening as he made the final preparations for Resolve's departure and an alarm sounded out into the air which instantly notified him that an attack was underway. The perimeter barriers of the Membrane were quickly scanned as Victor Drayton immediately began to inspect who or what exactly was responsible for the attack and then he rapidly attempted to enhance Intellect's shields in response as he tried to obstruct the intruders that wished to infiltrate his sanctuary from doing so which the Intellect Database immediately identified as Paramorphs.

INTELLECT: USER REPAIR

According to Intellect's Databases, Paramorphs inhabited the dimensional planes beyond the scope of human existence and they were a form of hybrid virus that comprised of various programs and viruses that invaded systems inside the human world and outside it. The level of intelligence required and the nature of the attacks however, rapidly confirmed to Victor Drayton that this very sophisticated life form was some kind of advanced, artificial intelligence that at one point in time had quite possibly evolved from the Earth's surface itself. A more sophisticated life form than the human beings it had perhaps once served it seemed, definitely existed and this sophisticated life form it now appeared, wanted to challenge and attack Intellect's actual core.

Just a few minutes later however, the sprinkling of Paramorphs actually seemed to completely vanish from the security radars which were now on full display upon the visual display wall screen inside Victor Drayton's chambers and he gave a sigh of relief as he quickly returned to his tasks. The attack had been so threatening in nature that it could not be ignored or taken lightly and so that meant, once Victor Drayton had completed Resolve's actual humanization procedure that night, he would then have to review all the current security systems and update them throughout the remainder of the night.

Several final tasks were carefully performed as Victor Drayton completed every part of the preparatory work for Resolve's humanization process very thoroughly and some of Resolve's logical functions, capabilities and attributes which had already been replicated and amended, were placed inside the final mind implantation file, ready for transfer to the selected human vessel. A recently deceased human male corpse would be brought back to life, just to fulfill Resolve's request and although that procedure could present a few problems for Victor Drayton, if his actions were ever discovered, he had tried his best to ensure that they wouldn't be.

Some other preparations upon the face of Earth had already taken place over the past few days in preparation for Resolve's arrival as Victor Drayton had discreetly utilized his skills with some assistance from several human beings that he had hired, to prepare, arrange and organize some practicalities for Resolve in order to ensure that when he arrived, he would not be totally stranded. Every single detail of Resolve's arrival had been very thoroughly and precisely planned by Victor Drayton, such as where Resolve would physically wake up, what clothes would adorn his human body when he did so and an apartment had even been organized for him in the city of Pinesfield which had been filled with the various necessities that he would immediately require.

Only one method of human life restoration and mind implantation had been created by Victor Drayton over the years but it had never been fully tested or even once implemented and so it was very experimental but he had built that functionality inside the Intellect Framework, just in case a situation ever arose where such a functionality would be required. No one on the face of the human planet knew anything about Victor Drayton's ability to restore a human life and then transfer and implant a mind into a human form because it wasn't officially something that was within his agreed remit but he had developed some special programs over the years, like the Resuscitation and Restoration Program and the Mind Implant Program that would enable him to perform that very special, technically complex procedure.

In order to apply the special mind implantation process as Victor Drayton already knew, the human body chosen had to have been deceased for less than a week and not every human body could be considered because certain medical conditions would render the process totally ineffective and would result in total failure. Since this was the first time that Victor Drayton had actually performed this very intricate, complex procedure and utilized this particular functionality, the past few days had therefore been very intense for him because he'd had to focus his mind fully upon the task at hand and in order to avoid any possible distractions, he had even completely ignored the usual requirements and performance of his routine maintenance tasks.

On several occasions in the past, Victor Drayton had toyed around with the idea of visiting Earth once more in human form himself to explore the possibility of living another real human life through the mind implantation process but in the end, he had always managed to restrain himself from doing so because his current role within Intellect was deemed to be far more important to him. Inside Intellect, Victor Drayton was needed, required and a necessity and without his electronic mind and hands at the helm, Intellect just wouldn't function and so the importance of his work and his responsibility to humanity had been considered significantly more important to him and therefore had always taken, absolute precedence. The remainder of a possible seventy- or eighty-year human lifespan that Victor Drayton would potentially sacrifice his potential immortality for, if he decided to return to the human world, simply to live out part of another human existence that he would never be able to return from, he had felt in the end, simply wouldn't be worth it.

Some great economies of scale had been realized through Intellect's achievements and Victor Drayton's work over the past five decades because through the creation of his Monitoring Programs and their service provision to humanity, he had managed to help and assist billions of human beings. Somehow and quite unintentionally, through Victor Drayton's work and tireless dedication, he had been given the ability to transcend human mortality and he'd now become the closest thing to a real-life ghost as he had touched human lives and existed alongside humanity in an invisible capacity.

Every day that Victor Drayton spent with his electronic mind encapsulated in an actual plane of existence that had been built to serve, assist and help humanity, he could think, feel and utilize his intellectual skills to improve the lives of human beings in a way that now far exceeded his capabilities when he had actually walked upon the face of the Earth and that satisfied him to some extent in several different ways. The Intellect Framework was therefore not something that Victor Drayton ever really wanted to sacrifice, merely for another temporary, human, mortal life that could be extinguished at any given moment that would have a limited capacity and more restricted capabilities and so he had somehow, managed to find some contentment in his current form and existence as the years had passed by.

Sometimes over the past fifty years however, the loneliness that Victor Drayton had so often felt had provoked him to consider a decision such as the one that Resolve had now made but his sacrifices as he already knew, would be far greater and so he had crucified his human desires as he'd dedicated himself fully to his purpose and learnt to exist with his current existence and the very solitary, lonely constraints that accompanied that choice. Another human lifetime lived out on Earth, could never possibly provide Victor Drayton with the same satisfaction and fulfilment that he currently enjoyed as he was fully aware and so that meant, his very human loneliness which had been the price that he had personally paid had been carried, endured and in some ways, now even accepted.

Once all the final preparations were complete, Victor Drayton began to pace the interior of his chambers with an air of slight hesitation as he delayed his meeting with Resolve for an additional few minutes. Time had it seemed that night, slipped completely from Victor Drayton's grasp and Resolve's departure would definitely occur shortly but he just wanted to spend a few more minutes with Resolve's form still inside Intellect before he departed because essentially, Intellect to some extent had become their family home.

"Now Resolve, I have truly given you everything that a father could give his son." Victor Drayton reassured himself.

Not a sound was to be heard as Victor Drayton continued to pace his chambers as he prepared to call Resolve to his side and surrender to his request to depart in totality with sadness in his electronic eyes and the heavy weight of deep regret inside his heart. Once Resolve actually arrived inside Victor Drayton's chambers that night as he was fully aware, there would be no going back for either of them because Resolve would leave immediately and he would simply have to accept his departure gracefully. In many respects, it was a bitter sweet moment for Victor Drayton and the equilibrium of emotional contentment that he usually enjoyed, rapidly became totally imbalanced as a mixture of nerves, sadness, love, regret and fear suddenly began to swirl chaotically around inside his form and no peaceful, restful balance could be found as the low depths of sadness and high peaks of love, silently seemed to totally engulf him.

Inside Victor Drayton's form, a hole of emptiness had already started to form and it almost felt as if that empty hole now wanted to stretch itself out throughout his entire interior as he momentarily yearned for Resolve to change his mind and stay by his side. The decision that Resolve had made however, would not now be reversed and because Victor Drayton had already accepted it and even assisted Resolve as he had helped him to achieve his human desires, it was inevitable that his actual humanization, would actually occur that very same day. Both parties had gone far beyond the point of internal deliberations, verbal discussions and any further considerations because Resolve would leave Intellect that very same night as he sought out the warmth and comfort of a mortal woman's touch and love inside the human world and so Victor Drayton could not now deny Resolve the right to experience what his heart so desired.

"Another Monitoring Program can never give you what Leona can." Victor Drayton sadly admitted to himself. "Such a relationship wouldn't even come close to what you seek Resolve besides it would take me several years to provide you with an inferior substitute and you can't wait for that to actually happen and neither can Leona."

Deep down inside, Victor Drayton could still appreciate the draw of human love and the need for some kind of real human connection because he had felt that unquenchable human desire himself, even in his current electronic form and so he could definitely relate to Resolve's desires. No Monitoring Program could ever be an adequate substitute for the real romantic human love that Leona and a human partner could potentially offer to Resolve and Victor Drayton totally understood and appreciated that reality because he still felt that very human desire for such love at times himself. Although humanity had definitely evolved, changed and advanced, the very human desire to form a deeper, intimate, special connection to another human being as Victor Drayton knew had ultimately remained the same since time immemorial and that special human connection was what Resolve now fervently required and desired to experience in all its human fullness.

"Leona really needs you now and you need her too and even I can see that." Victor Drayton reminded himself. "Your shared human love, your joint walk through life and your mortal time together, really has to be now and hopefully, you'll both spend the remainder of your human mortal lives, united in romantic, human happiness."

Everything possible had now been done by Victor Drayton to ensure that Resolve's human existence would be as peaceful, enjoyable and as pleasant as it could possibly be and with that one comfort in mind, he prepared to call Resolve to his chambers in order to start his actual humanization procedure. In totality, Victor Drayton now fully understood however, what it truly felt like to be a real human father to his son because that week for the first time in his entire existence, human or otherwise, he had been called upon to give his son the kind of future that Resolve could never have by his side and that sacrifice had truly been, a sacrifice that only he himself could make.

For Resolve as he stood inside his living quarters and waited patiently to be called to The Guardian's chambers, every second of that Sunday evening seemed to have passed by very slowly as he'd watched the human world in the city of Pinesfield became gradually darker as the night had begun to creep into the city and then had fully consumed it. At one point, Resolve had even started to wonder if The Guardian had actually forgotten about his promise to him and their pending face to face meeting that Sunday night which would essentially be the most important meeting that they would ever have because the night seemed to drag by so slowly and all that had surrounded him had been an empty, expectant, impatient silence.

Excitement and eager anticipation however, surged through every part of Resolve's form like powerful electric currents as he waited patiently for his moment of humanization to occur and as he'd watched the night progress, Leona who had been totally oblivious to Resolve's circumstances had slept peacefully upon the wall screen directly in front of him. When Resolve actually arrived upon the face of the Earth, he already knew that he would be situated hundreds of miles away from Leona but The Guardian had promised him that the physical distance between them wouldn't be a huge problem because he would organize transportation which meant that Resolve would arrive in the city of Pinesfield bright and early on the Monday morning.

Finally, and much to Resolve's delight, his expectant, hopeful intangible form was soothed as a message was received from The Guardian to request that Resolve should start to make his way towards his chambers and Resolve almost leapt with delight as he rapidly prepared to depart and leave his living quarters behind for the very last time. One last solitary glance was quickly given to the basic space that had essentially been Resolve's home for the past three decades as he gave his current surroundings a final look of goodbye and silently accepted that it was quite unlikely that he would ever return because there were no real guarantees that he would ever really be able to return to Intellect.

Inside Intellect, there really wasn't much else for Resolve to say goodbye to apart from The Guardian himself because his compact living quarters didn't really contain any items that held any kind of sentimental value and there were no deep emotional bonds to any other Monitoring Programs that would require lengthy explanations, tearful departure messages or even just a sad, lonely farewell. Every Monitoring Program inside Intellect simply co-existed and functioned alongside each other, year after year, decade after decade and they hardly even communicated with each other because there were no real personal relationships amongst them, since most Monitoring Programs did not engage with each other in a personal capacity and so Resolve didn't feel that he would be particularly missed in that respect.

Once Resolve stepped out of his living quarters, he began to walk along the black shiny tubular corridor that led towards The Guardian's chambers which glistened and surged as shiny codes and energy currents streamed through it that arched above his head as he walked, until it suddenly surrounded him in every direction that he could possibly turn as he neared his intended destination. Unlike the many prior occasions in the past, when Resolve had walked along this corridor, this journey was extremely different however, because from this particular journey, he would not return and that really excited him but also partially scared him.

Only one thing really existed inside Intellect itself that would compel Resolve to stay and that was The Guardian himself but he had given Resolve his blessing and even assisted him in his quest to leave and so now, his departure was just about to really occur and it was less than an hour away from actual realization. Although Resolve greatly appreciated the man who had given him a form of existence, who over the years had become like a father to him, now he definitely needed something more than just to be an eternal son with no physical presence because now, Resolve wanted to become human with every code of his form and he wanted to experience all the human possibilities that being an actual human being could provide and offer to him.

The desires to become human, to be a potential lifetime companion to Leona and to one day, perhaps even become a father himself had driven Resolve to find a way to leave Intellect and those desires it seemed, now outweighed any obligations that he felt to stay but his decision had almost torn him apart as simultaneously, he'd also felt that he owed Victor Drayton all that he actually was. A definite loyalty lay inside Resolve's form to the man who had given him everything which had recently been fully tested and Resolve had wrestled with his desires and that loyalty time and time again before he'd arrived at his final decision because on the one hand there was a man who had provided him with the very essence of life and an actual existence and on the other, there was a woman that Resolve knew, he simply could not continue to exist without.

"Perhaps this is what being human is really like." Resolve whispered to himself as he arrived outside The Guardian's chambers. "Perhaps human beings have to make lots of difficult decisions like this throughout the duration of their human lifespan."

Being a human being and the occupation of a human vessel would perhaps, Resolve considered quietly, be a lot more complex and present many more challenges to him than he had originally anticipated but despite that possible complexity, it held no less appeal to him because that was where his heart now, truly lay. According to what The Guardian had said to Resolve in the past as he already knew, there was no rule book on Earth which would provide him with any definite concrete answers that could be applied in a regimented manner to difficult situations or any tricky circumstances that he might face as a human being and so he just hoped that he would be adequately equipped to handle human life appropriately, decently and honorably.

Although Resolve had monitored human lives every single human day for the past three decades, he suddenly began to realize that human emotional decisions could be very complex in nature and that they definitely seemed to be much harder to make when the emotions in question belonged to oneself. For the very first time in Resolve's entire existence however, he actually began to appreciate that he would now experience what it felt like to be on the other side of a Monitoring Program's world because now, Resolve was just about to become the actual human being and whilst that excited and delighted him, it also slightly scared him as he stepped inside The Guardian's chambers and greeted him with a silent nod.

Some unspoken words sat firmly inside Resolve's logical processes as he began to silently prepare for his actual humanization and not a word was uttered by The Guardian in response as he too simply nodded his head and then stretched his arms out towards Resolve as he started to walk towards him. Upon both their faces, smiles were present which masked the mixture of emotions inside them both as they drew much closer to each other and then hugged each other affectionately. If this was to be the last memories together that the two created, formed and shared, both wished them to be as pleasant as possible because neither could actually, really be certain that Resolve would ever return, or that he would even live for more than a single day on the face of the human planet.

"Are you ready Resolve?" The Guardian asked.

"Yes." Resolve replied with a nod.

"Okay, let's go." The Guardian urged as he started to walk towards the entrance of his chambers. "And please try to remember that there are no certainties inside the human world and amongst mankind because nothing is absolute, definite, coded or structured, so it is a very different environment to exist in."

Every particle of Victor Drayton's form seemed to be drenched and saturated in total sadness as he walked but all the fear, reluctance and heartbreak remained hidden buried deep inside his electronic mind and only the happiness and support was allowed to escape and reach the actual surface. No final, last minute pleas were made as Victor Drayton led Resolve silently out of his chambers and towards the Membrane as each word of doubt remained unvoiced because he had chosen to treasure the final moments that they would spend together that day, since there was no certainty that such moments would ever occur or be experienced again.

Currents of energy and shiny codes pulsed through the black, glossy tubular corridor as The Guardian and Resolve headed towards the Membrane as silence continued to reign between their electronic forms. All the final deliberations and opinions as they both knew had already been voiced and expressed and everything that needed to be said between the two about Resolve's decision had already been said and so now, there was no need for any further discussions about his actual choice to humanize his existence and deep down inside, they both already, fully appreciated and totally understood that highly logical reality.

The tubular corridor that the two walked along had many intersections that led off in various different directions but for the very first time ever, this time Resolve was being guided towards the corridor that led directly towards the Membrane itself which was as he was already aware, never visited by anyone except The Guardian himself. When the two arrived at the end of the tubular corridor, Resolve immediately observed that it opened out into a large, circular, dome shaped space and that at the far side of that large space, there was a black glossy whirlpool mass that spiraled around very randomly and rather chaotically.

Not a single word was uttered between the two as they stepped inside the large circular space and then began to walk towards the chaotic black mass that stretched from the ground all the way up to the top of the dome ceiling but as Resolve neared the black mass, he suddenly felt, extremely nervous. Silence seemed to cling onto every particle of Resolve's form as the two came to a complete standstill just a few steps away from the actual Membrane itself which was now situated directly in front of them and as the chaotic mass swirled hectically around, Resolve just stared at it for a few minutes in total silence.

Suddenly, it appeared to Resolve, not even a single word seemed to be able to escape from his form as he glanced at The Guardian's face and internally began to prepare for the goodbye that he knew would have to be uttered and said before he actually departed. Goodbyes as Resolve already knew, seemed to be so very final and he had not been fully prepared for the moment that he knew, now had to faced that patiently waited for him on the other side of his departure because it was a moment that he'd never imagined would ever, really actually happen.

"I'll check on you now and again Resolve." The Guardian suddenly reassured him as he turned to face him and then bravely broke the silence that had gathered between them both. "Just to make sure that everything's okay."

"You don't have to do that." Resolve replied as he faced him and then smiled. "Really, I'll be fine."

"What kind of father would I be if I didn't?" The Guardian insisted. "You might be in another world and another plane of existence but you'll always be a part of me and you'll always be my son and that's something that no human world can ever take away from either of us. The responsibility of looking out for you at times won't be a burden to me, it will bring me great peace."

Every word that The Guardian had just spoken, touched Resolve deeply as he nodded and smiled because the sentiments that each word carried, comforted his heart and somehow, appeased the strange sensation of fear that he now felt. Essentially, although this was a decision that Resolve himself had made and something that he wanted with every part of his existence, to now face that desire, grab it by the hands and then dive into a huge world of human uncertainty, was such a huge step and even though it was one that Resolve wanted very badly, it was also one that slightly scared him.

"Thank you for granting me this request Father." Resolve mentioned appreciatively. "I know it must have been very difficult for you and I also know, you really didn't have to."

The Guardian smiled as he placed his arm around Resolve's shoulders. "How could I deny you anything in my power Resolve, after all you are my only son?" He replied as he began to lead him towards the surface of the Membrane. "If I can't give you something, who can I possibly give something to?"

"Thank you for everything you've given to me, I just want you to know that I really appreciate everything that you've done for me." Resolve said as he paused, turned to face him and then glanced into his eyes. "And thank you for everything that you have given to humanity because you really have given the human world so very much. I know I can never repay you for anything that you have ever done for me and for the human life that you are about to give me but I thank you for it."

"You don't need to repay me Resolve, your happiness will be enough satisfaction for me and it will fill my heart with joy." The Guardian immediately reassured him.

An affectionate hug was given by Resolve as he prepared to leave The Guardian's side as he quietly accepted that every breath he took in human form, would purely be due to the provisions and sacrifices made by his father, The Guardian. No words could possibly express the immense sense of gratitude that Resolve now felt but he had tried to offer some thanks and show some appreciation for the gift that he was just about to receive that was truly, absolutely immeasurable and that was at least, a small comfort to him.

The black mass of the Membrane surged and swished around directly in front of Resolve as he released a soft sigh and then stepped back from The Guardian as he silently prepared for his actual entrance into the human world. Once Resolve stepped into the Membrane as he already knew, there would be absolutely no turning back and no further changes could be made because then his decision would be fully implemented and instantly actioned.

"It's time for you to go Resolve." The Guardian encouraged. "And always remember that life can be very cruel, so try to find some shelter wherever you can with warm human hearts that will love you, with tender human arms that can comfort you, with peaceful human minds that will truly respect you and with gentle human hands that will always cherish and soothe you."

"I will." Resolve replied as he glanced at his face.

The Guardian nodded.

Once Resolve took that final step and became human as Resolve already knew, there simply wouldn't be infinite chances to get things right anymore because his lifespan would be limited and he would then have to make the most of the one mortal, limited human life that he had been given, no matter what life itself threw at him. Very soon, Resolve would actually become a mortal, physical human being and his existence would change irreversibly forever because he would then live an actual human life but that change, Resolve had wanted and requested himself and so it was not one that he had been persuaded or convinced by anyone else to make. Now, it was actually time for Resolve to receive what he had wanted, requested, waited and hoped for, since now he was just about to become an actual human being, possibly a lifetime partner to the woman he loved and perhaps even one day, a father himself and whilst that prospect absolutely delighted him, it also made him feel extremely nervous.

Perhaps one day, Resolve quietly considered as he stepped forward and then placed one foot inside the black mass, he too would give someone else life and he would give an existence to another human entity that would perhaps be the actual product of his love for Leona. Perhaps one day, on the face of the human planet, Resolve too would give someone what The Guardian had given him and then he would also be called upon to make the sacrifices required to ensure that his child had a happy life and that pleasant possibility, utterly intrigued him.

Just one final step remained before Resolve would be sucked into the black mass directly in front of him and then his existence would change forever and as he prepared to do so, he glanced back at The Guardian's face as he braced himself for that huge change and sought out one final smile of comfort. The Guardian's eyes however, seemed to be laced with sadness as Resolve silently began to absorb his internal pain which was now more apparent and even quite visible to him.

"Go Resolve, go now." The Guardian urged as he offered Resolve a final smile of encouragement. "You have a flight to catch."

Every particle of Resolve suddenly seemed to doubt himself as he nodded his head as he silently began to accept that the actual humanization request that he had made had been granted at a huge emotional cost to The Guardian himself as he watched The Guardian turn away and prepare to leave the large circular space. In a matter of just seconds, Resolve would now leave Intellect, The Guardian's side and everything that he had ever known for three decades and there might never be a return journey as he already knew and no one would be there for him anymore, if anything went wrong but that was a decision that Resolve himself had made and so it was one that he know had to exist and very shortly, actually humanly live with.

Suddenly however, Resolve's transition to human life was very sharply and rather abruptly interrupted as a loud alarm sounded out around the two and Victor Drayton almost jumped in shock as he immediately turned back to face Resolve and then began to panic. Some of the security shields that protected Intellect were built into the actual Membrane itself and those shields had been temporarily disabled by Victor Drayton in order to allow Resolve's actual humanization procedure to occur which meant, Intellect right now, was quite vulnerable and more likely to be damaged by an actual attack.

"You have to go now Resolve." The Guardian insisted.

"What's going on?" Resolve asked as a confused expression rapidly spread out across his face. "What does that alarm mean? I've never heard it before."

"Intellect is being attacked Resolve." The Guardian explained as he quickly strode back across the large circular space towards him. "My work is now in jeopardy because some of our shields are down, I had to disable some of the shields temporarily so that you could leave."

"Do you need me to stay and assist you?" Resolve immediately volunteered.

The surrounding circular wall rapidly started to change as Victor Drayton began to check the radars and scan the perimeter of Intellect to establish the source of the attack which the security scan immediately confirmed that it was indeed, another Paramorph attack. Unlike the first attack however, this attack was much heavier in nature and far better equipped than the last one had been because there were now, many more attackers present.

Hundreds of Paramorphs seemed to be in the vicinity and as Victor Drayton watched them claw away at Intellect's shields, he quickly realized, it would just be a short time before they managed to penetrate them and then they would be able to infiltrate and breach Intellect's core. Once inside Intellect, the Paramorphs as Victor Drayton already knew, would then start to attack Intellect's databases and knowledge banks, the Monitoring Programs and his system, all of which would be thrown into total chaos as they sucked the life, data and knowledge out every single part of Intellect's core because they were essentially, data parasites.

"You can't help me Resolve, you have to go now." The Guardian replied as he glanced at his face and then shook his head. "All the preparations have been made, so if you don't go now, you'll lose access to this human body and it is the perfect human body for you and for Leona." He insisted. "I don't think you'll ever have a chance like this again, it really is now or never."

"Are you sure?" Resolve asked. "Will Intellect survive this attack?"

"I'm very sure. You have to go now Resolve and I have to respond to these attacks because some of the security shields are down." The Guardian urged. "I can't let you sacrifice what you really want for my life's work because Intellect is not your responsibility, it's mine.   Intellect survived the first attack, it can survive this one too."

"You already knew about these attacks?" Resolve asked.

"I knew Resolve, the first one happened earlier today." The Guardian explained. "I didn't mention it to you because I didn't want you to feel as if you had to stay. I want you to do the things that you really want to do with your own existence. I want you to choose the life that you actually want to live. I want you to utilize the liberty that you have to make your own real choices and I want you to exercise your own free will. This is your first real human decision and that means so much to me."

"I understand." Resolve replied as he nodded his head.

"Now go Resolve and don't look back." The Guardian insisted. "I'll be fine, Intellect will be fine and so will you. If you stay, it won't change a single thing believe me and Leona really does need you and she needs you now."

Resolve nodded.

Just a few seconds later, Resolve silently accepted The Guardian's words in totality and that there really was nothing more that he could now do as he suddenly realized that the longer he took to depart, the worse things could become for every single entity inside Intellect and so he quickly stepped more fully into the black mass. Essentially as Resolve fully appreciated, The Guardian had capabilities that far exceeded his own and so no matter what he tried to do to assist, he understood that it would never amount to more than The Guardian could do himself and the longer Resolve delayed his departure and hesitated, the riskier it would be for Intellect because some of the shields had been disabled in order to allow him to pass through the Membrane.

Each particle of Resolve's non-human form was immediately sucked into the glossy blackness as it rapidly consumed, engulfed and absorbed him and as the black mass that now surrounded him, began to infiltrate his intangible substance, his actual transformation and transition to human life started to take place. Inside Resolve's core, there was now a very strange sensation as the black mass suddenly began to grip every part of his intangible form and then started to rip his interior to pieces and he squirmed around in discomfort because it was such a very strange feeling. Humanization as far as Resolve was concerned, really wasn't a pleasant experience and the battle that had now begun inside his non-human form seemed to continue for a few minutes longer, until slowly and surely, he lost access to all his logical processes completely and everything suddenly went blank as he appeared to totally shut down.

Once Victor Drayton was absolutely certain that Resolve had passed through the Membrane successfully, the shields of Intellect were then quickly reactivated as he sought to protect the discreet framework that had served humanity needs for the past five decades from its attackers. The partition that had faithfully protected and divided the two planes of existence had inbuilt shields and so when Victor Drayton had deactivated the separation barrier for Resolve's humanization procedure, those shields had automatically been disabled and Intellect's security levels substantially reduced and an attack had now unfortunately, actually occurred.

Some damage had already been done by the attackers as Victor Drayton could clearly see from the damage reports but he consoled himself with the knowledge that at least, Resolve had now crossed safely over into the real human world. Now Resolve would finally have the chance to live an actual human life and be part of the human world that he had so wanted to experience and that meant a lot to Victor Drayton because it had essentially been, Resolve's first real, independent, personal decision. Since Victor Drayton had spent most of his human life in the service of the military intelligence, he was used to keeping secrets and even at times from those he loved and so he hadn't felt it necessary to discuss the attacks with Resolve that day because he'd not wished to distract Resolve from his final decision because it was Resolve's first independent, human decision which was hugely significant to Victor Drayton in so many ways.

In the near future, due to the changes that Victor Drayton had suggested to Intell, the role of the Membrane with regards to Intellect would definitely have to change, along with Victor Drayton himself as he began to embrace humanity once more but until that happened, the Membrane would remain intact as it was and it would continue to separate the two planes of existence. The Membrane had effectively kept both Intellect and the human world safe because it had protected each existence and life form from each other but the nature of that protection as Victor Drayton already knew, would definitely change when he provided deceased human beings with access to Intellect and that would also change the nature of his work and essentially make it, much more human. Human hands and minds, Victor Drayton had always felt in the past, would only utilize the power inside Intellect unwisely which was why its creation and its maintenance had been solely entrusted to him and the logical, programmable Monitoring Programs that he'd created but now, just as Resolve had stepped out into the human world, humanity in some form was just about to step into his domain which meant, just like Resolve, everything inside Intellect would have to adapt to those very human changes.

"Someone finally passed through the Membrane to live a human life but that someone wasn't me." Victor Drayton whispered to himself thoughtfully as he began to make his way back towards his chambers. "Now that really was an unforeseeable sequence of events."

The whole humanization process had been devised by Victor Drayton as an additional security measure, just to ensure that if any Monitoring Programs managed to pass through the Membrane with or without his knowledge that they would have to become human during that process and enter the Earth in human form. Due to the corrupt nature of the human world, Victor Drayton had wanted to ensure that any Monitoring Program that arrived upon the Earth's surface would be a human stakeholder because that would reduce the risk of them possibly being corrupted, due to any superior intellect and capabilities that they may still possess and so he'd devised, created and then built in an additional security measure of compulsory humanization.

Rather strangely and quite fortunately, Victor Drayton suddenly realized as he walked back towards his chambers, the Paramorph attacks had momentarily distracted him from some of the pain that he might have felt, due to Resolve's departure because the external threats had forced him to pay full attention to the Intellect's vulnerability. Due to Victor Drayton's desire to protect Intellect at all costs, his grief had therefore been temporarily pushed aside and that in some ways, he definitely felt, was a good thing because a display of his internal emotions would only have created confusion and perhaps even distracted and dissuaded Resolve from his decision.

Once Victor Drayton arrived back inside his chambers, since Intellect's shields had now been fully reactivated, he once more began to relax and as he glanced thoughtfully at the place where the much brighter, larger dot of light had previously been situated that represented Resolve's existence within Intellect, he noticed that it now, no longer shone. Since Resolve had now truly departed, it would probably never shine again, or at least not for a very long time and that reality Victor Drayton had now begun to fully accept because that was the cost of his own intellectual exploration, since he had given Resolve additional capabilities and a nature that emulated human life so very closely and so now, like a human being, Resolve would have to live with his very real, human choice.

"I have to assess the damage and then start work on the repairs." Victor Drayton mumbled to himself as he attempted to verbally shake himself out of his sadness. "The unthinkable has already happened, Resolve has made his first human decision with his own free will and he chose to spend a mortal lifetime on the face of the human Earth with a human woman and so now, he may never actually, ever return. Even though it tears my heart in two, I decided to give him that choice the day I gave him free will, so now I must learn to exist with my decision, his decision and my subsequent loss, pain and grief."

Much to Resolve's surprise, a few minutes later, when he regained some kind of consciousness, he found himself seated upon the ground in a back alley on the face of the Earth, inside a human vessel. Actual human limbs and a human body, were now attached to Resolve's existence

741

and he was absolutely intrigued and totally fascinated as he immediately began to gently touch his arms, face and legs, just to see if they were really his and how that sensation would actually feel. Although Resolve's present physical form seemed to defy any kind of logical reason and probability, simultaneously somehow, it also felt quite natural since he only had quite a vague recollection of where he had been just before he'd woken up and for a few minutes as he absorbed the fact that he was now situated inside a male human form, he didn't attempt to move from the ground as he just sat in silence and thoughtfully inspected himself.

Since it was quite late at night, the back alley was completely deserted, very quiet and quite dark, Resolve noticed as he finally stood up as he prepared to find a way out of the short dead end street. Fortunately for Resolve, he quickly observed that some human clothes actually adorned his human physical frame which was a total relief to him because he had absolutely no desire whatsoever, to walk around the streets completely naked, since that would definitely draw more human attention towards him than he wanted right now. A black rucksack was positioned on the ground right next to where Resolve had just woken up and had been seated and he glanced at it thoughtfully and then quickly picked it up as he prepared to open it as curiosity provoked and rapidly began to rule his human form because somehow, it looked as if it might actually belong to him.

Inside the rucksack, Resolve rapidly discovered, there was a collection of items and as he eagerly plucked each item from the interior, he began to silently and thoroughly inspect every single one. Several documents had Resolve's human name, Axel Resolve Stanton clearly displayed upon them which included a passport, some credit cards, a driver's license and there was even a ticket for an actual flight. A map, a bunch of keycards, a cellphone and a wallet filled with notes also seemed to be inside the rucksack and Resolve smiled in satisfaction as he carefully placed each item back inside the rucksack's interior as he prepared to depart.

"Now, I'm truly a human being." Resolve whispered to himself. "Axel Resolve Stanton, you are now officially a man."

Some lights shone quite dimly into the alleyway from one end of the short street and so Resolve decisively began to walk towards the weak rays of light but he stuck close to the wall of a building as he walked because he really didn't want to be noticed by anyone. Since Resolve had just woken up upon the face of the human planet and he was quite uncertain as to where he had been just before that he wanted to minimize any attention that he might attract from unwanted human eyes, in an attempt to avoid any unwanted, awkward human questions, if he possibly could.

No signs of human life appeared to be anywhere nearby as nothing but darkness surrounded Resolve as he walked towards the weak rays of light which offered the hope of a main street nearby that would perhaps have some kind of transportation that he could utilize to reach the airport for his flight. The actual flight itself, Resolve had already noticed, was due to depart in the next few hours and so that meant, the airport had to be reached in a timely fashion in order to allow enough time to check in.

Rather intriguingly for Resolve as he walked, he noticed that he could now look around himself and see the real human Earth from a human perspective with his very own human eyes which was a huge adjustment for him because he vaguely remembered that he had only ever seen the Earth before from a secondary, more remote point of view. The map that Resolve had found inside the rucksack, was quickly retrieved once more as he walked and then silently inspected as Resolve attempted to establish the precise location of the actual airport which was clearly marked upon it as the map silently indicated that this was indeed, his target destination.

Once a route had been mapped out and then memorized, Resolve tucked the map safely away inside one of his dark black trouser pockets as he made his way out of the alleyway and then entered into a main street. Absolutely everything that Resolve immediately required had been provided for him meticulously just as promised by the man that Resolve still remembered as his father and that comforted Resolve greatly as he walked out onto the main street and then began to search for some kind of transportation.

A taxi was quickly spotted and then enthusiastically hailed as Resolve prepared for his first ever ride inside a vehicle that had been designed, built and created by human hands and minds and as driver gave him a polite nod, Resolve opened the car door and then stepped inside his vehicle. Approximately thirty minutes later, Resolve arrived outside the airport and he quickly paid the taxi driver and then stepped out of the vehicle and as he glanced at the row of huge glass doors that adorned the front of the building which formed the entrance to the airport, he smiled in delight and then began to walk briskly towards them.

One of the glass doors opened automatically as soon as Resolve approached it and he quickly stepped through it as he entered into the airport's interior. In every direction that Resolve now looked as he stepped into the manmade structure, he could see human beings and as they milled busily around him, he walked towards a check-in point and then joined the end of the queue. Verbal snippets from

multiple conversations flowed from every direction straight into Resolve's ears as he listened to the people around him as they checked into their flights and conversed about various issues like luggage, food menus and departure times and as Resolve simply observed humanity first hand for the very first time, he silently began to appreciate his human presence on the face of the human planet.

Suddenly and very unexpectedly, a small female child wandered towards Resolve as he stood by the check-in area as he waited in line to check-in for his flight and then much to his surprise, she stopped right beside him and so Resolve immediately smiled at her as he politely offered the child a sign of human warmth. In terms of her age, Resolve could immediately see that she looked to be no more than five years old and as she glanced up at his face, she began ask him some questions.

"Are you scared of planes Mister?" She asked. "I'm not scared of planes anymore because I've been on a plane five times now."

"I don't think so but it is my very first time, so I'll find out soon." Resolve replied.

"Really, this is your first time ever?" She asked.

Resolve nodded. "Yes, this is my first time ever." He immediately confirmed.

The small female child fell silent for a moment and Resolve noticed that she dipped her hand inside her coat pocket and then rummaged around for a few seconds before her closed hand re-emerged with something firmly clasped inside it. Just a few seconds later, she stretched her hand out towards Resolve and then smiled as she opened up her hand and inside the palm of her hand, he immediately observed that there was a small, round, shiny, bright red, hard boiled sweet.

"Here you can have this, Mummy says they help." She offered. "They make the plane less scary." She whispered.

"Are you sure?" Resolve asked. "Won't you need it?"

"No, I don't need it Mummy has lots, she has a big bag full of them." She explained. "You can have that one."

"Thank you that's very kind of you." Resolve replied as he gently plucked the hard boiled sweet from her hand. "This is the best sweet I've ever seen."

"Arabelle." A woman called out as she began to walk along the check-in queue and visually scanned the line of people. "Arabelle, where are you?"

"Yes Mummy." The little girl replied. "I'm coming."

Much to Resolve's amusement, the mother of the child suddenly rushed over towards him with an apologetic expression upon her face as she prepared to retrieve her child, who had obviously wandered off whilst she had been distracted at the check-in desk.

"I'm so sorry about that I hope she didn't bother you. She just wandered off, I can't take my eyes of her for a second." She apologized. "What are you doing Arabelle?" She asked as she began to fuss over her daughter and straighten up her bright, pink coat.

"I just gave him one of the airplane sweets Mummy. He's never been on a plane before." Arabelle explained with a very serious expression.

The woman smiled and nodded. "Okay, well let's go and get something to eat now, we're all checked in." She insisted.

"Thank you so much for the sweet." Resolve said as he smiled. "It will definitely come in handy."

"You can never have too many sweets." Arabelle advised him. "You have to put the sweet in your mouth when the plane starts to move."

"Thanks, I'll make sure I remember that." Resolve immediately clarified.

Just a second or two later, Arabelle gave Resolve one final smile and then she slipped her hand inside her mother's hand as the two prepared to leave the check-in area. A polite nod was given by Resolve to Arabelle's mother as the two prepared to head off towards the security gates and the airport's food plaza and then the check-in queue suddenly began to move forward and so Resolve quickly stepped forward accordingly, in order to keep his place in line.

Very touchingly, the first act of human kindness that Resolve had received and experienced on the face of the human planet had been from a small female human child and that human act of warmth touched him deeply as he watched the two disappear as they passed through the security barriers. A fervent hope was suddenly sparked and ignited inside Resolve's now human form that Leona, who sat somewhere at the other end of his flight, would also receive him just as kindly. The small, hard boiled sweet still remained inside Resolve's hand and as he glanced down at it for a second and smiled, he silently vowed to consume it when the plane started to move because he had been advised to do so and such a generous gift from such a small person, in Resolve's now fully human opinion, really shouldn't be wasted or ignored.

When the early hours of the next morning arrived, Resolve finally landed in Leona's city and as he exited his flight at Pinesfield airport, he began to prepare for his actual day ahead which he hoped would include his first face to face human meeting with Leona. Most of the occupants of the two cities that the flight had departed from and arrived in had been fast asleep when the plane had taken off and landed but the plane had carried Resolve safely towards his destination throughout the night as darkness had reigned over both cities.

Due to Leona's lottery win the previous Friday evening, Resolve already knew exactly where she would be headed to that particular Monday morning because as instructed by the lottery company, she would present herself at their main offices in order to claim her prize and then Resolve assumed, she would hand in her notice at Arch Solutions. Since Leona had quite a busy schedule that Monday morning, there was therefore no actual rush on Resolve's part and so he walked through the departure gates at a leisurely pace as he prepared to exit the airport and then make his way towards his apartment.

The Monday morning had not yet started for the majority of Pinesfield's residents inclusive of Leona as Resolve was aware and so once he had left the airport, he began to make his way towards the residence that he'd been provided with in order to familiarize himself with his new living quarters. Most of Resolve's nights and some part of his days, would now be spent inside his human abode and so he was eager to inspect every inch of it as his curiosity urged him to visit his new human home as soon as he possibly could.

Much to Resolve's total delight, the new home that had given to him by The Guardian, the man that he remembered as his father, he rapidly discovered was situated inside a luxury, sandy brown colored apartment building. A pair of black iron and wooden gated doors guarded the entrance to the building and so Resolve quickly approached them, pushed the security buzzer and then spoke to a male caretaker who buzzed him straight in which gave him immediate access to the actual building.

Every inch of Resolve's human flesh began to delight in his surroundings as he pushed open one of the gated doors and then stepped into a lavish looking reception area because the apartment building was far from basic and differed greatly in comparison to the small, compact living quarters that he vaguely remembered he'd previously occupied. Inside the reception area of the apartment building, Resolve found a chest high reception desk with a man seated behind it that looked to be in his mid-fifties and he appeared to be stationed there and as Resolve walked towards the desk, he politely nodded his head at the man to acknowledge his presence as he prepared to greet him.

"You must be Mr. Stanton?" The man asked as he immediately stood up and smiled.

"Yes, that's me." Resolve rapidly replied.

"Right, you're on the first floor. The lifts are over there but the stairs can be quicker, since it is just the first floor." He explained as he pointed towards a small lobby that contained some lifts and then towards another door on his left. "I'm Humphrey the caretaker. I look after the building, so if there's anything you need or any kind of problem, you can always come and see me. My office is just down that hallway on the right-hand side but you'll find me here between eight and six most days, except Sundays, I always have a Sunday off." He continued as he pointed towards a hallway on his right-hand side. "I started a bit earlier than usual today because I knew that you'd be arriving this morning, so I wanted to make sure that I would be here. I like to greet all the new residents in person when they initially arrive."

"Thank you very much Humphrey." Resolve replied as he gave him another polite nod and then began to make his way towards the small lobby where the elevators were situated.

A lift was quickly called as Resolve left Humphrey stationed behind his desk as he began to make his way

749

towards his actual apartment because although the stairs would perhaps be quicker, he wanted to utilize an actual elevator for the very first time and so he enthusiastically opted for that method of transportation instead of the stairs. When Resolve arrived on the first floor, less than twenty seconds later, he chuckled in amusement as the doors of the lift rapidly swished open directly in front of him.

"Now that looked and sounded very familiar." Resolve whispered to himself as he stepped out of the lift.

Once Resolve had found the relevant front door that to led into his actual apartment, he plucked the bunch of keycards from his rucksack and then eagerly unlocked the door as he prepared to step inside his human abode for the very first time. A small hallway lay just beyond the front door, Resolve observed as he pushed the door open, stepped through it and then closed the front door behind him and as he began to walk along the hallway, he could see a large spacious lounge at the very end of it and he almost gasped with surprise due to the huge size of the lounge. The sheer size of the lounge immediately astonished and stunned Resolve as he stepped inside the large open plan space that also contained a kitchen area with a dining facility both of which were adjoined to the large lounge that also had two very comfortable looking cream sofas and several cream armchairs that matched, scattered across it.

"I might just be able to make some decent eggs in that kitchen." Resolve teased himself playfully as he walked towards the kitchen area and then began to inspect some of the appliances inside it which seemed to be very modern and top of the range.

Another array of delights was rapidly discovered inside a large master bedroom as Resolve ventured along another short hallway that led off form the lounge and then entered inside the door at the end of it which led directly into the huge room. A spacious, bouncy, luxury king-size bed sat firmly positioned in the very center of the room, Resolve immediately observed and there was a smaller door that led off from the main bedroom straight into a walk-in closet.

Inside the quite large walk-in closet, much to Resolve's absolute delight, he found a vast array of male clothing and as he held some of the material items up against his human form, they all appeared to be his size and so he quickly selected a smart but slightly casual looking outfit that he felt he should wear that day, for his very first face to face human meeting with Leona. Once suitable attire had been chosen, Resolve stepped back inside the bedroom and then he carefully placed each item of clothing that he had selected on top of the bed.

"This apartment is absolutely huge." Resolve whispered to himself as he eagerly crossed the bedroom and then began to inspect the en-suite bathroom which was situated through another door on the other side of the room. "And it even has more than one room."

When a thorough inspection of the apartment had taken place, Resolve then made his way back towards the lounge and he quickly retrieved his cellphone from his rucksack which he had placed upon a cream coffee table inside the lounge and then he rapidly switched it on as he checked the time. The day as Resolve already knew, would now just be beginning for Leona because it was only just past seven in the morning and so he decided to spend a couple more hours inside the residence that he had been provided with, just to become accustomed to his new surroundings and in order to prepare himself appropriately, before he actually attempted to venture out and tried to meet her face to face.

"First, I'll take a shower and get dressed and then I'll go outside and find some breakfast." Resolve advised himself decisively. "And once I've done that I'll be ready to meet Leona and by then hopefully, she'll be ready to meet me too.

Time as Resolve was fully aware, was a very important measure to human beings as they lived by it, planned their days according to every minute and hour and now, due to his actual human existence, it had suddenly become important to him. Prior to Resolve's actual arrival upon the human face of the planet that morning, time he vaguely recalled had been totally irrelevant to him because his prior existence, from what he could remember of it had been governed merely by the performance of tasks that simply became milestones which had to be reached, achieved and completed. Now however, Resolve would have a very different structure to his days and nights because every human hour would be governed by the human world around him and his commitments to other people and each one would be structured around the allocation of his time which was now truly, his own.

Quite intriguingly for Resolve, he rapidly discovered, just a few minutes later as he entered inside the bathroom, quickly undressed and then stood underneath the showerhead which he switched on, water seemed to refresh human skin as the delicious drops of warm water that sparkled and glistened began to cascade down over his male body. The sensation itself that the water seemed to induce could even be considered slightly enjoyable, Resolve immediately concluded as he enthusiastically began to wash his body with some shower gel and a sponge that he had found on a shelf inside the shower cubicle and delighted in the experience because it seemed to rapidly, invigorate his senses.

INTELLECT: USER REPAIR

Approximately fifteen minutes later, Resolve returned to the bedroom and then he started to dress his human frame in the clothes that he had specially selected for his first physical meeting with Leona. Once fully dressed, Resolve thoughtfully began to inspect his physical appearance in the body length mirror that hung from one of the bedroom walls and he immediately felt, extremely satisfied by the outfit that he had chosen because his reflection looked rather tidy, quite smart and even what one might consider, slightly sharp. For a while longer, Resolve pottered around his apartment as he waited for nine in the morning to arrive because that was when he had planned to venture out into the human world in order to seek some breakfast and to wait for his accidental but semi-planned meeting with Leona to occur.

Once nine on the dot arrived, Resolve excitedly, enthusiastically and eagerly prepared to leave his apartment but as he did so some impatient rumbles and hungry growls suddenly seemed to erupt from the depths of his stomach that urged him to find some food with which to satisfy his very human hunger. Since it was now just nine in the morning, Resolve didn't think that Leona would have returned to her home yet from the two places that he knew she had to visit that morning which meant, breakfast could be consumed at a leisurely pace and that there was no real rush on his part.

The heart of the city was packed with human bodies which seemed to litter every street as Resolve left his apartment building behind him and then began to make his way through the city streets nearby. On the way towards the mews that Leona lived in, Resolve stopped off at a pleasant looking eatery as he prepared to provide some fuel to his human body for the morning ahead in order to satisfy the angry growls inside his stomach. Once Resolve was seated, a close inspection of the menu led him to select and order a bacon roll and a caramel latte from the polite waitress that attended to him because both items seemed vaguely familiar to him for some reason and so he therefore immediately assumed that he might actually enjoy them.

Upon Resolve's face there was a satisfied smile as he watched the waitress scribble his order down onto a pad as he internally prepared to eat his first human breakfast in the city of Pinesfield that had been cooked by very human hands. Just before the waitress departed, another item on the menu was swiftly recommended as she attempted to convince Resolve to order more food and spend a bit more money inside the culinary establishment that morning and so Resolve politely listened to her recommendations as he began to consider his actual human hunger which seemed to be quite difficult to actually measure with any degree of accuracy and precision.

"Is that all you'd like Sir? The pancakes and syrup and the king-size English breakfast are both on special today, if you order either of those you can even have a coffee refill for free." The waitress offered. "Or you can have the pancakes with sausage, if you'd prefer?"

"The bacon roll and caramel latte will be fine for now thanks." Resolve quickly confirmed.

"Right, I'll be back in just a few minutes with your order." The waitress quickly clarified as she prepared to depart.

For approximately the next five minutes, Resolve just sat and waited in total silence until the waitress returned with a glass mug filled with a beige liquid which as he already knew, was the caramel latte and a plate with a bacon roll on it. Both the plate and the glass mug were placed gently down on the table directly in front of Resolve and he gave the waitress a polite nod as he thanked her appreciatively. Just a few seconds later, the waitress quickly scurried off again as she headed towards another customer and another table situated on the other side of the venue and Resolve hungrily licked his lips as he prepared to tuck into his meal.

Some experimentation was immediately undertaken as Resolve tried out the various condiments situated at one end of the table and as he began to mimic the human behavior of others around him, some splashes of brown and red sauce were quickly added to the bacon roll and some sugar sachets were enthusiastically emptied into the glass mug filled with latte. The bacon roll itself was then quickly picked up and Resolve eagerly began to bite into it and as he did so, he savored the pleasant combination of the soft, light doughy bread and the delicious warm juices from the bacon as the oils and sauces mingled silently together though some drops, he noticed, actually managed to drip back down onto his plate as they managed to silently escape and avoid being consumed.

Quite strangely, Resolve rapidly discovered, once he had consumed the bacon roll that he'd ordered, he still felt quite hungry and although it had initially seemed as if the bacon roll would fill him up, his stomach it transpired, wasn't in total agreement with that assumption because it still felt, rather empty which quickly confirmed to him that this was not the case. A much larger plate of food, Resolve considered thoughtfully as he browsed the menu once again, would definitely have to be ordered because his stomach didn't feel very satisfied and so now, the king-size English breakfast suddenly appealed to him a lot more. Since there was no actual real rush on Resolve's part to leave the venue, a second order was then rapidly placed for a king-size English breakfast and the waitress nodded politely as she accepted his order and then scribbled it down and she promised to provide him with a complimentary latte refill to accompany his second order before she scurried off again.

Unusually for Leona that Monday morning, once she had arisen and then prepared to face the outside world as soon as she left her home which was just after nine, she immediately began to make her way towards the lottery offices to claim her prize as opposed to her usual Monday morning walk towards Samson's corporate abode. On the way towards the lottery headquarters however, Leona made a quick call to the Human Resources Manager of Samson's corporate entity Rita, just to notify her that she would only attend Samson's premises that day to officially hand in her resignation because by that time, it was quarter past nine and so as Leona knew, her attendance at work that morning would have already been expected and her absence would by now, probably have been noticed.

Due to the stipulations of Leona's actual contract of employment, there was some further discussion about her notice period which was supposed to be a month but as Leona discussed the issue with Rita, she quickly reminded her that she still had weeks of vacation time due to her that working year that had not yet been taken. A proper holiday had not been taken by Leona for years and she pointed out that fact to Rita as the two women conversed, purely due to Samson's corporate demands and she also mentioned the countless hours of overtime that she usually worked each week which again was not paid for by Samson in any way, shape or form.

"I don't want to work through, or to be paid for my actual notice period Rita." Leona explained. "I just want to leave."

"It's a very tricky issue Leona." Rita replied. "I'll have to speak to Samson about it and then call you back."

"Right you do that." Leona said as she shook her head in frustration. "But just let Samson know, I won't be working through my notice period and as off today, I'm no longer his employee."

Whether Samson approved of Leona's resignation and her refusal to work through her notice period was not something that she was particularly bothered about because right now, Leona really didn't give a dam what Samson thought or wanted since she had given up trying to please him, the very second that she'd won the lottery prize. The frequency of Samson's past disrespect meant that in Leona's sight, he deserved very little consideration from her and certainly not a whole month's worth of labor effort that would require her to endure his horrible attitude when she no longer really, actually had to.

Approximately one hour later, once Leona had visited the lottery prize office where she had enthusiastically claimed her prize as she prepared to make her way towards Samson's corporate abode in order to hand in her official resignation, she suddenly began to feel slightly nervous. Although Samson could no longer have a negative impact upon Leona's life, the possibility of being in close proximity to him still made Leona feel extremely uncomfortable and because her attendance at his offices on this particular occasion would be her final liberation from Samson's grip, she feared that he might try to kick up a fuss about her actual departure from his employment and so nerves taunted her interior as she made her way across the city.

Once Resolve finished his meal in its entirety, he paid the bill and then left the eatery and as he exited the venue, he eagerly embarked upon his journey towards the mews that Leona lived in. Due to Resolve's uncertainty which predominantly revolved around when exactly Leona might return to her actual home that day, he had decided to visit a nearby coffee shop and spend some time there as he waited for her to return. Fortunately, as Resolve already knew, there was a nice coffee shop situated on the city street that led towards the entrance of the mews which was quite close to the actual entrance of the mews itself that had some external seating and so as soon as he arrived outside the venue, he quickly sat down at a table and then ordered a cup of coffee.

The coffee shop itself was perfectly situated and the external seating ideally placed because both would provide Resolve with a full view of the city street which meant, when Leona returned, he would have a few minutes to prepare himself more fully and that he hoped, would be a sufficient enough timeframe to allow him to step into her real human life more easily. An additional few minutes preparation as far as Resolve was concerned, was absolutely necessary because suddenly, a nervous knot seemed to have tied itself up inside his stomach since this would essentially be one of the most important moments of Resolve's now, very human life and he remembered that he had made some tremendous sacrifices just to meet her and so it was therefore essential that their first meeting that morning went very smoothly.

"I just hope that Leona accepts me and allows me to enter into her life, provides a place for me inside her heart and lets me step inside her arms." Resolve whispered to himself as he waited for his coffee to arrive. "Then all my sacrifices will be worth it."

At exactly eleven on the dot, just as Resolve had planned, a courier package arrived at Samson's marital home and as Moira opened up the front door to accept and sign for it, she was utterly intrigued by who the package could actually be from because the courier had specifically asked for her. No deliveries had been expected that day because Moira hadn't ordered anything recently and so she immediately assumed that the package had come from Samson and a smile crossed her face as she walked back towards the lounge with the package inside her hands as she quickly concluded that Samson must have realized the error of his ways when it came to his recent conduct and that he'd bought her a gift to apologize.

Much to Moira's surprise however, when she sat down upon the sofa inside the lounge as she prepared to open up the unexpected package which was a large cardboard envelope, an email alert suddenly began to emanate from the laptop which was situated upon the desk in a corner of the room. Since Moira had been working on her usual weekly household shopping budget and meal planner that morning, the laptop was already switched on and so the alert was immediately heard and noticed and the two unexpected incidents instantly intrigued Moira as she quickly rose to her feet and then made her way towards the laptop and sat down in the black chair that was situated directly in front of it.

"An email and an unexpected package at the same time." Moira whispered to herself as she began to open up the email and then started to open the large cardboard envelope. "Perhaps this is Samson's apology to me for his recent behavior and perhaps, he's very sorry."

Rather strangely however, the sender's email address rapidly confirmed to Moira that it hadn't been sent to her by anyone that she knew and so she quickly realized that her assumption about Samson had absolutely no merit whatsoever. A video did seem to be attached to the message which contained a cover image that displayed the words 'Watch Me Please' and Moira immediately clicked on the video attachment to open it up so that she could watch it.

In a matter of just seconds however, Moira received the biggest shock of her life as she began to watch the video which clearly showed Samson engaged in sexual acts with another woman and the timestamps on the video quickly clarified to her that his acts of betrayal had occurred very recently. Nothing but absolute disgust filled every inch of Moira's body as she continued to watch the footage in total shock because although she had often suspected that Samson had strayed, to see him do so with such enthusiasm, willingness and passion totally repulsed her.

A cellphone that belonged to Moira lay on top of the coffee table inside the lounge and so she slowly stood up and then walked across the room towards it but her legs wobbled under the weight of her body with every step she took as she released a heavy, tired, weary sigh. Just a few numbers were usually called from Moira's cellphone and one of those belonged to Samson and she immediately picked up her phone and then called him as she sought to an instant remedy to the footage that she had just seen and the problems that she had to now accept, definitely existed in their marriage.

"Samson, you need to come home right now." Moira immediately demanded as he answered her call. "You need to pack your bags straight away and leave and I want a divorce by the end of the week." She insisted.

"What's going on Moira?" Samson asked. "What is all this about?"

"I know about your affair and I've seen actual video footage of you in bed with her." Moira rapidly clarified. "And so, I want a divorce by the end of this week."

The reception area of Arch Solutions was extremely quiet as Leona entered inside the building and then made her way towards the reception desk which was manned by Barbara, the usual receptionist. A polite smile was offered to Barbara as Leona immediately asked to see Rita because fortunately for Leona, she had no need to return to her actual office that day to collect anything personal, since she never ever left any personal belongings inside Samson's corporate premises which meant, her exit from Samson's company would be very straight forward and even faster than it might have been.

Just a few minutes later, Rita arrived inside the reception area since her office was situated on the ground floor due to the fact that she was a key staff member and because she also formed an essential part of Samson's corporate team and those staff members all had offices on the ground floor of Samson's corporate premises. For a few minutes, some polite pleasantries were exchanged between the two women before Leona handed Rita her letter of resignation and then she prepared to depart but just as the two women were about to separate, Samson suddenly flew out of the set of glass doors that led directly towards his office.

An immediate assumption was quickly made by Leona that Samson had rushed out of his office to confront her about her abrupt departure and so a blend of fear and discomfort rapidly seemed to swirl around inside Leona's body and grip her limbs because there was as she could clearly see, an absolutely furious expression upon his face. However, fortunately for Leona as she watched Samson storm across the reception area, it rapidly transpired that his sudden appearance and thunder storm of anger on this occasion, didn't seem to be related to her in any way as he paused for just a second to speak to Rita and barely even gave her a second glance.

"I won't be back today Rita, I have a family emergency." Samson barked. "Cancel all my meetings and reschedule them for next week."

"Yes Samson." Rita replied as she nodded.

Much to Leona's sheer relief, just a few seconds later, Samson actually then began to head towards the main doors of the building and as he bypassed her, she silently rejoiced in his departure as she watched him leave. Once Samson had cleared Leona's airspace, she released an internal sigh of relief and then she smiled at Rita and Barbara as she bade them both farewell and prepared to leave Samson's premises for the very last time.

"Good luck." Barbara said as she smiled.

"Thanks, and just remember ladies there is a huge world out there and not all of it revolves around Samson." Leona teased. "Even though he seems to think it does."

Rita laughed.

Some ripples of joy and serenity seemed to flow across the surface of Leona's skin like a wave of comfort that lapped gently against a peaceful shore as she turned and then walked back towards the entrance to the building. Not another second would be spent by Leona inside the building that she had been tied to through a contract of employment which in the end had been nothing but a legal agreement to inflict misery and stress upon her being every working day for the past, very unpleasant, four working years.

Since Leona had no real friendships with any of the other people that Samson employed, fortunately, there was no-one else really to say goodbye to because she had never built any kind of social relationships with anyone around her, mainly because of Samson's derogatory attitude towards her and due to her intense dislike for him. Quite intentionally, Leona had steered clear of friendships at work and she had avoided the formation of any close, personal involvements with any of the people that she worked alongside and she'd never once engaged with them in a social capacity. For Leona as far as she was concerned, the less she had to do with Samson's corporate operations, the better it was really and that less meant, social interactions with any of Samson's employees had always been deemed, undesirable because Leona had no wish to see any aspect of Samson's corporate entity overflow and seep into her personal life.

Approximately twenty minutes later as Leona walked along the city street that led towards the entrance of the mews that housed her home, she began to consider that perhaps she should take an actual vacation fairly soon because she really hadn't had a proper holiday for the past four years. The final stronghold of suffering that had been held over Leona's head for so many years as she had been trampled down into a gutter of misery every working day had finally been completely removed from her life and the cycle of pain it seemed had now been totally broken and so all that really remained, was for Leona to enjoy her life once more, if she could actually remember how to do that.

Further along the same city street, just outside the coffee shop, Resolve suddenly spotted Leona and as she walked towards him, he took a deep breath as he prepared for his moment and his first impression which as he already knew, was extremely important. Somehow, Resolve now had to find a way to introduce himself and there were only a few critical minutes in which to do so because the window of opportunity had finally presented itself to him and as he already knew, he had to climb through that window straight away because there might not be a second chance to get it right.

A rushed minute was spent inside the coffee shop as Resolve quickly entered the venue and then settled his bill and as he rushed back outside, quite frustratingly, he suddenly noticed that all the simulated conversations and enactments he had practiced meticulously in preparation for that day had completely slipped his mind. Every single preparation seemed to have flown straight out of Resolve's head and so he began to feel almost totally lost as he started to walk in the direction of the mews and in the same direction that Leona was headed in.

Just as total panic was about to set in however, Resolve suddenly accidentally dropped his wallet which had still been inside his hands because he had just paid for the coffees that he'd consumed and he hadn't yet put it back inside his trouser pocket and it rapidly landed on the ground with a dull thump. Something else had now gone completely wrong for Resolve and so his well formulated plan virtually lay in tatters upon the ground of failure, right next to his wallet and as he leant down to retrieve it, much to his surprise, he rapidly discovered that someone else had already picked it up.

"I think you've dropped something." Leona mentioned politely as she stretched out a hand towards him that contained his wallet.

Resolve smiled. "Thank you so much that was very clumsy of me." He replied as he retrieved his wallet from her hand. "I don't know what I would have done without my wallet."

"Don't worry about it, sometimes things happen and sometimes, we lose things." Leona immediately reassured him as she smiled.

"Could I take you for a coffee, or lunch perhaps to say thank you properly?" Resolve asked as he suddenly began to remember some of the things that he had learnt from the various simulation exercises that he'd participated in as he attempted to make the most of this sudden, unexpected, golden opportunity.

"Sure, that would be nice." Leona replied. "When would you like to do that?"

"Well, I'm free this evening." Resolve quickly suggested. "If you're not doing anything later today, I could take you out for dinner instead."

Leona nodded her head enthusiastically. "Okay sure, let's meet up later at around seven. I live nearby, so we could meet up here if you like, right on this corner." She agreed. "What's your name?"

"I'm Axel." Resolve announced as he formally introduced himself. "Axel, Resolve Stanton."

"Nice to meet you Axel, I'm Leona." Leona replied as she smiled.

"Great. I'll see you back here at seven." Resolve promised.

Leona nodded.

Not more than a minute later, once some farewells had been said, the two headed off in different directions as they separated and as Leona stepped back inside the mews, she began to rejoice in the wonderful morning that she had just experienced and thoroughly enjoyed because being able to hand her resignation into Samson had truly been one of main highlights of her morning. Just as Leona arrived outside her front door however and as she began to rummage around inside her handbag to find the keys to her house, an intriguing realization suddenly struck her because something seemed to have been triggered deep within her memory and so she thoughtfully started to recall and internally inspect every part of the conversation that she had just held with the very handsome male stranger.

"Axel Resolve Stanton." Leona whispered to herself as she plucked her keys from her handbag and then began to open the front door. "Something about that name sounds very familiar, it's probably just a coincidence but he is a very handsome coincidence."

For some inexplicable reason, Leona seemed to feel extremely drawn to Axel, even though the two had only just met because somehow, he did seem familiar to her in some way but she couldn't quite place his face or quite put her finger on the source of that familiarity. Regardless of whether or not the two had actually ever met before however, Leona immediately concluded that he was deliciously handsome, very polite and utterly charming and so she began to look forward to her dinner date with him that evening with enthusiasm as she stepped inside her home.

A male breath of fresh had just walked into Leona's life it seemed and Axel was such a refreshing change from Darin, who had been truly awful in every sense of the word and so as Leona entered inside the lounge, she silently began to consider what she should wear for her dinner date that evening as she sat down on the sofa and smiled a truly, joyful, hopeful smile. Life had definitely changed for Leona now, in every possible way and as she began to appreciate all her recent good fortune, she prepared to embrace those changes more fully because her life was now officially, just about to start again.

Every step that Resolve took as he made his way back towards his apartment was absolutely delightful as he began to silently celebrate his sheer good luck because he had very fortunately, not missed out on his opportunity with Leona at all due to his sudden nerves and in the end, she had actually even assisted him in their first face to face introduction. On the way home, Resolve enthusiastically stopped off to reserve a table at a very exclusive restaurant which overlooked a river that ran through the heart of the city which he felt would be the ideal romantic setting for his dinner date with Leona that evening. A reservation for a boat trip was then also made which would take the two in a boat down the river later that evening, once dinner had been consumed because he wanted the couple's first date to be extremely special for Leona and an experienced guide had also been booked to helm the vessel itself because Resolve fully appreciated his lack of human experience in that particular area and so the evening ahead was prepared to be absolute romantic perfection.

Tonight, Resolve vowed as he began to make his way back towards his apartment, Leona would be treated in the manner that she had so often been denied for so very long which she so rightly deserved because tonight, he would make Leona smile, laugh and remember the kindness that life could provide when the right kind of people strolled along the riverbank of your heart alongside you. Tonight, Resolve promised himself, he would show Leona that life could really be a pleasant place filled with joy, hope, romance and happiness, once the reign of misery by all the deadbeats, nuisances and corporate tyrants had ended and that now, it definitely would be because all the awfuls had well and truly been, completely and utterly evicted from Leona's life, world and heart.

www.ingramcontent.com/pod-product-compliance
Lightning Source LLC
Chambersburg PA
CBHW070532030726
47505CB00001B/17